FAVORITE SON

STEVE SOHMER

FAVORITE SON

BANTAM BOOKS
TORONTO • NEW YORK • LONDON • SYDNEY • AUCKLAND

FAVORITE SON is a work of fiction and is entirely the product of the author's imagination. Names, characters, places, and incidents in this novel are fictitious or are used fictitiously. Any similarity to persons living or dead or to any American political party is pure and unintended coincidence.

FAVORITE SON
A Bantam Book / November 1987

All rights reserved.
Copyright © 1987 by Steve Sohmer.
Book Design by Jaye Zimet.

Library of Congress Cataloging-in-Publication Data
Sohmer, Steve.
    Favorite son.
    I. Title.
PS3569.043F38 1987   813'.54   87-47563
            ISBN 0-553-05205-5

Published simultaneously in the United States and Canada

Bantam Books are published by Bantam Books, Inc. Its trade-mark, consisting of the words "Bantam Books" and the por-trayal of a rooster, is Registered in U.S. Patent and Trademark Office and in other countries. Marca Registrada. Bantam Books, Inc., 666 Fifth Avenue, New York, New York 10103.

PRINTED IN THE UNITED STATES OF AMERICA

FG   0 9 8 7 6 5 4 3 2 1

For Abram Sohmer and Millie Braunstein Sohmer,
the light that never failed

"For I have sworn thee fair, and thought thee bright,
Who art as black as hell, as dark as night."

—William Shakespeare,
Sonnet CXLVII

President Samuel Baker
and
Vice President Daniel Eastman

were elected to office on
November 4, 1984.

TUESDAY, AUGUST 9, 1988

THE FIRST DAY

7:55 A.M. THE GROUND FLOOR hallway of the Capitol was choked with yellers and shovers. The staffers yelled, the Secret Service shoved, and Sally Crain was stuck in the middle, wondering why all the power and the glory of the United States government couldn't keep the welcome reception for Colonel Octavio Martinez from turning into a riot. She was one of those earnest, honest women who began to appear in Washington under Carter. Her fair hair was her own, and her eyes were blue and wide-set. She had healthy, ruddy skin, like a freckled kid who has grown up slow and easy. And she had a long, loose gait, the way tall women do when they're confident in their sex.

Sally did her best to push her way upstream, smiling and nodding her apologies, trying to work her way to Martinez. But the crush and the summer heat were stifling. At last, she stepped into a doorway, leaned out of the way, and waited while the noisy mob oozed down the hall, bringing Martinez to her.

She could just make him out at the far end of the corridor, dark and handsome in his beret and fatigues, trying to shake every eager hand, flashing fine white teeth under his thick mustache. She had followed his campaigns in the Nicaraguan jungle with a mixture of professional detachment and sentimental pride. He was the stuff of legend—a high school algebra teacher who had watched his sweaty little country evolve from an oligarchy of the rich to a tyranny of the poor to a dictatorship of *Comunistas*. All that while, he had gone on patiently unraveling the mysteries of sine and cosine to classes of disinterested adolescents. Year by year, the textbooks grew more tattered and the rows of empty seats crept forward toward his desk. Until one day he realized that the seats were empty because boys who should have been in high school were in the hills of Jinotega Province, carrying M-16's and bleeding to death in the mud. So, he kissed his wife

3

and sons, put some socks in his old briefcase and rode a wheezing yellow bus to the end of the line, and walked into the jungle to find his students.

The first man he killed, he killed with a machete, and the blood spurted out of the man's neck into Martinez's face and made him vomit. After that, they gave him a pistol, and when the next Contra died, Martinez inherited his M-16. That winter, he led the raid that took the town of Ocotal and held it three days against a government battalion. The grateful Contras made him a major in their ragtag army. And in the end, the peasants adored him, the CIA pushed him, and he became *Colonel Reynaldo*—the leader, the inspiration, the fox.

Now, President Baker and his administration pointed to Octavio Martinez and his war as the true popular revolution that would bring representative democracy to that turbulent isthmus in the middle of our hemisphere. And the one-time algebra instructor, who now taught teenage boys how to plant Claymores and ambush recon patrols, had been flown to Washington to do the rounds of the committees with his tales of barefoot freedom fighters in the jungles, praying to the Blessed Virgin that the *Yanquis* would heed their cry for aid. Heroic Colonel Martinez would be the perfect counterpoint to the bitter memories of Colonel North, Irangate, and the illegal diversion of funds.

The crowd swirled by and Sally saw her chance. She held her clipboard to her bosom, stepped quickly between the Secret Service men, so close to Martinez that she almost bumped him, shouting to be heard above the din.

"Colonel, I'm Sally Crain. I'm Senator Fallon's press aide."

Martinez shot her that quick, dazzling smile, but waved his hand beside his ear to show her that he didn't understand.

Sally fought to keep her place beside him as the noisy mob slid down the hallway toward daylight and the exit to the Capitol steps. She switched to Spanish.

"Por favor. Me llamo Sally Crain. Soy assistante periodista del—"

In the din, Martinez shrugged, baffled.

Sally caught her breath and shouted in Portuguese, *"O meu nome é Sally Crain. Sou journalista assistante—"*

Martinez only smiled and shook his head. And as they reached the doorway, he left her behind, trying hard to look like a lady and shouting *"Je suis Sally Crain, une assistante-presse . . ."*

But he was gone, through the door into the daylight, far out of earshot.

Sally surrendered to the swell of the crowd rising behind her, let the pushing, jabbering mob carry her out. She stood blinking, blinded by the harsh daylight, letting the sea of humanity sweep past her on both sides. And she said, half aloud, half to herself, "Dammit—what language does he speak?"

Suddenly, as if from nowhere, Martinez was swept past her. Gently, he caught her arm and drew her against him so that the crowd bore them along the promenade like rising surf. She looked up, astonished, as the thronging well-wishers pressed them together. She could feel the rough canvas of his fatigues against the backs of her arms. She could sense his body moving under the cloth. His eyes were dark and glinting, and his voice deep under the chatter of the crowd. It was as though, for an instant, they were intimately alone.

"I speak all of them," he said. "Your Spanish is excellent. But your Portuguese. . . ." He shook his head and clucked his tongue.

Sally stopped where she was, speechless. And as she stood gaping, the surging crowd bore Martinez away down the steps toward the rostrum and the impatient television news crews.

She stood, feeling punctured and ridiculous. Then Martinez looked back up at her and winked. That made her laugh out loud.

"Shit," she said, and trailed after him down the steps, feeling girlish and silly and charmed.

Martinez was shaking hands down a long line of well-fed, dark-suited dignitaries by the time Sally climbed the stairs to the wooden rostrum. She checked her watch: 8:09. She knew that in NBC Studio 3B in New York, the *Today* show's Willard Scott was just wrapping up the weather report. In Control Room 3B, Steve Chandler, the producer, was on the intercom to Bryant Gumbel, reminding him to tell the audience that, after the next commercial, *Today* would switch live to Washington.

Sally knew it because she had guaranteed Chandler that Senator Terry Fallon would get up and welcome Martinez at 8:11 on the button. She'd also promised him an exclusive Gumbel interview with Terry and Martinez on Wednesday—provided Chandler would agree to cover the welcome live. Chandler took the deal, even though he knew he was being used.

He knew—and so did Sally—that if one network morning news took the event live, the other two had to follow suit or let *Today* have an exclusive. The welcome on Tuesday and the interview on Wednesday assured Terry of national exposure on two successive days. And the morning ratings were small enough that, if it were a slow news day, the welcome could be replayed on the noon and evening news.

Chandler knew all that—and he knew that Sally knew it, too. He knew she was using the competition among the three networks to advance Terry Fallon's career. But Chandler went along because he also knew that Sally would get the Secret Service to set the rostrum at the Senate end of the Capitol so that the morning sun would be behind the speakers, haloing their hair instead of glaring in their eyes. He knew that Sally would get Fallon out of his chair at exactly 8:11 come hell or high water. He knew that whatever Fallon had to say would run twenty-five seconds or less, the ideal length for an audio bite in a news feature. And he knew that Sally would coach Fallon to play it to the camera with the peacock. In fact, Chandler was so confident that Sally would manage it down to the second, he was not at all surprised to see her standing at the podium behind the Great Seal of the United States of America when *Today* went to commercial and the Washington feed came up on the line.

When the red tally light on the NBC camera blinked on, Sally stood at the podium, looking down at the busy news crews and gossiping print reporters ringing the rostrum. Twenty microphones stared her in the face. She checked her watch: 8:10. She began. "Senator Fallon will make a brief—"

Then she realized that her mikes were dead and she was talking to herself. "Audio, open number 4, please," she said.

Suddenly, the whistle of electronic feedback cut through the air. Instinctively, people ducked and held their ears.

Sally's voice boomed *"Thank you. . . ."* Then the sound man cut the gain to normal levels. Sally smiled as the crowd settled down. The gambit always worked.

"Thank you," she said, and her voice echoed between the Capitol and the Russell Building across the street. "Senator Fallon will make a brief welcoming statement. White sheet with blue border."

She held it up and gave the reporters a moment to find their copies.

"Then Colonel Martinez will respond with this text—"

She looked at the sheet—then over her shoulder at Martinez. There was a puckish twinkle in his eye and, despite herself, she smiled back.

"—in *English*," she said. "Red border." She held it up. "Translations are in yellow." She held up one of those. "Foreign press, if you need one, see Betty." Sally waved, and Betty, her secretary, waved back from behind the cameras. Four or five foreign reporters hustled for a copy of the translation.

Sally let her eyes sweep down across the news crews. They were all there: NBC, CBS, ABC, the BBC, the CBC, TF1, every country in Latin America, a dozen Iron Curtain countries. What Terry would say would be carried to every city, every hamlet in America, virtually every country on earth. She had organized it, she had arranged it, she had planned it down to the last detail. The morning light glistened in her eyes. The reporters and cameramen stared silently up at her. The only sound was the soft breeze off the Potomac and the snap of the flag before the Capitol dome. Sally raised her face into the wind, and her eyes were slits of satisfaction.

"Roll tape," she said.

In the television mobile units, directors parroted her command.

On the NBC television network, Bryant Gumbel was looking into the camera and saying "—to the steps of the U.S. Capitol where Senator Terry Fallon will welcome the Nicaraguan freedom fighter who—"

Sally smiled. "Ladies and gentlemen, the senator from Texas, the Honorable Terrence Fallon." As the applause started she made her way to the side of the rostrum, then down the stairs to where she could stand looking up at Terry.

He crossed the boards with a loping, easy stride. There was so much of the boy in him, so much of the athlete, that she had to remind herself he was a senator now, one of the hundred who guided the destiny of the nation. When Julio Ramirez, the Contra spokesman-in-exile, had requested Terry make the speech welcoming Martinez, Sally had jumped at the chance. And the White House had two reasons to hasten to agree. First, Senator Fallon had leadership on Central America. He wouldn't roll over for Castro, Ortega, or the Sandinistas. He wanted to fight the good fight the same way the White House and the voters did: our money, our guns, our advisors—their blood. The other reason was even more apparent: the dimpled, open-handed, kid-from-Texas grin that had been Terry's hallmark since he entered the House of Representatives from Houston in 1978.

Some people wondered if he could ride his good looks and moderate-conservative ideas all the way to the Senate. But he didn't have to. When the ABSCAM net caught Senator Caleb Weatherby in 1984, the governor of Texas appointed Terry to fill the unexpired term. Overnight, Representative Fallon became Senator Fallon. And Washington took note; he was a young man on his way.

Bryant Gumbel said, "—live from Washington, Senator Terry Fallon." In Control Room 3B, Steve Chandler said, "One on the line," and, on cue, the NBC network fed America a picture of Terry at the podium. In the dark of the control room, a technician whistled through his teeth, and someone else said, "Amazing . . ."

Chandler laughed out loud. "Supercunt," he said, and the technicians knew that in his mouth it was the ultimate professional compliment.

The applause for Terry was warm, sustained. In fact, it began to build—until Terry raised his hands for silence. "My fellow Americans," he began, in a loud declamatory voice. The crowd settled down. Then his tone changed—as Sally had taught him—to something approaching tenderness, and a warm light came on in his eyes. "My fellow Americans. . . . For more than 200 years, the brave men and women of this hemisphere have carried the flag of freedom against the forces of oppression. Since 1981, Colonel Octavio Martinez has led the daring and historic struggle to free his Nicaraguan homeland from Communist dictators.''

Sally looked up at Terry as he spoke, watched the soft breeze lift the ends of reddish hair from his temples. She watched the way his eyes moved from face-to-face among the crowd, how they greeted people, spoke to them alone, one by one, how his smile was ready and how you knew by the way he held his shoulders that the world would be all right. She glanced over at Martinez.

But the colonel wasn't watching Terry or listening to his remarks. He was staring straight at Sally. Then he nodded toward Terry—nodded to tell her he understood how she felt about the thin young man at the podium. There was something sweet about this hero, something powerfully seductive. Shyly, Sally lowered her eyes.

Fallon said, "I am proud to welcome you, Colonel, in the name of the people of the United States. And in the name of all people everywhere who love freedom and peace.''

Steve Chandler looked up at the clock on the control room wall. Twenty-five seconds on the nose.

Martinez rose and walked to the podium. The dignitaries, the onlookers, even the reporters broke into hearty applause. Terry clasped Martinez's hand and then his arm. The applause rose higher. The dignitaries on the rostrum stood, pounding their hands together. Then the handshake became a warm embrace as the two dashing young men threw their arms about each other. The crowd below the rostrum came to its feet. And the roar swelled so loud that the gunshots would have gone unnoticed, would have sounded like Chinese firecrackers in another street, if it had not been for the way the bullets seemed to explode as they struck.

There was a moment just after the last shot was fired, as the applause was choking into silence, when the two men clung together like drunken dancers propped on one another's shoulder. And if it had not been for the blood that stained their jackets and trousers and streamed down their pant legs; had it not been for the bare bones showing in Martinez's back where the rounds had torn away his flesh; had it not been for the blood and tissue that spattered on the clothes and collars and faces of the horrified dignitaries behind them—had it not been for those grotesqueries, the crowd would have thought they had witnessed a burlesque turn, not a political assassination.

Steve Chandler said, "What the fuck . . . ?''

When the two men fell, the scream of the crowd pinned the audiometer in Control Room 3B into the red.

*   *   *

Rear Admiral William Rausch, the director of the CIA, was reading "Heard on the Street" in *The Wall Street Journal* when the red phone in his bedroom rang.

"Yes, sir?" he said.

"Are you watching television?"

"No. . . ."

"You should be."

Then the line went dead.

Rausch slid out of bed and snapped on the set. He had seen men shot before, had ordered men into combat, to their certain death. But what he saw before him on the nineteen-inch screen struck him with a terror beyond all knowing.

In the NBC mobile unit at the bottom of the Capitol steps, the director was screaming into his headset, "Grant! Get up there! Get on the stage! Get the stiffs! Fight for your shot!"

The monitor in the center of the console showed swirling images of pandemonium on the rostrum as the NBC cameraman fought to climb up onto the platform. Two Secret Service men with Uzi sub-machine guns rushed through the crowd. One of them pointed to the Russell Building across the street.

"On the roof! Move out! Move out!" he shouted into his walkie-talkie.

The NBC cameraman pushed past the Secret Service, pushed into the center of the melee on the rostrum. The bodies of Terry Fallon and Octavio Martinez lay side by side, slack as broken dolls. In the puddle of blood spreading around them, medics and Secret Service knelt and feverishly administered first aid. But reporters and still cameramen and news crews had surged up onto the platform, making it almost impossible for the medics to work. Secret Service men with drawn sidearms struggled to push back the mob of newsmen.

On the center monitor, a blond woman—Sally Crain—fought through the ring of reporters, looked down at the bodies at her feet. Her scream of desperation cut the air.

For Sally it was as if her whole life, her whole future, her whole being climaxed in that momentary roar of gunfire. She had raced for the stairs only to be knocked to her knees and almost trampled by the dignitaries fleeing down and away. By the time she had gathered herself, reporters were rushing the platform and the swell of them carried her up toward the ghastly scene of death. A ring of still photographers and video cameramen had gathered around the bodies, weaving and shoving and fighting each other for a clear shot of the fallen men.

Sally had tried to push through them. Then she tried to fight through them. Finally, she beat at their backs with her fists until they made room for her. Then she had caught sight of Terry.

His suit was saturated with blood. A medic was cutting away his jacket. In the right side of his shirt, just above his beltline, was a pumping wound. Frantically, the medic tore the shirt away, struggled to close the wound. A Secret Service man tried to push the reporters and Sally back. But she knew where her place was. She went to her knees and took Terry's head in her lap and held him as though by pressing his white face against her body she could force her strength into him.

The last person on the Capitol steps who realized what had happened was Terry Fallon. One moment he was embracing Martinez, the next moment Martinez seemed to jump up and land on him with his full weight. Terry staggered backward a step, trying to help Martinez regain his balance. Then a piercing pain in his right side made his leg buckle, and he fell backward into a row of empty folding chairs. The back of his head hit the bare boards of the rostrum, and his forehead filled with a dull, numbing pain. He felt his stomach churn with nausea. And then his jacket and trousers were damp and hot as though he had wet himself. It was only when he looked down and saw that his shirt and pants were drenched with blood, that he realized he had been shot. His eyes rolled back in his head, and he blacked out.

Then, a moment or an eternity later, he heard a distant voice calling his name. It was Sally's voice, and it was full of pain. He wanted to sleep, wanted to stay in the dark region beyond the agony. But it hurt him to hear the pain in Sally's voice, hurt him more than the pain of the wound in his side. He kicked back at the darkness and rose to the sound as a deep swimmer rises to the light, and he turned to the sound and opened his eyes to see if he could find Sally and console her.

Sally was on her hands and knees beside him, holding his head to her body, her skirt and hands covered with blood. There was such stark terror in her face that he thought for a moment she had been shot. But when she saw his eyes open, a wave of relief swept the terror from her face. Then he knew that he was the one who was wounded, who must be brave, who must carry on despite the pain.

He grasped her hand and tried to rise. But the wound in his side dragged him down like a great weight and the throbbing in his forehead blinded and humbled him.

"Senator, stay down!" a man's gruff voice commanded beside him.

But he wouldn't stay down. He fought to rise on one elbow. "Help me, Sally."

And despite the Secret Service clustering around him, despite the medics trying to hold him, Terry Fallon rose and looked around. What he saw was chaos.

Like jackals, the cameramen and reporters ringed the body of the fallen Martinez with glaring tungsten lights and flashing strobes. The colonel lay on his back in a puddle of blood and shattered tissue, his head thrown back, his eyes and mouth open, while a medic worked frantically at CPR. But the fluid in his eyes was already beginning to cloud and dry, and Terry could tell that Octavio Martinez was dead.

Terry pushed away from the hovering Secret Service, shouldered past the shouting cameramen, stumbled through the line of still photographers in front of him. He steadied himself on Sally's shoulder and pushed past all of them toward the podium and the microphones.

Steve Chandler was screaming into the intercom that connected him to the director in the NBC mobile unit in Washington. "Stay on him! Stay on Fallon! Jesus Christ, somebody get me that wound!"

Suddenly, the torn edge of Terry's bleeding shirt appeared in close-up on the monitor.

Chandler shouted, "His eyes! Holy Christ! Shoot his eyes!"

And they were there in the monitor, burning resolute through the pain as Terry groped his way to the podium.

"Home base!" Chandler shouted. "The podium! Take one! Open his mike!"

Terry clung to the podium, trying to maintain his balance. Sally held him under the elbow. Her hands and face were covered with his blood.

Terry tried to speak, and his voice cracked with pain. ". . . can you . . . hear me? . . . anyone . . . ?"

In the rush and dither of the crowd clambering onto the rostrum, in the madness of shouting men and women, his thin, pained voice went ignored.

Terry gripped the podium, steadied himself. "How can we . . . turn our backs . . . while our friends . . . lie dying?"

In the mobile unit the director was shouting, "Chandler? Are you getting this?" And Chandler's voice roared back in his headset, "You're live on network from coast-to-coast!"

No one who was watching television that day ever forgot what he saw. Decades later, you could ask an old man or a middle-aged woman, and he could tell you where he had been, what he was doing at the very moment Terry Fallon was shot. It was like hearing the news of Jack

Kennedy's death, or Bobby's or Martin Luther King's. It was an event that froze the moment in time so that the rest of the day and the month and the year vanished from memory.

Into some 75 million homes that day came the image of a tall, young American, his white shirt and red tie stained to bloody scarlet. There were streaks of blood drying on his face, and it took a young, blond woman and a graying Secret Service man to support his elbows while he struggled to find words for what he and they and every American was feeling at that moment.

There was a haunting, distant burning in his eyes, like the eyes of a voyager who has returned from the unknown with a revelation. Behind him, a priest with bloody hands was administering the last rites to a fallen soldier. Behind him, armed men and shocked reporters rushed to and fro. But at the podium, above the Great Seal of the United States, Terry Fallon stood and pieced together the words that would make his country understand.

"This man . . . was not a politician. He was . . . just a man . . . with a simple man's dream . . . that his children should live free."

In his commentary on the *NBC Nightly News,* John Chancellor recalled his first meeting with Terry Fallon this way: "It was hard to believe that anyone could rise to a seat in the Senate of the United States without the patronage of special interests, without the taint of political compromise, without the smell of cigar smoke and back-room deals clinging to his clothes. But Terry Fallon had."

Everywhere you turned that day—television, radio, newspapers—Terry's words rang and his face stared back, an accusation and a challenge.

"Octavio Martinez died . . . to bring us the truth," Terry said, and clung to the podium against the rising dizziness. "His fight is our fight. His cause . . . is our cause. And his dream . . . must not be buried with him."

Dan Rather and Diane Sawyer watched the replay together that night on a CBS Special Report: "Death of a Hero." Rather had once visited the Contra staging areas in Honduras, had once interviewed Martinez among his army of teenagers and *campesinos.* "But is it our fight, Dan?" Sawyer demanded. "Is it ours—or is it the politicians'?" Rather held the bridge of his nose for a moment. Then he said, "Diane, either it's our fight—or it's our children's. . . ."

It was after midnight when Ted Koppel wrapped up his interviews with Secretary of State Cranston and Tomás Borge, the interior minister of the Republic of Nicaragua. The two men had exchanged half an hour of bitter recriminations and angry accusations. Koppel had wanted to close *Nightline* by asking the central question that had emerged from the melee—so he reran the last words Terry Fallon had spoken before the medics forced him to lie down on the stretcher that took him to Walter Reed Hospital.

It was a familiar image by now. The milling crowd of Secret Service men and reporters had fallen still and silent in a ring around the three people standing at the podium. The gray-haired Secret Service man to Terry's left was weeping openly. Sally Crain's clear blue eyes and brave face looked up at Terry with trust and adoration. With bloodied hands they held his elbows, sustaining him. Over his shoulder, the flag before the Capitol snapped in the rising breeze.

"How long, America?" Terry said, and his pain-ridden voice rang with courage. "How long will men like this suffer and die before we're willing to listen? How long before we lift our heads . . . and hearts . . . and fists . . . so that their children—and our own—can live in freedom in a world at peace?"

When he finished, there was only silence. But it was the silence of the ages.

A man named Lou Bender watched it all.

To him, Martinez's assassination was an awkward inconvenience—an inconvenience that would have to be dealt with quickly, decisively. But it was an inconvenience that could be managed.

To him, Terry's words were simply the jangled rambling of an idealist drifting into shock.

To him, the deluge of network coverage—the *Special Segments, Special Reports, Nightline, Today, Good Morning America,* and the *CBS Morning News*—were a textbook example of how the three networks gorged themselves on violence, until they bloated the insane act of one illiterate terrorist into an event of international consequence. When Lou Bender turned off his television set at 7:30 the next morning, he was disgusted with the whole pathetic circus.

But he was the second person in the world to understand that if Terry Fallon survived his wounds, he was destined to become the most powerful man on earth.

WEDNESDAY, AUGUST 10, 1988

THE
SECOND
DAY

8:40 A.M. LOU BENDER MARCHED past the president's secretary without so much as a nod and pushed through the door into the Oval Office. Sam Baker swiveled around in his chair to greet him.

"What is it, Lou?" he said.

Bender slapped a copy of *The New York Times* on the desk between them.

"That's our man," Bender said.

President Baker looked down at the banner headline:

COLONEL MARTINEZ ASSASSINATED ON CAPITOL STEPS

And beneath that:

Senator Fallon's Heroic Address Stuns Nation

There were two photographs, one, the fallen Martinez, and the other, Fallon at the podium; his image was nothing less than messianic.

"Because he's able?" the president said.

"Because he's famous."

"But what kind of man is he? What's he made of?"

"The same thing all good running mates are made of. Ink."

The president leaned back in his old desk chair. He had known Lou Bender for twenty-nine years. Through six congressional and senatorial campaigns and one long run for the White House, Lou Bender had been there, and had been right.

Now, Bender was a grizzled old politico in a black suit, a starched white shirt, and a thin black tie that didn't reach his belt. He was a short, small man with a taut little face, a shock of loose white hair and busy,

17

miniature hands. The coming presidential election, their bid for a second term, was Bender's last hurrah. Win, lose, or draw, it was the last hurrah for both of them. They were behind. They knew it. The nominating convention was eight days away.

"We've got a vice president," the president finally said. "His name's Dan Eastman. What about him?"

Bender put his hands in his pockets, looked down at the shine on his shoes. "What about him?" he said, as if he didn't give a damn.

The president could see that Bender believed Terry Fallon was a gift from the gods—a gambit that could clinch a second term. Bender had that look in his eyes that a pit bull gets when it locks its jaws and even death can't break its grip. It was a look that President Baker admired, and mistrusted. Because he knew it meant shortcut, compromise, expediency.

Four years before, they had forged a coalition with Dan Eastman, the burly governor of Pennsylvania, a trolley car mechanic's son with hands as big as a catcher's mitt. Eastman was a brawling, two-fisted, sell-and-repent politician, a throwback to Tweed and Daley. He was the perfect running mate for Senator Samuel Baker, the Virginia planter and white-shoe Wall Street lawyer. Lou Bender had said so. And in these matters, Bender was infallible. The election was a Baker-Eastman landslide.

But that night—November 4, 1984—had been the high watermark of their popularity. From that day on, almost without remission, their approval scores began to slide. It was like running on a treadmill that moved at gradually increasing speed. For a short while, they won as many new constituents as they lost. But, as the months rolled by, the lingering problems of the country resisted treatment like a stubborn rash. Each day, Sam Baker ran a little faster, a little harder. But the treadmill whirred on, accelerating.

The once-congenial newspapers blinked, then inexorably began to turn their faces away. The rhetoric of the television commentators became less conciliatory, more strident and judgmental. And the polls—*The New York Times*/CBS poll, the NBC/Associated Press poll, the ABC/*Washington Post* poll, the NOW poll, and the Gay Men's Caucus poll—the all-powerful polls showed Baker-Eastman losing ground as the third year of their administration juddered to a close.

In December of last year, a high-level party delegation had come to the Baker ranch in Santa Fe, six awkward men in blue suits and white shirts with the red desert dust on their black wing-tip shoes. Old Charlie O'Donnell, the Speaker of the House of Representatives, spoke for the group. He ticked off the accomplishments of the Baker-Eastman administration. He was perhaps too lavish in his praise for the success of tax reform, the rejuvenation of the space shuttle program, the progress on international trade and industrial recovery. But in the end, his soliloquy came down to one simple question: for the good of the party, would President Baker step aside at the nominating convention?

Sam Baker knew O'Donnell was right. He knew he was in for an uphill fight, a fight that he might not be able to win. But he couldn't see himself retired: an old man in a rocking chair, yarning away a string of interminable afternoons that unraveled to the grave.

"I'm sorry," he had finally said.

Then O'Donnell turned to Dan Eastman.

"Drop dead," Eastman said.

Now, eight months had passed, the nominating convention was only eight days away, and O'Donnell's prophecy had come true. The party was divided. It probably could not deny renomination to an incumbent president. But there was a growing sense of indolence and ennui among the regulars. Everyone said so—even George Will. "All President Baker needs to be re-elected," Will wrote in *Newsweek,* "is 50 million votes and a miracle." In politics there were no miracles, only ploys.

But he had no appetite for expediency. There was an ugliness about expedient politics, like a deformed infant that was undeniably a monstrosity, but nevertheless one's own. It was useless to deny its paternity. But it was impossible to embrace it without revulsion.

"I've ordered class one Secret Service protection for Fallon," Bender was saying. "The same as Eastman and you."

But Sam Baker stared out the window, lost in his reverie.

"Mr. President?"

At last, he looked back at Bender. "I'm sorry, Lou."

"I said, I've ordered class one Secret Service protection for Fallon."

"Why? He wasn't the target."

"He just made himself a target." Bender took a cigar out of the humidor on the president's desk. "A lot of your constituents want us out of Central America." Bender bit off the end of the cigar, spit it into the wastebasket. "Besides, he's just become the party's favorite son. Got a light?"

"No."

Bender stopped. He stared at the president. "What's your problem?"

"Dan Eastman."

"No problem."

"It stinks, Lou."

Bender went to the president's desk, opened the top right-hand drawer and found a pack of matches. It was not the first time they had disagreed. "I'll tell you what . . ." He wet the end of his cigar with the tip of his tongue. "We'll do it this way. You ask Fallon to give the keynote speech at the convention next week. After what's happened, the delegates will hand him the number two slot by acclamation.''

"What about Eastman?"

"If the delegates want Fallon, what choice has he got? He's got to step aside." Bender shrugged and smiled. "Fallon is in, we get our second term, and Eastman is out with no fingerprints on the body. Right?"

"We'll see." The president sat down at his desk. "Now please excuse me.''

But Bender didn't move. "Right?"

"Lou. I said we'll see."

The president's intercom sounded. He pressed a button.

"Yes, Katherine?"

"It's Speaker O'Donnell, sir."

The president looked at the buttons on his telephone; none was lit.

"Which line, Katherine?"

"He's here in the reception room, sir."

The president shut off the intercom. He looked at Bender. "O'Donnell? At this hour? What do you think he wants?"

Bender struck a match. "Vultures like to hit before the body gets cold."

Now Sam Baker understood what he had to look forward to—a day-long parade of pundits and power brokers all peddling the same idea—dump Eastman, grab Fallon. He would have to sit and listen to them, hear them out, acknowledge their logic. But he alone could make the decision to replace Dan Eastman—if it had to be made. And he alone would live with it forever on his conscience.

Lou Bender lit his cigar, rolling it slowly between his fingers. Then he blew a huge puff of acrid smoke into the air.

"Let's not be dainty, Mr. President. One martyr is enough for this campaign."

8:50 A.M. FOR YEARS, SALLY Crain had worked to build the popularity of elected officials, to give them an image, to make them stand for something in the public mind. She had relished success and tasted failure. She had seen her ideas realized and dashed.

But nothing she had experienced even approached the events of the past twenty-four hours.

When the medics hustled Terry down the steps of the Capitol toward the waiting ambulance, she clung to the cold steel rails of the stretcher, running alongside. All around her, men and women were weeping. An old woman tossed her rosary on the stretcher as Terry's gurney rolled through the street.

At first, the Secret Service wouldn't let Sally board the ambulance. But she wouldn't let go of the stretcher, and she saw that they didn't have it in their hearts to deny her.

As the ambulance wove through the streets of Washington behind the wailing sirens of the police escort, the medics worked like men possessed, cleaning and stanching Terry's wound. They started an I.V. on radio instructions from Walter Reed. Sally held Terry's hand until he lapsed into unconsciousness. When he did, one of the medics pressed Sally's head to his own chest and held her all the way to the hospital.

In the emergency room, six doctors were waiting to rush Terry into the O.R. There were fifty aging men from the MacArthur Post Number 101 of the American Legion in the blood bank wearing blue caps and campaign ribbons, some of them in wheelchairs, all waiting to be typed so that they could give the blood Terry needed, bickering with each other over who had arrived first, who had seniority, who might be chosen for the honor of being a donor. A monsignor from the Washington archdiocese arrived ten minutes later to tell Sally that the Pope would say mass for Terry's recovery at Evensong in Rome. He brought two nuns who went upstairs to the chapel to hold a solemn vigil through the night.

Nothing in Sally's experience had prepared her for the outpouring of love, the willingness to sacrifice, the selfless kindness of the people about her. She sat in the small, private waiting room, staring out at the traffic passing silently on the streets below. At eleven o'clock, the surgeon, an army colonel, came to tell her that Terry was out of the operating room. His wound was painful and bloody, but no major organs were damaged. He would need rest. But he was safe. Sally went home and changed her clothes. When she came back in the afternoon they let her see him.

An army sergeant and a corporal flanked the door. They checked Sally's likeness on her ID, noted her name on a clipboard. Then she went inside.

The sun cast a dull orange glow through the drawn curtains. The army nurse beside the bed rose silently, and Sally took her place. The only sound was the soft, repetitive ping of the cardiac monitor. In the massive mechanical bed, Terry seemed so small, the sheet lay almost flat. He had been catheterized. His face was pale, almost ashen; his face looked damp and cold.

Sally sat a long moment, staring dully at the bed. Then she stretched her hands forward on the top sheet until she felt Terry's body under the covers. She lay her head on her arms and drifted into sleep.

She did not hear the nurses come and go during the night. She was not aware of the doctors who came by on their rounds. All night long she lay, head down, arms outstretched like a supplicant, fingers in delicate contact with the warm life beating beneath the sheets. She did not hear the noise of the reporters in the corridor the next morning. It wasn't until she felt Terry move under her hands that her eyes opened. For a moment, she could not remember where she was. Then she sat up abruptly. Terry was looking at her. It was only then that she remembered what had happened, where she was, and that it was over.

She looked toward the muffled sound of reporters' questions that filtered through the door.

"They woke you," she said, and started to rise. "I'll have the police move them back into the lobby."

He moved his lips as though he wished to speak; they were dry and badly cracked. "No. Don't go . . . just now."

She went to the sink, dampened a tissue, and touched it gently to his mouth. He licked the moisture gratefully.

"Am I . . . all right?" he asked.

"Mending."

"Is it . . . serious?"

"No." She sat beside him. "You'll be fine."

Then a shadow seemed to pass across his face. "How . . . how could this happen?"

She took his hand in both of hers. "I don't know. I don't understand it."

Then that grinning little boy looked out from inside him. "What are the papers calling it? A nick? The proverbial flesh wound?"

She squeezed his hand, held on as though if he slipped her grasp he'd be lost to her forever. "They're calling you a hero."

He raised his other hand and cupped the side of her face. "Are they?" he said, with a soft, ironic smile.

And she buried her face in the hollow of his palm and, for the first time in a very long time, she began to cry.

9:05 A.M. JUST THEN, THE president was leaning forward, his elbows on his desk, listening intently to the two men seated before him. He was sure that one of them was lying.

The bald one, the wiry little man in the dark blue suit was Admiral William Rausch, director of the CIA. The other, the chubby, cantankerous

Irishman in the tweed jacket was Henry O'Brien, director of the FBI. There was no love lost between them. Lou Bender stood near the windows neither in nor out of the conversation.

"How do you know it was Petersen?" Rausch finally said.

O'Brien referred to a little spiral notebook. He was a cop, had always been a cop, had never stopped being a cop. He was methodical, meticulous, persnickety—a compulsive compiler of facts. He could be infuriating.

"Our agents got a positive ID," O'Brien said. "Two secretaries passed the perpetrator in the north hall near stairway six to the roof."

"The FBI's been wrong before," Rausch said.

"Come on, Bill. They picked his mug shot."

"Together?"

"Separately. He was CIA for five years," O'Brien said. He flipped his little notebook closed. "He's your man and that's an end to it."

Rausch slouched down in his chair. "He *was* ours. Until he went freelance."

"Why?" the president said. "Why did he go freelance?"

Rausch shrugged. "Drugs. Money. Who the hell knows why these guys do what they do?"

"Conscience?" Bender said behind him.

Rausch looked back over his shoulder. "In the case of Petersen, you needn't worry about conscience." He turned and looked at the president. "He's a mindless, flawless, cold-blooded killer."

"Working for whom?" the president said.

Rausch opened his hands.

"I see. Where is he now?"

O'Brien said, "We'll find him."

And then, softly, to no one in particular, Bender said, "Do we want to find him?"

It was very quiet in the room for a moment. Then O'Brien blinked and looked at Bender as though he wasn't sure what he had heard.

"I'm just wondering out loud, Henry," Bender said. "Just wondering what our Latin American allies will think if they find out that Martinez was gunned down by a former member of our own CIA."

Rausch said casually, "Speaking for the Company, if we never see him again, it'll be one day too soon."

O'Brien sat up. "Let me get this straight. An ally of the American government was shot dead on the steps of the Capitol. And you're telling me you don't want to find his killer?"

Bender's voice behind him was soft, oily. "No one said we didn't want to find the killer, Henry."

O'Brien could smell whitewash, and the odor burned his nostrils.

"Now, listen to me," he said. "I'm telling you there has to be an investigation by the FBI. Or there is going to be a congressional circus that will make the Warren Commission look like a kangaroo court."

He glared at Rausch. But the CIA director sat silent, looking straight ahead. Bender came up behind O'Brien and put his hand on the back of his chair.

"Of course, there are investigations . . . and then there are *investigations*. . . ."

O'Brien said, "I don't believe what I'm hearing. This was cold-blooded murder!"

He looked to the president. But now Sam Baker understood. There was another dimension to this murder, some terrible secret. It was something Lou Bender might know, but the president must not.

The president rose. "Thank you, gentlemen," he said. Rausch stood. Only O'Brien sat, blinking and bewildered, looking among the faces of the three men. The president's intercom buzzed.

"Yes, Katherine?"

"Vice President Eastman is on the phone, sir," she said. "And Mr. Flaherty is here."

"All right," the president said, and pressed the button that would put Eastman's call on the line when he lifted the receiver.

Bender cleared his throat and the president looked up. Pat Flaherty was the White House political pollster. If he had come to the president's office without an appointment, he must have news of enormous importance.

The president looked again at the blinking light on the phone that indicated Eastman's call. Then he pressed the button for the intercom instead. "Katherine, send Flaherty in."

Almost in that very instant the door opened and Flaherty burst in waving a computer printout. "A 91 awareness and an 88 Q! This guy Fallon is bigger than Cosby! There's no doubt about it, Mr. President. He's the guy you can win with!"

The president stared at Bender. Bender put his hands in his pockets, looked down at the shine on his shoes.

The president pressed the button on his intercom. "Katherine—" Then he stopped. He was about to take a step—and it was an irrevocable step, one that he could never retrace. "Katherine, tell the vice president I'll call him back."

O'Brien got to his feet. He glared at Bender. Then at Rausch. Without saying a word, he shoved Flaherty aside and pushed out through the door.

10:05 A.M. "FUCK YOU!" JOE Mancuso shouted. He shoved so hard that Dave Ross bounced off the glass wall at the rear of the court and had to charge back to hit the ball on the carom. It was more like hand-to-hand combat than handball.

"Cocksucker!" Mancuso roared, as Ross's lob arced back over his head. He turned to run it down, smacked into Ross again, shoved the younger man aside. "You're blockin'!"

"Your ass!"

Mancuso barely caught up with the ball, slapped it backhand off the sidewall toward the front. He pushed off the rear wall and doggedly headed back the other way.

"I'll kill you," he panted, as he went by Ross.

"Try it!" Ross squared in position in the forecourt as Mancuso's weak return bounced at his feet. He cut a delicate little drop shot into the right corner.

Mancuso smacked into him, shoulders down. "Move it!"

Ross almost lost his balance, barely recovered to chase Mancuso's save into the far left corner. Now he had Mancuso trapped in the forecourt. Ross hit a savage cross-court return.

But the older man took it on the volley and slapped it down the right-hand wall. Ross leaped for it.

Mancuso stuck his leg out. Ross went flying on his face, skidding in his own sweat across the shiny maple floor. The ball bounced past his outstretched hand, died in the far corner.

Ross rolled over, angry fists clenched. But when he looked up, Mancuso was laughing.

"You rotten old crook," Ross gasped, breathless.

"You're bitchin'. But you're buying." Mancuso gave him a hand up.

Ross laughed, too. In two years, handball was the one thing they had found in common. In fact, Ross was no handball player—he was a squash player who learned the game at Yale, perfected it at Georgetown Law School. One day in the gym in the basement of the Hoover Building, he had run into Mancuso in the lockers, changing into shorts.

"You play squash?" Ross had said.

"Handball."

"Try squash?" Ross held up the light, elegant racquet.

"That's for pussies." Mancuso threw him a dirty old pair of handball gloves.

25

More out of cussedness than curiosity, Ross had learned the game. These days they were well matched: the dark, muscular kid who looked like he was still in prep school, but hit sixty miles an hour off either hand, and the aging, stubborn bull who chased down every shot, who always seemed about to drop but never did.

Ross knew what he was getting into when the Bureau handed him Mancuso as his partner. Mancuso was a lifer, a thirty-year man, a misanthropic, saturnine old dick who had nothing to show for his career with the FBI: no family, no friends, no stripes. He was still only a grunt agent when all his contemporaries were either special agents-in-charge or memories. He was a mean, silent hulk of a man. And as his time drew on toward retirement, he had become even more private and withdrawn. Ross appealed. He even volunteered for immigration enforcement. No soap. He was Mancuso's, Mancuso was his—until death or retirement them did part.

Ross picked up his blue Ralph Lauren gym bag, and threw Mancuso's towel in his face.

"One round, then I'm back on duty."

But something outside the court caught Mancuso's eye. "Chickie. The bulls."

In the hallway beyond the rear glass wall, Supervisory Special Agent Barney Scott stood in his double-breasted brown pinstripe, hands in his pockets, glaring.

Mancuso and Ross came out.

"Hiya, Chief," Ross said, and wiped at the sweat pouring off his neck.

"Your shift don't break till noon, Ross."

"He took an early lunch," Mancuso said.

Scott sneered. "You been out to lunch since '79, Joe. Why don't you take your pension and give the Bureau a break?"

"I got three months till fifty-five-and-out, Scotty. Then I'm history. And in the meanwhile, fuck you."

He started to walk away. Scott poked his index finger in Mancuso's shoulder to stop him.

"I'd love to bust your pension for insubordination."

The two men stared at each other. They had thirty years of grit between them, and it rubbed hard.

"I didn't hear anything," Ross said.

Scott turned on him. "You watch your step, Ross. You got a long way to go before you cash in. And until then, your ass is mine."

"Eh, fongool!" Mancuso said, and gave Scott the Italian salute and laughed. "Come on," he said to Ross, and the two started down the corridor toward the lockers.

"You can skip the shower," Scott called after them. "Man on the sixth floor wants to see you two."

Mancuso snorted. "Sure, he does. And he's gonna send us on vacation to Acapulco." He elbowed Ross, who elbowed back, and they both laughed out loud.

"It's about the Martinez assassination," Scott said.

That stopped them, dead.

They looked back.

"Up yours, guinea," Scott said. And he shot them the Italian salute.

10:10 A.M. "YOU TWO LOOK like a couple of clowns," Henry O'Brien said. Ross with his blue gym bag, Mancuso with his towel, stood sweating and feeling ridiculous in the middle of the long, oak-paneled office of the director of the FBI. A small gray-haired man sat in the far corner.

"Mancuso, I'm assigning you as agent-in-charge of the Martinez investigation. Ross will be your backup," O'Brien said.

There was a long silence. Mancuso shuffled his feet. "Yeah," he said. "Well, I'm out of here in three months, Boss." He called O'Brien "boss" to keep from slipping and calling him "Blinky," the nickname the guys had hung on O'Brien when he joined the Bureau in 1957.

"I understand that," O'Brien said. "When you move on, we'll assign another senior agent if the case is still open."

That made Mancuso raise his head. "If?"

But O'Brien ignored him. "You are to keep the facts of this case and particularly the name of the assailant strictly confidential for—" he wet his lips "—for reasons of national security."

Mancuso thumbed back over his shoulder. "Then how do we—"

"Just do your best," O'Brien said. "That's all."

Mancuso and Ross stood, silent.

"I said, that's all."

"Yes, sir." They went out and shut the door behind them.

Ross could barely contain his excitement as he followed Mancuso into the hall. When they were alone, he caught his arm.

"Jesus! The Martinez gig."

"It's a setup," Mancuso said.

"Huh?"

Mancuso waved him silent, walked on.

10:10 A.M. PLUMP, EAGER CHRISTOPHER Van Allen backed into Terry's hospital room. When he turned around, Sally saw that his arms were full of newspapers.

She had borrowed a yellow pad from a supervisor to log the telegrams and flowers and fruit baskets that had begun to arrive before nine o'clock. An hour later, the room was awash in roses, chrysanthemums, pineapples, and Godiva chocolates. Terry was sitting up, sipping orange juice through a straw, still shaky but gathering strength.

Chris was elated. "Three—count 'em—three network special reports. Every newspaper." He tossed them on the foot of the bed. "New York. Chicago. L.A. Detroit. Did I tell you Barbara Walters called for an interview?" He spilled the whole pile of papers at Terry's feet. Then he grabbed the handkerchief from his breast pocket and wiped his pudgy, grinning face. "Jesus, Terry, you're a household word!"

Exhausted, Sally picked up the *Detroit Free Press,* absently scanned the headline and photographs of Terry and Martinez. Terry stared blankly into the distance.

Chris looked as if he would burst. "Jesus, can't you even smile?"

Terry said, "And just forget Octavio Martinez lived and died?"

Chris stood where he was, deflated, ashamed.

The phone rang.

Sally answered it. "Yes?" Then her face went slack. She covered the mouthpiece. "It's the president." She handed the phone to Terry and stood up, away from the bed.

Terry cleared his throat. Then he put his ear to the phone.

"Yes, Mr. President?" He paused and listened. "A lot better now, thanks. Yes. Yes, sir. As soon as I'm able."

He handed the phone to Sally and eased back into his pillow, staring at the ceiling. Sally and Chris stood in silence.

But when he could hold his peace no more, Chris whined, "Aw, Terry, tell us."

Terry did not look at them. His voice was mechanical. "He says he must speak to me as soon as I'm up and around."

Chris kept a straight face as long as he could. Then he clapped his hands once, hard. "Fuckin'-ay!" he shouted, and he didn't care who heard him.

11:55 A.M. DOCTOR PAUL SUMMERS wore an impeccable white lab coat and thick, round, rimless glasses. He looked like a zoology professor Ross had studied with at Yale. Ross always felt like he was back at school when he sat in the operating theater of the FBI forensics lab. Now, he sat taking notes while Joe Mancuso sat beside him, his feet on the chair in front of him, absently picking his ear.

"In all respects, a very elegant shoot," Doctor Summers said.

"How so?" Mancuso said.

Summers held up a photomicrograph of a shell casing. He used his pencil as a pointer. "From the markings on the casings, we know that the rifle was a Heckler & Koch HK-91. These horizontal striations—"

"Yeah, sure," Mancuso said. "What kind of gun is that?"

Summers stopped, looked over the tops of his glasses at Mancuso. Then he quietly put the photoprint down and picked up the rifle from the table before him. He pulled the bolt to; it rang with a sharp metallic clang.

"Automatic," he said. "Five-shot standard or twenty-round box clip. Fires ten rounds a second."

"Whose issue?"

"Nobody. It's for specialists."

"Yeah?"

"NATO snipers."

Ross looked up from his notes.

Summers put the rifle down and picked up another photoprint, this one a bullet. "Fires a 7.62 high-velocity slug. An experienced shooter can hold down the trigger and still keep the whole burst in the black."

"What kind of slug?" Mancuso said.

"Name it. Soft-point, hollow, flat-nose, Teflon, full-steel jacket. It depends on how your target is protected—and how hard you want him to die."

"How hard did Martinez die?" Ross said.

"A near miss on the first one was enough to do the job. The rest of the clip was—" he shrugged "—extreme prejudice."

Summers folded down the picture of the bullet. Behind it was a photo of another bullet, one that had struck its mark. The point was mushroomed and deformed, the metal flattened, spread wide, a dozen razor-sharp edges gleaming.

"This load is Tauride. It's manufactured by Arms Ariadne in Deauville. It mushrooms to four diameters on impact. Cuts a tiny entry wound, then

29

rips the guts to shreds. If it hits bone, it fragments. So does the bone. Fallon doesn't know how lucky he is." Summers put the picture down. "Here's the brass." He tossed a plastic evidence bag to Ross. "SID found those on the roof of the Russell Building."

Ross held the plastic bag up to the light. The empty cartridges jangled. He opened the zip-lock and spilled them into his palm. They were light as air to be so deadly. They were also heavily scratched.

"These been used before?"

"Pro hitters load their own. All the casings are reloads."

Six of the cartridges were identical brass. The seventh was black.

"These don't match," Ross said.

"Same caliber, mixed brass," Summers said. "You see that a lot with home loads."

"What else, what else?" Mancuso said, impatient.

Summers picked up his clipboard, sat down on the edge of the table, and began to thumb through it. "I performed an autopsy on Martinez. Want to hear about it?"

"Fuck that," Mancuso said. "Guy shot him, he died."

"He was going to die anyhow."

"How do you mean?" Ross said.

"Colonel Martinez had AIDS."

Ross stopped writing.

Beside him, Mancuso said, "So he was a fruit. Lots of spics are fruits."

Summers shook his head, sighed. He turned to another page. "The man was married. He had three . . . no, four children."

"So, he was acey-deecy."

"He was a devout Catholic. A daily communicant."

Mancuso got up from his chair. "Listen, Doc. Lots of old altar boys play hide-the-weenie where they shouldn't."

Summers put his clipboard down on the table. "You know, Mancuso, you're a real scumbag."

Mancuso shrugged, straightening his tie.

"What are you getting at, Doc?" Ross said.

"Two days ago, this colonel goes to Walter Reed for a physical. They did the whole workup: G.I. series, heart, blood, everything. Yesterday, some shooter blows him to kingdom come."

"So?"

Summers took off his glasses. "On Monday, the results show he wasn't AIDS-positive. Tuesday he was. There's only one explanation."

"Yeah?"

"Somebody at Walter Reed juiced him with infected blood."

There was a long silence.

"Cute," Mancuso said.

12:10 P.M. TERRY WAS FEELING better; his hands had stopped shaking and his vision had cleared. He was sitting up in bed, reading glasses down on the end of his nose, a pile of telegrams in his lap. Sally sat beside him, her yellow pad resting on the edge of the bed. She was struggling to read her own shorthand, but she was fading.

"I'm sorry," she said. "That senator . . . was it Fulton or Fulham?"

Terry took off his glasses.

"You're tired," he said, gently.

There had been a flood of calls that morning—until she asked the switchboard to take messages. There had been an endless stream of nurses carrying baskets of flowers, chocolate, and fruit—until she pleaded with the supervisor to deliver the cards but distribute the gifts to other patients. And Chris Van Allen kept rushing in and out with telegrams from senators, from foreign heads of government, from governors, constituents, and friends—until Sally's head began to swim.

"I'm not tired," she said. "Not really."

Terry smiled and laid his hand on hers, made her put her pencil down. He grinned. "How'd you like to slip out and get us a pair of ice cream sundaes?"

She smiled, too. "I would. But they've got guards on the door."

Terry lay back. "Know what I want more than anything in the world?"

"What?"

He looked at her. There was such caring in her eyes, such tenderness, that he knew she would give him anything he asked for, if only it were hers to give.

He scratched his chin. "A shave."

She smiled and ran her fingertips down the stubble on his cheek. "You look just right." They jumped apart at the sound of the door.

"Jesus Christ," Chris Van Allen said, and his eyes were bulging. "Speaker O'Donnell is coming up the hall!"

He swung the door wide open and Speaker Charlie O'Donnell rolled in. He was a huge, grayed, lofty man, big everywhere—big smile, big feet, big jowly face, but little steely gray eyes.

"Terry, Terry, my boy, how are you?"

"I'm getting along, sir," Terry said. "Forgive me not getting up. Sally, give the Speaker a chair." He tried to push himself higher against his pillow, but the effort drove the I.V. needle deeper into his arm and he winced.

"Are you in pain?"

"No, no," Terry said, waving it away. "They've got me so full of needles and tubes I can't scratch without something tearing loose."

Sally turned her chair for O'Donnell. "Thank you, dear." He plumped himself down. "Terrible tragedy. Just terrible." Then, abruptly, he said, "Could we speak privately?"

His tone was startling, preemptive.

"Sally?" Terry said.

"Of course." She went out the door.

Chris Van Allen was waiting in the hallway.

"Jeeze," he said. "O'Donnell himself." Then he looked at Sally. "You're whipped. Come on, I'll get you a coffee." He took her arm.

There were two things in Washington that Chris Van Allen loved being near: politics and Sally Crain. On the day of his graduation from Dartmouth, he had taken the train to New York, changed for the Metroliner, and reported for work on the staff of Caleb Weatherby, senior senator from Texas.

Weatherby was glad to have Chris Van Allen on his staff. Hiring Chris cemented a relationship with Van Allen, Burns and Company, the investment bankers at 30 Wall Street. In fact, Weatherby told his friends that he "wouldn't touch the little pansy if it wasn't the only way to float $160 million." Most of Weatherby's office staff felt the same way. They were first-generation Texas money who wore Gucci cowboy boots to prove they'd made it. Chris was a genuine Eastern aristocrat with the right name, right family, right connections, and the wrong sexual preference. About the only person in the office who took him seriously was Sally Crain.

Sally understood that Chris Van Allen gave Weatherby's office entree to society—and society was where it had been at under Reagan. Chris was old money, and his family had laid a lot of pipe down the generations. Their genealogy and their tentacles reached into the social and political Olympia of the cities of the East, the Old South, Grosse Pointe, Shaker Heights, all the way west to San Marino and Bel Air. A lot of people who wouldn't return Bunker Hunt's calls had to pick up the phone for a Van Allen. It was a calling card that Caleb Weatherby needed—anyone needed—if he really wanted to be vice president.

They spent a lot of time together, Chris and Sally. She knew about him and he knew she knew and it was fine. Many a night they ordered-in Chinese, sat in front of the fireplace in her Georgetown apartment, drinking Beaujolais and spinning dreams. There was a deep-running kindness in Sally, and Chris felt closer to her than he had ever felt to any woman, closer than he ever dared hope he could. But the house of cards came crashing down when Caleb Weatherby was indicted.

Weatherby was an oil speculator who was worth $40 million—but he never got the dirt out from under his fingernails. When a phony wildcatter offered him $150,000 cash against shares, he tried to push the EPA to loosen oil leases in plot WT11915. Weatherby was on camera when he agreed to the scheme and again when he took the briefcase full of cash. A moment later, the wildcatter and his partner revealed themselves as FBI agents. A moment after that, Weatherby was in handcuffs, and his career was buried in plot WT11915.

A year later, a picture of Weatherby flashing the "V for victory" sign appeared on page fourteen of *The New York Times*, with a caption that read: "Former Senator Caleb Weatherby entering the federal minimum security facility at Lewisburg to begin serving a seven-year sentence for bribery and collusion." By then, Texas Governor Wendell Taylor had already appointed Terry Fallon to assume Weatherby's unfinished term.

Fallon blew through Weatherby's office like a whirlwind. Nepotism and ward-heeling came to a grinding halt. The first month, eleven of twenty-three staffers were pink-slipped. Some were replaced by seasoned professionals, others by longer hours and hard work. The good people rose to it, and Chris Van Allen was one of those.

Terry Fallon didn't seem to care that Chris was gay. If anything, he took a kind of fatherly interest in the young man, and made him his political liaison with the party functionaries. That gave Chris entree to the gut politics of Washington. It also opened a new world of sexual opportunity and Chris made the most of that. A lot of what he learned, he learned from pillow talk. And the tidbits and secrets he gathered made the Fallon office one of the most tuned-in on the Hill.

The only disappointment that Chris had to face was sharing his friend Sally with the senator. Both Sally and Terry came from Houston and had made a nodding acquaintance somewhere up the trail. They began to spend a lot of time together, working, talking, planning. Fallon's wife was in an institution for the emotionally disturbed in Cleveland. Sally was an ideal surrogate at dinner parties and galas—articulate, attractive, widely recognized and respected around town through her years as a reporter on the *Post* and as press secretary to the Weatherby office. There was little idle gossip; it was said that once a month Fallon went to Cleveland to visit his deranged wife. If anything, social Washington wanted Fallon to divorce his wife and make Sally the next Mrs. Fallon. But they knew he wouldn't. He wasn't that kind of a man.

Chris didn't feel that way at first. He was worried about Sally. Terry Fallon was smooth, seamless. Sally was a hardworking career girl with little time for herself. If someone as charismatic as Terry took an interest in her, it was sure to turn her head. But Terry kept a respectful distance. And the more Chris watched them together, the more he realized that Sally could be a friend to both. That was good. While that arrangement lasted, Chris would do everything he could to further Terry's career. But if he ever thought Terry was taking Sally away from him. . . . If he ever thought that, he might become jealous. And if he did, there was no telling what Chris Van Allen might do.

Now, he steered Sally into the chow line of the hospital cafeteria. She rested her hands on her tray and her shoulders sagged with exhaustion.

"You're dead tired," he said.

"I'm okay."

"Check into the Mayflower and take a nap."

She yawned and put the back of her wrist to her mouth. "When this settles down."

Chris drew two cups of black coffee from the urn. "Sally, this won't settle down for five more years."

"You think he'll get it?"

"Could be." Chris put the cups on the tray, gave the cashier a dollar, led the way toward an empty table. They sat. Sally held her coffee mug with both hands, staring down at it as though she hadn't the strength to lift it.

"The president's in trouble in the cities," Chris said. "He's got a record on welfare that's criminal. The media think he's a doddering old fart. And they may be right. Terry's young. He's a veteran. He's GQ. Women and nonwhites think he's Rambo in pinstripes. As far as Baker is concerned, Terry was born to run."

Sally put her elbow on the formica tabletop, resting her chin in her palm. She listened patiently, but her eyelids fluttered with exhaustion.

"All of which means we're on our way to four amazing years." Chris stopped and looked at her. "For Pete's sake, Sally. I'm telling you Terry is going to be vice president, and you're falling asleep!"

12:20 P.M. IN A CALCULATED, oblique, but leading way, Speaker Charlie O'Donnell had just finished saying the same thing.

"That's the lay of it, Terry," he said. "That's what the party leadership is thinking. The president has reached no decision. But the party needs to know if you'd accept."

Terry eased down into his pillow. "What do you think, Charlie?"

"I believe a man who is called by his country must serve his country. But not if he knows his life is in danger."

"You think it's that bad?"

The old man put his hands together. "All of us, everyone in public life is a target. But you've already had one close call. No one would blame you if you didn't want to go on."

Terry knew that he was under observation. Finally, he said, "I have to follow my conscience, Charlie. Tell the leadership I'll think on it."

O'Donnell's eyes shone with admiration. "God bless you, son," he said, and rose heavily from his chair. "Terry, one more thing." He leaned over the bed. "We need to know . . . is there anything, any background we should talk about? Anything that might come out?"

Terry stared gravely. "Well," he said, "you know I never miss *Donahue*."

The old man laughed and Terry laughed with him. Then, his tone changed.

"Harriet," Terry said. "You know about my wife."

"Yes, poor soul, we do," O'Donnell said. "Terry, you know we'll be checking. Is there nothing more?"

"Absolutely nothing more."

O'Donnell stuck out his hand. Terry looked at it. Then he turned slightly in the bed and clasped it in his own. It was as though a momentous decision had been reached.

O'Donnell shook Terry's hand once firmly, then began to let go. But Terry held him fast.

"What about Vice President Eastman?"

"Yes," O'Donnell said. "Well." He nodded to himself. "Dan Eastman has served his party for fifteen years. If he has to, he'll serve his party now by stepping aside."

Terry gripped the old man's hand. "But how will he feel? How will he take it?" The concern in his face was genuine.

"Not well," O'Donnell said.

2:40 P.M. DAN EASTMAN KNEW something was up—and he had no intention of taking it well. It had been five hours since he had called the president. His call had still not been returned. He stood, leaning his fists on his desk while Ted Wyckoff, his political analyst, led him through the long sheets of computer runs.

"The good news is your scores haven't budged." Wyckoff pointed to the numbers as he ticked them off. "Most people know Dan Eastman is vice president of the United States." He ran his pencil down a row of numbers to the next boldface entry. "And most people rate you good-to-excellent. Here's the problem."

Wyckoff turned to the next page and the numbers jumped up and hit Dan Eastman in the face.

"A Baker-Eastman ticket, 47%. Loser," Wyckoff said. "A Baker-Fallon ticket, 53%. Winner."

"I can read," Eastman said darkly. He studied the sheet a moment longer. "Goddamit!" With an angry sweep of his arm, he cleared the desk. Then he dropped into his chair. Wyckoff bent to retrieve the documents scattered across the floor.

Eastman swiveled his chair and looked up at the official photograph of President Baker on his wall. He liked Baker, but he didn't trust him. He didn't trust him because he was a rich man's son, a Virginia gentleman, a Harvard graduate, a Wall Street lawyer, and a Unitarian besides. Sam Baker was everything that Dan Eastman had grown up envying and despising. Their political coalition had always been an uneasy one. Less than a year after they were elected, they tangled.

By then, Dan Eastman had become one of Washington's outspoken independents. He called former President Carter "a clown" and told Henry Kissinger to his face that he "single-handedly lost the war in Vietnam." When interest rates had gone up, he gave an interview to the *Washington Post* in which he said "the Federal Reserve is pimping for the big banks, and the American home buyer is taking the fall."

For a while it seemed that President Baker's phone was ringing off the hook with complaints about Eastman. Complaints from politicians, from congressional leaders, cabinet members, from the Pentagon, and the social doyens. Sam Baker finally took Eastman over the coals.

"You're embarrassing us," Baker said.

"I call them as I see them."

"You're costing us support on the Hill. If enough petty men turn against us, we won't be able to move the legislation the country needs."

"I don't like fakers," Eastman said. "I don't like rip-offs. I don't like liars."

"There are white chips and blue chips," Baker reasoned. "Let them have the white chips."

"No, Sam. You let them have the white chips. I know the difference between right and wrong."

Sam Baker stared at him a long moment. "I wish I believed it was that simple."

"You used to," Eastman said.

Now Dan Eastman saw that fate had handed President Baker a trump card—Terry Fallon. And he was sure that the ruthless men around the president would force Baker to play it.

Ted Wyckoff had gathered the fallen computer papers, set them on Eastman's desk. "You think the president would replace you on the ticket?" he said.

Eastman swiveled around in his chair. "He sent O'Donnell to see Fallon. What do you think they talked about? The weather?"

Eastman got up and paced to the far end of the room in angry strides. "We've got to break Fallon," he said. "I want Niles working on his voting record. Tell Davis to cross-check issues that—"

"Forget it," Wyckoff said.

Eastman looked up.

"There's no time. The convention starts in a week. He can't be taken on his voting record."

"What are you talking about?"

"You're not competing with the man," Wyckoff said. He put his hand on the stack of computer printouts. "It's the polls."

"But you said Baker and I can't win."

"You can't."

They stood a moment like that, staring at each other.

Then Wyckoff said quietly, "You just have to prove that Baker and Fallon can't win either."

"And how do I do that, smartass?"

"We get something on him. Something dirty. Something we can slip to the papers. It's his fucking record, not his voting record that we have to go after."

Eastman went around the desk, stood so close to Wyckoff they were almost touching. Then he stuck a finger in the smaller man's face, and his voice was a hoarse whisper. "Listen to me, you little bastard. We're not playing their dirty, shit-ass games."

Wyckoff smiled. "No, sir," he said.

6:30 P.M. THE SHADOW OF the Lincoln Memorial lengthened in the early summer evening, crept across and down the steps toward the Reflecting Pool. Mancuso walked along the edge of the still water. He was an aging gumshoe with spots on his tie, sagging polyester socks, and a cheap brown suit from Sears. His face was leathery and wrinkled, and he needed a shave. Beside him, Ross looked like the tweedy young lawyer that he was.

"Well, what do you think?" Ross finally said, as if he couldn't contain himself any longer.

"I think it sucks."

But Ross was elated. "Man, what an assignment. Somebody doses the guy with AIDS. Then Petersen shoots him. One victim, two murders. That's got to be a first."

"Yeah," Mancuso said. "And the big boys are into it."

"Huh?"

"That guy in O'Brien's office. Bender. He's from the White House. This is a command performance, kiddo."

"Well, I'm ready," Ross said and rubbed his hands together. "Which way do we go?"

Mancuso walked to the edge of the water and looked at his own reflection. "Maybe both. Maybe neither."

Ross did a take. "What do you mean, neither?"

"Clerical work. Go through the motions. Don't make waves. That's all they want."

Ross couldn't believe his ears. "Come on, Joe. . . ."

"A lame duck and a green kid on a hit like this? Use your head. If they wanted it busted, they'd assign a whole division."

"I don't care. I want to try to break it."

"Sure you do. Sure you do." Mancuso turned the corner of the pool, began to walk the perimeter east. "The trouble is, there's two horror shows out there. And I got a bad feeling that one of them knows we're coming."

He looked eastward the length of the Reflecting Pool. The Washington Monument stood glowing gold against the sky in the failing summer light. As long as he had been in Washington, as long as he had walked the Mall when he needed time to think, that image had stirred Joe Mancuso's heart. This evening was no exception.

Mancuso turned his collar up against the rising breeze. It would be night soon, and it was going to rain. He knew they would never solve this murder. He knew that if they really tried, they'd be lucky to come out of this alive.

He looked up at the perfect obelisk of the Washington Monument. He said, "If government worked the way it looked, this would be a great place to live." Then he shuffled his feet. Then he walked on.

6:40 P.M. IT HAD ALREADY begun to rain in Baltimore. The dripping soot blurred the outside of the dirty motel window. It was a different rain they had in North America, different from the rain in the tropics. A hard rain, a cruel rain, a numbing, beating, freezing rain that dulled the senses and chilled the blood.

Rolf Petersen lay naked on the damp, tangled sheets. He was forty-two, blond, and his muscles rippled his fair skin. At his fingertips lay a loaded .44 Smith & Wesson revolver, its safety off. He was thinking about the rain in the jungle north of Managua, remembering the soft tattoo on the roof, the way the warm mist brought the earth smell up through the bare board floor. He remembered how the smell and the damp mixed with the lust odor of his lover, how she writhed and bent in the night, and arched her back and raised him from the cot. He thought, and he grew hard.

After they fought and killed, they fucked. Savagely. It was as if the orgasm affirmed their survival. They walked on the bloody faces of their fallen enemies, then rolled together, seething and panting until they came. Then they rubbed his semen on their bodies, as though reanointing themselves with life.

Now, he lay in a motel room south of Baltimore, remembering the jungle 2,000 miles away. Only one person in the world knew where to find him. He touched the cold handle of the revolver. God help anyone else who tried.

THURSDAY, AUGUST 11, 1988

5:25 A.M. AROUND MIDNIGHT, SALLY had wrapped herself in a blanket and curled in the armchair beside the bed where Terry lay sleeping. Long after the cafeteria dinner, long after Chris Van Allen trundled home to bed, she sat watching Terry, listening to the soft brush of the rain at the windows, listening to the repetitive, reassuring *ping* of the cardiac monitor. She thought of her own comfortable bed, thought of going home and crawling into it. But she knew he might wake in the night and she wanted to be there for him if he did. At 2 A.M., a nurse roused her, showed her to the vacant room across the hall, laid a fresh gown and robe for her, and turned the covers down.

Sally arranged to have their calls routed to the room, undressed and slid between the cool sheets, let her body sink back into the thick, sustaining mattress. Her shoulders ached and her hands were stiff with writer's cramp. She lay back and shut her eyes. But she did not sleep.

She kept thinking of Speaker Charlie O'Donnell and the look on his face when he'd entered Terry's room. There was such haste in his eyes, such portent of things to come. She had always felt uneasy around O'Donnell. There were smarter men in Congress—shrewder men, too. But O'Donnell was the "master of the game." No one in Washington had more clout—not the president, not the chairman of the Joint Chiefs. No one was better informed—not the director of the FBI, not Ben Bradlee of the *Post*. No one had more stature—not even the chief justice. And no one could be more dangerous.

Charlie O'Donnell could make careers and break them. After thirty years on the Hill, his network of informers and his wealth of favors-owed gave him power and influence that approached omnipotence. He could move legislation or table it. He could advance "comers" or bury them.

Maybe he couldn't pass any law he wanted—but he could line up enough votes to defeat any bill, even—so they said—the Bill of Rights.

And now he had come to Terry Fallon's sick room, carrying a message from the president. . . .

Silently, under the cover of thickening darkness, Sally lay still in her bed, thinking of O'Donnell and the days to come. She was stepping over, she knew, into the realm of absolute power. She was crossing the threshold. Her eyes slowly closed, and behind her lids another iris opened—first in rays of gold and yellow, then in a dizzying spiral of white heat that soared and swelled until she was looking into a blast of blinding light, looking into the fusion of power, into the very furnace of energy that drives the stars. It seared her skin and raced her heart to bursting, it roared through her hair and made her gasp to catch her breath. It was all terror and all glory and all being. It was everything she feared. It was all she'd ever wanted.

It was the phone ringing.

"Yes, Chris?"

"You're gonna love this," he said.

Sally and Chris talked every morning at 5:30. He always called her. That way, she wouldn't know where he was sleeping unless he wanted her to. This morning, he wanted her to.

"Ted Wyckoff," Chris said. "Can you believe it?"

Sally pushed herself up on one elbow. "The guy who works for Eastman?"

"The same."

"You're right. I don't believe it."

Chris was sitting at the white wrought-iron table on the leafy little patio behind his townhouse in Georgetown. The first streaks of light were pinking the sky, and the early summer morning was heavy with the scent of jasmine. His slinky Jamaican houseman, Maurice, swept out the back door in his white linen caftan and put a cup of *cafe au lait* and a packet of gold-tipped cigarettes on the table before him.

"He's snoring away upstairs," Chris said. "Quite a pretty picture."

"But he always came on so . . . straight."

"Darling, you simply don't understand these things," Chris said. "Maybe I just bring out the beast in him." He giggled. "I can be such a queen."

Sally had to laugh.

"I'll give you three guesses what he wanted to talk about," Chris said. "And your first two don't count."

"Terry."

"Terry, Terry, only Terry. How he admires him. How he respects him. How much he'd love to be a part of the team when Terry is vice president."

44

That made her sit up. "You didn't say anything . . . Chris? Did you?"

"Sally, honestly. Don't you think I know when I'm being made?" Chris took another sip of coffee. "Now hear this. Wyckoff says he's had it on authority that Terry's brain-damaged from loss of blood, incapacitated, dysfunctional—a vegetable."

"What? That's ridiculous."

"Maybe. But that's what the town will be chewing this morning with their bacon and eggs. Remember. This is Foggy Bottom."

"Who the hell would spread a rumor like that?" Sally said, her anger rising.

"My guess . . . ?" There was a smirk in Chris's voice. "He's snoring away upstairs."

Sally sat a moment, silent. So it had begun. The Eastman team wanted the nomination—and if they were going down, they were going down hard. This was the opening skirmish, a fire-fight before the main battle. From now until the nomination was won or lost, Eastman's forces would probe Terry's lines looking for weakness. And if they found weakness, they would attack ruthlessly. Sally knew she had to move.

"Bedside press conference?" Chris said.

"No chance." Sally swung her legs out of bed and pulled on the hospital robe, changing the telephone from ear to ear to keep the conversation going. "Doctors and hospitals scare people out of their wits. I don't want the country plastered with pictures of Terry looking like an invalid. We've got to get out of the sick room before we get in front of the cameras. How soon can you be here?"

"Gee, boss, I was just going upstairs for a daybreaker."

"Twenty minutes."

"Yes, *bwana*," Chris said. He hung up.

Sally held down the button on the telephone and looked at her wristwatch. It was coming up on 5:30—soon, the network morning news shows would go on the air. This was Washington, and rumor was no pastime. It was a game for professionals: vicious, wicked, deadly. She punched the 212 area code, then the number of Steve Chandler's private line.

"How's your boy?" Chandler said.

"A-okay."

"What about this brain damage thing?"

So, the word had already hit New York. "Red herring," Sally said.

"Show me."

"We will."

"What about the number two spot?"

"No comment."

"O'Donnell went to see him."

45

"Just a courtesy call."

Chandler didn't buy that.

"Can you give me anything on background?" he said.

"Not today."

"Deep background?"

"Sorry."

"You owe me an interview."

"Steve, I can't."

"We made a deal."

"Terry's too hot. Stringer and Arledge would cut my throat."

Chandler didn't like it, but he knew she was right. The stakes were a lot bigger now. "Okay. What have you got for me?"

"We're rolling out at 7:30."

"Who else are you calling?"

"Nobody."

"Thanks," Chandler said, and punched the button that connected him to the NBC Washington Bureau.

Terry was still drowsy when she told him.

"We have to move to the house."

He looked up, blinking. "Why?"

"I'm sorry. We have to. Can you read this?" She handed him a white card. "Learn it."

He forced a smile. "Whatever you say."

At 6 A.M. Sally broke the news to General DeVane, the hospital administrator.

"That's idiotic," he said.

"Is the senator in any danger?"

"No. But he should stay a week for rest and observation."

"I'm sorry, General. We don't have a week."

He straightened. "We take no responsibility."

"Thank you, General."

Five minutes later, Agent Browning of the Secret Service was in the hallway outside Terry's room, asking to see her. Like all the men in the Secret Service, he was tall, muscular, colorless.

He was also startled. "Seven-thirty?"

"Yes."

"This morning?"

"Yes."

"That's—" he looked at his watch "—an hour and a half from now, ma'am."

"Right."

"Miss Crain, I have to insist—"

"Please don't."

He tried to reason with her. "This is a secure environment. The senator's home is not."

"Since when is the senator's home considered a security risk?"

"Miss Crain, the senator has been upgraded to class one protection. His home has not been surveyed for—"

"Upgraded? By whom?"

"The White House." He let the words hang there for emphasis.

"Seven-thirty," Sally said. "On the dot."

Browning shook his head. "Yes, ma'am," he said.

It was 7:25 when Browning returned to give his lecture. Sally and Chris stood at Terry's bedside.

"Senator, I'm Agent Browning of the Executive Protection Division. In class one protection, you will be traveling in a defensive bubble. There are advance men and flankers who will precede your party, and a close escort of six officers around your person. In case of emergency, these rings will fold in to protect you and your party. But we cannot guarantee your safety without your complete cooperation. Please follow my instructions without hesitation. You must now regard every moment you spend in public as a life-threatening situation." Then he said, "Thank you," without waiting for an answer, and nodded to the Secret Service man at the door.

"We need a moment for the press," Sally called after him.

"I'm sorry," Browning said as he went out. "No unscheduled stops."

It gave Sally an eerie feeling, traveling that corridor under the control of the Secret Service. It was reassuring and disturbing at the same time. The six officers surrounding the wheelchair wore bulletproof vests under their jackets, carried sidearms, and were never more than arm's length from Terry. The flankers carried stubby Uzi submachine guns for close combat or carbines for defense against snipers. And they all moved as a unit, timing each part of the trip so that doors were opened, elevators waited, hallways cleared just as Terry got there. It was very much like a "bubble" as it slid along around them.

Sally had never encountered anything like it. It gave her a bizarre, remote, separated feeling. The people whose votes might put them into office were pushed back, aside, held at a distance. Hospital orderlies and nurses simply shrank away. The barrier of Secret Service protection surged down the corridor ahead of her, silencing conversation like a cold wave of alienation. This, she suddenly realized, was the great paradox of power: that those who have the most power have the most to fear.

About the only people the Secret Service couldn't intimidate were reporters. Reporters had rights above and beyond those of mere mortals, and they pushed those rights to the limit if they were good reporters. So, they were there, even at this early hour—reporters, photographers, and news crews—hanging over the yellow police barriers in the driveway.

Agent Browning paused his men inside the door, waiting for a sign from outside.

"Excuse me, Agent," Sally said softly. "We really do need a moment for the press."

Browning had enough. "Miss Crain, if you interfere with the Secret Service, you are subject to arrest and detention—without bail—until we perceive that any danger to Senator Fallon is past."

Sally smiled. "You know, I've never been arrested on network television. Excuse me." She walked past Browning and out the door.

The roar of reporters' questions hit like a sonic boom.

"Sally, will Fallon accept the nomination?"

"Has he received death threats?"

"Will Eastman step aside?"

Sally smiled and scanned the group until she spotted Andrea Mitchell and the camera with the NBC peacock.

"May I have your attention!" Sally said, and the din quieted down. "Senator Fallon will have a brief statement. I'm sorry, no questions today. I'm sure you understand." She turned and waved toward the doors, as though cueing Terry and his escort.

Behind the solar glass, Browning stood watching her. "Goddamit," he muttered. An agent outside rapped on the door and nodded. "Move out," Browning ordered. Two agents swung the doors open and Terry's wheelchair rolled into the sunlight.

Sun-guns switched on. Strobes fired. The roar of questions mounted. As the wheelchair and its entourage hustled toward the open doors of the ambulance, Sally stood, seemingly nonchalant but squarely in the path of Browning and his men. The group rushed down upon her; Sally stood her ground. For a moment, it seemed that the group would run her down. Then, suddenly, Browning lifted his arm. The convoy stopped.

He glared at Sally. "One minute."

"Thanks." Sally turned Terry's wheelchair to favor the camera from NBC. All the reporters shouted for his attention at once.

Terry sat, unmoving, under the barrage. He didn't speak, didn't try to outshout them, didn't raise his hands for silence. He gave no indication that he would speak to them at all. He sat, patiently staring at the reporters waving and shoving behind the yellow police barrier. He stared at them in silence. Then something odd happened, something Sally had never witnessed before.

The reporters began to quiet down. One by one, they stopped shouting until they had all fallen silent, some shuffling their feet, some readying their notebooks, some simply wide-eyed and gaping.

Sally studied their faces. They were the same hacks, the same stringers, the same field crews who had covered the Martinez welcome and had become eyewitnesses to murder. But in their faces she saw something that had not been there on the day of the assassination: respect, reverence, even a sense of awe.

She could see that, to them, Terry Fallon was no longer a politician. He had become something else—the dream that all reporters live to cover: a genuine hero. Sally had been a reporter, and she knew how they thought.

In 1974, Sally had gone to work at the *Houston Post*. She had come back from two years in the Peace Corps, hoping to help make the Americas a better place. But what she had found in Houston was statutory theft on a scale that staggered her imagination. Oil money was pouring into the city like a Niagara. The city fathers and the rich-and-powerful decreed that the city would make a "great leap forward" to international prominence. That demanded a skyline. And for the sake of a skyline, all decency had to give way. Through a cabal of condemnations and demises, the barrios of the city were swept away by the great backhand of the courts. The lives of the poor were tossed up on the rubbish heap with the cinder blocks and tin roofs of their shanties. Sally walked through rubble that was worse than anything she had seen in Central America, listened to the wailing women, the bitter crying of the children. She wrote the stories that dogged her heels and wracked her nights with angry dreams. Then, every morning, she scanned the columns of the paper looking for a word, a sign, a signal that someone gave a damn. In the end, at the point of rage and hysteria, she confronted her editor with a sheaf of unpublished stories. He rolled a yellow pencil between his chubby fingers and heard her out.

"Miz Sally," her editor said—he always called the women on the staff *Miz*. "Miz Sally, you just don't get the joke. Buildings come and go. But Houston and the Hobbys go on and on." In that moment, he taught her the bitter lesson that every young idealist learns: only those with power have the power to change the world.

One man seemed willing to speak out for the poor. His name was Terry Fallon. He was a history instructor at Rice who was running for the city council in the very heart of the barrio. The old politicos snorted and ignored him. The media wouldn't even take him as filler. Even the Hispanics used him for a joke; they called him *El Gringo*.

But this Fallon was a tireless campaigner who spent every free minute walking the streets and alleys of the barrio, telling anyone who would listen that their fight could be won. His Spanish was flawless. His smile was engrossing. And he had a vision of a better way. Inevitably, his path crossed Sally's. Inevitably, they saw how much they had in common. Inevitably, he was engaged to be married to someone else. But she didn't care. She adored him and wrote about him anyhow. He was elected. Then Sally quit her job and headed north.

A friend who worked on the *Washington Post* got Sally a five-minute interview with Ben Bradlee. He took the first three minutes to thumb past her tearsheets and scan her sheaf of unpublished tirades. Then he squeaked back in his chair and got hold of his suspenders. "I wouldn't print this sentimental crap either," Bradlee said. He turned back to one of her published stories about Terry, tapped his finger on the photograph. "Were you screwing this guy?"

"No."

"Don't screw any politicians while you work for me," Bradlee said. "When a Washington politician fucks you, you stay fucked. See personnel. Welcome aboard."

She went back to Houston, closed her apartment, stuffed her things into her car and headed north. On her last day in Texas, the *Houston Post* carried the story of the fairytale wedding of heiress Harriet King to dashing Councilman Terry Fallon. Fourteen months later, the Deb-of-the-Year was in an institution. In 1978, Terry Fallon came to Washington as Congressman Fallon. That same year, Sally quit the *Post* to become press liaison for Texas Senator Caleb Weatherby. When Weatherby went to jail for bribery, Governor Taylor appointed Terry to fill his unexpired term. For Sally, their reunion was the fulfillment of a consuming dream. But, then again, she had always believed he would come. He was the man the people needed. He was a man to be followed. That is what she saw reflected in the wondering eyes of the reporters lining the driveway of Walter Reed Hospital.

Like Sally Crain, they believed.

In the silence, Terry spoke. "Today, all Americans mourn the death of Octavio Martinez," he said, his voice clear and fresh as a trumpet call. "Colonel Martinez was a patriot and a hero to free people everywhere. I speak now to his brothers-in-arms in the jungle. *Estará vengada su muerte.* His murder will be avenged." Terry was looking right down the barrel of the NBC camera. "To all of you who have expressed so much caring for my pain, thank you and God bless you. This wound is nothing," he said. "It's an honor to carry it."

Sally nodded to Browning. Instantly, the Secret Service escort rushed the wheelchair toward the ambulance.

Andrea Mitchell shouted, "What's next for you, Senator?"

Terry laughed. "I'm going to the convention. Aren't you?" He gave the thumbs up as the Secret Service whisked him aboard and slammed the ambulance doors behind him.

Sally turned to face the bank of cameras. "Senator Fallon will be recuperating for a few days. He will attend the presidential nominating convention as co-chairman of the Texas delegation. Thank you."

Agent Browning grabbed her arm and hustled her toward the last black Oldsmobile.

"Thanks," she said as they ran. "I owe you. And I don't forget."

"Neither do I," Browning said, and she knew he meant it, too.

The convoy of cars and ambulance rushed off with a squeal of tires and blaze of sirens. The reporters dashed to their vans to follow. In a moment, the driveway was deserted, except for two men.

One of them was Mancuso. He watched the ambulance and its escort disappear down the street. Then he spit on the pavement. "Hope Fallon skipped the blood test."

"Jesus, Joe!"

Mancuso turned toward the door of the hospital. He had a name written on a three-by-five card. He handed the card to Ross. "You do it," he said.

7:45 A.M. IT WAS HARD to drink coffee, read *The Wall Street Journal,* watch television, and go to work at the same time. But Howard Stringer, the president of CBS News, had the limousine and the knack. He had watched the live report on Senator Fallon leaving the hospital with a mixture of curiosity and pride. It always gave him a lift when his guys were on the spot where news was happening. Then Stringer remembered that he had tuned to Channel 4 and was watching NBC's *Today.*

"Shit," he said, and picked up the car phone and punched Recall-6.

Dave Corvo, producer of the *CBS Morning News,* answered almost immediately. "Yes, Howard?"

"Did we have that?"

Corvo was sitting in the West 57th building, just across from the set of the *CBS Morning News.* But he had all three networks on the monitors before him. "You mean Fallon?"

"Yes, I mean Fallon."

Corvo knew from the sound of his voice that his boss was at the limit of his patience. "No. We didn't have it."

"Well, goddamit, why not?"

"Sally Crain must have tipped Chandler."

"Sally who?"

"The blond. The press girl."

"For Christ's sake, she practically did a stand-up for them!"

"Look, Howard," Corvo said, and he was beginning to lose his composure, too. "Chandler's got her in his pocket. What do you want from me?"

"Get to her!" Stringer shouted into the phone. "Reach her! Am I the only person in this fucking organization who realizes that Terry Fallon is going to be vice president of the United States!"

7:50 A.M. MANCUSO SAT IN the corner office of General Green, the hospital administrator, listening to Ross's long string of dull questions. Walter Reed was an army hospital and full of uniforms and brass. Mancuso had been in the army. And he hadn't liked it a bit.

Mancuso's educational deferment had expired when he graduated from law school in May of 1952. A month later, he was drafted. He had just started looking for a job. There was an Irish girl who lived on Ocean Parkway—Mary Louise Dugan—with whom he'd been keeping company for a year, too. But the Korean War was ending in an uneasy truce. Mancuso was called, and he thought he was needed.

After basic at Fort Bragg, he was transferred to Scofield Barracks on Oahu, not far from the site of Pearl Harbor. When he got his first weekend pass, he went down to Pearl and took the harbor tour.

It was one of those bright, breezy tropical days that you see on all the travel posters. There was a warm sun, flying clouds. The tour launch stopped near the old battleship docks on Ford Island, and the guide led everyone to the port side, pointed down into the water. Beneath his feet, lying just below the surface of the bay, Mancuso could make out the shape of the battleship *Arizona*. Tiny bubbles of oil rose from the sunken ship, and a blue slick hazed the surface of the sea. Eleven hundred men were entombed there, a few fathoms down, trapped when Japanese torpedoes struck the ship at her moorings. The ship's aerial protruded from the water, and the Stars and Stripes flew from its tip, standing out stiff in the westerly breeze. The tourists on the launch gawked, goofed, and chattered among themselves. But Mancuso pressed his lips together. He found it hard to swallow. Under the water of the bay, among the ghostly shadows of the *Arizona*, he thought he saw what it meant to serve his country. The army had other ideas.

They assigned him as assistant gardener for a two-star general. Mancuso trimmed hedges, pruned bougainvillea, and spread manure. He finally made sergeant and transferred to the military police. That was skunk work, too: breaking up fights, carrying drunken marines out of whorehouses, raiding dice games. Two months before Mancuso's hitch was up, a recruiter from the FBI came to see him.

The man had a great spiel—engrossing stories of lone agents with only their guts and gumption to go on, hunting notorious desperadoes. The 1950s were going to be an era of rapid expansion for the Federal Bureau of Investigation, he told Mancuso. The FBI was evolving into a sophisticated national police force, our front line of defense against domestic communism. McCarthyism was rampant, the House Un-American Activities Committee was big news, the Hollywood blacklist was growing. The FBI was a great career for a young lawyer who wanted excitement and a chance to serve his country.

It sounded right to Mancuso. He signed up, grabbed his discharge, and went to San Francisco. That Irish girl from Ocean Parkway—Mary Louise Dugan—was waiting for him in a hotel on the Embarcadero in a white linen shift and nothing else. Four days later, they took a bus to Reno and got married. They had their picture taken in front of a huge, six-tiered, plaster-of-paris wedding cake. Then they flew east and Mancuso reported to the FBI training camp in Quantico, Virginia, for a three-month course. He signed up for specialist training in electronics. After the first lab class, he realized that meant wire-tapping. Mary Louise found a studio apartment for them. They had a mattress on the floor for five months before they could afford a bed. Back then, a mattress on the floor was all they'd needed.

In those days, clandestine microphones were still the size of silver dollars and miniaturized tape recorders were science fiction. The only way to pull an effective electronic surveillance was to put a tap on every phone line that a suspect used. Mancuso was transferred to Los Angeles to set taps for the HUAC surveillance of the entertainment business. He spent a lot of time in the basements of buildings on Wilshire Boulevard and Canon Drive. He particularly liked tapping the lines of the William Morris agents. They had the best jokes—and they had them first. The FBI guys used to argue about who got the Morris office and who got Jack Warner. They were the only people in town who were always good for a laugh.

On his first assignment, Mancuso asked to see the authorizing warrant. But the special agent in charge brushed him off, said the warrant was "on file." After a while, Mancuso realized there weren't any warrants. The taps were unofficial. They were just a way for Hoover to sop up Hollywood's filth and find a few tidbits he could feed to McCarthy. And Hoover kept the investigations unofficial so that, if McCarthy went down, the Bureau wasn't dragged down with him. McCarthy went down in 1954 and the Bureau moved on to civil rights.

Mancuso had nothing against blacks. But he had no affinity for them either. So when all the black power agitation began in the winter of 1955, Mancuso couldn't figure what all the shouting was about. In February of 1956, he was transferred to the zone office in Montgomery, Alabama. It was an angry time. The blacks said if they couldn't ride the front of the buses, they wouldn't ride the buses at all. Normally, the white folks didn't give a whit if the blacks rode or walked or stayed home. Except most of the people who rode the buses in Montgomery were black, and twenty black nickels made a dollar just like twenty white nickels. And without all those millions of black nickels, well, running the buses in Montgomery would break the city bank. So, the city fathers were pissed but powerless.

All this consternation was due to a young black preacher named King. He wasn't doing anything illegal by organizing the bus boycott. But, then again, he wasn't exactly helping to build brotherhood and community spirit in Montgomery, either. So, Mr. Hoover decided that the Bureau should get to know Dr. King a little better. And the quickest way to do that was to tap his phone. That, Mancuso did for seven weeks, listening to King and his wife organize rallies, gossip about their neighbors, order pizza, and generally conduct the monotonous life of a happily married couple. King was not a Communist. He was not a traitor. He was not a drug addict. He was simply a man with a different idea about the way things should be. Mancuso recommended the tap be terminated. Instead, the special agent in charge of the Montgomery field office called him in for a chat.

"Joe, you and me, we need to have a come-to-Jesus meeting," the man said. His name was Griffiths and he wore suspenders and a bow tie and yellow buckskin shoes. "You not from around *heah*, but most of the boys kinda like you. Which is unusual for a fella from New York and a *Eye-talian*."

Mancuso sat across the desk in a double-breasted suit with a crisp white handkerchief in his pocket showing three points. He'd been told that Mr. Hoover liked a man who showed clean linen and he never went to work without a nice fresh pocket handkerchief.

"These *nigras* is up to no good and you don't seem to want to find them out," Griffiths said.

"King's no criminal," Mancuso said. "He's a reverend."

"He's as reverend as my monkey's uncle," Griffiths said. "And Mr. Hoover'll decide who's a criminal and who ain't. How'd you get so sweet on *nigras* anyhow?"

"I'm not."

Griffiths fingered a stack of typewritten transcripts. "Well, your reports sure make 'em sound like you over there keeping company."

"If those are no good, why don't you make up your own and send them in?"

They sent Mancuso west to Nevada, where he could eavesdrop on white people and his fluency in Italian might be of some use.

It was the start of a long series of bad bounces and lateral moves that took him everywhere and nowhere, until he sat listening to Dave Ross ask a routine, boring set of questions in a doctor-general's office at Walter Reed Army Hospital.

General Green handed a thick file to Ross. "This is the workup on Colonel Martinez."

"Including the names of the doctors who conducted the tests?"

"Yes, yes," Green said. "It's all there."

Ross thumbed the file. "The blood tests, for example?"

"The yellow form. Yes. That one."

Ross found it.

Mancuso watched Green. There was no hesitation in him, no flicker of emotion when Ross mentioned the blood tests. If anything, Green was impatient and as bored as he was.

"This . . . Captain Beckwith," Ross said. "He drew the blood and ran the tests?"

"Yes."

"Would he be in the office today?"

"No. I told you. Thursday's his day off. He's probably home."

Ross started to page back through his notes, looking for the reference to Thursday. But Mancuso reached over and flipped his notebook closed.

"Thank you, General," Mancuso said, and stood up to go. Ross didn't understand. But he knew enough to take his cue.

Mancuso swung his black Ford across the 14th Street bridge. The address in Captain Beckwith's file was in Arlington—and that bridge to Virginia was like a passage to another world.

Once, the hills west of the Potomac had been a patchwork of forests and fields from Leesburg to Mount Vernon. Mancuso used to take a drive there every now and then when Mary Louise was alive. Now, government and urban sprawl had gobbled up the farms and fields and memories, and the forests around McLean hid the headquarters of the CIA. What was left for human beings was street after street of cookie-cutter houses stamped across the bulldozed, treeless hills. The human evidence—a bike here, a hedge there, a limp basketball hoop hung over a garage—only added to the unreality. Mancuso turned his car north on Cadwell Drive. But it could have been Carson Drive or Carlisle Drive or Canter Drive. It was all the same now. He looked down the street and shuddered. It was contemporary civilization.

Ross studied the numbers stenciled on the curb.

"3121, 3123. There it is," Ross said. "The white one. 3125."

"They're all white," Mancuso said. He drove on by.

"Hey? Where you going?"

"See the front door?"

"What about it?"

"It was open."

Ross twisted around in his seat, looked back at the house. The door was ajar.

"Uh-oh," Ross said.

Mancuso turned the corner and parked in the next block. They walked up the street until they could see the rear of the Beckwith house. Mancuso looked around. The street was perfectly still. It was 8:45. Husbands and other workers had left for their offices, children for school. Housewives were still hanging around their kitchens over a second cup of coffee. There was an eerie stillness. It might have been a ghost town.

"Come on," Ross said, and walked up the driveway.

Mancuso followed him. There was a six-foot cyclone fence between the two backyards.

"What do you think?" Ross said.

Mancuso looked through the fence at the rear of the Beckwith house. The blinds were drawn in the upstairs bedroom windows. An air conditioner in one of the windows was humming. The downstairs louvered windows of the kitchen were open. There was a girl's bicycle leaning against the side of the garage. A Buick with a blue U.S. Army officer tag was in the driveway.

"Looks quiet."

They stood a moment.

"Well, we're here," Ross finally said.

"Yeah."

Mancuso leaned against a fence post.

"I'm going over there, Joe," Ross said.

"Yeah. I figured." Mancuso raised his foot. "Gimme a lift up."

Ross squatted down, locked his fingers, and made a step for Mancuso. When the older man caught hold of the top of the fence, Ross straightened up quickly, lifted him up and over. Mancuso lost his grip and fell ass-over-teakettle on the other side.

"Jesus Christ!"

"Are you all right?" Ross couldn't keep from laughing.

Mancuso got up, brushing himself off. "What are you, a fucking comedian?"

"I'm sorry. I didn't mean to—"

"Goddamit," Mancuso said. He slapped at the stubborn dirt on the knees of his trousers. "Come on."

Ross pulled himself to the top of the fence, swung a leg over. Then his trousers caught on the bare wire at the top. There was a long, loud sound of ripping as he jumped to the ground. He landed on all fours.

"Christ, I almost tore my balls off." He felt the back of his pants. "Aw, shit."

"Keep it down." Mancuso grabbed his arm and turned him around. "Let me see."

Ross's trousers were torn up the back from the crotch to the belt.

"They're ripped, aren't they?" Ross said.

"What a fucking clown."

"Oh, Jesus, they are ripped," Ross said, feeling the length of the tear. "Shit, I just got these. Forty-seven bucks."

"Take them back. Tell them they leak. Come on," Mancuso said. They hunkered down, hurried to the back of the house, and knelt below the kitchen window.

Mancuso stopped to catch his breath. He felt ridiculous. He was a middle-aged man with dirty knees and a partner with his pants torn clean up the back. They were sneaking around the back of a perfectly middle-class house in a perfectly middle-class neighborhood like a couple of kids on Halloween. If anyone spotted them, he thought the embarrassment would kill him. He was three months from retirement. And he knew it was time his years with the Bureau should draw to a close.

"What about it?" Ross said.

"Lemme take a look."

Mancuso raised his head to the windowsill and peeked inside. It was a typical boring modern kitchen in a typical boring development house: there were notes pinned to the refrigerator with magnetic fruit, a hanging plant in a macramé holder, a tall glass jar filled with different kinds of pasta. There was a pot on the stove. It was boiling over.

Mancuso stared at the pot. And as he did, his body went wet and clammy all over. He ducked down.

"Trouble," he said, and drew his revolver. Ross did the same.

"What is it?"

Mancuso leaned back against the aluminum siding of the house. He didn't answer. Ross watched him carefully. There were little beads of sweat on Mancuso's forehead.

"Are you okay?" Ross said.

"Yeah, yeah," Mancuso said. "Come on." He pressed his body against the wall of the house, slid forward toward the back door. Ross inched along behind him. When they reached the door, Mancuso stopped. He seemed to be staring at the knob. Ross didn't understand; he nudged him. Finally, Mancuso reached up and tried the knob. It turned easily in his hand.

Mancuso sat back down, resting on his haunches.

"Fuck," he said softly. "Fuck. Fuck. Fuck."

"What's the matter?"

"Nothing." Mancuso reached for the door knob again. "Cover."

Ross caught his arm. "You cover."

Mancuso stopped, looked back at the younger man. "Thought I told you never volunteer."

"Thought I told you to go fuck yourself," Ross said and smiled.

Mancuso sat where he was a moment. Then he slid back to let Ross take his place at the door. "Keep your head down," he said. He cocked his revolver and turned to the window.

Ross cocked his revolver. He looked back at Mancuso and took a deep breath. Mancuso inched up until his eyes and the barrel of the revolver cleared the sill. Then he whispered, "Go."

Ross slowly turned the doorknob. The lock clicked free and the door swung slowly back, revealing the empty kitchen. Ross got down on his hands and knees and began to creep across the threshold. As he did, Mancuso caught sight of his undershorts sticking out of his torn trousers.

"What a fucking sight you are," Mancuso hissed.

But Ross didn't answer. He crept forward across the linoleum floor, leaning against the cabinets. He had done this drill a hundred times at the FBI rookie camp at Quantico. They had taught him that a startled assailant was more likely to fire his first shot at waist level or above, and that the kick of the gun would send his second shot higher. They had trained Ross to come in low. They had also issued him a Colt .45 automatic. Mancuso made him leave that in his locker, made him buy and carry a Smith & Wesson .38 revolver. Automatics jammed, revolvers did not. Ross reached the end of the row of cabinets. Around the corner lay the hallway to the front of the house. His heart was pounding. He stopped to catch his breath. He could not see Mancuso at the windowsill; the cabinets and sink were in the way. But he knew Mancuso was watching the hallway. Ross crept to the edge and peeked inside.

Just around the corner was a young girl, maybe ten years old, wearing a pink cotton nightie with a ruffle at the neck. She was lying on the linoleum, staring straight into Ross's eyes. He jumped back. But when he looked again, he could see the pool of blood under her cheek was already drying, already turning black. Her mouth was open and there were bumps in her forehead, as though something had tried to break out from inside her brain. Then he saw that she had been shot twice in the back of the head, just below the rubber band that held her blond pony tail.

Ross felt his stomach churn. He clapped his hand to his mouth to cover the sound of his gasping breath. His head spun on a wave of nausea and a rush of vomit burned up his throat. He gasped and gulped it down. Then something stirred behind the swinging door to the dining room. He whirled and leveled his revolver and he screamed at the top of his lungs.

"Stop where you are!"

The door swung open and a black-and-white Cocker spaniel trotted into the kitchen. It stopped, looked at Ross. He was drenched in sweat. He didn't know whether to laugh or cry. He lowered his revolver. The dog trotted past him to the body of the girl. It sniffed her face. Then it began licking the blood from the floor.

Ross puked.

Ross was hanging on to the toilet bowl in the hall bathroom of the Beckwith house when Mancuso came downstairs. Mancuso holstered his revolver and started picking through the contents of a wallet. He pulled out a U.S. Army ID card. Ross lay his cheek against the cold porcelain of the toilet, gulping deep breaths of fresh air.

"Captain Arnold Beckwith," Mancuso read. "Hema . . . hemato . . . fuck, who cares?" He stuck the card back in the wallet.

Ross took a handful of toilet paper, wiped his mouth. "Is he dead?"

"Does the Pope wear a beanie? In the den. Guess the dog didn't like him."

"Why?"

"It took a leak on his corpse."

Ross puked again.

"College boys." Mancuso said, and went out into the hall until Ross was done.

"This isn't murder," Mancuso said, when Ross finally flushed the bowl and came out of the bathroom. "This is butcher work."

The body of a middle-aged woman in a flowered housecoat was spread-eagled on the stairs, head down on the second step, legs above her, akimbo. There were streaks of blood on the wall behind her and blood soaking a dark patch into the rug where her head lay.

Mancuso had it cased.

"Shooter came in the front door, went to the den, said 'Hiya, Doc,' and iced him." Mancuso pointed to the stairs. "Wife heard the noise, came running down. Shooter steps into the archway, pops her in the eye from over there. Not a bad shot."

Ross followed Mancuso back up the hallway to the kitchen. "Little girl tries to run out the back door. Pop-pop. Very neat. Very pro."

Mancuso turned off the flame under the boiling pot. Then he sniffed the rising steam. "Minestrone. My favorite."

Ross leaned against the door, dizzy and sick and angry. "Who the hell would do a thing like this?"

Mancuso just stared at him as though he had said the dumbest thing in the world.

Ross was just about to ask him again when the loudspeaker from the street opened up.

"You in the house! Attention!"

Ross and Mancuso went to their knees. They looked at each other.

The loudspeaker roared again. "This is Captain Brewster of the Arlington police. You are surrounded. Throw down your weapons and come out with your hands over your head."

"Fuck me," Mancuso said softly.

Ross shrugged, stood, opened the back door, and began to raise his hands.

Mancuso sighed. "Don't do that . . ."

A burst of automatic rifle fire from the backyard cut through the kitchen windows, shattering the venetian blinds. Ross dove for the floor. Then a cross fire of automatic weapons opened up from outside the front of the house. The bullets stitched through the kitchen walls, shattered the glass of the stove, blew the refrigerator open, broke the bottles inside, shattered the dishes in the cabinets above the sink. Mancuso and Ross clung to the linoleum, covering their heads as the salvo went on and on and glass and plaster showered down upon them.

"Christ!" Ross shouted over the firing. "What the hell is the matter with them?"

"They're scared," Mancuso shouted back. "Somebody told them the guys in the house just killed three people."

"Who told them that?!"

"The guy who killed the three people, asshole!"

The roar of the automatic weapons rose to deafening. The kitchen became a whirling storm of splintered wood and shattered china.

Finally, Mancuso rolled over on his back and drew his revolver.

"What the hell are you doing?" Ross shouted.

"If it's okay with you, I'm going to surrender." Mancuso threw his revolver out the empty window frame. "We give up!" he shouted. "Hold your fire!"

Eventually, the shooting stopped.

9:05 A.M. TED WYCKOFF WAITED in the anteroom outside the vice president's office. He had no news—and that was bad news. At last, Dan Eastman excused himself from his meeting with the NASA planning group and came out.

"What have you got?" Eastman said.

"Nothing."

They walked down the hall to Eastman's private study.

"Did you see the *Today* show?"

"No," Wyckoff said.

"Moron! They beat you to the punch."

They went inside and Eastman slammed the door.

"I told you no games," Eastman said, and there was a cold, deep-running rage in his voice. "I told you to get into his voting record."

"We did," Wyckoff said, and he wasn't backing down. "There's nothing there."

"So, you put the word out that Fallon's a vegetable? Goddamit!"

"I didn't do it."

"You're a liar."

They stood, staring at each other. Then Wyckoff smiled. "Sure I am," he said. He put his hand on the bar built into the paneled bookcase. "Mind if I have a drink?"

"For Christ's sake, it's nine o'clock in the morning."

"I said, do you mind?"

"Do what the hell you please," Eastman said. He went over and sat on the couch and slapped his feet up on the coffee table. "Shit," he said.

Wyckoff measured out a stiff belt of Scotch. "Let me tell you about our friend Mister Fallon. . . ." Then he raised his glass in a toast. "Success." But Eastman ignored him. Wyckoff took a drink. Then he propped himself on the edge of the desk and crossed his legs.

"Yesterday, I pulled in all the sources, squeezed every contact, called every marker. And you know what I found out about Fallon?"

"What?"

"Nothing." He took a long drink. "Not a goddam thing."

Eastman sat silent. He watched Wyckoff. The man was grinning like the Cheshire cat.

"Make your point," Eastman finally said.

"The guy taught history at Rice. He was a goddam instructor at Rice in 1976, for Christ's sake. Now he's in the Senate of the United States, and if we're not careful, he's going to be vice president and we'll be on our way back to South Philly."

"What are you talking about? Make sense."

"I'm telling you it's a fairy tale."

"So what?"

"Fairy tales never happened."

Eastman didn't understand.

"Listen to me, Dan. I'm telling you there's nothing to find. The guy's Mr. Clean."

"So?" ·

"Nobody's that clean," Wyckoff said. "Not even Santa Claus." He came over and sat at the other end of the couch. "I've talked to everybody I can find. I was on the phone to Texas half the night."

"And what did you do the other half?"

Wyckoff started to answer, but Eastman abruptly held up his hand. "Forget I asked."

"You know who put him into Congress?" Wyckoff said.

"Who?"

"Nobody. His congressional district in Houston is a barrio. There's no special interest money even if Fallon wanted it."

"So, the guy campaigned. He worked. He won a seat fair-and-square."

"What about Governor Taylor?" Wyckoff said. "Why did he pick Fallon to serve out Weatherby's term?"

"Everybody knows why. Taylor was looking for a white knight."

Wyckoff began to laugh.

"What's so funny?" Eastman said.

But Wyckoff couldn't stop laughing. Then Eastman reached over and grabbed his lapel.

"I said what's so goddam funny?"

"You are," Wyckoff said. "You really believe in the American dream."

Eastman threw his lapel back at him. Then he got up and went to the door and yanked it open.

"Get out," he said.

But Wyckoff didn't move.

"I said, get out."

"It's pussy," Wyckoff said softly.

"What?" Eastman said. Then he shut the door.

"Fallon's wife's in a looney bin. She's been there since 1977."

"And?"

"Who's he been screwing in the meanwhile?"

"Who?"

"Nobody."

"Nobody?" Eastman said, and he was beginning to get the drift.

"Nobody." Wyckoff took another sip of scotch.

"I don't believe it."

"I don't believe any of it."

"What about that blond?" Eastman said. "The press girl who works for him?"

"Sally Crain? No."

"You're sure?"

"I got it straight from that creepy little fuck, Van Allen. Anyhow, it's too obvious.'' Wyckoff stood up and went back to the bar. ''No. With this guy it's going to be something real dark and real secret and real, real ugly.'' He put his empty glass down. ''Now, if you have no objection, I think I'll find out what it is.''

He waited. Dan Eastman stood where he was a moment. Then he opened the door and went back down the hall to his meeting.

''Thanks for the drink,'' Wyckoff said to the door closing behind him.

9:35 **A.M.** MANCUSO HAD TO say one thing for Arlington, Virginia. They had a nice jail, and the chow wasn't bad. It was a better breakfast than he usually got in the Bureau cafeteria. Ross didn't feel like eating, so Mancuso ate his, too.

''How the hell can you eat?'' Ross said in disgust. ''Jesus, it was a slaughterhouse.''

''Yeah, right,'' Mancuso said, his mouth full.

''Fuck.'' Ross hung on the bars of the cell door. ''When are we getting out of here?''

''What's your hurry?''

Ross turned on him. ''You really don't care if we break this thing, do you?''

Mancuso went on eating.

''You didn't want to go in that house,'' Ross said.

''Give it a rest.''

''When you saw the back door was open, you sat down on your chops and didn't want to go inside.''

Mancuso looked up. ''Come on,'' he said wearily, and bit into another sausage.

''Hey, Joe. I got eyes. I saw it.''

Mancuso went on chewing until he had finished the sausage. Then he wiped his mouth. ''So?''

''How come?''

''What do you care?''

''I want to know.''

Mancuso sat a long moment on the edge of his bunk. In his dirty pants and open-collar shirt, he looked old to Ross, older than Ross had ever known him. The jailers had taken away their belts and shoelaces and their neckties. Sitting there with the tongues of his shoes hanging out, Mancuso seemed a shadow, a memory, an old man with no place to go. ''Maybe I was scared,'' Mancuso said.

"Scared of what?"

Mancuso shrugged, looked down at the tin plate on his knees. "Maybe I'm not up to it any more."

Ross looked down at the older man and there was much kindness and compassion in his face. Then he said, "You know, Joe, you're full of shit."

Mancuso went back to his breakfast.

"You weren't scared when the Arlington police opened up," Ross said. "I was looking right at you. They could have made chopped liver out of us. You weren't scared at all."

Mancuso waved it away with his fork. "Those locals can't hit a cow in the ass with a bucket."

Ross said softly, "Cut the shit, Joe."

But Mancuso wouldn't answer.

Ross sat down on the opposite bunk. "Somebody got to that general at Walter Reed before us, didn't they?" he said quietly. "Somebody else got Doctor Beckwith's name and address."

Mancuso shrugged. "Maybe."

"Somebody's trying to cover this up—and they're half a jump ahead of us."

"Maybe."

"Who is it, Joe?"

Mancuso shook his head.

"I think you know," Ross said, and he was starting to lose his temper.

"I don't know," Mancuso said. "And if you've got any sense, you don't want to know either."

Ross stood up. He was angry. "Well, if you thought somebody was laying for us in that fucking house, why didn't you call for some goddam backup?!"

And in the next moment he realized that he had answered his own question.

They stayed like that a while, Mancuso looking at the tin plate, Ross staring down the hallway. Then Ross said, "Jesus Christ. . . ."

"I don't know," Mancuso said. "But we gotta have a plan."

"What plan?"

The heavy steel door at the end of the corridor slid open. Supervisory Special Agent Barney Scott of the FBI was standing behind it, hands on his hips. He wasn't happy. The police lieutenant next to him said, "That them?"

Scott scratched his balls.

"Okay. Turn 'em out," the lieutenant said.

Somewhere out of sight, a guard flipped a switch and a huge groaning of metal sounded as the bolts on the cell began to move. Ross handed Mancuso his jacket.

"I was scared, too," Ross said. But the noise of metal on metal was so loud that Mancuso didn't hear him.

9:45 A.M. BY THE TIME the Secret Service had swept Terry's home in Cambridge, Maryland, for internal bugs, microwave transmission, explosives, clandestine microphones and cameras, sniper angles and salients, they had compiled a list of do's and don'ts that would have satisfied a Jewish mother:

Don't answer the phone or front door; the Secret Service will do both. Don't sit in the front parlor until the glass is replaced with bulletproof. All mail, gifts, foodstuff, and parcels that enter the house must go through an X-ray and an electronic sniffer to detect explosives. The two front upstairs bedrooms are off-limits (too vulnerable to snipers). The rear patio and swimming pool, too (until the adjoining neighbors can be vetted and the block secured).

Terry stretched wearily on the curving leather sofa in his robe and pajamas, listening to the director of the security survey unit. Sally listened, too—and as she did, a new life took shape before her.

There would be men in the house from now on; armed men who took turns watching the children on bicycles and the milkman and mailman on Crescent Drive. Men in dark, nondescript suits would begin knocking on the doors of unsuspecting people who were family and friends of Katrina, the tubby Danish housekeeper, and Jenny, the cook, asking a lot of questions about their politics and their habits. Someone would stop by to visit Roy, the gardener, and ask a long list of questions about the men who cut the lawn and pruned the fruit trees. And Matsuda, the pool man whose Nisei parents were interned in 1942, would get even more of the same.

Everyone who came to the house, whether lifelong friend or party associate or visiting dignitary or member of the clergy—all would have to present credentials and be identified, all would pass through an airport-style metal detector, all would be videotaped coming and going, their automobile license plates noted and checked.

Sally listened to the litany of rules and regulations with a growing feeling of sadness and alienation. It was another bubble of protection, but one that would constantly lie upon their shoulders like a smothering blanket. It was an end to accessibility, it was an end to privacy. It was the start of a life in retreat.

When he was finished, the director put a copy of the typewritten list and his card on an end table. Then he said, "Thank you, Senator," and left. Agent Browning followed. When they had gone, Terry put his head back on the pillow and sighed, let his eyes roll shut.

Sally waited. She looked at Chris. Chris shrugged. They watched Terry together until they were sure he was asleep. Then Sally nodded to Chris. They rose and began to tiptoe toward the door.

"Are you going?" Terry's voice said behind them.

Sally turned. "We thought you were—"

"No, no," he said, and there was a little weak smile in the corners of his mouth. "It's all the tension. The security. The men-at-arms. There's never been a gun in this house before. What's happening to this country?"

Chris took a long breath. Then he stared at the floor without trying to answer.

But Sally went to Terry, knelt beside the couch, took his hand in hers. "We have to change it. We have to make it better."

"I don't know," Terry said. "I don't know any more."

"We can if we believe we can. We can if we start today."

Terry smiled. He touched her arm. "Not today. Today I'm going to sleep until tomorrow. You do the same."

"There's so much to do."

"No," he said. "We all need a rest. Take the day off. Come back tomorrow."

"I'll go downtown and get my things. I'll stay in the guest house until we go to the convention," she said. "Chris will take me."

"Sure," Chris said from the door. "In my bulletproof Toyota."

Terry smiled at her and lay his hand against the side of her face. She snuggled into it, into the warm hollow of his palm. And she heard him say, half-aloud, to no one and to everyone, "What's the matter with this country? Have we all gone mad?"

10:10 A.M. ". . . COUPLE OF FUCKING dopes . . . whole fucking house shot to shit . . . be filling out those fucking goddam reports until Christmas, for Christ's sake." Barney Scott muttered as he paged through the Martinez autopsy report. Mancuso and Ross, in a pair of cotton work pants, stood in the center of his office, shifting from foot to foot, uneasy.

"I don't see nothing about AIDS," Scott said, and slapped the file closed.

"It's in there," Ross said. "I read it."

Scott threw the file across his desk. "Show me."

Ross thumbed through the papers and found the yellow form. Mancuso plunked himself down in the corner looking very bored. Scott stared hard at Mancuso.

"Shot up the fucking house like a goddam fucking cheese," Scott said.

"Wasn't my idea."

"Did I ever tell you you're a shmuck?"

"Yeah," Mancuso said. "You're real free with the compliments."

Ross looked up. "I don't get it. It was right in—"

"In your fucking imagination," Scott said.

Mancuso sat, picking his ear. "Call the Doc," he said. "He'll tell you."

"Which Doc?"

"What's-his-name. Summers. Forensics. The four-eyes."

"Yeah. I'll do that," Scott said and made a note to himself. "I'll do that."

Ross glared at Mancuso.

"Although . . ." Mancuso scratched his chin. "Maybe he was talking about hearing aids."

That got Scott's attention. "Hearing aids?"

"Yeah," Mancuso said. "You get it from listening to assholes."

Scott sat back, really angry. "Get the fuck out of here!"

They did.

Ross caught up with Mancuso in the corridor.

"What did you do that for?"

"What?" Mancuso kept walking.

"Set up Doc Summers. Goddam it, Joe, you just fed him to Scott."

"Gimme a break."

"Don't fuck with me, Joe." Ross was really angry. "You did it. I heard you."

They stopped at the elevator. Mancuso pushed the button.

He said softly, so softly Ross could barely make out the words, "We got to find out if Scott's on our side."

But Ross was hot. "What happens to Summers if he isn't?"

"Shut up, Dave," Mancuso said, and looked up and down the hall.

"What happens to him?"

Mancuso shrugged. "Life's a bitch."

Ross looked like he wanted to spit. "For Christ's sake, Joe."

The elevator doors opened. They stepped inside. Mancuso pressed the button for the lobby.

Ross said, "Now, listen to me, Joe—"

But Mancuso smiled and took hold of his arm, his grip like a vise. Ross broke off in midsentence. His eyes followed Mancuso's to the front of the car. Above the control panel was a small black speaker grating. Above that, the lens of a television camera.

"Don't you think you're overdoing it?" Ross said when they were out on E Street.

"You listen to me," Mancuso said. "In 1954, the Bureau had me catching Commies for McCarthy. Now they say McCarthy's a dirty word. In 1956, they sent me to bug some black preacher in Alabama. Now his birthday's a national holiday. In 1971, I went to Canada after conscientious objectors. Then Carter gave them amnesty and a party at the Kennedy Center. Every time the Bureau waves the flag, you can bet they'll hand you the shitty end of the pole."

They stopped at the corner.

"You don't believe in anything, do you?" Ross said.

"Lots of things. But not people."

Ross shook his head.

"No heroes, kid," Mancuso said. "Only sandwiches."

They walked their separate ways.

11:50 A.M. CHRIS HAD DRIVEN Sally back to Georgetown to pack. And she had almost finished when she went into the bathroom and realized that she was out of everything. So, she pulled a sweater over her yellow sundress and ran down the cobbled hill to the Peoples Drug on Wisconsin Avenue.

She grabbed a cart and rattled up and down the aisles, picking up hairspray and hand lotion, plus a big bottle of Scope that was on sale. And she was so busy looking for toothpaste that she ran smack into someone else's cart at the end of the aisle.

"I'm sorry," she said. "I wasn't watching."

The young man was rubbing his knee. "You really ought to—" Then he looked up at her. "Sally?"

She blinked and stared at him.

He stood up. He was tall, over six feet, fair-haired and blue-eyed, and dressed in a crisp blue blazer and button-down shirt, gray slacks, and loafers. He was gorgeous.

"Sally Crain?" he said.

"Yes?"

"Hey, it's me. Steve Thomas."

But she couldn't place him.

"Steve Thomas. You know. Emory University. Dooley's Frolics, 1968."

She smiled the best she could. "I don't—"

"The Deke House."

She laughed and opened her hands. "I must be getting senile. I just can't—"

"Your girlfriend Angie was dating Jerry Kamer."

"God," she said, and laughed out loud. "I haven't thought of Angie and Jerry for—"

"Got time for lunch?"

"Gee, no, I'm sorry," she said. "I just ran out to grab a few things and—"

"Gotta eat sometime."

He really was gorgeous.

"A quick one," she said.

Noon "TWO WITH EVERYTHING," Mancuso said, and handed a five-dollar bill to the pushcart vendor. He didn't like driving all the way back to Arlington in the midday traffic, but it was halfway to McLean and there was always a crowd around the Iwo Jima Monument in summer. It was a good place to get lost. While he waited for the dogs, he watched the families taking Polaroids in front of the bronze statue of the flag-raising on Mount Suribachi. Some of the families were Japanese tourists. Mancuso stared. Fucking Japs taking pictures in front of a memorial to a battle where they got their ass kicked. Funny how time turned things upside down.

"Easy on the kraut, Mac," Harry Wilson said, behind him. He reached past Mancuso and took his hot dog.

Mancuso got his change, followed Wilson to a bench and sat down beside him.

"Got to ease up on spices," Wilson said. "Burns me at both ends."

"Ulcers?"

"Bullshit," Wilson said. "I'm so fed up with bureaucratic bullshit, I smell like a cow when I fart."

Mancuso had known Wilson a long time, and he knew what he meant. Wilson had joined the CIA in 1961, in time to help kick the Vietnam mess into high gear. He was infiltrating peace groups in Chicago in 1968 when he met Mancuso, who was doing the same thing for the FBI. They used to get together on weekends and go to the south side and eat deep-pan pizza and drink beer. After the Democratic convention riots, Mancuso was sent off to chase draft evaders and Wilson was promoted to deputy station chief in Teheran because the shah wanted an expert on infiltrating radical groups. Wilson was on leave in Paris in 1978 when some of the "students" he was watching overran the embassy and began the seige that hamstrung Jimmy Carter. So, Wilson came back to Langley as a member of "the intelligence community"—in other words, he was a spook who made no bones about it. Now, he was too old and too well recognized for field work. He hadn't made deputy director or even section chief, so he wound up a recruiter. There were a lot of guys like Wilson in the CIA, older guys who couldn't be pushed out and had to be treated with a certain respect. They knew too much. It didn't pay to let them become disgruntled.

"Why don't you get out?" Mancuso said.

"I'm sixty-two in February, Joe. Then I'm a memory. If I cut out early, they may think I'm going freelance. The company doesn't like guys who go into business for themselves."

"Like Rolf Petersen," Mancuso said.

"Like Rolf Petersen."

They sat a while, eating. Mancuso watched Wilson. He was a spiffy dresser. Nice brown suit with a nice neat crease in his trousers and a nice shine on his shoes. He wore a silk necktie and a white-on-white shirt. And he always wore steel-rimmed sunglasses. Mancuso could see why Wilson hadn't made it to the top. He looked like a fucking spy.

"I got trouble, Harry," Mancuso said.

"How come?"

"I got to find Petersen."

Wilson wiped his mouth with his napkin, wrapped the end of the hot dog in it, and dropped it in the wastebasket beside the bench. "You got trouble," he said.

"You know where to look?"

"No. And I'm not curious." Wilson sat back in the sun, slouched down, and adjusted his glasses on his nose as though he were going to take a nap.

"Can you get me a picture and service record?" Mancuso said.

Wilson leaned his head back, closed his eyes. "This an official request?"

"No."

"I'll try."

Mancuso chewed the last bite of his hot dog.

"Where you gonna go after you retire, Harry?"

"Me and the wife got a little place in Vero Beach," Wilson said. "It's a motel. Twenty units, room for twenty more. What about you?"

"I don't know. Got no plans."

"Shame that you lost Mary Louise."

"Yeah." Mancuso sat a while, thinking about that. Then he stood up. Wilson's eyes opened. "Hey, Joe. . . ."

"Yeah?"

"Petersen's a real mean fuck. You're gonna have to kill him. You know what I mean?"

"Yeah," Mancuso said, and his voice was old and tired. "I seen his work."

Slowly, he walked away.

12:25 P.M. "TO A QUICK lunch," Steve Thomas said and held up his glass of burgundy.

"You're a devil," Sally said. "I'll die if anyone I know comes in and sees me like this." She held the front of her sweater closed over her sundress and touched her glass to his. They drank.

"Don't be silly. You're beautiful."

"Oh, sure. No makeup. Big, dark rings under my eyes. Dressed like a teenager. I don't even have stockings on."

In fact, the maitre d' had raised his eyebrows when they walked into Clyde's. But Steve gave him ten bucks, and he found a corner booth in the back. Now, Sally hunched down in the booth, feeling silly and out of place amid the trendy Georgetown lunchtime crowd.

"I'm in real estate," Steve said. "In Golden, Colorado."

"Anywhere near the university?"

"Er . . . yeah. What about you? What about the girl I met at Dooley's Frolics a thousand years ago?"

Sally tasted the burgundy. It was sweet and dark and heavy with the smell of fruit and France. "Oh, I don't know. She wandered around for a long time before she found herself. The Peace Corps, a couple of weekly papers, and the *Houston Post*. Then up here to the *Washington Post* and politics."

"I'm impressed," he said, and she could see he was.

"I was press aide for Senator Weatherby 'til . . . you know."

"Weatherby, Weatherby? Wasn't he the one that—"

"Yes," Sally said.

"Hey, that must have been something to live through."

"Like the song says, I've seen fire and I've seen rain."

"I guess," Steve said. There was tenderness in his eyes, and caring. She liked him.

"Now I work for Senator Fallon."

Steve had a mouthful of wine. He coughed and almost choked. "Jesus," he said, wiping his mouth. "You mean the guy who—"

"Yes."

"My God! I saw the whole thing on television!" Then he stopped himself. "God—that was you! Holding his arm."

"Yes."

"It must have been terrifying."

"Yes."

"Are you all right? I mean, is he all right? Is he—"

"He's recovering. We're working out of his house while he recuperates. That is"—she looked at her wristwatch—"if I can get my shopping done today."

"Gee, I'm sorry. I didn't understand. Let me get a waiter." He twisted around in his chair.

She looked down at his left hand on the tablecloth. It was a strong hand, tanned, with neat, rounded fingernails. There was no wedding ring, and no suntan line where a ring might have been removed. It looked like a gentle hand. It was the kind of hand she needed. Maybe she could afford just one day off.

5:35 P.M.   Joe Mancuso sat at the end of the bar at Gertie's, at the corner of 11th and F Street. He sat there for an hour or so after work every weekday. Some people said there were only three days in the last thirty years that you couldn't find Mancuso on that bar stool at six o'clock: the day Jack Kennedy was shot, the day after the Redskins won the Superbowl, and the day after Mary Louise died. If Mancuso was sober enough to stand, you'd find him sitting in that chair.

Gertie put a double of Jack Daniel's on the bar in front of him.

"Whatcha workin' on now, Joey. Somethin' big?"

"Yeah." Mancuso took a belt. It felt good going down.

Gertie leaned forward, put her elbows and her tits on the bar. "No kiddin'?" she said. "Lemme hear."

"Well . . ." Mancuso looked up and down the bar. The regulars were there: a few old FBI guys, some of the lifers from the Labor Department. There were three or four hookers, including his friend, Mandy, working the weekday evening trade. He leaned in toward Gertie. "Somebody's been stealing quarters out of the prophylactic vending machine in the president's office."

"No! You don't mean it?"

"Yeah," Mancuso said gravely.

"The president's own office," she said, and her voice was full of wonder.

"Shhhhh."

Gertie shook her head. "Some people." She was still shaking her head when she went down the bar to set up another drink.

Ross slid onto the stool beside Mancuso.

"Whatcha find out?" Mancuso said.

"Gertie, gimme a gin and tonic," Ross called. "No. Better make it a gimlet."

"When are you gonna stop drinking that pussy stuff?"

"Fuck you."

"Bad news, I gather."

"Shit." Ross turned on his stool. "Doc Summers doesn't remember anything about AIDS."

Mancuso snorted. "How about that?"

"Yeah. How about that?"

Gertie put Ross's drink down on the bar. He gulped it gratefully.

Mancuso said, "And when you called he had a lot of appointments and not much time to talk."

"Something like that."

"Which means Scott ain't on the side of the angels."

"Who do we see about that?" Ross said.

"Nobody."

"Yeah."

They sat a while, staring at the row of bottles on the back bar.

Then Ross said, "Are they gonna kill us?"

"Only if we poke too deep," Mancuso said. "Three months of clerical work. That's what they want. Then I'll be on the beach, you'll be transferred, and the trail will be as cold as Kelsey's nuts."

Ross took a long swig.

"Meanwhile, they're telling us to go the other way," Mancuso said.

"Which way?"

"After the guy who shot Martinez."

"Who's telling us?"

Mancuso stopped and stared at him, just like he had done in the kitchen of the Beckwith house, with the body of the murdered little girl at their feet.

"Is that a serious question?" Mancuso finally said.

"Yes."

Mancuso shook his head. "Yale. . . ." he said. "Didn't they teach you nothing?" He got down off his stool, tossed a crumpled five-dollar bill on the bar. "The same people who brought you tax loopholes and Selective Service. The rich. The privileged. The powers that be."

Ross sat, speechless, watching Mancuso walk away.

At the end of the bar, the hooker, Mandy, reached out and plucked Mancuso's sleeve.

"How about a date, Joe?"

"Sorry, kid," Mancuso said. "I already got one."

He went out.

10:10 P.M. IT HAD BEEN lovely. It had been fun. It had made Sally feel like a girl again. They had lunched in Georgetown, then driven down the George Washington Memorial Parkway to Mount Vernon in Steve's convertible with the wind blowing in her hair and the trees heavy with green and the sun darting in and out between the branches. On the way back, they had stopped and walked along the Potomac. They had dinner by candlelight in an old coaching inn on Willow Tree Road.

It was after ten when Steve brought her back to the door of her townhouse in Georgetown. The old-fashioned gas lamps were flickering and the breeze shook a pattern of leaves and lamplight on her doorstep. She dug in her bag for her keys, and he hung over her, keeping his distance, but looking for a kiss.

"Sure you don't want me to come in for a nightcap?" he said.

"I do," Sally said. "But not tonight. I have to finish packing."

"I'll only be in Washington five days . . . and nights."

"I'll bear that in mind." She found her key, slipped it into the lock. "Good night, Steve. Thanks," she said. "It was a real nice day. I needed that."

She got up on her toes, gave him a peck on the cheek.

He stood a moment, a little glad and a little disappointed at the same time. "I'll call you," he said. And he walked back down the red brick steps into the night.

Sally went inside, locked the door behind herself, and snapped on the light.

There was a gruff-looking man sitting in an armchair in her living room. He stood up and went for his pocket.

Sally dug in her pocketbook for her can of Mace. She seized it, flung her purse aside.

"Stop right there!" she commanded.

"Mancuso," he said, and held up his shield and ID card. "FBI."

She looked at him. "Put it on the table."

He did.

"Back away."

She waited until he had moved to the other side of the room, then she picked up the folder and looked from the likeness to him. "What's your office address?"

"Tenth and Pennyslvania."

"How many floors in the building?"

"Seven on the Penn side, eleven on E Street. And three basements."

She thought a moment. Then she dropped his ID on the table. "Okay," she said, and went and got her purse and put the Mace away. "What do you call this?" she said.

"Last guy I went to talk to about Martinez, somebody killed him and his whole family."

Sally looked up.

"Let's take a ride," Mancuso said.

As they drove down M Street, Sally leaned against her door, watching Mancuso in the lights of the oncoming cars. He was a stoop-shouldered man in an old brown suit with narrow lapels, frayed cuffs, a pot-belly and a double chin. He was just the kind of lock-step, civil service dullard that she had expected the FBI to assign to the investigation. Just the kind of drudge who would never turn up anything that would make an embarrassing headline before the nominating convention. She looked at him and realized that the White House had decided to bury the investigation along with Martinez. And she wondered if the White House had its reasons.

"Have you any idea who killed Martinez?" she said at last.

"You think Aaron can turn the Braves around this year?" Mancuso said.

"What?" For a moment, she didn't understand. Then, she suspected that she did.

Mancuso parked near the Lincoln Memorial. He led the way up the long flight of marble steps. It was 10:30, but it was a warm night, and there were tourists taking flash photographs, talking in whispers.

Sally climbed to the top of the stairs behind the slumping figure of Mancuso, followed him between the towering columns to the foot of the statue. It glowed a warm, granite yellow, and the great head of Lincoln looked down, weary and benign.

Sally was impatient. "Now, what can I do for you, Agent?"

"How come Fallon loves the greasers so much?"

Sally blinked and stopped short of an answer.

"What's your problem?" Mancuso said.

"I don't like your choice of words." She walked past him.

"Have it your own way." He followed her.

"Senator Fallon believes that we can only have peace in this hemisphere if the United States supports popular revolutions to—"

"Okay, okay," Mancuso said. "I get it."

She was growing irritable. "What are your politics, Mr. Mancuso?"

"I haven't voted since Truman went back to Independence." He took
out a pack of cigarettes, offered her one. Brusquely, she waved it away.

As he cupped the flame of the match before his face, he watched her.
She was a good-looking head, cocky and bossy and full of herself. He
knew the type. She was probably one of those dames who hung around
classy parties until somebody with a little power took her for a tumble.
Once a woman like that got her hooks into a guy, she used his dick as a
rung to clamber up the ladder until she got the job or the ring or the
settlement she wanted. Mancuso knew the type all right—and he didn't like
her a bit.

"All right," she said. "I haven't got all night. What do you want?"

"A lead." He snuffed the match between his fingers, put it in his
pocket.

She studied him a moment. He was a rumpled, worn-down nub of a
man—and a bigot in the bargain. "Suppose I had a lead to give you? What
then? What do you do? Write a report and sit around for a week until
somebody with some authority finds the time to read it?"

"You give me a lead, I follow it up. That's the way it goes."

"If you don't mind, I'd rather talk to the agent-in-charge."

He flicked an ash to the marble floor. "I'm agent-in-charge."

"You're in charge?"

"Yeah. Look, Sis', what's your beef?"

Sally laughed out loud. "The most important political crime of this
decade and they put *you* in charge of finding the killer?"

He was starting to get angry. "What's so funny?"

"Forgive me," she said. "I always knew justice was blind. I didn't
know she was stupid."

She had a real sharp mouth on her, and Mancuso was getting good and
pissed. But he knew he'd get a lot more out of her if she thought she had
the upper hand. "You having a good time?" he said softly.

"All right," Sally said. "All right. I give you a lead—you run it down.
That how it goes?"

"Yeah. That's how it goes."

It was just what she expected from the Baker administration—a passive investigation in the hands of incompetents with no possibility of catching the killer or punishing the guilty. It wasn't a cover-up. Not exactly. Washington had learned a lot since Watergate. There was more than one way to suppress evidence; the best way was not to uncover it in the first place. It was the kind of thing that Terry Fallon would change when he got the chance.

"I may have a lead for you," she said. "A man came up to me in a drugstore today. A man who claims he knew me in college. He was very friendly."

"So?"

"He said he lives in Golden, Colorado. Near the university."

"So?" Mancuso said.

"There's no university in Golden. It's in Boulder."

Mancuso put his hands in his pockets. Oh, yeah—she was a real piece of work, this one. She could say one thing and mean another while her hands or her eyes did something cute to throw you off the track. And she had that open, fresh-as-clover beauty that made men want to believe her.

"What do you think about that?" she said.

"What do you think about it?"

"Could be something," she said. "Could be nothing. Just some enterprising reporter trying to get some pillow talk about Senator Fallon."

"Is there pillow talk about Fallon?"

"No."

"You screwing him?"

She looked back again, and this time her eyes flashed with anger. "Listen, you filthy little—"

"All right," Mancuso said, and he knew that he had hit her hot button. "So, you're screwing him. I don't give a shit."

She turned on him and she was practically shaking with rage, so much rage that she couldn't speak.

"All right, all right," Mancuso said. "You love him." He walked away from her and leaned against a column. All of a sudden, he was feeling pretty cocky himself.

She stepped close to him. "What the hell do you care?"

"Like I said, honey . . ." He took a pull on the cigarette. "I don't."

They stood a long moment like that, eyeing each other.

"His name's Steve Thomas," Sally finally said. "He's staying at the Four Seasons Hotel."

"Come on," Mancuso said. "Let's make a phone call."

11:30 P.M. THERE WAS A *WELCOME NAB* sign hung in the lobby of the Four Seasons Hotel. The lobby was busy with overfed, middle-aged men in dark business suits with badges on their lapels. The badges said "Hi, I'm Fred" or "Hi, I'm Dick" and the men were a noisy bunch of back-slappers, telling each other old blue jokes.

Mancuso and Sally hung in a corner until Ross came hustling through the revolving door, still struggling to knot his tie.

"You took your time," Mancuso said.

"Hey, I was asleep." Then Ross saw Sally beside Mancuso and stopped dead.

"This is Ross," Mancuso was saying. "He works with me. This is Sally Cain."

"Crain," she said.

"Yeah, hi," Ross said, and he couldn't take his eyes off her.

"Whatever," Mancuso said. "Now here's the thing—"

The elevator doors opened and three conventioneers carrying plastic highball glasses waltzed off. Behind them, Steve Thomas stepped out and started across the crowded, boisterous lobby toward the cocktail lounge.

"That's him," Sally said. Instinctively, Mancuso and Ross turned away.

"Did he make us?"

"No."

Mancuso looked back over his shoulder. "Which one?"

"The tall man. With the sandy hair."

Mancuso took Sally's arm. "You just keep him talking fifteen minutes. We'll see what we can find."

"Find where?"

"In his room."

"Now, hold on a second." Sally took a step back. "I said I'd call him and point him out. I never said I was going to entertain him while you search his room."

"You want to find Martinez's killer or don't you?"

Sally looked back and forth between the two men.

"Look, lady," Mancuso said, and took his hat off. "Breaks like this don't come along every day. You got to give us a hand."

"But you don't have a warrant. Don't you need a warrant?"

"Only if we get caught. Now, please. What do you say?"

But she didn't move. She looked at Ross. He shrugged.

"Okay, okay," Sally said. "Fifteen minutes. But if he lays a hand on me, I'm out of here."

"Deal," Mancuso said.

She threaded her way across the lobby, and disappeared into the cocktail lounge.

"Kinda pushy with her, weren't you?" Ross said.

"She's tougher than she looks. Come on." They walked to the elevator.

Mancuso said, "You watch, I'll search."

"I'll search," Ross said. "I'm neater."

"Okay." Mancuso nodded in the direction of the house phones. "One ring means move out."

Ross got into the elevator. Then he stood, looking at Mancuso.

"So?" Mancuso said.

"You gonna tell me the room number?"

"Oh, yeah, 724."

"See you." Ross pushed a button and the elevator doors closed between them.

Sally walked through the busy cocktail lounge. There was an unbroken line of conventioneers down the length of the bar, punctuated here and there with hundred-dollar hookers. A man on a settee at the far end of the room stood up and waved. It was Steve Thomas.

"Hi, Steve."

"Come. Sit. Have a drink." He looked smart and crisp and preppy, not a hair out of place. He smiled and Sally could see the anticipation—and lust—in his eyes.

"I'm glad you called," he said. He let her sit down, then slid in close beside her.

"I had to run an errand," Sally said. "Took me right past the front door. I thought I'd see if you were still up." As she spoke, she saw Mancuso standing in the entrance to the lounge. He glanced at her, then took the last open seat at the farthest end of the bar.

"My lucky night," Steve said. He motioned to the waiter. "How about a double for openers?"

The lock on the hotel room door was a three-channel Schlage, the kind with a teflon insert in the bolt. Ross had straight A's in locks at Quantico; he passed it like it was open. Then he used the knuckle of his index finger to switch on the lights in the room and shut the door behind him.

He put on the rubber surgical gloves and started on the dresser. He pulled out a pair of shorts and looked at the label. He got a jolt right off. Steve

Thomas might be from Colorado, but his underwear was from Woodward and Lothrop.

"Must be tough being a beautiful single woman in Washington," Steve Thomas was saying in the cocktail lounge downstairs. He leaned toward Sally, so close that they were almost touching.

"Oh, I don't know."

"Guess everybody you meet tries to hit on you."

"Not really."

Steve Thomas was pitching his heart out. "Hard to meet somebody you can really care about, I guess. Somebody who really cares about you."

"That's true everywhere, isn't it?"

Sally was beginning to lose patience. She felt idiotic. She looked toward Mancuso. He eyed her without emotion.

"Yeah. Yeah, you're right," Steve was saying. He raised his glass. "No friends like the old friends, right?"

"Sure . . . right."

He drank deeply. Sally took a sip of whisky. It was smokey and bitter and she wasn't much of a drinker.

"Hey, Sal," Steve said. "Bottoms up." He drained his glass. Just then, Sally needed a drink. She did the same.

Upstairs in the hotel room, Ross pushed the desk drawer closed. He looked around. What was missing was more interesting than what was there.

There was no raincoat, no umbrella in the closet. There were no airline baggage stubs on the empty suitcase—and the suitcase was too big to be a carry-on and too big for the few articles of clothing he had found in the dresser. But, most important, there was no briefcase, no notebook, no manila folders, no pocket calculator, no call-back numbers written on the bedside pad. There were none of the paraphernalia of a traveling business-man. Now, he knew what Steve Thomas was not—he was not a developer from Colorado. He was not a reporter. Ross looked for clues to what he was.

Quickly, he went to the bed. Someone had been lying there, reading this month's issue of *Penthouse*. Ross turned up the spread, slipped his hands between the mattress and the box spring. He was running out of time and he hadn't got it done.

Sally looked at her watch as the waiter put fresh drinks down before them. It was quarter to twelve.

"Got to make this my last one," she said. "Some of us have to work tomorrow."

Steve Thomas was feeling the liquor. He slouched against the back of the settee. "Hey, I thought we were just getting started." He raised his glass; some of the liquor splashed on the table. "Here's to long nights." He drained it, slid over against her, and put his hand on her knee. "Hey, look, Sally, what do you say we have a fresh round sent upstairs? Maybe talk a while in my room? What do you say?"

Gently, firmly, Sally removed his hand. "I don't think so."

He leaned against her, coaxing. "Come on. Half an hour. What can it hurt?"

She leaned away. "I said, I have to go." Exasperated, she looked down the bar toward Mancuso. He seemed happy enough, ordering another belt, chomping on a handful of peanuts. She realized that she had let herself be cozened, had let Mancuso use her. Before she realized it, he had conned her into the middle of something. She had underestimated Mancuso. He had foxed her. She had to be certain she didn't let that happen again.

Steve was looking at his watch, trying to read the dial in the half-light, through the haze of alcohol.

"Hey, it's only eleven-thirty," he said. "You can stay till twelve, can't you?"

"No, Steve. Five more minutes and I—"

"What the hell did you come for then?" he said, and she could hear the disappointment and irritation in his voice. "Hey? Get me down here for—"

Suddenly, he broke off in midsentence. He stared at her like he was seeing her for the first time.

"Jesus Christ," he said and pushed the table back abruptly. His glass fell over and ice scattered everywhere. He shoved himself up off the couch, pushed roughly through the conventioneers, and rushed out of the lounge.

Sally looked anxiously toward Mancuso.

Mancuso got down from his stool. He dropped a ten-dollar bill on the bar. "Shit," he said, and followed Steve Thomas out the door.

When he reached the lobby, Mancuso could see Steve pushing his way toward the elevator, shoving through the crowd of conventioneers. Mancuso hurried after him. Steve pushed two men aside, grabbed the closing door of the elevator, and pushed his way in. The door clapped shut in Mancuso's face.

Mancuso turned to the house phones. Conventioneers and wives were using every one—and a knot of others were waiting.

"Fuck," Mancuso said. He looked at the elevator bank; the indicator showed both cars heading up. He turned for the door to the fire stairs and ran smack into Sally.

"I couldn't help it. He—"

"Go home," Mancuso said. "Forget you were here."

He opened the fire door and began to run up the stairs.

There was nothing hidden under the mattress, nothing under the pillows. Ross turned the Gideon Bible over and shook it out. Nothing. He threw it back in the drawer of the night table and slapped the drawer shut. He checked his watch. Then he turned toward the bathroom.

Mancuso ran up the gray steel fire stairs, pulling himself along with a hand on the railing. His footsteps clanged and rang in the shaftway, and he could hear the grating of the elevator cables through the wall as the car carrying Steve Thomas slid smoothly up toward the seventh floor. "Fuck," he said, under his panting breath. "I'll be a cock-sucking, mother-fucking, son-of-a-bitching, bastard cock-sucking son-of-a-bitch. . . ." And his curses punctuated every step.

Just then Ross clicked on the light in the bathroom. There was a can of Rise and an Atra razor on the counter, a tube of Crest, and a toothbrush in one of the glasses. On a shelf above the sink, there was a large black leather toiletries kit. Ross picked it up. It was heavy. He shook the kit. Some small metal items rattled around inside. Ross unzipped it.

Mancuso swung himself around the fourth floor landing and pounded up the steel stairs toward the fifth. He was breathless, panting, his collar sweated to his neck. "Mother-fucking, shit-eating, cock-sucking son-of-a-bitching bastard cunt-licking fucking asshole. . . ." He made the turn halfway to the fifth floor.

The elevator door opened, and Steve Thomas stepped out into the silent hallway. He walked quickly to 724. Then he leaned against the door and listened.

Inside the room, Ross turned out the contents of the shaving kit and they clattered on the formica counter beside the bathroom sink.

Dimly, almost imperceptibly, Steve heard the sound through the heavy hall door. He bent down, drew the .38 caliber revolver from his ankle holster, took the silencer from his jacket pocket, and eased it over the barrel of the gun until it clicked into place. Without making a sound, he slipped the key into the lock.

Ross quickly began to replace the contents of the kit: aftershave, deodorant, a bar of Equipage soap in a plastic box, a matchbook sewing kit. All that remained on the bathroom counter were five collar stays, two buttons, and four little lapel pins.

He pushed the pins together in a bunch. One was the American flag. The other three were a circle, a square, and the letter "S". Ross stared at the pins. Suddenly, his jaw went slack and his eyes opened as if someone had slapped him hard across the face. Just as Mancuso pushed, sweating and panting, through the fire door at the end of the seventh floor, Steve Thomas silently turned the key in the lock and stepped into room 724, and slammed the door behind him.

"Freeze!" he shouted at Ross.

Ross wheeled around in time to see a man level a pistol at his chest. With all his might, Ross flung the heavy shaving kit backhand across the room. Steve jumped back, pulling the gun up. The shaving kit hit the bottom of his wrist and the gun fired. There was a soft *pock* and a sudden surge of air pressure in Ross's eardrums. The bullet was discharged upward, entered Steve's neck just below his jaw and exploded out the top of his scalp. It blew the cap off his skull and splashed blood and tissue on the ceiling. The bullet ricocheted down off the concrete under the plaster, up off the concrete under the rug, back down off the ceiling, and buried in the mattress. Steve's body fell onto the bed, writhing and twitching, spewing blood on the bedspread, the lamps, and end tables. It jerked in gruesome spasms, rolled over, and fell onto the floor.

Breathless, his shirt sweated to his back and belly, Mancuso reached the door of 724. He heard a body hit the floor. Without hesitating, he stepped back, drew his revolver, and kicked the door with the flat of his shoe just below the knob. The frame holding the striker plate shattered and the door crashed open as Mancuso crouched, ready for combat.

Ross was leaning against the door frame of the bathroom, his hand over his eyes. Mancuso stepped into the room, quickly pressing the door closed behind him. At his feet, Steve Thomas's body jerked and quivered on the floor.

"Jesus Christ," Mancuso said. Then blood dripped down from the ceiling. He ducked out of its way and looked up at the spattered tissue on the plaster. "Jesus Christ."

Ross was hyperventilating, struggling to catch his breath. "Motherfucker . . . motherfucker . . . he almost killed me."

"Must have lost his head." Mancuso holstered his pistol, took a pair of latex surgical gloves from his pocket, and began to pull them on.

"Very funny," Ross said, catching his breath. He was angry. "Where the hell were you?"

Mancuso loosened his collar where it was sweated to his throat. "I had to take the local." He bent over Steve's twitching corpse, began picking through his pockets. He took Steve's money and wristwatch.

"What the hell are you doing?"

Mancuso patted down all of Steve's pockets. "No wallet," he said. "You find a wallet?"

"No."

"I'd like to know who this son-of-a-bitch is. And make this look like a robbery for the D.C. cops."

"Forget it," Ross said. He pushed himself away from the bathroom door and made his way across the room, stepping over and around the spattered blood.

"What are you talking about?" Mancuso said.

"Forget it, Joe." Ross stood over him. He opened his hand and dropped the four little lapel pins into Mancuso's waiting palm.

Mancuso looked down at them. "What the fuck?"

Then he stopped, and the sweat ran cold into the small of his back. The tiny pins glinted on the white latex glove. He looked up at Ross and saw that he, too, understood. In Washington, only one kind of man would carry an array of pins like those: an agent of the United States Secret Service.

FRIDAY, AUGUST 12, 1988

THE FOURTH DAY

7:50 A.M. TWO DESKS WERE stuffed into Room 4776A in the north-west corner of the fourth floor of the FBI Building. One was neatly laid with a leather desk pad and two ballpoint pens in a holder. There was a Sony VHS player and a television monitor with a headset plugged into its speaker jack and a stack of videocassettes in black plastic boxes.

The other desk top was invisible, awash under a sea of old newspapers and magazines, memoranda, candy wrappers, and empty orange juice cartons. It was easy to tell which desk belonged to Mancuso, even when he wasn't sitting there. But just now he *was* sitting there, feet up in the middle of the pile, staring at the front page of the *Post*. The three-column headline read:

FALLON CALLED FRONT RUNNER FOR V.P.

Beneath the headline was a photograph of Fallon leaving Walter Reed Hospital in his wheelchair. He was making the "thumbs up" sign. When Mancuso was a little boy, he'd once made that sign to his grandmother— and had gotten a swift crack in the face. In Italian, that sign meant something else.

Mancuso folded the newspaper and tossed it on the pile on his desk. He sat back in his chair, watching Ross shuttle back and forth through the videotape of the assassination. On the glowing face of the television monitor, Martinez and Fallon, like two spindly marionettes, fell to the wooden rostrum and leaped back up as if yanked by invisible strings.

Finally, Mancuso reached over and tugged on the wire to Ross's headset.

"What do you want?" Ross said when he lifted the phones away from his ears.

"Mind telling me what you're doing?"

"Looking for answers."

"There are no answers."

"Only sandwiches." It was plain that Ross was in no mood.

"Yeah," Mancuso said. "Right." He sat back and folded his arms.

Ross was pissed. "We tried doing it your way last night."

Mancuso sat up and leaned forward and he spoke in a whisper that only Ross could hear. "What do you want? The guy was too smart for his own good. Sue me."

Ross put his headset down. "Anything in the paper?"

"You kidding?" Mancuso said under his breath. "He never lived and he never died. That's how they do things."

Ross just stared.

They jumped when the door of the office opened.

It was Jean, the big blond from the typing pool, carrying a large manila envelope.

"Hello, Cookie," Mancuso said. "How's your chops?"

She sneered at him. "You'd pay to know."

"Would I ever." Mancuso rubbed his hands together.

She dropped the envelope into Mancuso's lap, then slammed the door as she left.

Mancuso sat up, dug under the papers on his desk until he found a yellow pencil, and used it to tear the envelope open. "Man I love the jugs on that honey."

"You're a class act, Joe."

Mancuso spilled the contents onto the desk. There were two folders with the crest of the United States Central Intelligence Agency and a red overstamp that said *Confidential Eyes Only*.

"Looks like your friend Wilson came through," Ross said.

"Yeah. Interagency cooperation. Sweet." Mancuso slit the seals on the first folder and opened to a black-and-white photo of Rolf Petersen.

"What an ugly fuck." He handed the photograph to Ross.

"Look who's talking." Ross cocked the photo of Petersen up against the VCR, put his elbows on the desk, and sat forward, staring at it eye-to-eye. Mancuso started flipping through the other contents of the folder.

In fact, Ross could see that Rolf Petersen was anything but ugly. He had a straight, aquiline nose and an almost pretty mouth that bent double into a little smile, the way an English longbow bends, so that the corners turn down. He had straight, blond hair, parted close to the middle, and long, elegant lashes. But the most arresting thing about the photograph were his eyes. They were light as morning and cold as stone.

Ross stared at the photo, committing it to memory, as he had been trained to do. Yet he knew, even at first glance, that it was a face he could never forget.

Mancuso was half-mumbling. "Born Hampton, Virginia, March 16, 1946. Enlisted U.S. Marines, August 1965. Recruited by the CIA, January, 1967. This son of a bitch did some mean years—Salvador, Chile, Paraguay . . ."

Ross was intent on that immobile, imponderable face. "Wonder what he did there."

"Training, probably."

"What training?"

"Security. Interrogation."

"Interrogation?"

"Torture."

That made Ross look up. Mancuso leafed on into the folder. "Then he fell off the world." Mancuso let the folder flip shut. "Freelance."

"For who?"

"It don't say." Mancuso slit the seals on the other folder. "Aw, shit," he said.

"What's the matter?"

"Listen to this." Mancuso ran his index finger down the page. "Small arms. Pistol. Shot expert. Rifle and carbine. Shot advanced expert. Third in his class."

"Well, maybe it was a small class." Ross was getting the idea and he didn't like it.

"Field weapons. Light and heavy machine guns. Mortars. Mortars? T-O-W. What's that?"

"Some kind of rocket."

"High explosives. Demolition. Scuba. Karate. Tai-chi. What the fuck is tai-chi?"

"Chinese karate."

"Handy guy to have around the house."

"Yeah—if you're expecting a revolution."

"Poison. Holy shit—poison," Mancuso said.

"Jesus Christ, Joe. I thought these guys were only on television."

"Listen to this, I was right. Specialist course in interrogation—advanced instruction."

"Torture."

"Fuck," Mancuso said, and threw the file on the pile of papers on the desk.

"How are we supposed to take a guy like that?"

Mancuso looked at Ross as though he didn't believe his ears. "Are you kidding me? You heard that rap sheet and you still want to find him?''

"Yes, goddamit. Yes, I do."

"Well, you are a fucking nut," Mancuso said, and got up and went to the water cooler. "A crazy fucking nut." He took a tiny paper cup of water. "You know, when they gave you to me as a partner, I knew they were stuffing it up my ass. Some fucking Jew-boy from Yale full of bullshit ideas about saving the world."

"Fuck you, Mancuso," Ross said.

"Big fucking ideas," Mancuso went on. "So, they plopped you into Records and Stats as my partner. Which had to tell you what they thought about me and what they thought about you." He started to drink the water, then stopped and threw it, cup and all, into the wastebasket beside the cooler. "And anybody with shit for brains could see that when they put us on this fucking case we were supposed to come up dry and let the politicians get on with whatever the fuck they're up to."

"That's your idea, Joe. Nobody told me we were just supposed to stick our thumbs up our asses and whistle."

"Then what about this?" Mancuso snatched up the photograph of Petersen and waved it in Ross's face. "How come this isn't in every newspaper? Why don't they slap it up in every post office? How come the papers say 'assassin or assassins unknown'?" He threw the photo on the desk. "If they really wanted this guy, they'd stick his face out there so that some civic-minded citizen would spot him . . . or some *friend* of his would turn him in."

Ross couldn't answer that.

Mancuso leaned over the desk, but he was practically shouting. "Now what the fuck is so hard to understand about that?"

"Nothing," Ross said and he wasn't going to knuckle. "Nothing. Only I'm not going to play."

"So, what are you going to do?"

"I'm going to find the guy who juiced Martinez with AIDS."

"Oh, shit." Mancuso walked across the room. "Are you back to that again?"

"I never got off it."

"Didn't you see what they did to Beckworth or whatever-the-fuck-his-name-was?"

"I got eyes."

"Sure you do. And when whoever it was finds out you're still on the case, it won't be the Arlington locals who are shooting at you, asshole. It will be some high-priced pro hitter who don't miss."

Ross wasn't taking any shit. "First, I'm gonna find out who juiced

Martinez. Then I'm going to find the guy who shot him. If that's Petersen, then that's Petersen.''

''Oh, you fucking crazy bastard. I suppose you actually want to track this madman down?''

''That's right. I do.''

''For Christ's sake, Dave!'' Mancuso stuck his index finger in the middle of the face in the photograph. ''Look at him! He's a fucking pathological killer!''

''I want him,'' Ross said softly. ''I want the answer.''

''What answer?''

''Why he shot Martinez.''

Mancuso started to laugh, and his laugh was bitter. ''Only two reasons, buddy boy. Somebody paid him—or somebody ordered him.''

''What do you mean 'ordered'? The guy's freelance. Murder for money. O'Brien got it straight from the director of the CIA.''

''Oh? Really now?'' The sarcasm in Mancuso's voice was sharp and angry.

''Yes, really now. Jesus Christ, Joe. It's in the report. The president was in the room when he said it.''

''Yeah,'' Mancuso said. ''And next you're gonna tell me that the CIA don't lie to the president.''

That stopped Ross cold.

''Dumb son-of-a-bitch,'' Mancuso said. ''Don't you see this is some big boy's play? And you're nothing but a dollar chip in a high rollers' game?''

Ross looked at Mancuso through a veil of frustration and rage. ''You poor, cynical bastard. . . .'' he finally said.

''Go fuck yourself.'' Mancuso went over and started pulling on his jacket. ''Come on. We got Fallon at nine.''

''I'll get the car,'' Ross said and grabbed up his jacket and went to the door. ''And Joe?''

''Yeah?''

''Go fuck yourself, too.'' He slammed the door behind him.

Mancuso waited as Ross's footsteps disappeared down the hall. Then, he shook his head and snorted. When he could hear the footsteps no more, he began to hum—quietly, absently, no tune in particular. He looked around the office. Gently, he opened the top drawer of his desk. As he had expected, the red light on the electronic surveillance detector was blinking. It told Mancuso that there was a hidden microphone somewhere in the office. He stopped humming. In a moment, the red light blinked out and the green light beside it blinked on. So, the microphone was wired to a voice-activated tape recorder. Mancuso started humming again, the red light blinked on. He switched the detector off, dropped it in his jacket pocket, and closed the drawer. He was still humming when he swung out of the office and shut the door behind him. Now, whoever was listening knew that Joe Mancuso would do just what was expected of him. And that Ross was a dangerous fool.

8:10 A.M. THERE WAS NOTHING very special about the two businessmen breakfasting together in the rear booth at the Dutch Treat cafeteria on 19th and L Street. In their plain dark suits, white shirts, and narrow, undistinguished neckties, they could have been accountants with the GAO, or GS-10 drudges with HUD or DOT.

The waitress who served their poached eggs and coffee and toasted English didn't recognize them, didn't take notice of their conversation. But they were just the kind of "invisible men" one spotted from time to time on the periphery of "official" Washington, talking deeply together in the kinds of places reporters didn't frequent.

They were the kind of men who knew that phone lines could be tapped. Offices—even the Oval Office—had been bugged. Homes could be wired. The only real privacy was obscurity and anonymity, outside in the real world of working people and private citizens.

The small, graying man on the left was Lou Bender, special assistant to the president. He was never quoted, rarely photographed. He had no known authority in the White House, no recognized responsibility. Yet it was said that nothing important happened in the White House unless Lou Bender knew about it and endorsed it.

The other man—the thin, flinty one—was Rear Admiral William Rausch, director of the CIA.

"He can't just disappear," Bender was saying. "That's a crock of crap."

"Lou, either you can't understand or you don't want to." Rausch knew Bender was scrambling. That gave Rausch an opportunity, if only he had the guile to seize it.

"I can't *and* I don't want to."

Rausch stirred his coffee. "Lou, the man doesn't work for us anymore. He's been out in the cold for years."

"So you've said. . . ."

"Petersen's a trained guerrilla. Now he's here, in his native country, with somebody bankrolling him and looking out for him. He can blend into the background and vanish without a trace. We can't find him unless you let us put his mug shot in the papers."

"Forget that," Bender said abruptly.

"Then we have to wait until he makes a move or—" Rausch caught himself and looked up.

"More coffee, gents?" the waitress said.

Bender shook his head. He watched Rausch as he lifted his cup for a refill. He didn't trust Rausch. But they were bound up together so tightly in this conspiracy that he didn't have any choice. He had to rely on Rausch until he found a way to cut his throat and separate himself from Rausch forever.

When the waitress left the table, Bender said, "All right. Where's Petersen going?"

"How should I know?"

"I mean, where's home for him now?"

"We can't be certain. Nicaragua maybe. Maybe Panama. Moscow, for all we know."

"Well, wherever home is, he's got to get there. Stop him. Kill him before the FBI or anyone else finds him. That's the only way we can bring the Martinez investigation to an end."

"Lou, be reasonable. It's illegal for the Company to conduct operations within the continental United States. We're doing the best we can. There's three-and-a-half million square miles out there. He could be anywhere."

"But he isn't anywhere," Bender said. "He's somewhere—and he's on his way home."

Rausch sipped his coffee. Bender was really desperate. He was ripe for shaking, and Rausch had the perfect ploy. "I don't think that's a safe assumption," he said softly.

Bender squinted, trying to catch his drift. "Why not? He did his job."

"Maybe," Rausch said.

"What do you mean *maybe*?"

"What makes you so sure he did his job?"

"Don't be ridiculous," Bender said. "His job was to kill Martinez. He did it. Now, all he wants to do is get the hell out of here."

"But what makes you so sure?"

Bender leaned forward. "Bill, talk plain. What are you saying?"

Rausch leaned forward. "Do you honestly believe that Ortega and the Sandinistas sent Petersen to shoot Martinez?"

"Of course I do."

"Why?"

"Goddamit, Petersen is the perfect assassin," Bender said, and he was getting huffy. "He's American, he's CIA—at least he was, and to the newspapers and our allies in Latin America, *was CIA* is the same as *is*

CIA. So Martinez visits the United States and gets blown away by an American CIA agent on the steps of the Capitol, 2,000 miles from Nicaragua. Ortega is clean. He gets what he wants and every newspaper in the Western Hemisphere vilifies the CIA—for a change.'' Bender knocked the ash off his cigar and stuck it in the corner of his mouth. ''What could be simpler?''

Rausch just smiled. ''But why would Ortega want Martinez dead?''

''Because he believed killing Martinez would cripple the Contras.''

''Will it?''

''Of course not,'' Bender said. ''Don't be a fool.''

Rausch picked up half an English muffin and slowly began to butter it. ''From what you know about Ortega, would you say he's a fool?''

''He's a shrewd little rat.''

''Exactly.'' Rausch ate his muffin and waited.

Bender just stared. ''What the hell are you talking about?''

Rausch dabbed at his lips with his paper napkin. He was playing Bender and taking his time. ''Lou, there are just two problems with your theory,'' Rausch said. ''First, Ortega knows that killing Martinez won't slow the war. And whatever the press may believe, Petersen isn't our man. We know it—and Ortega knows we know it.''

''Meaning what?''

''Ortega didn't send Petersen to kill Martinez. We certainly didn't send him. So that only leaves one possible conclusion.''

''What?''

''That Martinez wasn't the target.''

''Oh, for Christ's sake,'' Bender said, and his patience was clearly exhausted. ''If he wasn't the target, who the hell was?''

''Fallon.''

For a moment, Bender just stared. Then he snorted. ''That's the dumbest thing I've ever heard.''

Unruffled, Rausch continued. ''Lou, you don't know your Sherlock Holmes. Once you eliminate the impossible, what remains is the solution—no matter how improbable it may seem.''

Bender crossed his arms and sat, sneering. But Rausch could see that he was worried.

''What if the Martinez hit was only a cover—and the real target was Fallon?'' Rausch went on chewing and talking. ''Lou, think it through. If Ortega hired Petersen to shoot Martinez, he'd be risking our reprisals. Who's to say we wouldn't send hit squads after Ortega?''

''What? Hit Ortega?'' Bender said. ''For Christ's sake, we'd have the fucking United Nations up our ass like a hot poker. And none of our diplomats in Latin America would be able to take a leak without half a dozen security guards lining the john.''

''I'm just saying that if Ortega broke the rules, we might break the rules.''

Bender stirred his coffee for a long moment.

''It just doesn't make sense for Ortega to hit Martinez this way,'' Rausch said. ''He has nothing to gain and everything to lose.''

Bender's face slowly darkened with anxiety. ''In other words . . . In other words, you're telling me the Sandinistas didn't pull the trigger?''

''I'm suggesting that the murder of Martinez was incidental,'' Rausch said. ''The real target was Terry Fallon.''

Bender sat perfectly still. He was thinking hard; Rausch knew he had him now. Like all men who worshipped power, Bender was devious, crafty, subtle, and merciless. He was capable of convoluted plotting and sudden, ruthless acts. But he was also paranoid—because he knew his enemies were capable of the same. Now, Rausch had pricked that paranoia. Because what he was suggesting put Bender's whole Baker-Fallon dream-ticket strategy in danger.

Bender motioned to the waitress.

''I will have more coffee. Thanks.'' And when she had poured him a cup and left, he said, ''You can't find Petersen?''

Rausch was point-blank. ''Not unless he shows.''

''And you think he might?''

''If his job's not done—yes. He might.''

''Where?''

''Wherever his victim is.''

''You think it's Fallon?''

Rausch shrugged; he never overplayed a winning hand. ''Maybe.''

''Why?''

A dark little sneer flickered in the corners of Rausch's lips. ''Fallon's a big mouth when it comes to Central America. He's more dangerous to Ortega than Martinez ever was.''

Bender knew that Terry Fallon was a sharp critic of CIA blunders in Central America. Rausch couldn't disguise the fact that Fallon had enemies in the CIA—and he didn't try.

''You take it easy on Fallon,'' Bender said. ''The Company fucked up in Nicaragua. If you hadn't dropped the ball, there would be no Ortega, no Sandinistas, no fucking Contras. The Cubans put one past you and Fallon called you on it.''

''Bullshit,'' Rausch said. ''Every goddam administration since Roosevelt backed the Somozas—the Somozas and United Fruit and the Chase Manhattan Bank. That was all the American government wanted to know about

Nicaragua. And if a Somoza were still there, you'd be backing him right now and you know it.''

Bender steamed—but didn't reply. Rausch was right; on that issue, they had a standoff. ''Okay,'' he said. ''Make your point.''

''This has nothing to do with me and Fallon,'' Rausch said. ''I know you need him to get Baker a second term.''

''I said, make your point, goddamit.''

Rausch balled his napkin and put it on his plate. ''Fallon wants to hang tough in Central America. Nobody in the Senate has shouted louder or done more to get money and arms flowing again to the Contras. Maybe Ortega figured that if he silenced Fallon he'd close the bank.''

''Do you believe what you're saying?'' Bender said.

Rausch shrugged. He had Bender where he wanted him. Now was the time to let him make up his mind for himself. ''I believe it's one possible scenario,'' he said. ''Anyhow, it makes a hell of a lot more sense than Martinez being hit by Ortega.''

Bender shook his head. He said, half-aloud, as though reminding himself, ''We can't lose Fallon. We can't.''

''He's your boy, isn't he?'' Rausch said, solicitously. He'd won. It was only a matter of time before he got what he wanted.

''Not my boy. But he's a winner. We can't let anything happen to him.''

''Of course not,'' Rausch said, and there was a wisp of condescension in his voice. ''But you know, Lou—there's no such thing as perfect security.''

Bender sat silent. Rausch let his thoughts darken and ferment.

''The son-of-a-bitch,'' Bender finally said. ''Is Ortega smart enough to know that Fallon is on his way to becoming vice president?''

It was the moment. Rausch reached down into his briefcase. ''Don't you think he reads the *Post*?'' He pushed a copy of the paper across the table to Bender. Terry Fallon's picture blazed from the front page. ''If he's out to silence Fallon, he knows he can't afford to miss again.''

''Fuck,'' Bender said. He sat back, relit his cigar and chewed it mercilessly. ''All right, all right. Who's your new boy in the Contras?''

''His name's Carlos Bevilaqua—Father Carlos to you.''

''What's he about?''

''He's a renegade Jesuit—a seminary dropout.''

''Another looney-tunes,'' Bender said wearily. ''Can't you find a real soldier to run the goddam war?''

Rausch smiled. ''Lou, there's a lot about guerrilla warfare you don't understand. Bevilaqua is fighting the Commies in the name of the Father, the Son and the Holy Ghost. He's a practical mystic, leading a holy war. The peons think he's Saint Michael incarnate. He believes the end justifies the means.''

"Can he run the war?"

"And offer Communion every Sunday besides."

"Who picked him?"

"We did."

"Will he do what he's told?"

"Poverty, chastity, and obedience—that's all he knows. That and killing with piano wire."

"Let's send Ortega a message," Bender said. "Let him know what will happen if he tries for Fallon again."

This was the pay off. "Like what?" Rausch said.

"Kill someone he cares about."

Rausch sat where he was. Bender blew a long plume of blue smoke in the air and the morning light filtered through it in lacy, elegant shafts.

Rausch snickered. "Who? His mother?"

"Anyone you want," Bender said. "Make it look like an accident."

Rausch smiled. He had what he wanted: brutal escalation. "You're a cold little fuck, aren't you?"

"Spare the compliments," Bender said, and folded his paper napkin and lay it neatly on the table. "Do it tonight."

8:25 A.M. ROLF PETERSEN STOOD in the phone booth in the 7-Eleven parking lot and listened once more to the recorded message. Then he slammed the receiver back in its cradle and pocketed his quarters. He picked up his brown paper bag of orange juice and donuts and walked to the edge of Route 2. The highway was still busy with morning commuter traffic heading from Annapolis and the shore into downtown Baltimore. He waited for his chance, then dodged to the other side and walked quickly across the parking lot of the old Holiday Inn to the door of cabin 108.

Whether he was in or out of the room, he always left the television set on and the Do Not Disturb sign hanging from the doorknob. That discouraged visitors. While he drank the juice from the container, he watched the *Today* show.

Fallon was the lead story—the fallen hero, fighting his way back to health. Fallon, the talk of the nation. Fallon, the sun-child of his party, the name on everyone's lips for vice president. Party leaders were interviewed: O'Donnell noncommittal but laudatory, acknowledging Fallon's competence for high office. Fallon recuperating. Flocks of well-heeled well-wishers making a pilgrimage to the Fallon house in the Neck District of Cambridge, Maryland. Convoys of television news vans and battalions of reporters invading Crescent Drive in the hope of catching a glimpse of their new idol.

Petersen drank his juice container dry as he watched. Then he flung it angrily into the wastebasket and got the map from the top of the dresser, yanked it open, and spread it on the bed.

It only took him a moment to locate the township that was known as Cambridge. And only another moment to pinpoint Crescent Drive.

8:50 A.M. WHEN MANCUSO AND ROSS pulled up at the bottom of Crescent Drive, the street was closed with police barriers and they had to show their IDs and park around the corner. Then they had a long walk uphill toward Fallon's house. Both sides of the street were lined with news vans and reporters doing stand-ups for mini-cam crews, interviewing Fallon's neighbors, or just chewing it over with each other.

There was another set of barriers at the end of the driveway to the house. Those were controlled by the Executive Protection Division, a bunch of pretty boys from Secret Service who played nursemaids for the biggies. Mancuso looked up at the splendid Georgian mansion. Congressmen and senators worked for wages just like he did, but somehow they always managed to get their hands around big money.

When pudgy little Chris Van Allen showed them into the library, Mancuso almost couldn't believe his eyes.

Terry Fallon was seated like some kind of crown prince on a big leather sofa at the far end of the room. He was wearing blue silk pajamas and a blue silk robe with a belt that ended in a long, fringed tassel. His velvet slippers had little shields embroidered in gold on the toes. Behind him, Sally Crain stood in an expensive gray suit and pearls.

Terry barely waited for the door to close.

"I want to make it clear that I deplore what you men did last night," he said. "You put Miss Crain into a very awkward and potentially embarrassing situation."

Mancuso and Ross stopped where they were, just inside the room.

"Yeah," Mancuso said. "Well, it seemed like a good idea at the time."

"I want you to know that I called the Four Seasons this morning to apologize to Mr. Thomas."

Ross shifted uneasily from foot to foot.

"I bet the guy was really touched," Mancuso said.

"Unfortunately, Mr. Thomas had already checked out."

"Yeah? Pity."

Terry took hold of the arms of the sofa. "That's right, Agent. And if you do anything else that might embarrass this office, I'll call Director O'Brien and see that you're removed from this case."

Mancuso and Ross stood in sheepish silence.

"Am I making myself clear?"

"Yes. . . er, Senator," Mancuso said. "Perfectly clear."

"Now, what is it you want?"

Mancuso nudged Ross.

"Senator, we have a photograph of a man who may have been your assailant," Ross said.

"Let me see it."

"It's confidential," Mancuso said, and he was looking right at Sally.

"That's all right." Terry opened his hand for it.

"Look, Senator, we've been instructed not to—"

"Agents, I'm getting a little tired of your shenanigans." The irritation was rising in Terry's voice. "Miss Crain has access to all the private papers of this office. You—"

"Show him," Mancuso said, and put his hands in his pockets. This Fallon was a smug bastard—smug and stuck-up, just like the bimbo standing behind him.

Ross took the photo of Petersen from the folder and gave it to Chris, who walked it down the length of the room and put it in Terry's hand. Sally looked over his shoulder.

"Have you ever seen that man, Senator?" Ross said.

Terry shook his head. "No. Never." He looked up at Sally. She shook her head and shrugged.

Ross couldn't take his eyes off Sally. This morning there was a glow to her skin or a glow to her hair or a glow to her eyes or something about the weight of her breasts under her white silk blouse. Last night she had been pretty. Now, she was ravishing.

"Why should I recognize this man?" Terry was saying.

"He was with the CIA," Mancuso said. "Martinez have any kind of beef with the CIA?"

Terry stiffened. He looked up at Sally, then at Mancuso. "Are you telling me that Octavio Martinez was murdered by an agent of the CIA?"

"Nah. The guy's freelance now. And anyhow, he ain't elected yet—just a candidate."

The joke wasn't funny. Terry sat forward to reprimand Mancuso. But before he could, Ross spoke up.

"Senator, did President Ortega want Martinez dead bad enough to risk direct American reprisals if the assassination could be traced back to him?"

Mancuso looked sidelong at Ross, impressed with the question. Terry looked up at Sally. They were impressed, too.

"I don't know," Terry said. "That's interesting. I don't know."

"Who would know?" Ross asked.

"Ramirez."

"I'm sorry, who?"

"Julio Ramirez," Sally said. "He was secretary of state before Ortega ousted the Somoza government. He's their spokesman-in-exile. He arranged for Senator Fallon to make the speech welcoming Colonel Martinez to America."

Ross smiled. She was not only lovely, she was articulate and bright with a low, easy voice.

"Where do we find this guy?" Mancuso said.

"He's gone into hiding in Florida."

"Yeah." Mancuso rubbed his chin. "And you wouldn't know how to find him?"

Terry looked up at Sally; she shook her head no.

Then Terry said, "Yes. We can make contact. Miss Crain will arrange a meeting with him."

That startled her. "But there's so much to do here," she began. "There's only six days—"

"A great man has been killed," Terry said. "I want his killers brought to justice. We all want that."

Sally lowered her head for a moment. When she looked up, she said very softly, "As you wish."

Ross just stared. When she pouted, she was breathtaking.

"Thank you, gentlemen," Terry said. "Please leave your card. We'll call you when we've made arrangements."

"Today," Mancuso said.

"When we've made arrangements. Now, good day."

At last, Ross caught Sally's eye—and when he did, he smiled his very best smile. She simply nodded back, all proper and correct.

Chris Van Allen saw them out.

9:15 A.M. SOMETIMES WHEN HE had a decision to make, Sam Baker would get into the tiny White House elevator, and punch the button for B-3. Then he would stand against the back of the car while it slowly slid away from the family level, past the executive level, past the street level with its ceremonial receiving rooms and endless line of tourists thronging the East Wing. He would watch the indicator lights blink from 2 to 1 to G and then B-1. He could always sense it when the car passed ground level. Somehow, the cool, damp scent of the earth seemed to pervade the air of the car as it slipped underground, down toward the level where the Secret Service operations center was located, and then onward, to B-2 and the hardened meeting rooms where Jack Kennedy had slept during the Cuban missile crisis in 1961. There was always a little final jolt when the light of B-3 came on and he knew that the elevator had stopped thirty feet underground, deep in the cold, wet earth of the Potomac shoreline.

He put the silver key in the lock, twisted it to the right, and the elevator doors hissed open. He stepped out into a dim, narrow corridor of reinforced concrete and filtered air. At the end of the corridor was a darkened room, carpeted and soundproofed, where three armchairs were bolted to the floor. He sat down in the middle chair.

Before him, panoramic one-way windows looked down upon the White House Air Defense Command Room. A triptych of huge, illuminated displays showed three electronic views of the earth.

A red light began blinking on the telephone at his elbow. He raised the receiver.

"This is General Gaynor, Mr. President. May I help you?"

The president leaned forward. On the floor of the Air Defense Room below him, he could see General Gaynor standing at attention, telephone to his ear, looking up toward the mirrored windows, not quite in the president's direction.

"A little to your left, General," the president said and smiled.

"I beg your pardon, sir." Gaynor turned slightly. He was a major general, a fiftyish career officer with five rows of campaign ribbons on his chest. Sam Baker had met him once at a cocktail reception for the Joint Chiefs.

"You're the officer in charge of the War Room," Sam Baker had said. "You'll be down there if the time comes, won't you?"

"Yes, sir," Gaynor had said softly. "I'll be there with you."

"I hope I never see you again, General."

"I pray I never see you again, sir."

But Sam Baker did see General Gaynor again—even if Gaynor could not see him—through the one-way glass of the Air Defense Room. From time to time when he had a difficult decision to make, Sam Baker would come down to the ADR, sit alone in the center chair, and look out at the electronic vision of a world at peace. When the marines landed on Grenada, or when the FB-111s from Gresham Common struck Libya, it was possible to sit in the ADR and get a sense of the drama unfolding through satellite projection. Then the floor below would bustle with crisp, alert men in uniform.

But, somehow, when the room and the plotting boards were quiet as they were just then, the wonder of it made a deeper impression on Sam Baker. He looked out at the known world, half of it sleeping, half of it getting on with life, and he mused at the perfect stillness of a world at peace. And although the displays were only electronic representations of national boundaries, in his mind's eye he could perch himself in the deep space of the satellites and look down upon a globe of blue water and dun-colored continents and swirling, sun-silvered clouds and he could see the wonder of God's creation.

Some day, he might have to sit in that very chair and make a decision of indescribable terror—perhaps the last strategic decision that any human being would ever make before The Last Judgment. So, it was good for him to sit in that chair in moments of peace. That way, he knew he would have a last memory of the world that was—if he ever had to give the order to destroy it.

"Excuse me, sir," General Gaynor said softly through the telephone at his ear.

"I'm sorry, General. I was daydreaming."

Gaynor looked at the display boards. "I do that, too, sir. Some-times."

It was remarkable to Sam Baker how well they understood each other.

"Tell me one thing, General."

"Yes, sir."

"How do you know when I'm here? Do they call and let you know I'm coming down."

"No, sir. It's your seat."

"My seat?"

"Your chair, sir. It's hot. When you sit down, an alert light blinks on my console."

"I see," the president said, and he knew the irony was not lost on either of them.

"Thank you, General."

"Yes, sir."

He put down the phone.

At the far end of the corridor, the bronze elevator doors hissed open and Henry O'Brien, director of the FBI, stepped out into the semidarkness. He stood, blinking, as the doors slid closed behind him.

"Hello?" he said into the dim light. "Anybody there?"

The president sat up in his armchair and looked around.

"I'm over here, Henry."

"Mr. President, I—"

"Come. Come sit here." The president patted the armchair beside him.

O'Brien sat, wide-eyed and blinking at the plotting boards in the Air Defense Room below. He never seemed at ease around the president. His beer belly dipped over his belt and his shirt collar was always unbuttoned. He wore the same styleless, thick tweed jackets summer and winter. He was just a cop, wanting nothing more than to be a cop. He was a very smart man and Sam Baker hoped he could trust him.

"So," O'Brien said. "So." He nodded to himself and set his jaw. "This is the place."

"This is the place," the president said.

"Hail Mary, Mother of God," O'Brien said quietly. "Pray for us sinners, now and at the hour of our death. Amen." He crossed himself.

"Amen," the president said.

They sat a while looking at each other.

"Any progress?"

O'Brien knew what he meant. "No, sir."

"I see." The president leaned back in his armchair. "The men you've got working on it," he said. "Will they find anything?"

"It's unlikely."

"Will they find the assassin? Petersen?"

"No. I don't think so. There isn't much to go on."

The president thought about that.

"Of course, if we released his picture to the papers. . . ." O'Brien said.

"Henry, is your oath of office sacred to you?" the president said.

The question startled O'Brien. He took a breath. "It is, yes."

"Would you break that oath? If I asked you to?"

"I hope you wouldn't ask me, Mr. President."

"I won't," the president said. "But I will ask you to keep faith with it, whatever happens this week. Will you do that?"

"I will. Yes, sir."

"Then tell me—why are there only two men working on this case?"

O'Brien stared at the president.

"I asked you a question. Why are there only two men working on the Martinez assassination?"

O'Brien looked at him as though he were speaking in a foreign tongue. "Henry?"

"It was—" O'Brien stammered. "It was—an order."

"An order? Whose order?"

O'Brien sat dumb. Then he shrugged his shoulders. "Well, it was yours, Mr. President."

"Mine?"

"I got it straight from Mr. Bender."

The president stared at him. The light on the phone at his elbow began to blink, but the president didn't seem to notice.

Now, Sam Baker knew. It was deep water. Dark, deep water boiling with treacherous undercurrents that could drag a man down deeper than his death. He was in it, swimming, kicking, not knowing where to reach for help. O'Brien sat before him—a slippery rock in a tormented sea.

"Mr. President. . . . The phone, sir."

"Stay close to me this week, Henry, will you?"

"Count on me, Mr. President."

"I will." He picked up the receiver. "This is the president."

It was his secretary, Katherine. "Mr. President, you have the ambassador from Gabon at 11:30. He'll present his credentials. There will be a brief photo session."

"Thank you, Katherine." He was just about to put the phone down when she said, "Vice President Eastman called to say he'll join you."

8:25 A.M./CST TED WYCKOFF WAS still perspiring. He swabbed his glistening forehead with a handkerchief and loosened his collar. "Well, what are we waiting for?"

Arlen Ashley smiled a southern smile, but his eyes were angry points of green. "*Mistah* Wyckoff," he said, "I been instructed to show you what you askin' for. And I'm obliged to do it. I'm just a little fretful about it, is all. Now, do you understand me, *suh?*"

"If that's the way you want it, fine."

"You know, our published newspapers are on microfilm and available to the public. Even to you, *suh.*"

"If you don't mind, I'm in a hurry, Mr. Ashley."

"I know that, *suh.* And if my management wants you to see our editorial reference—" He rolled his pencil between his fingers. "Well, it's my pleasure to extend our hospitality." He got up and went to the door of the newsroom. "Will you follow me?"

Ted Wyckoff followed him into the newsroom of the *Houston Post.* It was very different from the newsroom in which Ted Wyckoff had begun his career fifteen years before. He had parlayed a 3.8 grade average and his extracurricular work as an editor of the Bowdoin College *Lit* into a trainee job at the *Trenton Times.* It was pure intoxication for a comparative literature major with aspirations to writing the great American novel. His heroes were Hecht and Hemingway; that was just the kind of barnstorming reporter-turned-novelist that he fancied to become.

But after two years of warfare with an old black Royal typewriter, the growing stack of rejections from *The New Yorker, Paris Review,* and other smart publications were sending him a message that was hard to ignore. To make things worse, his college roommate, Dick Stanton, had already been promoted to reporter on the city hall beat of the *Philadelphia Inquirer.* It had taken Wyckoff all freshman year to seduce Stanton, and by senior year he was still sharing him with coeds. Now, Stanton was a full-fledged reporter, thanks to a girlfriend at city hall who was feeding him a lot of inside stuff. And Wyckoff was writing obituaries for the *Trenton Times.*

Then, in 1974, a Philadelphia councilman got into a battle with the governor over the Philly Fire Department, and Ted Wyckoff found himself devouring the *Philadelphia Inquirer* and *Daily News* and *Bulletin* while his copy of the *Trenton Times* lay unread on the front porch of his parents' home.

One day he drove to Philadelphia and camped outside an office until the burly man who had tweaked the Governor's nose came out the door.

"What the hell do you want?" Dan Eastman had said after Wyckoff followed him into the elevator.

"A job."

"What can you do?"

"Find out things."

"Like what?"

"Like who's leaking your memos to the *Inquirer.*"

Eastman reached over and hit the Stop button, and the cage juddered to a halt between floors.

"Who?" he demanded.

"If I tell you, I'll need a job. Because it will cost me the one I've got."

Eastman looked him over. "How old are you?"

"Twenty-three."

"Get it right and you're hired."

"Paula Turner."

"Bullshit," Eastman said.

"Have it your own way." Wyckoff reached over and pressed the button and the elevator started to descend.

Eastman hit the button and the elevator stopped again. "How do you know that?" The veins were bulging in his neck and he was barely controlling his fury. He was a man capable of intense anger—extreme physical intimidation. But Wyckoff was neither impressed nor intimidated. He was excited by Eastman's rage.

"I told you," Wyckoff said flatly. "I'm good at finding out things."

"We'll see." Eastman started the cage down again. "Call me next week." The door opened at street level. "What's your name, kid?"

"I'll tell you when I call."

That Friday the *Inquirer* carried a short item on page twelve about Paula Turner's resignation from Dan Eastman's office to pursue interests in the private sector. On Monday Wyckoff called Eastman's office.

"May I tell him what it's in reference to?" the secretary asked.

"An elevator ride."

When the secretary came back on the line, she gave him an appointment on the following Friday and when he turned up, Eastman was ready for him.

"You went to Bowdoin, work on the *Trenton Times*, and think you want to be a novelist."

"You've been checking me out," Wyckoff said. "I'm flattered."

"What else should I know?"

"I'm a homosexual."

Eastman screwed up his mouth in distaste. "Jesus," he said.

"I'll admit it's not for everyone."

"How do I know I can trust you?"

"Two reasons."

"Yeah?"

"I want to win."

"What else?"

"I have no conscience."

Eastman snorted. "You're a nasty little fuck for twenty-three years old."

"I have other redeeming qualities."

"Like what?"

"People can't tell when I'm lying."

"I don't want any faggot bullshit in this office," Eastman said.

"Agreed."

"A hundred and fifty a week. That's it. Take it or leave it."

"When do I start?"

"You've started."

But when the news of his appointment to Dan Eastman's staff got around, Dick Stanton put two and two together, and called him on the phone.

"You miserable fucking little faggot. You sold Paula out."

"It was just politics, Dick. Nothing personal."

"I'd like to beat the shit out of you."

"How'd you like your bowling buddies to know you suck cock in your spare time?"

There was a long silence on the other end of the line. Then the receiver slammed down.

Now, fourteen years later, Ted Wyckoff was in Houston to find what he could in the files of the *Houston Post* to silence Terry Fallon.

At the far end of the newsroom was an empty cubicle with venetian blinds drawn to shield it from the staff. Ashley sat down at the desk, switched on the IBM terminal, and waited for the CRT to glow unearthly green. It challenged with the message ACCESS CODE PLEASE.

Ashley typed a string of letters and numbers. The machine cycled and responded with KEY WORD PLEASE.

Ashley typed FALLON TERRY SENATOR.

The screen blinked, then displayed a chronological list of entries dating back to 1976, each with a brief précis of story content. The first was headlined:

RICE INSTRUCTOR SEEKS COUNCILMAN'S SEAT

"There you are," Ashley said and rose, offering the chair to Wyckoff. "You type the index number and press the Enter key and the story will be displayed. If you want hard copy, press the button marked Print Screen. When you finish and want to go on to another story, press the Escape key."

Wyckoff sat down. "Thanks."

Ashley smiled. "*Y'all* don't mention it." He shut the door behind him.

9:40 A.M. "MIAMI?" BARNEY SCOTT said. "What the fuck is this? A vacation?" He held up the travel voucher as though it were a fish that had gone to stink.

"Ramirez is in Miami," Mancuso said. "We want to talk to him— somebody's got to go. What do you want from me?"

Ross leaned against the far wall of Scott's office, watching, listening.

"And what are you gonna get from this wetback? Tell me that."

"He knows who had the knife out for Martinez," Mancuso said. "He's a governor in exile—something like that."

"Sounds like a crock to me." Scott studied the voucher. "Four hundred and ten bucks out the window."

"Listen, Scotty, for my two cents, the guys from the Miami zone can handle it. I don't give a shit."

"No, sir," Scott said. "It's your case and you two are gonna handle it. Leave the guys from the zone out of it." He signed the voucher and held it out to Mancuso.

"Thanks," Mancuso said. "Here's the one for the girl."

"What girl?"

"The girl. The press girl. She's the contact. Without her, we get squat."

Scott signed the second voucher. "What a fucking rip-off! You guys don't give a shit about the taxpayers' money, do you?"

"Yeah. Jesus. I'm all broke up about it, Scotty. Honest to God," Mancuso said as they went out the door.

In the hall he passed the travel vouchers to Ross. "You're it," he said.

"Me? Why me?"

"She don't like my vocabulary."

"Who does?" Ross said. He tried to look petulant, but what Mancuso was saying delighted him.

Mancuso pressed both buttons for the elevator. "I'll tell Jean-with-the-big-tits to order the tickets. You go home and pack."

"What makes you so sure they'll set it up so fast?" Ross was staring at the vouchers and trying to keep from smiling.

"Trust me."

Ross folded the vouchers into his pocket. "What are you going to work on?"

"Fallon."

"Why him?"

"He's too true to be good."

"No heroes?"

"No heroes."

The white light indicated an elevator going up. The doors opened and Ross stepped inside.

"You know, Joe, there are days when you make me sick."

The doors slid closed between them.

11:25 A.M. HAMILTON TATE, THE State Department's chief of protocol, led the way down the stairs toward the Blue Room on the second floor of the White House. The president followed him and as he did he thought through the bits of information about Gabon that he had retained from his last night's reading. There was really only one salient fact: Gabon was 150 miles north of Angola, a West African country where thousands of Cuban military advisors were billetted.

At the door to the Blue Room, Tate stopped and looked back at the president. "They speak French and Bantu," he said.

"What do you think?"

"I'm afraid it will be Bantu, sir. It's that *Roots* thing. It's very strong there now."

"Oh, well." The president sighed. "Bantu banter it will be."

The Gabonese ambassador certainly did look the proper diplomat in his morning coat and stiff collar. He was a tall man with wavy scars on both his cheeks like the whiskers of a cat. He was just shaking hands with Dan Eastman when the president was announced.

"Missa President," he said and put his hands together and bowed.

"Good morning, Mr. Ambassador. And welcome to Washington on behalf of the people and the government of the United States."

The ambassador leaned toward the interpreter, hanging on his whispered words.

Dan Eastman stepped forward. "Good morning, Mr. President. I've been trying to reach you."

"Good morning, Dan." The president shook his hand.

Tate took the president's elbow, positioned him between Eastman and the ambassador, turning his good side toward the cameras.

"Missa President," the ambassador said as the strobes began to flash— and then proceeded to a long speech of greeting in Bantu.

But on his other side, Eastman said, "You know what I want to see you about. Now, when do we talk?"

"Later," the president said through gritted teeth, smiling for the camera.

Eastman was smiling, too. "It's the goddamnedest thing I ever heard of."

The interpreter began, "Our revered president, El Haj Omar Bongo, sends you felicitations and the thanks of our people for the bounty of—"

"Damit, Sam," Eastman hissed, "you're not shutting me out."

"Keep your voice down."

"Excuse me, sir," the interpreter said, baffled.

"No, not you," the president said, still smiling. "Please, please continue."

"—for the bounty of economic development, which the great people of America have—"

"You think you're going to put Fallon past me, you're crazy," Eastman said, under the noise of the strobes and cameras.

"I'm doing nothing of the kind."

The interpreter stopped, gaping, his mouth open.

"No. Please go on," the president said. And then aside to Eastman, he said, "You come here tomorrow, we'll talk it out."

The interpreter said something to the ambassador, who grinned broadly.

"He will be here tomorrow with pleasure," the interpreter said.

"No, not him," the president said. "Him." He pointed to Eastman.

"The hell I will," Eastman said. "We can settle this today or never."

The interpreter began to speak to the ambassador.

"Don't translate that, dammit!" the president said. "Look, Dan, we'll discuss this tomorrow."

"Perhaps a picture or two with the vice president," Tate said. He stepped back, pulling the ambassador and Eastman together. Strobes flashed. The ambassador grabbed Eastman's hand, pumped it eagerly.

"You're not getting away with this," Eastman said, partly turned to the camera, partly to the president behind him.

"The press is here, Dan," the president said softly, but there was a steely edge to his voice.

"The hell with the press." Eastman dropped the ambassador's hand as though it were a dirty rag. He turned on the president. "You're dumping me out of this campaign over my dead body. If I go down, you go with me."

"Whatever you say, Dan," the president said and tried to smile. "You do have a way of making me ashamed of you."

The ambassador and the interpreter looked back and forth between the two angry men. Across the room, the cameras blazed away.

"Goddamit," Eastman said. He pushed past the photographers and out the door.

Sam Baker stood looking after him, a sad smile brushing one side of his face.

10:40 A.M./CST TED WYCKOFF DIDN'T like to admit it, but there it was. The story of Terry Fallon's rise from an $11,000-a-year history instructor at Rice to the U.S. Senate was a fairy tale come true. On the screen of the computer terminal—before Wyckoff's very eyes—the man walked through the pages of the *Houston Post* like a Lincoln for our time, a knight-errant who stood single-handed against the power brokers of Houston, and who led his dirty, polyglot band of tired-and-poor to a resounding constitutional victory in the Texas State Supreme Court.

It had all the sentimentality and melodrama of a television mini-series: Fallon's life had been threatened; a cross had been burned on his lawn; someone had fired rifle shots into his office. But through all that turmoil, he never swerved, never veered even one degree from his course toward equal justice under the law. And in the end, he brought together the whites and the Latins of Houston, and united them in a semblance of brotherhood.

Ted Wyckoff took off his glasses, and rubbed his eyes. No wonder Fallon's work in the barrio had catapulted him onto the city council and into Congress. No wonder Governor Taylor had chosen him to serve the unexpired term of the convicted Senator Weatherby. And it was certainly no wonder that Sam Baker might think he would make a superb candidate for vice president.

But there was something else—a kind of subtext that was equally enlightening. Almost all the stories about Fallon's ascendancy, his struggle, his indomitable will, his commitment to the people—almost all those stories were under one byline: Sally Crain. To hear her tell it, she had run across him—discovered him, so to speak—as he walked amid the rubble of barrio tenements that were being razed over the screaming protests of the occupants.

Tall he was, and lean. His tie was loose, his collar open, and the sleeves of his pristine white shirt rolled up past his elbows. His reddish hair had a boyish wave—the way it fell across his eyes reminded you of Jack. He comforted a grandmother, and shook the hand of one disconsolate man after another. He spoke Spanish as if it were his mother tongue and his message was a simple one: *valentia*—courage; *persistencia*—persistence; *esperanza*—faith.

In Sally Crain's words, Fallon's campaign for a seat on the Houston city council unfolded like a mystery play.

Wyckoff paged on into the computer's record of Fallon's congressional campaign. But the tone of the stories had changed, had become more businesslike, more reportorial. Then he realized that the byline had changed. There were dozens of stories, but none by Sally Crain.

"What happened? She stopped writing about him in 1976. Why?"

Arlen Ashley studied Wyckoff over the tops of his reading glasses. "She moved north. To your part of the world."

"To Washington?"

"To the *Washington Post*. To 'Pravda on the Potomac,' as we call it here."

"Was she that good a reporter?"

"No." Ashley laughed. "No. She was a better writer than reporter. I told her once that she should try her hand at fiction. But she was a believer. And Washington is a place for believers—and for fools."

Wyckoff let that pass. "Was she in love with Fallon?"

"Oh, I suppose so."

"Were they lovers?"

"Now, I ask you—why would I care to answer that question?"

"So, she left for a better job?"

"No. She left because he married."

Wyckoff leafed through his handful of reprints until he found the right one. "Yeah, I got your society blurb. 'The Prince and Princess of Light.' " He snickered. Then he read, " 'The bride glided among them like faint music heard in the stillness of a summer day. Even the mockingbird forgot his song. And the prairie held its breath.' " Wyckoff shook his head, folded the paper and sat smirking. "A year later, the bride was in the booby hatch. And the prince was on his way to Congress. End of fable."

Ashley said, "Sally wrote that."

Wyckoff's mouth fell open. He looked down at the story of the wedding in his hand. "You're kidding."

"She was on her way to Washington. Wanted to make this her last assignment. I thought it would be okay."

Wyckoff gaped at the text in wonder. "Why, do you suppose? Out of love? Or out of hate?"

Ashley stood up. "Well, if there's nothing more you require. . . ."

Wyckoff stopped at the door. "This 'enchanted castle'—where is it?"

"In Wharton County," Ashley said. "Fortunately, you'll find it on your way out of town. *Y'all* come back and see us."

12:05 P.M. IN THE BEDROOM of the guest house behind the Fallon mansion, Sally unpacked her cases and put her things away. She had spent many nights in that bedroom. It was a place that felt like home.

Many a time she had dragged herself down the flagstone walk to the little ivy-covered cottage after a long night of wrangling with a position paper. Sometimes, when all the power brokers and wise men had crushed out their cigars and slid into their long limousines and headed back through the darkness toward the District, she and Terry would walk out the back door of the main house together, around the edge of the swimming pool, past the barbecue pit, following the soft circles of light that the stubby, low-voltage lamps dripped on the stone. They seldom spoke. They were weary of the complicated, endless problems of government—the struggle to find positions that would reconcile judgment and popular opinion with the Constitution. Terry always relied on her in those meetings; he knew she never lost focus on the kernel of the idea, and she always understood the economic implications before anyone else. The others might ramble and their conversation wander, but Sally never forgot the objective. With her beside him, Terry Fallon could always find a way.

When those meetings finally broke up, Terry's fat Danish housekeeper, Katrina, would stand in the window of the main house until she saw the two of them reach the cottage. She was a good woman, not snoopy. And when she saw Terry and Sally reach the door of the guest house, she would always turn away from the window.

Then Sally would stand with Terry in the darkness, listening to the crickets calling in the night, hearing the east wind off Chesapeake Bay moving in the branches of the elm trees. In the dim light, she could see how tired he was, how the years and days and nights of Washington had aged him, had toned him with sadness, had brushed him with regret. For all his magnetic qualities, he was still a frail, aging man, nearing the threshold of middle age. Sometimes, while they were standing there, he would bend his head and kiss her—not the way friend kisses friend, but the way a man kisses his wife of twenty years, with gratitude, and reverence. There was such tenderness in his kiss that it made her want to weep, and the pain of being separated from him was like a needle in her heart.

But they were separate. And as she watched him walk back up the path toward the house, sometimes with the dawn rising red behind him, sometimes with his shoulders so stooped with care that he seemed bent and old, she mourned for all the might-have-beens of her life and his, and she cherished him.

But today, armed men with walkie-talkies sat under the beach umbrella beside the pool, ever watchful. Through the open window of the guest house bedroom, Sally could hear the dim crackle of their walkie-talkies.

The phone rang.

"Miss Crain?" It was the Secret Service man at the portable switchboard in the main house.

"Yes?"

"I have a Mr. Benson from the Associated Press on the line. Will you take the call?"

"Yes, thanks."

"Sally?"

"Yes, Bob."

"Don't miss the noon newscast."

"Why? What's up?"

"Baker and Eastman had it out in the Blue Room in front of a bunch of still photographers. Pictures are on the wire right now."

"What are you talking about?"

"Baker went down to greet some African whim-wham, Eastman shows up for the photo session, has words with him, and walks. You gotta see the pictures. They were really pissed."

"I don't believe it," Sally said.

"Care to comment."

"No comment."

"Background?"

Sally shrugged. "Boys will be boys."

Benson laughed. "Call you later." He hung up.

Someone rapped at the door.

"I'm almost ready, Chris," she called, struggling to fit the back on the post of her pierced earring.

"That's what you said twenty minutes ago."

"Well, this time I mean it." Sally swung the door open. "Anyhow, what's the rush?"

"It's twelve-ten and you're due at Maison Blanche at twelve-thirty and I—" he turned and started up the path "—I have a lunch date with a lovely fellow from William and Mary."

"Don't you ever think of anything else?"

"My mother taught me sex was dirty," Chris said. "And I love it because it's dirty."

They nodded to the Secret Service at the back door and went into the house.

"He's asked for you," Katrina said.

They went into the study. Terry was sitting in the window seat in his blue silk robe, his feet drawn up on the cushions, the telephone on the floor beside him. He was holding the curtain aside so that the May sunlight haloed his face. He looked for all the world like a wistful little boy.

"Did you want to see me?" Sally said softly.

"Oh . . . yes," Terry said. "Good morning, Chris."

"Senator."

"Baker and Eastman—"

"Yes, I just heard," she said.

Terry shook his head. "Sad," he said. "Two fine men like that."

"Yes."

"I had a call from Ashley," Terry said.

Sally cocked her head. "Not Arlen Ashley? At the *Houston Post*?"

"He said that someone we know visited him this morning."

"Who?"

"Went through all the files about me, asked a lot of questions about you."

"Someone we know did that? Who?"

Terry looked straight at Chris. "Ted Wyckoff."

Chris swelled up like he was fit to burst. "That . . . that filthy little Georgetown queen! I'll bust his dirty little balls!"

"It's all right, Chris," Terry said. "It's all right. What's in the paper is on the record. We have nothing whatsoever to hide."

But Van Allen was furious. "It's . . . it's—"

"No one likes to feel used," Terry said. "It's just politics and part of growing up."

"Shit," Chris said. "The little bastard."

"That's what it's going to be like around here until the convention," Terry said. "Maybe for a long time after that. But the main thing to remember is we're proud of what we are and what we stand for." He rose, favoring his side. "We've got nothing to hide"—he took hold of Chris's shoulders— "and we trust and care about each other."

They stood like that a moment, Terry holding the chubby little man's shoulders, Chris staring at the floor.

"Right?" Terry said.

Chris nodded. "Right."

"Okay, you two," Terry said. "Have a nice lunch downtown. Sally, don't let Tommy Carter peddle you any of his applesauce."

"Don't worry, boss."

"And, Chris, you just be a little more careful."

"Right. Yes, sir." Terry clapped him gently on the back and started him for the door.

"Did Ashley say what Wyckoff was going to do?" Sally said.

"He thinks he might go to visit Harriet's parents," Terry said. Sally stood where she was, staring. "Not—I wouldn't think—a very good idea."

Sally shook her head.

"See you around two." Terry waved them out.

They made their way through the cluster of political types and Secret Service in the foyer, and out the front door. At the bottom of the drive, news crews were clustered, hoping for a glimpse of Terry Fallon. Some of the reporters who knew Sally called out.

"Sally, has Fallon seen the pictures?"

"What does he say about Eastman and the president?"

"Has Baker called him?"

Sally waved them off. Chris gave his ticket to a Secret Service man, who went to get their car from the secure garage.

"Sally, come on!" the reporters shouted. "Hey! Give us a break!" But she smiled and waved "no comment."

"I feel like an asshole," Chris said, when they were in the car. "A complete asshole."

"We've all got a lot to learn," Sally said.

The Secret Service cleared the reporters at the end of the driveway and swung back the barrier. Chris's blue Toyota bumped over the curb into Crescent Drive. As it did, he shifted gears and hit the accelerator.

"Next stop, Maison Blanche."

Suddenly—with a wrench that almost hurt her neck—Sally turned in her seat, peering out the rear window of the car. For an instant, there was the flash of a face in the crowd, a face among the reporters that didn't belong there, a face she seemed to remember with dread.

"What is it?" Chris said. "Someone you know?"

Sally turned around. "No," she said. "I guess not." But the color had drained from her cheeks.

12:20 P.M. ROSS DIDN'T GO home to pack. He took a cab to 23rd and E Streets, went up the driveway to the Navy Bureau of Medicine and Surgery, and identified himself to the chief petty officer at the reception desk. Then he sat awhile amid the old wooden furniture and recruiting posters. A few minutes later, an imposing black shore patrolman in snappy navy-and-white called his name.

"Agent Ross?"

"Yes?"

"I'm Seaman Brown. I'll take you up to Captain Fairchild's office." All the way up in the elevator, he stood at parade rest at the back of the car. At the door to Captain Fairchild's office, he snapped to attention. "I'll wait for you here, sir."

"Suits me." Ross shrugged and went inside.

"Hey, Davy," Tim Fairchild said when the door opened. He was a navy captain, an internist who had gone to Yale and Yale Med on an ROTC scholarship and was paying off his commitment with a residency in internal medicine. He and Ross had played a lot of squash in their time. "Come in, man. Come in. Sit down." He offered the chair across from his desk.

"Jesus, Pam is on my case once a month at least. What happened to Dave Ross? How come he never comes to dinner anymore?"

"I don't know. I don't get around much."

"Working hard?"

"Hardly working."

"Still partnered with the guy—what's-his-name—Mancuso?"

"Yeah. Same crap."

"Why don't they give you a break? Get you into something exciting?"

"Yeah. I've been asking myself the same question."

"Well, don't lose heart," Fairchild said. "When the old guy retires, they'll put you onto something important maybe."

"Yeah, I'm hoping," Ross said.

"Well. . . ." Fairchild put his hands on the desk blotter. "Something I can do for you today?"

"Yeah, actually there is. I've got some questions about AIDS."

"What?" Fairchild laughed out loud.

"Hey, hey! Hold on a second. I'm not talking about myself."

"Jesus Christ, I should hope not."

"Hey, Tim. Come on. How long we known each other?"

"Long time."

"Well, you think I'd ever go the other way?"

"No." Fairchild shook his head. "Not you, the old Davenport cocksman."

"Anyhow—let me ask you a hypothetical question."

"Hypothetical," Fairchild said, nodding. "Sure."

"Guy gets a blood test. Guy is straight. But two days after a clean blood test, he's got AIDS. How does that happen?"

Fairchild opened his hands. "I give up. How?"

"No, come on," Ross said. "I'm asking *you*."

Fairchild shook his head. "Can't happen."

"What do you mean *can't*?"

"Can't happen. You can't get AIDS like that."

"I thought a lot of druggies got it from using dirty needles."

"Sure they do," Fairchild said. "But without prior exposure, it would take thirty days before a primary immune response showed up."

"Yeah?"

"Yeah."

Ross sat a while, thinking.

"This is no hypothetical," Fairchild finally said.

Ross looked at him a moment. "Yes. Tim, it's hypothetical. You understand?"

Fairchild nodded. "Okay. Hypothetically . . . I'm speaking hypothetically here, somebody told you that a guy developed AIDS two days after he got a blood test?"

"That's the concept."

"Now, this hypothetical guy who gave you this hypothetical diagnosis—he could be a doc?"

"Sure."

"What kind of doc?"

"Forensics."

"Well. . . ." Fairchild rocked his head back and forth. "Could be an honest mistake. Lots of autopsy cutters don't know the first thing about AIDS except that it kills you. But that's not the real question."

"No?"

"No. You've got to ask yourself why they tested for AIDS in the first place. Hypothetically, I mean. No way a test for AIDS is part of a standard autopsy."

"This wasn't your standard hypothetical victim."

"Oh. Well, even hypothetically—believe me, Dave—you can't get AIDS in two days from a dirty needle or infected blood. The only way he could turn up with AIDS after two days was if someone injected him with a pure strain of the AIDS virus. And that sure didn't happen.''

"How do you know?''

Fairchild laughed. "Come on, Dave. Are you serious? A pure culture of AIDS virus? You know how deadly that is? Little pipette of that in the New York City water supply, you could kiss the 10 million people bye-bye. Growing that in a lab is like having a hydrogen bomb in the room with you.''

"Nobody's growing it?''

"Well, sure, they're growing it. They have to if they're ever going to find a vaccine. Polio vaccine is actually polio virus in a weakened state. It's strong enough to make the body create its own antibodies, but too weak to do any damage. They're doing the same thing with the AIDS virus right now.''

"Where?''

"Only one place I know of—the National Institute of Health in Bethesda. The French claim to have isolated the virus at the Pasteur Institute in Paris—you know, the place Rock Hudson went before he died. A lot of people don't believe the French claims.''

"Is it possible that someone could have stolen the AIDS virus from NIH?''

"It would be easier to steal an atomic bomb.''

"How come?''

"There are more of them.''

Ross got up to leave. "Listen, thanks a lot for—''

Then Fairchild said, "There might be one other place.''

"Where?''

"Fort Deitrich.''

"What's that?''

"It's something called the Headquarters of the U.S. Army Medical Research and Development Command.''

Ross took out his pad. "Who would I see there?''

"Nobody. Forget it. The place is top secret. You might as well ask for a tour of the headquarters of the Strategic Air Command. No fucking way.''

Ross was writing. "You said U.S. Army Medical Research and—''

Fairchild reached over and caught the hand holding the pen. "Dave, they're not going to tell you anything. These R-and-D guys aren't like regular soldiers. They're not docs who serve their hitch and go into private practice as pediatricians. They're ideologues who believe there's a war on right now. And they don't care about the body count as long as they win.''

Ross just stared.

"Anyhow, I wouldn't go down there if I were you,'' Fairchild said.

"How come?''

"You might catch something."

"So, how do I find out about what they're doing down there?"

"That's the idea. You don't."

"You're a big help."

"Hey," Fairchild said. "I thought this was a hypothetical question."

Ross stood still, not saying anything.

"I know one guy who might be able to help you," Fairchild said finally. He took Ross's pen and scribbled an address.

"Who is he?"

"A doc who used to work there. Did two tours and couldn't take the heat. Had kind of a short circuit and walked."

"Thanks." Ross pocketed the note.

"Dave . . . look." Fairchild came around the desk. "Be careful, will you? This is the real army you're fooling with. These people mean it. Watch your step."

"Sure," Ross said. "Did I tell you you're a good guy?"

"Not in a long time."

"Will you say something to Pam?"

"What?" Fairchild said.

Ross shrugged. They shook and Ross went out.

11:35 A.M./CST   AFTER HE PASSED the last Houston suburb and turned off the expressway, Ted Wyckoff drove for more than an hour. The dusty Texas plains slid by, all mesquite and tumbleweed, and solemn saguro cactus. Then his rented Ford humped over a single-line railroad track and a neat ribbon of macadam began. A crisp red-and-white sign read PRIVATE ROAD, and a hundred yards down the track he could see deserted stock pens and a loading chute. There was another red-and-white sign. This one read KIMBERLY.

He drove on, following the barbed wire fence that separated the grazing land from the road, drove a good five miles before the fence became white picket and the grazing land turned to grassy horse pasture, and then another mile or so to the brick arch and driveway that led toward a distant group of buildings under a grove of trees. He got out and picked up the telephone beside the gate.

A Texas drawl at the other end of the line said, "This is the Kimberly family residence. How may I help you?"

"I'm Ted Wyckoff. From the vice president's office. I called for an appointment with Mr. Kimberly."

"Just a moment, Mr. Wyckoff."

He stood, holding the phone. Just beyond the fence, there was a long strip of concrete and a pair of white hangars and a taxi pad large enough to accommodate a commercial airliner.

The phone clicked in his ear. "Mr. Wyckoff, I'm so sorry, but Mr. Kimberly's calendar is very busy today as you can likely understand. Would it be possible for me to set something up for you early next week? Or perhaps the week after that?"

"I'm afraid that wouldn't work," Wyckoff said. "Would you—just tell Mr. Kimberly I want a quick word with him. Tell him I'm on my way to Cleveland."

"One moment, please."

There was a beat—then the iron gates silently began to swing open. Wyckoff hung up the receiver, jumped back in the Ford. Halfway up the drive, three cowboys were setting a fence post. They were grizzled and dusty, their leathers worn and stained with rain and sun. They went on with their work, but their eyes followed him from under the wide brims of their hats.

At the end of the drive, there was an enormous spreading oak. Beyond it, a white Gothic revival mansion stood in a grove of nut trees, its six gleaming columns supporting a gracious portico.

A young woman with long dark hair was standing at the bottom of the stairs. She wore jeans, a blue denim workshirt, and lavishly tooled boots. Behind her, a Spanish boy in crisp, white uniform stood holding a tray.

"Mr. Wyckoff," she said as he got out of the car. "I'm Susannah Brown, Mr. Kimberly's secretary." She put her hand out and shook his. "Welcome to the Kimberly home. Would you like some ice water or iced tea?"

"Thanks." Wyckoff took the frosty glass of tea. "God, it's hot, isn't it?"

"Summertime in Texas, Mr. Wyckoff. It's hot—and it can be sticky." She smiled at him. "Mr. Kimberly can see you now if it's convenient."

But she didn't turn back into the house. Instead, she led him across the thick lawn to a large, low wooden building. A brass plaque on the door read TOPPING BARN. She held the door ajar.

He stepped into the dim, cavernous room. The walls were paneled in teak and covered with paintings of horses. The floor was a square of hard red earth. In the center of the square, two grooms wrestled with a mare. One had a long stick with an iron ring through her nostrils, the other bent her left foreleg up off the floor so that she had to balance on three legs. There was a red leather blanket strapped to her withers, and above her a huge white stallion loomed, the blanket gripped in his teeth, his huge, dark penis banging in and out of her rump. The snorting and groaning of the two beasts built to a scream as the mare's contractions spilt the stallion's semen on the hard red ground.

Across the way, a group of ranchers were shaking hands. Then the snorting stallion was led away, while the mare stood, shaky and wondering, as her groom patted her flanks to calm her.

"I'm Dwight Kimberly." The big stockman gave Wyckoff his hand. "Thank you, Susannah," he said, and the woman said, "Mr. Wyckoff," and turned back for the main house.

They walked into the sun.

"Well, what brings you out our way, Mr. Wyckoff?" Kimberly said, and got his boot up on the bottom rail of the pasture fence. They watched as the grooms turned out the white stallion, watched him bob his head and snort and gallop away.

"I'm interested in your son-in-law," Wyckoff said.

Kimberly stared out across the plains. "I reckon he's an interesting man," he said, and there was an edge in his voice.

"I'd like to know about his marriage. About your daughter. What happened to them, why she got sick? How could she be Houston's leading deb one year and in an institution the next?"

"Mr. Wyckoff," Kimberly said, and took his boot down from the rail and brushed himself off. " 'Round *heah*, some people still think marriage is a holy vow. Husband and wife become one flesh. Some folks wouldn't take kindly to you asking a lot of questions about Harriet. I reckon you ought to let well enough alone. Do you catch my meaning?"

"Let me be frank, Mr. Kimberly." Wyckoff wasn't concealing the threat in his voice. "I've got a ticket to Cleveland and a reservation for tomorrow morning. Now, I don't want to disturb your daughter. I don't want to set the Washington press to speculating about why her marriage to Terry Fallon put her in the nut house. But if I have to, I will. Now, do you get *my* meaning?"

Kimberly looked down at him and smiled. The skin of his face was weathered, and there was a harsh, hard quality to his eyes. "Mr. Wyckoff, I'm just a big-footed farmer and you're a smart boy from the city. But I'm gonna give you a piece of friendly advice. Don't stick your peter in other people's business. *Y'hear*? Now, you have a good day."

He put his thumbs in his belt loops and stood smiling.

"Thanks for nothing," Wyckoff said. He poured his iced tea out on the ground, and set the empty glass on a fence post. Then he crossed the lawn toward his car.

12:45 P.M. THE RESTAURANT WAS Maison Blanche—the place where official Washington went to be seen. And when a fellow reporter invited Sally to lunch there, something more than conversation was in the air.

The maitre d' showed her to a booth, but she didn't sit down. "Now, you're buying—right?" she said to the bearded man with the soft gray eyes who offered her a place opposite him.

"Right," Tommy Carter said. He was a network news bureau chief in Washington, but Maison Blanche was off his beat.

"And New York approved it?"

"Yep."

"So, I'm not going to get a call next month with 'Hey, Sally, the American Express bill came and your share is—' "

"No way, no way." Carter laughed. "Now, come on. Sit down."

She did.

"God, I haven't seen you in a long time," he said. "You look great."

"You're a liar."

"Okay, I take it back."

"Drop dead."

The maitre d' leaned in beside her. "Would *mademoiselle* care for an aperitif?"

"Une Kir Royale, s'il vous plaît."

"Merci, mademoiselle."

"So, you're on your way to the big time," Carter said. "I'm happy for you. A long way from Zacatecoluca."

"You're the only *gringo* I ever met who could pronounce that name without stepping on his tongue."

"You were happy there."

"I failed there," she said. "We all did."

The waiter set her drink down. Carter tapped the empty glass in front of him. *"Una más,"* he said.

"Pardon?" the waiter said.

"Un autre."

"Oui, monsieur."

"Snob," Carter said to the waiter's back. "Anyhow, you're making it big in Washington, Sally Crain."

"I'll drink to that." They raised and touched their glasses.

"What about Fallon? Is he for real?"

"He's real, he's honest, he's decent—he's just a good man with an idea that it can all be put right. End of bio."

"Was he hurt bad?"

"Yeah," Sally said. "He was."

"None of this brain damage bull though?"

"No. Just a big hole right here." She pointed at her right side.

"I was amazed, you know." Carter sat back in the booth. "I was amazed how articulate he was. Guy with a bullet wound in his side, losing blood, and going into shock. Said all the right things. Amazing."

"He's an amazing man."

"Yeah. You ever wear your hair in braids anymore?"

"Braids?"

"Yeah. You used to wear your hair in braids. Remember? Two braids down the back with rubber bands and little bows. I watched you midwife a *Ladino* woman once and I kept thinking, man, she's going to get blood on those braids if she bends over any more."

Sally sat back, folded her arms across her chest. "Hey, Tommy. What is this? *I Remember Mama?*"

"Just reminiscing."

"Tommy, please. I've known you too long. You're setting me up. Come on. What do you want?"

He sighed. Then he laughed. "Okay, okay. Word's out that NBC has Fallon in their pocket. Nobody else can get him in front of a mike. My guys in New York want me to offer you a proposition."

"Why you? They figure I can't say *no* to you?"

He shrugged. "I remember a time when you couldn't say *no* to me."

"Yes," Sally said, and looked at the little bubbles in the bottom of her glass. "Well. That was a long time ago in a galaxy far, far away."

They sat for a while like that, not speaking. She knew that, unintentionally, she might have hurt him. She had been a very young girl, a virgin when they became lovers. He had been something more than a boy, less than a man.

Back then, the Panama Canal Zone had been an American outpost—a major staging and training area for Peace Corps volunteers. She had come from Memphis, he from Andover, Massachusetts. She was a blond, braided, Fundamentalist-Baptist choir girl with nurse's training. He was a bearded, seedy, down-at-the-jeans, guitar-playing Amherst poli-sci B.A. who had spent two years in the Maine woods as a subsistence farmer. They had a wildfire case of instant loathing.

Bad luck, complementary skills and the Peace Corps computer packaged them together and packed them off to Lagrimas de Cristo, a dirty little village in the hills of western Honduras, on the border with El

Salvador, where the Rio Nua rose. On an old pink bus named *Ave Maria*, they rode among the screaming *niños* and squawking *polluelos* as far as Esperanza. Then a Peace Corps van took them as far as San Marcos. From there, it was a truck to Coroquin. After that, there was only the jungle and the red dirt road.

Walking into that jungle with a barefoot *Ladino* boy breaking trail in front of her had been the most frightening experience in Sally's life. One step into the jungle, and it closed about her, separating her as though forever from the dirt road that was the only scratch of civilization in the immense green wilderness. It was as though the civilized world she had known hung from the slender, almost invisible thread of the road. And as the palm fronds swung shut behind her, the thread snapped and she was lost to the eternal jungle.

It was high jungle—over 5,000 feet. Sally was breathless with exertion before they'd gone half a mile. Every mile they went, they had to stop and rest, while the *Ladino* boy perched on his haunches on the trunk of a fallen log, watching them. They walked all day and around them the jungle changed and yet remained the same—hills rolled into hills, thicket blended into thicket, stream trickled into stream—and all the while the sweet stench of rotting vegetation rose about them and insects hissed incessantly in the treetops.

Finally, they descended into a valley where a lively little river flowed east from the mountains. The floor of the valley had been cleared and the shanties of Lagrimas de Cristo dotted the crescent north of the stream. There were forty or fifty thatched huts, each with its pen of goats or swine. On the other bank, fields of stunted corn spread south until they butted the solid green wall of the jungle.

The *Ladinos* of the village were straight-haired, round-faced, beardless brown men just over five feet tall, the women shorter and wider. When they saw that Sally wore a little gold cross at her neck, they crossed themselves and held up the bronze crosses they wore on leather lanyards. They did not understand why Sally did not cross herself; to them, the great white world outside was Catholic.

She had come with the best of intentions: to bring health and a little more prosperity to this poor and benighted corner of the world. But by September, she was growing numb with the routine of inoculating children against smallpox and typhoid, tending their small hurts, midwifing the birth of infants and burying half of them in the first trimester of life.

For entertainment, they had a World War II surplus radio. At night, they would take turns at the pedals so that they could talk to the Peace Corps office in Tegucigalpa and occasionally raise the volunteers in the hills north of San Miguel. Once a month, a lean old Jesuit from Santa

Rosa walked into the village to hear confessions and say Mass. He rarely spoke to Tommy, never to Sally. He believed they were living in sin.

It was, in fact, a long time before she let Tommy have her. And then it wasn't that she loathed him less or liked him more. It was the boredom. After four months, the stultifying monotone of village life settled over her like a cold ground fog. As winter came on, it rained every afternoon. Their little hut with two hammocks and an iron stove was like a prison. She simply needed to be held.

The first time, he came before he entered her. She had to wipe him out of her pubic hair.

"I'm sorry," he said. And she remembered he was barely out of his teens, and still a boy. "I couldn't help it." He lay on his back trying to catch his breath, trying to hide his shame. So, she kissed him through his thick, fuzzy beard.

"It's all right," she said. "Never mind."

In a few minutes, he was hard again and this time he penetrated and broke her. It gave her no pleasure and she was sore all the next day and for three days after because he wouldn't let her alone. On Saturday, she hitchhiked into Coroquin and went to the Red Cross Family Planning Center and was fitted for a diaphragm.

Whatever she feared sex might be, she realized those fears in her first nights with Tommy Carter. She'd had no formal sex education—only what she had overheard around the house and picked up from her friends. She had eavesdropped on the married women talking in her mother's parlor in Memphis, had listened to their occasional whispers about bedroom matters. And what she overheard as an adolescent told her that sex was an act of submission to a man's needs, a man's mouth, a man's hands. Once she and Tommy became active, she bore it as well as she could.

The first time he turned her over on her hands and knees, she felt like a beast. She was ashamed, kneeling there naked with her breasts pushed against the blanket on the floor, listening to him grunt. Even though they rolled down the blinds, even though the scattered huts below were dark and silent, she sensed the eyes of the villagers penetrating the thin straw curtains. And she felt like a sideshow.

The next morning, she walked to the pump in the middle of the square feeling the eyes of the women burning into her and the eyes of the men ravishing her.

It was a long time—many long nights of shame and humiliation before she learned to listen to the soft sounds of love-making from the other huts below without embarrassment. It was only when she finally threw away her last modesty and went to the river to bathe with the women that she came to understand.

She had always washed alone in the jungle behind the hut with a pail of water from the pump. But the fast-running waters of the river were so enticing and the laughter of the bathing women that drifted downstream so engaging . . . that one day she took her soap and shampoo and marched up to where the river turned, to the women's private place of bathing. They stopped their splashing and fell silent when they saw her. They gaped as she undressed. And then one little girl came up and touched her blond pubic hair as though it could not be real and an old woman touched the pink of her nipple as though it must be paint and Sally realized that they were not curious about how she made love, but how she looked. And she knew that she was one of them. Then, in a startling moment of clarity, she realized who she had sensed watching them make love.

It was Tommy.

One night while she was on her hands and knees, she caught sight of him in the mirror on the washstand. He was leaning back, one hand on his hip, staring down in deep concentration, watching their coupling. She found that she was excited to know that he was watching. That awakening changed everything.

Half out of lust, half out of curiosity, she began to pander to Tommy's appetite for watching her.

Sometimes, she would take her mirror and hold it beneath her, let him watch the way her body opened to admit him. Some mornings, after he awoke she would draw away from him. Then she would lean back in her hammock, raising the cotton shift to reveal herself. But she wouldn't let him have her. She'd rub herself lazily and move her hips until he was hard. But she wouldn't let him enter. She'd make him kneel between her legs and masturbate until he came on her belly. Sometimes she'd come, too. But, more and more, she took greater pleasure in seeing the desperate look in his eyes as they followed the movements of her groin. And in the end, she could make him crawl to her. She would only have to throw one lazy arm across his back and whisper, "Come to me." Then she'd raise one knee and let him put his face to her while he masturbated. It gave her more than an orgasm. It gave her something she had never dreamed she would find in sex: a sense of absolute power.

One day after they had been in Lagrimas for eight months, she came across him lying atop a *Ladino* woman in the ditch beside the corn field. That was the last time she let him touch her. That was almost twenty years ago.

Now, he sat before her, the same boy-inside-a-man, his beard flecked with gray, his hair thinning a little at the crown, and his gray eyes crinkling when he smiled. And it seemed impossible that he had ever touched her at all.

"I'm going to make you an offer Fallon can't refuse," Carter said.

"That I'd like to hear."

"We've got an hour of prime time," he said. "Give us an exclusive and it's yours."

It was not merely an offer—it was a breathtaking offer. It took all her concentration to keep from gasping, and she struggled to maintain her composure. She knew that she would start to lose her bargaining power the moment she showed even a flicker of real interest.

"Which hour?" she said, skeptically.

"Thursday at eight."

"Sure. Right up against *The Cosby Show*. Tommy, we both know your network might as well be airing the test pattern for all the audience you get."

"Hey, listen. You know the news division doesn't get its pick of prime time. We always get the tough time periods."

"It doesn't matter," Sally said. "We don't want to play."

"How can you pass an hour of prime time on the night before nominations begin at the convention?"

"We don't need it." It took all her concentration to say that with a straight face. What she might be gambling away was priceless.

For a moment, Carter didn't answer. Then he said softly, "You're kidding me."

"Nope."

"You mean it?"

"Yep."

"Fallon's got it wrapped up? He's got the number two spot?"

Sally smiled. "The words are yours. Now, how about feeding a working girl some lunch?"

"I gotta make a call." Carter slid out of the booth. "Order me something." When he went around the corner, she sagged against the back of the booth, drained.

She was finishing her salad when he came back to the table. He was in a lather. "Jesus Christ. Did you hear about Baker and Eastman?"

"What?" Sally said, as though she hadn't.

"Christ, they almost had a shoving match in front of a whole bunch of still cameramen."

Sally clucked her tongue.

"Christ," Carter said again.

"Well, what have you got?" Sally said, trying to sound like she didn't care.

"You pick the hour, we pick the interviewer."

She just shook her head.

"Hey, Sally, what do you want? Fallon to anchor the evening news?"

She was ready for him. "Three vice presidential debates in prime time."

Carter gaped. "Aw, gimme a break, Sally. You gotta be kidding. No network can deliver that."

"You start the ball rolling, NBC will climb aboard."

"Never."

"Bet a dollar?"

"You haven't got that kind of hold on them. I don't believe it."

"I have no hold on them. None at all. But I promise you—if your management starts campaigning for three prime time vice presidential debates, it'll happen."

"And if we come out for that, you'll deliver Fallon for an exclusive hour?"

"Yes. Provided the hour and interviewer are mutually agreed."

"You really think big, don't you?" Carter said.

"I do love my work," she said, and smiled and ate her salad.

1:40 P.M. THE ADDRESS WAS a filthy run-down brownstone in the worst ghetto in D.C. There were three mean-looking teenagers smoking in the downstairs hallway. They looked up and snarled when Ross came up the steps of the front stoop.

"What do you want, motherfucker?" the tall one said.

"I'm looking for—" Ross checked the note "—Doctor Bruce McCarran."

"Maybe he ain't here," the fat one said.

"Maybe he don't want to see your white fucking ass," the one in the leather jacket said.

Then the tall one walked up to Ross and poked him in the chest. "Maybe you should pack it down the street, motherfucker."

"Maybe you should shut your mouth," Ross said.

The boy's eyes widened with anger. "What? You talkin' to me? You motherfucking—"

He drew his fist back. Ross stuck his .38 revolver in the tall kid's crotch. The boy froze where he was, his mouth open, his fist in the air. Ross thumbed the hammer back.

"Now, you want me to blow your fucking balls off? Or you gonna call Doctor McCarran for me?"

"There's no need for that," a weary voice said in the corridor behind them. "All right, Frisco. I'll take care of it. What do you want, man?"

"My name's Ross. I'm a friend of Tim Fairchild. Can we have a talk—in private?"

McCarran had a frizzled black beard and long frizzled hair tied in a pony tail. He wore an old white shirt, white pants, and dirty white buck shoes. He looked like a forty-year-old refugee from Haight-Ashbury. They went upstairs to the bare front room. There was a pair of old couches and mismatched chairs arranged in a circle for group rap sessions, and an old single-element electric hot plate. McCarran had some water on.

"Want some tea?" he said.

"Sure."

"Where do you know Tim?"

"College."

"You in the navy?"

"No. I'm with the FBI."

McCarran started.

"This isn't official," Ross said.

"No, huh?"

"No."

McCarran poured some of the steaming water into chipped china mugs, handed one to Ross. He sat on the couch across from him, plucking lightly on the string of the tea bag.

"Okay, what do you want?"

"I want to know if the AIDS virus can be used as a lethal weapon," Ross said. "I want to know if the army is developing it as a weapon at Fort Deitrich."

McCarran put his head back and laughed.

"What's so funny?"

"Look, man," McCarran said. "You take your ass out of here right now. I ain't talking to you. I don't want to see your face. I don't want nothing to do with you. Good-fucking-bye."

Ross went on sipping his tea. "How about I go downstairs and bust those three kids for carrying grass?"

"They ain't carrying."

"You want to bet? They'll close this fucking clinic up and throw away the key."

McCarran stared at him. "Prick," he finally said.

"What about it?" Ross said.

"Hey, look, my man," McCarran said, "I'm out of that. Eight years ago, I kissed the U.S. Army goodbye. I don't know what they're doing. I don't care what they're doing. And next time you see my dear friend Tim Fairchild, you tell him that—"

"Are they working with the AIDS virus at Fort Deitrich?"

129

McCarran sipped his tea. "Hey, look. I tell you what they're doing there, I go to Leavenworth on a long vacation. Anyhow, eight years ago, nobody had ever heard of AIDS."

"All right," Ross said. "But is it possible?"

"AIDS as a strategic microbe? Who knows?"

"What's that—strategic microbe?"

"That's what they look for. A germ that can immobilize enemy troops rapidly. Something that infects a small area. That can be masked to avoid detection. You give your own people the antidote and then turn the little fucker loose."

"How?"

McCarran shrugged. "Aerosol. That's what they do with anthrax and Q-fever. Those affect the epidermis and disrupt the pulmonary function."

"Meaning what?"

"First you itch, then you choke. Then you croak."

"Jesus." Ross put down his cup of tea like he had lost his appetite.

"Then there's—let's see. . . ." McCarran was warming to his subject. "There's tularemia. It's a sweet little killer—*pastorella pestis*—the only organism that can infect a human being through his skin. Causes bleeding in the lungs and guts. Makes you not-quite-the-perfect-weekend-guest."

"They've got that?"

"In six-packs, ready to go."

"What about AIDS?"

"I wouldn't know."

Ross sat forward with his elbows on his knees. "But could they be developing it as a weapon? Could they be breeding pure cultures of the AIDS virus?"

"Hey, you're talking about the United States Army. They're capable of anything."

"Even that?"

McCarran shrugged. "Shit, I don't know." He put his head back and stared up at the broken light fixture that dangled from the ceiling. "Maybe. It's such a horrible fucking disease. You ever seen anybody die of AIDS?"

"No."

He got up and poured more hot water onto the tea bag in his cup. "Well, usually, you start off with Kaposi's sarcoma. Kind of a patchy, purple skin cancer. It's painful. And mutilating. Of course, once that's diagnosed, you're a pariah—an outcast. Your friends desert you, you lose your job, your relatives ignore you, even your parents are disgusted with you. Because everybody thinks you've been taking it up the ass. Then you wait." Slowly, savoring, he sipped the tea.

"Wait for what?"

"For the killer. One of those diseases that your body can't fight off any more. Meningitis, if you're lucky." He tapped his forehead. "It puts your lights out. The sniffles, if you're not."

"Why?"

"Because sniffles turn into pneumonia and when you have pneumonia and you can't be cured, your lungs slowly fill up with fluid and you drown. That's how most AIDS victims go. First, it's exile. Then it's death."

Ross sat a moment. Then he took a deep breath. "Well, would they be developing it?"

McCarran shook his head. "Nah. Wouldn't make any sense. The incubation time is anywhere from six months to five years before the victim shows any symptoms." He swirled the dregs of his tea around in his mug. "Wouldn't make any sense as a strategic weapon. Not when you figure the next war will be over in thirty days. Or thirty minutes."

Ross sat, thinking about that.

McCarran fished around in his breast pocket and came up with a joint. "You mind?"

Ross shrugged.

"You ain't gonna bust me?"

"Burn," Ross said.

McCarran lit up and took a long toke and held it down. "Of course, it would make a great political weapon," he said breathlessly, trying to hold the smoke in his lungs.

"What does that mean?"

McCarran sat back, spinning out the idea. "Suppose—just suppose they had a foolproof way of infecting a target individual." He blew the smoke out. "Ooh, man." He held up the joint admiringly. "This is heavy shit."

"I don't follow you," Ross said.

McCarran took another hit. "Gorbachev. Castro. The Ayatollah. Just imagine a world leader—any world leader—struck down by AIDS. Imagine the outrage in his own country. Imagine the disgrace. Even his most loyal followers would turn on him." He blew the smoke out. "Sure. As a political weapon, it would be perfect. Impossible to trace. Symptoms don't appear for months. Once the disease is diagnosed, the victim is reviled by everyone around him." McCarran offered Ross the joint. "Hit?"

Ross waved it away. "How much would it take?"

"By injection?"

"Yes."

McCarran took a deep drag. "Just enough to wet the tip of the needle."

"Suppose they were developing the virus as a weapon at Fort Deitrich? Could some of it be stolen?"

McCarran started to laugh. He coughed and the smoke burned his throat. "Nope. No way. That's where your theory runs off the tracks. Anything like that would be in maximum security. Locked in a sealed growth chamber, only handled by remote control. No one would have access. No one could work in the lab alone. Nobody could get to it."

"Even if a high-ranking officer ordered it used?"

"Only one officer could order it used."

"Who?" Ross said.

McCarran took a long drag and shrugged at the obvious. "The commander-in-chief," he said.

2:35 P.M. CHRIS WAS WAITING in the little blue Toyota at the end of the canopy when Sally and Tommy Carter came out of Maison Blanche.

"Thanks for lunch," she said when they reached the curb.

"Do we have a deal?" he said.

"I'll watch the papers. Show me when you've got it done."

"Suppose we could get two vice presidential debates?"

She offered her hand. "Lovely seeing you." They shook; she smiled and got into the car.

Chris pulled out into the back-from-lunch rush hour traffic.

"Jesus Christ," he said. "The war between Baker and Eastman is all over town."

"Wait till you see what the media does with it." She peeled off her suit jacket. "They'll be like sharks in a feeding frenzy." Sally sat back in her seat, feeling well-fed and satisfied with herself. Now, all she wanted to do was get back and tell Terry.

Chris threaded north through the traffic. "How did you make out with Tommy Carter?"

"He offered a one-hour interview in prime time."

"What? Jesus, that's great!"

"I turned him down."

"No!"

"I told him we wanted three vice presidential debates in prime time."

"Holy shit!" Chris said. "I wish I could have been there. I wish I could have seen it. He must have choked."

Sally shrugged. "He got up and called his office in New York."

"No kidding?" Chris glanced over at her. "And . . . ? And . . . ?"

"And we'll see."

"We'll see! Jesus Christ, Sally, you think there's a chance?"

"I don't think they have any choice."

"Jesus, Sally, you're a genius!"

"Maybe. Now, what do you know?"

"Compared to that? Nothing. Wyckoff's in Texas and nobody's talking. I think Eastman's going for broke. He's trying to get something on Terry that he can slip to the press."

"I'm not so sure. Eastman's a tough cookie, but he's no sleaze."

"Wyckoff's got enough sleaze for both of them. And if Eastman gets bumped off the ticket, they're both out of work. You know what that makes Wyckoff."

"Yes," Sally said. "Dangerous."

They drove the rest of the way in silence. When they got to Cambridge, they found chaos.

The elegant suburban streets were swarming with police from the township, police from Chevy Chase, the Maryland State Police, and the Highway Patrol. On every street, people had come out of their homes and stood on their lawns and at the bottoms of their driveways. At every corner, patrol cars with spinning cherry tops were swung across two lanes, blocking the access toward Crescent Drive.

At each intersection, Chris and Sally had to show their Senate staff ID's to plainclothes detectives, while uniformed patrolmen with drawn sidearms stood beside the car.

"Excuse me," Sally called, anxiously. "Officer, what happened? What's wrong?"

But they brusquely waved her ahead in silence.

"Oh, God, Chris . . ." Sally said. "Oh, my God."

At the bottom of Crescent Drive, the street was barricaded by two armored personnel carriers of the National Guard. Sally's hand trembled as she held out her ID. A gruff guard captain with his hand on his holster ordered her out of the car.

"This street is closed to all nonessential traffic. Please give your keys to the sergeant. Your car will be returned when you leave the area."

Sally was desperate. "I'm Senator Fallon's press aide. Please . . . what happened?"

"There's been a shooting," the captain said. "A policeman's been killed."

"Oh, no." And she barely dared ask the question. "Senator Fallon . . ."

"The senator is safe, Miss. Please move along."

Sally pressed her hand against her chest to still the pounding of her heart. "Come on, Chris," she said. And she began to run up the hill.

Katrina was waiting with two Secret Service men just inside the door. "Miss Sally, they—"

But Sally didn't stop to hear her greeting. She rushed down the hallway to the study and flung the door open. Terry was sitting on the couch with two young men from the party political staff. A blueprint of the convention hall in St. Louis was spread before them on the coffee table. As she entered the room, they rose.

Terry said, "Sally, you remember—"

But she was across the room before he could finish, and her arms were about his neck and she was crying, not the way a woman cries, but as a child cries, bitterly, desperately.

At first he stood with his hands at his sides, nonplussed, completely taken aback, as though embarrassed by her outburst. And then, gently, his arms folded about her and pressed her to him.

"Gentlemen," he said softly, "would you please excuse us?"

They nodded, backed away, and quietly went to the door.

"It's all right," Terry said. "It's all right." He looked up at Chris standing in the doorway. "It's all right," he said again. Chris shut the door. They were alone.

She went on weeping a long time, weeping out all the feelings of the past four days, all the anxiety of the years they'd worked together, all the moments of doubt and fear they'd shared, weeping until her sobs were hollow coughing and her eyes could cry no more. Then she felt him reach down to lift her chin.

"I'm all right," he said. "Really. Not to worry, pretty face."

"I was so . . . Terry, I was so frightened."

"I'm all right. I'm safe."

"I love you so much."

"I know."

"Terry, I love you. I love you," she murmured as he pressed his mouth on hers.

Then he was dabbing at her eyes with the handkerchief from his breast pocket.

"Don't," she said. "My mascara. It won't wash out."

"No matter. Let me see that smile."

She tried to smile and then she managed to smile. And then she took his handkerchief and wiped her tears away. "I'm such a fool. What I must look like. What you must think of me."

"A tender fool," he said. "Eastman's a real fool."

"Yes," she said. "Come here." And she made him lean down so that she could wipe her lipstick off his cheek. "It'll be all over the news tonight. It's bound to help us."

"How do we play it?"

"In public, no comment. Privately, it's a shame."

"A disgrace."

"A shame will do." She straightened her skirt. "I'm a mess. I'm all perspired. Let me go change and I'll—"

"You'd better go to your apartment and pack."

That surprised her. "Pack for what?"

"Ramirez."

"Did you reach him?"

"You're flying to Miami tomorrow morning. You'll call our friends when you arrive. They'll make arrangements."

"Terry, I can't go now. This thing between Baker and Eastman could blow the convention wide open."

He took her shoulders. "You have to go. We have to see this through. Do you understand?"

She nodded. "Yes. I understand."

He let her go. "Thank you," he said. "I knew I could depend on you."

He put his hands in his pockets and walked to the window. And when he spoke, his tone had changed, the tenderness and gentleness gone. "What about this shooting? A policeman killed two blocks from here. What do you think?"

"Either a lunatic or. . . ."

He turned on her. "Or what?"

The look on his face startled her. "What do you mean?"

He touched the place at his side where his wound was bandaged and stiff. "Could it be related?"

"No. That's ridiculous."

He crossed the room and stood very close to her. "Is it?"

"Yes, of course. Why would anyone want to hurt you?"

He lifted her face and looked into it, and he chuckled softly to himself. "So wise—and so innocent at the same time. That is the quality in you that drives men mad."

He frightened her when he talked like that, and she turned away.

"All right," he said. "All right. Go home and pack. Call me after supper."

"I will."

When she reached the guest house, Sally threw herself down on the sofa, kicked off her shoes, and let the wave of nervous exhaustion roll over her. There were only five days left before the convention began—five days until Terry would stand before the screaming delegates and receive the nomination that would catapult him to national office. Now, Eastman had practically severed his bonds with the president. He was handing them the nomination on a silver platter. It was an opportunity that had to be seized—and seized with vigor.

She lay back, but her mind raced ahead. She had worked so hard. She had waited so long. She didn't want to alarm Terry. But she couldn't—and she wouldn't—let anything go wrong now.

She sat up, dug through her purse until she found the business card she was looking for. Then she took up the receiver and dialed the number.

3:25 P.M. "HOT OUT THERE," Ross said when he came off the elevator. "Any calls?"

"No," the secretary, Jean, answered. "But I got your honeymoon tickets."

"Very funny." Ross took the airline folders from her outstretched hand.

"And you better read this." Jean held out a green sheet of teletype paper. "A town cop got killed out near the Fallon place."

"You're kidding!" Ross grabbed the teletype, read it as he walked toward the office. "Mancuso in?"

"Nope."

"He call in?"

"Nope."

Ross went into the office and shut the door. The telex didn't tell him much. A local cop had challenged a suspicious man in a side street near the Fallon house. The man had pulled a gun, shot the officer twice in the chest. The only witnesses were more than a block away. They described the assailant as a Caucasian male, approximately six feet tall, wearing a baseball cap and leather jacket. That was as good as no description at all.

Ross dropped the telex on Mancuso's desk and sat down at his own. Mancuso was out, had left no message, but Ross didn't give a damn. Something was bothering him and he wanted to work it out. He switched on the VCR, put up the tape of the assassination, and fast-forwarded ahead to the moment of the shooting. Then he let the tape roll and watched for the hundredth time as the bullets tore Martinez to shreds. It was an amazing feat of marksmanship—it really was. One shot in a target at that range was phenomenal. Seven shots placed so close together in rapid fire almost defied imagining. Seven shots had been fired, five bullets and fragments of others had been recovered, all bearing striations that indicated they were fired from the barrel of the same gun. Seven shells were found on the roof. Ross unlocked his desk drawer, found the plastic baggie that contained the brass—six bright casings, and the seventh, which had been painted black. It all pointed to a single assassin, one weapon, one trigger, one trigger finger. But standing on the roof of the Russell Building that afternoon, the people walking up and down the steps of the Capitol were smaller than the fingernail on his thumb and the target area would have been smaller than the letter "o" on his typewriter. Flushed with the heat of killing, swept with the fear of capture and death, what assassin could screw his concentration to a target so small and kill without a flicker of hesitation? Only a man who cared nothing for his own survival. Or a man who knew that powerful forces would protect him.

The phone rang.

"Agent Ross?"

"Yes."

"This is Sally Crain."

"Yes," Ross said and sat up abruptly. He shuttled the remote control of the videocassette player and let the tape creep forward until the picture cut to the onlookers. There, in the front row, her hands over her face in horror, was Sally Crain. He froze the image of her face and hands, her panic-stricken eyes. "Miss Crain—" He cleared his throat. "I have the tickets for—"

"Something's happened," she said. "I thought I should call you."

"Yes. I heard. A policeman—"

"It was that man," she said.

"Which man?"

"The man in the photograph you showed us this morning. That man from the CIA."

Ross looked at the photo of Petersen leaning against the television set. "What about him, Miss Crain?"

"I saw him today."

"You saw him? Where?" Ross grabbed a pencil, opened a yellow pad.

"In front of the house as I was leaving for lunch. I caught a glimpse of him from the window of the car. I thought he was someone I knew—but I couldn't place the face. Then when I came home and heard there was a shooting. . . ."

"What time did you leave the house, Miss Crain?"

"Please. Call me Sally."

"All right—Sally."

"I left the house at noon. He was standing with the reporters at the end of the driveway—" She broke off there. "I feel so stupid. If only I'd thought."

"That's all right. It happens. We'll go to work on it. Thank you very much for calling."

"You're welcome," she said.

"I guess . . . I guess I'll see you tomorrow at the airport."

"I guess so."

"I'll look forward to it."

"Thank you."

He held the receiver until he heard her put down the phone. Before him, her eyes shone on the television monitor, beautiful and afraid. Beside the monitor, leaning against it, was the photograph of Rolf Petersen. Ross looked back and forth between them, and he tingled with the desire to protect her and to have her.

3:45 P.M. PAT FOWLER, THE CIA's deputy director for Operations, sat quietly smoking his pipe while his boss, Admiral William Rausch, read the decoded cable. When he had finished, Rausch fed it into the paper shredder behind his desk. The shredder hummed and was silent; the cable was no more.

"The girl's dead?"

"Very dead."

"Who did the hit?"

"Friends," Fowler said. "Our friends."

"It said that the car was registered to an Argentinian businessman."

"Stagecraft. A little trick the Israelis taught us. They hire Jordanians to hit Syrians and Moroccans to hit Lebanese. Just enough to point the media and the police in the wrong direction."

"Do you think Ortega will get the message?"

"I've found that a coffin makes a greater impression than a telegram." Fowler sat back, puffing on his pipe.

The secure phone rang. It was Bender.

"Goddamit," he said. "A policeman was just shot to death two blocks from Fallon's house."

"What?" Rausch said. "When?"

"A little over an hour ago. It was Petersen."

"I don't believe it."

"For Christ's sake, we got a positive ID. Fallon's press girl just called those jerks at the FBI."

"How do you know that?"

"Never mind how I know it. Goddamit, you've got to find that son-of-a-bitch and kill him!"

"Listen to me, Lou," Rausch said and leaned forward in his chair. "Everything we're doing, the guys at the airports, the men who are checking out his old haunts—it's all illegal. If it blows, it'll bring the house down."

"Then I want you to let Ortega know we're holding him responsible. Make him understand."

"Lou, we killed his daughter this afternoon."

There was silence at the other end of the phone.

"You did?"

"At 5:08 Geneva time. She was DOA at the hospital. Hit and run."

"Could Ortega have known?"

"Ten minutes later. We got word."

"And you think this thing with Petersen is his answer?"

"Could be."

"Goddamit," Bender said again. Then he was silent for a while. Then he said, "Turn up the heat on him. Way up."

"We need more money, Lou. The Contras—"

"You'll get it. Don't worry. You'll get it." He hung up.

Rausch put the phone down. He shook his head. "This guy Petersen. . . ."

"We're doing our best to find him," Fowler said.

Rausch began to laugh.

"What's the joke?"

But Rausch couldn't control himself. He laughed, pitched forward in his chair, and slapped his hand down on the desk with laughter. "Call off the search," he gasped.

"What?" Fowler said in disbelief.

"Don't you see? As long as Petersen's out there, Bender will give us everything we need to fight the war in Nicaragua. Ha-ha-ha-ha-ha."

5:40 P.M. MANCUSO ONLY SPENT fifteen minutes in the Library of Congress reading Terry Fallon's biography. But it gave him a very strong hunch. So strong, in fact, that he had to follow it up. So, he got into his car and drove all the way to Pimlico after lunch and put all the cash he was carrying—$56—on Too, Too Lucky in the fourth. She ran out of the money.

By the time he got back to the office, Ross had been and gone. He read the telex about the murdered Cambridge policeman, and then went down to Gertie's Bar to see if Ross was there. He wasn't and Mancuso didn't feel like going home to Mrs. Weinstein's rooming house on 37th Street, where he lived. So, he asked Gertie for the keys to Mandy's place.

But when he opened the door to the tenement apartment, there was a young john with a blond crew cut sitting in the parlor. He couldn't have been more than nineteen or twenty, and he was wearing a *Star Trek* T-shirt. He put his drink down and stood up when he saw Mancuso.

"Hey," Mancuso said. "Don't mind me." He hung his coat behind the door. But the kid just stood there, staring. "What are you looking at?" Mancuso said.

"Nothing."

"Then sit down and drink your drink." Mancuso went into the bathroom and washed his hands. Through the thin wall, he could hear a couple humping in the bedroom. Mancuso went back to the parlor and poured himself a bourbon, took a copy of *Reader's Digest* and sat on the old brown velour sofa. And he was just thumbing to "Humor in Uniform" when the bedroom door burst open and Mandy started shouting, "You dirty little pig! I ought to kick your ass! Filthy snot-nosed—"

Another college kid came running up the hallway, naked, his arms full of clothes and sneakers, laughing hysterically.

Mandy came after him, pulling on her robe. "Hey, Joe," she said when she saw Mancuso. "This little fruitface just pissed my bed."

Mancuso tried not to laugh.

"Hey, fuck you, lady," the kid shouted back, juggling his clothes and putting them on. "You'd be lucky if I pissed on you."

"Why you little pink bastard!" Mandy started swinging. The kid raised his arms to cover his head.

"Fuck," Mancuso muttered. He put his drink down and got to his feet. "Come on, come on," he said wearily, and caught Mandy's arm. "He's not worth the trouble."

"Who the fuck asked you?" the kid said. "Go blow it out your ass." His buddy got up to back his play.

"Hey, that's not nice," Mancuso said. "Go on. You two do yourselves a favor and take a walk."

"That fucker didn't pay me!" Mandy shouted.

"And I ain't going to!"

"Aw, come on. Don't be an asshole," Mancuso said. "People got to eat."

"She can eat shit for all I care."

Mandy struggled to get free of Mancuso. "Let me at him, Joey. I'll tear his balls off."

"Now, you shush," Mancuso said, and threw his arm around her. Then he said to the kid, "Go on. Be a good guy and pay up."

"Big fucking mouth you are," the kid said. "Maybe I ought to bust you one."

Mancuso held the front of his jacket open so that the kid could see the .38 in the holster on his hip. "And maybe you ought to suck on this."

The kid's eyes almost fell out of his head.

"Now put the money on the table and beat it."

The kid dropped his roll and the two blew out the door.

"Cocksucker," Mandy said. She straightened her robe, put the money in her pocket and poured herself a whisky. "Ain't no fucking way to earn a living no more."

Mancuso sat down. He sighed and picked up his glass. Three men were dead already—Martinez, the Secret Service agent, and a Cambridge policeman. Whatever it was, it wasn't over and it wouldn't go away.

Mandy sat beside him, fussing with her hair. "World ain't nothing but weirdos and faggots," she said.

He took a long pull on the bourbon. "Tell me about it," he said.

7:40 P.M./CST THE FIRST THING Ted Wyckoff did when he got back to his hotel room was shower off the South Texas dust and heat and driving stiffness. He felt like he could stand under that shower for a week and not get all the prairie out of his hair. But it was getting late and he had to make a call.

Dan Eastman was having dinner with his wife and teenage son when the steward called him to the phone.

"What did you find out?" he said.

"Something. Nothing. I don't know." Wyckoff was standing beside the bed in his room at the Marriott Hotel, wiping himself dry. "But I'll tell you one thing: there's no love lost between Terry Fallon and his in-laws."

"Great," Eastman said. "So, he's a walking mother-in-law joke. That's the big news?"

"It's the father-in-law. And it's no laughing matter." Wyckoff caught the phone under his chin and wrapped the towel around his waist. "Anyhow, the wife is in a place called—" He reached over and shuffled through the papers on his nightstand until he found the note. "Some place called the Carmelite Nursing Hospice. It's in Cleveland. I'm going up there in the morning."

"I don't think you should do that."

"It's no problem. I've got my reservation."

"Now, listen to me," Eastman said. "I don't want you bothering that woman. She's sick and deranged and I don't want her disturbed."

"How do you know?"

"What do you mean?"

"How do you know she's nuts? Have you ever seen her? Has anyone?"

"For Christ's sake," Eastman said, and he was losing his temper, "she's been in an institution for—what?—ten, twelve years? She's a psychotic, goddamit. Everybody in town knows that."

"If she's in a rubber room, I want to see the room for myself," Wyckoff said.

"Listen to me, you little bastard. I don't want you badgering Fallon's wife."

"Why not?"

"Why not?" There was a long pause. Then Eastman said, "Suppose the papers get hold of it. They'll tear us to shreds."

"Who says they'll get hold of it?"

There was a pause. Then Eastman said, "You haven't seen the evening news—or have you?"

"No."

"Something happened today."

"What?"

"Between me and Baker."

"What happened?"

"Watch the late news and call me and let me know what you think," Eastman said.

"That bad?"

"Maybe."

"All the more reason to get the truth out of Cleveland," Wyckoff said.

Eastman was seething and his voice was a dark and menacing whisper. "I'm telling you for the last time. Don't go." He hung up.

Wyckoff was smiling when he put the phone down. It was ever thus: all the wrong men were elected to high office. He got dressed, went out to get a burger and a beer, then downtown to the bright lights and found a country-western bar called Fillies. It was smokey and loud and full of real cowboys and girls dressed like Dale Evans. He listened to a couple of twangy sets—"Your Cheatin' Heart" and "Tennessee Waltz"—and drank three bottles of Lone Star. Then he looked at his watch, saw that the late news would be on in twenty minutes, paid his check, and went into the john to take a leak.

Two cowboys came into the john behind him. One punched him in the back of his neck, and Wyckoff's face hit the tile wall behind the urinal and knocked out his front teeth. He lost his balance, grabbing the steel partition between stalls, but the other cowboy hit him across the ear with a sock filled with sand and ball bearings. He was too startled to cry out and he bashed his forehead on the lip of the urinal when he fell. After that, they beat him and kicked him with their steel-tipped boots until he was unconscious and for a long time after that.

10:50 P.M. THE FALLON OFFICE had a strict "no comment" on the friction between Baker and Eastman. But they had to comment on the murdered policeman, and that afternoon Sally was in no shape to do it. So, she had written it out for Chris and watched from the window of the house as he went down the steps to stand before the gaggle of news crews and reporters. He was so excited, he was like a kid. And he was flushed and almost giddy when he came back up to the house fifteen minutes later and insisted on buying her dinner. At seven o'clock, they went out. But there was no flavor to her food and no lilt to the conversation. She was wrung out dry and she felt like she had nothing more to give. Like she had been running on empty for a very long time and only now noticed that her gauges were low.

Sally excused herself before dessert and went home to pack for Miami. But something quite extraordinary happened when she reached her house.

There was a white florist's box with a bright red ribbon leaning against the front door. Inside were a dozen long-stemmed red roses and a handwritten note.

> I had forgotten how tall you are.
> And how much I love you.
>
> Tommy

It was so simple and so unexpected that she sat down in the living room, took a pillow from the sofa into her arms, and began to cry.

Somehow, she had become a stranger to herself—a shrewd, driven woman who manipulated people, used her friends, was using Tommy Carter now. She had become so premeditated. How had it happened? What had changed her? How had she become so calculating and cold?

She crumpled the tear-stained note in her hand. However it had happened, she had no time for it now. Terry was only five days from the vice presidential nomination. Once he had the power, there might be time to set things right.

She fluffed her hair and sniffed back her tears. It was no time for sentiment. She must do what had to be done. This was her one chance to win or lose a world.

11:40 **P.M.**   WHEN ROLF PETERSEN entered the motel room, the phone was ringing. He shut the door, locked it, and walked across the room. For a moment, he stood over the phone. Then he lifted the receiver.

The voice at the other end said, "You stupid, stupid bastard. . . ."

"I couldn't reach you," Petersen said. "I wanted to get your attention. I gather I did."

"Shut your mouth and stay put," the voice said. "Or I swear I'll kill you myself."

The line went dead.

SATURDAY, AUGUST 13, 1988

1:35 A.M. SALLY COULDN'T SLEEP. She lay in bed and listened. From the patio below, a clatter rose of hard rain falling. She could hear the wind flinging sheets of rain across the shingles of the house, and the yellow glow of the gas lamps in the street outside her window threw a pattern on the wall of branches switching madly in the wind. She looked out through the parted curtains toward the city.

The glimmering torrent of rain slanted down, in and out of the flicker of the lamps. And she thought of Washington coiling uneasily in the darkness. It was alive and churning tonight, she knew—slithering through the blackness, glistening in the damp, its multicolored, scaly back catching pinpoints of neon from the M Street bars. Tonight there was no sleeping in this city, no repose.

Tomorrow, the photographs of Baker and Eastman would be everywhere—on every network, on every local news, on every newspaper. The confrontation had occurred on Friday morning, just before *Time* and *Newsweek* locked their Monday covers. She could hear the stop-press alarms ringing at the printing plants in Dallas and Livingston, New Jersey. She could imagine the coverage that the photographs would receive this weekend when the network news divisions found their footing: the snappy repartee on *Meet the Press*, the sympathetic hand-wringing of Charles Kuralt on CBS. . . . She could hear Sam Donaldson and George Will on *This Week* with David Brinkley, cackling like the three Weird Sisters, "Double, double toil and trouble/Fire burn and cauldron bubble . . .'' The journalists had unmistakable slants, even if their networks swore they hadn't.

Next week, when all eyes were focused on the nominating convention in St. Louis, the photographic proof of the rift between the president and vice president would be a subject of more debate than any plank of the party platform. In caucus rooms and hotel suites around that sweaty, overcrowded city, state delegation leaders and their strategists would read the columnists and argue the implications.

Lying there, listening to the hard rain falling, she began to understand that it was impossible for Dan Eastman to be renominated now. At least, it was impossible for him to be renominated for the vice presidency on a Sam Baker ticket. If the photographs said nothing else to America, they said that the Baker-Eastman axis had failed. There was nothing that disturbed Americans more than watching a family quarrel in public.

Sally stared out the window into the rain-swirling night. If it could not be Baker-Eastman, it could only be one other combination. Or was there more than one . . . ?

She pulled up her sticky nightgown, lifted it over her head, and tossed it on the floor beside the bed. Then she turned her pillow over to where it was cool and dry and lay back, thinking. She was not the only one weighing the possibilities, she knew. All along Constitution Avenue, lamps were burning late. In the mansions of Chevy Chase and Fairfax and Falls Church, coffee was brewing, worried men and women sat at their desks or alone in the corners of their studies or with a small circle of friends in agitated, whispered conversation. Everywhere about her in the night, political minds were turning over in the darkness, plots were hatching and unhatching, schemes were thrusting out invisible tendrils in the dark. From this moment until the convention ended, it was her against them—mind against mind.

She knew that tomorrow morning Washington would look the same, but would be different. It would have changed beyond recognition from the Washington of yesterday. Eastman would be discarded—forgotten but not gone. A vacuum of power would have opened, and like a black hole that draws with enormous gravity, it would suck and swirl people and ideas into it with the draft of banshee winds. Meanwhile, Sam Baker would slouch on toward the nomination, gored and bleeding, but still the leviathan of the party. And the petty politicians who rode his coattails would flail about to find a running mate who could cauterize the wound and hide the scar. Who was there besides Terry Fallon? Sally wondered. And she knew that others were wondering, too.

Her eyes fell on her suitcase near the door. It was just the worst time to be leaving Washington. She felt ridiculous, being packed off to Miami with an incompetent FBI agent to question an old recluse who probably couldn't name his grandchildren, much less put them on the trail of the killer of Octavio Martinez. It was a fool's errand. A charade. Terry knew that as well as she did. In the morning, she would have to persuade him that she shouldn't go.

She looked out the window again and listened to the steady hiss of the rain. Somewhere west of the city, somewhere in the Shenandoah Valley, lightning was splitting the sky. She could see the distant flashes, hear the thunder rolling like a drum—like a drumbeat heralding the future.

It was time of infinite possibilities.

1:50 A.M. "I'M VERY SORRY, but Senator Fallon has retired for the night. May I take a message and have him return your call in the morning?"

"This is Dan Eastman—vice president of the United States. Now you wake that son-of-a-bitch up and have him call me. And I mean right now!"

There was a pause and stammering at the other end of the line.

"Mr. Vice President . . . I'll have to confirm—"

"Just do it!" Eastman slammed the receiver down. The early editions of the morning papers cluttered the floor about his chair. "Let me see that." He stuck out his hand.

Rob Moorehouse, Ted Wyckoff's secretary, handed him the ragged sheet of telex paper. Moorehouse had been crying.

"How the hell did this happen?"

"We don't know," Moorehouse said. "He went to a bar, went into the men's room. Now he's in the hospital."

"They beat him bad?"

"Savage."

"Lumbar . . . thoracic vertebrae—what's all this?"

"They say . . . they say he may not be able to walk."

"Shit." He looked right at Moorehouse. "Goddam bunch of pansies. Get him medivaced. Get him out of there."

"We've arranged a charter. He'll be in Walter Reed by morning."

"Goddamit, I don't want him in Walter Reed. Put him in—I don't care—somewhere where the press can't find him."

"I don't know where that is, sir," Moorehouse said, and his upper lip was trembling with hurt and anger.

"Then find someone who does. And get out!"

"Yes, sir."

The phone rang. "Mr. Vice President, I have Senator Fallon for you." He pressed the lighted button.

"This is the vice president."

Terry's voice was groggy. "This is Senator Fallon. What can I do for you, sir?"

"I want to talk to you, Fallon."

"I'm sorry, sir. With this wound . . . I'm not able to leave the house."

"That's all right. I'm coming over to you."

2:05 A.M. LOU BENDER WAS a creature of habit. The next-to-last thing he did every night before going to bed was to scan the bulldog editions of the papers: the *Post* from Washington, *Times* and *Wall Street Journal* from New York, the *Sun* from Baltimore. He had discovered a long time ago that a person who read those four papers before going to bed rose a wiser, better person on the morrow—and, more important, half a step ahead of ordinary mortals who read one morning paper over breakfast.

Tonight it had taken less time than usual to scan the papers. There was only one story—and it was page one everywhere: Dan Eastman's outburst toward President Baker. Bender thumbed through one paper after another, and his lip curled into a smirk. From every front page, the same series of photos glared: Eastman pointing an accusatory finger at Baker; Eastman raising an angry fist to Baker; Eastman storming out of the Blue Room of the White House while Baker stood abashed. It was absolutely outrageous behavior for a national leader. But, worse than that, a public display of anger in the White House was sure to startle and frighten the Great Middle Class. And anything that frightened them, they shunned. Clearly, this was going to cost Sam Baker votes. Bender studied the photographs and pondered. He felt like the luckiest man alive.

Yesterday's polls had made it unmistakably clear that Sam Baker could not win a second term as president with Dan Eastman as his running mate. The trouble was that, with Sam Baker, polls were not the issue. Loyalty was the issue. Integrity was the issue. His understanding with Dan Eastman was the issue. In all likelihood, Sam Baker would never have cut Dan Eastman loose—even at the risk of losing the election.

But now, with one childish outburst of temper, Dan Eastman had effectively erased his name from the Baker slate. There was no way a president of the United States could condone that kind of behavior, no way a president could tolerate such insolence and disrespect for his office. Now, no one would blame Sam Baker for dismissing the renegade with the uncontrollable temper and replacing him with cool, reasonable Terry Fallon. In fact, right-minded people everywhere would be appalled if Baker showed any tolerance at all. They would perceive it as a lack of esteem for the presidency, or worse—weakness.

Bender folded his newspapers and smiled. He'd had one insurmountable task to perform before the election—now Dan Eastman had performed it for him. It could not have happened better had he choreographed it himself; Dan Eastman's vice presidency had just died of self-inflicted wounds.

The secure phone rang.

"Yes?" he said.

"Eastman just left the Observatory."

"Headed where?"

"To see Fallon."

"Let me know what they say."

"I'll have a transcript on your desk in the morning."

"Don't wait for morning. Bring it here as soon as it's ready."

Bender hung up. Then he said, "The son-of-a-bitch."

So, Eastman had a plan of his own. Now, he was out of the liability column. He had just moved himself onto the enemies list.

Bender picked up the receiver and dialed *09, the speed dialing code for Pat Flaherty, the White House political pollster.

"Wha—what is it?" the sleepy voice said.

"What are you doing?" Bender said.

"Lou? Lou, it's . . . Jesus, it's two o'clock in the morning! What do you think I'm doing?"

"Listen," Bender said, "I need a flash poll on this Eastman fuckup by close of business tomorrow."

"A damage report?"

"A death warrant."

"All right," Flaherty said. "I'll take care of it."

"Two thousand calls. I want stable numbers—none of this asterisk bullshit. I want him coffined and cremated."

"Lou, I said I'll take care of it. Now can I go back to sleep?"

"Be my guest."

Bender hung up and snuggled down.

2:35 A.M. "THEY PRACTICALLY BEAT him to death," Eastman said.

Terry Fallon shook his head. "I'm very sorry."

"He was in Houston. He'd been out to see your father-in-law."

"About what?"

"About your wife."

"My wife's in a hospital. She sees no visitors."

"Except you."

151

"Except me."

Eastman sat in the armchair by the fireplace, still wearing his London Fog. He was a big man and he filled the chair and his hands looked huge on the knobs of its arms. Outside, it was raining hard. Inside, it was cold.

"Shall I light the fire?" Terry said.

"Got any whisky?"

Terry rose stiffly and went to the liquor cabinet. Eastman could see that he moved the way an old man moved, keeping his back straight as he rose from the chair, shuffling and favoring his right side as he walked.

"You in pain?"

"Some. Scotch or bourbon?"

"Got any Irish?"

Terry poured a good strong shot of Powers into a snifter and handed it to Eastman. There was sweat on Terry's face, and Eastman could tell the pain was intense.

"Having one?" Eastman said.

Terry poured his own. They raised glasses and drank.

"What about it?" Eastman said.

"You think the beating is related to his visit to Dwight Kimberly?"

"Don't you?"

Terry sat down. He drew his robe about him. "Mr. Vice President, I have no way of knowing what or who—"

"Fallon, let's drop this Mr. Vice President crap, all right?"

Terry watched him. "If you wish." He folded his hands.

"I'm in trouble. You're circling like a vulture. One of my guys decides to try to get something on you and he winds up in traction. What is that supposed to make me think?"

"I don't know," Terry said. "But I suspect you're going to tell me."

"You bet your ass I'm going to tell you. I think you've got something to hide."

"And what is that?"

"I don't know. But I'm going to find out."

Terry smiled a cool little smile. "Is that some polite form of threat?"

"You're a real cutie pie. You know that?"

"I'll tell you what I know," Terry said, and it was clear he wouldn't be intimidated. "I've done some research on you, too." He opened a leather folder on the table beside his chair. Before him lay the detailed notes that Sally had prepared.

"I know you don't make deals. I know you don't put your hand in the till. I know you don't have an office full of relatives—never have had. I know that when you leave Washington, you want to leave with your reputation intact."

Eastman just stared.

"And I'm sitting here wondering," Terry said.

"Yeah?"

"I'm wondering why you want this so much that you're ready to throw away everything you are—to sell your soul if you have to—to hang onto your job."

Eastman raised one tough finger like he was going to come up out of his chair. And then he didn't. Instead, he took a swig of whisky and sat with his hands wrapped around the snifter in his lap.

"You know, Dan, we're all ambitious," Terry said. "We wouldn't be in Washington, in any of these jobs, if we weren't driven by a passion to succeed. Some have made it here by conniving and double-dealing. Others have made it on character and merit. I think you're one of those. So, I'm wondering. . . . I'm just wondering why you're prepared to throw that away for four more years."

Terry winced against the pain in his side as he got up. He knelt by the fireplace and struck a long wooden match and touched it to the end of the newspaper balled under the kindling and logs.

"My father-in-law is a violent man," Terry said as he watched the flames begin to rise. "We don't speak. I've done what I can to make Harriet comfortable. It's a tragedy. There's no more to be said."

The logs began to hiss and crackle, and the orange glow of the fire climbed the wall behind them. Eastman said nothing.

"Events chose me," Terry said. "Fate marked the place. But I was ambitious. And I was there. And I was lucky enough to survive. I can't apologize for that."

"No," Eastman said. "I realize that."

"And I'm sorry about . . . Ted Wyckoff? Is that his name?"

"Yes."

"I'm sorry about him." Terry sat down and folded his robe tightly over his knees. "But you'll forgive me if I say that you shouldn't have sent him to Houston."

"I didn't send him." Eastman swirled the liquor in his glass and looked into it. Then he shrugged. "But I didn't stop him either."

They sat a long while like that, both of them staring into the fire.

Finally, Eastman said, "I want an arrangement. You and me. We go to St. Louis together. As a ticket."

Terry didn't move, didn't look up. "And President Baker?"

"Baker takes a walk."

Terry sat a while, watching the fire. Then he said, "Dan, I'm sorry. I'm not for sale."

Eastman finished his drink, said goodnight, and shuffled to the door. When he was gone, Terry sat a long time, alone.

5:20 A.M. "OH, HE'S GOOD . . . he's really good," Lou Bender said. He thumbed the transcript of Terry's conversation with Dan Eastman to the end, then flipped the folder closed. It was still dark outside, but he was wide awake and on his game.

"Couple of fucking Boy Scouts," he said. "But this Fallon is real slick." He put his hands on the formica top of the kitchen table. "He's a real slick son-of-a-bitch and Dan Eastman just wrote himself into recent ancient history."

Agent Browning of the Secret Service stood against the far wall of the kitchen, holding his cup of instant coffee in two hands for the warmth. "Anything else you need?"

"Nope," Bender said. "You think there's any chance they could spot your bug?"

"It's our bug and we're doing the surveillance checks. Who's going to spot it?"

"Suppose they had their own people in?"

"Then they'd find it. But they wouldn't know whose it was."

"But they'd know you missed it," Bender said. "Don't you think that would give them a hint?"

Browning shrugged. "Do you want me to pull it?"

Bender thought it over. "Perhaps you should."

"It'll be out of there in a hour," Browning said.

"Thank you, Agent Browning," Bender said. He went on smiling until the man put down his cup and went out the door. Now he knew that what he would say to Terry Fallon would not be recorded.

5:40 A.M. "IT'S PANDA—, PANDA—, pandemonium!" Chris Van Allen shouted into the receiver. "Earth calling Sally Crain. Are you awake?"

He needn't have shouted. Sally was already on her second cup of coffee, sitting up in bed with the morning papers scattered about her. "Have you seen the *Post*?" she said.

"It's already pressed in the pages of my diary. Have you heard about Wyckoff?"

"No."

"Somebody beat his brains out in the men's room in a bar in Houston."

"What?!"

"The Gay Political Caucus is trying to decide whether to hold a march or just give a party." Chris laughed out loud.

"Chris, behave yourself." Sally swung her legs out of bed. "Listen, I want to see Terry first thing this morning."

"Sweetie, the flight's at ten o'clock."

"I may not be going."

"How come?"

"A lot is going to happen today."

"Like what?"

But instead of answering she said, "Can you pick me up at seven-thirty?"

"No problem. With an iced bucket of *Cristal* so that we can celebrate on the way to the airport."

"Make mine a black coffee. And don't be late."

"Me? Late?" He hung up.

The photographs were everywhere. Eastman's burst of anger was front-page news around the world. By comparison, the shooting near Terry's house was barely a footnote. But the article that Sally was really looking for was in one newspaper only—on page thirty-five of *The New York Times*.

NETWORK ENDORSES THREE VICE PRESIDENTIAL DEBATES

It was only a twenty-four-point head at the bottom of the television page. The article ran less than a third of a column. There were "no comments" from the other two networks and something evasive from the League of Women Voters. It was short and inconclusive. But it was there. And it told her that feeding NBC and starving the other two networks had been more effective than she could have hoped. Yesterday her bluff had worked. But the three debates would only help Terry after he got the nomination. She still needed a launching pad to get him there. But did she dare push Tommy Carter all the way?

At 6:35 the phone rang and Sally put her coffee down on the Dallas *Morning News*. It was Carter.

"You saw?"

"Yes. I saw," Sally said, trying to sound not-very-impressed.

"Do we have a deal?"

"Almost."

He was annoyed. "Listen, Sally, you got what you want. Pay up."

"Let's talk about that," she said gently.

"Goddamit, Sally—"

"Tommy, be nice. You know Dan Eastman just dropped out of the running."

He was startled. "Eastman dropped out?"

"Not officially."

"Oh," he said. "The pictures."

"Yes."

"You think they're that destructive?"

"I think the word is *catastrophic*."

"Three little pictures could do all that damage?" There was musing and wonder in Carter's voice.

"Mightier than the sword. . . ."

"Yes," he said. "And as long as we're on the subject of the news media, what are your other extortionate demands?"

"Nothing much."

"I'll bet."

She drew a breath. "Wednesday. The night we arrive in St. Louis. One hour, eight to nine. One interviewer, mutually agreed."

"Wednesday at eight? Don't be ridiculous."

"Why? Terry will outrate anything else on the air."

"Forget the rating. The other party will kill us if we don't give them equal time."

"Fallon's not a candidate yet. Equal time doesn't apply until after he's nominated."

"In theory, sure," Carter said. "Sally, we're not talking law here. We're talking politics. If we don't give them a matching chunk, they'll get even."

"They can only get even if they get elected."

"Shit," Carter said.

"Tommy," she said, "are we friends?"

"I used to think so."

"Tommy, we've received another offer." She held her breath. It was the final bluff.

He was silent. Then he said, "Fuck."

"Is that your answer?"

"I'll call you back."

"I'm going to Miami."

"You call *me* back."

"When?"

"Five o'clock."

"Done. Tommy?"

"What?"

"I loved the flowers."

"Why?"

He hung up. Then she dialed Terry's private line.

"Have you seen the papers?"

"Eastman was here last night."

That made her sit up. "What? When?"

"Two-thirty in the morning."

"My God! What did he want? What did he say?"

"I think he wanted me to understand what he was feeling," Terry said. "I think—in a strange way—he wanted to apologize."

"He should apologize to the president."

"I don't think he can."

"Is that all he had to say? I'm sorry?"

"I'll tell you more when I see you."

"Terry . . . I have a feeling you may get another visit from Speaker O'Donnell today."

He was silent for a moment. "I have the same feeling."

"We have to talk. I'm coming over."

"Don't miss your plane."

"It's crazy for me to go out of town today."

"Don't miss your plane," he said again.

"I'll be there in an hour."

She hung up. But the phone rang as she was putting it down.

"Three vice presidential debates in prime time? Is that what you're angling for?"

It was Steve Chandler from NBC and he was pissed.

"It was something we dreamed up together," Sally said.

"Bullshit," Chandler said. "Carter isn't that smart. Or that stupid." Then he snorted. "You guys must have been real close friends down there in Guatemala."

"Honduras," Sally said. "And it's none of your business."

"I'm in the news business, lady. You're news."

"Terry Fallon's news."

"You're news if I say you're news."

"Steve, go open a window," Sally said. "I think you've been breathing some stale air."

"You heard about Ted Wyckoff?"

"What about him?"

157

"He and his boss self-destructed on the same day."

"Yes. It's a shame."

"I can hear that you're all wrung out over it."

"Steve, I'm just going to a meeting," Sally said. "Is there something I can do for you?"

"Yeah. Stay out of bed with Tommy Carter." He hung up.

8:05 A.M. THE INTERCOM BUZZED. "Mr. Bender, the president would like you to join him in his meeting."

"I'll be right in."

Bender went out his back door, across the corridor to the Oval Office, knocked once, and entered. The president and Speaker O'Donnell were seated over coffee on the sofas near the fireplace.

"Mr. Speaker."

"Lou."

"Sit down, Lou," the president said and smiled. "The speaker was just warming up to harangue me about Dan Eastman."

Bender sat.

O'Donnell was loaded for bear. "You've seen the news," he said. "You've seen the papers. I don't think there's more to be said. The man has got to go."

"Why?" the president asked.

"Why!" O'Donnell puffed up like a bullfrog. "For God's sake, the man is an affront to his office. He's made your administration a laughing-stock."

"Lou?"

Bender said, "With all due respect, Mr. Speaker, I think you overstate the case." He picked up the coffee pot and poured. "My personal assessment is that Eastman has crippled himself—and hurt us in the bargain. My guess is that, if we move quickly and decisively, we can avoid significant damage." He looked at O'Donnell's empty cup. "I've asked Flaherty to run a survey. We should have the results by five o'clock. More coffee, Mr. Speaker?"

The president listened carefully. Bender was certainly taking pains to sound dispassionate and uncommitted.

"You and your polls," O'Donnell said, and held out his cup. "Statistics are no substitute for judgment."

"I'm not suggesting they are, Mr. Speaker," Bender said. "I just think we should have the facts in hand before we make any decision."

Baker watched Bender with a mixture of curiosity and contempt. No one—not even Charlie O'Donnell himself—was more convinced and determined that Dan Eastman must go. The morning after Terry Fallon was shot, Bender had been the first to suggest they dump Eastman. Now, Eastman had given a provocation that cried out for his dismissal. Yet, in front of O'Donnell, Bender was all reason and fairness and patience. It was a disturbing spectacle, disguising nothing, misleading no one. It was politics.

"You can have your polls and your statistics," O'Donnell said while Bender poured. "But I'm bringing you the message. Sam, you can't win with Dan Eastman."

Before the president could answer, Bender said, "We know that, Mr. Speaker. But what alternative do we have? Cream and sugar?"

"Fallon. We have Fallon. And thank God we do." O'Donnell put two lumps of sugar in his cup.

Sam Baker sat back and looked at the two men sipping their coffee. "Charlie, why are you so high on Fallon?"

"For goodness sake, Sam. Look at the polls."

"I'm aware of them," Baker said. "But I don't think you give someone the job of vice president of the United States just because the research says he can be elected."

O'Donnell put his cup down. "I'm not concerned about Fallon being elected, Sam. It's you I'm worried about."

"Well, that's very kind of you."

"Sam, you can't win with Eastman," O'Donnell said. "And the plain fact is, you may not be able to win at all." The quiet words struck like a thunderclap.

In the silence that followed, Sam Baker stirred his coffee. He felt their eyes on him. So, it had come to this at last. Now, if O'Donnell and Bender had their way, a pair of printed images—the wounded Fallon at the podium, an angry Eastman raising his fist—those two images would tip the scales and take out of his hands one of the most important decisions of his political career. Because in choosing his vice president, he might well be choosing his successor—the person who could eventually become the forty-second president of the United States.

Lyndon Johnson had warned him about the awesome power of images. The day after Johnson announced that he would not seek re-election, Sam Baker had gone to see him. The two men sat on the sofas in the Oval Office and Johnson took off his shoes and put his feet on the coffee table. He looked older, and his big head was bowed and brooding, and he reminded Sam Baker of Lincoln on his pedestal in the Memorial.

"You were right to let go," Sam Baker said.

"I was right about *evathin'*," Johnson said. "I was right about the war.

I was right about the rockets. I was right about the *po' folk*. I was even right about the *nigras*." That was how Lyndon Johnson summed up his achievements: the space program, the Great Society, civil rights.

"But you know somethin', Sam?" Johnson said. "You know how I'll be remembered? As the *sumbitch* who lost the war—and picked up his *dawg* by the ears."

Now, Sam Baker knew that, once again, Lyndon Johnson had been right. The pictures of him hoisting his beagle by the ears and the savage cartoon of Vietnam as his gall bladder scar *were* the images that had endured. So, too, would the images of Dan Eastman raising his fist to the president in anger.

Why did images have such power? Sam Baker thought of others: MacArthur wading ashore on the Philippines, Nixon poking Khrushchev's chest, Rockefeller giving the press the finger. Somehow the public believed those photographs projected the character of the men. Like Terry Fallon, bloody but unbowed above the Great Seal of the United States.

But Sam Baker didn't believe in images, even though he had come to respect their power. Because he knew that images, like men, could lie.

"Sam, you may not be able to win at all," O'Donnell said again. "With Dan Eastman or without him."

"I'd like to wait for the polls," the president said.

"And then what?"

"And then I'll think about it."

O'Donnell looked at Bender, then at the president. "That's your final word?"

"That's my final word right now, Charlie. And you must accept it."

O'Donnell shook his head. "Don't be a fool, Sam," he said. He stood up and straightened his jacket. Then he went out.

8:15 A.M. CHRIS PULLED UP at the Secret Service barrier at the bottom of the driveway to Terry's house.

"I'll be right back," Sally said.

"I'll wait." Chris tapped his watch. "Eastern Airlines won't."

She showed her ID and hurried up the walk to the house.

"He's still upstairs," Katrina said. "Shall I—"

"That's all right," Sally said. She was breathless when she reached the landing and knocked on the bedroom door.

Terry was sitting up in bed, making notes on a pad. The breakfast dishes were on a tray near the window. "Are you packed and ready to go?"

"I think it's crazy for me to go out of town today." Sally shut the door and went to the bedside. "Taking that jerk to Ramirez is a total waste of time."

He put his finger to his lips to silence her. She stopped, cocked her head to one side as though she weren't sure what he meant. Then he turned the yellow pad to her and she saw he had printed

SOMEONE MAY BE LISTENING.

She straightened up and looked about the room. "Who?" she said.

But he waved his finger at her and tapped it against his mouth for emphasis. Then he said, "I want you to ask Señor Ramirez to give the FBI his full cooperation. Tell him I believe that we must never rest until we find the killer of Octavio Martinez."

She shrugged and nodded, confused. "Of course, I will. But he'll just—"

Terry turned the covers back and got out of bed. He was wearing gray silk pajamas.

"—he'll be reluctant," Sally said. She watched, baffled, as Terry crossed the room and locked the door. He motioned to her to keep talking. She said, "After what's happened, he . . . he has a natural suspicion of anything our government—"

Terry came back to her, took her by the shoulders, and sat her on the edge of the bed.

"—of anything our government does." Sally opened her hands to him in bewilderment and her mouth formed the word *what*?

"That's why it's so important that you be there," he said, and lifted the hem of her white cotton skirt to her knees. "He knows I'll never rest until our government finds the killer and brings him to justice."

"Yes. But—"

Terry ran his hands up the outside of her thighs and caught the elastic at the top of her panties.

"—but I'm not sure what he can tell us," she said, trying to hide the surprise in her voice. She shook her head and tried to push his hands away, but he persisted and tugged downward on her panties until she had to raise her hips and let him slide them down her legs.

"That's why it's very important that you go with the agent," Terry said. He wet the tips of his fingers. "When Ramirez sees you, he'll know that he must cooperate."

She tried to fend off his hand, but he pressed her knees apart and touched the wetness on his fingers to her. It hit with the force of an electric shock.

He put his other hand on her breast and pushed her down. Reluctantly, she lay back in the bedclothes. Then he drew up one of her knees and pushed her legs apart.

"Do you understand?" he said.

"Yes, yes," she said. "All right. But even if he does, he—" Terry unhooked his pajama bottoms and they fell about his ankles. She could see him raise himself toward her. "—he doesn't have access to . . . oh . . ."

She gasped as he entered her.

"If he doesn't want to cooperate, you'll have to convince him," Terry said. He lay down on her, moving in small stabs that slid him into her. "Remind him that we have a common cause, a common brotherhood."

In spite of her resistance, he pushed her knees up, slid her legs around him. Then he made her move with him, tightly, silently. "Will you do that?" he said.

"Yes," she said, but her voice was almost a gasp.

"And then call me and let me know if anything promising develops."

"I will."

"Good. Very good."

He went rigid and she could feel the first spasm. He pressed his mouth on hers, wet, sucking, wrenching. She almost cried out and he had to clamp his hand over her mouth and hold it there, pressing her back into the mattress.

When he was spent, she looked up, between his fingers, watching the aftermath of passion lidding his eyes. And then he took his hand away from her mouth and said, "Good. Very good."

Soundlessly, she said, "I love you. I love you, Terry."

He nodded, slipped off her, and stepped into his pajama bottoms again.

"Well, you have a good trip," he said.

She took some Kleenex from the box on the end table beside the bed, padded it into the bottom of her panties. Then she slipped the panties on and smoothed her dress.

He opened the door for her. "Call me when you get to Miami?"

She was on the landing and the door was closed behind her before she was able to catch her breath.

8:30 A.M. THE WAREHOUSE WAS near Andrews Air Force Base, southeast of the District, just off the Beltway. The lot was almost deserted and Mancuso parked in one of the four spaces marked Visitors. He went in the access door and pushed the button under the security camera.

"You got authorization?" the tinny voice said through the little speaker.

"I don't need no authorization," Mancuso said. "Goddamit, Fatsy, you know I got a C-2 clearance."

"Hey, we got regulations here," the voice said. "I got procedures to follow. Lemme see your clip-on."

"Hey, fuck you."

"Fuck you and let me see your clip-on. Or you can stand out there until tomorrow for all I care." Then the speaker clicked off.

"Pèzzo da mèrda." Mancuso muttered, but he dug in his pockets for his clip-on ID and pushed it through the slot. A moment later the steel door at his right buzzed and clicked and the green light above it came on.

"Step through the door at your right and wait," the voice said.

Mancuso did. The door clicked shut behind him and he was in a wire cage facing an old formica counter.

"Hey, Joe," the fat man behind the desk said. His name was Lodovico Carnivale, but all the guys called him Fatsy. He was huge, well over 300 pounds, and his flesh hung in layers. He was wearing a Washington Redskins jersey. He always reminded Mancuso of the roly-poly Michelin tire man.

"Hey, Fatsy, *cosa dice?*"

"Niente. I been okay. What you working on?"

"Same crap. Records and stats. Want to know how many burglaries there were in Michigan last year?"

"Nah." He handed back Mancuso's ID and then swung the book around for him to sign in. "So, what'll it be?"

"ABSCAM."

"Could have saved yourself a drive, Joey. It's all in the computer." He tapped the screen of the IBM unit on the counter.

"They want some entries checked against the originals."

"What a jerk-off."

"Yeah. Same old make-work shit."

Fatsy swung the computer keyboard around until it was pushing up against his belly. "Got a case number?"

Mancuso dug in his pockets for the piece of yellow foolscap. He went through every one before he thought of the breast pocket of his jacket. That's where he finally found it.

"Same old Joey," Fatsy said. "Imagine you keepin' records. You'd lose your dick if it wasn't hung near your balls."

"Yeah, big laugh, huh?" Mancuso leaned across the counter while Fatsy punched in the case code. The screen on the computer terminal scrolled and stopped.

"Okay," Fatsy said. "Eighth level, rear . . ." He reached for a pencil.

"Here. Lemme write it down for you. Eighth level, rear, section 418, row 11, shelf 2 through 6. Want me to show you?"

"I can find it."

"Hey, remember your way back. We close at two on Saturday and I sometimes forget who's up there."

"You're a real kidder." Mancuso went to the elevator.

"Joey, don't make a mess, huh?"

"You won't even know I was here."

"And don't take nothing 'less you sign it out."

"Trust me."

The elevator stopped at the eighth level. There in tier upon tier of shelves were the files of the ABSCAM investigations and prosecutions. Mancuso checked the case number on the slip of paper, then made his way down the corridor until he stood before the cartons stenciled: The United States of America vs. Caleb Collin Weatherby (Senator).

He slid a carton out of the bottom shelf, and sat down on it. Then he opened Box 6248-05/LO.

He had an idea of what he would find inside: some of the 13,000 pages of trial transcript, thousands upon thousands of pages of depositions, and a stack of videocassettes. All that material was catalogued, numbered, cross-referenced on the massive computer that serviced the Bureau's Department of Records and Statistics.

But Mancuso was looking for something that wasn't in the computer's memory or in the court reporter's record of the trial. He was looking for something that had never come up in court. He was looking for probable cause.

When the ABSCAM indictments had hit the nightly news in 1984, the television public was treated to an on-camera performance of bribery by Senator Caleb Weatherby that left nothing to the imagination. Television convicted him long before a federal jury ever found him guilty. And the videotape made the issue of probable cause moot.

But Mancuso had reason to be curious. Sunbelt senators were usually conservatives—and the Bureau numbered conservatives among its strongest friends. And there was an old saying at the Bureau—"Enemies first." Given the choice between investigating a friend of the Bureau or an enemy, every assistant director and every agent knew which choice to make.

Mancuso knew that somewhere in that row of huge, overstuffed cartons there had to be a compelling reason why Caleb Weatherby was chosen as an ABSCAM target. Mancuso took his jacket off. He looked up briefly at the Absolutely No Smoking sign. Then he loosened his tie, lit a cigarette, and went to work.

8:45 A.M. SAM BAKER COULD remember meetings of the National Security Council that had gone better.

"I just want to ask one question," Arthur Cranston said. He was secretary of state, a man with all the subtlety of a rectal thermometer. "Who sets the foreign policy of this country? The president and the State Department—or the goddam CIA?"

Secretary of Defense Zack Littman sat back, chewing his thumb. He loved to watch Cranston when he was pissed off. He reminded him of George Steinbrenner.

Admiral William Rausch was trying to keep his cool. "Arthur, you exaggerate."

"Bullshit," Cranston said. "You think anybody believes that story of the drunken Argentinian businessman? You killed that girl. The whole goddam intelligence community knows it. Ortega knows it. The Swiss know it. *Pravda* has half a page on it. I had the Argentinian ambassador in my office for half an hour today yelling at the top of his lungs that we're endangering their diplomats, too."

"Tell your Argentinian friend to spend his time looking for the 'Disappeared Ones' and keep his fucking nose out of Nicaragua," Rausch said.

"Did we murder that girl?" the president said. "Yes or no?"

Rausch stared back at the president for a long moment. "No," he said.

"You're a liar," Cranston said.

"Arthur," Rausch said softly, "your charm is wearing a little thin today."

"I'm sick and tired of your spooks stirring it up everywhere I turn," Cranston said. He got up and stalked up to the far end of the table and stuck his finger in Rausch's face. "Listen to me, Admiral. If you escalate this thing in Central America, you blow it. The whole strategy is attrition. Grind their economies, squeeze their currency, keep the insurgency alive to keep their military off balance and drain their treasuries. But if you press too hard—if you create a critical state of emergency in Nicaragua or anyplace else in Central America—you bring in the Cubans, you have the OAS up our ass, and we'll be arguing till doomsday in the U.N. and the World Court while Russian freighters pile up arms on the docks of Corinto."

Rausch folded his hands before him on the table. "I'd like to express my gratitude to the secretary of state for his lesson in political economics. But his idealistic portrayal of the goals of the American government in this hemisphere does not alter the fact that the Central Intelligence Agency had nothing—I repeat, nothing—'' and his voice rose ''—nothing whatsoever to do with the death of Consuelo Ortega.''

''Jesus,'' Cranston said, and threw up his hands. ''Next, you're going to tell us you didn't mine the harbors.''

That got Rausch's goat. ''We mined the fucking harbors because we all agreed—agreed right here in this room—that we had a clear shot at knocking Ortega off his horse. It didn't work. We were wrong.''

Rausch was right. The men around the table sat, sullen, silent.

''As long as there's a lull in the festivities, I'd like to ask a question,'' Defense Secretary Zack Littman said. ''Who shot Octavio Martinez?''

No one spoke.

''You see, I have a very simple-minded approach to the subtle questions of intrigue that seem to delight some of my colleagues. I see a crime like the Martinez assassination and I say, *cui bono?*—who benefits? And then I make a short list of people who would be better off without Martinez, and I start looking for the guilty party.''

''What are you getting at, Zack?'' the president said.

''Well, we're going on the assumption that Ortega ordered Martinez's assassination. And that Admiral Rausch, our stalwart director of the CIA, decided to put Ortega on notice that it's not nice to murder our allies on television. And the quickest, most memorable way for the CIA to do that, was to exchange tit-for-tat and bury Ortega's daughter.''

''So what?'' Cranston said, and his patience was exhausted.

''But there's no logic to that at all,'' Littman said. ''Ortega didn't order Martinez's assassination.''

All heads turned.

''How do you know that?'' the president said.

''Because Martinez was losing the war,'' Littman said and fingered a stack of papers before him. ''Read the casualty reports. Read the counts of declining Contra strength. Look at the divisions Ortega is putting into the field. He's got Soviet T-62 tanks and HIND helicopter gunships. Why would Ortega want the Contras to have a new leader when he was beating the pants off the leader they had?''

He slid a copy of the documents across the table. Cranston stood behind the president's chair, reading over his shoulder.

''Now, if you were to tell me that the CIA murdered Martinez so they could replace him with this lunatic Father Carlos—''

''That's a goddam lie,'' Rausch said.

Littman went on imperturbably. "—with this lunatic Father Carlos, who puts us on the same side with the Catholic church in Nicaragua, then I'd say you've got a scenario that makes sense."

Rausch stood up. "Zack, that's the dumbest—"

"Sit down, Bill," the president said sharply. "Now."

Rausch did as he was told.

"Go on with what you're saying, Zack," the president said.

"Suppose Martinez was losing the war. Suppose it was time for him to step aside. Suppose he wouldn't go. Suppose he came to the United States, in part, to persuade you to continue supporting him. He never got the chance to speak his piece."

The president looked at Rausch. "Bill, is that true?"

"I have no information to that effect," Rausch said. "And no reason to believe it."

"Was Martinez winning the war or losing it?" the president said.

"It was too early to tell."

"Answer the question, dammit. Was he winning or not?"

"No," Rausch said. "No, he wasn't winning. But he wasn't losing either."

"Go on, Zack," the president said and turned back to Littman.

"Perhaps General Gabriel would care to comment," Littman said.

Gabriel was a four-star from the air force, and chairman of the Joint Chiefs of Staff. "Our assessment was that Martinez was losing. He wouldn't take logistical or tactical suggestions from the Special Forces advisors we've got down there. His kill ratios were too low. Ortega was grinding him instead of the other way around. In our view, Martinez was a candidate for replacement."

"Thank you, General," Littman said. "Clearly, the man had to go. I don't argue that. I just think the way we dismissed him was a little—" he searched for the word "—primitive."

Rausch spoke up, and he was barely able to control his temper. "I want to say categorically that the CIA did not—I repeat, did not—order the shooting of Octavio Martinez."

"But you were ready to get rid of him?" the president said.

Rausch hesitated. "Yes," he finally said. He looked at the faces of the men around the table. "But not by shooting him to death on the steps of the United States Capitol."

"Then how?" the president said.

Rausch lowered his head.

"How, Admiral?"

"Poison."

There was a long, terrible silence.

The president said, "Admiral Rausch, are you telling us that if Colonel Martinez hadn't been shot, the CIA was prepared to murder him with poison?"

"Jesus Christ," Cranston said. "You make me want to throw up."

"You dare talk to me like that?" Rausch said. He pointed at Cranston. "You sent the marines to Lebanon." Then he pointed at Littman. "And you put them in a barracks where a crazy Moslem with a truck full of dynamite could blow them to kingdom come."

Cranston turned, fists clenched and started back up the room.

"Stop it!" the president said, and slapped his open hand down on the table. "Stop it right now!"

The men froze where they were.

"Admiral Rausch," the president said. "You know that Executive Order 11905 provides that no employee of the United States government shall engage in, or conspire to engage in, political assassination."

Rausch nodded. "Yes, sir, I do."

"Then tell me how you could even contemplate the murder by poison of Octavio Martinez."

Rausch drew a long breath, and sighed.

"Admiral, I'm waiting for your answer."

Rausch spread his hands before him on the table. "Because he was losing the war, Mr. President. For Christ's sake, we all know it's a war this country can't afford to lose. Because if we lose the war in Nicaragua, our children will have to fight in Guatemala. And their children will have to fight in Mexico. That's why. And if anyone at this table thinks I'm mistaken, let him speak now or forever hold his peace."

They sat a long moment in silence—as though each could hear the judgment of history.

Then Littman spoke up. "As I was saying, gentlemen. We haven't any idea who ordered the assassination of Octavio Martinez."

11:10 A.M. "HOLY SHIT!" FATSY said. "What the fuck is goin' on here?" He tromped up the aisle, trying not to step on any of the documents, but making a bad job of it. "What the fuck are you doing scattering everything every which way? Jesus Christ, Joe, how the fuck do you know what goes where in all this shit?"

"It's all the Weatherby case," Mancuso said. "What's the difference?"

"What's the difference? Fuck you!" Fatsy shouted. "This is all chronological files."

"Yeah? Chronological how?"

"See this?" Fatsy slapped his hand on the code number stenciled on the carton. "This here—FO—that's the sixth. This here, EO, is five—"

"And that's number one up there?"

"AO? Yeah, sure. Whadya think?"

"Fatsy, you're a fucking genius," Mancuso said. He reached up and began to wrestle the heavy carton from the top shelf.

"Not so fast, motherfucker!" Fatsy put his bulk in the way and pushed the carton back up on the shelf. "You put all this shit away, you can open anything you want. But first you put it all back where it come from."

"Aw, Fatsy, gimme a break."

"I give you sweat off my balls," Fatsy said. "Clean it up."

"Fuck you."

"Fuck you."

"Ahhhh. . . ." Mancuso showed him the back of his hand.

Fatsy got his two fists up, began to bounce on his pins and his layers of fat shook and jiggled. "Come on. Come on. Just try it. I'll cockalize ya'."

Mancuso stared at the sepctacle before him. Then he started to laugh. "All right. You win. Don't hurt nobody." He raised his hands in surrender.

"Better." Fatsy stopped bouncing and hitched up his pants. "I'm gonna order pizza for lunch. You want?"

"Sure, sure. Sausage and mushrooms," Mancuso said. "I'll put this stuff away, then I'll look some more."

"Great. Thanks a lot. You're all right, Joe."

"Thanks," Mancuso said. He waited until the elevator slipped down out of sight. Then he pulled the AO Carton off the shelf and tore the top open.

It took Mancuso less than five minutes to find what he was looking for. It was in a file marked D/FBI Correspondence Confidential, and it was the last item in the folder, which made it the first exhibit in the case. It was on the director's memorandum stationery, dated 12/21/83, and addressed H.O'B. to Maximum Security File/No Copies.

Mtg w/M.C. re Senator Caleb Weatherby. Alleged improp in SRA Petroleum appeal EPA ruling WT11202. Verbal to A/DCA R&R ASAP.

It was signed Henry O'Brien, Director. And in the lower right-hand corner, someone had written the letters ABSCAM/OK, followed by four different sets of initials—O'Brien's and three associate directors of the FBI.

Attached was a notarized copy of O'Brien's meeting calendar for December 21, 1983. Mancuso scanned the list of names until he found the one he was looking for. Then he shook his head and laughed softly to himself, not because he was surprised but because he realized that nothing that happened in Washington could surprise him any more.

"Mother-fucking son-of-a-bitch," he said softly, and folded the two documents and put them in his pocket. "Mother-fucking son-of-a-bitch. . . ."

Then he kicked the carton down the aisle so that papers and cassettes and folders flew everywhere, kicked it all the way down the corridor to the elevator, and kept kicking it until he was sweating and panting and his rage was spent.

Then he rang for the elevator.

12:35 P.M. THEY LOOKED LIKE any vacationing couple you might see arriving at Miami International Airport. He was wearing a brown jacket and slacks, a white shirt, a red and brown striped tie. She wore a white cotton dress with patent leather shoes and patent bag. When he stood beside her, you could tell she was older—maybe ten years older, maybe more. But Sally was a beautiful vision in white to Ross as she shimmered in the glare of the Miami sun.

Through the flight down from Washington, Sally had sat beside him but somehow managed to keep to herself. She read *The Wall Street Journal* after breakfast. Then she took a nap. Then, when they were an hour from Miami, she excused herself and went to the washroom and when she came back she was fragrant and fresh and perfect and when he rose and let her by she brushed close to his body and that excited him.

But Sally hadn't been thinking of Ross; she had barely been aware of his presence in the seat beside her. All through the first hour of the flight, she had been rolled up inside herself, thinking about what had happened that morning. Her body kept the ache where Terry's hips had forced her thighs apart, and she could feel the rawness in her. The act had been so sudden and so unexpected. She was almost ashamed. It had been a long time since Terry had touched her that way.

From the beginning, from the early days in Houston, she'd had to hide her feelings for him. She was a reporter for the *Post;* he was a critic of city government and then a candidate for office. Any hint that their relationship was anything but professional would have been intolerable to editor Arlen Ashley. Any indication that she had lost her objectivity, and he would have immediately reassigned her. It was the beginning of a pattern that became permanent. In all the years that she had known Terry Fallon, she had never once let her feelings for him show in public.

In fact, it wasn't until Terry's engagement to Harriet Kimberly that Sally realized what her discretion had cost her.

Sally's stories about Terry's work with the poor had made him a source of curiosity among Houston's rich. He was a dashing, personable young man, well-mannered, well-educated. He was just the kind of acquisition that added so much to a dinner party or a social afternoon. What began as a trickle of invitations became a deluge.

It was a part of his life that excluded Sally. But she didn't mind. She followed it in the society pages of the *Post*—the parties, the balls, the cotillions when Houston society wintered in Palm Beach.

Then, one Saturday afternoon in February, Terry asked Sally to meet him at his apartment on Faculty Row.

"I have something to tell you," Terry said. "Something that may hurt you. I'm going to get married."

"Oh," she said. "To whom?"

It was such a proper question, so poised and so correct that he knew at once how deeply she was stricken.

"Harriet Kimberly."

"The heiress."

"Yes. When she comes back from Palm Beach next week, we're going to announce it."

"I see," Sally said. "Well, congratulations. I wish you all the best. I really do."

She went to the movies that afternoon. She saw *Annie Hall* for the second time or maybe the third. Then she went home and did her laundry in the fifty-cent machine. Around eleven o'clock that night, she got into her car and drove back to the apartment complex on Faculty Row and rang Terry's doorbell. He was wearing a yellow cotton robe when he answered the door.

"I want to stay the night," she said. "Please don't send me away."

In the morning, he said, "This doesn't change anything."

And she said, "I never want it to change."

It never had.

There were times since when she wished with all her heart that she had married. There were times she wondered what sort of wife she might have made. But she had the life she'd chosen. And all the time she'd been in Washington without him, she was merely waiting, marking time, counting the days until he would come. And when he did come, it was everything she'd ever dreamed it could be—like a roller-coaster ride that never ended. And now the vice presidency was almost in their grasp. It was like a dream come true.

It was only that—at times like this morning—she felt so guttural, so exploited, so used.

When the plane was an hour out of Miami, Sally excused herself and went past Ross to the washroom. She hiked up her skirts and took her panties off and discarded the Kleenex. She wet her handkerchief with warm water and washed herself. Then she smoothed down her dress and stood at the mirror and brushed her hair and smartened her makeup and sprayed some Shalimar on her wrists and behind her ears. Before she went back to her seat, she balled her handkerchief and panties and threw them away.

By the time the cab pulled up in front of the Miramar Hotel, Ross's shirt had sweated to his back and his pants were sticky with perspiration at the crotch. But Sally was still crisp and smart as she followed the bellman with their cases up the stairs into the shabby lobby.

"Not exactly a new standard of elegance," Sally said when she looked around at the chipped marble floor and sagging scheffelera. She was wasting her time in Miami, and third-class accomodations made it worse.

"Best the taxpayers would go for." Ross gave a buck to the bellman and followed her to the registration desk. "Crain and Ross," he said to the clerk. The man put down two registration cards and went to get their room keys.

Sally began to fill out her card.

"You don't like Joe, do you?" Ross said beside her.

"Who?"

"Joe Mancuso. My partner."

Sally looked him straight in the eye. "He's a vulgar, bigoted, primitive slob. Other than that, he's fine."

Her rancor took Ross off-guard. "I'm sorry if he's offended you."

"What is this? Good cop, bad cop?"

"No. I just thought . . . we're going to be down here together for a couple of days. No reason we can't be friendly."

"Yes, there is."

The clerk held out a key and a stack of papers to Ross. "I have quite a few messages for you, Mr. Crain."

"Miss Crain," Sally said and took the key and message slips out of his hand. "Those are mine," she said to the bellman, and pointed to her bags.

A middle-aged man in shorts and a polo shirt looked up from reading his *Miami Herald* and watched her cross the lobby. Ross caught his eye. They exchanged a shrug that said, simply, "Women. . . ."

Ross was in his hotel room unpacking when the phone rang. It was Mancuso and it sounded like he was in a bowling alley. "How's Miami?"

"Hot. Where the hell are you?"

"In a phone booth on the Beltway."

"Taking the day off?"

"I've been over to the dead storage warehouse."

"For what?"

Mancuso caught the phone between his chin and shoulder, dug the ABSCAM documents out of his jacket pocket, and unfolded them.

"I've been doing some homework on your friend Fallon."

"Jesus, Joe, give it a rest."

"Listen to this," Mancuso said. "Here's O'Brien's memo-to-file on probable cause in the Weatherby investigation. 'December 21, 1983. Meeting with member of congress regarding Senator Caleb Weatherby. Alleged impropriety in SRA Petroleum appeal of Environmental Protection Agency ruling on WT11202.' "

"WT—what?"

"Some oil lease thing. After the meeting, O'Brien made a verbal to the assistant director for congressional affairs to review and recommend as soon as possible."

"And?"

"And he recommended ABSCAM and that was all she wrote for Senator Weatherby."

"Joe, that's absolutely fascinating," Ross said. "I'm glad to know that dead storage isn't as dead as some people think it is."

"Listen, asshole," Mancuso said. "I got the name of the member of Congress who brought O'Brien the case." Mancuso flipped to the copy of O'Brien's meeting calendar. "It was Terry Fallon."

Ross was surprised, but he still said, "So what?"

"So what? Don't be a jerk. Fallon fingers Weatherby for ABSCAM and the governor of Texas rewards him with Weatherby's unfinished term."

"Joe, get to the point."

"Don't it strike you a little neat?"

"I don't see anything wrong with it."

"Look, use your head," Mancuso said. "Fallon didn't start the Weatherby investigation by sending an anonymous letter. He made a personal visit to the director of the FBI. A personal visit, asshole."

"Meaning what?"

"Dave, think about it. The man voluntarily made an appointment with the director of the FBI and sat in his office and told him that a United States senator was a crook."

"Well, Weatherby *was* a crook. He was guilty as hell."

"But Fallon couldn't prove that when he went to see O'Brien. He was making a potentially libelous allegation."

"Maybe he thought he was doing his patriotic duty."

"Bullshit. He made a personal visit because he wanted to put pressure on the director to act. And because he wanted to be on record for full credit when the sting went down. Do you think he would have done that if he wasn't sure he had Weatherby cold?"

Ross thought about that. "No."

"And there's only one way he could have been that sure about Weatherby. He had to have inside information—real deep inside information on who was paying him off and why and how. And to get that, he either had to be in on the payoffs, or he had to have somebody who was real close to Weatherby."

From where Ross was standing with the phone, he could look out through the nylon curtain that hung across the sliding glass door to the terrace. On the terrace of the room next door, Sally was stretched out on a chaise in a yellow one-piece bathing suit. She had rubbed her body with oil and it glistened in the sun.

"Are you listening to me?" Mancuso said.

"Yeah, yeah."

"That Sally Crain dame worked for Weatherby before she worked for Fallon. She was on Weatherby's staff when the sting went down."

"Joe, you're making something out of nothing."

"You better keep your eye on that bimbo. She's more than she's cracked up to be."

"Yeah, sure, I will," Ross said. "Listen, Joe. You ever hear of a place called Fort Deitrich? It's in Maryland."

"What about it?"

"It's where the army does biological weapons research. I think that may be where they got the AIDS to shoot up Martinez. Hello? Joe? You there?"

But Mancuso had hung up. There were some things he didn't want to know about—particularly over the phone.

When they arrived, Sally had gone into her room and shut the door and looked down at the pile of messages—messages from Chris, from the AP and UPI, from reporters whose names she recognized at *Newsweek* and *Time* and the *Journal* who liked to think of themselves as her "friends." But she didn't want to talk to anyone—not while she felt so soiled and dirty. So, she left the pile of messages on the end table and threw off her clothes and showered.

Then she pulled on her bathing suit, rubbed her body with lotion, and went out on the terrace. And she was lying there feeling bitchy and rigid and used when Ross put his elbows on the railing and leaned over to make conversation.

"Are you sleeping?" he said.

The last thing she wanted to do was talk. But she stirred, raised a hand to shade her eyes, and looked at him. "No," she said. "Just being lazy."

"What's happening?"

"We have to wait for them to call."

"And?"

"They'll see us when they're good and ready."

"Okay." Ross smiled at her.

He was young and rather attractive, she thought. He had a kind of curious, open face and boyish blue eyes. She felt embarrassed for the way she'd behaved in the lobby.

"I'm gonna get a paper," he said, and turned back for his room.

Sally sat up. "David?"

"Yes?"

"I'm sorry. I was wrong."

He looked back at her. She was all glitter and sheen and soft curving flesh. "About what?"

"Being rude to you downstairs. I guess I got out on the wrong side of the bed today."

Ross shrugged. "I thought you were angry about the other night."

For a moment, she couldn't think what he meant. Then she remembered Steve Thomas and the Four Seasons Hotel. "No, no," she said. "That wasn't your fault. I shouldn't have snapped at you."

He shrugged it off. "Forget it."

"As long as you let me apologize."

He went back to the railing. "Me, too. For Joe. He's just been at it too long. Okay?"

"Okay. We're even."

"You have freckles," he said.

Self-consciously, she put her hand to her throat. "Wh—what about them?"

"I love freckles," he said. "Want to take a walk on the beach?"

1:15 P.M. "WHAT AM I running here? A fucking travel bureau?" Barney Scott held up the voucher. "You gotta be kidding."

"The woman's in a nut house in Cleveland," Mancuso said. "What do you want me to do? Call her on the phone?"

"Is this goddam trip really necessary?"

"Nah," Mancuso said. "I'll just make up the report. Stick in an old Marvel comic, something like that."

"Fucking sense of humor." Scott signed the voucher. "Your fucking sense of humor's gonna get your ass kicked outta here one day, Mancuso."

"Yeah, that's what they say." Mancuso got up to go.

"You're gonna be—" Scott studied the carbon of the voucher "—at the Sheraton Motor Inn on Route 422?"

"Yeah," Mancuso said. "Gimme a call if you get lonely."

He went back to his office and gave all the information to Jean. He was going to leave an indelible trail—a trail so obvious, a trail that led so clearly away from the Martinez assassination and down a blind alley, that no one in his right mind would bother to follow.

"Anybody wants me, give 'em the number," Mancuso said.

"Who'd want you?"

"Ah, you do, honey. You just can't admit it to yourself."

1:55 P.M. THE SAME MIDDLE-AGED man in shorts and polo shirt was sitting in the lobby reading the *Herald* when they went downstairs. He looked up and saw Ross walking with Sally, and Ross saw him and they shrugged to each other as if to say, "Can't live with 'em, can't live without 'em."

But Sally was oblivious to the exchange and to the way Ross was looking at her. She was just glad to get out of the hotel, out on the beach where people were sunning and playing and sleeping and the telephone didn't ring. It was as though she could breathe for the first time that day. The sky above her was a pale, transparent blue and the sun was almost directly overhead so that there were no shadows, only streaming sunlight and hot sand on the bottoms of her feet. And she held her arms away from her body so that the breeze could ripple through the cotton wrap and cool her.

They turned south, walking on the high ridge of sand that rolled down to the waterline. To her right, the long row of beachfront hotels stretched toward downtown Miami, to her left there was the surf and the green sea. She felt achy inside, wounded—and she realized it was more than the rawness from the sudden act of sex. Something was unraveling inside her. She kept binding up the ends. But it kept fraying—and she felt as if somewhere inside her the close-knit fabric of her life was pulling apart. It was a feeling that she didn't understand.

"This must be a very exciting time for you," Ross said.

That brought her back.

"I'm sorry. What?"

"With the convention coming up in a few days and all. I said it must be very exciting."

"Oh. Yes," she said. "Yes, it is."

"What's he like?"

"Who?"

"Your boss. Terry Fallon."

The word chafed in her ears, and she realized how deep the confusion went.

"What do you think he's like?" she said.

Ross shrugged. "I don't know. I'd say he's pretty lucky."

"You mean about the shooting?"

"Yeah."

"Do you think he'd make a good vice president?"

"I haven't thought about it." He kicked at the sand with his bare toes. "He's gotten pretty famous in a hurry. Is he that special? Or did you do that?"

"Some of it."

"You're very good at that, aren't you?"

"I don't know," she said. "I guess so. They say I am." She walked on and he followed her.

"How did you get into this?" he said. "Politics and all."

"You mean, why didn't I stay home and have babies and get a man's supper ready every night?"

"I didn't mean that, but you can take it that way if you want to."

"I'm sorry," she said. "That was dumb."

They walked like that a while. She rarely talked about her past. In fact, she rarely thought about it. Now, here was this awkward, unpolished young man asking questions. And, suddenly, she felt she wanted to answer. It was that same feeling of unraveling coming over her again. She felt vulnerable. It frightened her. She hadn't felt that way in years.

"Most of my friends married right out of college," she said. "That wasn't for me."

"Why not?"

"I wanted to see the world. I thought I had a calling."

"A calling?"

"A kind of Christian duty. An obligation to serve. You're not a Christian, are you?"

He was surprised by that. "I'm a Jew. Does it matter?"

"Jesus was a Jew." She put her hands in the pockets of her wrap. "Anyhow, I had my nursing degree and I didn't know what to do with it. I wanted to do something worthwhile. So, I joined the Peace Corps."

"You're kidding."

"What's so odd about that?"

"I don't know," he said. "I didn't mean anything. It's just that, well, the Peace Corps . . . it seems like something from another age."

"It was the last refuge for true believers. After the Chicago riots and Kent State and all, some of us didn't feel at home here any longer." She looked at him. "How old are you?"

"Twenty-seven."

"You would have been—"

"Eight."

"Eight?"

He nodded.

She smiled and shook her head. "You were eight years old. And I was sleeping in a hammock in the mountains of Honduras, trying to save mankind."

"There's a *but* in here somewhere," he said. "I can feel it."

"Well, the trouble with the guerrillas was already starting. I took it for two years. Then I went home and worked my way to the *Houston Post* and a condo in Oak Creek."

"That where you met Fallon?"

"He was just a schoolteacher running for city council. But even then, he had ideas. He had vision."

It was part of the little stock speech she gave when people—mostly women—asked how she had met Terry. But now it tasted strange on her tongue.

"So, you fell for him," Ross said.

The statement was so blunt and unadorned, it stopped her. She stared at him. But there was no malice in his eyes. She learned something about him then. She learned that he was a very young man with a lot of life still hidden in his future, promising the way bright young people are, but without an acquaintance with pain.

They walked up the beach a little farther. Then Ross said, "I hear his wife went nuts."

Sally cleared her throat. "Schizophrenic. She's in an institution."

"Why doesn't Fallon divorce her?"

"He's Catholic."

"Why doesn't he get an annulment?"

She didn't answer him, and he said, "Am I asking too many questions?"

"No," she said. "No. But if you knew Terry, you'd know the answer to that one."

She went down to the waterline and stood so that the final frothy reach of the surf slid up around her ankles. He watched her standing there with the wind tossing the soft folds of her wrap and fluffing the ends of her long blond hair. And then it came to him that she was hurt, deeply hurt in a way that he could not fully comprehend.

He went and stood behind her.

"You love him a lot," he said.

She started to answer. Then she realized she was going too far.

She slipped off the belt of her wrap, stripped it off her shoulders, and turned on Ross. "Do you swim?"

"Well . . . yeah," he said, taken by surprise.

"Then come on." She threw the wrap back into his startled hands and ran down into the water.

"Wait up!" Ross started to unbutton his shirt.

But she had run down into the surf, out to where a big green roller was gathering, and as it began to arch and fall, she dove in under the crest, slicing through it like a clean, yellow arrow. The wave broke and crashed and Ross looked up and saw Sally pop out the other side, waving. Then she turned and swam out, a strong swimmer with a good smart kick and a long overhand reach with both arms.

Ross spread his shirt on the sand and folded her wrap neatly on it. Then he ran down toward the water. But the next big wave caught him in the chest and knocked him on his fanny, and it took him three waves and a lot of paddling before he got out past the rollers to where she was floating on her back.

179

"You made it," she said.

Ross was breathing hard, busily treading water with all fours. "Barely. I almost lost my suit."

"That would be fun. Can you float?"

"I can try." He did try, but his legs kept sinking and pulling the rest of him down.

"No. Look. Watch me," she said. "You have to roll your arms, keep a little movement."

He tried it her way and it worked, and they floated together like that.

"Oh, God, I'm relaxed," she said after a while. "It's like swimming in a bathtub."

"It's the Gulf Stream."

"Is it?"

"That's why it's so blue out here."

It was blue and it was warm and it was the Gulf Stream. She understood. It was the same water that warmed along the coast of Venezuela and drifted slowly north from Panama. It was the water she had swum in off the east coast of Belize in the winter of 1970 when she made the trek to see her school friend Maryanne Crosby, the archaeologist, on her dig at Altun Ha.

They had met during Sally's first year at Memphis State, and had become great friends, even though Maryanne was a year older. She was a short, dark, wiry girl, a P-E minor and as physically strong as a man. She was a chain-smoker who didn't bother too much with make-up. She was on the tumbling squad and persuaded Sally to go out for the cheerleaders. When Sally made the team, Maryanne bought her the skirt-and-sweater set as a gift—and then hemmed up the skirt half an inch to better show off Sally's thighs.

Sally became an economics major—a brilliant one. But, like other students in those years of dissent, she turned her back on theories of supply-and-demand, and looked for something practical, something that would give to the world, rather than take. She turned to nursing. It was Maryanne who first piqued Sally's interest in Central America, who first suggested Sally join the Peace Corps and do her nursing in the jungle. Sally's visit to Belize was more than a reunion—it was reaffirmation.

But when Sally got off the bus at Belize City, she hardly recognized the woman who welcomed and embraced her—a dusty, square little tank with her dark hair tied in a dirty red kerchief.

They went to the upstairs bar at the Hotel Bellevue and sat where they could see the muddy waters of Haulover Creek spill into the blue Caribbean.

"Couple of beers," Maryanne said. She wore a long-sleeved khaki shirt and pants and leather sandals with a thong between her toes. "I assume you drink now," she said.

"Yes."

"And fuck."

"Well . . . yes."

The boy put down two bottles of Beliken and two glasses. Belize had been a British colony and the bars served warm beer without compunction. Maryanne wiped the neck of the bottle and drank from it.

"That's all there is to do out here," Maryanne said and wiped her mouth on her sleeve. "Drink and fuck and wait for the mail. What's it like in the hills?"

"They're killing each other." Sally said.

"They're killing each other here, too. I don't give a shit."

"How can you say that?"

"Ah, babe." Maryanne shook her head. "Once upon a time there were great civilizations south of the border. The Mayan astronomers in Chichen Itza. The Aztecs with their calendar. A thousand years ago, the Incas built Machu Picchu. Now their descendants can't even wipe their ass."

"Is that what you found up here?"

"Yeah. That and crabs in my crotch." She kicked back with her boot on an empty chair. "Would you ever let me fuck you?"

"No."

"Well. It doesn't hurt to ask, I guess." She went back to drinking her beer.

Sally stayed three days and saw the dig on the plateau behind the city with the grid of white string and the square patches of orange clay where the topsoil had been turned and screened. Maryanne explained how the ancient Indians had driven back the jungle to build temples and cities. And how, in time, the jungle crept back, oozing like a green tide through the deserted marketplaces and fortresses, toppling stone from stone until all was eradicated, buried under soil.

In a temporal way, Sally had watched that process at work in the village of Lagrimas. Each day, the men cut back the jungle around the corn-fields. And each new morning, the jungle had crept back—a foot here, a meter there—as though it were jealous of the men and their corn. She had watched the work impassively, as though it were a game of give-and-take. But squatting in the prehistoric sites, she realized the game was played in earnest. Because the jungle was relentless— relentless and insatiable. And, in the end, it retook all a man could borrow and changed it back into itself.

When she got back on the bus for Tegucigalpa, Sally was sad to be leaving. She was sad because she knew she was saying goodbye to her friend forever.

Maryanne kissed her goodbye and shook her hand, a good friendly kiss and a good, firm shake. And all the way back to Honduras, Sally sat in the back of the bus and watched the jungle and thought about how the jungle makes its changes. She remembered Maryanne as a tumbler who worked in front of the cheerleaders at the Memphis State football games. The jungle had changed her to a stubby, sloe-eyed lesbian with the shadow of a mustache on her upper lip. How will it change me? Sally wondered, and looked out at the endless wall of green flashing past the windows of the bus. What will it make of me?

Now, she lay floating on her back in the same Gulf Stream under the harsh Miami sun. The wavelets washed across her body and her mouth held the bitter taste of salt. She was thirty-eight years old—and she had lived to see her question answered. She was a canny, competent, driven woman—a woman admired and respected—but perhaps a woman in name only. She had no close friends, no husband, no children. She had no drawer filled with old snapshots and fading *billets doux*, no menus saved, no theater ticket stubs, no pressed and dried corsages.

She had nothing but her job, her ambition, and Terry Fallon. And there were days when those were not enough.

Sally imagined herself lying there on the warm surface of the water, her arms stretched out like an imitation Christ. And as she looked down at the woman she had become, the understanding lapped over her like the blue hand of the Gulf Stream, and she trembled with the shock of recognition.

"Are you cold?" Ross said when he saw that she was shivering.

"No." she said. "No."

She knew now that the hills of Honduras had only been a rain forest. It was Washington that was the jungle.

2:10 P.M. EVERY SATURDAY AFTERNOON, Lou Bender played bridge in the card room at Burning Tree Country Club. The card room was stuffy and oak-paneled, full of smoke and famous faces. Lou Bender's game was Chief Justice William Rehnquist, Don Graham, and Russell Long. They were about as far apart politically as the four points of the compass. So, they never talked politics. But today they were talking about the convention because everyone in Washington was talking about it and nothing else.

"Four spades," Rehnquist said when the bidding came around to him again, and the other three men passed. Don Graham led the queen of hearts and Bender laid down his dummy. "The president has a devilish little problem," Rehnquist said. He covered the queen with dummy's king.

"So do you," Long said. He trumped with the three of spades.

"No heart?" Rehnquist said.

"No heart."

"The senator has no heart," Rehnquist said. "Lou, we should have known."

"The senator is renowned for having no heart," Bender said.

"Why, thank you," Long said. He led the ace of spades.

"Lou," Rehnquist said, "we are in trouble."

"Well, what's he going to do?" Graham said.

"He's going to go down two tricks," Long said.

"I mean the president. What's he going to do, Lou?"

"He's assessing that now."

"The thing with Eastman was a scandal," Graham said. "An outrage."

"I notice that you published the pictures," Bender said.

"His only hope is Fallon," Long said. "He should get on with it before someone starts a draft."

"I'll tell the president you said that, Russ. I'm sure he'll be grateful for your advice and continuing support."

Rehnquist went on playing the hand, but he said, "Testy today, Lou."

"A little," Bender said.

Rehnquist laid down his last four cards. "Six to the king, back with the ace sloughing the diamond, two cross-ruffs, and out."

"And down two," Long added and threw in his cards. "Which gives us the last rubber."

Lou Bender put three dollars on the table. "Thank you, gentlemen." He stood up.

"I'm starved," Don Graham said. "Let's grab a bite."

"I think I'll take a walk," Bender said. "Have a nice day, Russ."

He went down the path to the back of the eighteenth green and watched one foursome play their approach shots. After they had putted out, a twosome played up. That was the group he was waiting for.

One of the golfers hit a wedge to the center of the green. The ball bounced once, and when it landed again, the backspin drew it six feet from the hole. Bender applauded politely. The golfer handed the club back to his caddy, took his putter, and walked up onto the green. It was Admiral William Rausch.

"Didn't know you were a golf groupie," Rausch said, and stuck out his hand.

Bender shook it warmly. Then he dropped the bombshell. "Did you hear that the FBI traced the AIDS virus to Fort Deitrich?"

Rausch went white. "What?!"

"Be careful," Bender said softly, and tightened his grip on Rausch's hand. "People are watching."

The other golfer waved from the far side of the green and called out, "How are you, Lou?"

"Hello, General," Bender called back. Then he waited until the general took his sand iron from his caddy and climbed down into the sand trap, far out of earshot.

Rausch's voice was barely a whisper. "You told me they couldn't possibly—"

"I was wrong." Bender let Rausch's hand drop. He had something he wanted Rausch to do, but he knew he couldn't get him to do it by ordering or asking—only by playing on his fear.

"My God," Rausch whispered.

"Don't panic," Bender said. "There's no corroborating evidence. The autopsy report's been altered. For humanitarian reasons." He stood, smirking. "To preserve the memory of a fallen hero."

"Then how could they—"

"Unfortunately, the two fools O'Brien assigned to the case saw the report before it could be fixed."

"Goddamit," Rausch said.

Then Bender dangled the bait. "And one of them—the young one, Ross—turns out to be a real go-getter. He's the one with the ideas about Fort Deitrich."

"How the hell could he—"

"If you really want to know, it was dumb blind luck."

"I don't believe in luck," Rausch said coldly.

"Then call it a miracle. Call it whatever you please. It's a reality."

"Somebody talked."

"Who?" Bender said. "Captain Beckwith and his family?"

Rausch didn't answer. Bender could see that Rausch knew he was in real trouble. Bender savored the spectacle, "You assured me those two FBI agents couldn't find their balls in the bathtub," Rausch said.

"Even a blind pig occasionally finds an acorn."

Rausch was desperate. "Have they filed a report?"

"No," Bender said, and dropped the bait again. "At this point, it's just this guy Ross and a bright idea."

"All right, all right," Rausch said quickly. "What's the plan?"

"My plan? My plan is containment."

"Containment?"

"In five days the president leaves for the nominating convention in St. Louis. My first priority is to keep the lid on until the convention's in our pocket."

"But what about—"

Bender cut him off. "You've got to find Petersen," he said. "That's our best hope. If he's offered up as the killer, the FBI will mark the case closed and those two fools will fold up their theories and go back to counting paper clips." He knew that he was asking the impossible and promising the improbable.

Rausch was growing frantic. "Lou, I told you. There's no way we can find him. Not unless he comes out of hiding."

Bender shrugged and smiled. "Then you just may have to start looking around Washington for another drunken Argentinian businessman."

"What do you mean?" Then Rausch understood. "You're crazy. Goddamit, Lou, you're insane."

"I'm trying to re-elect a president of the United States," Bender said calmly.

But Rausch was losing control. "Lou, listen to me." He took the smaller man's arm and walked him back down the cart path, away from the green and the club house. Then he spoke more softly, more urgently. "Listen to me. We can't start killing FBI agents."

Bender made it sound so simple. "Only one of them is a problem. The young one—Ross. He went to Miami this morning with Fallon's press girl. That old fart Mancuso is just marking time to his pension."

"Maybe for you Ross is the problem. But they both saw the report. They're both a problem for me."

"Bill, you're right," Bender said. "Maybe you'd better hit them both."

"Lou. Stop it. Watch my lips. You're not talking about national security anymore. You're talking about unvarnished, premeditated murder."

At last Rausch had come to the point. Bender smiled. "Bill," he said, "you do make rather fine distinctions." Then he patted Rausch on the shoulder. "But . . . I guess you're right. It was a dumb idea." He glanced down at his watch and clucked his tongue. "Look at the time. I'd better hot-foot it back to town."

"Lou, I just don't want to take any more chances," Rausch said. "We're on real thin ice."

"There's an ugly rumor that some guy from Secret Service got his head blown off at the Four Seasons Hotel,'' Bender said. He was fishing, but Rausch didn't blink.

"Yeah. I heard that.''

They stared at each other.

"Well, not to worry,'' Bender said and smiled, and walked away.

Rausch stood looking after him. But Bender was certain that Rausch had already decided what he had to do. After all, the man had a lot of friends in Miami.

4:20 P.M. WHEN MANCUSO LANDED in Cleveland, he lugged his carry-on bag through the terminal, went down to the curb, and caught a cab. But when he gave the cabby the address, the man said, "What are you, Mac? A bible salesman?''

"No. I'm the archbishop of Canterbury. And what's it to you?''

The cabby laughed, put the flag down, and swung out into the traffic. "Those nuns don't see nobody,'' the cabby said. "They don't talk or nothin'.''

"How'd you get to be such an expert?''

"I lived in Cleveland all my life,'' the cabby said. "Ain't nothing about Cleveland I don't know. I know where to get a good steak and a bottle when the bars are closed and a piece of ass—any color, any shape.'' He shot a glance at Mancuso in the rearview mirror. "Of course, this offer is void where prohibited by law.''

"How many nuns they got up there?'' Mancuso said.

"Millions. Some just do the beads and some run the funny farm.''

"They got a big hospital?''

"Nah. Not too big. It's just for swells. You got to be rich and crazy. Otherwise, you go on the state. My brother-in-law went on the state. My sister drove him nuts.''

The convent was on the outskirts of town, west of the city. There was a long gray wall and a short gravel drive that ended before massive wooden gates. The cabby pulled up and shut off his engine.

"You gotta pull that bell thing up there,'' he said.

"Wait for me, will you?'' Mancuso got out.

He walked to the gates, and then he thought and dropped his cigarette and ground it out. There was dust on his shoes and he wiped them on the backs of his pant legs. Then he pulled the bell cord.

After a moment, he could hear slow footsteps on the other side of the wall. A tiny grating in the door slid open.

"Hello," Mancuso said. "I'm—"

The grating slapped shut. And in a moment he heard the shuffling steps on the other side of the gate, walking slowly away. He reached for the bell cord again. Then he saw a little plastic sign: Visitors 10 A.M. to 11 A.M. ONLY.

"Shit," he said.

The cabby was hanging out his window. "They only see people for an hour in the morning. Sundays and feast days, they don't see nobody."

"Now you tell me." Mancuso got back into the cab. It was Saturday and tomorrow was Sunday.

"Well, how did I know? Maybe you had an appointment or somethin'."

"I ain't got no appointment."

"Well, you're shit out of luck till Monday, Mac."

"Tell me about it."

"Where to?"

Mancuso dug the papers out of his inside jacket pocket. "The Sheraton Inn. On Route 422."

"Oh, you're gonna love that place," the cabby said, and swung the car out of the driveway. "They got a great bar there—The Trapper."

"Yeah?"

"Yeah. Lot of action. Saturday nights, the place is really jumpin'."

But when they got to the hotel, Mancuso didn't go to the bar. He told the cabby to come for him at 9:30 the next morning, and then went to his room and thumbed the phone directory until he found the number of the convent. He listened to the message and the blessing and the electronic beep. Then he said, "This is Agent Joseph Mancuso of the Federal Bureau of Investigation. I must see the Mother Superior tomorrow, Sunday August 28. I will be at the gate at 10 A.M." That sounded very official and good. He started to put the phone down. But he didn't feel right, so he put it to his ear again and said, "I know you got your big Mass and all tomorrow, Mother. But I hope you can see me. It's real important. Thanks a lot." When he put the receiver down, he felt better and ridiculous.

4:35 P.M. SALLY HAD SHOWERED off the salt and sand and blown her long hair dry. She was putting on her face when the phone rang.

It was Ross, calling from his room. "I'm thirsty."

"I'm not ready."

"How long?"

"Five minutes."

"Five minutes?"

"No more than ten."

"Fifteen at the outside?"

She laughed. "Maybe."

"Knock on my door," he said. "I'm going to read *War and Peace*."

She laughed and put the phone down, sat at the vanity, and tilted the mirror to catch the light. But the laugh was still in her eyes and it startled her to see a young girl in the looking glass again.

Something was stirring in her. She could feel it—but she couldn't quite grasp it. Something about Dave Ross was touching her in a way she hadn't been touched in a long, long time. Something about his youth or his inexperience or his open-hearted smile. Whatever it was, it was taking her back—and making her wonder what happened to the girl she once was, and what had made her the woman she'd become.

There were experiences that mark the heart, yet leave the face unblemished—like a blow that neither bruises nor breaks the skin, but leaves a lingering soreness in its aftermath. For her, Honduras had been the blow.

When she graduated from college at twenty her father took her by the hand back to the Baptist church where she had been christened. He made her change her miniskirt and cotton socks for a long cotton shift, walked her down to the baptismal pool in the stream behind the churchyard, made her wade into the icy water beside Reverend Haley. He was an old man now, thin and gristled like a Giacometti. He seized her head and pressed his thumbs into her eyes so hard that the pain shot through her limbs and he cried out, "I baptize you in the name of the Father and the Son and the Holy Ghost! I baptize you in the name and the work of the Lord!" She clasped her hands and laced her fingers. Then he pushed her back until she lost her balance and fell backward, and he thrust her down into the cold, quick flowing water.

It was not what she had expected.

She had gone with her father out of filial duty, nothing more. She had agreed to be baptized again because he wanted her to go into the world with her faith in Christ and His in her, renewed. It seemed silly the first time he suggested it—and it was only when he persisted that she understood it was important to him.

But when she fell backward into the grip of the icy stream, when the freezing, rushing waters closed around her, it was as if her heart stopped and her soul flapped like a limp white cloth in the current. It washed her body. It washed her blood and marrow. It washed her petty life. It washed away the whisky sours at Silky Sullivan's, and the petting party at the Summer Twin Drive-In, the feeling of rubbing up and down on the crotch of a boy's denims until he went all tense and limp and a little round stain darkened the fabric.

Deep it was, and cold—a burning, merciless cold that wrapped her soul and drew the sin like fluid from her mind. She *was* slain in the spirit— burned and healed, bruised and raised, crucified and resurrected. And as Reverend Haley wrenched her up from the deep, she rose, gasping, into the light, her lungs filled with cold air as a newborn babe's—flushed with new, untainted life.

That is how she came to the Peace Corps in 1969—a virgin in Christ, a soul with a mission to meet other souls at the point of need. There was no fear in her, no anxiety at stepping into the unknown. She was a hymn-singing postman's daughter when she went to Honduras. She was an idealist. And when the savagery of the "Football War" erupted around her, she thought the whole world had gone insane.

Through the first months of her assignment with Tommy Carter in the hills of western Honduras, she had become aware of the steady stream of landless *campesinos* who slipped across the border from El Salvador. Ten years of ceaseless migration had made the border a tense, armed camp. Then something unbelievably trivial sparked a shooting war.

The Honduran and Salvadoran national teams were competing to qualify for soccer's World Cup. An official's disputed decision favored the Hondurans. El Salvador was swept with fury at this "stain" upon its national honor. By nightfall, the army had mobilized and crossed the Honduran border in force. Before the Organization of American States had arranged a truce two weeks later, more than 2,000 had died.

At first, *La Guerra del Fútbol* did not come to the village of Lagrimas. It began by enveloping the road and some of the low-lying border towns. In Lagrimas, it was only a rumor—and the dull thudding of artillery in the distance at night, like rolling thunder.

Then, bands of armed and desperate men began to make their way through the village under cover of darkness. Sally and Tommy Carter had stood in the door of their hut and watched in horror at the inhumanity. Stores of food were stolen. And whatever money could be had. Sometimes a girl was raped or worse, taken. The villagers did not resist. They had no arms, no inclination to violence. Instead, they prayed that the madness would pass them by. It didn't.

In the winter, the Peace Corps sent a Jeep for them and she went down with Tommy to Tegucigalpa to be briefed—warned, really. They gathered the dozen or so volunteers who were based in Honduras in the assembly hall of the American grammar school near the embassy. The Peace Corps station director was there, but he only made the introductions. Instead, the briefing was conducted by a U.S. Army Special Forces major in combat fatigues. He showed them a map of the district that surrounded Lagrimas, showed them the routes of infiltration that the *Comunistas* were using to spread unrest throughout the mountain country along the border with El Salvador. He gave a long explanation of the kind of counterinsurgency operations that the Honduran army and their American advisors would be conducting during the next year. Sally looked around the room. At the far end were a group of American civilians, men in white short-sleeved shirts and dark glasses. There was something sinister about them, something unspoken and dangerous. She could see what was happening.

She realized that soon the Peace Corps volunteers and staff would leave Honduras. Soon the Red Cross would curtail its missions and the church groups would be encouraged to go home. Then these sinister men in white shirts and khaki pants—these *advisors*—would become the American presence in Honduras. And, gradually, the level of violence in the hill country would increase until the indigenous population would have to choose sides between the insurgents and the army. It had the makings of another Vietnam, she knew. It was 1970. She was 20 years old. But she knew it was happening again.

When the major finished, the Peace Corps station director took his place. He explained that all volunteers were advised to leave Honduras within thirty days. Those who wished to move on to a new assignment would be reassigned. Those who wished to terminate their service would be flown home. Those who stayed would have to resign from the Peace Corps and would no longer be under the protection of the American government, but would be supplied by the government of Honduras. He asked those who wished to stay to rise. Sally stood. So did a handful of others. Tommy did not. He looked up at her standing beside his chair, as though he were looking for a sign. But she looked down at him with only forgiveness. And in a moment he turned his face away.

The Honduran army had insisted that all volunteers who remained take small arms training. Sally refused. The insurgents had never threatened her. But they asked her religion, and when she answered Baptist they told her she had no choice. They taught her to clean and load and fire a revolver and how to wrap her arm through the sling of a carbine to steady it against the kick. She trained and went back to Lagrimas, this time with a dark-haired, silent Mormon woman who was exempt from using firearms. For three months, Sally slept with the revolver locked away in a drawer. For three months, life in Lagrimas went back to normal. Then one afternoon, the

Honduran army came up into the hills on a counterinsurgency sweep. They burned the huts of Lagrimas and the store of corn and slaughtered the pigs and goats and shot two men. When the children screamed, the soldiers beat and kicked them.

Sally pushed through the rowdy soldiers to the captain who was leading the operation and screamed her protest at him. He slapped her across the face and knocked her down. Two enlisted men dragged her into the jungle. She thought that they would rape and kill her. But they threw her and her knapsack on the road to Coroquin and left her there. The Mormon girl took a penknife and cut the sign of the cross into her own forehead. Then she went into the jungle with the villagers. Sally never heard from her again.

Sally went to the American embassy in Tegucigalpa to file a formal complaint, and the chargé d'affaires listened sympathetically while his secretary made notes. They gave Sally a typewritten transcript of their conversation and a copy of a letter that was hand-delivered to the Honduran minister of the interior. Then they put her up in the hospice across from the embassy and she waited.

In October of 1972, Sally returned to the United States. Her friends oohed and aahed at her adventures, but she couldn't convince them that Central America was going mad. She knew she had to find a way to change their minds and fix things. In 1975, after a frustrating three years on a Harte-Hanks weekly in Corpus Christi, she went to work at the *Houston Post*. And just as she was about to give up, she met Terry Fallon. He was the inspiration and the way. For her, he was the road—her way through the jungle.

The phone in the hotel room rang again, and Sally got ready to apologize for being late. But it wasn't Ross. It was Tommy Carter and he wasn't mincing words.

"Let's talk interviewers first," he said.

She understood in a flash. It was all she could do to keep from shouting for joy. A television network was about to offer Terry Fallon a choice hour of prime time. It was something no candidate for office—not even President Baker himself—could have dreamed a network would do. And it was happening on the very eve of the convention. It was the kind of exposure that a nominee would kill for.

Sally could barely concentrate on what Tommy was saying as he reeled off the names of the three proposed interviewers.

When he had finished, Sally gathered all her courage and said, "Pass."

"Pass?"

"Not the right flavor," she said. "You're looking to turn this into

Roger Mudd versus Gary Hart or Rather versus Nixon. We're not available for that."

She had fully expected the news division to propose their toughest interviewers—and they had. Accepting any one of them would be asking for trouble. But she knew in her heart that the offer was there. Except for the details, the deal was done.

Tommy's voice was bitter. "Listen, Sally. Maybe you should sell your interview to David Frost. You might make a few bucks."

She knew exactly who she wanted—and she said so: "What about Walter Cronkite?"

"Aw, kid, grow up," Tommy said. "We're talking major network news special here, not Joe Franklin's Memory Lane. They're never going to go for that."

"Will you put it on the table?"

"No, goddamit," he said. "No. I'm not going back to my management with that dumb fucking proposal. Now, get serious."

"I am serious. Walter Cronkite is a big tune-in. Terry's a tune-in. It's a forty share."

"Listen, Sally," Tommy said, and his tone had changed. "If you think I don't know what you're trying to do, you're wrong. First of all, Walter Cronkite is still Mr. Middle America. You want him to bring you all the older voters, all the whites, all the corn-fed rurals who won't like where your man stands on Hispanic immigration if they ever find out about it. Second, Cronkite isn't a working newsman anymore. He might not ask those nasty, probing follow-on questions that candidates dislike the most. You're setting us up to bring in the demographic you need—and then have Cronkite throw an hour of soft pitches your man can hit over the fence. Now, if I can work that out in my little brain, don't you think my management can, too?"

"Tommy," she said, "I'm sorry you don't have the faith in the American voter that we do."

"Sally," he said, "you're as cold a piece of flesh as ever came down the freeway."

"So, we agree to disagree?" She hung, waiting.

"Fuck," Tommy Carter finally said. "I'll call you back."

"You're a sweetie," she said, but by then the connection was already broken.

Someone knocked at the door.

She called out "Yes?"

It was Ross. "I'm up to the part where Smerdyokov commits suicide."

"That's *The Brothers Karamazov*," she said, and laughed. "I thought you were reading *War and Peace*?"

"I thought you were putting on your makeup—not painting the Sistine Chapel."

"I'll be right out."

"I'll believe it when I see it."

But when she came out into the hallway, he just stood there, staring at her.

"What is it?" she said, and looked down at her halter and shorts. "Is something wrong?"

"No," he said and shook his head. "No. I just can't get used to how pretty you are."

She put her hand to her face. For if she hadn't, she would have burst out, either laughing or crying.

They walked down the beach to a place called the Grass Shack. It was just a bar with a stone floor and bamboo walls and a patio that looked out on the ocean. It was empty, except for the bartender and one man who drifted in after them and sat at the bar. They ordered two mai-tais that came in tall frosty glasses decorated with little pink paper umbrellas.

"Why do they do that?" Sally said, and held up her little umbrella and rolled it between her fingers.

"I don't know."

"Perhaps it's supposed to make the drink more exotic?"

"The juice comes from Ocala and the rum comes from Puerto Rico," Ross said. "It's a real exotic drink."

"I see you're a true romantic."

"I have my moments." He raised his glass. "Luck."

They drank.

"You married?" she said.

"Nope. Engaged once. It didn't work out."

"How come?"

"She was the sister of my roommate at college. She was special. She just didn't like the idea of me working for the FBI."

"Why not?"

"She didn't see why I should work for a salary when I could be chasing big fees and making partner in a Wall Street firm."

"Why the FBI?"

"I don't know. Campus recruiter. He made it sound—well—exciting, different. Something a guy could do for his country without wearing a uniform."

That made her smile. "We're a great pair of idealists, aren't we? I joined the Peace Corps. You joined the FBI. Fifteen years changes a lot, doesn't it?"

"Yeah. It does."

She looked at him with a kind of gentleness he hadn't seen in her eyes before.

"You're a nice guy, aren't you?" she said.

"I'm okay."

"Let me buy you dinner?"

Ross laughed and shook his head. "Can't."

"Why not?"

"You're the subject of an official investigation," he said, being funny and serious at the same time.

"All business, aren't you?"

"Not all." He thought about it a moment. "I'll buy the dinner. You buy the drinks."

The sun was low in the west when they started back up the beach toward the Miramar. She felt restored, as though she had been on vacation for a year and a day. Her arms and her chest were rosy from the sun. She felt cleansed, healing. And as she walked across the sand with Ross, she felt that she wanted to hold his hand.

After they left, the man at the bar settled his tab and followed them.

5:45 P.M.   WHEN SAM BAKER returned to the Oval Office, Speaker O'Donnell and Lou Bender were sitting on the sofas near the fireplace, hunched forward, whispering to each other. Pat Flaherty, the political pollster, stood in the far corner of the room.

O'Donnell and Bender fell silent when the president entered. Then they slowly got to their feet.

"Well?" Sam Baker said. "Well, what is it?"

"It's on your desk," Bender said.

Baker went to his desk, and sat down. He put on his reading glasses and picked up the single green sheet of computer paper. He looked down the single column of numbers. Then he took off his reading glasses.

"As bad as that?" he said to Flaherty. But Flaherty didn't reply.

"Gentlemen. . ." the president cleared his throat. "Could you please excuse me?"

Nodding, they went out.

O'Donnell followed Bender across the hall into his office. They said goodnight to Flaherty, then shut the door.

"Goddamit," O'Donnell said. "You told me we'd have a decision before now. This Eastman thing is like an albatross around his neck. He has to cut clean or be dragged down with him."

"What do you want from me?" Bender said, with an angry wave in the direction of the Oval Office. "He's dug in."

"You mean he's buried."

Bender bit the end off a cigar. "We've got to get to Fallon."

"You get Sam to agree to offer him the vice presidential nomination. I'll talk to Fallon."

"We can't wait for Baker to agree," Bender said.

That stopped O'Donnell. "Meaning what?"

"If Fallon's doing the same research we are, he's getting the same numbers we are."

"So?"

"Yesterday he had promise. Today he's got leverage." Bender lit his cigar. "Either we move now, or Fallon may start thinking about slipping past Baker. How would you like that kind of a fight at your convention?"

O'Donnell looked grim. He hooked his thumbs around his suspenders. "You're proposing that we offer Fallon the vice presidential nomination without the president's approval?"

Bender rolled the cigar around on his tongue. "Perhaps you have a better idea?"

"Lou," O'Donnell said, and he picked up a little brass White House paperweight from the desk. "Lou, I've been in politics all my life. And that's either the smartest or the dumbest thing I've ever heard."

6:10 P.M. BY SIX O'CLOCK that night, it was all over Washington. Sally was in the bath when Chris called to tell her.

"You won't believe it."

"Try me."

"Baker-Eastman, 41%."

"My God," she said. "They dropped six points in three days."

"Baker-Fallon, 53%. Exactly the same score they had before."

"What?" She stood up in the bath, naked and soapy. Water splashed everywhere. "Do you realize what that means? It means that, strong as Terry was, he's still gaining. Whatever the Eastman episode cost Baker, Terry's compensating for the loss."

Then, finally, the excitement swept over her and she let go. "My God," she said. "Baker hasn't got a choice any more. He's got to give it to Terry!"

"Hey, Sally," Chris said. "Do you have any clothes on?"

She grabbed a towel to cover herself. "No. Why? How did you know that?"

"I can hear it in your voice." He began to laugh and she began to laugh and it was laughter from deep inside where she didn't know that she could still laugh.

"Chris, listen to me," she said, and she was gasping with excitement. "Nothing to the press. No statement, no confirmation. Blackout. That's what's working for us. They're starving for news about Terry. And the longer we hold him out, the more they want him and the brighter his image gets."

"But how long can he hold out?"

"Until he steps to the podium and accepts the nomination for vice president of the United States."

6:40 P.M. THEY ARRIVED WHILE Terry was having dinner alone in the study—Bender and O'Donnell, without an appointment, without so much as a phone call. Terry balled his napkin on his plate and stood up slowly to greet them.

"Are we intruding?" O'Donnell said.

"Not at all. Gentlemen, please sit down."

They did.

"We'll be brief," O'Donnell said. He looked at Bender, who nodded. "You've seen today's polls?"

"Yes," Terry said. "Yes, I have."

"Do you know what they mean?"

"All research is open to interpretation," Terry said. "I could read it several ways."

"It says that on the right ticket, you'd be a major asset to the party," Bender said. "That's beyond dispute. Don't you agree?"

"Yes. I do."

"Well, we need to know if you're prepared to serve," O'Donnell said.

Terry sat back gingerly on the sofa. "In what capacity?"

"Answer the question," Bender said.

"I will when I hear it, Mr. Bender."

"Terry," O'Donnell said, and leaned forward and rested his elbows on his knees. "Terry, I want to talk to you tonight about unity. About the unity of our party. I don't think any of us want to see that unity threatened at the convention."

Terry nodded. "Mr. Speaker, I want you to understand something. The party may be the most important thing in your life. It's not in mine."

"What is?" Bender said.

"This country. The Constitution. My conscience. My sense of— "

"Look, Fallon, if you want to make a speech, hire a hall. You wouldn't be sitting here if the party hadn't—"

"Excuse me, Mr. Bender, but I won my seat in the House on my own. The Houston regulars told me to go back to teaching history. Governor Taylor put me in the Senate, not you—and definitely not the party machine."

Bender stood up. "Well, that's the goddamnedest—"

"All right, Lou," O'Donnell said. "I'll handle this."

Bender walked across the room and leaned against the piano, his back to them.

"All right, Terry," O'Donnell said. "What's it to be?"

"I want to talk to the president."

"I'll arrange a call."

"No. I want to talk to him face-to-face. Tomorrow. Just the two of us. For half an hour."

"We'll set a time," O'Donnell said. He rose. "Tomorrow."

"You'll have your answer then."

O'Donnell shook his hand. Bender just walked out.

7:05 P.M.   "WHAT'D YOU SAY the name of this restaurant was?" Ross asked when the cab pulled away from the front door of the Miramar.

"Cafe Chauveron."

Sally sat back. She was wearing a yellow silk dress and pearls and her skin had begun to tan and she looked dark and her blond hair glittered.

"You look great," Ross said.

She smiled. "Is that the man talking? Or the federal agent?"

"Hey." Ross tapped the crystal of his watch. "It's after seven. I get off at five."

They both laughed and Sally rolled down the window of the cab, letting the sweet night breeze sweep in on them, carrying the soft scent of the sea.

"God, I feel good," she said.

"It's amazing what a mai-tai can do."

"No, no," she said. "I'll tell you the truth. I didn't want to come down here today. I thought I'd be hysterical if I had to be away when so much is happening. I went to see Terry this morning to ask him to let me cancel this trip."

"I'm glad he didn't."

"Funny," she said. "So am I."

They drove on past the point where hotel row ended, and then the taxi humped over the bridge into Bal Harbour. Then it turned west across the causeway and into the parking lot of Cafe Chauveron.

"Bon soir," the maitre d' said when they came to his desk.

"Evening," Ross said. "You have a reservation for two for dinner. The name's Ross."

The maitre d' ran his finger down the page. He looked at Ross over the tops of his glasses.

"When did you make your reservation, *monsieur?*"

"Oh, I don't know," Ross said, and looked at his watch. "Maybe a couple of hours ago."

"But, *monsieur*, we've been fully booked since yesterday."

"Now, listen," Ross said.

And then Sally said, *"S'il vous plaît, annoncez-moi à Monsieur André Chauveron. Mademoiselle Sally Crain, l'assistante-presse de Senator Fallon à Washington."*

The maitre d' picked up the phone.

"What was that all about?" Ross said. "That son-of-a-bitch is just scrounging for a tip."

Sally patted his arm. In a moment, a door at the rear of the restaurant opened and André Chauveron came out, straightening his jacket.

"Miss Crain," he said, and shook her hand warmly. "Welcome. We're honored. And how is Senator Fallon?"

"He's just fine. This is Mr. Ross," Sally said. "He's a friend of the senator's."

"Ah, Mr. Ross!" He warmly shook his hand. "Delighted to have you. Come. Table *vingt-cinq.*" He leaned in toward Ross. "By the water. It's a lovely night."

It was, indeed, lovely, and romantic—a little white cluster of candlelit tables on the verandah overlooking the marina. From where they sat, Ross could see the tips of the masts of the sailboats gilded with the last light of the setting sun. There were a few men and boys along the docks, crabbing with dropstrings. A funny little beast, the crab, Ross thought. When a crab closed its claw on a meal, it wouldn't let go—even when it was pulled up and out of the water. Its tenacity was its death.

When the candle on their table was lighted and the waiter went off to fetch their drinks, Ross said, "Okay. I'm impressed."

"Ten years in Washington. A girl has to learn a little about how the game is played."

The waiter set their drinks before them, and Sally thought about how he didn't seem to mind that she had stepped in with her connections and delivered the table. There were a lot of men who would have taken offense.

"Would you let me pay the check?" she suddenly said.

"No. I can't."

"I mean, if this were a date? Would you let me pay the check?"

He shrugged. "I don't know. If you wanted to. Why not?" He looked around the swanky room. "I sure as hell wouldn't want to."

She laughed, but then she pressed on. "Suppose I came to pick you up in my car?"

"When?"

"I mean, if this were a date. Suppose I called you and said, 'Dave, I'm taking you to dinner at Chauveron tonight. Wear something sexy and I'll pick you up at seven.' How would you like that?"

"Yeah. Well, that would be a problem," Ross said.

"Oh? What problem?"

"The truth is—I don't have a thing to wear."

That made her laugh again, but she said, "Be serious."

"Sally, you can pick me up and take me to dinner any time you want. And I'll wear my sexiest blazer." He slipped his jacket back off his shoulders, wrapped it around his chest as though it were a low-cut bodice. "Tell me, darling. How do I look?"

They laughed together. The waiter brought the menus. But she wasn't done.

She said, "You wouldn't mind if I picked the restaurant, made the reservation, invited you, drove my car, and paid the bill?"

He looked at her, and he could see that she was only half playing.

"No," he said. "I wouldn't mind."

She seemed satisfied with that. Then she said, "Why not?"

Ross laughed. "You're really intent on getting to the bottom of this, aren't you?"

"Bound and determined."

"Okay," he said, and sat back. "I'll give it to you straight. You've got a better job than I have, you make more money than I do, you're more sophisticated—I think you're even taller than I am."

"Not taller," she said.

"I wear lifts."

She was startled. "Do you?" She leaned over to look at his shoes.

"Only kidding."

"You," she said, and wagged her finger at him. "Now, be honest. Are you saying that you wouldn't find that"—she picked the word carefully—"intimidating?"

"Interesting, maybe. Intimidating, no."

"On the level?"

"Sally, believe me. If you were just another pretty girl and I was just a guy—I'd let you pick the place, pay the bill. I'd even let you sleep on the side with the telephone. Okay?"

"Okay," she said, and laughed. But it was the kindest thing a man had said to her in as long as she could remember.

"You're the one who said that fifteen years changes a lot."

"Eleven," she said quickly.

"Eleven?"

"I'm thirty-eight. You're twenty-seven."

"I'll be twenty-eight next month. And there are laws in this country against age discrimination. So don't pick on me."

"You either."

"Deal." Ross opened his menu. "Now, what's this here—*moules marinières*?"

She helped him through the menu, but when the captain came to take their order, Ross said, "I'll have the gefilte fish and the hot dogs."

"*Comme? Er . . . pardon, monsieur. Je ne connais pas. . . .*"

"Right here," Ross said and pointed at the menu. "The gefilte fish . . . and the hot dogs."

Sally tried to keep from laughing.

The captain took his reading glasses from the pocket of his tuxedo and leaned over Ross's shoulder.

"*Ah . . . oui, monsieur. Les quenelles de pike, sauce Nantua. Et le saucisson Auberge de l'Ill, garni. Parfait. Et pour madame?*"

When she had ordered and the captain had gone off toward the kitchen, she said, "I'll kill you."

Ross was laughing. He opened his hands. "What did I do?"

She was laughing, too. "They'll throw us out of here. And we'll deserve it."

"Ah, you see," he said. "You're the one who's worried about form."

That brought her up short. "You're right," she said. "My God, you're right. It's not you. It's me." And she sat, staring.

Then the captain stepped in and offered Ross the wine list.

"The lady will pick the wine," Ross said. "As a matter of fact, she just might pay the bill."

The captain looked surprised, but Sally just looked grateful. She pressed the red leather folder closed without a glance. "Louis Roderer *Cristal*," she said. *"Soixante-seize."*

"Oui, madame!"

"Hey," Ross said, when the captain had gone. "That's big money."

"We agreed," Sally said. "You buy the dinner. I'll buy the drinks."

And when the champagne was uncorked and poured into the chilled crystal flute, she raised her glass and studied the lacy strands of rising tiny bubbles and savored the bouquet and tasted. Then she nodded.

She held her glass aloft while the captain poured for Ross.

"Well," she said, "what shall we drink to?"

"L'chaim," Ross answered. "Life."

"Life," she repeated, and from the sound of her voice, he knew she really meant it. "God, that's good," she said when she put her glass down.

But suddenly—quite suddenly—Ross grew distant and preoccupied. She wondered if she had finally gone too far. She wondered if he were thinking about her and, if so, what he thought. And she realized that how he felt about her mattered to her very much.

But Ross wasn't thinking about Sally. He was staring at the last man crabbing off the dock across the harbor. There was no way he could have recognized that man. But, for some strange reason, he was certain that he did.

7:30 P.M. CHARLIE O'DONNELL AND Lou Bender sat in the limousine on the way back into the District, each pressed against his window, staring out into the rainswept night, each with his own thoughts. Finally, Bender lit a cigar.

"What do you think?" he said.

"I've always thought Fallon was a fine young man," O'Donnell said. "I didn't know he was quite that smart."

"How smart is he?"

"He's smart enough to know he's got you by the short hairs, if that's what you're asking."

"He's got us all."

O'Donnell shifted uneasily in his seat. He reached over and flopped down the jumpseat and put his big brown wingtips on it.

"If Sam doesn't act soon, if he keeps slipping in the polls, well, things could become—shall we say—unpredictable."

"Unpredictable?"

"There's talk of a draft."

"I heard it at lunch today. It's just talk."

"So far."

Bender snorted. "That's impossible," he said. "Fallon has no state organizations. He's never made a speech outside of Texas and Washington."

"You're right. He has no state people," O'Donnell said, and he was pondering that. "And yet he has a huge national following. What do you make of that?"

"What do you mean? It's the television. Just a—"

"Rather a phenomenon, wouldn't you say?"

Bender looked over at the old man. As the limousine swept through the streets of the District, the street lamps threw patterns of light and dark across his long, graying face. And he could see that the meeting with Terry Fallon had made a deep and lasting impression on Charlie O'Donnell.

"What we may be witnessing here," O'Donnell began, and he was nodding to himself, "is a resurgence of pure, popular democracy in a fundamental form that hasn't existed since the colonial town meeting. Television allows everyone in the national community to watch events as they happen. Everyone reacts at the same time. And the result is a spontaneous outpouring, a wave of support that can carry a little-known man to national office."

"You're not serious," Bender said.

"Perfectly serious."

"You mean, a wave of hysteria."

"Call it what you will. It's a force to be reckoned with."

"Why, Mr. Speaker," Bender said with sweet and biting sarcasm. "You sentimental old faker. . . . You really believe in democracy, don't you? You really believe that government of, by, and for the people—"

O'Donnell pressed the intercom to his chauffeur. "Harvey, take us to the Cosmos Club." Then he sat back.

"I think you'd better drop me at the White House," Bender said.

"No, you should come along with me, Lou. I asked a few of the boys to stop around for a chat."

"I think it's a little early to go public with this."

"It's already public." O'Donnell patted him on the arm. "Lou, you're just running one candidate for office in November. The party's running hundreds. Congressmen and governors and mayors and aldermen in big cities and little towns from here to Honolulu. The party needs a ticket that can win. But more than that, we need to remain in control. We can't have candidates using television to go over our heads to the public. Once they start doing that, the Republican and Democratic parties are on their way to being forgotten, like the Whigs and Tories."

"And *unity*?"

"Unity . . . unity is a polite word for control."

Lou Bender began to laugh. "Well," he said, "that's better. For a moment, I thought that bullshit about a wave of popular support was—"

"Oh, I believe in the wave, Lou. I believe we either steer it or we drown. I'm just trying to warn you that there may be a fork up ahead. A place where the river divides."

It was more than "a few of the boys" gathered in the Cosmos Club. There were Senators Longworth from Alabama, deFrance from Louisiana, Swartz from Arizona. And there were three congressmen—Wickert, Johnson, and Brown. It was as much clout as either party could stuff into a twenty-by-twenty room: the chairmen of Senate Finance, Appropriations, Judiciary, House Armed Services, Foreign Affairs, and Ways-and-Means. Congress was on vacation but they looked ready for work. They sat in a rough circle of leather armchairs. There wasn't much handshaking.

"Charlie, you got a hell of a mess on your hands with Eastman," Longworth said. He was a baby-faced little man, sixtyish, with a soft southern drawl, and it was plain he was speaking for the group.

"It's an awkward situation," O'Donnell said.

"I'd say it was a pain in the ass," Bill Wickert said. He was a seven-term congressman from Buffalo, New York, and nobody was right of him.

"Where's your man on this?" Longworth said to Bender.

"He's evaluating."

There was a pause. Some of the men looked at each other.

"What the hell is he evaluating?" Wickert asked. "He can't win with Eastman anyhow. We told him that last fall."

"Now, Bill," Longworth said.

"Ah, for Christ's sake—"

"Shut up, Bill," Longworth said.

Wickert crossed his arms and legs, slouched in his chair.

Swartz said, "Let's not lose sight of our objective." He was the richest and maybe the smartest man in the Senate. "We want to go to St.

Louis with a candidate in place. We want to avoid a floor fight. We want a unified party in November. That means sacrifices will have to be made.''

"Brilliant," Wickert said.

"Bill, I'm going to ignore that," Swartz said. "Lou, is Sam Baker willing to accept Terry Fallon as his vice presidential nominee?''

"At this moment?"

"Yes."

"No."

The group sat, silent.

Then deFrance said, "Perhaps there's a more diplomatic way to approach this."

"What?" Wickert said.

"Perhaps Dan Eastman might be persuaded to accept a new assignment?''

"Gentlemen," Bender said. "Gentlemen, you had this conversation with the president and vice president at the ranch in New Mexico."

"What kind of new assignment?" Johnson said. He had studied for the ministry and was all for peace on earth.

"Oh, something could be found," deFrance said. "A federal judgeship, ambassador to somewhere."

"It's entirely possible that Dan Eastman could make the worst judge in the history of common law," Senator Swartz said. "And I wouldn't vote to confirm him ambassador to Detroit."

"I say we kick the son-of-a-bitch out on his ass and be done with it," Wickert said. "And if Baker won't do it, then both of them have to go."

In his most courtly way, deFrance said, "Bill, there are moments when I believe you are an asshole. And there are times when I know it to be true."

"Fuck you," Wickert said.

"Living proof," deFrance said with a nod.

Then Archie Brown said, "I'd like to ask a question. What happens if Fallon reaches for the presidency?''

The room grew very quiet.

Finally, Longworth cleared his throat. "If that happens, boys, then I'd say we're sitting on the wrong side of the shit and the fan."

When the meeting broke up, O'Donnell motioned Bender to stay. And when the others had left, O'Donnell ordered a Napoleon brandy. He swirled it around in the snifter while Bender sat opposite on the couch, jawing his cigar.

"So, you see how it is," O'Donnell said.

"Clearly."

The two men sat in silence.

"Fallon's a slick son-of-a-bitch," Bender said. "I'm just beginning to realize how slick he is."

"You don't know the half of it," O'Donnell said.

And Bender added, "Maybe I do."

They sat, neither willing to play the first card. But it had become plain to Bender that he had been invited to sit among the party's powers-that-be and listen to the debate tonight for a purpose. And now Bender understood what that purpose was. O'Donnell was making him an eyewitness to history. He'd put Bender in a grandstand seat as the party leadership decided, for once and for all, to force Sam Baker to hand the vice presidential nomination to Terry Fallon. Now Bender could report that Charlie O'Donnell couldn't stop the bandwagon—even if he lay down in front of it.

Finally, Bender said, "You know Fallon put the FBI on Weatherby," and it was more than a question and less than a statement.

O'Donnell looked at the fingernails of his right hand for a moment and Bender could see that he was thinking about his answer. "Lou, how did you find out about that?" O'Donnell said softly.

"I'd rather hear how you found out about it."

"No great mystery. The party has done a thorough check of Fallon's background. We do that with every candidate for national office, and we do it right. Presidential candidates who don't do it right wind up running with Tom Eagleton, or Geraldine Ferraro."

Bender knocked the ash off his cigar. "Charlie, I almost believe you."

Bender watched the old man press a button on the table beside him. A waiter in tailcoat stepped into the room and O'Donnell ordered another brandy. He was an extraordinary figure, O'Donnell was, sitting there in the great leather armchair with its rows of brass rivets. He was the Speaker of the House of Representatives of the United States, one of the great, gray men of power, the incarnation of authority and influence and guile. Lou Bender looked at O'Donnell as if he were only beginning to see him as he really was.

The waiter came in and put another snifter on the table, took the empty one, and went out.

"Oh, Charlie," Bender said. He got up and walked around the empty circle of chairs until he was standing opposite O'Donnell. "Charlie, you are the best. No doubt about it. You brought me in here to see that there's a groundswell building within the party. So that I'd tell Sam there was nothing anyone could do to deny the vice presidential nomination to Fallon—not even the great speaker himself."

"You saw," O'Donnell said. "You make your own judgment."

"How would it be if the ABSCAM story got out?" Bender said.

O'Donnell sipped his brandy. "Lou, what does *got out* mean?"

"If it got to the press. It would sure make pretty-boy Fallon look like a back-stabbing louse."

O'Donnell put his glass down. "Lou, you're a shrewd man. And you've spent a lot of time in Washington. But I see I'm going to have to give you a lesson in politics."

"Oh? Really?" Bender wasn't backing down.

"Terry Fallon is a phenomenon, Lou. He's like Eisenhower after the war, or Kennedy in 1960. He's all the things that every candidate dreams of becoming. Charismatic. Popular. Electable. He can be vice president for four years under Baker—and president for eight years after that. Which would put this party in the White House for sixteen unbroken years. Do you understand—can you grasp what a rare and priceless opportunity Terry Fallon represents for this party?"

Bender did. And he could not deny it.

O'Donnell got up and brushed off his trousers to indicate the conversation was over. And they stood like that, poised, confronting each other like David and Goliath.

"Go ahead," Bender said. "Go ahead. Say it."

"Lou," O'Donnell said, "I warn you. Don't cast the first stone."

10:30 P.M. SALLY HAD WATCHED Ross through the dinner and the coffee and cognac afterward, had watched him grow quieter and more remote. He still joked with her and his mind was agile and alert and followed her train of thought. But more and more as the dinner wore on, he seemed distant and detached. From time to time, she caught him staring out across the waterway, just staring into the empty darkness among the docks and bobbing sailboats, and she wondered if she were boring him, or if he were just tired and feeling the champagne, or if there were someone else in his life.

The captain brought separate checks—his for dinner, hers for the wine.

"Well, that's a first for me," Ross said, and there was no hint of irritation.

"Me, too."

The maitre d' phoned for a cab, and when they were headed south on A1A, Sally said, "How about a nightcap? My treat?"

But he said, "No, thanks. I'd better hit the hay. We might have a long day tomorrow."

She was disappointed, but she said, "Right," and slouched back in the seat.

Then Ross sat up and tapped on the partition. "Hey, buddy," he called out to the cabby, "take a right."

"The Miramar's on Collins Avenue, pal. It's down—"

"That's okay. Take a right."

"You're the boss."

The cab swung over the causeway, heading west toward Miami Shores. "Is this a shortcut?" Sally said.

"I just thought we'd get some air . . . burn off a few of those bubbles," Ross said. "Take a left here, buddy."

They turned south again. Then the road forked.

"Take the . . . er . . . left," Ross said, and when the cabby turned they pulled up at a stop sign. Ross looked around. "I don't know where we are. Do you?"

"Yeah," the cabby said. "This is A1A. Just like before."

"Okay. I give up," Ross said. He sat back with Sally. "Another bright idea out the window."

He shrugged and she forced a smile and they agreed to an early breakfast and a swim, and all the same, when he saw her to her door and said good night, she was certain she had lost him.

10:35 P.M. THE SECRET SERVICE was still on duty at the West Wing of the White House when Lou Bender went by in the limousine on his way home. So he asked the driver to wait and went upstairs.

The president was at his desk, reading. He was wearing brown slacks and his old brown cardigan sweater and a white shirt with an open collar and no necktie. When Bender came in, the president closed the leather folder on his desk and leaned back in his chair.

"More bad news," Bender said.

"What now?"

"O'Donnell had a meeting of the brain trust." Bender sat down on one of the sofas and put his feet up.

"Who?"

"Longworth, Swartz, deFrance. The powers that be. And Wickert. I forgot what a little bastard he was."

"The trouble with Bill Wickert is that he doesn't like himself. Well, how did it go?"

"They're determined, Sam. Absolutely determined. And O'Donnell's ready to go whichever way the wind blows."

STEVE SOHMER

"I see." Sam Baker put his reading glasses on the desk. "What options do we have?"

"One. And it's not optional."

"Give Fallon the number two slot?"

"Or else."

"Or else what?"

"There was talk of shit. And fans." Bender got up. "Anyhow, Fallon wants a private meeting with you tomorrow. Check your calendar. I'll set it up."

"All right." The president opened the leather folder on his desk and put on his reading glasses.

Bender went to the door. "I'll see you in the morning. Get a good night's sleep. You'll need it."

"Lou?"

"Yes?"

When Bender turned around, the president was holding up a sheet of paper.

"Do you know anything about this?"

Bender went around the president's desk and took the sheet. It was a form condolence letter, typed on White House stationery and ready for signature. It read:

Dear Mr. and Mrs. Thomopolous:

I want to express my most sincere condolences on the occasion of your loss.

As a father, I understand that no sentiment can ever fill the void this tragedy has left in your lives. But I hope you will find comfort in the knowledge that your son, Stephen, was a credit to his country, and to the Department of the Treasury, which he ably and valiantly served.

Sincerely,

Lou Bender shrugged and handed the paper back. "Search me," he said.

"No idea what this is about?"

"No."

"Find out."

"When I have time."

"Do it now," the president said. "Good night."

But Bender didn't move. "What's the matter with you, Sam?"

"What do you think?"

208

"I think this thing with Eastman is getting to you. I think you're worried about what might happen at the convention."

Sam Baker looked down at the condolence letter on his desk. "I'm worried about a lot of things. Now, good night."

Bender put his hands in his pockets, pulled his trouser legs back, and took a look at the shine on his shoes. Then he said, "Good night," and went out the door.

Sam Baker was worried about Bender. For the first time in thirty years, he was beginning to wonder if Lou Bender had crossed the line.

11:05 P.M. AFTER HE SAW Sally to her door, Ross went into his room and took off his shirt and tie, shoes and socks. He took the pint bottle of Beefeater out of his suitcase and poured himself an inch in a tumbler from the bathroom and slid open the door to the terrace. But before he could step out, the phone rang. It was Mancuso.

"What do you know?" Ross said.

"Nothing. Visiting hour is ten o'clock. Only they don't see nobody on Sunday."

"So, what are you going to do?"

"I'm gonna try to get in there tomorrow anyhow. If I can't, I guess I sit here till Monday and pick my nose."

"You're wasting your time."

"No kidding."

"I mean on Fallon. The guy's all right."

"Yeah. He's a prince among men, right?"

"You're not interested in the AIDS thing?"

"No," Mancuso said, and then abruptly changed the subject. "Where are you on Ramirez?"

"We're waiting for them to call and arrange a meet."

"How's the chickie-boo?"

That rubbed Ross wrong. "She's fine."

"Watch yourself," Mancuso said. "She's guilty until proven innocent."

"Get off her case, Joe."

"Oh . . . ? That how it is?"

"Good night, Joe," Ross said, and hung up. He turned out the room lights, pushed through the nylon curtains, and took his drink out into the darkness on the little terrace that overlooked the beach. He leaned over the railing, looking down at the ghostly white waves.

There was no doubt about it: he and Sally were being tailed. The man who was crabbing on the dock across from the restaurant was the same man who had been sitting at the bar when they left the Grass Shack that afternoon. And then there was that middle-aged man who had been sitting in the lobby, reading the same newspaper all afternoon. But what clinched it was the headlights of the car that had followed them over the causeway and around in a big circle back to A1A.

From the start, nothing had been straight about this gig. Mancuso had been right—it was a setup. One victim and two murders. Then the bloodbath at the Beckwith house. And the lingering, gnawing feeling that someone else was on the case, someone was half a step ahead of them, someone was laying for them in the darkness. But now, here in Miami, it was a sure thing that he and Sally were being closely watched. But by whom?

The railing was cold and the concrete floor of the terrace was damp under his feet and the breeze from the west was chilly on the back of his neck. Ross turned to go inside. Then something moved in the room next door and caught his eye.

The gauzy curtains were drawn across the sliding glass door of Sally's bedroom. Inside, two bedside lamps were on and there was a crack of light showing from the bathroom. As he watched, Sally came out of the bathroom and stood at the end of the bed. She began to unbutton the front of her dress.

Ross stepped back, out of the soft moonlight and into the shadows at the end of the terrace. He watched Sally unbutton her dress, slip it off her shoulders, and let it slide down around her ankles. Then she stepped out of it, hung it neatly over the back of her chair. Ross knew he shouldn't stand there. He felt he was spying. But he was powerless to go.

She turned to face the door, turned directly toward the place where Ross stood hidden in the shadows. Then she unhooked her bra and dropped it on the chair. Her breasts were round and high, and without the bra they were just a little wider than her chest so that her waist seemed very tiny. Her nipples were dark and pointed and when she moved, the soft flesh of her breasts followed the flow of her body. Ross was barely breathing and he could feel his heart racing in his chest.

She bent down and slipped off her panties and lay them with her bra. Then she stood up straight in her high-heeled shoes. Now he could see all of her. She had rounded, voluptuous hips and a tight little V of blond pubic hair. She was the kind of woman he had seen only in the magazines, all curves and fullness and soft, giving flesh, and his pulse beat in his temples.

She turned and walked toward the bathroom, and as she passed the end table, the light of the lamp played down the curve of her back and buttocks. Ross swallowed hard. Then she stepped into the bathroom and closed the door.

He stood there on the terrace, trying to catch his breath. He was hot and hard. He took a long belt of the gin, went inside, and sat on the bed. But he didn't want to sleep, so he sat in the chair and put on David Letterman. But he had never found Letterman very funny and tonight was no exception, so he shut off the television and looked around the room, realizing that, just then, the room was too fucking small and he was goddamned if he was going to have anybody following him around all day and night. So, he put on his shirt and shoes and jacket, put his revolver in his pocket, took the room key, and went out.

Mancuso sat by the phone for a long time, thinking about calling Ross back. He didn't like the way he sounded. Sally Crain was a good-looking woman with big tits and a sweet little ass. She was smart and shrewd and she'd been around plenty. She was too goddamned smart for Dave Ross and that was for sure.

He put his jacket on and went downstairs in the elevator and walked into The Trapper. The cabby had been right; there *were* a lot of hookers. He sat down at the bar near one little redhead who was on the downside of forty.

"Buy you a drink?"

"Bourbon," she said. "Make it a double."

"That's my drink."

The bartender set them up.

"You from around here?"

"Washington," he said.

"You work for the government?"

"Yeah. I find beauty queens to sleep with the president."

"Wise guy, huh?"

"You want to audition?"

"Maybe."

"What's your price?"

"A c-note."

"Come on," he said. "I'm not that horny—and you're not that good."

"I'm better than what you get at home."

"That ain't saying much."

They laughed together, and then Mancuso told the bartender to send a couple of rounds up to his room and they took the elevator upstairs, laughing all the way.

When he took his jacket off, she saw the revolver he wore at his hip.

"What are you? A cop?"

"Not tonight," he said. "This ain't my jurisdiction."

"I don't fuck cops." She started to put her dress back on.

He put a fifty on the bed. "Come on. What about it?"

She looked at the money and then she looked at him. "You ain't gonna bust me?"

"No. But I might make you pop."

"This I got to see," she said, and picked up the money and stepped out of her dress.

In the dark, she moaned once when he came, and when he was done, she put on the light and they drank another bourbon together.

"Wanna go again?"

"Fifty's my limit," Mancuso said. "I'm tapped out."

"That's okay," she said. "I'll give you one for love."

She did. And it was the only kind of love he understood.

Dave Ross went downstairs to the bar of the disco in the Miramar. He ordered a Beefeater in a plastic cup and went out the back door onto the beach.

In the soft moonlight, he could see up and down the long row of hotels. The beach was deserted. It had turned cold now, so cold that it surprised him—but it didn't stop him. Without looking back, he walked straight out to the crest of sand where the beach broke and sloped steeply down into the water. He stopped there, put his drink down on a flat spot in the sand, kicked his shoes off, and dropped his jacket on top of them. Then he peeled off his trousers and folded them on top of the pile and ran down the sand in just his undershorts and dove into the water.

He held his revolver against his body and swam sidestroke a long way out into the dark, swirling water, and then turned north and swam hard with the current half a mile or so, until he looked back and the neon sign atop of the Miramar was almost too small to read. Then he rode the rollers in and crept up on the beach.

There was a cold breeze blowing from the south and it turned the beads of water on his skin to icy points. He hunched down, hiding behind the contour of the dunes, and crept along the beach back toward the Miramar. His jockey shorts were soaking wet and freezing in his groin and he could barely control the chattering of his teeth. By the time he was within striking distance of the hotel, his heart was hammering with the exertion of the swim and he was trembling uncontrollably with tension and cold.

He got down on all fours and crawled up the side of the last dune. Gritty sand covered his body and chafed like ground glass against his belly as he slid up to the top of the rise and peeked over.

There was a lifeguard watchtower set on a promontory of sand about fifty feet away. In the lee of the tower, a man in a gray business suit and black shoes was standing—half in shadow, his back to Ross—standing so that he could watch the pile of clothes that Ross had left in the sand.

Ross inched back down, looked at the wet revolver in his hand. Like his hands and his belly, the gun was crusted with sand. There was no way of knowing whether the action was clogged with grit. And the gun had been immersed for fifteen minutes. Bullets weren't waterproof—and there was no certainty the gun would fire even if the hammer fell.

Ross rolled over on his back against the sand dune, trying to catch his breath, trying to figure the odds. His weapon might be useless. But that man might hold the key to everything—the murders of Ramirez, the Beckwith family, the stranger in the Four Seasons Hotel. Whatever the risk, Ross knew he had to try to take him. He looked down at himself and the wet revolver. Silently, he slipped the safety off. Then he crept up and over the crest of the dune.

Slowly, hardly daring to breathe, he crept forward on his belly. Just beneath the surface, the sand was still warm, and he was grateful for that. He crept until he was only a few yards from the man's back.

The man stepped behind the guard tower. Ross flattened on the sand. He held his arms straight out and peeked at the man over the front sight of the revolver.

The man yawned and leaned against the tower.

Suddenly, Ross jumped to his feet, ran three long strides, and as the man turned toward him, he leaped up and kicked him hard in the center of his chest with the bottoms of both his feet.

The man cried out and fell backward, and Ross was on him, pinning his arms and shoving the barrel of his revolver against his cheek.

"Move and I'll kill you!"

"Aw, Jesus," the man whined. "Take it easy, pal."

"What the fuck are you doing following me?"

"Hey! I was taking a walk."

"Fucking liar." Ross thumbed back the hammer of the revolver.

"Jesus, pal! Wait a second! Wait a second!"

"Who the fuck are you, Mac? What the hell do you want?"

"Woodville. FBI. Miami zone."

Ross's mouth fell open.

"What? Bullshit!"

"Look there. In my jacket pocket."

He started to point and Ross shoved the gun hard against his jaw. "Don't move, son-of-a-bitch." Ross dug into the man's pocket. "Goddamit. I said, don't move!"

The man lay still, panting desperately. Ross pulled the leather wallet from his pocket, flipped it open. In the moonlight, the familiar shield gleamed. He pushed it under the man's chin and looked at his face and the picture on the ID.

"Woodville, huh? Who's the head of your office?"

"The . . . ah . . . it's Lucas."

"What's his first name?"

"Ah, first name . . . Sawyer."

"And what do they call him?"

"W–W–Wimpey."

"Fuck," Ross said. He dropped the hammer on the revolver and stood up. He threw the wallet on the man's belly.

Woodville sat up, rubbing his jaw. "Who the hell are you?"

"Ross. Headquarters. Records-and-Stats."

"Aw, you're kidding."

"Fuck you, I'm kidding."

It was bitter cold and Ross was shivering. He walked away, over to where his clothes lay on the beach and started pulling on his trousers. Woodville came after him, brushing the sand off his clothes.

"Jesus, pal," he said, "how could I know?"

Ross flipped out his shield and ID.

"Shit," Woodville said. "Sorry."

"Fuck you." Ross went on getting dressed, pulling his clothes on for the warmth, not even bothering about the wet sand coating his skin.

"Listen, I'm just doing as I'm told."

"We all are." Ross picked up his shoes and started back to the hotel. Then Woodville grabbed his arm.

"Look, Ross—do a guy a favor. Don't report this."

"Why-the-fuck not?"

"Come on. You know. If they find out I blew the tail, I'll lose all my promotion points."

"Not my problem."

But Woodville wouldn't let him go. "Jesus, buddy, have a heart. You practically broke my jaw."

Ross stopped. "What was the rap on me? What did you think you were pulling?"

"The usual. Dealer from out of town looking for a few keys of smack. That's all we do around here."

"Shit," Ross said and walked away.

"Hey, you won't turn me in, will you?" Woodville called after him. But Ross was too angry to hear. He realized why Mancuso had given him the trip to Miami and why he had been so circumspect on the phone. Mancuso had known they were being watched.

11:45 P.M. HENRY O'BRIEN STOOD with the Secret Service man in the hallway on the second floor of the White House, just outside the door to the family quarters. He adjusted his tie. Then the door opened and the president said, "Come in, Henry, please."

The president was wearing his bathrobe and green velvet slippers. He stood in a small sitting room, plainly furnished in the colonial style.

"I'm sorry to disturb you at this hour, Mr. President."

"That's all right. Please sit down."

"Thank you, sir."

They sat on a pair of straight-backed Shaker chairs.

"Well, what brings you here so late on a Saturday night, Henry?"

"We have the agents working on the Martinez assassination under surveillance," O'Brien said.

"You didn't tell me that."

"Mr. Bender requested it. It's not unusual in national security cases."

"I see."

"They've come up with something." But O'Brien didn't say what.

"Well?" the president said. "Is it something important?"

"I'm not sure."

Sam Baker sat a moment, waiting for O'Brien to speak. And when O'Brien didn't, he began to understand how important it might be.

"Well, Henry, if it could be important enough to bring you here at this time of night, let's talk about it. Shall we?"

"It concerns Mr. Bender."

The president sat back. "Has Mr. Bender broken the law?"

"I don't know."

"But you suspect he has?"

O'Brien didn't answer.

"Henry, none of us is exempt from the law," the president said. "Not me. Not you. Not Mr. Bender. I want you to understand that."

O'Brien nodded. "Yes, sir," he said.

"Now, what is it, Henry?"

"Our autopsy concluded that Colonel Martinez had AIDS."

The president just stared. "The . . . the disease, AIDS?"

"Yes, sir."

"Lord, what a tragedy. That poor man. His poor friends and family."

"Mr. Bender had me alter the autopsy report before it went to the Nicaraguans," O'Brien said.

"Alter it?"

"To spare his comrades and his wife. To spare the Contras from the publicity. We deleted the reference to AIDS from the report."

The president thought about that. "Well," he said. "Well, obviously, it was improper to alter the report. But, Henry—I don't know. I suppose there's a judgment to be made here. The man was dead. He had done much for his nation. I suppose the question is do we allow the Nicaraguan freedom fighters to keep their hero—or does history have a greater claim to truth?"

"Yes, sir, that's the way I felt. But then we monitored this conversation between our agents this afternoon." He took a sheet of paper from his pocket and handed it to the president. It was an excerpt from a transcript of a telephone conversation. Eight lines were highlighted in yellow. They read:

R: Yeah, sure, I will. Listen, Joe. You ever hear of a place called Fort Deetrick? It's in Maryland.

M: What about it?

R: It's where the army does biological weapons research. I think that may be where they got the aids to shoot up martinis.

M DISCONNECT

R: Hello? Joe? You there?

R DISCONNECT

The president stared at the phonetic spelling of Deitrich and Martinez. But it did not disguise the terrible message that the words contained.

"I'm not sure I understand," the president finally said. "Are you saying that someone injected Martinez with AIDS?"

O'Brien took out his little spiral notebook and leafed into it a few pages. "Colonel Martinez did not have AIDS at the time of his physical at Walter Reed Hospital last Sunday. Two days later, he had a severe infection. That could only be a result of an injection of the pure virus."

216

"But how could that have happened without the colonel's knowledge?"

"We assume it occurred during the blood test at Walter Reed."

"Have you questioned the people who conducted the blood test?"

O'Brien flipped a page in his notebook. "The doctor who conducted the test was U.S. Army Captain Arnold Beckwith. He and his wife and daughter were shot to death on Thursday, one hour before our agents arrived to question them."

The president sat up in his chair. "Shot to death? All three of them murdered?"

"Executed."

The president stood up. "What the hell is going on?"

O'Brien stood up. But he didn't try to answer.

"Do you connect Mr. Bender's instructions about the autopsy report to this phone conversation?" The president held out the sheet of paper.

"Not necessarily."

"Do you think they're related?"

"We have no way of knowing."

The president's voice rose. "But what do you think?"

O'Brien lowered his head. "Mr. President," he said, "you're asking me a question that I can't answer."

The president ran his hand through his hair. Then he sat down.

"All right, Henry," he said. "Monitor this closely. Keep me informed."

"Yes, sir. I will."

"Thank you for coming over. Good night."

But when O'Brien went out, Sam Baker did not go to bed. He sat in the stillness, remembering. He remembered what Rausch had said at the National Security Council meeting about "poison." He remembered how Rausch and Bender seemed to form an alliance against the hunt for Petersen.

If those incidents were more than coincidental, they could be the harbingers of a nightmare. And if they were what he suspected, the nightmare would not only be his. It would be the nation's.

11:50 P.M. IT HAD BEEN a long day. And Rolf Petersen had spent it waiting for a phone call.

At 5:55 A.M., he had awakened, switched on the television, and channel-hopped through the early morning network news shows. The big news of the day was still Vice President Eastman's explosive hostility toward the president. Even the longest report about the shooting of the policeman near Senator Fallon's house was little more than a one-liner. And even though it didn't matter how little space the media gave the shooting or how much, Petersen felt a twinge of disappointment. After all, he had been very thoroughly trained.

He knew that the primary objective of terrorism was publicity. The media could frighten and confuse the public faster and more thoroughly than any political campaign. The best acts of terrorism were the ones that lent themselves to visual presentation on the news. Even better were those with a novel twist that captured the imagination of reporters. Those threw off banner headlines.

But as he watched the television, Petersen admitted to himself that a murdered policeman was nothing new, and when *Family Ties* came on, he shut off the set and went across Route 2 to the 7-Eleven for a muffin, coffee, and the newspapers.

When he returned, he checked at the desk for messages. There were none. He went back to his room and watched the morning game shows impatiently until the local noon news. Their report on the shooting was more complete. There was mini-cam footage from the scene: the police-man's body covered with a blanket from a neighboring house, then body-bagged and taken away in an ambulance. There was the typical ID photo of the dead cop, expressions of outrage from the mayor and police chief, expressions of anxiety from Fallon's neighbors, the usual footage of the weeping family, and a few dry words of condolence delivered on behalf of the recuperating senator by a fat little faggot named Van Allen. Rolf Petersen was disappointed.

He watched the soap operas until late afternoon and then, at five o'clock, the local news came back on with a long review of the shooting incident including footage of the Fallon neighborhood today. The state police had moved in to reinforce the locals, along with what looked like half a company of the National Guard. A pair of M113 armored personnel carriers blocked the bottom of Crescent Drive. And, of course, many of the civilians on the street were plainclothes detectives and Secret Service. The network evening news shows didn't even mention the shooting. To them, there was nothing deader than yesterday's dead cop.

But by now Petersen knew what he needed to know about the level of protection around the Fallon home. He got out the Baltimore Yellow Pages and his map and cross-checked the private aviation fields that advertised helicopter rentals. There were only two—one at Essex Skypark on Rocky Point, and the other at Glenn Martin Airport off Route 150. They were both across the bay on the far side of the city, even farther from Washington than the motel.

The other alternative was to try to rent something out of College Park Airport, which was only two miles north of the District. That would cut his flying time to less than ten minutes—a big advantage, if push came to shove.

At 7:30 P.M., he went out and bought a Big Mac and large fries for dinner and checked for messages when he came back. Then he caught a John Wayne flick on one of the independent stations. The ten o'clock news had only a few lines about the shooting, and at eleven o'clock, the network affiliates gave it only a fleeting reference. And when the news ended at 11:30 and the phone still hadn't rung, he got up and went out to the pay phone in front of the 7-Eleven.

He dialed the familiar number and listened to the familiar message. But this time, when the electronic beep sounded, he said, "Either I see you with the money by midnight tomorrow, or Fallon won't be vice president. In fact, he won't even be shit."

Midnight   WHEN THE CIA courier dropped off the black dispatch case with the day's telexes, Admiral William Rausch took it directly into the study of his home in Bethesda and quickly locked the door. He hurriedly undid the combination locks, took out the blue folder marked D/CIA Eyes Only, and tore it open.

Atop the sheaf of cables from Europe and South America was a plain white envelope with his name and PERSONAL, PLEASE typed under it. It had been X-rayed and stamped in at his office in Langley at 2:14 P.M. that afternoon. It looked like another charity dinner invitation, so he tossed it aside and feverishly dug through the status reports. He was looking for one message, one brief message that would come through the Latin American desk, one short message that would tell him his worries about the FBI tracing the AIDS virus were almost ended. He found it at the bottom of a page:

MIAMI SPEC TO D/CIA: BABY HAS DOMESTIC NANNY.

He stared at the dim line at the bottom of the telex. It was trouble. Ross was under FBI surveillance, and that surveillance provided airtight protection. The Company's hired killer would have to bide his time. Rausch crumpled the paper in his hand. Why the hell was the FBI tailing its own man? Angrily, he fed the telex paper into the shredder and stuffed the other communiques in after it.

In fact, he had quite forgotten about the white envelope until he closed the empty briefcase and picked it up off the desk. Then he saw the envelope lying beneath it.

He was so irritated that he almost put it in the paper shredder unopened. But, at last, he decided to take a look in case the invitation was from someone important and he had to send regrets. In the envelope was a small piece of plain white paper, folded over. On the paper was typed:

Rolf Petersen
Cabin 108
Route 2 Holiday Inn
Glen Burnie, Maryland

He stared at the paper a long while, and even then he didn't believe his eyes.

SUNDAY, AUGUST 14, 1988

6:40 A.M. WHEN THE TELEPHONE rang, the sound felt like a long needle through her brain. The throbbing in her temples was louder than the bell and a lumpy migraine was thudding behind her eyes. The blackout curtains were drawn, and the hotel room was pitch-dark except for a few spidery rays of purple dawn light scattered across the ceiling. Sally rolled over and caught two handfuls of the rumpled sheets. She pulled herself across the bed and grappled the receiver to her ear.

"Y-yes . . . ?"

It was Terry Fallon, and his voice was crisp and clipped and crystal clear. "Eastman has called a press conference for 9:30 this morning," he said. "He claims he's going to make a major announcement."

"Wha—?" Sally sat up in bed; the migraine made her skull feel like it was filled with sloshing fluid. "Where did you hear that?"

"Chris just called me."

"Why didn't he call me?"

"Find out what it's all about."

"I'll try."

"Don't try. Do it." He hung up.

She sat up, switched on the bedside lamp, wiped the sleep out of her eyes, tried to clear her head. But the headache surged every time she moved, and she remembered last night and the candlelight dinner on the water and the champagne. She had never been much of a drinker; two glasses of white wine always made her giddy. But she had felt such relief talking to Ross, she had felt so gay. Even while those feelings had been coursing through her, she couldn't understand them. He was, after all, such an ordinary man. Perhaps that was why she felt so easy with him. He let her be a woman and asked for nothing more.

Now she had a hangover as a souvenir of her adventure—and an emergency bearing down upon her. She punched Chris's number in Georgetown.

"Why didn't you call me?" she demanded.

"You're there. We're here. Anyhow, I was just getting ready to call you when the phone rang."

He said that, but somehow he didn't sound convincing.

"What's it about?"

"Sally, you know as much as I do."

"Well, call around and see what you can find."

"I will."

"And Chris. . . ."

"Yes?"

"If you find out—call *me* first."

She held the button down. Then she punched Steve Chandler's private line at the *Today* show.

A voice answered, "Three-B."

"Steve?"

"Not in."

"May I speak to the line producer? This is Sally Crain from—"

"Hey, lady. It's Sunday."

She pressed the disconnect button and held it down. Then she straightened up and tried to pull herself together. There was no need to panic. It was quarter-to-seven on Sunday morning. The press conference wasn't until 9:30. If Eastman were going to make a major announcement, the network news divisions must be on the move.

She dug into her handbag for her Filofax and found Steve Chandler's home number in Darien, Connecticut.

"That's what I like about you, Sally," Chandler said when he answered the phone. "You're consistent. You've got no compunction about calling me whenever you want something."

"Steve, I think it's mutual. Fair?"

"Fair. What is it today? Or should I guess?"

"What do you hear?"

"Nothing," Chandler said. "Press conference at the Old Executive Office Building at 9:30. Something important."

"Is Brokaw on standby?"

For a moment, Chandler didn't answer. It was a kind of acid test. If the network news management really believed that Eastman's "major" announcement would be *major*, they'd heat up the main news set and put Tom Brokaw on alert so that he could be on the air with commentary before the other two networks. It was part of the childish tit-for-tat of inter-network competition.

"No comment," Chandler finally said. Which told her more than if he'd answered yes. NBC News clearly believed that something extraordinary was in the wind.

"Is there a handout?"

"Not yet."

"How are you going to carry it?"

"We're taking it live eastern and central with Andrea Mitchell covering. Now, how about letting me eat my breakfast?"

"What do you think Eastman's going to say?"

"Sally, how would I know? Why don't you be a good girl and watch the program and find out along with everyone else?"

"Steve, there are days you really piss me off."

"It's mutual." He hung up. She dialed Tommy Carter.

"I don't know a goddam thing."

"Tommy, please."

"Sally, believe me—I don't get out of bed until noon on Sunday unless war is declared. The guy's called a press conference, his people are telling us it's big news, and that's it for now."

"Do you think Eastman's bowing out?"

He didn't answer for a moment. Then he said, "He's either doing that—or going the other way."

"Which way?"

"Announcing for the presidency."

Sally swallowed hard. "That's not possible."

"Sally, America can put a man on the moon, they can put a fool in the White House."

"Where are we on Cronkite?" she said.

"Pending."

"Pending what?"

"Pending what Mr. Eastman says this morning."

Suddenly, she felt her whole strategy crumbling around her. "What's your next move?"

"My next move is to screw the Washington correspondent of *Jornal do Brasil*, who has just gone into the bathroom to reposition her diaphragm. She's a modern Catholic, you know. Only believes in removable birth control."

"Tommy, you always did set a standard for gallantry."

"Sally, do you know you were the first woman I ever really loved?"

That stopped her. "Was that supposed to be funny?"

"No. It was supposed to be special. It's only now—after all these years—that I realize it was funny."

"Bye, Tommy."

She dialed Chris.

"Nothing," he said. "Nobody's talking. It's a blank wall."

And for the first time since the day she met Chris Van Allen, she wasn't sure she should believe him. "What about what's-his-name—Rob Moorehouse—Wyckoff's secretary?"

"Gone. Vanished. Out-of-town. Wherever they've got Wyckoff stashed, Moorehouse is playing 'The Lady with the Lamp' at his bedside."

"Dammit, Chris. The hottest news break of the year and you're telling me we can't get a hint!"

"Yes," he said. "That's exactly what I'm telling you. And, while I'm at it, I'm telling you not to shout at me."

Before she could answer, he hung up.

She dialed Terry's private line.

"Well?"

"Nothing. And Chris is behaving like a little queen. Speak to him, will you?"

"It's jealousy."

"I don't like it."

"I don't like not knowing what kind of stunt Eastman is going to pull."

"You're the one who insisted that I go to Miami."

"You're the one who—" He broke off there.

"What?"

"It's not important. As soon as the press conference ends, call me with your assessment."

"Sure." She didn't try to hide the hurt in her voice.

"Sally?"

"What?"

"I wish you were here."

That got her right in the throat. She took a breath. "Thanks," she said.

7:05 A.M. AFTER HE GOT off the phone with Lou Bender, the president sat on the edge of his bed, considering. It was simply unthinkable for the vice president of the United States to call a network press conference without consulting the president. But it was happening. Whatever his announcement might be, Dan Eastman was clearly positioning himself away from the administration, separating himself from President Baker.

Bender believed that Eastman might announce his withdrawal as a candidate for the vice presidential nomination. Bender had a hunch that Eastman had offered Fallon the number two spot on his own ticket and that

Fallon had turned him down. Bender believed Eastman knew he'd had his turn at bat and struck out.

Sam Baker thought about that. It made sense. Almost.

The trouble was that Dan Eastman wasn't a quitter. He was a brawler and he lacked finesse, but he wasn't the kind of man to stay down just because he got knocked down.

Sam Baker picked up the phone.

"Yes, sir?"

"I'd like to speak to vice president Eastman, please."

"I'll put you through."

There was a single ring. "This is the vice president."

"Good morning, Dan. I hope I'm not calling you too early."

"No, sir."

"I understand you have a press conference this morning."

"That's right."

"Dan, is there anything you want to tell me about what you're going to say?"

"Not at this time."

There was a pause.

"Dan. . . ."

"Yes?"

"Don't turn a crisis into a tragedy."

"It's too late for good advice, Sam. But thanks anyhow."

The president hung up. He sat a while, staring down at his bare feet on the carpet, remembering what Richard Nixon had told him on the day he had left the White House forever: "Desperate men do desperate things." Nixon seemed to think that explained and apologized for everything.

7:25 A.M. THE LAST THING Lou Bender wanted for breakfast was a conversation with Admiral William Rausch. But the man was so insistent on the phone that Bender knew he was up to something. He told him to come to his apartment in the District—but only if he could get there by 7:30. Rausch just did get there before 7:30, and when the housekeeper opened the door for him, he came in beaming and disgustingly self-satisfied.

"All right. What is it?" Bender said. "I've got a lot to do today."

But Rausch wouldn't talk until they were seated in the kitchenette with muffins and coffee and the housekeeper had shut the door and left them alone.

"This will amuse you," Rausch said, and pushed the little white enve-lope with Petersen's location across the table to Bender.

Bender opened it and when he scanned the contents he almost choked on his English muffin. In fact, he went on coughing so long and so hard that Rausch had to get up and go around the table and clap him on the back. When Bender gathered himself, he drank a glass of water and coughed again.

He kept tapping his finger on the paper until he found his voice. "Where . . . where the hell did you get this?"

"It came in the pouch."

"From inside the CIA?" Rausch was playing him again—and Bender didn't like it.

"No way of knowing. It could have come from any branch of govern-ment anywhere in the city."

"Any prints?"

"Please, Lou. We're not dealing with amateurs. Anyhow, we know who sent it."

"We do?"

"It's from Petersen's employers. And they're telling us more than where to find him."

"They are?"

"Yes, Lou," Rausch said, and he took the note from the other man's hands and began systematically ripping it to shreds. "We were right about Ortega and the Nicaraguans hiring Petersen."

"How do you know that?"

Rausch dropped the shredded paper on his plate. "Ortega got our mes-sage and he's throwing in his cards."

Bender pointed at the pile of confetti. "This?"

"A peace offering."

Bender put an elbow on the table and rested his chin in his palm. "Why are they handing Petersen to you?"

"Because they know we'll punch his ticket and slide him into an unmarked grave."

"Letting you do their dirty work?"

Rausch buttered another muffin. "Like sending for the exterminator when you have vermin."

Bender snorted. "Nice line of work you're in."

"Lou, don't get sentimental on me." Rausch said. "Let's say there's a man in the KGB that we can turn. We feed him the name of one of our low-level informers. He denounces him or arranges his capture. We lose our informer, but we may get our man advanced to a position of real responsibility. It's like trading a pawn for a bishop."

Bender seemed to be listening. But he wasn't. He was thinking ahead. Rausch was dangling the Petersen discovery for a purpose—and Bender wasn't going to reach for it. He had to put Rausch on the defensive. He had to give him a scare or lose the initiative.

"Lou, it's just like politics," Rausch said as he chewed. "Only the losers get to die."

Bender said, "I don't want you to kill him."

"Excuse me?"

Bender leaned forward. "If Ortega hired him, Petersen is more valuable to us alive."

Rausch just smiled. "Maybe to you. But not to me. Lou, let's not get too clever about this. We need Petersen dead and the FBI investigation buried with him."

Bender waved him off. "Don't be a fool. The FBI investigation ends with the capture of Petersen in any case. But—" Bender sat back and tapped a finger against the side of his nose. "But if we get Petersen to tell the world that Ortega hired him. .... That's just what we need to stifle all the complaints about us picking on poor, innocent Nicaragua. You pick up Petersen and get him to sing and we've got a press bonanza."

"Forget it," Rausch said. "The Company can't pick him up. We can't operate within the continental United States."

"Well, then—" Bender knew how to hit Rausch's buttons. "Hand him over to the FBI."

Rausch bristled. Like other officers who had been in Naval Intelligence in 1984, Rausch had been embarrassed by the sensational revelations when the FBI broke the Walker spy ring. Rausch had been part of the task force that cleaned up the mess. To him had fallen the hairsplitting job of punishing the lax with transfers and early retirements. That had made Rausch a pariah among fellow officers—and left him deeply bitter toward the FBI. Bender had counted on that from the beginning.

"Let's not be petty," Bender said. "O'Brien can pull our chestnuts out of the fire. Let's use him for our own devices."

Rausch sat, brooding.

"This once. . ." Bender smiled his oily little smile. "Be reasonable."

"All right, goddamit. Have it your own way." Rausch checked his watch and stood up. "I'd better run. I want to be over at Langley before Eastman's press conference begins."

Bender kept smiling. He'd won this exchange. "Be a good sport, Bill. Maybe you'll get to kill the next one."

Rausch stopped halfway out the door. He had a strange look in his eye.

"What?" Bender said.

"You didn't believe me yesterday."

"Didn't believe what?"

"My theory that Ortega had hired Petersen—and that Fallon was the target. You didn't really believe it until Ortega caved."

"Oh, I don't know," Bender said. "I thought it was an interesting notion."

"So, you let me kill Ortega's daughter . . . what? On the come?"

Bender didn't answer.

"You know, Lou, I used to think I was a hard man."

"So did I," Bender said, and there was venom in his smile.

Rausch shook his head, chuckling. "You're a lucky little bastard, aren't you? Eastman bows out and Ortega hands us Petersen. Boom-boom, all your problems are solved." He made a big show of clapping his hands clean. But he wasn't smiling any longer.

After Rausch went out the door, Bender picked up the secure phone and dialed 301-555-1212. In a moment an operator came on and said, "Information. May I help you?"

"Yes. I need the phone number of the Holiday Inn in Glen Burnie, Maryland, please."

When she gave him the number, he wrote it down, thanked her, and hung up.

On his way across town to Langley, Admiral William Rausch sat in the back of the black Oldsmobile, chewing his left thumbnail, and thinking about his conversation with Lou Bender. You could never tell with a man like Bender. And in spite of every indication to the contrary, Rausch was convinced that Bender's real game hadn't yet surfaced.

Together, they had made a cold, closely reasoned decision to eliminate Martinez. They had a poison that couldn't be traced and a method of inoculation that couldn't be detected. In six months or a year, Martinez would develop sarcomas and be diagnosed with AIDS. His friends and brothers-in-arms would shun him. His wife would desert him. The Church would castigate him. And he'd stumble off to die in obscurity, never knowing who had murdered him. About one thing Rausch and Bender were determined—Martinez was not going to become another Che Guevara.

Rausch had seen photographs of the legendary Guevara when he was captured, during lulls in his brutal interrogation, and after his death. More than anything in his experience, those photographs told Rausch what the war for the Americas would be like. Che had died at the hands of his sadistic Bolivian captors. But, somehow, his spirit had survived. And it haunted the CIA and Latin America to this day. Rausch and Bender had decided to make certain that no such phoenix rose from the grave of Martinez.

But Martinez was truly a popular revolutionary—adored by his followers, worshipped by the *campesinos*. It was inadequate—and perhaps even impossible—to dismiss him from generalship. His identity had to be erased as well, so that at some unforeseen future date his mystique did not become a rallying cry for the enemies of the United States—as Augusto Cesar Sandino, the Nicaraguan guerrilla leader who died in 1934, had become the symbol of the modern-day Sandinistas. Bender recognized the AIDS poisoning as an elegant—even an inspired—solution. AIDS would not only kill Martinez, it would disgrace him.

The U.S. Army had been evaluating the potential of AIDS as a tactical biological weapon since 1982. Thanks to funding and facilities that far outstripped the private sector, the army had isolated the virus in December of 1983, when civilian research was still in its infancy. That created a nasty dilemma: the army had findings that could accelerate the production of AIDS vaccine by almost three years. Yet, the army could not provide the pure strain of the virus and technical assistance to the medical research community without revealing that AIDS was under evaluation as a weapon.

What's more, it was a superb weapon: silent, invisible, deadly, a weapon the Russians didn't have and couldn't defense, a weapon with the power to destroy not merely cities, but whole societies by neutering and ostracizing their leaders. But there were limits to how far the army could take its AIDS weapons research on its own.

Explosives and shells could be tested on cadavers of itinerants purchased from coroners' departments in big cities. But the AIDS virus had to be tested on living organisms and, although it was carried by a variety of other primate hosts, it produced its deadly immune deficiency syndrome only in humans and felines. There was only so far the army could go in testing their weapon on cats. At a point, they turned to people with overseas "field testing" capabilities. They turned to the CIA.

Neither Rausch nor Pat Fowler, the CIA's deputy director of Operations, gave anything but lip service to the idea of "testing." They never thought of the virus as anything but a new weapon for their arsenal. They had people who needed killing. If the weapon were operational, they intended to use it. In fact, it caused a lot of excitement among the old Company hands. A lot of them still remembered the "007" days of Operation Phoenix in the early 1960s, when Clandestine Operations had authorization to murder as an adjunct to counterintelligence work abroad. Now the AIDS virus added to the CIA's arsenal of weapons meant not just a new toy but a chance to return to the game of eye-for-eye with a superweapon.

Operations made a list of targets and started wading through it. When Octavio Martinez accepted the president's invitation to come to Washington he was moved near the top of the list. It was Lou Bender who tacked the comprehensive checkup at Walter Reed onto the President's invitation.

Yes, indeed, Lou Bender had teed it up and the CIA had hit the ball out of the park.

So, when Bender had called early on the morning of the assassination and Rausch turned on his television set and saw the chaos on the rostrum as Martinez lay dying with Fallon wounded beside him, Rausch could not believe his eyes. It was as though someone had decided to play an enormous, lethal practical joke. And then that joke was compounded by another: for no apparent reason, the FBI tested Martinez's corpse for AIDS. That had forced the Beckwith decision. What followed was one bizarre coincidence after another. Bender stepped in and had the autopsy altered for "humanitarian" reasons. But the two fools O'Brien had assigned to the case had already seen the original. Then one of them traced the virus to Fort Deitrich. And when Rausch tried to neutralize the man, he discovered that Ross was under surveillance by the FBI, which gave him an impenetrable ring of protection. Then the tip on Petersen's location arrived. And Bender reversed himself on the plan to kill Petersen and insisted he be captured by the FBI. It was one coincidence after another. And Rausch didn't believe in coincidence.

There was a common thread in all of this. Rausch knew there was— because there had to be one. Yesterday at the golf course, Rausch had realized that even if there were no conclusive evidence to identify the mastermind, there was one and only one recurrent player—like an actor who turned up in every scene: the ubiquitous Mr. Bender.

Was it possible that Lou Bender was the puppeteer jerking all the strings? Was he the ringmaster, viciously playing both ends against the middle? And if so, what possible motive could he have?

Rausch sat in the back of the Oldsmobile and looked out through the bulletproof window at the scattered cars and pedestrians. Even on a quiet Sunday morning, you could always spot the working people of the District: when they had to be somewhere by 8 A.M., heaven help anyone or anything that stood in their way. You could see it in the faces of the drivers hammering their horns at the timid and slow-footed. You could read it in the stiff lips and jutting jaws of the pedestrians on the street corners. And it was while he was staring at the faces of those determined pedestrians, that Rausch suddenly realized how he knew that Lou Bender was behind it all.

Without Sam Baker in the White House for the next four years, Lou Bender would have nowhere to go at 8 o'clock in the morning—except into a mean and bitter retirement. President Baker had family, money, position, distinction, a substantial federal pension, staff, friends. His retirement would be a graceful fade from the front line, cushioned perhaps by the writing of memoirs and the granting of interviews, gentled with directorships and honorary degrees, seasoned with travel and invitations to notable functions. When it was over for Baker, he could begin the richly textured life of an elder statesman—author, consultant, counselor to all, as well as father and grandfather.

But Lou Bender had lived his solitary life in obscurity and anonymity. He had none of those prospects. He knew nothing of writing books or running corporations. He had no family, no savings to fall back on, a modest federal pension, the prospect of Social Security. He could expect a directorship here or there, but nothing of any financial or social significance. The existence to which he would be condemned would be a life of scrupulous meanness—or, at best, asceticism. For Lou Bender, this November would be his moment of truth. While Baker reigned in the White House, Bender held influence second to none in Washington. But when a person fell from a position of influence, there was no safety net, no golden parachute—there was nothing, nothing but the mocking laughter of the envious and the darkness of the grave to break the fall.

Rausch thought about that. He, himself, had one dream when his stint as director of the CIA ended. He would put himself on active duty with the navy and follow the fleet to sea. But Bender had no such option. If Sam Baker didn't rest his hand on the Bible and swear in for another term on January 20, Bender would would suffer a fate—for him—worse than death. As long as he lived, he would have to sit on the sidelines and watch the world go on without his advice. And he would feel the keenest pain that anyone who once had influence could feel—that he was redundant, superfluous, unnecessary.

It was so obvious that Rausch had almost missed it. But now he dropped the last piece into the puzzle: when Terry Fallon was selected to welcome Octavio Martinez to the United States, Lou Bender had smoothly shifted gears and arranged the shooting to bring Fallon to national prominence and forge a Baker-Fallon ticket that would be invincible in November. Then Bender had cued the FBI to test for AIDS so that he would have a sword to dangle over Rausch's head. And he authorized the reprisal that killed an eleven-year-old girl to make Rausch believe that he bought the Ortega-Petersen theory.

But Bender had gone too far when he sent the tip on Rolf Petersen. Because sending that was the master stroke.

Anyone—anyone in the intelligence community who knew that Petersen was a former CIA agent—would assume that, if the Company could find him, they would stop at nothing to eradicate him.

Only Bender knew that Rausch would bring the note to him before he acted. Because Bender was the only other man on earth who knew that the White House and the CIA were tangled together in this web of murder. And when Rausch brought Bender the note, Bender acted surprised—and then pretended to come up with the idea of handing Petersen to the FBI. Clearly, that meant that Bender had made a secret deal with O'Brien to put protective surveillance on Ross and hang the whole affair on Rausch and the CIA. And Bender had left it up to Rausch to pass the information to the FBI and sever the last possible connection between Petersen and Bender forever.

There was only one flaw in Bender's plan. Right now, Rausch's agenda and Bender's didn't match. There were two FBI agents who had seen the original autopsy report and might go public. Silencing them was more important to Rausch's survival than capturing Rolf Petersen. Because if the FBI were to follow the trail of the AIDS virus, it would inevitably lead to Langley, Virginia, and the office of the director of the CIA. And there would be not one shred of evidence to connect Lou Bender with AIDS and Octavio Martinez. If the top blew off, Bender would be safe. Either way, Rausch and the Company would take the fall. That was why Bender had put the two fools from the FBI under surveillance—to monitor their progress and keep them safe from harm.

Rausch lounged back comfortably into the seat of the car. So, that was Bender's plan. It was Machiavellian. It was cunning. It was brilliant.

Well, Rausch thought, if Bender wanted the FBI to have Petersen, he'd arrange it. But he'd do it his own way, in a way that none of them could dream. As a matter of fact, he had just the men for the job.

8:10 A.M. THE TELEVISION WAS on in the bedroom, and Mancuso was in the bathroom shaving and listening to a special Sunday edition of NBC *News at Sunrise* with Connie Chung. She said:

> —and with only four days to go before the nominating convention, political insiders are now laying odds that the president will dump Vice President Daniel Eastman in favor of Terry Fallon, the young senator from Texas. This morning at 9:30 eastern, 8:30 central time, NBC will carry an urgent press conference called by the vice president amid speculation that—

The phone rang, and Mancuso hustled to answer it. But when he picked up the receiver he realized that he hadn't shaved that side of his face yet and that the receiver was covered in shaving cream.

"Aw, shit!" He wiped the receiver and then his hands on the bed-spread. Then he put the receiver to his other ear and told Ross, "You always call at the worst possible moment."

"Do you recognize my voice?"

He did—and it wasn't Ross.

"Yeah."

"Your friend is at the Holiday Inn on Route 2 south of Baltimore. He's in cabin 108. Have you got that?"

"Got it."

"He's a real mean fuck, Joe. You're gonna have to kill him."

"Yeah. Thanks. I owe you."

"I know." The caller hung up.

Mancuso signaled for the operator, and when she came on the line, he said, "I wanna call Miami Beach."

Ross was asleep when the phone rang. "Fuck you, you cocksucker!" he shouted when he realized who was calling.

"Get your pants on."

"Go fuck yourself."

"Get your fucking pants on," Mancuso said.

"Fuck you," Ross said, and there was a cold fury in his voice and Mancuso guessed why. "You slimy son-of-a-bitch. You knew they were going to—"

"Goddam you, Dave! Shut up!"

He did.

"Now write down this number." He rattled it off.

"What's that?"

"I said, write it down, goddamit!"

"All right, all right."

"It's a pay phone in the lobby of this hotel. You got five minutes to get to a pay phone on your end. Go now."

Ross got out of bed and into his slacks, shoes, no socks, and a pullover. He grabbed a handful of change, his wallet, and the key, and bolted out the door.

Mancuso wiped the shaving cream off his face and put on his bathrobe and slippers and took the elevator downstairs to the lobby. It was a busy lobby, filled with people checking out and heading for the airport. And Mancuso cut quite a figure in his blue slippers and blue-and-white striped bathrobe with only half his face shaved, leaning on the shelf by the pay phone, waiting for his call.

The phone rang. It was Ross and he felt twice as angry, standing at a pay phone on Collins Avenue with no shave and his hair uncombed.

"You slimy old motherfucker! You knew they'd tap and tail me."

Mancuso said nothing.

"Didn't you?!"

"Yeah, okay. So, maybe I figured."

"Maybe nothing. You knew, you fuck."

"Well . . ." Mancuso shuffled his feet. "Yeah, I figured they'd pull some shit. Anyhow, that don't matter."

"Fuck you, it doesn't matter! I'm going to bust your fucking head next time I see—"

"I got a line on Petersen," Mancuso said.

"What? How?" Ross's voice was breathless.

"A buddy of mine. Don't ask questions."

"Where is he?"

"According to this guy, holed up in Baltimore."

"What are you gonna do?"

"I'm gonna take a little detour over there on my way home. Just take a look for myself."

"Suppose he splits?"

"He's holed up. Waiting for his dough probably. You seeing the head spic today?"

"Hopefully. You?"

"I'm gonna try to talk my way in and see the Mother Superior at the nut house."

"With any luck, we'll both be back in Washington tomorrow," Ross said. "Maybe you and me, we'll pick Mr. Petersen up."

"Don't count on it," Mancuso said. "Meanwhile, you stay out of that snatch you got down there with you. The more I think about her, the more I know she's trouble."

"Excuse me, Joe," Ross said. "This is where I get off."

"I sent you the papers on Fallon fingering Weatherby. You try that on her. See if I'm wrong."

"You're wrong, Joe."

"Don't be a dope."

Ross hung up.

9:30 A.M. "LADIES AND GENTLEMEN, the vice president of the United States."

The conference hall on the fourth floor of the Old Executive Office Building was jammed with reporters and news crews. But when Dan Eastman stood up at the podium, the room fell into absolute silence.

"I have an announcement to make to you today—and to the American people. Due to the nature of this announcement, I will not be able to answer any of your questions."

There were a few grumbles among the reporters. But they knew the conference was being fed live on all three networks—and they didn't want the American public to think that the press would show disrespect to a man who was a heartbeat away from the presidency.

Eastman spoke without notes. "As you are no doubt aware, I have differed with President Baker on many issues during the course of our administration. As I'm sure you understand, strong and honest men may have differences of opinion on matters of state.

"But yesterday's papers carried clear evidence that my disagreements with the president have gone beyond differences of opinion between teammates. Events have created an environment in which I can no longer keep silent. And this morning I have decided to take my case to the American people."

They were all watching. Sally, curled up with a croissant and coffee on the edge of her bed in Miami. Ross, in the room next door, listening to the television set over the hum of his electric razor. Bender, Rausch and Tommy Carter in their offices in Washington. Steve Chandler watching his tummy-television on the redwood deck of his house in Darien. The president was watching on the console in his private dining room. Rolf Petersen sitting in cabin 108 at the Holiday Inn on Route 2, chewing an Egg McMuffin. Even Joe Mancuso, still in his blue-and-white striped bathrobe, picking his toes at the Sheraton Inn on Route 422, east of Cleveland. And Terry Fallon, in the drawing room of his mansion, with Chris Van Allen perched on the arm of the leather sofa.

Eastman held up an envelope. "I am today sending this letter to Representative Charles J. O'Donnell, Speaker of the House of Representatives—"

"Goodbye, Dan Eastman," Bender said, half-aloud.

Sally crossed her fingers.

So did Chris Van Allen. But Terry Fallon sat, unmoving.

"I am sending this letter to Speaker O'Donnell to request that he and Senator Luther Harrison, the majority whip of the Senate, form a bipartisan, bicameral committee to investigate the assassination of Colonel Octavio Martinez. And along with the assassination, I am demanding that the Congress investigate the foot-dragging, inadequate, and unconscionable way in which this administration has obstructed the investigation of this terrible crime."

Lou Bender's jaw dropped.

At the CIA offices in Langley, Admiral William Rausch was sitting with his feet up on his desk. He threw his head back and began to laugh out loud.

In his bathroom in Chevy Chase, Charlie O'Donnell opened the medicine cabinet and reached for the Bufferin.

There was intense stirring among the reporters in the hall.

Eastman held up another sheet of paper. "According to this internal FBI document, only two agents have been assigned to this investigation. And these two agents are not experienced field operatives. They are clerks from the FBI's Department of Records and Statistics."

In the Hoover Building on Pennsylvania Avenue, Henry O'Brien put his elbows on the desk and buried his head in his hands.

Eastman went on. "There is also indisputable evidence that an agent of the United States Secret Service was shot to death to prevent him from conducting inquiries that might have led to the arrest of the killer of Colonel Martinez." He held a blown-up ID photo of the man.

When Steve Thomas's picture filled the screen of her television set, the coffee cup fell out of Sally's hand.

Ross folded his arms across his chest. "Shit," he said.

Mancuso closed his eyes and rapped his knuckles against the side of his head.

"This man, Steven Philip Thomopolous, was murdered as he followed the trail of the assassin of Octavio Martinez. His death has never been acknowledged to the press. The District of Columbia police have been investigating it as a routine hotel room burglary and homicide."

There were audible gasps from the newsmen.

"Please . . . Please!" Eastman raised his hands to quiet them. "Today I call upon Congress to act where President Baker has not. I believe that this country and those who lead her must put justice ahead of politics. The killer of Colonel Octavio Martinez must be found and brought to trial. And I for one will press the search—even if it leads into the very inner sanctum of power. Thank you."

The reporters leaped to their feet, screaming their questions. But Eastman turned his back on them and walked briskly from the stage.

On the porch behind his house in Darien, Steve Chandler clapped his hands, swiveled around in his chair, and yelled through the open kitchen window to his wife. "Well, that's show biz!" And he was wearing a shit-eating grin a mile wide.

Sally grabbed the phone and punched the number of Terry's private line. Chris answered.

"Sally? Holy cow!" was all he could say.

Then he passed the phone to Terry.

"That's the man."

"Yes. Terry, how was I to know? He—"

"I don't want to discuss this over the phone," he said abruptly. "When do you see Ramirez?"

He was so angry that it frightened her. And she was ashamed that she could have been such a fool. "I'm . . . I'm waiting for his call now. Terry, please don't—"

"Let me know as soon as you make contact. And get back as quickly as you can."

"All right, all right," she said. "Let me talk to Valerie. I'll dictate your statement for the press."

"Chris and I can handle that," he said sharply. "You get your meeting with Ramirez done and get back here. And stay the hell out of trouble."

The hang-up rang in her ear. And a hollow emptiness opened in the pit of her stomach.

She punched a local number.

A man with a deep voice answered. "Yes?"

"Hello, this is Sally. I must see our friend this morning."

"No es posible," he said sharply.

"I must. I must see him now. *Ahora mismo.*" She knew she sounded desperate, but she couldn't help herself.

"What is the meaning of the vice president's remarks?"

"Nada. They are politics. They have nothing to do with us."

"We must consider this. We call you."

"Please. *Es muy urgente.* I must see him right away."

But he had already hung up.

She put the phone down and as she did, it rang. It was Ross.

"Did you see the—"

"Yes."

"Let's talk," he said.

"Give me five minutes."

She put down the phone and when she looked at her hand resting on it, she could see that her hand was trembling.

She sat on the edge of the bed and tried to get a grip on herself, tried to think it through.

So, Steve Thomas had been Steven Thomopolous. He had been a Secret Service agent and now he was dead, and she sat on the edge of her bed in a Miami hotel room and realized that she bore some responsibility for his death. She had been the diversion so that Ross could conduct a search. But when she wouldn't accept Steve's advances, he caught on and rushed back upstairs. That's when Mancuso told her to go home and forget she was ever at the hotel. What happened when Steve got upstairs to his room? She had assumed Mancuso had warned Ross, who made a clean escape.

But now she realized Steve Thomas had caught Ross in the act, and Ross or Mancuso had shot the man to death. And the crime had been covered up until now. The implications were terrifying.

Mechanically, she looked down at the large brown stain where she had dropped her coffee cup on the carpet. Then, like a sleepwalker she went into the bathroom and dampened a towel with cold water and went back and knelt beside the stain and rubbed as hard as she could.

She had two choices. She could keep silent. But if she did—and if the circumstances of Steve Thomas's death were discovered—her silence would create a presumption of guilt. If she kept silent, she risked losing her freedom. But the alternative could be worse.

She could go to the police and explain how Mancuso had used her. But she could imagine the headline:

PRESS AIDE LURED SECRET SERVICE MAN TO HIS DEATH

If she came forward with her story, the media would rake her with innuendo. Still, she could endure that if it were only herself at risk. But it wouldn't be—because the headline would read:

FALLON AIDE LURED SECRET SERVICE MAN TO HIS DEATH

That's the way the headline would be written; that's the way the story would be read. If she stepped forward now, Terry's chances could be destroyed. At the very least, he would have to disavow her actions. At worst . . . She could barely bring herself to contemplate the worst. Terry would have to put her on leave until the matter was resolved. That might take months. Just the thought of being separated from him made her stomach roll. It was a risk she couldn't take.

But if she didn't speak up, could she be discovered? She rubbed at the stubborn stain and considered the possibilities.

Ross and Mancuso couldn't talk. She wasn't a lawyer, but she knew that Steve Thomas had been killed during an illegal search. They didn't have a warrant. That probably made Mancuso and Ross guilty of a serious crime— maybe even murder. She was an accessory, but one of them had pulled the trigger. Whatever her punishment, theirs would be worse. That was probably enough to guarantee their silence.

Terry. Terry would never betray her. She knew that as she knew her own name.

She stopped scrubbing the carpet and sat back on her haunches and tried to control the jangling of her nerves. She was not completely out of jeopardy, but—for the moment—she was safe from exposure. She stood and balled the dirty towel and started for the bathroom.

Chris.

She thought of Chris, and she stopped dead in the doorway.

Her mind flashed on how pleased Chris looked yesterday speaking to the press, how he basked in the gaze of the cameras as if in the light of the summer sun. She thought of that—and of how surly he had sounded on the phone this morning. "Jealousy," Terry had said. And he was right. If she were out of the way, Terry would have to rely on Chris. Then Chris might become what he had always wanted to be—Terry's spokesman and confidant.

But Chris would never speak out. No. That would alienate him from Terry forever, and that was a risk Chris would never take. She dropped the dirty towel in the bathroom, went to the dresser, and pulled open the drawer that held her lingerie. She stopped there.

But suppose Chris realized he didn't have to speak out? Suppose he leaked it instead? Suppose he dropped a hint to one of their enemies? Suppose he simply wrote an anonymous letter to a radio station? In Washington, there were a thousand ways to cut someone's heart out and never bloody your hands.

She leaned against the dresser. The fit of nausea was coming on again. Her breath was labored, her face flushed, and her stomach turned.

Chris could be dangerous. Chris would have to be watched.

Someone knocked on the door. And then she heard Ross out in the corridor saying, "Are you decent?"

"I'll be right there." She left the drawer open, went into the bathroom and dampened another towel with cold water, and pressed it to her face. Then she pushed her hair back off her forehead, straightened the front of her robe, and went to the door.

Ross was barefoot, wearing only his blue bathing suit and carrying his room key. She let him in and they stood staring at each other.

Then she said, "You killed him."

Ross stood where he was a long moment. Then he opened his hands. "Look. It was an accident. He pulled a gun. It went off. That's the truth."

She sat on the edge of the bed, folded her arms, and turned her face away. "If they connect me with the shooting, they'll use it against Terry."

Ross touched her shoulder. "How can anyone connect you?"

She pulled away and didn't answer.

"The only people who know are Joe and me. We're not going to say anything."

"Terry knows."

"Well, he's not going to say anything, is he?"

"No."

"Well then, what are you worried about. Come on," he said. "Put your suit on and we'll get some sun."

She turned on him. "How can you be so matter-of-fact? The man's dead."

"Sally, look at me." He pointed a finger at his face. "The man pulled a gun and shot himself."

"It was still a crime. You didn't have a search warrant."

Ross sighed heavily. "Okay. You're right. What do you want me to do about it?"

"How serious a crime is it?"

He didn't answer.

"How serious, David?"

"Second-degree murder."

She put her face in her hands.

"Jesus," Ross said, and stood there and didn't know what to do. Then he sat on the edge of the bed and put his arm around her shoulders.

"It's going to be all right," he said, softly.

And through her fingers, she gasped, "I'm just . . . so . . . frightened."

"Sally. Please. Listen to me. Everything will be all right."

She was breathless. "How? How can it be all right?"

He didn't really have an answer. "I don't know. But I'll make it right. Somehow."

She leaned against him and he put both arms around her and held her. A tear fell from her cheek and ran hot down the bare skin of his chest.

9:40 A.M. THERE WAS ONE thing you had to give Lou Bender credit for: he could get things done faster than any man in Washington, including the president. Five minutes after the Eastman press conference ended, he had the District of Columbia police reports on their way to the White House, he had located Treasury Secretary Richard Brooks at breakfast in the men's grill of the Congressional Country Club, he had ordered a presidential helicopter into the air from Andrews Air Force Base, and had informed the country club manager to clear the parking lot. Ten minutes later, Brooks was in the air, on his way to the south lawn of the White House, and ten minutes after that, Bender was opening the police report on the shooting and Brooks was coming up the stairs to the Oval Office, wearing cleated shoes and green-and-pink checkered pants and a tam-o-shanter. And, boy, was he pissed.

"Mr. President, what can I do for you?" he said without sitting down.

But before Sam Baker could answer, Lou Bender cut in. "Why the hell was the Secret Service running its own investigation of the Martinez assassination?"

"We were not."

He said it so flatly and with so much authority that the conversation stopped. Sam Baker had known Richard Brooks a long time. He was a trustee of the Harvard Business School, an elder of the Presbyterian church, and a ranked seniors tennis amateur. He was also no-bullshit, no-nonsense, and no-prisoners.

"Your man was killed," the president said. "I signed the condolence letter for his parents."

"An unrelated formality. The man was on leave. He put in for the time on the day after the Martinez assassination."

Bender opened the folder from the D.C. police. "Then what the hell was he doing getting his head blown off in the Four Seasons Hotel?"

"Moonlighting."

"Moonlighting?"

"Some agents do private investigations in their spare time. Chase husbands for divorce lawyers, that kind of thing."

"Is that legal?" Bender said.

"No. But it's done."

"Who was he working for?"

"We don't know. We've only got one lead."

"What?"

"A used airline flight ticket found at his home."

"To where?"

"Cleveland."

"Cleveland?" Bender said. "Did you say Cleveland?"

The president said, "How did he die?"

"Apparently, he shot himself under the chin with his own revolver. There was no evidence of a struggle."

"Suicide?"

"No. The door to the room was kicked in."

Bender said, "He thought someone was in his room and kicked the door in to surprise them?"

"No," Brooks said. "There were wood splinters on his body. The door was kicked in after he was shot."

"No other clues?"

"He was seen in the bar just before the shooting with a blond woman. Probably a hooker."

Bender said, "Or someone else's wife."

"Perhaps."

"So you think this was a robbery?" the president said. "Or a crime of passion?"

"Personally, yes. Murder for gain or a tawdry little crime of passion, and your vice president is and always has been a four-star ignoramus." Brooks looked at his watch. "Must we dwell on the obvious? I'd like to pick up my foursome when they make the turn."

"Just one other thing," Bender said. "What sort of cases was he working on for Treasury?"

"He wasn't," Brooks said. "He was EPD."

"EPD?"

"Executive Protection Division."

"Guarding whom?"

"I thought you knew," Brooks said. "He was on the vice president's staff."

10:05 A.M.   WHEN MANCUSO CAME out the door of the Sheraton lugging his carry-on bag, the cabby was waiting for him.

"Hey, sorry I'm late," Mancuso said. "I was watching something on television."

"No problem," the cabby said, and flicked his butt away. "I turned the meter on at nine-thirty."

He took Mancuso's bag and tossed it into the trunk. When Mancuso got into the cab, the meter read $8.90.

"How'd you know I'd be here?" Mancuso said. "Maybe I took another cab or something."

"Nah." The cabby pulled out into the traffic. "You're a *paisan*, right?"

"Yeah. So?"

"I knew you ain't gonna stick me. One guinea don't stick another guinea. See what I mean?" He put on a white cap. "Lookit this here."

A printed legend on the crown of the cap read: *"If you ain't Italian you ain't shit."*

"Capisce?"

"Cute," Mancuso said. "You gonna wear that to the convent?"

"Nah. Them nuns ain't got no sense of humor."

When they got to the convent, Mancuso told the cabby to wait and he went to the gate and pulled the cord. In the distance, he heard a small bell ringing. And then he heard the slow, shuffling footsteps coming toward him on the other side of the wall. The footsteps halted and the little grate in the door slid open.

"Morning," he said. "I'm Joe Mancuso. The one who called—"

The grating slapped closed.

"Now wait a second, goddamit!"

Then one huge oak door began to swing open. On the far side, an elderly nun stood, glaring at him.

"Jesus, Sister, I—" Then he caught himself. "Aw, shit." Then he snatched off his hat. "I'm sorry. I. . . ."

Behind him, he could hear the cabby laughing. Mancuso turned and silenced him with an angry wave. Then he followed the old nun up the path, feeling like a jerk, feeling for all the world like an awkward little boy.

10:20 A.M. CHARLIE O'DONNELL TOOK his Bufferin, tightened the belt of his terry bathrobe, and went downstairs into the library of his Chevy Chase house. There was something droll about his shaggy, white-haired, big-nosed bulk wrapped in bright green terry cloth with a pair of spindly legs descending to his bright green slippers.

Ciaran, his old houseman, brought in the silver coffee service. "And how is your worship this morning?"

"I've had better mornings."

"*Biodh an diabhal aige.*"

"You can say that again."

Ciaran shuffled out.

For Speaker Charlie O'Donnell, what Eastman said had changed everything.

Until the moment of Eastman's press conference, O'Donnell's primary objective was uniting the party behind an electable slate—the incumbent and a vice president who could help him win. But if it were clear that Sam Baker couldn't win in November, O'Donnell's second preference would be a presidential candidate who could capture the convention and seize the nomination by acclamation—as Terry Fallon might.

Eastman's allegations, if true, had eliminated option number one.

The allegation that a sitting president had instigated or abetted a plot to obstruct justice in the Martinez assassination investigation was, clearly, the first salvo in an explosive exchange. Even if there were no direct hits, the fallout would cripple all survivors.

O'Donnell knew what the party regulars were thinking that morning—if there were even a shadow of a doubt about Baker's innocence, they should disavow him right now and line up behind someone else—Fallon or anyone whose reputation was unsullied and who might make a decent showing in November.

But did the facts support the allegation? O'Donnell wondered. Was it possible that Sam Baker, a gentleman, a lawyer, a man with vision and depth of character—a man who had himself sat at Sam Ervin's elbow during the Nixon hearings—could he have tried to cover up the truth behind the death of Octavio Martinez?

It didn't seem possible. What motive would he have? Only one: that he had ordered—or at least had prior knowledge of—the assassination. But was that conceivable? Had Sam Baker any motive for ordering the murder of Octavio Martinez? Because if he had a motive he might—he just might be culpable. And if he were guilty, it would fall to Charlie O'Donnell to assemble the committee that would drive him from office.

The intercom sounded.

It was Ciaran. "Your worship, Senator Harrison is on the phone." Harrison was the canny one—calling him before Eastman's letter was delivered, before receipt of the formal allegation put their conversations on the record.

"Tell the senator I'll call him back within the hour."

"Yes, sir."

O'Donnell didn't like to do it, but he had to get the facts. He had to know if the president had a motive for eliminating Martinez. He turned his Rolodex to the card for Bill Wickert, the chairman of the House Armed Services Committee. But when he picked up the receiver, he hesitated. He knew he was about to make a call that would send a signal—a signal that the House would comply with Eastman's demand.

He hadn't any choice. He punched the number.

"Wickert."

"Bill, it's Charlie. Let's go to church."

10:30 A.M. RAUSCH HAD BEEN expecting the call.

"What took you so long?" he said.

"We had a meeting with Brooks," Bender told him. "Look—we've got a problem."

"Tell me about it," Rausch said. He pulled out a drawer of his desk and leaned back and put his feet up. He liked it when Bender was scrambling.

"You've got to grab Petersen right now."

"Before lunch?"

Bender hesitated. Then he said, "What do you think this is? A fucking joke?"

"Lou, don't get exercised. It's being handled."

"I want Petersen right now—with enough evidence to positively connect him to the assassination. Do you understand?"

"You think that will prevent a congressional investigation?"

"I think so."

"What about the Secret Service guy?"

"He was freelancing."

"For who?"

"Who knows? He was down in the bar with some bimbo. Half an hour later, he was dead."

"A pimp?"

"Or an outraged husband."

"So, Eastman's confused—"

"Or up to something." Then Bender's tone changed. "Listen to me, Bill," he said. "This thing is almost out of control. If we miss Petersen now, it could mean disaster."

"Lou, I understand."

"Make sure."

"Lou, I will."

"Keep me informed." He hung up.

Rausch put the phone down. Clearly, the wheels were coming off for Bender.

Bender needed action now because his convention was only four days away and he knew Baker probably couldn't get the nomination if Congress was preparing to investigate him. That wasn't an issue Rausch had to be concerned with.

The embarrassment of the less-than-zealous FBI investigation wasn't Rausch's problem, and he had no intention of making it his. If Congress wanted to hoist the president and Bender on that one, he wanted no part of the necktie party. In fact, the last thing he wanted to do was take an active role in the cover-up. That would only expose him to prosecution if the milk turned sour.

And right now there was no reason he should take part in the cover-up. Right now he was in a win-win situation. If, by some miracle, the buffoons from the FBI bagged Petersen, the FBI investigation would be closed, Congress would calm down, and there would be peace in the valley. But if Petersen blew away the fools, the secret of the altered autopsy report would be buried with them. In either case, the White House and the FBI could argue that they had a positive ID and location on Petersen and were trying a small, surgical strike to capture him alive.

The only disappointment in all this was that now he'd probably never be certain who had hired Rolf Petersen in the first place. That was a pity. Because it could have been a useful bargaining chip in a real emergency. Meanwhile, Bender's call had given him another option.

He reached over to the button that signaled his secretary and pressed it three times. The door opened a moment later and she came in carrying her steno pad.

"Yes, sir?"

"Memo to private file, Sarah. Mark it Secret/No copies."

She sat and opened the pad.

"Call from White House aide LB requesting assistance in search for alleged assailant of Octavio Martinez. Cited Rule 303 re prohibition against CIA domestic operations Ref 2161. Request denied. Got that?"

"Yes, sir."

"When you finish typing it, stamp it with date and time and countersign it, please."

10:40 A.M. HER HOTEL ROOM seemed empty. But it was not. In the corner under the window, wedged between the nightstand and the wall, Sally sat on the floor in a white silk nightgown, her knees pulled up against her bosom. Her cheeks were streaked where her mascara had run. She looked like a lost child.

She was thinking then of the leather sofa in the library of Terry's house. She was thinking about herself leaning over the arm of the sofa—laying across it, really—with her head and her hair hanging down. She remembered how her skirts were rucked up behind her, pulled all the way up, so that she could feel the hem of her dress brushing the back of her neck. She had been wearing four-inch heels and her feet were planted on the carpet behind her, set wide apart so that the elastic bands of her garter belt gapped a little reaching from her hip bones to her thighs.

She had heard Terry put the receiver down in the front room, and start up the hall toward her. In spite of herself, her knees had begun to tremble. Then she heard his hand on the doorknob and her heart was beating with such a fury that she couldn't catch her breath.

He came in, shut the door behind him, and although she didn't dare look up, she could sense him in the room. She could smell his aftershave.

She could smell the paraffin in the oxblood polish on his shoes. She could hear him open the desk drawer and fish about and then a little grating sound as he uncapped a jar. The excitement ran so high in her that she had to open her mouth to breathe. Then she heard the whisper of his zipper coming down. It was a sound she never heard without her pulse leaping, and she could imagine him stroking himself and the warmth of his body and fingers liquefying the Vaseline.

There was a soft sound, a tiny clicking-sucking sound. And then she felt him close behind her. She could hear his breath deep in his chest and feel the warmth radiating from his body to her buttocks. She felt his thumb and index finger open her and she could feel the oily vaseline. Then she felt him.

It was always hard for her when he took her that way. But she let her legs go limp as he pinned her against the sofa and penetrated. It was so painful that it almost made her scream and it was all that she could do to push her knuckles into her mouth and bite down hard and shut her eyes and keep the screaming in her brain. She arched her neck and groaned, gulping for air. Then he fell on her, tearing the shoulder of her dress away and sank his teeth behind her shoulder until the pain of that was equal to the one in her buttocks. He thrust in and out and the burning was like fire down inside her. He pulled her head back and wrapped the fingers of his hand around her throat so tightly she could barely breathe. And then she heard him whisper in her ear, "Don't . . . don't ever do it again. Don't."

"I promise. . . ."

"Don't. . . ."

"I promise. I promise."

"Never."

"Terry."

"God."

"I love you. Terry . . ."

"God. Oh, God."

Then she felt him strain and grow rigid and his hotness shot up into her. His hand closed so tightly around her throat that she couldn't speak, and he jammed himself deeper inside her, and just as suddenly pulled away and out.

It was as though she had lost all spine; she went limp, sagged over the arm of the sofa, trying to catch her breath, feeling the wet silk of the dress plastered to her back and body. He turned her head, and pushed himself against her face, and she shut her eyes and opened her mouth and let him have her. She closed her eyes, pressed their lids down as if shutting out the light could drive it all away. Then she realized that he was going to come again and she let him push far down her throat until all of him ran down inside her.

When she opened her eyes, he was at his desk, reading.

He looked over the top of his glasses at her.

"Don't ever get pregnant again," he said.

Now, she was huddled in the corner on the floor of the Miami hotel room while the tremors came and went, feeling the same nausea and lassitude diffusing through her body that she'd felt the day the doctor told her that she was pregnant. It was an emotion compounded of excitement and alarm, anticipation and panic, hope and fear, love and dread.

The night after she'd seen the doctor, Terry had come into the guest house while she was undressing. She had gone to his arms and snuggled there, her cheek and the soft flesh of her breasts brushing the bristled tweed of his jacket. It made her nipples hard and he noticed that and kissed her on the forehead and then pressed down on her shoulder until she submitted and knelt before him and unzipped his slacks.

There was always a musty smell under the band of his white Jockey shorts. She liked it when he was soft and tiny like a baby. She liked to feel him swell and harden in her mouth. She liked it when the pushing movements in his hips began so quickly, when he couldn't stop himself and grabbed her head as though it were her hips. She liked it when he came so quickly. She liked it when he made her submit.

"On your face," he said between gritted teeth. And she'd pumped him, listening to the click and gurgle of the saliva between him and her fingers, and shut her eyes and let the heat spatter on her. Then she turned her face up and let him look at her.

"I missed you this afternoon," he said. "Where were you?"

"I had to go to the doctor."

"Are you ill?"

"I'm going to have a baby."

"Get rid of it."

She remembered the doctor's office on Rhode Island Avenue, the tubby little nurse who hung her dress so carefully in the closet of the dressing room. The doctor was the same one who removed her IUD three months before and he was puzzled.

"He didn't want one?"

"No."

"I suppose you should have asked him first."

"I suppose." She lay back and put her heels in the stirrups.

But that had happened only months after Terry had come to Congress, before she'd understood what their relationship would be. His coming was like a bolt of electricity that set her nerves upright. She couldn't sleep. She all but stopped eating. The flurry of her press work became a drudge, and she watched the clock incessantly, agonizing as the sluggish hours slouched by, anguishing through the languid afternoons, only breathing and alert as night began to fall over the District. Then, as the lights of the Capitol dome set its cupola in relief against the reddening evening sky, she'd hurry to the parking garage, start her Honda, and drive to Cambridge, park in the driveway, make her way through the gathering dusk to the guest house, change to her peignoir, and wait. When she heard the screen door slap closed on the back door of the house, she'd jump up. And she'd stand there, hearing his hard heels clicking on the flagstone walk that circled the pool, hearing him humming as he crossed the lawn, waiting for his fingers on the doorknob, and his tall, boyish presence in her arms.

"Divorce her."

"I can't. You know I can't."

"Divorce her."

"I can't. Not now. Not ever."

"I love you."

"I know. And we won't change."

"Never?"

"Never."

She wanted the things that many women wanted. To wake up in the morning and slide her fingertips between his body and the sheets and feel the deep night-warmth in the fibers of the mattress. To hear him moving in the house around her while she curled beside the fire, reading.

Some nights, he was so tender that she wept for joy. He'd sit up in the narrow double bed of the guest house and watch her rub the jelly on him and on her thigh. And then she'd simply lay her hand down flat and press him against her flesh and rub him up and down while she ran her tongue across his belly. He would spend then almost without moving, impassively, just a boyish spurt in the hollow of her palm, and a sigh of relaxation.

Then he'd be asleep and she would softly make her way to the bathroom and leave the door open so that she could see his form beneath the blankets on the bed. She'd sit back on the seat and hold her knees apart and lubricate and stroke herself. Sometimes, the little gasps she couldn't hide would wake him and he'd roll his head and look dully back across his shoulder at her. Then she'd close her eyes and lay her face back and push her toes against the tile and lift her heels and show him. Her orgasms were explosive.

Nothing in her life aroused her like those moments of total, abject surrender to him. And there was nothing—no one—nothing in heaven or hell that would ever take him from her.

Sally got up, ignoring the stiffness in her arms and legs, and looked out through the sliding glass doors of the hotel room, down at Miami Beach and the sea.

She went to the phone and punched a local number. The deep-voiced man with the Spanish accent answered, "Yes?"

"This is Sally."

"*Espere usted. Llamaremos—*"

Angrily, she cut him off. "You tell our friend that either he calls me with an appointment in one hour, or I'm going back to Washington. And six months from now, when Terry Fallon is vice president of the United States, we'll pull your visas and ship you back to Nicaragua to stand trial for treason."

There was silence at the other end of the phone.

"*¿Comprende?*" she demanded. "*¿Entiendes, hombre?*"

She slammed the phone down. No one was going to come between her and Terry Fallon. She went into the bathroom and threw two fistfuls of cold water in her face.

10:50 A.M. HENRY O'BRIEN WAS surprised to be summoned to the White House on Sunday. When he arrived, the president's secretary showed him into the private waiting room beside the Oval Office. For a little while, O'Brien stood at the window, looking at the gardens edging the south lawn. When he retired in a few years, he would spend his summers in his own garden in Swampscott, behind an old, rambling saltbox house where he could smell the sea. Then he would put all of Washington behind him, but most particularly, the secrets.

It was, after all, the bearing of the secrets that was the great ordeal, and after six years as director of the FBI, his secrets hung heavy about his neck like a great chain of office. There were secrets he could not tell his wife, secrets he could not share with his confessor. There were things he knew that no one—no one—should ever know. Things that could never be told, not to the living or the dead.

When the president came in, he said, "Henry, I'm sorry I kept you waiting."

O'Brien stood up, but when he looked at the president, he was startled. The man looked tired and drawn, his face pale, almost gaunt.

"You wanted to see me?"

"Yes, Henry. Please sit down."

They did, on a small sofa under the window.

"I'm afraid there may be a congressional investigation."

"I understand."

"If it comes, it will probably begin in September and run into the winter."

O'Brien nodded.

"I'm sure you'll come through it all right, Henry."

"Thank you, sir."

The president folded his arms across his chest.

"I want to ask you about this fellow Terry Fallon," he said.

"I've just been through our files on him."

"You have?"

"Yes, sir."

"At whose request?"

"Mr. Bender."

"I see. And what did your files tell you about Terry Fallon?"

"INS wanted him checked out when he was teaching at Rice and meddling in the Latino problems in Houston. They wanted to know whether he had any foreign connections."

"And?"

"Nothing. He was just a—what-do-you-call-it—a liberal."

The way O'Brien said that made Sam Baker smile. "Henry, I understand Fallon made the original allegation about Senator Weatherby's misconduct."

"Yes. He did."

"He came to see you personally?"

"Yes."

"And based on what he told you, you ordered an ABSCAM sting on Weatherby."

"I asked the assistant director for congressional affairs to review the matter. When he recommended a sting and the other assistant directors agreed, I approved it."

"With whom did your assistant director review the matter?"

"The majority whip of the Senate. And the Speaker of the House."

"With Charlie O'Donnell?"

"Yes. It's a courtesy."

The president muttered in distaste. "I thought those courtesies ended after Director Hoover."

O'Brien lowered his eyes.

The president leaned forward in his chair. "I want to ask you something about your meeting with Fallon. Was he—did he seem at all nervous or apprehensive?"

O'Brien considered the question. "No. Not as I remember."

"Did he seem—embarrassed?"

"No."

"Did he show any signs of diffidence about bringing you an allegation about a colleague?"

O'Brien shook his head. "No."

"Then how would you describe his manner?"

"Very . . . matter-of-fact."

"Confident?"

"Yes. Confident."

"What precisely was the nature of the allegation?" the president asked.

O'Brien opened his hands. "He told me Weatherby had accepted a bribe to press the EPA for oil leases on a particular plot of land."

"But did he give you any specifics?"

"All the specifics. Who paid the money. How much. When. Where."

The president sat back in his chair. For a moment, he was silent. Then he said, "Did you investigate that allegation?"

"No. Bribery is almost impossible to prove after the fact. We went for ABSCAM."

"I see. How much of this did you report to Mr. Bender?"

"All of it."

The president stood. "All right, Henry. Thank you very much. We'll speak again tomorrow."

But when O'Brien was at the door, the president said, "By the way, whom did Fallon accuse of bribing Weatherby?"

"Dwight Kimberly. His father-in-law."

For a moment, the president was speechless. Then he said, "Did you tell that to Mr. Bender?"

"Yes, sir. I did."

When O'Brien went out, the president buzzed his secretary.

"Yes, sir?"

"Katherine, tell Mr. Bender I'd like to see him, please."

"I'm sorry, sir. Mr. Bender has gone out."

"Gone where?"

She paused and he heard the rattling of papers. Then she said, "I'm sorry, sir, there's no destination in the log."

"Put him on the beeper, please."

"Yes, sir."

The president switched off his intercom. So, Lou Bender had requested a search of the FBI files on Terry Fallon. The president shut his eyes and ran his hand back through his thinning hair. It was going too far now. It was like a time bomb. It was ticking. And if he didn't cut the wires, it was going to explode.

Lou Bender didn't answer the page—because his beeper didn't detect it. By the time the White House Communications Room sent the signal, the helicopter he was traveling in was eighty miles away, just passing over York, Pennsylvania, and far, far out of range.

11:00 A.M. THERE WERE TWO good things about St. Matthew's Parish Church in Chevy Chase. For one, it was only about a two-minute walk from Charlie O'Donnell's house. The other was that it had a robing room just off the nave where O'Donnell could hold a private conversation in hearing of the Mass. That way, he got both businesses done—Caesar's and the Lord's. That little room was notorious in Washington. O'Donnell's detractors called the church "St. Matthew-in-the-Woodpile."

When he arrived, O'Donnell crossed himself, sat down in an old pew beside Bill Wickert, folded his hands, and said his quick devotion. He didn't like Wickert, didn't like to have to turn to him for answers. But the man was chairman of the House Armed Services Committee, and the shortest distance between Congress and the inner workings of the Pentagon.

When he lifted his head, he got right into it. "What about the war in Nicaragua?"

"What about it?"

"Was Martinez winning or losing?"

"Who the hell cares?" Wickert said. "What are you going to do about Eastman?"

"What am I going to do? Or what would I like to do?"

"He's got us up shit's creek without a paddle, hasn't he?"

"For crying out loud, Bill," O'Donnell said in a harsh whisper. "We're in church."

Wickert folded his arms and legs, slouched down uncomfortably against the hard back of the pew.

"Answer my question," O'Donnell said. "Was Martinez winning or losing?"

"Losing. Ortega was beating him six-ways-from-go. The Joint Chiefs had written him off. The CIA wanted him out."

"How bad did they want him out?"

"Bad."

"Was Martinez willing to step out?"

"Was Diem?" In his snide way, Wickert was referring to the Kennedy-CIA coup that murdered Diem and toppled the South Vietnamese government.

"You think Rausch might have—"

"I shudder to think what Admiral Rausch is capable of," Wickert said. "But if you're asking me if he ordered Martinez shot on the steps of the Capitol in broad daylight, the answer is no."

"What makes you so sure?"

"Charlie, the man is nothing if not subtle. And I'll tell you something else," Wickert said. "You better do this right."

O'Donnell looked up sharply. "How so, Bill?" he said very softly to indicate he didn't like the other man's tone.

"Because you've got the party in the shitter. You're four days away from the convention and you haven't got your slate. Some of the boys are starting to wonder if you've lost it."

O'Donnell was astonished at his boldness. "Is that right?" But he knew that Wickert was not speaking for himself alone and that the challenge ran deep.

"You bet your ass that's right," Wickert said. "Last week we had an incumbent president and a boat ride to four more years in the White House. Now we've got nothing but some pretty boy from Texas and a month of televised dirty laundry to look forward to when the Select Committee gets rolling."

"You know, Bill," O'Donnell said, "I'll bet your mother didn't like you."

Wickert sat forward. "Some of us don't want you choosing our side of the committee, Charlie. You might as well get used to the idea."

"You little bastard. . . ."

Wickert stood up, brushing the creases out of his trousers. "You've been warned, Charlie. Get this right or get the next Amtrak to Boston." Then he turned toward the nave, quickly knelt and crossed himself, and went out.

11:10 A.M. FUNNY HOW NOTHING HE SAID seemed to surprise her. The Mother Superior fingered the edge of her cowl and listened impatiently until Mancuso had finished. Then she said, "There are no circumstances that can justify this intrusion, Mr. Mancuso. None in what you've told me, none I can imagine." She was a pudgy little woman, short and wide, with puffy little hands, and a round, white face wound tight in starched linen. When she stood up, he could see that she was barely five feet tall. "Now, if you'll excuse me. It is Sunday—or have you forgotten?"

Mancuso knew she was just rubbing it in. He got up, grabbed his hat, and followed her out the door of her office into the hall. "Look, Sister—"

"Mother."

She moved fast for all her bulk, and he had to hustle after her down the long corridor that divided the office block from the convent.

"Mother, this is a capital crime. The guy killed a man. He shot up a United States senator."

"So you keep saying."

Mancuso stopped. So did she.

"What's that supposed to mean?" he said.

She looked up at him with those squinty eyes that nuns put on when they try to look right through you. "How do I know that's why you're here?"

"The . . . er . . ." Mancuso shrugged and shifted from one foot to the other. Shit, nuns were just too tough. "Look—"

She pushed the door open and walked out into the courtyard.

"Look," Mancuso said and went after her. "You can sit there when I talk to her. You can keep a stenographic record."

She kept walking while she answered him and didn't look back. "Mr. Mancuso, twelve years ago Harriet Fallon came to us to be hospitalized. For twelve years, she has chosen to stay among those who keep the vow of silence. Like us, she has turned her face from the world. She has seen no newspapers, no television. She has not listened to the radio. She has concerned herself only with salvaging her mind and her spirit."

"Yeah," Mancuso said. He practically had to run to keep up with her and he sounded out of breath. "But this is about her husband."

She stopped so suddenly that Mancuso almost bumped into her. "Mr. Mancuso, on the day I told her that her husband was appointed senator, she prayed for his wisdom and courage. On the day I told her he'd been shot, she prayed for his recovery. Other than that, she has never mentioned his name.''

''What about when he visits her?''

''Senator Fallon has never come here.'' She said that and glared at him like it was his fault.

Mancuso blinked his eyes. ''He's never been here?''

''Never.''

She turned and walked on down toward the gate. Mancuso stood a moment trying to grasp what she had told him. Then he trailed awkwardly behind her.

The Mother Superior was saying, ''At her request, Mrs. Fallon sees no one. She has left her husband behind with the rest of the world. I don't think she would recognize a photograph of him. I'm sure you understand what I mean.''

''Yeah.'' He understood better than she knew.

He stopped a moment in the center of the old gravel courtyard and looked back at the convent. It was a low stone building, timbered and roofed in slate, impenetrable and mysterious as all convents seemed to him, full of secrets and whispers. He could imagine Harriet Fallon behind one of those many shuttered windows, a chalky little woman, her head cleanshaven under her mantle, down on her callused knees on the bare, hard boards every evening, sleeping alone every night in a narrow bed under the sign of the cross.

''Well, Mr. Mancuso?'' When he looked, the other old nun was holding the gate ajar for him.

Mancuso dug in. ''Look, Mother. I'm not leaving.''

She didn't seem the least impressed. ''Mr. Mancuso, may I ask you a question?''

''Yeah?''

''Why are you here?''

He fingered the brim of his hat. ''I told you. We're looking for the guy who shot—''

''Please don't lie to me.''

That stopped him. They stood a while like that, him holding his hat, she with her hands folded and hidden in the great black sleeves of her habit.

''I can't tell you,'' Mancuso finally said. ''But I need to talk to her. It's real important.''

''You've said that.''

''I'll get a court order. A federal bench warrant.''

''Your order's no good here, Mr. Mancuso. Unless you can prove that Mrs. Fallon is a material witness to a crime. Church and state—remember?''

She nodded to the old nun and swung the gate wide open for him.

Mancuso looked at the old nun; there was nothing but disdain for him in her eyes and he felt like he deserved it.

"Good day, Mr. Mancuso," the Mother Superior said. "And God bless you."

He stepped outside. Then he turned back. "You knew I was coming," he said. "Didn't you? Somebody told you I was coming."

The Mother Superior stared at him through the closing gate. And he saw something in her eyes that hadn't been there before. Clearly, she was thinking about her answer. "The man who was here on Wednesday," she said.

Then the gate slammed closed.

Mancuso told the cabby to wait, and walked around the long granite wall of the convent to where it curved west toward Lake Erie. There was an open field that ran down to the water and some mossy boulders. He sat down on a big round rock and lit a cigarette.

So, it was all a lie—the whole bullshit yarn about the loving, loyal husband who honored his marriage vows to the deranged wife. It was an ugly, cynical, unmitigated lie. The marriage was a farce and Terry Fallon was a liar. And if he could lie about that, who could say where his lies ended and truth began? Five people were dead. And Eastman had told America that the Secret Service was conducting a parallel investigation. But Mancuso knew better. No fucking way the Secret Service was conducting an authorized investigation into the shooting of Martinez. They had no jurisdiction.

Mancuso reached into the change pocket of his jacket, took out the four little lapel pins Ross had found in the dead man's room at the Four Seasons Hotel. He laid them in the flat of his palm and pushed them around with his index finger. Circle. Square. The letter "S." And the American flag.

It was the same old game after all.

For the first time, everything was becoming clear.

11:35 A.M. AFTER LOU BENDER had signed in and walked through the metal detector, a guard showed him through the gate in the tall cyclone fence and walked him down to a bench under a grove of trees near the empty softball field. The guard left him there, and Bender sat down and threw his arms back over the bench and looked around at the compound.

There was a ring of simple wood frame bunkhouses, a long, low building that could have been the mess hall. There were four hard tennis courts, four paddle tennis courts, and a running track that circled the ballfield. The place could have been a park or a boys' school or a summer camp—except for the cyclone fence topped with barbed wire and the watchtower near the gate and the federal detention guards who strolled outside the perimeter.

This was the federal minimum security prison at Lewisburg, Pennsylvania—"Club Fed" they called it. And its list of distinguished members had included John Dean and John Mitchell and now former Senator Caleb Weatherby.

Bender didn't recognize Weatherby at first—and it wasn't just the jogging suit and Nike running shoes. It was the suntan and the twenty pounds he'd lost and the spring in his step. The Weatherby Bender remembered was a beaten, cornered felon who held up a newspaper to hide his face from the glare of the cameras. The man who was coming up the gravel walk looked years younger, leaner, fitter, and full of self-confidence. Bender hoped to hell Weatherby hadn't found Christ and gone born again in prison like Chuck Colson. He hadn't made the long trip to listen to a sermon about why he should accept Jesus as his personal savior.

He stood up and held out his hand. "Cal. . . ."

"Lou—" Weatherby smiled and took his hand warmly, firmly. "Lou, how you been keeping?" He still had that vote-getting smile and lilting drawl.

"Not as well as you."

Weatherby patted the flat of his stomach. "Yep. I'm lean and mean as a junkyard dog."

"You're not . . . uh . . . born again, are you?"

"Hell, no," Weatherby said. "But there ain't much to do up here, 'cept jog and Nautilus. Pity this place don't have a golf course. You should tell the president. Put a golf course in and the whole Congress would confess their sins and queue up for the joint."

"I'll mention it. But if everyone in the Senate confessed his crimes, I don't know how they'd ever get a quorum."

They laughed and then they sat.

"Well, you're probably wondering what brings me out here," Bender began.

But Weatherby cut him off. "No. You're here about Fallon."

Bender stopped.

Weatherby just smiled. "Lou, we do get the papers here—and the television."

"Okay," Bender said. "Let's talk about Fallon."

"In a minute, Lou, in a minute." Weatherby sat back. "Now, you know, I seem to remember that you smoke cigars. . . ."

"Sure," Bender said. He dug two Monte Cristos out of his jacket.

Weatherby put one in the pocket of his sweatshirt. Then he ran the other back and forth under his nose, savoring the aroma. "Hello, Havana," he said. "How sweet it is!" He bit the end off. "Got a light, cousin?"

And while Bender held up his lighter, Weatherby said between puffs, "Before we . . . talk about Fallon, let's talk about . . . talking about Fallon."

"Go ahead." Bender put his lighter away.

Weatherby sat back and crossed his legs and blew out a long, twisting strand of smoke. "Mother, I've come home to die," he said with deep appreciation.

"Let's talk," Bender said.

"Lou, you know what the trouble with you is?"

"No. What?"

"You're in a hurry." Weatherby nodded to himself. "That's it, plain and simple. You're in a hurry. Rushing here—rushing there like a pissant. You never take time to smell the roses."

Bender shifted uneasily on the bench.

"Now, me," Weatherby said. "Me, I've got time." He rolled the cigar admiringly between his fingers. "Here I am, a prisoner in a federal *penile* institution, as it's called. None the worse for wear, I grant you. But cut off from the world of high finance, sippin' whisky, and young, tender pussy. And here comes a *heli-a-copter* with a distinguished visitor, a gentleman from Washington who's known to have the ear of the president himself. Well, what shall we talk about, Lou?"

"I can't get you a pardon," Bender said flatly. "That's not on the table."

Weatherby nodded once. "Understood. However, I do have thirty-one months and nineteen days left in this vacation. And frankly, cousin, I don't see any benefit to the taxpayers in me serving all that time. Now, do you?"

It was exactly what Bender had expected. "All I'm authorized to say is . . . that if you help us, we'll be disposed to help you."

"Sam Baker said that?"

"Yes."

Weatherby took another long drag on the cigar. "Lou," he said, "you know a good cigar. But you are a lousy liar."

Bender nodded. Then he set his jaw. "All right, Cal. Let me be blunt."

"Go to, son."

"You want a ticket out. I'm the only travel agent in town. You talk, I'll try. That's the news."

Weatherby smiled. "Now you're talking, son." He got up. "Lou, let's take a walk."

They went on down the gravel running track to where it turned behind the backstop of the softball diamond. Weatherby leaned against the chain link fence, puffing on the cigar. "Now, as I see it, you and Baker are trying to decide whether to get on the pony," he said. "But you don't know if it's a pony you can ride—or one that's going to buck you off on your ass."

"So to speak."

"Well, you've hit an itchy little patch, ain't ya?"

"Yes."

Weatherby chuckled darkly to himself. "Terry Fallon is the cutest little buttfucker since Hero was a pup," he said. "And his right hand ain't seen his left hand in twenty years."

"Meaning what?"

Weatherby spit on the ground.

"For instance?" Bender said.

Weatherby looked at Bender and pondered. Then he seemed to brighten. "Ah, Lou," he said. "Now I see what it's all about. You're not trying to decide whether to put Fallon on your ticket. You want something that will give you a hammerlock on Fallon so he won't try an end run at the convention."

Bender didn't say anything.

"Sorry, Lou," Weatherby said. "You can't get that answer for a couple of cigars and a promise."

Abruptly, Bender said, "You know Fallon fingered you for ABSCAM."

Weatherby put his hands in his pockets and stood there, kicking at the ground. "Yep. Didn't know it then, but I know it now."

Bender got up. He stood close to Weatherby and put one finger in the middle of his chest. "Fallon and his father-in-law set you up for ABSCAM."

Weatherby snorted. "Fallon and Dwight Kimberly?"

"Set you up."

"Lou, Dwight Kimberly wouldn't piss on Terry Fallon's grave if he had *dia-beatus*. Shit, Fallon broke the back of Kim's plan to stretch the Houston skyline clear to Galveston. Cost him millions. Then he *ruint* his daughter."

"The woman in the nut house?"

"That's right, cousin."

"I hear she's psychotic."

"Harriet Kimberly psychotic? My, my, Lou, you are an innocent boy."

Bender stood toe-to-toe with him. "You're telling me that Fallon and his father-in-law didn't make a deal to get you?"

"Lou, my . . . my arrangements with Dwight Kimberly go back before

Terry Fallon was out of diapers. Somehow he got onto it. He buried me and he's been blackmailing Kim ever since.''

"Blackmailing him?"

"Yes indeed."

"For money?"

"To keep him quiet."

"Quiet about what?"

"Oh. . . ." Weatherby tapped the ash off his cigar. "Cousin, you sure want a lot for a couple of smokes."

Bender grabbed Weatherby's arm. "If you've got something on the son-of-a-bitch, give it to me and I'll see you get even."

"Not today, son." Weatherby tried to walk away, but Bender wouldn't let him go.

"*Shee-it*," Weatherby said and pulled free. "I want to see him burn more than you do. The *sumbitch* wiped me out. Grabbed my seat, gobbled up my office. That little faggot, Van Allen, shined up to him in a hurry. And Sally Crain." He shook his head. "She sure was a disappointment to me."

"Sally who?"

"Oh, you know, the little press bitch." Weatherby smiled. "I treated her all right. Even threw a fuck into her couple of times a week to keep her on her feed."

In the distance, the PA system crackled to life and a recorded trumpet call sounded.

"Well, that's recall," Weatherby said. "Time to get my nose counted. Come on, Lou. I'll walk you back to the gate." He turned to go.

Bender didn't move. "Listen, Cal, I'm asking you for the last time—"

"Lou, you go get *sumthin'* to put on the table and we'll do business," Weatherby said. "But don't come back empty-handed. *Y'hear*?"

They stopped at the gate and the guard swung the door open for Lou Bender.

"And, Lou. . . ."

"Yeah?"

"I think you'd best hurry." Weatherby waved and grinned. "You have a nice day now."

Noon LUTHER HARRISON, THE Senate majority leader, pushed his plastic goggles up on his forehead and took off the leather gloves and put them on the bench with the tools and went to the door of the garage to greet Charlie O'Donnell.

"Can't shake hands," Harrison said, and turned up his greasy palms.

"How are you, Luke?" O'Donnell said.

"Been better."

"What you working on?"

"Come in. I'll show you."

Under the banks of fluorescent lights that hung from the ceiling of the garage, the chassis of an old roadster sat, stripped to its guts of stainless steel and iron. The floor of the garage was carpeted, except for a trench that the wheels of the car straddled. On the workbenches around the perimeter, tools and testing devices were ordered, impeccably clean, laid out like instruments in an operating theater.

"Now this—this is a Bugatti Tipo 35," Harrison said. "Someone once told Bugatti that the brakes on his cars were lousy. Know what he said? '*Signore*, my cars are built to go—not stop.' How about that?"

O'Donnell patted the flank of the car tentatively, as though it were a strange beast. "Handsome," he said.

"We got a major problem here, Charlie," Harrison said.

"I'd noticed."

"This thing with Eastman is a nightmare."

"Agreed."

"Is Baker guilty?"

"Is that the issue?"

"Nope." Harrison rubbed the lid of his eye with the back of one knuckle. "Did you get the letter?"

"Not yet. You?"

"Nope."

"Let's have a meeting."

Harrison peeled off his leather apron and washed his hands, and they went out of the garage and up the steps to the patio behind the house. Frances Harrison was sitting at the white wrought iron table in her housecoat, doing the crossword puzzle in the Sunday *New York Times*.

"Hello, Charles," she said. "Coffee?"

"Thank you, Fran."

She looked back and forth between the two men. "Well, I see I'm about to be in the way." She gathered up her papers.

"Thank you, Frannie," Harrison said.

"I'll send Blanche with fresh coffee. You boys have a nice talk." She went inside.

O'Donnell sat down and rubbed his knees through his trousers.

"I'd like to kill that son-of-a-bitch Eastman," Harrison said.

"Take a number," O'Donnell said.

The maid put their coffee down and left them alone.

"Well, we've got two choices here, Charlie. Give him his investigation or not."

"What have you heard?"

Harrison poured the coffee. "Nobody on our side of the aisle wants any part of it. The other side wants a full-scale witch hunt. Were you expecting something else?"

"I can't say I was." O'Donnell stirred his coffee and looked down the cherry walk to the three greenhouses at the bottom of the garden. "I think we ought to see Sam."

That surprised Harrison. "About what?"

"I want to ask him if it's true."

"You'd better go by yourself," Harrison said.

"I can't do that, Luke."

Harrison thought about that. "Wickert busting your balls?"

"I will never understand why the decent and responsible people of the archdiocese of Buffalo would send such a cocksucker to Congress."

"Perhaps it's the only way they could get him out of town."

They smiled and nodded together. But Harrison was watching O'Donnell, and O'Donnell knew it.

"You're going to ask Sam to resign," Harrison said at last. And when O'Donnell didn't answer, he added, "Aren't you?"

O'Donnell folded his big hands on his belly. "If he's guilty, yes."

Harrison cleared his throat. "Maybe we should take Rehnquist."

"He'll never go."

"He's got nothing to lose. He's on the court for life."

"No," O'Donnell said. "This is not official. It's three friends talking. I want a chat, not an exorcism."

"If he quits—then we've got Eastman," Harrison said, and he was taking no pleasure in saying it.

"Only till January."

"He'll make a run for the nomination at the convention."

"I suppose."

Harrison put his cup and saucer down. "Are you that sure of Fallon?"

"Yes," O'Donnell said. "I'm that sure."

Harrison folded his arms and sat back, thinking. "Suppose . . . suppose Sam says there's nothing to the charges?"

"Right now," O'Donnell said, "that's the worst thing that could happen."

Harrison shook his head. "Jesus Christ, it's a crummy world."

"I didn't invent Washington," O'Donnell said. "I just work here." He shifted his great bulk in the chair and stood up. "Well, let's get it over with. Mind if I use the phone?"

1:40 P.M. WHEN LOU BENDER got back to the White House, he headed directly for the Oval Office, but the president's secretary held up her hands when she saw him coming down the hall.

"He's not in."

"Where is he?"

"He asked not to be disturbed."

Bender stood a moment, shifting impatiently from foot to foot. "Buzz him," he finally said.

"Mr. Bender—"

"It's important."

She sighed. "He's in the ADR."

"Tell him I'm coming down."

Reluctantly, she pressed the button on her intercom. Bender took the elevator to B-3.

The president was sitting in the middle armchair of the observation room, looking out at the electronic plotting boards. He didn't look back when Bender stepped off the elevator. "Where've you been?"

"Visiting."

"O'Donnell called. He's coming by this afternoon with Harrison."

Bender shook his head. "Goddam Eastman. Somebody should cut his balls off and stuff them down his throat."

The president ignored that. "You asked O'Brien to check the FBI files on Fallon."

"I thought we'd better make sure he pays his taxes."

"I don't believe that, Lou."

"No?" Bender took the cigar out of his mouth.

"No. I believe you were looking for some way to blackmail Terry Fallon out of reaching for the presidential nomination."

Bender looked at the end of his cigar. Then he blew on it to make it glow. "Blackmail is rather a strong word."

"What would you call it?"

"Preparedness."

The president shook his head.

"We need him on the ticket as vice president," Bender said. "I want some insurance in case he gets greedy."

"Lou, sit down here," the president said. And when he had, the president said, "I want you to stop it."

"What?"

"What you're doing about Fallon."

"And do what instead? Roll over and give him a shot at the presidential nomination?"

"We're not giving Terry Fallon anything," the president said. "But we're in trouble and anything you do now could make it worse."

"What trouble?"

"The investigation."

"Sam, we've got a lead on the assassin. A very good lead. We expect to pick him up within twenty-four hours."

That turned the president's head. "Is that true?"

"Absolutely."

The president leaned back in his armchair. "How sure are you?"

"Sure. And if we capture the assassin, Eastman looks like an idiot and the congressional investigation goes away."

"What about the Secret Service man?"

"A red herring. Eastman's up to something."

"What?"

"I don't know. But I'll find out."

Sam Baker studied the little white-haired man beside him. A long time ago, he'd learned to rely on Lou Bender's judgment and it took an effort to doubt him now. "Let the Fallon thing alone," he finally said.

"I can't just now. I'm close to something."

"What?"

"I don't know. There's something there. I just can't touch it yet."

"Don't expose us any further."

"I need a presidential pardon for Weatherby," Bender said.

The president just stared at him.

"I went to see him, Sam. He's got something that can help us. We've got to pay his price."

"No."

"Then reduce his sentence. Knock a year off. What's the difference?"

"No."

"Goddamit," Bender said. "We've got to put a leash on Fallon. Otherwise, the son-of-a-bitch could stampede the convention."

"Lou, did you know the CIA was planning to poison Martinez?"

Bender sat, cold-eyed, glaring. "Who said they were?"

"Answer the question."

"Sure, I'll answer it." He leaned over and put his face near the president's and spoke very softly. "What's the difference . . . if you don't get the nomination?"

The president bowed his head and shut his eyes and rubbed the bridge of his nose. "Lou, for God's sake."

Bender got up and went to the windows overlooking the ADR. Beneath him, the desks and consoles stood empty, the ready lights burning a cool green. He stared out at the electronic projections of the western world before him and chewed his cigar and looked at South America dangling from their own continent by the delicate filament of Central America. And he said, quietly and with musing, "The whole thing's hanging from a slender thread, Sam. Do you want to be remembered as the man who lost the hemisphere?"

"No," the president said behind him. "And I don't want to be remembered as the man who trampled the Constitution, either."

Bender looked back at him.

"Stop it, Lou," the president said. "Right now. Leave Fallon alone. Or else."

Bender put his hands in his pockets and looked down at the shine on his shoes. "You're the boss," he said.

1:35 P.M. ALL MORNING ROSS had been thinking of Sally Crain. He had stretched out on the terrace in his blue swim trunks, facing the curtains behind the sliding glass door to her room, waiting for her to come out on the terrace. But all morning her curtains had remained drawn, impenetrable.

He had gotten her into serious trouble. There was no way around that. She was an accessory to a felony. If it came to a trial, she might get off with five years' probation by turning District's evidence. But her career in politics would be over, and she'd be shut out of serious journalism forever.

Given the nature of the Secret Service man's charade and the importance of the Martinez investigation, it was unlikely that any of them would actually go to jail. But Mancuso would probably lose his pension. And he, Ross, would be looking for another job. He lay on the chaise and wondered if he'd be disbarred from practicing law. It hadn't occurred to him until that moment. If he were disbarred, what would he do?

Well, he was a long way from having to face that decision, and it didn't pay to waste time brooding about it now. What was plain to him was that they were locked in a conspiracy of silence: Sally, Mancuso, and him. If any one of them cracked and threw the others to the wolves, that one individual might be saved from a criminal conviction but not from the notoriety.

In a way, he knew that he had the best chance of surviving. He was twenty-seven, on his first field assignment, and he had inexperience on his side. Searching the man's room hadn't been his idea. He could probably get off with a formal reprimand and ninety days suspension without pay if he copped a plea. Probably Mancuso would have to take the fall. Not that Mancuso had many friends at the Bureau. But if Ross talked, he knew how every other agent in the Bureau would look upon him. He would become a pariah, an outcast. No one would partner with him. No one would speak to him. He would save his job and end his career. It wasn't hard to figure that out. So, they were stuck, trapped, locked together. None of them had an easy way out. Worst of all, he wanted her. And he might have lost his chance with her.

Ross was drowsing, half-asleep when Sally knocked at his door. He thought it was the maid.

He pushed himself up on one elbow and called, "Can you come back in half an hour?"

"David?"

"Sally?"

He bounced off the chaise and across the room and pulled the door open. "Gee, I'm sorry."

She had her hair tied in a ponytail and she was wearing a bronze, one-piece bathing suit that squeezed and rounded out her bosom, and khaki shorts. She looked girlish and young and bright as a penny.

"Oh, God, look at you," she said.

But he was looking, appreciatively, at her. "At me?"

She touched his arm. "You're red as a lobster. What have you been doing?"

"Lying in the sun." He looked down, and where she'd pressed her fingers to his flesh, little white dots were fading back into the deep pink of his sunburn.

"You'll ache tonight," she said. "You'd better get some cream."

"Are you feeling better?" he asked.

"Better."

"It'll all work out."

"I hope so. But can we not talk about it?" There was such pain in her eyes. "Can we just take a walk or something? I need to get out for a while."

He got his shirt and put on his sneakers and took the room key and they caught the elevator to the lobby. The same middle-aged man was sitting in the corner of the lobby, but this time he was reading the paperback of *Iacocca*. He looked up casually and watched them pass. Ross lowered his head in disgust. Clearly, the Miami FBI didn't know their stakeout had been blown. No wonder coke and smack poured through Miami like a sieve, with a bunch of clowns like that guarding America's borders.

They went out the door into the sun and crossed Collins Avenue, walking along the quay where the cabin cruisers bobbed at their tethers on the Inland Waterway. And as they did, Ross saw a gray Ford with two men inside roll to the front of the hotel parking lot and stop.

"God, it's a beautiful day," she said, and raised her head and breathed deeply. "I had to get out of that room."

She seemed relieved. And that made him feel all the worse because he was deceiving her.

"Look, Sally," Ross said suddenly.

"What?"

"Just keep walking."

"What's the matter?"

"I've got to level with you. Dammit," he said, "I have to tell you something."

"What's the matter?"

"Listen. We're being followed. No. Don't look around."

"Followed? By whom?"

"We've been followed ever since we got off the plane. There's a guy in the lobby. There were men watching the restaurant last night. A car followed us back to the hotel."

She was shaken. "Who—?"

"The FBI."

"What? But why?"

"It's a national security case. They do it sometimes. When the stakes are this high. They're always afraid someone will get bought."

"They're watching you?"

"They're watching us."

"God," she said softly. They walked on. Then she said, "Why are you telling me?"

"Hell, I feel like a louse for getting you tangled up in that hotel thing. It was a stupid stunt."

"It wasn't your fault." She walked the steps down to the white board-walk dock that floated on a row of empty oil drums. The wavelets from the passing powerboats clicked against the bottom of the boards and made the gangway roll.

"Listen. I've been thinking," Ross said. "About the . . . you know, the situation."

"I haven't been able to think of anything else."

"That guy in the Four Seasons Hotel—no way he could have been official. The Secret Service doesn't have jurisdiction."

"I don't understand."

"He must have been on his own or working a private gig."

"For who?"

"Search me. But the thing is"—he took hold of her elbow—"the thing is that if we find the guy who shot Martinez, this whole thing may simmer down and fade away."

She looked back at him. "You're sweet," she said. "I know you care. But how can you believe you'll find the assassin?"

Ross shrugged and kept on walking. "We might. You never know."

She sighed and shook her head. "I don't see how you'll ever find him."

"Hey, don't be so discouraged. We've got ways."

"What ways?"

"You know. Detection. Informants. That kind of thing."

"Excuse me, Agent," she said, and she was teasing him, "but isn't that just a lot of macho talk?"

"No."

"I wish I could believe it."

"Think what you want."

"David," she said, "I know you don't want me to worry, but—"

"Look," he finally said. "We've got a line on him. We might have a definite make on him by tonight."

She was genuinely surprised. "Really?"

"Really."

"How?"

He grinned and held up one hand. "Sorry. Trade secret. Score one for the FBI."

"Okay," she said. "Okay. I'm impressed. But I still think I'll wait and see."

They had come to the end of the dock. Ross looked around. "Now what?"

Then he heard a noise behind them. When he looked, two tough-looking men had jumped down from the fantail of one of the cabin cruisers at the dock. Both wore jeans and white T-shirts, the short one carried a billy club.

"Hey, guys. . . ." Ross said. But they came swaggering down the rolling dock, walking shoulder to shoulder. Then Ross saw that the bearded one was carrying a baling hook.

"Get back," Ross said to Sally, and put his arm out and pushed her around behind him. Then he turned and squared to fight them.

"Buenos días," Sally said. *"¿Cómo está nuestro amigo viejo?"*

Ross straightened, but he didn't drop his guard. "Friends of yours?"

Sally winked at him. "Just in case we were being followed."

Ross stood with his mouth open. "Why, you little—"

The taller deck hand waved for Ross to put his hands down. He did, and let the man frisk him. The diesels of the cabin cruiser wheezed and turned over and the dual exhausts coughed black smoke. The shorter man gave Sally a hand up the ladder and over the rail onto the boat. Ross stood on the dock, hands on hips, more charmed than annoyed.

"Come on, David," she said, and held her hand out to him, laughing. "Score one for me."

He jumped the widening gap of green water and clambered up the side of the boat as the captain hit the throttles. And as Ross swung his leg over the railing, he caught a glimpse of the gray Ford up on Collins Avenue and a man who got out and slammed his door and looked angrily after the wake of the cruiser.

2:05 P.M. THE PHONE RANG again. And again. Then the operator came back on and said, "I'm sorry, sir. Mr. Ross is not in his room. Would you like to leave a message?"

"Shit," Mancuso said.

"I beg your pardon."

"No . . . I mean—look, just say Joe called. Okay?"

"Yes, sir," she said cooly and broke the connection.

Mancuso put the phone down and looked at his watch. The next plane to Baltimore was at 6:30. Which Mancuso knew meant sitting around the Cleveland airport with his thumb up his ass for hours. The cab fare had been $37.30—and he gave the cabby five, which meant that he had six bucks left, so he went to the cafeteria and stood behind the stack of trays and silverware dispensers and looked up at the colored pictures of the food behind the counter. Two bucks for a hot dog. Shit, he used to go to Ebbets Field with his father in the old days and the ticket was a deuce and dogs a quarter, same for beer, and peanuts salted-in-the-shell a dime. Fucking world was crazy. Two bucks for a hot dog, dollar for a Coke. Three left three. Pack of smokes was a dollar thirty-five. He got the smokes first, then went back and took a tray and got on line.

The public address announcer said, "Paging Mr. Joseph Mancuso. Mr. Joseph Mancuso to the white courtesy telephone, please."

"I'm coming," he muttered and left the tray and walked three-quarters of the way back around the building before he saw the white phone on the wall.

"Yeah, I'm Joe Mancuso."

"Just a moment, please," the operator said. There was a lot of clicking.

"Mr. Mancuso?"

"Yeah?"

"Could you come to the American Airlines courtesy desk, please?"

"Yeah, where's that?"

"To your right."

He looked around and all the way down the end of the terminal. A girl in an American Airlines uniform was holding a telephone and waving at him.

"Do you see me?" she said over the phone.

"Yeah, yeah, I'm coming." He hung up and slouched in her direction. But when he got to the counter, she showed him into a little VIP waiting room behind it and shut the door.

There was a fancy big-screen television at one end of the room. Beside it was a rolling bar with a lot of brand name liquor and mixers and a bucket of ice and some cigarettes in shot glasses and trays of pecans and walnuts. Mancuso grabbed a handful of pecans. So, this was how the biggies traveled. There were fancy leather armchairs and a rack with a bunch of classy magazines. And wedged into the far corner, on a straight-backed chair, sat a woman dressed in the flowing white habit of a convent novice, her face turned away from him. Mancuso straightened up and stared.

"Are you . . . Mr. Mancuso?" she asked.

"Er . . . yeah."

"From the FBI?"

He snatched his hat off. Then he looked around for a place to put the pecans and finally put them in his pocket. "Sister, I— "

"I am Harriet Fallon."

He stood, silent, his hat in hand. Then he took a breath. "Mrs. Fallon, I—"

"Please do not attempt to engage me in conversation," she said softly.

He dummied up. He brushed his hand on his trousers to shake off the salt from the pecans. Then he leaned over to try to make her out around the corner of the cowl that wrapped her cheeks and chin.

"And please do not attempt to see my face."

"Yeah . . . sorry."

He stood, waiting.

"The man who came on Wednesday said he was from the Secret Service. Is that the same as the FBI?"

"No. Did you—"

"Mother Superior sent him away. But she said you could get a court order to question me. Can you do that?"

"Well, yeah. Sure. I mean, if I have to, yeah."

"You are trying to find the man who shot my husband?"

"That's right. Now, what I need to—"

"But that's not why you're here."

273

He didn't answer her.

"Is it?"

He sighed. "No. It isn't."

She raised her head slightly, as though preparing herself. But when she spoke it was without hesitation. "Mother Superior told me that I may speak to you about my husband if I wish. She said my husband might become vice president of the United States."

Mancuso shrugged. "It's . . . it's a possibility. Yeah."

"I do not think my husband should be vice president of the United States."

Mancuso blinked. "Well, he—"

"I want it understood that you will never try to see me again," she said. "That you will never try to call or contact me again in any way. Is that understood?"

"Sure. But why—"

"My husband is a very unhappy man. Unhappy and disturbed. He needs help."

Mancuso had listened to just about enough. "Look, the main thing here is—"

"He could have had any girl in Houston for his wife. But he chose me. And I did not understand it. When we were married, my parents sent us to Palm Beach for our honeymoon. I was a virgin."

Her voice was flat, without emotion.

"On our wedding night, he raped and sodomized me. My arms and legs were so bruised and beaten, I couldn't go out on the beach. The second night, he did it all again. He stuffed my panties in my mouth to stifle my crying. Even so, the assistant manager came to our hotel room."

Mancuso stood frozen in astonishment.

"After we returned to Houston, he brutalized me three or four times a week. He would tie my ankles and my wrists, put adhesive tape over my mouth, and assault me until I bled. He blackened my eyes and battered my face so that I couldn't walk in the street."

Mancuso cleared his throat. "Why didn't you—"

"Then, one night, he brought a friend home for dinner. And after we had eaten, I realized that he intended for me to have sexual relations with both of them. At first, I wasn't sure what he was asking me to do. I couldn't believe women did such things. Then he showed me those. . . ."

She nodded to her right and on the table near the wall, resting atop a pile of magazines, there was a yellowed envelope tied with string. Mancuso put his hat down on his carry-on bag, took the envelope and untied it, and leafed through the photographs inside.

274

"When I saw those pictures, I became hysterical. That only seemed to arouse them more. They tied me up. They hit me. They used me. Hour after hour. All night long."

Gently, almost as though he were a man walking through a dream, Mancuso eased the photographs back into the envelope.

"In the morning, I was incoherent. My husband called a doctor, had me sedated. But I couldn't stop crying. It went on for weeks. In the end, he called a priest and when he left us alone together, I confessed. The priest wouldn't believe me. I had to find those pictures and show him. When he saw them, when he saw my bruises, he went to Terry and pleaded with him to go for counseling. Terry refused. When the priest begged him, Terry suggested I come here, to the convalescent home of the Carmelites. After I was here two years, the court made Terry executor of my estate." She paused, and then she said, "I kept the photographs."

When she had finished, Mancuso stood, listening to the silence.

"Now, will you kindly go back to Washington and let me be?"

"Yes." He bent and took his hat, took up his carry-on bag.

"Mr. Mancuso?"

"Yeah?"

For a moment, it seemed as though she were about to turn to face him. But she didn't.

"If you . . . if you see Terry, will you tell him I forgive him?"

Mancuso stood a long moment, staring at her back. Then he put his hat on.

"No," he said.

2:30 P.M. THE CABIN CRUISER bore northward through the channels of the Inland Waterway, and Ross and Sally sat in two sling chairs on the rear deck. In a third chair, one of the deckhands sat with his back against the cabin of the boat, a double-barreled shotgun resting across his knees. He watched them, and Sally watched him.

He was a young man—a boy really—still in his teens. He had the stubby build and wide shoulders of the Central American *Ladinos*. He had a gold cap on one incisor and a little shadow of a mustache and dark-slitted eyes that seemed more suited to the night.

The cruiser gradually worked its way toward the verges of the Everglades. The lavish, pink stucco mansions with their white-stepped roofs faded in the distance, and the thickets of wisteria, ferns, and plane trees crept down to the banks and tangled with the reedy waterline.

Sally remembered the rusting river steamer that had carried her south in the winter of 1970 when the Red Cross found a nursing assignment for her in Santa Amelia on the Rio Coco. It was the farthest part of Honduras from the border with El Salvador, the farthest they could send her from the village of Lagrimas and her memories of the Football War.

She had settled stubbornly in the hospice across from the American Embassy in Tegucigalpa, waiting to be called to press her complaint against the officer and soldiers who had raided Lagrimas and shot two men and burned the village. But by late November it was clear to her that the embassy wanted the incident forgotten.

She went twice a week to the office of the chargé d'affaires. Sometimes she sat all day in the sticky waiting room with the slow fan grinding overhead. He was always cordial, always most attentive. Sometimes, his secretary took detailed notes. Sometimes, Sally received a copy of a letter he had written to the minister of the interior or to the provincial governor-general in Santa Rosa de Copan. Sometimes another man—one of those sinister Americans in khaki slacks and short-sleeved white shirt and sunglasses—would sit in the corner of the room and listen. That man never spoke, but he never took his eyes off her.

Finally, in the first week of December, she found a note under the door of her room at the hospice. The American ambassador would see her at 9 A.M. the next morning.

She washed and curled her hair and put on her best white cotton blouse and skirt and used the nub end of her lipstick and wore her wide-brimmed straw hat. But when they showed her to the ambassador's office, he was wearing his tennis clothes and kept looking at his watch.

"I know you've had a bitter disappointment," he said. "But there's no remedy for that."

"What about Lagrimas and the—"

"There's been an investigation. The case is closed."

"Who investigated?"

"The army."

"The army?"

"Miss Crain, there's no purpose to you staying any longer in Honduras. I think it's time for you to go home and take up your life again."

She had been expecting that. "I'm not going," she said.

He opened a folder on his desk. "I've been in correspondence with your parents." He held out a letter. "They want you to come back. Perhaps you can resume your study of economics."

She didn't even glance at the sheet of paper. "I'm done with economics," she said. "I'm a nurse."

"Your visa will expire."

"I renewed it. It's good until next August."

"You'll be arrested and deported."

"Only if you order it. If you do, I'll go to the newspapers. I'll tell them what I saw."

"What makes you think they'll care?"

"I'll make them care."

"No one cares about two little Commies who were hanged somewhere in the middle of the jungle."

"They weren't hanged. One was shot in the ear. The other was shot in the mouth. Then their genitals were cut off."

The ambassador crossed his arms and sat back, his head cocked to one side, staring at her.

"How old are you, Miss Crain?"

"Twenty. And I'm not going home."

The next day, a car and driver from the embassy came for her at lunchtime and drove her through the yellow dust and crumbling stucco streets of Tegucigalpa to the Red Cross office in the Paseo Bolivar.

A long-faced, shag-eared old man named VanDoren interviewed her about her nurse's training and showed her a map.

"I'll take it," she said.

"You *vill* be on your own."

"Better," she said.

They sent her to *El Lugar de Tranquilidad*—the Place of Silence—the sleepy villages of the Miskito Indians in the region where the border with Nicaragua was lost in the mud and quicksand of impenetrable bogs and marshes along the sluggish Rio Coco. The village where the river steamer left her standing on the dock with her three footlockers of Red Cross supplies was called Santa Amelia, and the bamboo hut provided by the Red Cross thrust out over the water on creaking stilts of cedarwood.

The Miskitos were dark and small, descendants of Incas who had mated with the English-Portuguese and black bloods from Africa. They had been brought to Christ through the husbandry and martyrdom of Moravian missionaries from Pennsylvania, who had proselytized among them since before the Civil War. They had a language of their own, and English.

Sally taught herself the words she needed in Miskito and to fish with dropstrings tied to nailheads where the floorboards of her hut jutted out across the river. She had an old woman named Arundel who cooked her meals and did her wash and swept the floor of the hut with a handful of plantain fronds. There were no crops. The only food was fish and fowl. The Miskitos traded alligator skins for corn and rice from Panama when the diesel boat came up the river from Cabo Gracias a Dios every other month. Sally didn't like the way the Portuguese river trader and his *Ladino* deckhands looked at her. They used to blow their air horn when they passed her hut so that she would raise her bamboo blinds. But if she did, they'd squint at her body under her shift. Once, when she went to the market to buy some rice with Arundel, the trader came over and stood beside her, so close that she could smell the dry sweat under his arms and the diesel oil in his beard.

"You lonely?" he said. "Come Cabo with me."

"Get away from me," she said in Portuguese.

She put her hand on the butt of her pistol.

He smiled at her and chuckled in his throat.

That night, she made her bed alongside Arundel under the lee of the roof outside the hut. And when she heard him push the bamboo door aside and heard the floorboards creak under his boots, she sat up beside the window and aimed her revolver at his back.

"*Fillo da puta,*" she said quietly, and there was menace in her voice. "*Fora dagui.*"

He was startled. He straightened up and turned and looked at her.

"Out," she said and flicked the barrel of the gun in the direction of the door. "And don't come back."

He made that chuckling sound in his throat and scratched his belly and took a step toward her. She fired and the bullet hit the floor in front of his boots. He jumped back and put his hand on the pommel of his sheath knife.

She extended her arm and took dead aim at his forehead.

"Right now," she said. "Out!" He turned and pushed through the bamboo curtain and shoved his way through the crowd of Miskitos that had run down to the river when the gunshot sounded. They laughed and hooted after him all the way back to the dock.

There were few occasions for laughter in Santa Amelia. There was malnutrition and scabies and ringworm and impetigo and dysentery and, of course, malaria. She took her quinine pills three times a week. She had diarrhea for the first two months until her system got used to the amoeba in the water. But she had little time to worry about herself. There were so many things that killed the children: tuberculosis and tetanus, black water fever, appendicitis. The nearest clinic was in Cabo Gracias a Dios, a hundred-and-fifty river miles away.

Every month or so, a Capuchin priest would come up the river in a dugout with two Miskitos on the paddles and say mass for the living and the dead. He was a Frenchman from Provence named Pere Jean-Baptiste, a flinty old priest in a dirty brown cassock and old leather sandals. Sally would sit in the door of her hut, under the crooked Red Cross sign and watch him lay his altar cloth and chalice on the upturned bottom of a barrel. There were only five Catholic families in Santa Amelia; the others were Moravians, and they held their prayer meetings in a long hut near the edge of the jungle. In the year Sally stayed at Santa Amelia, she and the priest never spoke. She never understood why.

In February, the steam packet from the west brought a letter from VanDoren saying that Sally was to have a two-week furlough and free passage, either to Tegucigalpa or, if she preferred, to Cabo Gracias a Dios. The boat was heading east and Sally didn't much care which way she went, so she booked on to Cabo. It was a two-day trip and she slept in a hammock on the deck with her revolver under her pillow, and each night the soft swaying of the little steamer and the steady drone of the engine rocked her to sleep under a blanket of cypress trees and peeping stars.

Cabo Gracias a Dios was a low, coastal town in the delta where the Rio Coco spilled its silt into the Atlantic on the Honduran-Nicaraguan border. It was an evil-smelling port settlement of 3,000 with a mill and waterfront bars and whorehouses that catered to the crews of steamers that tramped the coastline between Venezuela and Belize. Sally took her duffel bag across her shoulder and humped it up the hill to the Red Cross mission while knots of dirty sailors and longshoremen stood on the street and shouted ¡Mira! ¡Mira! and made kissing sounds and catcalls after her.

The director of the Red Cross was an Englishwoman named Christina Brown. She was very tall, over six feet, and her long black hair was tied behind her head. Her husband had brought her to Nicaragua when he came to run the timber farms and mill in Bluefields, 300 miles to the south. But he'd started drinking mescal and spending weeks in the bordellos near the harbor. He got a rash and she made him move out, and a year later he was stabbed to death after a card game. For the last five years, she had held the Cabo station together, while a tug-of-war went on between the Capuchins and Moravians for the souls of the Miskitos, and the bars and whorehouses along the waterfront dispensed stab wounds and gonorrhea.

All this she told to Sally as they sat with Minton teacups and linen napkins on their laps in a drawing room that might have been in Chelsea— told her plainly and without compunction, as though it were a story she'd read somewhere in a magazine.

"You know they call you *La Putita*," Christina said.

Sally was startled. "But why?"

"The captain of the *Esmerelda* started it. Because you shot at him."

"I didn't shoot at him. I shot the floor."

"You should have shot his John Thomas off."

"I will next time."

"I reckon you might."

Christina stood up. "You'll stay tonight for dinner. I'll have Steadman put your belongings in the guest room. And you won't need that at dinner," she said, pointing to the butt of the revolver sticking out from under Sally's shirt.

They were four at dinner. Christina, Sally, Monsignor Silha of the Moravians, and a fragile little Spaniard named Carlos Fonseca, who smoked during the meal of ceviche and a kind of local paella made with eel and grouper, washed down with liter bottles of *Victoria*. They talked a kind of shifting patois of English sliding into Spanish and back again. Monsignor Silha was from Alexandria, Minnesota, a town called Clitheroe near Annie Battle Lake.

"How do you find your work at Santa Amelia?" the old priest said.

"Hard," Sally told him. "The babies die. That's the hardest thing."

"It's a form of natural birth control," he said and took another helping of paella.

Sally's neck got red and she was about to answer when Christina said, "More *cerveza*, Carlos?"

"*Gracias.*"

"I was alarmed when I first learned of you," the monsignor said.

"Why?" Sally had always wondered why the missionaries had shunned her. And then she saw Christina turn and touch the bun where her hair was tied behind her head.

"I'd heard you were a very pretty woman," Silha said. "A woman who . . . attracts attention."

"Would it be better if I were plain? If I were ugly?"

"Infinitely."

"I disagree," Fonseca said. "I find her beautiful. If somewhat dangerous."

"Carlos has been to Russia," Christina said. "He's a bit eccentric, you'll discover."

"Eccentric how?"

"He believes in Lenin and in the Second Coming of Our Lord," she said, and the monsignor added, "At least, he claims to."

"Really?" Sally said.

"He wrote a book about it."

"What was your book called?"

"*Un nicaragüense en Moscou.*"

"Have you been to Moscow?"

"*Si.*"

"What was it like?"

"I froze my *cojones* off."

"Carlos!"

The monsignor tried to keep a straight face, but couldn't. Sally laughed behind her napkin.

"Forgive me, *señora*, but it's true," Fonseca said. "It would be better to study Marxist-Leninism in Hawaii. But there are no classes yet."

"Carlos fought at Panascan," Christina said. "He was almost killed at Panascan."

Sally shrugged. "What is Panascan?"

"Oh, the old battlefield where Sandino made his stand," the monsignor explained. "Sandino made a deal with President Sevilla-Sacasa in the thirties. He was going to turn the whole Miskito coast into an agrarian utopia, don't you know. They coaxed him out and killed him. Now these young fools call themselves Sandinistas and they dream of *Nicaragua Libre*."

"Do you?" Sally said. "Is that your dream?"

"Yes," Fonseca said and lit another cigarette with the butt of the last. "That—or an early death."

The next day Fonseca came for her and took her on the back of his motorbike into the hills behind the town. From the lookout where he stopped, they had a vista of the dusky little harbor and the ring of shanties with corrugated roofs that climbed the hills. The other way was nothing but the rain forest, spreading like a deep, green blanket away to three horizons.

"It's lovely here," she said.

"Only with your back to civilization."

"Are you a revolutionary? Really?"

"*Sí.*"

"Against Somoza?"

"Against all the landed people—and the exploitation."

"But can you ever hope to win?"

He pushed his glasses back on his forehead and scratched the whiskers on his chin. "Do you hope to save the babies in the jungle?"

"Some. If I can."

"I hope to save the babies' babies."

She stayed with him that night and he was a gentle lover. He was the second man she'd had and he was uncircumcised. The next morning, she went back to the Red Cross hospice and took her duffel bag. Christina stood in the doorway of her bedroom, her arms folded, watching Sally pack. When she saw her take the revolver from beneath the mattress, Christina said, "Don't take that with you if you're going to stay with him."

"Why not?"

"He's a hunted man. If they find you with a gun, you'll go to jail. Or worse."

Fonseca was stopping in a room over a cantina called El Parador. There was a wooden cross over the bed and three stacks of books in a corner and a table under the window where he wrote. There was also a picture on the wall of three young men-in-arms. They carried rifles, but they were only boys. One of them was Fonseca.

"Tomás Borge. He's a big mouth," Fonseca said, and pointed to the little man with the big cigar. "And Silvio Mayorga—another fearless hero." He shook his head and laughed with tender irony.

"When was this taken?"

"In 1960 or '61, back in Tegucigalpa. We were full of talk and grand ideas. We were young and stupid. We trained not far from Santa Amelia. And in 1962, we went across the River Coco to Wiwili. But we lost our way in the jungle, attacked the wrong village. The army tracked us back across the border and killed twenty men before we got away."

"Was that Panascan?"

"No," he said. "That was later—in 1966 and '67. It was Silvio's idea. He was going to organize the *campesinos* to start a popular revolt. But all the peasants wanted was to be left alone to their tortillas and *cerveza*. They shot Silvio. They almost got us all."

"He was killed?"

"Yes. Killed."

She looked again at the photo. Mayorga had been a bright-eyed young man who seemed so full of hope.

"Why don't you give it up?" she said.

"Why don't you?"

It was an earnest question and he waited for an answer.

"Because I'll be goddamned if I'll give up," she said with such conviction and determination that it startled her.

He smiled and put the back of his fingers against her cheek. "You'll find what you're looking for in Nicaragua," he said. He kissed her and she let him fumble between her legs.

After she had lived with him a week, she decided that she wanted to cook him dinner. So, she went out and bought a stack of tortillas and a bream and a bottle of *Flor de Caña* and a bunch of dried wildflowers and a little red terra-cotta vase to put them in. But when she came back to the cantina, there was a Jeep parked outside and soldiers with fixed bayonets standing at the entrance to the alley. She kept walking, and when she turned the corner, she threw the groceries down and ran straight up the hill to the Red Cross hospice.

"They found my bag. They've got all my things."

"Your passport?"

She touched her purse. "No, thank God."

"Go to the port," Christina said and pressed a roll of bills in her hand. "Take whatever boat is leaving. Here." She gave her the revolver wrapped in a tea towel.

Sally stuffed it under her shirt.

"And there's one more thing you must do," Christina said. She got a pair of shears from the kitchen drawer. "Sit down." Then she cut Sally's hair to within an inch of her head.

The old woman, Arundel, cut it for her after that and, in time, the close-cropped girl in the mirror didn't seem a stranger. And although she stayed in Santa Amelia and worked tirelessly at her nursing, somehow she never left Fonseca and the room in Cabo behind. Then, in March of 1971, the trading boat from Tegucigalpa brought another American to Santa Amelia.

He was tall and very fair and very quiet and after she knew him, she understood that Carlos Fonseca had changed her life forever and that she would never, never be the same.

The channel through the Everglades began to widen, and Sally saw Ross standing on his tiptoes in the stern of the cruiser, looking over the cabin at the mansion on the shore. Its walls were the color of ivory and overgrown with bougainvillea, so that they seemed washed with crimson. Sally had been there before, and she knew it well.

It was the Somoza mansion—or, more exactly, the Debayle mansion, because it had been the Florida home of Salvadora Debayle, wife of Anastasio Somoza Garcia, the man who ordered the murder of Sandino in 1934, seized the presidency of Nicaragua from Sacasa in 1936, and begat a dynasty of terror.

The original Somoza held the presidential palace until 1956, when a dour, metaphysical poet named Lopez Perez shot him to death. After his death, his swollen bank accounts passed to his son, Luis. When Luis died of a coronary in 1967, all his chattels—including La Reserva, as the Miami house was now called, an airline, a shipping line, enormous holdings of land throughout Nicaragua, the presidency and close ties with the Johnson administration in Washington—became the property of his younger brother, Tacho.

By the time Tacho Somoza had been overthrown by the Sandinistas and assassinated in Asuncion in 1980, Sally had left Honduras and the Rio Coco far behind. She had worked in Houston, and had already moved on to Washington. People who thought they knew her talked of her as a dreamy, impractical idealist. When she could find anyone to listen, she liked to sit up late over coffee and talk about everything that was wrong with American policy in Central America.

Because she knew that, somehow, Carlos Fonseca's wistful ideas had miraculously triumphed in Nicaragua. But they had been twisted into a cruel garrote around the nation's throat. And now in that tiny, sweltering country, the roles of liberator and oppressor had curiously reversed. The ideological heirs of Carlos Fonseca—Daniel Ortega Saavedra and his Cuban-trained Marxist guerrillas—now held the presidential palace and tyrannized the Miskito Indians with their schemes to collectivize their land. Fonseca's boyhood campaign buddy, Tomás Borge, had become the ruthless minister of the Interior. The CIA-supplied, right-wing former Somoza guardsmen haunted the swampland of the Rio Coco. And Julio Ramirez Blanco, the aged former foreign minister for Tacho Somoza and his dynast father, sat in La Reserva deep in the Florida Everglades, plotting the counterrevolution.

Eight years later, the old man was still there, still implacably anti-Sandinist, still the spokesman of the government-in-exile when he received Sally and Ross. He was pale and very thin, deep in his seventies, and the milky cataracts that filled the lenses of his eyes gave him the look of statuary, as though he were wearing his own death mask. He was quite blind and had to feel for the saucer on the table, and then gently run the hooked, arthritic tips of his fingers around the rim until he found the handle of the teacup. But his English was precise and his voice was clear.

"In the end," Ramirez said, "there is no winning and no losing. There are only battles—and women who cry over the graves."

Ross looked at Sally. She was sitting forward, her elbows on her knees, her chin resting on her clenched hands, listening intently as Ramirez rambled on.

"If one revolution succeeds, others will take to the hills. And when their revolution succeeds, another generation will rise to fight. And so it goes for centuries, long after the reason we fight is forgotten." Ramirez felt for his cup of tea, and with two hands, brought it to his lips.

Ross was growing impatient; he wanted to get to the point. "Mr. . . . that is, Señor Ramirez, we're trying to find the man who killed Octavio Martinez."

The old man twitched his head as though he were trying to sense Sally's reaction. Then he felt for the saucer and put the cup down. "No, no," he said. "Tavito was no soldier. He was a teacher. Did you know that?"

Puzzled, Ross looked at Sally.

"Well, yes, I did," Ross said. "But, actually, we're—"

"Then he went to the jungle," the old man said and broke off. He sat a long while with his face turned to the light, until Ross began to wonder why the old man seemed so uneasy, so reluctant to speak.

"Señor Ramirez. . . ."

The old man started and said, "*Sí?*"

"Señor Ramirez, would Ortega send someone to America to kill Martinez?"

The old man shook his head and chuckled to himself. "No, *muchacho*. Ortega wishes to appear a statesman, not a soldier. Ortega has friends at *Time* magazine. He has friends at the Associated Press. He believes that if he can win the war in the American press, in time he will win the war in the jungle."

"Then who ordered Martinez's death?" Ross asked.

There was a long silence. Then the old man shrugged. "Simple people are the prey of men who lust for power."

Ross looked around. Sally's eyes were fixed on Ramirez, shining cold as ice. Although he could not see her, Ramirez seemed to cringe under her stare.

"The lust for power is a dark beast," Ramirez said haltingly. "The more it is fed . . . the larger it grows—and the larger grows its appetite. Those who have power hunger for more. And those who have absolute power are insatiable."

"But who?" Ross said. "Who are they?"

"Young man, are you blind as well?" Ramirez felt for his cane. Then he pressed down on the arms of the chair with the heels of his hands and rose and straightened himself. Sally got to her feet. Ross did, too.

"Now, you must excuse me," Ramirez said, and began to shuffle away.

"Gracias, Colonel," Sally said.

The old man stopped and suddenly went rigid. He hesitated and wet his lips as though he were about to speak. But instead he put his hand out and raised his crooked fingers until he found her face. His palsied hand trembled as he caressed her, as though he were afraid. "So, you are still beautiful," he said. *"Vaya con Dios, La Putita."*

"Jesus Christ, what a waste of time," Ross said when they were sitting in the stern of the boat and La Reserva had disappeared behind the curtain of the Everglades.

But Sally sat, folded within herself, in the sling chair at the far corner of the deck. She didn't answer.

"That guy's a basket case," Ross said. "No wonder they can't win the war." He leaned back in the chair. "What was that he called you?"

She looked at him blankly for a moment. *"La Putita.* Just a name. Something they called me when I worked with the Red Cross. I didn't think anyone remembered."

"What does it mean?"

She turned away from him and sat, staring out into the evening darkness gathering in the jungle. "It means 'Little Whore.' "

5:40 P.M. THEY LOOKED LIKE three old cronies—the kind of old men you see chattering away the afternoon on a park bench. They wore shirts with open collars and old cardigans, their pants baggy at the seat, pushed out around the knees. They were the kind of old men you saw in the reviewing stand at a military parade on Memorial Day, soldiers from another era in the blue-and-gold caps of the VFW, old men who took a long time getting up when the flag went by, but who stood straight with their age-dappled hands over their hearts, and you knew they'd paid a price beyond all reckoning for the privilege.

But the three men sitting in the small room tucked away on the second floor of the White House weren't pensioners. They were the president of the United States, the Speaker of the House, and the majority whip of the Senate.

"Sam, what we have here is a serious situation," O'Donnell said. "You know that."

"Yes, I do," Sam Baker said, and leaned back in his rocker.

"Is there any truth to Eastman's allegation?"

"Some."

Senator Luther Harrison tamped his pipe and watched O'Donnell. But O'Donnell didn't follow up.

"Some?" Harrison finally said.

"It's true that there are only two FBI men working on the shooting. That much is true."

"Now, why the hell would O'Brien do a thing like that?" O'Donnell said. "He ought to have a hundred agents on the case."

"Lou Bender asked him not to."

"The little bastard," O'Donnell said. "Kick his ass out, Sam. Do it right now."

"It's not that simple," the president said. "There have been other killings."

"What? When?"

"And evidence has been found of a crime that could undo everything we've accomplished in Latin America."

O'Donnell just stared.

Harrison struck a match and put it to the bowl of his pipe. Between puffs, he said, "Sam . . . I owe you an apology. I didn't expect such candor."

"Luke, I'm not telling you everything."

"What does that mean?" O'Donnell said.

"There's something else to this," the president said. "Something I can't talk about just yet."

"Something that's happened—or will happen?" O'Donnell said cautiously.

"Something that's happened. Something that might involve the Intelligence Oversight Board."

"Christ!" Harrison almost dropped his pipe and had to jump up and brush the fall of glowing ashes from his cardigan.

"The Oversight Board?" O'Donnell said. "Mary, Mother of God."

The IOB was the civilian review board that had been established in the wake of the Nixon excesses to prevent illegal activities by the United States intelligence services.

"So, we have a problem that goes beyond anything Dan Eastman has imagined, gentlemen," the president said. "And when it blows, it could blow a mile high."

"When does it blow?" O'Donnell said.

"I don't know. This week, next week. . . ."

"Goddamit. During the convention?"

"Perhaps."

O'Donnell slouched down in his chair. "Sam, for God's sake, is there no way to—to manage this thing?"

"You mean, cover it up?"

Harrison rapped his pipe empty in an ashtray. "Gentlemen," he said, and looked at his wristwatch, "it's late. I think I'll be going."

"Luke, sit down," O'Donnell said.

"The hell I will," Harrison said. "This conversation is taking an ugly turn. I think you'd better have it without me."

"Your exception is noted," O'Donnell said. "Now, goddamit, sit down."

Harrison perched on the edge of the desk.

O'Donnell said, "That man, Petersen, the one they're looking for. You're not telling us he's still on active service with the CIA?"

"Nothing like that," the president said. "And I'd appreciate it if you didn't question me further, Charlie. Please."

Sam Baker got up and went to the window and looked out at the gates and guard posts where heavy concrete barriers stood against the threat of terrorism. There had been a time, he knew, when President and Mrs. Coolidge waited in the White House door on Christmas morning and shook hands and exchanged greetings with every passerby. How long ago that seemed. How much the world had changed and grown uneasy with itself. Perhaps he would be better off next year at Lockhart Hill on the Virginia River with his grandchildren and his books.

"Sam, if things are really this bad. . . ." O'Donnell began. Then he stopped himself.

Harrison said, "Sam, with all of this. You're not going to seek renomination? Are you?"

The president sighed. For a moment, he stood silent. "I don't know, Luke. At this point, I don't know."

It was very quiet then in the Rose Room. Three old men, each alone with his thoughts.

"Perhaps . . . well," O'Donnell said, and didn't go on.

"Yes," the president said. "I think we ought to talk about succession, don't you?" He went back and sat on the sofa alongside O'Donnell.

"Not Eastman," Harrison said.

"No," the president said. "I used to think he'd grow into the office. But he hasn't. And he's made a fool of himself."

"I guess that leaves us Fallon," O'Donnell said.

The president shrugged. "He's an enigma, isn't he?"

"He is that," Harrison said. "And if you don't seek the nomination, it's his."

The president touched the sleeve of O'Donnell's cardigan. "But, of course, he doesn't know that."

O'Donnell looked at Harrison. Then he looked back at the president.

"I'm going to see Fallon this evening," the president said. "We'll decide after that."

"Luke?" O'Donnell said.

Harrison puffed his cheeks and blew a breath. "All right," he said. "I agree."

7:45 P.M. THE FIRST THING Sally did when she got back to her room was to punch the number for Terry's private line.

"This is Chris Van Allen."

Sally sat down. "That's how you answer Terry's private line? What happened to 'Hello, this is Senator Fallon's office'?"

"It was Terry's idea."

"Oh? Well . . . may I speak to Terry, please?"

"He's not here."

"Where is he?"

"He just went out."

"Out where? Chris, am I pulling teeth or what?"

"He went to see the president."

"What?" Sally stood up. "When?"

"He left at seven-thirty."

"Dammit, Chris. Why didn't you call and let me know?"

"I would have, Sally, but Terry said not to tell a soul."

"Well, since when do you and Terry have secrets from me?" She was really angry.

"Sally, look. I just work here—same as you. The man said 'tell no one.' I told no one."

"All right, all right. What's it about? Did he say anything else?"

"No."

"Chris—damn you—"

"He said he was going to see the president. Period. Look, Sally, that's all he said, okay?"

"Okay, Chris. I'm catching the next plane home. And when I get there, I'm coming to your apartment and—"

"I'm staying in the guest house."

She sat, seething.

Then he said, lightly, "Sally, did you see the network evening news?"

She glanced at her wristwatch. It was almost eight. "No," she said. "I missed it."

"Shame," he said.

"Why?"

"Terry wanted you to watch the evening news and call him before you head back."

"Why? What are you talking about? What's happened?"

"Sally . . . just do as you're told."

She cocked her head. "Chris, what did you say?"

He paused a moment—but when he spoke there was no apology in his voice. "I'm just following instructions."

She slammed the receiver into its cradle, and she stood there, rigid, her fists clenched in rage. She was so full of hurt and anger that when the door slammed in the next room, she paid it not the least bit of attention.

It was Dave Ross who slammed the door of the next room. He slammed it, and then tore open the blue-and-red Express Mail envelope he had signed for at the front desk. He already knew what was inside: the FBI memo about the tip-off on Weatherby, and a copy of O'Brien's appointment calendar page with Terry Fallon's name. It was the material Mancuso wanted him to use to test Sally, and he dreaded what he had to do.

At precisely 7:59, Sally picked up the telephone and punched a number in New York. It was 5:59 in the mountain time zone and NBC was about to feed the Sunday evening news via K-band satellite to a handful of stations near the Rockies. The number was the line that NBC's foreign correspondents could call to listen to the audio of the broadcast so that they would know which parts of their reports actually made air.

She sat down and held the phone under her chin and opened a yellow pad to make notes. There was music and the voice of Danny Dark, the network promo announcer.

. . . and come home to NBC Monday night when Daniel J. Travanti

and *Knots Landing*'s Michele Lee star in "Smoke and Fire" on the
NBC Monday Night Movie.

The music buttoned out.

Then the ponderous John Williams theme began, and she imagined
the computerized animation of the sun setting behind the Statue of Liberty
that opened the news, then dissolved to the standard shot of Chris Wallace
at the anchor desk.

> Good evening, I'm Chris Wallace. Vice President Daniel East-
> man's rift with President Baker turned into a yawning chasm
> today when the vice president accused the administration of foot-
> dragging in the investigation of the assassination of Nicaraguan
> Contra leader Colonel Octavio Martinez. Andrea Mitchell reports.

In her mind's eye, she could see Andrea Mitchell standing on the
north lawn of the White House with her name and the NBC logo supered
below her.

> At a hastily called press conference this morning, Vice President
> Daniel Eastman issued a stunning challenge to President Baker that
> is unprecedented in the history of American politics.

The audio cut to a sound bite of Eastman at the podium.

> I am sending this letter to Speaker O'Donnell to request that he and
> Senator Luther Harrison, the majority whip of the Senate, form a
> bipartisan, bicameral committee to investigate the assassination of
> Colonel Octavio Martinez. And along with the assassination, I am
> demanding that the Congress investigate the foot-dragging, inade-
> quate, and unconscionable way in which this administration has
> obstructed the investigation of this terrible crime.

Sally shook her head and sneered. She remembered Eastman at the podium
with the seal of the vice president of the United States, his hand raised
above his head, clutching the envelope containing the letter. It was such an
absurd grandstand play—just a weak, transparent attempt to cash in on the
furor about the killing, to steal some of Terry's thunder.

Andrea Mitchell's voice continued.

> The vice president also alleged that the murder of Secret Service
> Agent Steven Thomopolous on Thursday night in his room at

Washington's posh Four Seasons Hotel was part of a coordinated
cover-up designed to frustrate the investigation. The FBI has now
joined the search for the agent's assailant. District of Columbia
police have released this composite sketch of a woman who was
seen with Thomopolous in a bar at the hotel shortly before he was
shot to death. She is described as a blond Caucasian female,
five-feet-six to five-feet-eight inches tall, who may be a prostitute.

While Speaker O'Donnell and Senate Majority Whip Harrison
were unavailable for comment today—

Sally put the phone down. She had heard enough. It was as though her
heart had stopped.

8:10 P.M. SAM BAKER SAT across the coffee table in the Oval Office
from Terry Fallon, the phenomenon from Texas who had rocketed from the
Houston city council to the threshold of the White House. And Baker
realized that no interview he had ever held had been quite so important—
because what was said in the next few minutes might determine who would
be the president of the United States for the next four years—and for eight
years after that.

Fallon was a lanky and attractive man, smartly and conservatively
dressed in a dark blue suit, white shirt, and regimental tie. He had an easy
smile and ruddy highlights in his hair and a good strong jaw. His attire
revealed no secrets, but he favored his right side when he walked.

"I know the Speaker of the House has asked you if you're prepared to
serve," Sam Baker said.

"Yes. He has."

"Have you considered what he said?"

"I told him I'd respond when there was something to respond to."

Sam Baker poured them both another cup of coffee.

"Well, Terry . . . may I call you Terry? There is some prospect now that
we might have a chance to work together. I thought it would be wise if we
sat down and exchanged ideas."

"I'd like that."

"I've admired what you've said and done about Central America. But I
don't know how you feel about, say, Subic Bay. Or Kandahar. Or UN
Resolution 242." Sam Baker sat back with his coffee cup and waited to see
if Terry Fallon had done his homework.

"Let me tell you, broadly," Terry said. "I favor unilateral action where
coordination with our allies and trading partners fails. I think if you apply

that concept, you'll understand I'm predisposed to an active policy in any theater where our interests are threatened or infringed.''

Sam Baker watched and listened. It was easy to see why this striking young man had so captivated the media and the public. He was articulate, he was confident, he was smart.

"For example," Terry said. "I would favor supporting the Afghani Mujahideen through Pakistan, as we've done with the Khmer Rouge through Thailand. And as for the Philippines, I think we should assert our treaty rights with President Aquino, but restore SEATO as our counterforce against the Soviet Pacific fleet.''

Sam Baker thought about that. Terry Fallon knew the players—and he had ideas.

"As to Resolution 242, I favor the creation of a Palestinian homeland on the West Bank of the Jordan as a neutral state with an elected parliament. But with its foreign policy and defense administered by a joint council of Israel and Jordan, Egypt, Syria and us—a sort of Austrian solution to the Middle East.''

"And the Soviets?''

"Freeze out.''

"The Israelis would never go along. Neither would the Syrians.''

"I wouldn't give them any choice.''

The president folded his arms. It was a visionary concept, but it was not beyond the realm of possibility.

"How do you feel about our tariff agreements with Canada?''

"I'd let them protect their basic industries as we would ours. Paper, timber, uranium—they've got resources we can't match. But I'd stop all shipments of asbestos. And I'd be tough on manufactured goods and encourage them to open markets in the southern hemisphere.''

"Cuba?''

"No direct negotiations until after Castro.''

"Taiwan?''

"No forced repatriation to the mainland.''

"Would you supply them F-16's?''

"For what? If they're attacked, we're in it. They don't need anything but a radio to call for help.''

Sam Baker nodded. Terry Fallon had passed the first part of the test with flying colors.

"Can we spend a few minutes on domestic programs?" the president said.

"Fire away.''

"Food stamps.''

"I'd sell the program to a consortium of banks, let them administer it by credit card for a fee, make it semiprivate like the post office. That saves printing and distribution, discourages counterfeiting, minimizes abuse. It would eliminate an entire government agency and reduce federal employment by 20,000.''

It was an extraordinary idea—and it was not his only one. They continued a long while—and the longer they talked, the more Fallon shaped and molded a utopian economy before Sam Baker's astonished eyes. He would create a cabinet-level secretary for Minority Affairs; he would create a corporate investment tax credit for on-the-job internships, private day-care centers and retraining programs. He would protect steel, textiles, and leathers, and press for expanded free export markets for high-tech hardware, wines, grain, meat, and dairy products. What he laid before Baker was a glittering highway to prosperity, driven by growth and individual initiative. It not only sounded good, it sounded like it would work.

"Terry, I'm delighted," the president said when he finished. "Absolutely delighted."

"Thank you, sir."

"I'd like to ask you something else. It's personal. I hope you won't mind."

"Please. Go ahead."

"They tell me you're ambitious—that you've seized upon a happenstance and you're trying to ride it to the White House. Is that true?"

Terry didn't miss a beat. "Mr. President," he said, "we're all ambitious. We wouldn't be in Washington, in any of these jobs—if we weren't driven with a passion to succeed. Some have made it here by conniving and double-dealing. Others have made it on character and merit. I think you're one of those. I've always admired you for that."

"Why, thank you, Terry," Baker said, and he was genuinely touched.

"But as to . . . what you call a 'happenstance' . . . well, events chose me. Fate marked the place. But I was ambitious. And I was there. And I was lucky enough to survive. I can't apologize for that."

"Fate?" Baker said.

"Yes."

Baker put down his coffee cup. He smiled. "You're not saying you believe in fate?"

"Yes. I believe in fate. I believe in destiny. And I mustn't be embarrassed that I've been chosen."

"No. Of course not," Baker said softly. "You shouldn't be embarrassed about that." But it was odd that a man so pragmatic in foreign affairs and so practical in economics should believe that there were transcendent mysteries that steered the world.

Terry smiled at him. "Anything else?"

"Yes. One more thing. If you were offered the vice presidential nomination, would you accept?"

Terry nodded, smiling, as though it were a question he had waited a long time to hear. Then he said, "No."

Baker stared at him. "Well, that's straightforward enough. May I ask you why?"

"Because you've failed."

"I have?"

"Yes, Mr. President. You have."

"We, none of us are perfect. I've made mistakes. But 'failed'? Isn't that a little harsh?"

"No, I don't think so," Terry said. "You've lost the war in Nicaragua—or, at least, you're losing it. You've lost the military initiative in Africa, from Cairo to the Cape. You've lost your play in Lebanon and in the Persian Gulf. Everywhere our arms are in retreat."

"And what would you propose to do?"

"Mr. President, you know the old saying—those who do not study history are condemned to repeat it?"

Sam Baker nodded.

"I taught history at Rice, Mr. President. And it has always been a source of wonder to me how little America's leaders have learned from the history of the Second World War—and the Russian domination of Eastern Europe in its aftermath."

Baker cocked his head, listening.

Terry sat forward, put his hands together in earnest. "Hitler wanted to set Germany *über alles*—to make white Aryans the rulers of subservient nations in his hemisphere. Our banks and our jingoists want America to do that in this hemisphere. It's wrong. It's dangerous and it's wrong."

His sincerity and his caring reached out to Baker and touched him. "Terry, you know I agree with you. Like you, I feel—"

But Terry got to his feet, paced to the president's desk. "The nations Hitler conquered, he disemboweled and enslaved. And created the Holocaust to exterminate their minorities. It was a crime beyond words to deplore."

"Terry," Baker said, gently. "I've heard you speak about this before. I know how deeply you feel a commitment to Latin America. I know that—"

"The work sapped Germany's strength," Terry said.

Baker was silent a moment. Then he said, "What?"

"In the final confrontation, partisan forces and underground movements rose among the conquered nations and struck at the German army's flanks." Terry turned around, leaned back against the desk, stared down at Baker. "But Stalin learned from that, you see. He armed the nations he controlled. And they became his bulwark against the West. And made Russia the dominant force in their hemisphere.''

Baker sat rigid. ''I'm afraid . . . I don't understand.''

''I'm saying we use Grenada as the template. That's the policy that will win the war for the Americas.'' Terry paced back to the couch, stood over the president. ''The great international questions of our generation aren't going to be settled at the conference table. They're going to be settled in the streets, with steel.''

When Baker answered, his voice was a whisper. ''Surely, you don't believe that . . . ?''

''I believe it as I believe my Redeemer liveth,'' Terry said. He smiled. ''Mr. President, it's so plain. It's history staring us right in the face.'' Then he chuckled. ''The Soviets want an end to Star Wars, and a total ban on nuclear weapons. Of course they do. That would leave them with an overwhelming superiority in conventional forces.'' Terry leaned forward. ''I'd begin a massive arms and training program among our allies in South and Central America. I'd build their forces as the Soviets have the Poles and the East Germans. And I'd deploy crack units around the world just as the Soviets have with the Cubans.''

''You're talking about making the Americas an armed camp,'' Baker said.

''Yes,'' Terry said.

Baker slowly shook his head.

''I know you don't agree with me, Mr. President,'' Terry said. ''But that's because you don't have the spine to lead the Free World to victory. You're a decent man. But you're in the wrong job. And I hope you'll step aside and make way for the coming of the future.''

Sam Baker sat as he was, thunderstruck.

''I think that's all I have to say, Mr. President.''

''Yes. Of course.''

''Now, if you'll excuse me. . . .'' Terry went to the door. ''I hope you understand what I've said.''

''I believe I do.''

Baker sat a moment after Terry was gone. Then he turned his head and looked back the length of the Oval Office at the desk of the president of the United States. If he, himself, did not seek renomination, Fallon might well sit at that desk for the next four years. Baker reached in through his jacket and touched his shirt front over his heart. His undershirt was damp with perspiration, sweated to his body. Seated at that desk, Terry Fallon would be the most powerful and, clearly, the most dangerous man in the world.

8:50 P.M. WHEN THE PHONE rang and Sally heard Terry's voice, she almost lost her own.

"How . . . how did it go?"

He was all business. "You saw Ramirez?"

"Yes."

"And?"

"And nothing. Ramirez is Ramirez. He's a terrified old fool, troubled with bad dreams. You had a meeting with the president?"

"Yes."

"Well? Terry, for God's sake, tell me."

He hesitated. "Sweetie . . . Sally . . . do you remember that note I wrote when you came to see me yesterday?"

"A note?"

"I wrote it on a yellow pad."

Then she remembered he had written "someone may be listening," and she said, "Yes. I do."

"Well . . ." he said. "We need to talk, but we may have the same situation right now. Do you understand?"

"Yes." She sat down on the bed. "Go on."

"Did you see the evening news?"

"No. But I caught up with it. I know what you're referring to."

"Then I think you should come back tomorrow, and . . . and take a few days off."

She started. "But the convention—"

"Take a few days off and catch your breath. Do you understand me?"

"Catch my breath?"

"There'll be a lot of contact with the press during the next two weeks with the convention and all . . ."

"Yes?"

He was measuring his words. "And I . . . I want you to . . . well, I want you to work on press releases and my speeches. Do you follow me?"

"Yes. But what about the press announcements? If I—"

"You mean the stand-ups on camera?"

"Yes, of course. What did you think I meant?"

"Sally, I . . . I feel . . . for obvious reasons, I think that Chris should do the stand-ups. Don't you agree?"

"No," she said, "I don't."

"Sally, let's not have an argument."

"Let's not." But she could feel her temper rising. "Let's just remember—"

"Sally, use your head."

"Dammit, I—"

"Sally, wait until you see the picture we spoke about. Then tell me if I'm wrong. Let's not wave it in their faces. All right?"

That silenced her.

"Get a good night's sleep," he said. "We'll talk about it in the morning." And without giving her a chance to answer, he hung up.

When the phone rang again, she snapped, "What is it?" and Ross said, "Hey. It's only me."

"Oh. I'm sorry."

"I called the airline. The first flight out is at seven tomorrow morning. It gets in a little after nine."

"To Dulles?"

"National. How about some dinner?"

"Not for me."

"A drink?"

"David, I'm sorry. I'm not in any mood."

"I'd like to see you."

She sighed and let her shoulders sag. "All right. Come over for a drink, okay?"

"Sure. Make mine a large gin gimlet."

"Ten minutes?"

"Or call me when the drinks come."

She did that and when he came in and sat down, he was wearing a faded, blue Yale sweatshirt and gray sweatpants.

"What are you dressed up as?"

"The spirit of the class of '82. Did I tell you that I rowed stroke on the varsity and won the Yale regatta?"

"No."

"I didn't. But I'm a good liar."

They laughed and touched their glasses. Then they drank. It was odd how his simple presence relaxed her and made the problems with Terry seem to drift away.

"How come you're crazy?" She sat up on the bed and folded her legs under her and smoothed the pale yellow cotton robe around her knees.

"I don't know," he said. "I wasn't born this way. I'm a disappointment to my parents."

"Really?"

"My father says that I'm my mother's blood relation—but only related to him by marriage."

She laughed and had to hold her scotch and water with both hands to keep the drink from spilling on the bedspread.

"Were you always a closet clown?"

"Nope." He kicked his loafers off and put his bare feet on the coffee table. "I learned from Mancuso."

"I wouldn't think he had a sense of humor."

"He doesn't. But you need one to work with him. I learned the first year. He can be an awful bastard. Oops!"

"No, he deserves it. I don't know how you stand him."

"He's actually a good cop." Ross held his glass up to the light. "I'm going to need another one of these. You mind?"

"No. Not at all." She picked up the phone to call room service. "I buy the drinks. You buy the dinner. Remember?"

"You said you didn't want any dinner."

"I don't. But I wouldn't mind some quiet conversation."

She ordered—two more drinks each, a bowl of peanuts, and potato chips.

"I shouldn't eat these," Ross said, but kept on digging peanuts by the handful. "I used to weigh 200 pounds. Can you believe that?"

"Never." Sally was feeling the scotch and didn't care.

"Oh, I was fat," Ross went on. "I was out to here. A great big gut and jowls like an elephant."

She laughed and rocked and leaned back against the pillows. "You're funny. I don't know why I like you."

"Why shouldn't you?"

"Hey, I'm old enough to be your . . . well, your older sister. I was eighteen back in 1968. I'm a grown-up hippie in a Garfinckel's dress. You're a pig. Can this be chemistry?" All of a sudden, she was talking about her past again. And she felt like she had nothing to hide.

"A hippie?" he said. "You? Come on."

"No kidding," she said. "I was a flower child. Well, now wait. Not entirely. See, I was a virgin, too."

That made him laugh.

"Hell, what do you expect?" she said. "I was raised in Memphis where sex is referred to as original sin. Although I can tell you from later experience that there is nothing original about having sex in Memphis. But, other than being innocent of carnal knowledge, I was a full-fledged, bead-and-sweatband, feather-wearing hippie."

"You smoked pot?"

"Er. . . ." She looked at the ceiling and rocked her head back and forth. "Yes and no. It didn't do much for me. I got hungry and ate my head off at Colonel Sanders."

"You got any idea what old man Ramirez was talking about?" Ross said.

"Yeah." She leaned back against the headboard. "Ambition."

"Come on. What ambition?"

"Hey, listen." She got off the bed and put her empty glass down and took another. She realized that she was a little unsteady. "It's a disease that's epidemic where I live. It's not too pretty."

"Fallon's got it. Gimme while you're up." He held his empty glass out and she swapped him for a full one. "He's got it and you think he's pretty."

"No," she said, and got back on the bed. "He's different." She was getting drunk and she didn't give a damn.

"Different?"

"Sure. A lot of things mean more to him than . . . what were we talking about?"

"Ambition."

"Yeah," she said.

"Like what?"

"America. Loyalty. Our country."

"What?"

"Mean more to him than power."

"Who said *power*?"

"You said."

"I didn't."

"Yeah."

"I said *ambition*."

"Sure," she said. "Ambition." She was halfway through the third scotch and water, and right then it was hard to see the difference between power and ambition.

"I don't get the schizo wife," Ross said. "I don't get that."

"Terry's a man who keeps his promises."

"Maybe he still loves her."

That drew her up short. "Maybe . . ." she said softly, and looked down at the tumbler cradled in her hands.

"And maybe it's because he knows a wife can't testify against her husband."

She smiled. "Yeah, maybe not." And then she thought about that. "Testify to what?"

But Ross changed the subject. "He didn't run for the Senate, did he?"

She looked at him. "No, he was appointed. Why?"

"Why him?"

"Well, Weatherby was put in jail. They needed somebody to—"

"Yeah, I know. But how come Terry Fallon?"

She shrugged. "Terry was in Congress. He was qualified. They—"

"But there were other guys. Guys who'd been in Congress longer. Why did they pick Fallon?"

"Well, he was—"

"And why did they pick Weatherby to ABSCAM?"

She laughed and leaned forward on the bed and almost lost her balance. "Senator Weatherby was a star-spangled crook."

"But they didn't know that until they caught him in the ABSCAM. There are a hundred senators—how come they picked Weatherby?"

"I don't know why they picked Cal Weatherby," she said. "But I—for one—am pleased as punch they did." She was beginning to slur her words, and she was surprised how hard and fast the liquor hit her and how much she felt like letting go with Ross.

"Sally, do you really not know why they chose Weatherby? Look at me. Tell me," he said in earnest.

She looked at him, blinking. Then she clumsily opened her hands and grinned. "I give up. You tell me."

Ross said, "Fallon fingered Weatherby."

She sat that way, staring and blinking, as if it were taking a long time for the words to sink in. Then her eyes narrowed as if she were only beginning to grasp what she had heard. And then, in a voice so small that it was barely audible, she said, "What?"

"Fallon went to see O'Brien to tell him Weatherby was taking graft from wildcatters. The FBI built a scam around oil leases and Weatherby fell for it."

She rolled her head and tried to shrug it off. "Hey, that's not true."

He pulled up his sweatshirt and pulled out the papers he carried under the elastic of his pants. They were the documents from Mancuso. "Here's O'Brien's memo-to-file confirming the visit. The next page is his diary. You see the name that's circled?"

She squinted at the paper through the haze of intoxication. "Why would O'Brien write a memo like this?"

"Probable cause," Ross said. "Fallon's visit gave us probable cause to investigate. O'Brien needed that memo in case the scam blew up in his face." He reached for the paper. "I'm sorry. I need that back."

Her hand was trembling when she gave it to him, and so was her voice. "Even if Terry did that . . . that wasn't wrong."

"Sally, look." He sat on the edge of the bed and she eased back against the headboard, leaning away from him. "I know you worked for Weatherby before you worked for Fallon. . . ."

There was a long, terrible silence. She stared at him with the wide eyes of a frightened child.

"Sally," he said softly, "I need to know if Fallon used his . . . his relationship with you."

Then she turned her face up to the light and closed her eyes, and whimpered, "No . . . God . . . no."

He leaned to touch her and she pulled away, curled into herself. "Sally, listen to me," he said. "I got a bad feeling about all of this. I got a feeling something terrible could happen. Just . . . I just don't want to see you get hurt."

She looked so lost and helpless. He reached out and touched her arm.

"Please," she said. "Don't do that."

He pulled his hand back. "I was only—"

"Go," she said. "Please. Let me be."

He folded the papers up, put on his loafers and quietly went out the door.

She lay like that a long time after he was gone. He was a user. They were all users. And she was a vulnerable fool.

9:00 P.M. WHEN MANCUSO LANDED at Baltimore International, he went to the Hertz desk, rented a car, and drove to the Holiday Inn on Route 2. It was an old-fashioned motel—two rows of little green cabins and a parking lot on either end. Mancuso pulled up in front, took his carry-on bag and went into the office.

A little redhead came to the front desk.

"Got a room for tonight?"

"Sure."

"Gimme something on the first floor."

"It's all cabins."

He gave her a credit card and signed the form. "Check out 11 A.M.," she said. "Fourth cabin on your right."

Mancuso found cabin 117, went inside and locked the door behind him. It was cold in the bedroom and he fiddled with the old propane heater until the element caught. It crackled and groaned as the hot air filled it. He took his revolver from its holster on his belt and swung out the cylinder. He always carried the gun with an empty chamber under the hammer. He took one more cartridge out of the box in his carry-on bag and inserted it and snapped the cylinder closed. Then he holstered the revolver and walked out into the night.

He stopped at the soft drink machines behind the office and bought two cans of Coke, but instead of turning back to his room, he turned the other way, toward the even numbers: 124, 122, 120, 118. The curtains were drawn across the windows of cabin 108, but there was light seeping through them. He walked as slowly and quietly as he could. The Do Not Disturb card was hanging from the doorknob, and as he passed the door, he leaned

301

in slightly. He could hear music and it sounded like the television was on. He stopped in front of 104. From there he could see the darkened, half-filled parking lot. He could park his car back there behind somebody's big red camper. Then he could watch cabin 108 without being seen. It probably meant sitting up all night behind the wheel. But if he wanted to get a glimpse of whoever was in 108, it would have to be done. He sighed and let the two cans of Coke hang from his hands. He was getting too old for all-night stakeouts.

When Rolf Petersen got back from Pizza Hut, he was so preoccupied with picking his teeth that he almost walked past the office of the Holiday Inn. But he reminded himself what he was waiting for, opened the door of the office and stuck his head in.

"Anybody call?"

"Sorry," the little redhead said. She'd told him "no messages" so many times over the last six days it was getting to be a reflex.

He turned toward cabin 108 when he heard the door of the office open behind him.

"Hey, mister." It was the little redhead. "You did get a message."

He hurried back.

"The girl on the board just took it." She handed him the While You Were Out slip, folded over.

"Thanks a lot, kid." He gave her a dollar.

"Hey, all right."

He went around the corner of the building and stopped under the light near the soft drink machines to read it. The call had come in at 8:20 P.M. while he was out for dinner. The message was printed in pencil. It read:

MUST SEE YOU TONIGHT AT 11 P.M. WAIT FOR ME.

It was unsigned.

He looked at his watch; two hours to get ready. He smiled and folded the paper carefully, and when he walked back to his cabin, he was whistling.

It was the whistling that made Mancuso look up. And when he did, he saw that the man walking toward him from the motel office was Rolf Petersen, the Company assassin, the man who had shot Octavio Martinez to death. He was tall—well over six feet—muscular, and wearing the leather jacket and baseball cap that had been described in the reports about the murdered policeman. Petersen's hands were balled into fists and driven down into the pockets of the jacket. For a moment Mancuso thought he should draw his revolver and confront him. But he had a can of Coke in each hand and the front button of his jacket was closed, and just then Petersen said, "Evening," went by him, and put the key in the door of his cabin, and went inside—and, anyhow, who wanted to be a fucking hero and maybe get your ass shot off?

Even so, Mancuso was muttering when he turned the corner toward his cabin and walked right into the barrel of a .38 special that was pointed at his nose.

"Freeze!" a voice said, and Mancuso did.

"Hands up!" another voice said at his side. Mancuso raised his hands and stood there holding the two Cokes over his head. Someone started to frisk him.

"Shit! He's got a gun," the man who was frisking him hissed and the other man cocked the .38.

"Goddamit," Mancuso said. "I'm Agent Joseph Mancuso of the FBI."

"Shut up," the man holding the gun said.

The other one took Mancuso's revolver and dug his ID out of his jacket pocket and passed it to his partner. Then he pointed to the cans of Coke. "What have you got there?"

"What the fuck do they look like?"

"Listen, fuck you, buddy. On the ground. Hands behind your head. Spread 'em."

"You can suck my dick before I'm getting on the ground in this suit," Mancuso said.

"Listen, you asshole." The man beside him slammed his .38 into Mancuso's ribs.

Mancuso doubled over, gasping.

Then the other man stepped out into the light.

"Straighten up, pal," he said. And when Mancuso did, he held his ID photo near his face. "What do you think, Phil?"

Mancuso looked back and forth between the two of them. They were like something out of a movie, all dressed in black from head to foot and wearing black flak jackets. Their faces were smeared with black grease.

"Shit," the second man said, and snapped the ID wallet closed and held it out to Mancuso. "Give him his gun."

The other man did. "Sorry, friend."

Mancuso put away the wallet and holstered his revolver. "Fuck you," he said.

"Now beat it," the first man said. The walkie-talkie strapped across his chest crackled.

"Stiles? Roberts? What the hell is going on?"

"We got a guy here from the FBI," he said into the microphone.

"From where?"

"The FBI."

"You're kidding."

Mancuso grabbed the mike. "No, he ain't kidding. And I got a warrant for that bozo in 108. So, fuck off with your SWAT team."

"Bullshit," the voice said. "We got a warrant, too. Now you suck wind, mister, before you get hurt."

Mancuso dropped the microphone. "Where is that asshole? Where is he?"

"Over in those trees," the cop said, and pointed to the darkened corner of the parking lot beyond the row of cars.

"Don't do nothing," Mancuso said, and he hunched down and followed the line of cars into the darkness.

Rolf Petersen locked the door behind him, turned down the sound of the television set, laid his old suitcase on the bed, and undid the combination locks. Inside was a foam rubber pad cut to hold the stock, the action, the barrel, and the scope of the HK-91 sniper's rifle and its twenty-round box clip. There were two spare boxes of teflon-coated ammunition and three circular wells that held shiny black concussion grenades with their safeties filed away and their red pull-tabs taped down. He snapped the rifle parts together, pulled the bolt, and slapped the clip home. He stood the rifle against the bedstead, then turned his chair to the door and sat down with his .44 magnum revolver in his lap. He had just reached into his pocket and unfolded the slip of paper to reread the message when the phone rang.

The SWAT command post was behind the wall that separated the motel parking lot from the bar-and-grill next door. There were four men in blackout gear and flak jackets hunched together. One of them wore captain's bars.

"Who the fuck is in charge here?" Mancuso said when he clambered up beside them.

"I'm Captain Brower. What's your beef?"

"I got a warrant for that guy. He's a federal fugitive."

"We got a warrant, too. And this is our jurisdiction, so back off."

The walkie-talkie crackled. "We're all set, captain. When do we jump? Over."

"Goddamit," Mancuso said. "I need him alive."

"Stay out of this," Brower said.

The voice from the speaker said, "Whatcha say, captain?"

"Nothing. All units ready?"

Voices came back, "Unit two ready. Unit three ready."

"You cocksucker," Mancuso said.

Brower raised his head and peeked over the wall. "Okay. Let's go. Move in."

Rolf Petersen sat listening to the phone ring. Then he got up and went to the nightstand and lifted the receiver.

"Hello?" the voice said. "Hello?"

He didn't recognize the voice and started to put the phone down, when the voice said, "Don't hang up."

Petersen put the receiver to his ear.

"He sold you out. Your cover's blown. You—"

At that moment, the two SWAT cops kicked the door in, shouting, "Police! Freeze!"

In the time it took Rolf Petersen to turn his head to the door, he saw two men wearing flak jackets holding pistols leveled at him. The first shot he got off hit the first man in the throat, severing the carotid artery and blowing out the third and fourth cranial vertebrae. The force of the blast threw the man across the doorway, jarring his partner's arm as he raised his revolver to fire. His shots went into the ceiling of the cabin and Petersen's second bullet struck him in the chest. The teflon-coated cartridge cut through the fiberglass lining of the flak jacket, and when the bullet hit the man's sternum it shattered into a handful of coarse shrapnel about the size and weight of nailheads. The shower of red hot lead-and-steel alloy sprayed into his viscera, effectively shredding his heart and lungs. The impact of the bullet flung him back with a force equal to being struck by an automobile traveling at forty-five miles an hour.

Captain Brower screamed into his microphone, "Stiles? Roberts? Ah, shit! All units—open fire!"

Petersen was on the floor before the first salvo hit, a crossfire of M-16's cutting through the wood frame and plaster walls of the cabin as if they were paper. Petersen rolled on his back, fired one shot into the ceiling fixture that shattered the bulb and brought the glass bowl crashing down, and another into the television, which imploded in a shower of sparks, plunging the room into darkness. Then he scrambled to the bedstead, seized the HK-91, crawled to the door under a storm of plaster and splinters, and fired back at the flashes between the cars in the parking lot.

Brower and his men hunched down as a burst of fire from the cabin stitched the wall above their heads.

"Fuck!" Brower shouted into the walkie-talkie. "Give him the gas!"

Mancuso stood, hitched up the belt of his trousers and brushed the dirt off his knees. He turned his back and walked up the blacktop toward the door of the bar-and-grill. Behind him, he heard the loud, angry brat-brat of the automatic rifles and the dull whump as the tear gas launchers fired.

He pushed through the door of the bar and sat down at the end of the counter. The fat blond barmaid said, "What's yours?"

"Bourbon. Double."

She set him up, nodding toward the noise outside. "What's the racket?"

"Fireworks." Mancuso socked the drink down. "Gimme another."

When the first tear gas canister bounced in the door, Petersen slid over and kicked it back outside. But the second landed on the bed and the sheets burst into flame as though hit with a blowtorch. He lay on his back and looked up at the black smoke billowing against the ceiling. In a moment, he would have a smokescreen pouring out the door of the cabin and enough cover to make a break for it. He slid over to the bed, pulled the suitcase out and stuffed the spare boxes of ammunition into his pockets. The crossfire from the two sides of the parking lot was withering. But the flames were leaping off the bed now and he hugged the carpet, waiting for the black smoke to totally obscure the doorway. He could barely see the two dead cops on the pavement. Then the smoke enveloped him, and he gathered himself to spring into the night.

When the flames of the burning bedding reached the propane heater, the hot gas split the copper feed pipe, sending a bolt of flame back along the line to the vertical tank behind the cabin. When the flame hit the tank, the force of the explosion blew the back wall into the cabin ahead of the fireball and, when the four grenades detonated simultaneously, that explosion carried the front wall away with it. For an instant, the sidewalls of the cabin stood like a tunnel for the expanding globe of superheated gas; then they reached their flashpoint and disintegrated. The whole spherical mass of flame and debris lurched into the sky.

"Jesus fucking Christ!" Brower screamed. Then he and the other SWAT cops ducked and covered their heads against the rain of fiery ashes.

Mancuso turned his head toward the explosion. When it hit the sidewall of the bar-and-grill, it was like an earthquake. Rows of glasses and bottles seemed to fling themselves off the counter and crash to the floor. The barmaid squatted down and clutched her head and started screaming.

Mancuso watched the bourbon washing back and forth in the tumbler in his hand.

"Shit," he said.

11:25 P.M. IT WAS GETTING very late when the intercom finally sounded in Lou Bender's office.

"Yes?"

"I'd like to see you, please."

"Where?"

"Across the hall."

When he went into the Oval Office, the president was seated at his desk, but he had hung his jacket over the back of his chair, and loosened his tie. There were two tumblers of whisky on the blotter before him.

"Have one," he said.

Bender sat down. They touched glasses and drank.

"How did it go?" Bender said.

"Preconvention dinners with governors should be against the law. Like football players betting on their own games."

"I mean Fallon."

"Yes," the president said and nodded. "Badly."

"Oh?" Bender stiffened. He had hoped the president and Fallon would be love at first sight. Now, he saw the match would take some shoe-horning.

"As a matter of fact, Senator Fallon has some very good ideas. Ideas for domestic programs, trade, that sort of thing."

"Well, that's promising."

"As far as it goes." The president sat forward in his chair. "Lou, he's a fascist. Listening to him is like listening to Mussolini. Or worse."

Bender shrugged. "Sam, he's young. He needs to learn that—"

"Lou, he sat on that couch and told me that the international issues of this generation won't be settled by negotiation, but in the streets—with steel."

Bender waved his hand. "That's just talk."

"Dangerous talk. He'd like to lead us back into gunboat diplomacy and arm our Latin allies."

"Well," Bender said, "I see we're going to have to give Senator Fallon a little help with his keynote speech."

The president shook his head. "I don't think you're listening to me. Do you think I'd give Terry Fallon a nationally televised forum for spouting that nonsense?"

"Maybe O'Donnell and Harrison should talk to him."

"Forget it, Lou. Even if he were acceptable—which, believe me, he is not—Fallon doesn't want to be vice president."

"That's ridiculous. Of course, he does."

"He wants to be president."

"In four years."

"Not in four years," Sam Baker said. "In January."

Bender put his elbow on the desk and leaned toward the president. "Terry Fallon sat in this office and told you he's prepared to take you on at the convention? I don't believe it."

"He didn't say that."

"Then what did he say?"

"He told me to step aside and make way for the coming of the future."

Bender and the president stared at each other. "He said that?" Bender smiled. "Sam, he was pulling your leg."

The president's tone was dark. "He was . . . in earnest."

Bender folded his arms and sat, thinking.

The president rocked back in his chair. "How can a man so inexperienced in politics and so filled with destructive ideas be within reaching distance of nomination to national office? Terry Fallon is a demagogue. He's dangerous, Lou."

"Now don't get carried away, Sam. We need him."

But the president wasn't listening. "Until this evening, I thought Fallon was a bright young man who needed seasoning—who needed to be developed and encouraged. Now I realize he must be stopped."

"Not stopped, Sam," Bender said abruptly. "Housebroken."

The president looked at Bender out of the corner of his eye. "What are you talking about?"

"Fallon knows the media created him. He knows the media can destroy him. Give me a pardon for Weatherby. Let me find out what he knows. I'll teach Fallon to heel."

"Never."

"It's the only way, Sam. You've got to have Fallon on your ticket in three days if you want the nomination."

"Not at that price."

"Think of it as the eleventh commandment."

"What do you mean?"

Bender smirked and sipped his whisky. "Those who live by the press shall die by the press."

11:40 P.M. IF HE HAD a choice of going into the morgue or puking on his shoes, Mancuso would take the shoes every time. But he didn't have a choice and he could feel the chill of the cold room even before he started down the stairway from the county medical examiner's office. Captain Brower was still in his blackout suit and greasepaint, covered with ashes from the blast. And his chief had torn him a new asshole for blowing the cabin at the Holiday Inn and Brower wasn't talking to Mancuso, but making like it was all his fault.

Thank God, the bottle of Jack Daniel's hadn't shattered during the explosion. Mancuso had stood drinking doubles among a knot of the curious just beyond the yellow Police Line Do Not Cross tape, while the firemen came roaring up the highway and rushed all over the place hosing everything in sight, and the team from the coroner's office pieced together the remains from amid the rubble and drove them away. Now Mancuso just felt giddy and bloated and good all over. With Petersen in the morgue, he could go back to Washington, get a good night's sleep, and anyhow he didn't give a fuck.

But going down the stairs to the cold room sobered him enough to remember how much he hated looking at stiffs, and before he went in the door, he kind of turned away so that Brower couldn't see, and he crossed himself.

They followed a technician around the corner to another line of refrigeration units, and Brower said, "Who was this guy anyhow?"

Mancuso shrugged. "A social undesirable."

Brower stopped walking. "Listen, you son-of-a-bitch, he killed two of my men."

"Like I said . . ." Mancuso walked on. "Not a nice person."

The technician checked the hangtag on one of the stainless steel doors, yanked it open, and rolled out the slab. It was covered with a sheet—but there was something sticking straight up under the sheet about six inches high.

"Looks like he died with a hard-on," the technician said.

But when he pulled the sheet back, Mancuso could see that it was the burned stump of Petersen's arm that was sticking up. The hand had snapped off at the wrist and was lying on the steel slab beside the body, looking like an ugly black spider. The man's body had been burned black and there was a dim outline of a collar and breast pocket where his shirt had burned into his chest. The buttons were melted into the black skin like a row of little white M&M's. The heat of the flame and the dehydration of burning had shrunk his skin and tissue so that it was pulled tight across his bones. His eyes were burned out and his mouth was open as if to scream and his black lips were pulled back so that his white teeth were grinning. Through the shriveled muscles of his arm, the radius and ulna were visible, and the white dial of his wristwatch showed where it was baked into his forearm.

"Somebody order well-done?" the technician said.

Mancuso leaned in over the dead man. In spite of the cold, he could smell him—and the smell was the same as steak charred on a backyard barbecue. The face was a gnarled, gruesome caricature of a man now, but it was unmistakably Rolf Petersen. Mancuso hawked and spit in the corpse's face.

"Aw, Jesus," the technician said in disgust, and threw the sheet back over the body.

Brower stood a little way off. He was white as a ghost and looked like he was going to lose his lunch.

"What started this?" Mancuso said.

"Tip," Brower said mechanically.

The technician rolled the slab back into place and slammed the refrigerator door.

"From who?" Mancuso said.

"Anonymous."

"Don't bullshit me. You wouldn't roll SWATs on an anonymous tip. A black-and-white maybe. But not a SWAT team."

Brower focused his eyes on Mancuso. Then he just stood there, grinning maliciously, and Mancuso could see he wasn't going to answer.

"Fuck you," Mancuso said, pushed past him, and walked out the door.

THE SEVENTH DAY

5:30 A.M. THE FIRST THING SALLY thought of when she awoke was the police artist's sketch. She had not seen it. But she knew it. And she was afraid.

It was a drawing of her and it had been projected into some twenty-five million American homes. Now millions of people were wondering who she was and hundreds, if not thousands, of policemen were looking for her. And she realized that it had been a long, long time since she had been so frightened. Once, in Cabo Gracias a Dios, a rapist had pushed the barrel of his pistol against her forehead and asked her to remember him when she was with Christ in heaven. Even that had not made her so afraid.

She lay in the morning bed, silent, huddled around the pillow in her arms, pressing her face into the downy softness as though it could be a refuge. Then she thought of Terry, and she knew that she might lose him. That fear was even worse.

She threw back the covers and swung her legs out of the bed. The room was cool and damp, the way air-conditioned rooms are in Miami in the summertime. She slipped the shoulders of her yellow nightgown and let it puddle on the floor about her feet. Then she went naked into the bathroom, ran the cold water, and squeezed the toothpaste onto her toothbrush. But when she raised it to her mouth and caught its spearmint smell, she felt sick. So, she stood there in the bathroom, naked and cold with her gooseflesh rising on her back and buttocks, stood there in the clammy morning, clutching the edges of the white china washbowl and decided that she was going to hang on until she knew she wasn't going to be sick. And then she was going to take care of herself and fight her way out of the trap that was closing around her.

But it was a long time before her breath came normally. And it was a long time before the dizziness left her. And it was even longer before the fear receded in her mind.

Strange. It was strange that the phone didn't ring. It felt strange and hollow to have the day begin without her wake-up call from Chris. But after Sally had showered and dressed, she knew that her wake-up calls from Chris were over. That was clear in his voice last night. That was obvious from the situation.

Chris was living in the guest house now. He was writing Terry's press releases, and holding the regular 3 P.M. press briefing. Chris was getting the calls from Ben and Katherine and Dan and Barbara and Roone. Chris was staying on after the smoky, late-night meetings to sip brandy by the fire and tote up deal points won and lost, objectives gained, alliances exhausted or renewed. Perhaps that had always been his plan. Perhaps that was the only reason he had followed her lead so avidly, been so attentive to her. Because in a premeditated, calculating way, he was devouring her skills and style with only one objective: to replace her in Terry's office and his life.

She looked in the mirror. With her hair pulled back and the dark glasses and the broad brim of her Panama hat turned down, she hardly recognized herself. Instead, she saw a stranger—a cold-eyed, determined woman with a purpose. The bellman took her bags, and Ross was waiting for her in the lobby.

"Did you sleep?" he said.

"Sort of." She turned her face away from him.

He reached out and touched her arm. "Look," he said. But she wouldn't. "Sally, look at me." And when she finally did, he said, "I don't expect you to forgive me. But I'd like you to understand."

She stared at him. There was pain in his eyes, and gentleness. But now she was afraid to trust him.

"I have a job to do," he said, softly. "I was trying to do it in a way that might help you. I was clumsy. I was wrong."

She started down the stairs. "I want you to believe that," he said.

"David, I don't know what to believe."

They went down the steps into the clammy morning. Ross gave the bellman a dollar—and another when the man stood looking at the money in his hand—and they slid into the cab. When they had turned south on Collins Avenue, Ross was watching her. "Are you in disguise?" he finally said.

"They've got a police artist's sketch of the woman who was in the bar of the Four Seasons."

He was startled. "What? Who has?"

"I heard it on the news last night. Do you think we can find a Washington morning paper at the airport?"

He looked at his watch. "At this hour? I doubt it." Then he saw how anxious she was.

"Hey, don't worry," he said. "Those sketches aren't worth a damn. Besides, pretty people are real hard to get right."

"Thanks—I think," she said. "What should I do, David?"

"Do?" And then he understood. "Well, you'll have to wait and see. Lay low a while. Can you do that?"

"I think I have to."

"In a few days, there'll be another crime or another sensation. And everybody will forget."

"Do you believe that? Or are you saying it to reassure me?"

"A little of both." Then, rather impulsively, he reached out and took her hand. "I'll do anything I can to help you."

There was something so decent about him. There was so much compassion in him, so much fondness. She understood. He was a tender, gentle man who had a job to do. She understood better than he could imagine. Another time, another place—it might have been different. But events were driving them apart, as they had once torn another young man from her arms.

She sat back in the cab and watched the long, gray row of beachfront hotels slide past against the pink sky of morning. She was flying back into the unknown with only straws to grasp at—flying back into a rising wind. And when the PanAm 727 lifted off the runway and she heard the grind of the wheels coming up and the whine of the flaps retracting, she looked down upon the green, alligator-ridden Everglades. She thought of the week in Cabo Gracias a Dios and Carlos Fonseca kneeling on the board floor in the morning light through the open window, fingering his rosary and saying his prayers.

The nights they had together were spent sitting by candlelight long after the moon was down, and in his soft and patient voice he spun out for her the adventure that was his life—from the adobe hut where he had been born, the illegitimate son of a cook and a manager, on one of the many Somoza farms in 1935, a year after the murder of Sandino.

Fonseca might have grown up a field hand. But when he was fifteen, his mother enrolled him at the *Instituto Nacional del Norte*—the high school in Matagalpa, a city only sixty miles from the mountains of Cordillera Isabelia and the village of Panascan. The legend of Sandino was strong among the people there, and Fonseca came to hold the image of the little man in the oversized ten-gallon hat as *El Padre de la Resistencia* and a saint. At high school, he met Tomás Borge and Silvio Mayorga and learned of Marxism from Jose Ramon Guitterez, a twenty-year-old who had studied socialism in Guatemala. Together, they founded *Segovia*, a subversive student newspaper.

Sally had sat on the blanket on the bare board floor with her legs curled under her, listening to Fonseca talk. And as she listened, she wondered at her own snug, bourgeois life in Memphis. From kindergarten through college, her life had been an orderly progression. In fact, until she met Fonseca, she thought herself iconoclastic—abandoning economics for nurse's training, choosing the Peace Corps over graduate school, Santa Amelia over a ticket home. But listening to him spin the tale of his struggle, she realized that everything she had, she had been given. Every plan she made, someone had made for her. Every stream she followed was the mainstream.

In 1956, she had been a fourth-grader and Brownie scout when Fonseca enrolled at the National Autonomous University in the city of Leon. There he had been reunited with Borge and Mayorga. He edited the student paper, *El Universitario*, and used the editorial page to lash out at the government. After the assassination of Anastasio Somoza, the founder of the dynasty, the three friends were arrested along with hundreds of other leftist students. Fonseca was beaten with round bats and a strangling cord was tied around his penis and tightened until he screamed and fainted.

He told Sally of this without self-pity, calmly, without emotion. By the glow of the flickering candlelight, she could see the old welts and wounds under the smooth skin of his arms. He had been taken and beaten so many times that he had a kind of gentleman's agreement with pain. It had its place and he did not mock its power. But it was a power that did not touch his soul.

After a month of repetitive beatings and interrogation, they let Fonseca go and the socialist underground paid his way to Moscow, where he studied at Patrice Lumumba Friendship University and wrote his book.

After Moscow, Cuba had been a revelation.

Fonseca made his way there in 1959, in the wake of Castro's overthrow of Batista. To hear him tell it, the city of Havana had been a Lourdes for a twenty-four-year-old revolutionary dreamer. The rich and decadent were leaving—most fleeing with nothing but the clothing on their backs. Castro had closed the Yanqui-owned hotels, shuttered the casinos, pulled down the notorious whorehouses. The flags of *26 julio* flew everywhere. In the presidential palace, there were Castro and Che and committees of armed men in olive drab, laughing and drinking *cerveza* and arguing about the future of their country. It was as though the dry Leninist rhetoric Fonseca had studied in Moscow had suddenly leaped to life. And he was exalted. If Moscow had made him a believer, Cuba made him apostolic. Like Sally herself, Fonseca returned to Central America imbued. Yet, where all her well-supplied and well-intentioned plans had failed, he had worked a miracle. In 1960, he met with Borge and Mayorga in Honduras and formed the *Frente Sandinista de Liberación Nacional*—the FSLN which, almost twenty years later, was to drive the last Somoza from office.

Sally listened, awestruck. Hearing these exploits firsthand made her understand that what the American newspapers called "burglaries" and "hijackings" could be epic and heroic acts, extravagant and chivalrous. It made her own ideals seem condescending pedantries—and she felt foolish and naïve.

Somehow, the week Sally spent with Fonseca became the fulcrum of her life—and all events before and after turned upon it. It made her see the Peace Corps and her whining liberal friends for the sham they were. Fonseca became her inspiration as he was her lover.

Carlos Fonseca was a fugitive from the police of three countries when he had dinner with Sally at the home of Christina Brown in Cabo Gracias a Dios. He still nursed the bruises he had received during his interrogation in a Costa Rican prison. At night, he lay naked on the mattress on the floor with a candle at his head, reading while Sally stripped and straddled his narrow hips and kneaded his back and thighs with oil. Sometimes he would read aloud to her from what he had written. She liked that—particularly when he read his poetry. He wrote not in the classical Spanish that the schools and universities taught, but in the startling, idiosyncratic Spanish dialect of the countryside, rich with slang and alive with metaphor. One poem was her favorite, and she had painstakingly translated it into English. It was just a fragment in her memory after all the years, but it began:

I have a green home by the edge of brackish water.
I have a woman waiting by the fire where night touches earth.
I have a dark child who does not know my name.
I have three scars on my belly to remember them.
God guide them to my grave after I die.

After she had rubbed him deep and warm with oil, and after the harbor sounds had settled for the night and the guitar and laughter were silent in the cantina below the stairs, and after the candle had guttered to a black nub and there was only moonlight through the caseless window, he would turn her over on her back and straddle her legs and rub the healing oil up her thighs and coat her breasts and make her pull her knees up so that he could work his fingers into her. Then they would lie side by side, his erection caught between their rocking bellies, like a hot fist against her skin. And when he entered her like that, lying beside her with her one knee up on his hip, there was no weight of a man upon her, only the probing, thick mystery that grazed her body and made her tremble. It was like making love in a dream or at a distance. It made her feel remote and separate, a million miles from Memphis and America and everything that she had ever seen or known. He satisfied her and then himself. And she lay on her side after he had gone to wash, feeling the little round pool of him inside her, knowing that if she moved or stood, he would drip away and there would be nothing at all to connect her to him and to the sultry reality of life, nothing but the oil growing tacky on her skin. She was twenty years old, and profoundly, passionately in love.

Sally settled back in the seat of the airplane as it climbed through the Miami sky, feeling the tug of gravity pressing her earthward like the great burden on her mind. And she gathered her soul inside her and raised herself against the tether of the seat belt. The cruel and powerful of Washington would not break her.

She would not surrender.

The dream would never die.

7:10 A.M. LOU BENDER DIDN'T have to look far in the *Baltimore Sun* to find what he was after. There was a two-column headline at the bottom of page one:

THREE DIE IN FIERY BLAST
AFTER SOUTH SIDE SHOOT-OUT

And there was the typical police blotter story about a SWAT team investigating a suspicious man and running into a firefight. He scanned the story. There was speculation that the assailant might have been a terrorist. The blast had incinerated his body and belongings beyond recognition. Police were combing the wreckage, trying to fix his identity. An officer on the scene was quoted as saying, "We don't know. We may never know."

In the breakfast room of his home in Bethesda, Admiral William Rausch was bent over the table, holding his head in his hands and reading the same report when the secure phone rang.

"That's your idea of taking care of things?" Bender demanded.

"All right. It wasn't what I had in mind. But, look, it worked. It's over."

"What worked? We've got nothing but a dead John Doe. We're the only ones who know his name. And how the hell can we tell anybody?"

"Okay, okay," Rausch said, and he was scrambling. "I'll admit—it isn't perfect."

"Goddamit," Bender said, and his rage was rising. "Now we've missed our chance to tie him to the Martinez killing, give Ortega a black eye, and end the FBI investigation."

"Lou, I'll handle it."

"How?"

"Leave it to me. In a day or two, we'll drop a hint in the right place. They'll run ballistics on the weapon."

"Which weapon?"

"The rifle that he used on Martinez."

"Suppose he didn't have it with him?"

"Well . . . then we've got dental records."

"How the hell will dental records tie him to the assassination?"

"Lou, please. Relax. It's handled. Leave it."

"Goddamit!" Bender said, and slammed the phone down. He was more angry with himself than with Rausch. He had known of Rausch's antipathy toward the FBI. He had regarded it as an asset. But now that mindless anger had wrecked their chances of trapping Petersen, connecting him to the assassination, and breaking the back of Eastman's call for a congressional investigation.

Lou Bender sat back in his chair and stared at the telephone on the table before him. Clearly, Rausch had to go. He had to go tonight. And Bender would have to be more careful about his choice of allies in the future. He could not again afford to forget the most important lesson Washington had taught him:

LOVE IS NEVER SO BLIND AS HATE.

7:40 A.M. STEVE CHANDLER HAD a coup. Majority Whip Harrison and Speaker O'Donnell together in the Washington news room of the *Today* show on the very morning when they were obliged to respond to Eastman's demand for a congressional investigation.

As the 7:30 segment of the broadcast moved from Bryant and Jane to John Palmer at the news desk to Willard Scott with the weather, Chandler sat staring at the feed from Washington on Monitor 6. He drank his paper cup of coffee and watched the two gray-haired politicians trying to settle their outsized butts into the uncomfortable leather chairs in *Today*'s Washington studio. He listened to the rustle of the fabric of their neckties against the clip-on microphones, and to the whispering between them. It was remarkable that even sophisticated men could sit in a television studio with

319

microphones clipped to their clothes and, simply because they were not on the air, assume no one was listening.

"I want to get this over with and get back up the Hill in a hurry," Harrison said. "What time is O'Brien coming in?"

"I think it's 10 A.M.," O'Donnell said. "Or is it 10:30?"

"That S.O.B. better have some answers. If he beats around the bush, I'll—"

"Let's cross that bridge when we come to it, Luke."

"Yeah. Sure."

The makeup technician stepped in front of the camera and applied a little powder to the forehead of each man. Then they tugged their jackets down over their paunches.

"Is my hair all right?" O'Donnell said. He was looking off, trying to catch a glimpse of himself in the floor monitor.

"Just like an old sheepdog," Harrison said.

Chandler loved watching the powerful fidget as they sat waiting for an interview to begin. It embodied what his J-school dean had said in his commencement speech: "The job of journalists is to comfort the afflicted and afflict the comfortable." Chandler thought he did at least half of that well.

Today went to commercial, and Chandler watched the men settle as the floor director counted them down. Then Bryant Gumbel introduced them and said, "Good morning, gentlemen and thanks for joining us," and went in for the kill.

"Senator Harrison," Gumbel said, "can a committee dominated by the president's own party conduct an impartial investigation into the Martinez assassination and determine if President Baker has been guilty of obstruction of justice?"

"Well, Bryant," Harrison said, "the answer is yes if a committee must be called. But we're a long way from that point."

"But the vice president is demanding an investigation. Under the circumstances, can you decline his request?"

"We intend to evaluate the merits of his allegation to determine if an investigation by the Congress is required and justified."

"Well, doesn't the lack of a proper FBI investigation suggest that the Baker administration has been engaged in—and I'm using Vice President Eastman's words here—unconscionable foot-dragging? Speaker O'Donnell?"

Sam Baker sat in the overstuffed, green chintz chair in the corner of his study on the family floor of the White House with the *Post* open on the table before him and watched the broadcast. O'Donnell was a shrewd old fox, too smart to fall into Gumbel's trap.

"Bryant, you know the FBI has many ways of conducting an investigation. Some are apparent, others are not."

"Mr. Speaker, are you saying that the vice president was wrong when he alleged that only two agents were assigned to this investigation?"

"Senator Harrison and I will be meeting with FBI Director O'Brien this morning. I think we should have his assessment of the situation before we form a judgment."

"Senator Harrison," Gumbel continued, "leaders of the opposition are saying that, for political reasons, you and Speaker O'Donnell would like to delay the start of this investigation until after the nominating convention. Is that true?"

"As a practical matter, it would be impossible to assemble a Select Committee until after the convention," Harrison said. "There are ascertainment proceedings that have to be conducted first. Then nominees have to be selected by both parties from both houses. That couldn't happen overnight under any circumstance."

"But isn't the trail to the assassin of Colonel Martinez getting colder every day?"

"Bryant," O'Donnell said, "I want to assure you—and assure the American people—that this Congress will do everything in its power to see that the killer of Colonel Martinez is brought to justice. And I want to emphasize that, if the facts support Vice President Eastman's contention that a Senate and House Select Committee is required, we will establish an impartial committee and conduct a diligent and probing investigation."

"Senator Harrison, Speaker O'Donnell . . . thank you, gentlemen, for being with us this morning."

Baker clicked the television off. The boys had come through. He was pleased—and he was also, in a peculiar way, uneasy. He was facing a maze of dilemmas, like a labyrinth filled with tricky corners and blind alleys. And it might be a maze from which there was no exit.

He could probably prevent the party from forcing him to accept Terry Fallon as his running mate. But, paradoxically, he probably could not win the general election without him.

If he pressed an investigation into the poisoning of Octavio Martinez with AIDS, reports would leak out and terrify America's allies in Latin America—and those same leaks would drive the perpetrators of the crime under cover where they might never be found. But if he failed to press the investigation and the Select Committee uncovered the poisoning, the consequences could be worse. He would have conspicuously violated his oath of office in not prosecuting the crime.

Either way, if the trail of poison led to the CIA, his administration would be disgraced and Terry Fallon would walk off with the presidential nomination.

Sam Baker knew what he needed most was time—time to sort out answers, to seek the facts, to assess his options. But he knew the web was rapidly thickening about him. And with each successive day—each day of maneuver and artifice—the strands of deceit criss-crossed until the matrix became impenetrable and dark.

The president had the power to defer, to procrastinate, to stall—even to stonewall if he had to. But Sam Baker knew what consequences would follow if he did. He had seen, firsthand, what happened when President Nixon tried to bend the law.

Sam Baker had learned a lot about government by serving with Sam Ervin on the Senate Select Committee during Watergate. He had learned that the congressional investigative process once begun, grinds on in an implacable and merciless way. And as it grinds, it throws off sparks that ignite the interest of the media. The media made the Watergate hearings into a real-life *Dallas*—so engrossing and seductive that they blotted out all else that mattered in the world. And that led to the second—and the more important consequence—that now rested heavily on Sam Baker's mind.

The disproportionate coverage of Watergate that television and newspapers disgorged had dwarfed other critical matters of state. From the day the Watergate burglars were arrested in June of 1972 to the president's resignation, only two news events broke through to the American consciousness: the Yom Kippur War of October 1973, and the resignation of Vice President Spiro Agnew.

Few Americans took notice of the Afghan coup in July of 1973 that provided the "legal" basis for the Russian invasion fifteen years later. Few understood the significance of Libya's nationalization of foreign oil companies that September. And in April, who took notice when Arab guerrillas raided an Israeli border town, starting the chain of events that would lead to an invasion and the destruction of Lebanon as a nation?

In the rare lulls that marked the Watergate hearing calendar, Sam Baker spoke out on these issues, tried to raise his colleagues on the Senate floor, tried to open the eyes of his constituents to the near and present danger. But it was no use. He was a whisper in the wind. For more than two years, the media yapped after the retreating Nixon—and the nation looked on, mesmerized, utterly unaware as the larger world changed and darkened around them. And the ultimate revelations of Nixon's methodical abuse of power—as detailed again and again by the media—left Americans alarmed over the potential for evil in the awesome office of the presidency. Sam Baker knew it would be a long time before America would feel comfortable again with a strong leader in the president's chair.

The final legacy of Richard Nixon was six years of the incompetent Gerald Ford and the obsequious Jimmy Carter.

When he ascended to the White House, Sam Baker wanted to steer a middle course, to use the "carrot and stick" to move the Americas toward elective democracies and economic development. But soon after Baker's election, it became clear that Castro was intent on using Nicaragua as a springboard for the destabilization of Central America and, eventually, Mexico itself. That realization shattered most of Baker's options. What was left to him was the Contra war in Nicaragua—an ugly and quasi-legal undertaking. But, at least it meant that Ortega's people's militia was fighting in their own mountains, not exporting revolution north across the Honduran border. Baker was a man who had come to the White House with a dream of peace on earth. And he found himself the instrument of belligerence, the captive of crisis.

He had talked about it once with Jimmy Carter, when the former president visited Washington and the two sat down to a private lunch. Carter was working as a carpenter on a Christian inner-city redevelopment program. He was lean and fit and his eyes were clear.

"What do you think?" Sam Baker had said.

"The world is a child," Carter said. "It needs patience, love, and understanding. We're short of patience."

"I'm worried about Nicaragua," Sam Baker said. "It's going sour. It'll be another Cuba if we don't stop it."

"Can you stop it?"

"I don't know. I don't like playing God."

"You should try carpentry some time."

"Is it relaxing?"

"Our Lord did that work when he was a man," Carter said.

Sam Baker was tired of playing God, tired of the presidency and its staggering burden. As his popularity in the polls declined during his third and fourth years in office, he flirted with the idea of retiring after one term as Johnson had. It was an appealing notion.

But now he was trapped. He had a congressional investigation ahead of him, Fallon pressing him from behind, and he could no longer trust the men closest to him.

Had the CIA poisoned Martinez with the AIDS virus? Who had ordered the shooting? Was he surrounded by men whose "zeal had exceeded their judgment," just as Nixon claimed to have been in 1973? And would events now take the same course, driving his administration from office in disgrace and condemning America to another cycle of soporific, impotent leadership or, what was worse, to the perilous militancy of Terry Fallon?

Sam Baker leaned forward in his chair and laced his fingers together, resting his forehead upon them. And for the first time in many, many days, he prayed.

8:00 A.M. MANCUSO GOT IN early—but there was already a yellow Advisory in his mailbox. It read: SEE ME ASAP. SCOTT. When he went up to the FBI's zone offices on the second floor, Scott was reading the paper and eating a bagel.

"Where the fuck were you last night?" Scott said, and wiped his mouth with the back of his hand.

"Hey, you missed me," Mancuso said. "Sweet." He sat on the chair in the corner and rocked it back against the wall. He didn't take off his hat.

"Where were you, asshole?"

"I went to Baltimore to see a sick friend."

"Why didn't you call in?"

"My friend died."

Scott wrapped the end of the bagel in his napkin and threw it in the wastebasket. "You're a real cut-up, Mancuso. Some day your jokes are gonna get your ass kicked the hell out of here."

"You keep telling me."

"Whatcha get in Cleveland?"

"Nothing. She's a Carmelite. I couldn't talk to her."

"So, find somebody who speaks their lingo."

"For Christ's sake, Scotty. She's a nun. Talking's against her religion."

"Gimme a break." Scott folded his newspaper and stuffed it into the wastebasket after the bagel. "Where's your asshole buddy Ross?"

"How should I know? Flying back from Miami maybe."

"Did he see Ramirez?"

"Do I look like the fucking encyclopedia?"

Scott just glared. "You know, I wish I had a way to bust you and your pension together."

"You know, I believe you."

"Six days on this thing and you guys ain't got shit." Scott poured the cold dregs of his coffee into the wastebasket.

"We got Petersen."

"What Petersen?"

"The guy that blew away Martinez."

"What about him?"

"He's in the paper."

"Where?"

"The Baltimore locals burned his ass last night."

"What!"

"Take a look in your fucking newspaper," Mancuso said and straightened his chair and got up.

Scott made a face and fished around in the wastebasket and brought out the newspaper, soaked through, stained, and dripping with coffee.

Mancuso stood over his desk. "Right there." He pointed to the bottom of the page. "There lies Petersen. A crispy critter."

"This?" Scott squinted at the runny type. Then he looked up at Mancuso. "How do you know this was Petersen?"

"I went. I saw. I kissed him goodbye."

"You were in on this?" Some of the coffee ran off the newspaper and into Scott's lap. He shouted "Fuck!" and jumped to his feet. Then he grabbed the water jug on his desk and dampened his handkerchief and started rubbing furiously at the stain on his fly.

"You keep doing that, you're gonna need glasses," Mancuso said.

"Get the fuck out of here!"

"With pleasure."

The moment the door closed behind Mancuso, Scott reached for the phone.

8:50 A.M. THE PRESIDENT WAS in conference with the ambassador to Paris, when his secretary came into the office and put the folded slip of paper on his desk. It was a sheet of Lou Bender's memo stationery with one handwritten line:

PETERSEN KILLED GUN BATTLE IN BALTIMORE CONFIRMED FBI

The president stood up.

"Tom, you'll have to excuse me."

"Yes, sir," the ambassador said. He didn't wait for a handshake. Bender came in the door as he went out.

"Well," Bender said, and he was beaming.

"If it's true, it's a miracle," the president said.

"At the very least."

"Who knows about this?"

"Nobody. I put a cork in it. May I?" Bender reached for the cigar box on the bookcase behind the president's desk.

"How on earth did they find him?" It was impossible for Baker to hide his relief. But right behind that sense of deliverance came a wave of unease and culpability. Suddenly, everything about this affair cut both ways.

"Let's just put it down to good police work." Bender bit the end of the cigar and spit it out. He took a match out of the drawer in the president's desk. "What's the difference how they found him? The main thing is, they did. That gets us off the hook—and hangs Eastman out to dry."

"They got a positive identification? There's no possibility of error?"

Bender held up his hands for silence. Then, smiling, he opened the office door. In the waiting room beyond, Henry O'Brien, the director of the FBI, put down his newspaper and stood up.

"Come in, Henry," Bender said.

He did.

And when they sat, the president said, "I understand you have good news for us."

"Yes."

"Lou tells me that your man tracked down Rolf Petersen."

O'Brien shifted in his chair. "Well. . . ."

But before the president could ask another question, Bender said, "We want to know if you have a positive ID."

"We're checking dental records now."

"But are you satisfied the man is Petersen?"

"Yes." He opened his little spiral notebook. "Our agent saw him in the parking lot before the shoot-out. Then he viewed the body in the morgue. According to our agent, there's no doubt. The man is Petersen."

"And the rifle?"

O'Brien turned a page. "He used an HK-91 automatic rifle in the shooting that preceded the explosion. It's the same type of weapon used in the Martinez assassination. We'll have a ballistics report by three o'clock this afternoon."

"But what's your sense of it? What's your assessment?"

O'Brien closed his notebook. "It's him. And it's the gun. The case is made."

Bender turned and opened his arms. "Ta-da!"

"All right," the president said. "Thank you, Henry."

O'Brien stood. And then Bender said, "Mr. President, there's a little matter of the director's appointment on the Hill. . . ."

For a moment, the president wasn't certain what he meant. Then he remembered. "Yes, that's right. You're going to appear before the congressional leadership this morning?"

"Yes, sir."

"I think the director should cancel that appointment," Bender said.

The president thought about that. A cancellation without a word of explanation would ring like a fire alarm on the Hill.

"Definitely cancel," Bender said, hopefully, and the president could see where he was going.

"All right. Yes, please, Henry. Cancel your appointment."

"With what reason?" O'Brien said.

"On instructions from the president," Bender said. "Right?" He looked at the president.

The president nodded. "All right." Clearly, Lou Bender wanted to play the element of surprise to the hilt.

But when O'Brien turned for the door, the president said, "Henry, there's something about this that bothers you."

O'Brien stood, nodding. Then he said, "Yes, sir."

"Is it something we should know?"

O'Brien put his little spiral notebook in his pocket. "There's no way our agent could have found Rolf Petersen," he said.

The president looked at Bender, and then back at O'Brien. "But he did find him."

"Yes."

"I don't understand."

"He must have had a tip," O'Brien said.

"From whom?"

"I don't know. I haven't had a chance to talk to him."

"If you ask him, will he tell you?"

"He might. Or he might not. He might have someone he has to protect."

Then Bender broke in. "I think it's results that matter here. And the plain fact is—"

"Just a moment, Lou," the president said. "If your agent had a tip—what then? What does that mean?"

"It means that someone wanted Petersen captured or dead," O'Brien said. "And couldn't or wouldn't do it himself."

"I see."

"There's something else," O'Brien said. "Whoever tipped our agent knew his name and how to reach him."

There was an ominous drift to this, and Sam Baker could see it now. "And what do you make of that?" he said softly.

"Whoever hired Rolf Petersen is in this government—or has close ties to it."

It was very quiet in the Oval Office for a moment.

327

Then Bender said, "Poppycock."

The president ignored him. "Will you see this agent today?"

"This afternoon."

"And will you call me after you speak with him?"

"Yes, sir."

"Thank you, Henry," the president said. When O'Brien went out the door, Bender said, "This changes nothing. There are a million ways that information could have been passed to the FBI. And there's no reason to believe that—"

"I'm not so sure," the president said. "What about the Secret Service man who was killed?"

Bender waved that away. "There's nothing to connect him to Martinez, except Eastman blowing wind."

"Lou—"

"Now, listen to me, Sam," Bender said. "Listen to me." He came over to the desk and leaned on it with both hands. "We have to act. We cannot sit around and wait for all the ducks to line up and be counted on this one. We have to make our suppositions. And we have to move. The clock is ticking."

"What do you propose?"

"Maximum shock value. A live press conference in prime time tonight. All three networks. And no leaks. We'll have O'Donnell and Harrison on the rostrum behind you. Shit, the press will probably think you're going to beat your breast and do a *mea culpa*." He snorted. "Then you give it to them cold-cock. Hell, we'll even get the FBI agent to stand up and take a bow." He blew out a big cloud of smoke. "Sam, we're holding all the aces again."

9:10 A.M. THE FIRST THING they did when the plane landed in Washington was to look for a newsstand. And all the way down the long tunnel to the terminal, Sally's heart was pounding so hard in her chest and her pulse was ringing so loudly in her ears that she couldn't hear the swirling sounds of the terminal around her or the metallic chatter of the public address system or feel Ross's arm under her elbow, gently sustaining her. And when he paid the vendor and took a copy of the *Washington Post* from the rack and followed the jumped story to page four, her breathing stopped completely.

There, at the bottom of the page, was the police artist's sketch of the woman seen in the bar with Steven Thomopolous. Ross held it up to the light and they stared at the drawing together.

She could see at a glance that he had been right. Perhaps it *was* hard to draw pretty people. But the extraordinary thing about the likeness was that it did look like Sally—not as she looked now, but as she had looked years ago. Her eyes followed Ross's index finger down the text of the story to the source of the sketch:

> The waiter who served the couple described the woman as in her early twenties, tall, wearing a yellow sun dress and white sweater, probably a prostitute. The hotel was hosting the annual Newspaper Advertising Bureau convention. Although the management of the Four Seasons denied—

Ross folded the paper.
"Told you," he said.
She drew a long breath.
"Actually, it's kind of flattering," he said. "Early twenties?"
"Thanks," she said. "For nothing."
"Are you going to be okay?"
"Yes. I think so." And she was already breathing easier.
"Want me to see you home?"
"No. I have to go to work."
He didn't move on. "I'll see you . . . right?"
There was such hope in his eyes and such concern that it stopped her, and they stood together among the travelers swirling around the newsstand, stood as though they were quite alone. What she saw in his eyes were things that had been missing from her life for a long time. They were things she had stopped daring to hope for. But it was a desperate time, she was fighting for survival, and she didn't know how to respond.
"David," she said. "I don't know."
"Sally—"
"Not right now," she said. "Let me go."
"Will we talk?"
"Sure."
She got up on her toes and kissed him on the cheek, and then she hurried down the hallway toward the exit while he stared after her.

She took a cab from the airport to Terry's house in Cambridge. When the Secret Service passed her through the door, she went straight to his study.

"You look terrible," was the first thing he said.

"How do you expect me to look? I—"

Then she realized that he was fully dressed. He was lounging on the couch in brown slacks, a smart patterned Turnbull shirt and dotted yellow tie, and a beige cardigan. He didn't look like a man who'd been badly wounded, who had pulled himself back from death. He looked fit and healthy.

"You're dressed," she said.

"Yes. What about it?"

"What about your wound?"

"It's better."

She looked around. The medical bag on the table by the door was missing. "And the nurses?"

"I let them go."

"But we agreed—"

He stood up. "Why don't we take a walk in the garden?"

They went in silence, out past the Secret Service men at the back door, and sat in the white wrought iron chairs under the umbrella near the pool.

"What the devil is going on?" she said.

"You're upset."

"Of course, I'm upset. Terry, the whole idea was to use your recuperation as an excuse to stay aloof from politics. To make the public starve for news of you. Until you appear on the podium at the convention beside the president, ready to lead the party."

"Yes," he said. "Well. There's been a change of plan."

"But, Terry, my God, we—why didn't you call? Why didn't you discuss it with me?"

"You were in Miami. I didn't think we should take a chance on the phones. Did you see the sketch?"

Two Secret Service men walked by. They tipped their hats and nodded. Terry and Sally smiled back, silently.

When they had passed, Terry said, "Did you see it?"

"Not a good likeness."

"Perhaps," he said. "Can your FBI friends be trusted?"

"They're more at risk than I am."

He thought about that. "I don't know. It's potentially an explosive situation."

"It's been defused."

"I don't know," he said again. "It could blow up in your face. And mine."

"I don't think so."

"I think so."

"All right, all right," she said. "I'll be careful. Now tell me what happened when you went to see the president?"

"Oh, that."

He seemed reluctant to speak of it. "Yes," she said. "That."

"Well, you know how these things go."

"No. I don't." She sat forward on her chair. "Terry, why are you shutting me out?"

"Sally, you're not listening to me. I'm trying to tell you that you're in trouble. Having you close to me right now could be dangerous. To you. To me. To all of us."

"I'm telling you there's no danger," she said. "They're looking for a girl who's half my age."

"And your FBI friends?"

"Terry, for heaven's sake. If they admit what they did, they'll lose their jobs and go to jail."

"They could use it against me."

She just stared. "Terry, how can you be so selfish? My God, for ten years I've—"

"Okay," he said. "Okay, Sally. We won't worry about it for now. All right?"

"All right. Now, tell me about the president."

Terry sat back and crossed his legs. "Well, he grilled me. You know. A lot of silly questions about international relations, domestic affairs, that kind of thing."

"And?"

"And I gave him your concepts on food stamps and establishing an investment tax credit for industrial retraining."

"What else?"

He crossed his arms and looked very satisfied with himself. "And I let him know where I stood."

Her eyes narrowed. "What does that mean?"

"I told him I didn't want the number two spot."

When she spoke her voice was an airless whisper. "You told him . . . what?"

"I told him that I didn't think he was the man to lead the party—let alone the country—for another four years. I told him he should step aside."

Sally sat, speechless.

Terry chuckled. "And I did that bit you wrote about 'Fate chose the place'—you know."

She leaned forward and held her forehead in her hand. "Oh, you stupid man. You stupid, stupid man."

Terry got up. "Sally, I think you're tired."

"Terry, you just threw away—"

"You look tired and you are tired, Sally. I think you should go home and take a rest," he said firmly.

She looked at him and shook her head. "Have you any idea, have you any conception—"

"Sally, look at the polls," he said. "We're getting stronger every day. The—"

"Polls," she said, and the word was an expectoration. "Don't you realize how polls can change? You could be a nobody like that." She snapped her fingers in his face.

He sat back. "Sally," he said, and there was an edge to his voice now. "I want you to go home and rest. When I want you here, I'll call you. Do you understand?"

The screen door banged behind them, and when she looked up, plump little Chris Van Allen was coming down the back steps of the house.

"Hey, Sally, glad you're back," he said, but something in his voice said that he wasn't.

"Don't talk to me," she said. She pushed past him and ran up the stairs.

9:30 A.M. ADMIRAL RAUSCH GOT the last new can of tennis balls from the closet behind his desk, took the freshly laundered warm-up suit from the hanger and lay it across his arm. He was heading toward the rear door when his secretary buzzed. He frowned and went back to his desk and pressed the button for the intercom.

"I'm running late, Sarah. What is it?"

"It's Mr. Bender, sir."

"Tell him I'll call him after lunch."

"He's here in the waiting room."

That startled him. In four years, Lou Bender had never once come to Langley. "All right. Send him in." He set the can of balls and the bright red-and-blue warm-ups on a chair.

When Bender came through the door, he didn't waste any time. "You son-of-a-bitch," he said.

"Nice to see you, too, Lou."

Bender came around the desk and poked a finger in his gut. "You just couldn't stand to see the FBI get the bust. What are you—crazy?"

Rausch pushed the smaller man's hand aside. "I tipped the FBI. What the hell's the matter with you? If the FBI blew it, it's their problem."

"The FBI got the bust."

"What?"

"That jerk Mancuso. He was there."

"No. I don't believe it." Rausch sat down and shook his head and began to laugh. "The Lord works in mysterious ways His wonders to perform."

"This is no joke, Bill."

"No, Lou," Rausch said, and he was getting the drift. "It isn't. And now you're going to break Eastman's balls with it."

"A press conference. Tonight."

"So the matter's closed."

"Not exactly." Bender sounded like he was sharing a confidence—but he was preparing the final trap. "Baker knows the FBI was tipped. He's asked O'Brien to identify the source. O'Brien's going to see your friend Mancuso. Will he talk?"

"Talk?"

"Will he identify the Company as the source?"

Rausch thought about that. "I don't know. The two of them go back a long way. To Chicago '68."

"Is there honor among spies?"

"Is there honor among anyone?"

Bender started to sit down. Then he saw the tennis balls and warm-ups on the chair. "What's this crap?"

"Keeping in shape, Lou. You should try it."

"Christ." Bender slapped the stuff down onto the floor. Then he sat and waited. It wasn't long before Rausch took the next step.

"Why should the president give a damn who tipped the FBI?"

Bender shrugged. "He wants to know who hired Petersen. Does that surprise you?"

"Jesus Christ," Rausch said. "Ortega hired him. He's a hit man for the Nicaraguan government. Do they have to see it on television before they'll believe it?"

That gave Bender the opening he needed. "O'Brien doesn't buy that."

Rausch set his jaw. He loathed O'Brien and the FBI. It was an old wound, one Bender could depend on. "All of a sudden, O'Brien and the FBI are your best friends," Rausch said sharply. "What are you up to, Lou? Huh?"

Bender let that slide by. He leaned forward in his chair. Now, he moved into the closing gambit. "Bill, I'm going to ask you this just once: do you know who hired Petersen?"

Rausch waved him away. "Grow up, Lou. Ortega hired him."

"Do you know that for a fact?"

"No, goddamit, I don't. How the hell could I?"

"Can you prove it?"

"Of course not. If I could, don't you think—"

"Listen to me, Bill. Listen to me carefully. What I'm asking you is—can you prove it even if you can't prove it?"

Rausch cocked his head. "What are you getting at?"

Rausch was hooked and Bender knew it. "Baker's into this," he said. "I know him. Once he sets his mind on something, he digs in and won't let go."

Rausch was visibly shaken. "What does that mean?"

"He suspects that Martinez was poisoned with AIDS. He doesn't want that to get out any more than we do. It could shake the foundations of every alliance we have in Latin America. But"—Bender paused for effect—"but he'll have to press the investigation unless. . . ."

"Unless what?"

"Unless we give him incontestable proof that Petersen was sent to kill Martinez by Ortega."

"I just told you—we have no proof."

But Bender persisted. "Let Baker hang the Martinez shooting on Ortega and the Marxists, and he can let the AIDS thing drop. Otherwise, he'll be forced to press the investigation until the whole thing's public. And you know what that means."

Rausch did, and he feared it.

Bender said, "I want you to get irrefutable evidence that Ortega hired Rolf Petersen, supplied him with weapons and transportation, and sent him to the United States for the express purpose of killing Octavio Martinez. And I want you to get it tonight."

"How, goddamit?" Rausch said. "How am I supposed to do that?"

"Bill, you proved that Khadaffi blew up the nightclub in Berlin so that we could justify the raid on Libya. If you could do that, somehow I'm confident you can do this."

When Bender left, Rausch pressed the button for the intercom.

"Yes, sir?"

"Sarah, I need to speak with Fowler."

"He's not in yet, sir."

"Put him on the beeper."

In less than a minute, the phone rang.

"Fowler here."

"I need the poker game. As soon as possible."

"Mittleman is lecturing at Annapolis. And Boden's in Charleston. His mother is dying."

"Get them back here. Right now. When can you have the whole group assembled?"

"Six o'clock."

"Four o'clock."

"Is it that bad?"

"Worse."

9:50 A.M. MANCUSO WAS JUST putting on his jacket when Ross came through the door of the office, carrying his suitcase.

"I came straight from the airport."

"Come on. Scott just called."

They caught the elevator down to the second floor.

"What about Petersen?" Ross said.

"Dead."

"No shit?"

"A SWAT team got him."

"A SWAT team?"

"Tipped off."

"By who?"

"Santa Claus. How the hell should I know?"

They got off on the second floor.

"Anything in his room?"

"Burned. The Baltimore locals are very thorough. When they fuck something up, they fuck it nine ways from Sunday. Whatcha get out of the girl?"

"Zip," Ross said. "She's a dreamer. She loves Fallon. He can do no wrong."

"He just likes it wrapped in leather, that's all."

"Huh?"

Mancuso stopped outside the door of Scott's office. "Did you fuck her?" he said.

Ross set his jaw. "What's it to you?"

"Nothing." Then he looked Ross in the eye. "Did you?"

"No," Ross said angrily, and pushed him out of the way and opened the door.

"Now what about Ramirez?" Scott said to Ross.

"El flako grande. He's out there where there's no area code and no zip code."

"And Petersen's roast beef. Like I said before, you guys ain't got shit."

"We would, Scotty," Mancuso said. "Only our witnesses keep dying."

"What the hell is that supposed to mean?"

"We're not dealing a full deck."

"That's a cop-out, Mancuso. Just a fucking cop-out."

"Sure it is."

"You guys get me something or I'll pull you off this case and you can go chase crack in Harlem."

"Is that a promise or a threat?" Mancuso said. "Come on." He nodded to Ross.

"Just a minute, asshole," Scott said. He held up a sheet of paper. "Mancuso, I got instructions here to send you to the White House."

"Who? Me?"

"Seven-thirty tonight. In Mr. Bender's office." Scott stood up and handed him the sheet of paper with the presidential seal. "And for Christ's sake, go home and change your suit and don't go over there looking like a piece of shit."

"You kidding or what?" Mancuso stared at the paper and Ross craned his neck and gaped over his shoulder. It was for real.

"Hey," Scott said, and he was sneering at the irony of it. "You're a fucking hero, don't you know. The lone agent who tracked the killer of Martinez and fought him to his death. The great, shit-kicking Joe Mancuso."

Mancuso glared at him. "Hey, Scotty. Did I tell you? You got coffee on your pants."

When they went upstairs to their office, Ross said, "Jesus, the White House."

Mancuso balled the note with the presidential seal and threw it into the wastebasket behind his desk. Then he sat down and hung his head, and he was bitter and angry. "It's a crock, kid. Can't you see the whole world is a fucking crock?"

Ross looked back at the wastebasket. "Joe, you really suck, you know?" He bent over and plucked the letter from among the refuse and sat down at his desk, and tried to smooth out the wrinkles.

"They're just using us, you dumb son-of-a-bitch," Mancuso said. "Don't you see that?"

Ross looked down admiringly at the smeared ink, the cracks in the presidential seal. "You don't care about anything, do you, Joe?"

"Gimme that," Mancuso said, and pulled it away from him. He read it loud enough so that whoever was bugging the office and recording their conversations couldn't miss a word.

Agent Joseph F. Mancuso, you are hereby directed to report to the
White House and present yourself at the office of Mr. Louis
Bender, tonight, Monday, August 15, 1988, at seven-thirty in the
evening, to meet with the president and receive a citation for your
outstanding contribution to the rule of law in the United States of
America.

"Now don't that fucking beat all?" He looked about, as though waiting
for applause.

Ross said, "Joe, I never realized what an unhappy man you are."

"Aw, fuck." Mancuso dropped into the chair behind the pile of crap
covering his desk. Ross got up and took the note out of his hand and put it
into a manila folder and placed it on top of the pile.

"Thanks," Mancuso said.

"Forget it," Ross said. "What are you doing today?"

"I got an appointment. You?"

"I want another look at those tapes."

"What tapes?"

"The tapes of the assassination."

"Hey, give it a rest. For Christ's sake, the man's dead. Case closed.
Okay?"

"Not by me."

"Hey, Dave," Mancuso said. "When are you going to stop playing Boy
Scout and jerking yourself off?"

Ross stopped dead in his tracks and reached down and got a fistful of
Mancuso's jacket. "Look, Joe, I listened to your sad story about how the
Bureau handed you the shitty end of the stick. And I'm real sorry that your
whole career was a mistake. And I know you just want to get through the
next three months and fade into the sunset. But I want to crack this thing.
And I keep thinking that there's something we've missed that would break
it wide open. And if you don't give a damn, at least get out of my way and
let me do my job!" He threw the fistful of his coat back at him.

Mancuso stared. And for a moment there was a look in his eyes that
might have been affection. Then he laughed. "Aw, don't be a pussy."

"Fuck you," Ross said. And this time there was no doubt that he really
meant it.

10:00 A.M. STRANGE. WASHINGTON LOOKED strange to her this morning as the cab threaded its way to Georgetown from Terry's house. Sally looked out the window at the passing buildings, and for the first time in a long time, the buildings seemed inscrutable, yielding no secrets. For the first time, she felt doors in Washington silently closing against her.

When she had come to Washington in 1976, she quickly learned that this was a city of insiders. Only insiders could get things done. Others sat, cooling their heels in reception rooms all over town—or waiting for their petitions to grind through the sluggish mill of the bureaucratic system. But insiders had contacts. They could push buttons. They had Rolodexes stuffed with private line and home phone numbers. They knew secretaries by their first names, wives and husbands by their last affairs, and they could spot a personalized license plate in front of the wrong address by the dawn's early light. Insiders had relationships. In a secretive city of professional liars, those who had relationships nominally told each other the truth.

It was hard as hell to get inside from outside—but it was no trouble at all to slip through the grate and find yourself outside when you thought you were safely in. There was a mysterious current that connected everyone in the federal village, and signaled who was in or—on the same day, so it seemed—told everyone that so-and-so had fallen out.

Today, for some reason, Sally had that outsider feeling. And driving back across the city, she suddenly realized why. When she had arrived in Miami, the desk clerk had handed her a stack of telephone messages— urgent "Please call's" from *Time, Newsweek,* the *Washington Post,* CNN, CBS, and a long list of others—even *The Christian Science Monitor.* But when she'd come back from having dinner with Ross, there were no messages in her box. There were none yesterday morning—and none today. She'd been so preoccupied that she hadn't realized the deluge had stopped. And it happened the way all things happen in Washington: suddenly, without warning, and with numbing finality.

She paid the cab driver, took her heavy suitcase, and, despite its weight, ran up the steps to her front door. She dropped the case inside, tossed her hat and bag and sun glasses on the couch, grabbed the phone and punched a number.

"This is Audrey Pierce."

"Aud? It's Sally."

"Hello, honey. How's your ass?"

"Sagging. You?"

Audrey had been hired on the *Post* the same week as Sally. They had learned the ropes—and fought off the male reporters—together. They had a relationship.

"The same. What's cooking?"

"That's why I was calling you. Nobody's beating down my door for breaks on Fallon. What's the story?"

"We're talking to Chris. Word's around you're easing off."

Sally could barely get the words out. ". . . easing off?"

"Yeah. Moving up or something."

Sally thought a moment. "Can you forget we had this phone call?"

"Which call?"

"I love you, Aud."

"Me, too, sugar."

Sally hung up and dropped down onto the arm of the sofa. A kind of cold soreness poured through her. She didn't know whether to laugh or cry or get drunk or throw something heavy through a window. It was worse than she had expected. Terry had told Baker that he wouldn't accept the nomination for vice president. And Chris had made his move. And the District of Columbia police were looking for her, even though they didn't know it.

Everything was closing in and she felt not only trapped but cornered. It was three days before the convention would begin to assemble in St. Louis, three days before the gavel called the party to order to nominate a president and vice president. She was running out of options. She was running out of time. But she knew that, no matter how much it hurt, there was one luxury she couldn't afford—feeling sorry for herself. She stood up, tried to shake it off, and went to the foyer to collect the mail that had piled up behind the slot while she was away.

There were the usual bills and flyers, and one sheet of photostat paper, the kind the wire services use to transmit pictures. It was folded over and, oddly, unstamped—as though someone had pushed it through the mail slot. The slick side had a copy of the police artist's sketch of the young prostitute who had been seen with Steven Thomopolous, a woman in her early twenties, with long hair and high cheekbones and wide-set, pretty eyes. On the back of the photostat, someone had scribbled one line with a ballpoint pen. It read:

I THINK WE'D BETTER TALK. TOMMY

11:15 A.M. WELL, MANCUSO HAD to say one thing for the CIA: they sure knew how to spend the taxpayers' money. The FBI had a firing range at Quantico—an old sandlot thing with a lot of dead trees and a combat street with housefronts that had so many holes in them they played music when the breeze blew by. But the CIA now—they had a goddam gun club. A whole range for trap and skeet—in case the United States was ever attacked by ducks. And fucking Wilson really dressed like a gun club fashion plate. Mancuso felt a little foolish standing out on the firing pad of the skeet range in his baggy old Sears suit.

Wilson called "Pull!" and a loud spring thunked in the tower and a terra-cotta disc flew out toward the trees at the far end of the field. He fired one shot and the clay target disintegrated.

"You're a fucking killer, Wilson," Mancuso said. "I always knew that."

Wilson didn't turn around. He broke the action of the gun, ejected the smoking orange shell, and inserted another.

"Be brief, Joe," he said. "It's hot." Then he shouted, "Pull!" and another clay pigeon flew and he fired and broke that one, too.

Mancuso went over to the rack at the rear of the concrete pad and picked up a double-barreled 12-gauge. "You mind?"

Wilson broke the action and ejected the spent shell. Then he hung the gun over his arm and stepped back. "Be my guest."

Mancuso took a shell from the frame, put it in the left-hand chamber of the gun and stepped up. "This how you do it?"

Wilson craned his neck to watch.

"Pull!" Mancuso called. But the target flew through his field of vision so quickly that he fired at least six feet behind it and the kick of the shotgun against his shoulder almost made him lose his balance.

"Something like that," Wilson said.

"I visited your friend Petersen last night," Mancuso said as they changed places.

"Yeah? Where?"

"In the Baltimore city morgue."

"Pull!" Wilson called. A pigeon flew, he fired, and the pigeon shattered into dust. He ejected the spent shell and stepped back.

"Who got him?" Wilson said.

"Local SWATs." Mancuso chambered a shell and stepped up. "Burned him to a crisp. Pull!'' He fired—but the clay pigeon flew serenely on, curving in a soft wide arc. It fell, untouched, into the edge of the forest.

"Shit," Mancuso said and stepped back.

Wilson took the firing position. "He was a real mean fuck."

"So you said."

"Had to end that way. Pull!"

This time, two clay pigeons broke from the tower. Wilson fired twice and both targets burst into red dust. He stepped back alongside Mancuso.

"Did Petersen shoot good?" Mancuso said.

Wilson broke his gun, popped the two steaming shells.

"The best."

"Better than you?"

"Nobody shoots like a guy who kills for a living."

Mancuso put two shells in the twin chambers of his gun and stepped to the head of the pad. "Pull!" he shouted. He fired twice and missed twice.

"You don't shoot worth shit," Wilson said.

Mancuso ejected the spent shells. "I'm a thinker, not a hitter."

That made Wilson laugh. But when he stepped up to the firing position, Mancuso said, "Who tipped the locals?"

Wilson stopped with his shotgun halfway to his shoulder. "I figured a thinker like you would have all the answers."

"The Company tip them off?"

"Not the Company, Joe. The Company doesn't call the cops. That's not neat. It's important to be neat. Pull!"

He fired twice and broke both birds, but when he came back to the gun rack, Mancuso didn't move up to the firing line.

"You tell anyone else where he was?"

"Didn't have to," Wilson said. "Whoever hired him already knew."

Mancuso looked at him. Wilson touched the rim of his amber shooting glasses, pushed them back up his nose.

"You set me up, you fuck," Mancuso said quietly.

Wilson broke his gun, ejected the spent shells, and inserted two more. "Petersen was an embarrassment, Joe. He was an embarrassment to us and an embarrassment to his boss. We were all hoping you'd close his account. Apparently, somebody got impatient."

He stared at Mancuso, smiling. And Mancuso wanted nothing so much as to put his fist through Wilson's face.

"Who hired him?" Mancuso said.

Wilson shrugged. "Don't know." He snapped the action of his shotgun closed on the two fresh shells. "But if I were you, I'd sure find out how they knew you were on the way."

341

NOON "It's more than awkward, Sam," O'Donnell said. "It's got the whole Hill in an uproar."

They were sitting in the president's private dining room on the second floor of the White House and the table was laid for three.

"I'm sorry about that," the president said. "It can't be helped. Will you have some lunch?"

"Lunch? At a time like this?!"

The door opened and Lou Bender came in.

"Good morning, Mr. Speaker."

"Lou," O'Donnell said. "Lou, tell the president he cannot cancel an appearance of the director of the FBI before a meeting of the congressional leadership without an explanation."

But Bender merely smiled, sat, and said, "What's for lunch?"

"Am I in a madhouse?" O'Donnell polished off his martini.

"Another?" the president asked.

"Yes!"

The president rang the little crystal bell and his steward entered. "Michael, the Speaker will have another martini—dry, a twist of lemon."

"Yes, sir." He went out.

"Do I detect a note of levity?" O'Donnell said. "Is something that I'm saying funny?"

The president and Bender exchanged a smile.

"All right. What is it?" O'Donnell said.

"The FBI found the man who shot Martinez."

"What!" O'Donnell looked back and forth between them. "Where's that drink?"

The door opened and the steward brought in the frosted glass on a silver tray, set it before O'Donnell, and went out.

O'Donnell held up the glass as though it were an offering. "Thank God, His Holy Mother, St. Patrick, and St. Jude," he said and drained half of it. When he put it down, he said, "Sam, we're back in business."

"Lou," the president said.

Bender took the floor. "I've arranged a press conference for eight o'clock tonight. Three networks. The whole shebang. We feel that you and Harrison should be on the rostrum."

"Delighted," O'Donnell said.

"Not a word until then," Bender said. "We'll let the press speculate. It'll drive them nuts."

O'Donnell rubbed his hands together. "Ah, sweet revenge. Eastman will have to quit. You can appoint Fallon and go to the convention with the ticket all in place."

But the president didn't respond.

"Now don't tell me you don't want Fallon," O'Donnell said.

"I didn't say that."

"Then you'll take him?"

"I didn't say that either."

"Now, listen, Sam, don't be a reluctant bridegroom. With you and Fallon on one ticket, the convention will be a boat ride. Without that, it'll be a donnybrook. Say you'll take Fallon and let's get on with it."

"No."

"Why not?"

"I have my reasons."

"Such as?"

The president sighed. "Charlie, would you believe me if I told you that, under it all, Terry Fallon is a warmongering fanatic with a messiah complex?"

O'Donnell looked to Bender. "Lou, for Pete's sake."

But Bender only shrugged and opened his hands.

"I didn't think you would," the president said, "but I will offer you a deal?"

O'Donnell perked up.

"I'll go this far," the president said. "I'll consider Terry Fallon. But I'll consider not just the vice president he'll make, but the president he might become. Will you do the same?"

O'Donnell cocked his head and looked at the president from under that shock of white hair. "Sam, what are you talking about?"

"I think you know what I'm talking about."

They were quiet a while, the three of them, just sitting there in silence.

Then the president said, "I know O'Brien consulted you before the FBI approved ABSCAM for Weatherby."

O'Donnell kept right on smiling and Bender watched him and marveled. They said that O'Donnell had the best poker face in politics, and they were right. "Yes, he did that," O'Donnell finally said.

"And you approved the sting?"

"Why not? The man was a crook. He had no place in Congress. That's all there was to it."

"Not quite, Charlie," the president said.

"What else could there be?" O'Donnell looked as innocent as a cherub.

"I want to know if you encouraged Fallon to go to O'Brien with his allegations."

O'Donnell snorted, but the president went on. "I want to know if there was a deal to get Weatherby out of the Senate and Fallon into it."

"And what if there was?"

"Was there?"

"Sam . . . Sam." O'Donnell said and sighed. "When Governor Taylor appointed Fallon to fill Weatherby's unexpired term, the party gained a seat in the Senate without a primary, without an election, and without spending one dime of campaign money. Where's the dishonor in that?"

"Charlie, I'm asking you a question. Did you make a deal with Terry Fallon to put him into the Senate if he gave his evidence on Weatherby to the FBI?"

O'Donnell was still smiling, but the luster had gone out of his eyes. "Sam, you run the White House. I run the Congress. We'll both answer to God and our constituents for our sins. Let's leave it at that."

Lou Bender reached over and picked up the crystal bell. It summoned the steward and ended the round.

12:20 P.M. WHEN MANCUSO GOT back, Ross was hunched over his desk, his eyes glued to the video playback monitor, his left hand on the remote control and his right hand scribbling notes. He was wearing his headphones and didn't look up. On the desk before him was a three-foot strip of white cardboard divided by blue crayon lines into seven segments identified with large red numbers one through seven. In each of the first six squares lay one of the six brass cartridge casings from the assassination. The seventh square contained the cartridge that had been painted black. It looked like a grade-school science project and Mancuso shook his head and sneered. That made Ross look up.

"What do you want?" he said, and slipped the earphones down around his neck.

"Nothin'." Mancuso sat down and scanned the mounds of papers on his desk for anything that might look unfamiliar. "Anybody call?"

"Nope."

"Any mail?"

"It's in the in-box." Ross pointed to the filing cabinet behind the door.

Mancuso screwed his head around and looked. On top of the cabinet behind the door sat a new over/under wire in- and out-box with a double tray. The left set was labeled ROSS. The right set was blank. "Now, what the fuck is that?" Mancuso asked.

"That is how I mean to find my mail every morning from now on. Instead of digging through your pile of crap."

"Touchy," Mancuso said. "He's very touchy."

"Leave it, Joe."

Mancuso lit a cigarette. "Where'd you say you traced that stuff from the army?"

"What's it to you?"

"Nothin'. Just curious." He puffed and leaned back in his chair.

Ross studied him—a dumpy, aging flatfoot with the two ends of his necktie lying wrinkled and apart on his shirtfront and one wing of his collar turning up. His Benrus watch had a crystal so scratched that he could barely read the hands. His dun-colored hair was graying and there were age spots on his brow. Soon, Joe Mancuso would be another discard of the nation, a forgotten GS pensioner, sitting on an orange crate against a brick wall in Miami or Brooklyn or St. Petersburg, endlessly thumbing the newspapers, looking up and down the street for conversation. They would talk about him for a long time after at Gertie's Bar—talk about Joe Mancuso, the dour dick who hated his work and his life and liked his bourbon and got called to the White House at the end of his career to get a commendation that he hadn't earned and didn't want—a reward for doing nothing, for being in the wrong place at the wrong time. It was the capper to a career that was full of wrong turns and wrong times and wrong sides. Ross looked at him, sitting there at the threshold of old age and abandonment, and he could feel no anger toward him. Only pity.

"What are you going to do after you retire?" Ross said gently.

"Huh?"

"You got any plans after you retire, Joe?"

"What's it to you?"

Ross stared at him, rebuffed. "It's nothing to me, Joe. Not a fucking thing." He reached for his headset.

"You didn't tell nobody we had a line on Petersen, did you?" Mancuso said.

But Ross had already put on the headphones. He didn't hear what Mancuso said, and, even if he had, he wouldn't have answered.

2:25 P.M. SALLY HAD TORN the photostatic picture into tiny pieces. Then she had taken a hot bath and brewed herself a cup of decaf, and mixed it with a tablespoon of whisky. When her nerves were settled, she put on her pink cotton robe and called Tommy Carter. That was just before noon.

"You're back," he'd said.

"Yes."

"How about lunch? Maison Blanche at one?"

"Well, er . . . no, thanks. I'm a little tired from the trip. Thought I might stay in today."

"I figured that," he'd said. "I'll come over about two-thirty."

"Tommy, I've got a bunch of things I'm working on. Terry's speeches for the—"

"I'll see you at two-thirty. Don't worry. I can only stay a minute. Got a three-thirty deadline. *Ciao,* baby." Then he'd hung up.

Now, through the curtains at the front windows of her living room, she saw Tommy coming up the steps to her door. He was carrying a manila folder and she could hear that he was whistling.

When the doorbell rang, she stood a moment, composing herself. Then she drew a long breath and opened the door.

"Well," he said, and came in and took his jacket off and dropped down on the sofa. "How was Miami?"

"Uneventful."

"Too bad. You'd be amazed at what's been happening up here."

"I've heard."

"Vice president screaming for the blood of the president. Congress in an uproar. Did you know that Baker's going to address the nation at 8 P.M. tonight?"

She was startled. "No. . . ."

"People are saying he's going to tell all about the Martinez affair. Or maybe resign." Tommy glanced at his watch. "I've got to get back to the office in a minute. You got anything to drink around here?"

She went to the kitchen and got him some Canadian Club on the rocks. And while she was doing that, she realized that everyone in town probably knew that Baker was going on television that night. Everyone but her. And she realized that neither Terry nor Chris nor any of the networks had bothered to call her. And she knew that unless she acted quickly, the doors of Washington would shut tight against her, now and forever.

"Won't you join me?" he said when she handed him the glass.

"No."

"Suit yourself." He drank. "How'd you like your picture? I thought they missed the hair. Was your hair tied back that night?"

"What picture?"

"The picture I sent you. The picture of the woman who was with the Secret Service guy before he died."

She forced a laugh. "Don't be ridiculous. That wasn't me."

"Let's not kid each other, Sally." He opened the folder. Inside was a photoprint of the police artist's sketch. Unlike the stat that he had sent her, this drawing had the tones of her skin and hair, the soft shadows under her cheekbones, the warmth of her eyes. "This is the girl I lived with in Lagrimas," Tommy said. "This is the girl I loved."

He said that with such finality—and with such a spike of passion—that it startled her. But when she gathered herself, she said, "It's not true. I wasn't anywhere near that hotel that night."

"Where were you?"

"Here."

"With who?"

Two days ago, she could have said, "With Chris." But she knew she couldn't say that now. "Alone," she finally said.

Tommy closed the folder. He sat back. "You've been a reporter. You know how a reporter's mind works. A reporter sees two people together—people who shouldn't be together. And he asks himself, what are they talking about? What could they be talking about? Now, you and a guy from the Secret Service—what could you be talking about late at night in a hotel bar?"

"You're wasting your time. I wasn't there."

"Suppose . . . suppose Martinez wasn't killed by a lunatic foreign terrorist the way they're saying. Suppose Martinez wasn't the target at all. Suppose the target was Senator Terry Fallon," he said.

"That's absurd."

"Is it? Wouldn't that explain why the FBI wasn't all over this case? Wouldn't that explain why the Secret Service was into it? Wouldn't that explain why you were sitting in a hotel bar—and why the guy you were with got his brains blown out an hour later?"

"Oh, you're talking rot," she said and started to get up.

He caught her wrist. "You know, Sally, I could make a pretty good case that this whole thing is a conspiracy to protect Terry Fallon and get him the vice presidential nomination so that Baker can walk off with a second term."

"Tommy, I'm not going to sit here and listen to this." She pulled her wrist free and stood up.

"Maybe you'd rather hear it on the news?"

It was the threat she had been expecting—and she was ready for him. "What you're saying isn't news, it's fiction."

"It sure reads like news." He opened the manila folder again and handed her two typewritten sheets of yellow paper. She scanned the first page and blinked. "Sit down, my love," he said, and patted the cushion on the couch beside him.

Under the bold heading *Backgrounder* were 400 words of dirt, conjecture, and speculation. Her eye hung on the operative sentences:

Law enforcement officials who declined to be named believe the
mysterious woman seen with Thomopolous minutes before his
death may have been Sally Crain, press aide to Senator Terry
Fallon, who was assisting in the Secret Service investigation.
D.C. police may subpoena Miss Crain for questioning in the
murder.

"What a load of filth!" She threw the papers in his lap. "No network
would carry that. And no self-respecting newspaper would print it."

"Do they have to?" He smiled and shuffled the papers back into the
manila folder.

She knew that he was right. A story didn't have to be printed to be
damaging. Every big story starts with a rumor. And a background report
like that one, filed from the network's Washington bureau, was not intended for air. But it would set all the muckraking minds in the network
newsroom spinning the moment it came out of the telecopier. And it
wouldn't be long before someone picked up the phone and called the D.C.
police and asked if they were really going to bring Sally Crain in for
questioning. Of course, the police wouldn't have heard of Sally Crain—
but a call from the network would make them wonder if they should have.
And it wouldn't be long before she was called in for questioning and the
rumor would have turned into reality. She sat on the couch, shaken,
desperate.

"You . . . you wouldn't file that," she said. "Tommy, you wouldn't."

He leaned toward her and there was an angry little smirk in his
eyes. "You played me like a fish on the Fallon interview. Didn't
you?"

She put her hands in her lap and pressed her arms close to her body and
tried to control her trembling.

"Didn't you?" he said again, and his voice was dark.

"All right, yes."

"And you picked me because you knew I cared about you. Didn't you?"

It was true and she couldn't deny it. She had picked his network because
she knew that he still wanted her and probably always would. And she
knew that would make him more vulnerable. She had wept for shame about
it once, and now she might again.

"Yes," she said. "Tommy, I'm sorry. I know I—"

"Oh, I understand." He put his arm gently across her shoulders.

Her eyes were damp. "Do you?"

"Of course."

"I didn't mean to—"

"I know," he said. "But I think it's time we reconsidered our relationship. Don't you?"

"Reconsidered . . . ?"

He raised her face with his fingertips and kissed her once, very lightly on the lips. She stared at him. And then he began to unbuckle his belt.

"I think it's time we reached an understanding," he said. He unzipped his fly. "Don't you?"

"Tommy, no. Please. I can't."

He reached through the fly of his boxer shorts and lifted himself out. "Don't be shy. You used to like to do this once." He pushed her head down toward his lap.

"No," she said. "No. Please."

But he pushed himself against her mouth and reluctantly she took him, and when she breathed it was the sweaty, musky smell she remembered from long ago.

"There," he said and took her hand and curled her fingers around him and took his own saliva and made himself wet. She was leaning over on her side, half-sitting, half-lying on the couch now. He reached down and flipped back the skirt of her robe and pawed her thighs apart. "There," he said. "Let me see it. Don't be shy." And when she let her thighs sag, he made a V with his fingers and teased her apart. Then he moaned. "Pretty," he said, and stroked her. "So pretty. . . ." And then she felt the jerky little spasms, and she gagged and coughed and almost spit up.

"Oh, my," he said, and leaned her back against the couch. "We're a little out of practice." She lay back, wiping the back of her hands across her mouth, gasping to catch her breath as he adjusted his clothes. "This will be our little secret for a while." He stood up and took his folder and his jacket. "Now I have to run. But I'll stop by tomorrow around lunchtime. You wear something sexy underneath. Right?"

She lay back, her eyes closed, trembling all over with disgust and degradation.

"By the way," he said. "Did you know Fallon's accepted our invitation for an interview?"

That made her open her eyes.

He stopped to look back at her from the door. "Thursday at eight. Hell of a time slot."

She sat staring.

"Oh, you didn't know. Gee, you're a little out of touch. Better get back into the swing of things, Sally. Wouldn't want to miss the fun—would you?"

When he closed the door behind him, it was as if the whole house shook.

3:10 P.M. WHEN MANCUSO WAS called up to Director O'Brien's office, he figured it had something to do with the White House invitation bullshit and how he should get his shoes shined or not pick his nose before he shook hands with the president. O'Brien's secretary, Miss Tuttle, looked up from her typing and glared at Mancuso when he came into the reception room. She looked just about as glad to see him as he was to be standing there.

"What do you want, Agent?"

"He wants to see me," Mancuso said.

"Over there." She nodded toward the couch and picked up the phone. "Agent Mancuso to see you, sir. Yes, sir."

As Mancuso started to sit down, she snapped, "Don't sit there and keep the director waiting."

Mancuso almost fell on his face trying to sit down and stand up at the same time. "Make up your mind, will ya?"

But she just pressed the button that unlocked the director's door and turned away with a toss of her hair.

Behind her back, Mancuso gave her the finger.

"I saw that," she said without looking at him.

Mancuso looked around, but there wasn't a mirror in sight. "Yeah? How'd you see it?"

"I know you. You . . . ruffian." She went back to her typing.

Mancuso pushed the door open and stood at the end of Director O'Brien's long, wood-paneled office. Blinky O'Brien had always been a square, old-fashioned duck, and it didn't surprise Mancuso that he had worn-out foreign rugs when he could have had real carpets.

O'Brien got up and came around from behind his desk. "Joe," he said, and held his hand out, blinking like always.

"Hiya, boss."

They shook.

"Sit anywhere." O'Brien indicated a pair of leather armchairs. "Want a Coke? Or something stronger?"

"Thanks. I just ate."

O'Brien took the other chair, opened a cigarette box on the table between them. "Smoke?"

"I got." Mancuso tapped one from the pack in his pocket and lit up.

"Well." O'Brien put his hands on his knees and rubbed them. "We're marking a big one Case Closed thanks to you, Joe."

"Didn't do much." Mancuso didn't like it when any of his supervisors were nice to him. It always put him on his guard. And for the director of the FBI to be offering him Cokes and smokes and asking him about the price of peas really put his dukes up.

"It's nice," O'Brien said. "This honor and distinction. Coming to you at this time in your career. It sort of leaves you with a sweet taste, doesn't it?" He was blinking a million fucking miles an hour and Mancuso knew he was being set up.

"Yeah. Exactly."

"But, you know, I'm curious." O'Brien was trying like hell to sound off-hand.

"Yeah? What?"

"I'm curious about how you could pinpoint Petersen in Baltimore like that. I mean—" He shrugged. "Even giving credit where credit is due . . . You'll admit, it's an amazing piece of detective work."

"I had a tip," Mancuso said.

O'Brien blinked and looked at him, surprised that Mancuso had no false pride, startled that he was so matter-of-fact.

"Hey, you know I got a tip. You gotta know that. Right?"

"Well, sure." O'Brien tried to recover his footing.

"So, that's it." Mancuso puffed on his cigarette and looked around. When you got used to it, the place was a real nice office.

"Look, Joe." O'Brien ran his hand back through his hair. "I'm sorry I have to do this. But I've got to ask you. About the tip. Where did it come from?"

Mancuso shrugged. "Guy I know."

"Someone you have to protect?"

"Not necessarily."

O'Brien waited a moment. But when Mancuso didn't volunteer, he said, "Will you tell me who it was?"

"Not right now, boss."

O'Brien leaned back in his chair. "Joe, you've been here a long time. You know we've got policies. We've got rules."

"Yeah, I know all about the rules."

"This is a national security case. There are no protections for informants on this one."

"Say, I meant to ask you," Mancuso said. "You wired my office. Didn't you?"

O'Brien just blinked and stared.

"And you had my partner tailed in Miami."

O'Brien looked like he was going to answer and then didn't.

"Look, I'll make you a deal. For old time's sake," Mancuso

said. "You tell me who you bugged us for. I tell you who tipped me on Petersen."

"If you're making a joke, it isn't funny," O'Brien said.

"Okay, okay," Mancuso said. "If that don't suit you, how about this?" He leaned forward and spoke very softly. "You tell me who it was, or when I see the president tonight, I tell him the whole yarn—AIDS, wires, the Secret Service guy—the whole pastafazool."

O'Brien started. "For Christ's sake, man. That was you at the Four Seasons?"

"Hey, come on, Blinky. We were casing the guy's room. He walked in and shot himself in the fight."

"Jesus, Mary, and Joseph. . . ." O'Brien looked like he was already reading the headlines.

"Hey, hey—not to worry," Mancuso said. "The guy was doing an illegal investigation. He was assaulting one of our witnesses. If it ever got tried, it'd be thrown out."

O'Brien set his jaw. "Look, Joe, old times, the rest of it—they don't count for anything right now. I need to know who tipped you on Petersen." Mancuso didn't doubt the earnestness in his voice. "It's important. It's important all the way around."

"It's the White House, isn't it?" Mancuso said. "The guy who was sitting here when you put us on the job. What's-his-name—Bender. The guy who works for the president. Tell me I'm lying."

O'Brien leaned back and blew a breath and clasped his hands behind his head. "Joe, let me ask you a question. Do you care about the Bureau? Do you care about what we stand for?"

"What do we stand for?" Mancuso said bitterly. "Everything we were doing, everything we said. It was all going somewhere before we were. They knew we were heading to Beckwith's house. Somebody slid in and blew him and his whole family away."

"Joe, look," O'Brien said.

"You look!" Then he caught himself and didn't show his temper. Instead, he spoke very softly. "Jesus, Blinky, don't you see what you did?"

O'Brien didn't answer him. He looked away as though he weren't even listening.

"I thought it was all gonna be different when Hoover died," Mancuso said. "I thought this place was gonna, you know, *be* something. I thought it was gonna be like a clean place to work. I didn't think it would end up the same old shit pile. You shouldn't let 'em do it, boss."

O'Brien sat a moment, silent.

Mancuso opened his hands like he was going to say something else. But then he couldn't find the words. O'Brien got up and walked to his desk, pushed his chair back, and sat down.

They sat like that a while at opposite ends of the office, O'Brien behind his desk, Mancuso in the leather armchair.

Finally, Mancuso said, "Aw, shit," and crushed out his cigarette. "Who the hell cares?"

He got up and went to the door. And when he looked back, O'Brien was still behind the huge oak desk, his head turned away, his eyes staring at the floor, blinking like he was trying to remember something.

"For Christ's sake, Blinky, it was the Company," Mancuso said. "Who the hell did you think it was?"

He went out and shut the door behind him.

3:50 P.M. ADMIRAL RAUSCH UNLOCKED the door at the rear of his office and stepped into his private elevator. He pressed #868# on the keypad set into the front steel panel and the door hissed shut and the elevator began to descend. After Lou Bender had left his office that morning, Rausch had canceled all his appointments and waited. He had read the paper and looked out the window at the Langley woods and paced. But most of all, he had waited for four o'clock and the poker game.

At the lowest level, the elevator doors hissed open and two Marine sentries at the entrance to the corridor braced. "As you were," Rausch said, and went down the corridor.

There were six men sitting at the round table in the conference room when he came down the two last stairs. They were called the "poker game" because, with Rausch, they were seven— and because they set the ante and made the wagers and figured the cards that America held against its enemies in any confrontation.

There were three deputy directors—Fowler, Operations; Alexander Mittelman, former vice chairman of the Department of Physics at MIT, now Science and Technology; Hastings Brown, Intelligence, and a master cryptologist. The fourth man was a member of Brown's staff—Carl Boden, director of the Office of Imagery Analysis. Then there was Lewin Vander Pool, former Sterling Professor of Philosophy at Princeton, now director of the Office of Global Issues. The sixth was Jim Renwick, head of the Latin American desk. They were not all section chiefs; two were actually rather junior members of the hierarchy. But what they had in common was that they were, by consensus, the six smartest and most cold-blooded men in the Company.

"Gentlemen," Admiral Rausch said, and sat down in the empty chair beside the console that held the red telephone to the president.

There was some shuffling. Then there was silence.

"It is critical to the administration and to the Company that we know who hired Rolf Petersen to kill Octavio Martinez. It is crucial that ties to the government of Nicaragua be discovered if they exist. I want everything the Estimates Office has, everything the Latin American Desk has, and I want the H-and-A group to tear it apart and put it back together so that it makes sense. I need whatever you can give me. And I need it by midnight tonight. Questions and comments?"

Vander Pool raised the index finger of his left hand. He was sixty-six, grandfatherly, a droll, dumpy Dutchman who wore blue V-neck sweaters and bow ties. "If you wish," he said, in his retiring European manner, "I give you the answer right now."

4:20 P.M. WHEN TOMMY CARTER left, Sally locked the door after him, then leaned against it, trying to catch her breath. It was flooding over her, so much, so quickly that she could barely grasp it all. She felt as though her whole world were going haywire. She put her hand to her breast, and she could feel that the collar of her robe was damp with spittle.

She tore off the robe and threw it in the laundry hamper, then went into the bathroom, turned on the shower, and got under it before the water warmed. She stood under the icy spray with her face turned up and her mouth open, her body turning to gooseflesh and shaking in the cold. She hunched her shoulders and cringed under the icy needles, shaking her head so that the water cleansed her mouth and face until every sensation of Tommy Carter was washed away. And then the hot water came up and the shower warmed and steam began to rise around her, stilling her tremors.

She was in trouble—deep and deepening trouble. Carter would blackmail her sexually and politically. And it wouldn't end with the convention. It would go on—a disgusting, degrading series of encounters until she found a way to break his hold on her. But that would have to wait. She had more immediate problems now.

She stepped out of the shower and shut the water. Then she picked up the phone on the bathroom wall and punched Terry's private number.

"This is Chris Van Allen."

"I need to talk to Terry."

"He's busy."

"Tell him it's important."

"What he's doing is important."

She seethed. "Chris, put Terry on this phone right now."

He put her on hold, and she stood in the misty bathroom, naked, dripping wet, waiting.

Then Terry came on the line. "What is it?"

"You accepted a prime time hour Thursday at eight?"

"Why not?" he said. "It's the night before the floor opens for nominations."

"That means you'll be on against *The Cosby Show*. Terry, for crying out loud, Cosby does a fifty share. I can't believe that Cronkite would accept that time period."

"It isn't Cronkite," he said. Then he told her the names of the four interviewers.

"For God's sake, Terry! They'll tear you to bits."

"Don't be ridiculous. It's just like *Meet the Press* in prime time."

"Is that what they told you?"

"Look, Sally, it's done. End of discussion."

"Chris told you to do it, didn't he?"

"We discussed it. Yes."

"Terry, please—listen to me. Chris is a bright boy. But he's in over his head. The whole strategy was no exposure. Keep the mystique. Make them wonder. And take only the best, the surest shots. Don't change that. Please. It's working."

"I don't agree, " he said. "I think I need to step out a little, show them that I'm healthy and able."

"Okay. Maybe you do. But not against *The Cosby Show*."

"Dammit, Sally, I said the matter is closed. I'm doing that hour. I'm doing the governors' caucus dinner tomorrow night and—"

"The formal dinner?"

"Yes."

"But you'll be photographed."

"Sally, that's the idea."

"But you'll be wearing a tuxedo. You'll look like an aristocrat. That's not what you stand for."

"Maybe it's what I should stand for."

"Terry. Terry, please. Hear what I'm saying. You're the guy next door. You're a man of the people. Baker's the aristocrat. It's the matchup we've always talked about. It worked for Eastman. It'll work for you."

"Sally, I have to go now."

"Terry, you've got to let me back in. You're going off the track."

"Are you forgetting your little problem?"

She flashed on Tommy Carter. How could Terry know about that? "What . . . what do you mean?"

"Your two friends? I met them. Remember?"

Then she realized he was talking about Mancuso and Ross.

"If you find a way out, I'd love to hear from you." His voice was reassuring, but the message was ominous. "Think about it, dear," he said. Then he hung up.

But she didn't have to think about it. She already knew that Tommy Carter couldn't prove she was at the Four Seasons. Only Mancuso or Ross could do that.

7:25 P.M. MANCUSO WENT TO the West Wing entrance of the White House. A Secret Service man showed him to a little waiting room. He sat there, trying to be comfortable in his best tweed suit. But the fabric was too heavy for August and the tweed scratched his ass and the backs of his legs. He felt like some kind of a shmuck, sitting there in the White House and waiting to meet the president and receive a citation he hadn't earned and didn't deserve. A crisp young secretary stuck her head in at the archway, and he jumped to his feet.

"Mr. Bender will see you now, if you'll come this way." She walked out and left him to grab his hat and trail after her, plucking at the seat of his pants.

She showed Mancuso into one of those offices all paneled in expensive wood, with books that looked like they had never been opened. There was a big, shiny desk with nothing at all on top of it except a leather folder. Dozens of framed eight-by-ten pictures hung over every spare inch of the wall. They were black-and-white pictures mostly, celebrities and famous politicians, all standing with the same unsmiling, gray-haired little man. Mancuso spotted two popes, the queen of England, Adlai Stevenson, Frank Sinatra. The little gray-haired man looked the same in every picture. It was like he was never young and never grew older.

Bender was on the phone. "I'll call you as soon as the conference ends. Bye." Then he hung up and sat, staring at Mancuso.

"I'm Joe Mancuso. From the—"

"Yes, yes, I remember. Director O'Brien's office."

"Yeah."

"Sit down, Agent. Sit down."

"Thanks." Mancuso looked back and forth between the chairs and the sofa until Bender pointed to one. "Thanks."

"Have you ever been on television, Agent?"

"Television?"

"Yes. You're to be on television. Presented to the nation by the president himself as the man who tracked down the killer of Colonel Martinez."

Mancuso looked like he didn't understand.

"You did do that, didn't you?"

"Did what?"

"Track down the killer of Martinez."

"Oh. Yeah."

"Please, Agent. No undue modesty."

"No."

Bender stared at him a moment. Then he said, "Well, I think you'll find this evening quite exciting."

Mancuso felt like he had a burr stuck up his ass, sitting there with his tweed suit giving him itchy balls and this oily little fuck doing a routine on his head.

Bender got up from his desk and pressed a button on the console behind him. A panel slid back and a three-decanter tantalus emerged with a line of glittering crystal glasses. "Will you have a drink?"

"If you've got bourbon."

"Of course." Bender chose two glasses and began to pour. "The president will make some brief remarks about the Martinez matter. And the evidence linking Petersen to the crime. Then he'll discuss your involvement in the attempt to capture the man, and his unavoidable death. He'll ask you to stand and be recognized. That's about it." Bender looked back over his shoulder. "Any questions?"

"Yeah," Mancuso said. "Did the president order the army to dose Martinez with AIDS? Or was it the Company's idea?"

Bender stopped where he was, then turned to face Mancuso, a glass in either hand. "I'm sorry," he said with that slimy smile. "What did you say?"

"Did you send the SWAT team that killed Petersen?"

Without responding, Bender crossed the room and put Mancuso's drink in his hand. And when they were standing close together, Mancuso said, "You put the Secret Service on the case. Only the executive branch could do that."

"There are two limbs to the executive branch," Bender said. He touched the rim of his glass to Mancuso's. His eyes twinkled over the rim as he drank. "I see you're a man with a lively imagination, Agent Mancuso." He sat down on the edge of his desk and the smile never left his eyes. "You missed your calling. You should have been a writer."

"I'm writing an obituary for Martinez. Wanna help me?"

Bender nodded and chuckled softly to himself. "Martinez, eh?" Then he put his head back and rubbed his chin. "Sure. I'll help you. Colonel Octavio Martinez was a heroic casualty in a war of his own choosing. He—"

"You shot him up with AIDS so that he wouldn't be a hero anymore," Mancuso said. "While he was dying, you could pick somebody to take over. Somebody you had your hooks into."

"You're quite a political scientist, Agent Mancuso," Bender said.

"Then Petersen dealt himself in."

"This is fascinating. Did you see this in a movie?"

"What about Beckwith?" Mancuso said.

"Who?"

"You don't even know his name, do you? The doctor. What about him and his wife and kid?"

"I can't wait to hear."

"Your spooks did that, too. Otherwise, the AIDS thing might have leaked. So they killed three people to cover their tracks."

"Now, do you really believe the American government would commit a crime like that?" Bender said.

"Hey, mister, you're talking to the guy who put the microphone under Martin Luther King's bed."

Bender walked over to the wall map of the Americas. "Mancuso, you seem to like games. Let's play a game. All right?" Bender had his back to him and was looking up at the map. "Suppose—just suppose there's even the tiniest kernel of truth in your idiotic story. Suppose we wanted Martinez out of the way—which we didn't. Why didn't we just have him shot somewhere in the jungle?"

"Because the spics would never trust you again if they found out."

Bender snorted. "I see you're a great humanitarian as well as a fool."

"I got nothing against spics," Mancuso said. "I'm not putting them up to killing each other."

"Well, if you're right, then whoever hired Petersen almost lost us the whole of Latin America," Bender said.

"Who hired him?"

For a moment, Bender looked at him. Then he said, "Presumably the same people who snuffed him."

"Who?"

"I wish I knew. They do nice work."

Mancuso stood up and put his glass on the desk untouched. "Excuse me. But I have to get out of here before I puke."

"You wouldn't be the first," Bender said.

The intercom buzzed and Bender pressed the button down. "Yes?"

His secretary's voice said, "The president will see Mr. Mancuso now, sir."

"Thank you." Bender looked at Mancuso. "And even if you were right," he said, and there was a threatening darkness in his voice. "What do you suppose you could do about it?"

Mancuso took his hat. "Who said I want to do anything about it, Mac?"

It doesn't matter who you are. You get a funny feeling standing in a corridor, waiting for a door to be unlocked, knowing that the president of the United States will be waiting for you in the room beyond the door.

Mancuso stood in the hallway, shifting uneasily from foot to foot beside Lou Bender. He waited, and he felt those feelings coming over him—feelings he thought he was done with a long time ago.

He'd been undercover among the crowd at Jack Kennedy's inauguration in 1961. A brittle day it was, harsh and blustery through the sunshine, the way Washington can be in January. Mancuso was supposed to watch the crowd, but he didn't. Instead, he watched the rostrum with the other thousands of upturned faces, heard Kennedy tell Americans to ask what they could do for their country, watched him shade the papers for old man Frost when he tried to read his poem.

It seemed as though all of official Washington dreaded the coming of Kennedy, envied him and his glamorous wife, feared the sweeping winds of change that would blow through the Capitol behind him. Hoover was no exception. The old man didn't get along with any of the Kennedys—but particularly Bobby. And when Jack appointed Bobby attorney general, the hope was that the old man would resign. But Hoover's response to pressure from the Kennedys was the same as it had always been to anyone who crowded him—surveillance. Joe Mancuso was assigned to wiretap the president at home and at play.

But Mancuso grew to like Jack Kennedy—not that he ever got to meet him. But when you listened to a man's private conversations with people—his friends, his government associates, his wife, his mistresses. . . . You do that long enough and you get to know a man, even if you never once shake his hand.

Kennedy stood for things that Mancuso could understand—money, success, family. Kennedy was a Catholic. That was no big deal with Mancuso, but it was better than nothing. Like everyone else, Mancuso was sick at Kennedy's death. But unlike most people, Mancuso really missed him—missed him the way you miss one of the guys.

Standing at the doorway, waiting to meet President Baker, Mancuso thought of those Kennedy years. All through his career with the FBI, he had done as Jack Kennedy had wished. He had asked what he could do for his country.

He had not asked much in return.

And his reward for three decades of faithful service to the nation was to be as grotesque as his career, a facetious appearance on television—and a guilt that would pad softly behind him like a mangy dog, all the long way down the path to his grave.

The guard held the door ajar and Mancuso went into the Oval Office. It looked just like in the picture books. Then he heard a toilet flush and a door in the wainscoting opened and President Baker came out in his shirtsleeves, drying his hands on a towel. There were Kleenex tissues stuffed in around the collar of his shirt and he looked like he had a terrific tan.

"Mr. President," Bender said, "this is Agent Joseph Mancuso."

"I'm sorry you had to wait," the president said, putting his hand out. "I'm President Baker."

"Mancuso." They shook.

"Yes, I've heard about you, Agent Mancuso." The president went around the desk and took his jacket and slipped it on. "May I call you Joe?"

The president's secretary, Katherine, stuck her head in the door. "They're ready for you, sir."

"Come on, Joe," the president said. "Let's walk over together."

They walked across West Exec Avenue toward the Old Executive Office Building. It was really something to walk with the president, Mancuso discovered. All the way over, people stopped and stepped out of their way and marine guards braced and people nodded and said, "Good evening, sir." Mancuso looked around and watched the people bowing and scraping, like they were laying down before him. And he could see what an intoxicant power was and what it could do to a person.

"You've done us, done the country a great service, Joe," the president said. "I want you to know how grateful I am."

"I didn't do much."

"More than you know," he said so that only Mancuso could hear. "And I appreciate your candor in your conversation with Director O'Brien this afternoon. Do you understand? That was very helpful."

"Didn't cost me nothing." Mancuso looked over at the president, and the two men stared at each other, eye to eye. He was surprised then, because it occurred to him that, just maybe, the president wasn't in on it. Maybe it was only the men around him who were playing dirty and scrambling to cover their tracks.

"I'm sure your family's very proud," the president said.

"Don't have family."

"Well, your friends, then."

"Sure."

A Secret Service man was holding the elevator door for them and they stepped inside. When the door shut, the president said, "What do you make of all this, Joe?"

"All this?"

"What's happened, I mean."

Bender was leaning very close, listening to every word. But Mancuso shrugged and scratched himself behind the ear. "What's the difference what I think of it?"

That made the president smile. "Maybe no difference. Maybe just curiosity. When you sit where I sit, things sometimes get, you know, a little distorted."

"Where I sit, too."

They smiled together.

"I guess you do a lot of this kind of work," the president said. "I guess after a while it gets to where it's just a job."

"Is it for you?"

The president thought about that. "There are days when I wish it were only a job."

"Me, too," Mancuso said.

They exchanged a smile. And they nodded to each other, and to themselves.

The elevator door opened on a hallway full of hushed, hurried people rushing this way and that. A little bearded man in shirtsleeves and a bow tie was waiting right outside. He was wearing an earphone with a little antenna sticking up off his head. "Good evening, Mr. President," he said, and handed him a leather folder. Then he squinted at Mancuso's face and grabbed his arm and called out, "Dolores, give me a quick one here."

"I'll see you later, Joe," the president said, and went off with Bender and the floor manager.

A woman wearing a light blue smock and carrying a big box of cosmetics came over and put her fingers under Mancuso's chin and looked at his face in the light. Then she got him by the elbow and steered him toward a director's chair that was set up under a spotlight. "Sit right there, darlin'," she said. And when he did, she slopped up some gunk on a sponge and tried to rub it on Mancuso's nose.

"Hey, whatcha doing?" Mancuso pulled away and leaned back so far the chair almost went over.

"Honey, you're gonna be on television. You gotta have makeup. Otherwise, you're gonna look like a dead fish."

When she was done, the man with the headset walked Mancuso down the corridor and through an opening in the curtains and out onto the stage.

Mancuso had never been to a presidential press conference before. What struck him first were the lights. There was a battery of television lights across the top of the stage and two banks on aluminum standards set left and right of the rostrum so that the entire stage area was lit bright and flat. There were twenty rows of seats in the auditorium, rising toward the rear of the room where the camera crews were packed in on the floor and on scaffolding. Every seat was taken. Down front, Mancuso recognized a bunch of celebrities—Sam Donaldson, Bob Scheiffer, Andrea Mitchell, even Dan Shorr.

The bearded man with the headset took Mancuso by the arm and led him to a chair on the far side of the stage. There were two men seated there, and he recognized them as the Speaker of the House and the majority whip of the Senate. They nodded wordlessly as he sat.

Then a voice over the loudspeaker said, "Ladies and gentlemen, the president of the United States."

The first thing that surprised Mancuso was that everybody got up. He didn't know that he was supposed to get up. So he was the last person who did. And then he didn't know when to sit and was the last person to sit, and he had a feeling that everybody in the room was looking at him and thinking that he didn't belong there.

But the reporters quieted down as the president went to the podium, put on his reading glasses and opened the leather folder, and Mancuso could see that there were sheets of typewritten paper inside.

"My fellow Americans," the president said. "One week ago, this nation and civilized peoples everywhere were shocked and outraged by the murder of Colonel Octavio Martinez, leader of the Contra freedom fighters of Nicaragua. This brutal and cowardly act—this savage and vicious crime. . . ."

While the president spoke, Mancuso looked down at the reporters. Some were holding pocket tape recorders. Some were merely looking on. Mancuso watched their faces. They seemed to know that something big was in the air.

The president was saying, "Yesterday, Vice President Daniel Eastman wrote to the leaders of both Houses, requesting that they appoint a Select

Committee to conduct an investigation into the murder of Colonel Martinez. And in his remarks, the vice president expressed his frustration that the FBI investigation of this crime had failed, so far, to produce satisfactory results.''

Mancuso watched the president. He had his speech written out on the papers in front of him, but he barely looked down. He seemed to know it just about by heart. Then Mancuso watched the reporters. He could see them sitting forward like kids on the first day of school, as though they were trying to impress the teacher that they were straining to catch every word.

"Many of the things that Vice President Eastman told you were true. There were, in fact, only two FBI agents assigned to this case.''

Now, a palpable wave of excitement stirred the reporters.

"The vice president believed that the nature of this case demanded an all-out investigation. And I will admit to you that I agreed with him.''

Some of the reporters shifted in their chairs. Something was happening that Mancuso couldn't quite put his finger on. He looked over at the podium. Why was the president beating around the bush? Why didn't he just lay it out for them—what had happened, how Petersen had been killed, that the evidence that he had shot Martinez was incontestable.

"Like you, I was profoundly saddened by the cruel murder of this visionary, bold, young man,'' the president said. "Octavio Martinez was a hero to the freedom-loving people of his homeland. And, like you, I was impatient to see his murderers identified, captured, and punished to the fullest extent of the law.''

When he said that, Mancuso realized what the president was doing. He was playing the reporters—playing them the way a fisherman plays a trout. Mancuso looked back down at the reporters, and they had taken the bait, hook, line, and sinker.

Their faces were blank and their eyes round and staring. After all, they were only everyday men and women, and they were seated before the very fountainhead of power. The man who held the podium held them all. And it occurred to Mancuso that a person who could control that room could control the press. And a person who could control the press could manipulate the nation.

The president paused and turned a page on the podium before him. When he did, the reflection of the paper flashed in the two tilted panes of glass that stuck up on little black poles before the podium. Mancuso looked at them and blinked his eyes. There on the panes of glass, he could see the text of the president's remarks projected from television monitors lying face-up on the floor.

The president said, "Few acts in memory have so dramatized the violent nature of the enemies of freedom in this hemisphere,'' and Mancuso watched the words crawl up the glass. The president's text was marked with capitals and little squiggles. And as the president spoke, Mancuso could hear the cadence, the pauses, the raising and lowering of the voice for emphasis, and the continuity of a phrase from one line to the next.

The president spoke and Mancuso read along with him.

> WE believe that we ARE a nation of law.|
> WE believe that we ARE a government of>
> free men and women.|
> WE believe that we MUST set an example of>
> justice under the law for the nations of>
> our hemisphere AND the world.|

[PAGE TURN]

[BEAT]   [WARM]

The president turned a page and paused, and his tone changed. "But, my friends," he said, "if we are to remain a civilized and a free people, we must, ourselves, obey the law and act with moderation. Justice is not revenge. And the cause of freedom cannot be served by police state tactics, no matter how ghastly the crime nor how vigorous our appetite for retribution."

The words the president spoke were lofty. But, somehow, projected on the glass TelePrompTers, the words looked empty and hollow, like the meaningless patter of an advertisement.

Then the president began to explain how the FBI had tracked and trapped the assassin. Mancuso watched the words go by on the glass— words that overstated his own part in the investigation. And when the president told of the death of Rolf Petersen and his identification as the assassin, the reporters gasped on cue.

But Mancuso didn't hear that. He didn't hear the president's voice and he wasn't reading the words. He was simply sitting there, perspiring heavily in the heat of the lights and feeling like he hadn't any heart anymore. The facts and fancies of the hunt for Rolf Petersen slid by on the glass and, like everything else, the little truths were magnified and distorted by the glass and by the setting and by the reporters and their cameras, blown out of all human proportion and vaporized by the heat of the lights.

Mancuso sat there, feeling like there was nothing in the world he cared to hold or touch or believe in. Like there was nothing that meant anything.

Nothing true. Nothing real. And as the president talked on, Mancuso felt weary and drained. His perspiration was beading on his brow and on his upper lip. He rubbed the back of his hand against his mouth, and when he looked down at his hand, it was smudged with ochre makeup and he was sure that his face was streaked where the makeup had come off and he wasn't sure what to do. He slipped his hand up and took hold of the handkerchief in his breast pocket, trying to do it without drawing attention to himself.

The president was saying, "The identification of Rolf Petersen . . . the hunt for this depraved killer . . . and the heroic action that concluded in his death—were all the result of diligent, tireless detection by one agent of the Federal Bureau of Investigation. I'd like you to meet this man," the president said. "The man who identified Rolf Petersen. The man who followed the trail. The man who tracked him to. . . ."

Mancuso got out his handkerchief and mopped his forehead, and the makeup turned the folds of his handkerchief dark brown. He wanted to wipe it all off. He wanted to stand up and leave the stage. But he knew he didn't dare. He couldn't leave. He was about to be presented to the press.

He knew he was, after all, part of tonight's performance. In fact, he was the main attraction. He was on exhibition—a freak in a sideshow to murder. Tonight he was his government's trained bear. He was a clown, a curiosity, a gawk, a geek—a travesty before the television cameras. And he knew he was superbly cast. Because he *was* a bumbling, botching, fumbler— the butt of every Bureau joke. He was a stooge, a patsy for all the filthy, vicious little crimes that a government can conceive in its supreme contempt for people and the law. Hell, he was Joe Mancuso, the old reliable gumshoe with dirty fingernails who did what he was told and didn't ask questions. He was exactly what he had let himself be for thirty years—a scumbag and a fake, a grotesque, loathsome, corrupt, incompetent, a wretched little excuse for a human being. And what was worse, he knew now that he was no better than all the professional liars and manipulators. He was, after all, merely their accomplice.

"Ladies and gentlemen, the FBI agent-in-charge of the Martinez investigation, Joseph Mancuso."

Then there was silence.

Mancuso looked around and the reporters were staring at him and he didn't know why. Then he looked over at the president and the president was smiling, nodding and beckoning for him to stand and he did.

And suddenly the battery of cameras swung around toward Mancuso. Suddenly the lights turned, blinding him. Suddenly the strobes began to flash–flash so fast and so hot that he flinched and almost raised his hand to shield his face. And he could hear applause building in the room somewhere behind the glaring strobes—tumultuous applause, roaring, deafening, resounding applause. And he stood, blinking into the lights and half-turning from them, holding the back of the chair to keep his balance, trying to tell himself it was only a show, just a show, just some bullshit make-believe show.

And then, suddenly, the truth struck down on him like thunder, and he knew. He knew about Martinez. He knew about Petersen. As he knew the truth about himself, he knew the truth about them all.

8:20 P.M. DAN EASTMAN PRESSED the off button on the remote control and watched the television picture shrink to a hot white point in the middle of the screen. Then he settled back into the deep leather cushions of the chair, folding his arms across his chest.

The intercom buzzed and he looked down and saw that all eight lights on his telephone were lit. He pressed the speaker button. "Yes, Dale?"

She was flustered. "It's . . . it's everybody, sir. The AP, *Time*—"

"I'm not taking any calls just now, Dale," he said softly. And he was about to release the button when she said, "Mrs. Eastman is calling from Philadelphia on line three."

He thought a moment. "Tell her I can't speak with her now. And, Dale?"

"Yes, sir?"

"Tell her I miss her."

He released the speaker button and then pressed the one that locked the door. He leaned back and raised his arms above his head and stretched. Then he swung his legs out of the chair and padded in his stockinged feet over to his desk and sat down.

He took his key ring and fingered through it until he found the little brass key that fit the bottom right-hand drawer to his desk. When he opened the drawer, he took out the snub-nosed .38 police special that the Philadelphia PBA had presented him when he was named their Man of the Year. It had gold filigree up and down the barrel and a checkered rosewood stock, and it had his name engraved between the sights.

He lay the revolver on the maroon leather desk pad and put his hands down on either side of it. And he sat there, staring.

8:35 P.M. WHEN MANCUSO PUSHED through the door of Gertie's, somebody shouted, "There he is!" and a cheer went up like the Redskins had won the Super Bowl. And suddenly, they were all grabbing his hands and his arms and pummeling him from behind and pinching his cheeks and the hookers were lining up to throw their arms around him and kiss him big fat wet ones on the mouth and ears and it was all he could do to fight his way through the hand-shakers and back-slappers to his seat at the end of the bar.

Gertie ran down the length of the bar with a bottle of Jack Daniel's and a glass full of ice and slapped them down in front of him and pushed her big tits up on the bar and said, "Gimme one, Joe!" and kissed him. Then she pushed the bottle and glass at him and said, "Party's on me."

"You seen Ross?" Mancuso said.

"Hey, everybody!" Gertie shouted. "Everybody up to the bar and have one on me to toast the greatest cop in the history of the FBI!"

They all pushed up from everywhere, all the hookers out of the back room and the old drunks who had been sleeping it off in the booths near the kitchen, all shouting "Hey, man!" and "Hot shit!" and "Way to go, Joe!" and lining the bar. And when every glass was filled, Gertie got her stool out, climbed on top of the bar, raised her glass over her head and shouted, "Here's to Joe Mancuso—hero cop and television star!"

And they all cried "Yay!" and drank to him.

"Hey, Gertie," Mancuso said. "For Christ's sake—has Ross been in here?"

But Gertie was shouting, "Okay, everybody! Everybody! For he's a jolly-good fellow. Ready? One . . . two . . . three . . . For he's—"

And the whole bar sang at the top of their lungs.

Mancuso sat there, feeling ridiculous, but trying to go along with it. And when they finished, he called to Gertie again. But she got her fists up and started leading the cheer.

"Everybody! Hip-hip . . ."

"Hooray!"

"Hip-hip . . ."

"Hooray!"

"Hip-hip . . ."

"Hooray!"

Then they all cheered and clapped and Mancuso's hooker friend, Mandy, slid up on the stool beside him and grabbed him around the neck and kissed

367

him right on the mouth and looked at him with eyes brimming with happiness. "I'm so proud of you, Joey." She kissed him again.

He shook his head. "Nah, it don't mean shit."

"Maybe not, baby. But it mean something to me."

He took her hand and held it tight. "Thanks."

"Now, you looking for Ross?" she said.

"You seen him?"

"Nope. He ain't been in yet. Go call him up. I get a friend and we have a party."

"Yeah," Mancuso said. He slid down off the stool and made his way through the back-slappers and glad-handers to the phone booth near the door.

8:40 P.M.   WHEN WORD CAME DOWN at 7:45 that Mancuso would be on television, Ross had looked at his wristwatch—and then at the videocassettes and his notes and the seven cartridges from the assassination. He was surprised at himself, surprised at how he felt.

He knew that if he cleaned up just then, he'd have enough time to get down to Gertie's, kick one back and get himself a good seat in front of the television over the bar before the president's press conference started. It would be a hell of a show. First, the president announcing that the FBI had found the killer of Martinez. That would drop some jaws. But when the president introduced Gertie's own Joe Mancuso as the guy who got it done, the place would go up for grabs. Now, that would be worth the price of admission.

It sounded like fun. But when the time came, Ross was surprised to find that he didn't feel like wrapping it up and heading down toward Gertie's. He wanted to stay with the work. He didn't care what baloney the president said about Petersen or the Bureau or about Joe Mancuso. If Joe didn't give a shit, then neither did he. And it made him wonder if something of Mancuso—his indifference, his cynicism, his bitterness—was beginning to rub off. But, in the end, Ross switched his monitor from videocassette to channel 5 and watched the press conference. And when Joe Mancuso stood up to be recognized—stood up goggle-eyed and blinking like someone who'd gotten off at the wrong stop—he felt only pleasure, and an abiding tenderness.

At 8:45, he was still sitting like that, his hands clasped behind his head, watching Tom Brokaw's instant analysis, when Jean, the secretary, opened the door and stuck her face in.

"Hey, your partner's a hero."

Ross laughed. "Yeah. Maybe they'll name a sandwich after him."

"You expecting somebody?" Jean said.

"No."

"Well, she's here. . . ."

She swung the door a little wider and, behind her, Ross could see Sally in the waiting room, holding her big panama hat and dark glasses.

"Hey! Hello," he said brightly. And when she came into the office and the door was closed, he said, "God, I'm glad to see you."

"Am I intruding?"

"Are you kidding?" He reached out and took the hand she offered. "Did you see Mancuso? Did you see the press conference?"

"Yes. You must be very pleased."

"Hey. I told you we'd get the shooter. We got him. The heat's off."

"You don't think they'll press the . . . the other matter."

"For what? Now that Martinez is settled, the other thing is grade-B crime." But the last thing he wanted to do was talk business. "You look great," he said.

"You're sweet. I feel like I haven't slept in two weeks."

"Well. You've got to get that thing off your mind."

"I know," she said, and stood, staring at him.

"Is there . . . something I can do for you?"

"Oh. Well. . . ." She hesitated.

"Yes?"

"I leave for the convention the day after tomorrow. I was hoping we could have dinner tonight."

It was more than he could hope for. And he stood, gaping, until she stood on her toes and kissed him, bluntly kissed him on the mouth. He was so startled that he took hold of her shoulders, almost as if to protect himself. But there was no misunderstanding the message in her lips. They were soft and liquid and hot inside and her tongue moved under his upper lip and slid down the line of his teeth. He took hold of her shoulders and eased her against him. Then he could feel the warm mass of her breasts through the front of his shirt and her hips pushing against him. And the whole warm, sugar-scented presence of her surged over him.

The phone rang, but he ignored it. He slid his right hand down into the small of her back and made her hips bend up against him. And he put his left hand around the back of her neck, under the soft fall of her hair, pressing her lips to his. Her mouth opened for him and closed on his tongue, sucking.

The door opened. It was Jean. They jumped apart.

"What? What is it?" he stammered.

Jean looked back and forth between them, cocking an eyebrow. "It's Mancuso. He wants to talk to you."

Ross was trying to catch his breath, trying with all his might to keep the blush rising in his neck from choking him. "Tell him . . . tell him I'm out. Tell him I went home."

Jean took one more look at Sally's back, shook her head, and pulled the door shut.

Sally was holding her hands clenched against her chest. When the door closed, she put her head back and laughed.

"What's so damn funny?" Ross said.

She shook her head and looked at him with those gentle, confiding eyes. "I wasn't going to come here. I knew I'd get us into trouble."

He put his hands on his hips. "So, why did you come?"

"I had to," she said and she wasn't laughing anymore.

She stood quite still, looking up at him, and in the blue of her eyes he could see only a desire that was a mirror of his own.

"Let me wrap up here," he said.

While he hurriedly shuffled his papers together and slid the videocassettes back into their sleeves, she stood off to the side, looking at herself in the tiny mirror in her compact, touching at her makeup. Then she came up behind him and put her hand on his back as he bent over the desk, put it on his hip and slid it up under his shirt tail, all the way up to his shoulders, with her fingers spread wide so that he could feel the sharp edges of her nails sliding across his skin. That made him straighten and lean back against her and murmur.

"What are those?" she said, and nodded at the seven cartridges on the cardboard panel.

"The shells from the Martinez shooting."

Involuntarily, she shuddered. "God, they're gruesome." Then she slipped her other hand under the front of his shirt and ran her fingernails lightly up his chest until she had both arms around him, holding him to her. He was aroused and his breathing was labored with excitement.

"Why would one be black?"

"I don't know." He swept the seven shells into a plastic evidence bag and zipped it shut.

"Is it important?" She could feel perspiration breaking out on his back.

"Yes. I don't know," he said and shrugged. "I think so. It just bugs me." He pulled the drawer open and dropped the bag into it. Then she let him go as he tucked in his shirt and began gathering his stack of manila folders and sliding them, one by one, into his briefcase.

"Your partner—Mancuso?" She said his name as though she didn't like the taste of the word in her mouth. "What does he think about all this?"

"Him? He doesn't think about anything. He's got three months till he retires. He just wishes it would go away."

Ross took his keys from his pocket and locked the drawer of his desk. "Where would you like to go for dinner?"

But when he looked up, she was doing something he had never seen a woman do before. She was rubbing her index finger in a small circle on the front of her sweater, a small circle that surrounded the nipple of her left breast, and he could see the nipple, swelling and hardening under the airy wool. He stood, mesmerized, aching for her.

"I don't want any dinner," she said.

9:00 P.M. MANCUSO CALLED AGAIN in half an hour. But by this time, no one answered, and when he looked at his watch he realized that Jean and the other secretaries had cleared out by now and the office was deserted. So, he told Mandy that they'd have to party another time. Then he made his way down the bar through another round of free drinks and back-slappings and finally slipped out the door, leaving the celebration going full-blast without him.

He stood for a while, watching the last flight of homebound traffic roaring up E Street and thought of the harried, busy workers all hurrying home to their families as night began to fall. And he thought of the homes they were heading back to—mostly substantial, proper, middle-class homes. The men he saw would sit down to long tables covered with steaming dinners, say grace over God's bounty, and not mean a word of it. They took for granted all the enduring riches of life—wife, home, family, plenty—all the things that, somehow, in the rush and tumult of living, had eluded Joe Mancuso.

He could feel himself swaying and realized he'd had too much to drink. Then he focused on the corner street sign, and turned right down 10th Street toward Constitution Avenue and the Mall.

Ahead of him on the Mall, the night lights were on, playing up the colonnade of the Museum of Natural History. And he walked to the corner of Constitution Avenue, humming to himself no-song-in-particular. The light was red against him, and he stopped.

Behind him on the corner was a newsstand. He went over and leaned in under the fluorescent fixture. The seller was just cutting the tie on a fresh stack of the *Washington Post*. Mancuso leaned over his shoulder.

A headline ran the full width of the front page. It read:

KILLER OF MARTINEZ DEAD IN GUN BATTLE

And beneath it:

President Praises Hero FBI Agent

Through the mist of alcohol, Mancuso stared at the photographs on the front page. One showed the president speaking at the podium above the Great Seal of the president of the United States. He could see the president and the podium, but he couldn't see those glass reflectors that had the speech on them. At first, he thought that was too bad—everybody should know what a crock the whole show was. But then he thought, well, after all, people wanted to look up to a president. Why not let them? Who gives a shit?

He looked at the other photo. That was a picture of a man he didn't recognize—sort of a big, burly man in a funny dark suit that didn't fit him right, with his tie knot a little crooked and his sleeves too long down around his wrists and his hands held clumsily in front of him like he didn't know the picture was being taken. He was jowly, and his mouth had a kind of startled look like someone had pinched him in the ass. And then it occurred to Mancuso that the man looked like his grandfather. And then it occurred to him that the man was Joe Mancuso.

"You wanna paper?" the seller said.

"Huh?"

"I said, you wanna paper or what?"

"Yeah," Mancuso said. "Gimme a paper." He dug around in his pocket and found some change and paid the vendor. He took the first section, rolled it, and stuck it in the back pocket of his trousers and crossed the street to the Mall.

The Washington Monument was fully lit, and as he walked past it, he could see the ring of flags blowing in the breeze off the Tidal Basin. He went up on the grass and walked past the monument and down the hill toward where 17th Street cut through the Mall. It was all grassy knoll from there down to the Reflecting Pool, and he could see the Lincoln Memorial glowing yellow and warm against the last purple of the sunset sky behind it.

He went over and sat on a bench on the south side of the pool. Sitting there, he could really see it all: the Capitol far off to the east, the Washington Monument, the Lincoln Memorial. They were all lit and gleaming and he remembered the first time he had walked down by the Reflecting Pool at night. He had been a young man then—a new husband, a new agent of the FBI, a new face in Washington. So much had passed since then, so many seasons, so many lifetimes. But he remembered himself as he was then, in his heavy, lace-up, wing-tip shoes, his wide necktie and double-breasted suit that never closed right and the three-pointed pocket handkerchief he always wore because everyone said Hoover liked to see some linen on a man. He had not been much more than a boy then, a boy whose world whispered and glittered with promise.

Sitting back, he thought of the old fella on the newspaper front page and he didn't know how it had gotten so changed around. He didn't know and he probably never would know.

Everything had changed, had slipped out from under his feet the way sand banks dissolve in water. All he had ever wanted to do was to serve his country, to defend the Constitution and enforce the laws of the United States. But, somehow while he wasn't looking, someone kept shuffling the deck and making right into wrong, and wrong into right, and heroes into villains and vice versa until he really didn't know what was right and what was wrong. He had to stop listening to his conscience because it only confused him. And he listened instead to his superiors and did exactly what they said. Because he believed that if anyone knew right from wrong, it must be them.

It hadn't worked out, though. It hadn't worked out. All these years, he hadn't known why. Until tonight, when he'd been on television with the president.

Now he knew that it hadn't worked out because the president wore makeup and pretended that he knew his speech by heart when he was actually reading it off glass plates. It was all a show. The speeches, the presidency, the whole government. That's why guys like Bender thought they could do whatever they wanted and get away with it. Because all that mattered was how it looked to the cameras. Because the whole thing was just one big fucking television show.

He leaned over and a big bump in his back pocket goosed him—the section of the *Washington Post*. He took it out of his pocket. There wasn't enough light to read and he was real tired anyhow.

But it might be good for something. He opened a few sheets of the paper and lay back, stretched out on the bench, and covered himself with the broadsheets of paper. Then he put his two hands flat on the wooden slats and lay his head down and rested his cheek on them. And he started to hum no-song-in-particular. It was then he realized what song he was humming and then he thought of the words.

My country 'tis of thee, sweet land of liberty, of thee I sing. . . . He couldn't remember the rest. And it didn't matter. Because by then, he was fast, fast asleep.

9:20 P.M.   THE FUNNY THING was that once they acknowledged their desire, there wasn't much to say.

They went back to her place. And they hardly spoke at all during the drive across town. And then Ross couldn't find a spot to park and had to drive around the block again. But when he offered to drop her in front of her door, she said, "No. I'll stay with you," as though she didn't want to be apart from him. And when he finally found a parking place, it was three blocks away and they walked back to the row of townhouses with barely a word between them.

Once inside her door, the pretense ended.

She was in his arms at once, her mouth wet and open, taking his tongue into her. His hands were all over her body. And while they kissed, she unbuttoned his blazer, pulling it back and down off his shoulders, and tossing it on the sofa. As she started undoing his tie, he put his hands under her sweater, cupping and raising her breasts through the silky fabric of her bra. Her nipples had hardened to stone, and they were both so short of breath that she said, "Wait. Come with me." Then she led him into the bedroom.

It was white, with delicate blue-and-white flowers in the wallpaper and a chaise longue covered in matching fabric, piled with white and pale blue pillows. There were tiered, white ruffled curtains on the windows and wistful prints on the walls that had a childlike, cartoon quality about them. There was a wide brass bedstead, and two brass lamps on the end tables. The bed had a frothy white coverlet, heaped with pillows. He was so full of her by then that he would have barely noticed the room, but for the stuffed animals. They were everywhere: bears and rabbits peeking out of corners, puppies on the cushions in the corner under the windows, and one droll little koala plumped down in the middle of the bed. It might have been a little girl's room, not a woman's.

But it was a woman's bedroom and the woman was there with him, sitting him on the edge of the bed to unbutton his shirt and ease off his loafers. And while he did that, she stood a little bit off, unbuttoning her sweater. And when she shrugged it off her shoulders, he could see the soft, rounded fall of her breasts caught in her bra and the hard nipples pushing through the fabric. And when she unclipped the bra between her breasts and pulled it back and away, her breasts hung like large, soft pearls and her nipples were red and hot as her mouth. Then she unzipped her skirt at the hip, undid the buttons and let it spill down around her ankles, stepping out of it, naked but for her high-heeled shoes. And Ross looked up at the same naked woman he had seen through the sheer curtains as he stood out in the cool Miami night.

When she came to him and put her belly against his face, he could smell the Shalimar mixed with the scent of her body. He kissed her flesh and folded his hands behind her hips and he was surprised at how firm her buttocks were.

He was just the kind of lover Sally had imagined he would be. Attentive. Careful. Cherishing. Thorough. She set the cuddly, brown koala aside and turned the lacy comforter back and lay down on the cool sheets and cocked up one knee to let him see her. When he had finished undressing and came to the bed and looked down at her parted legs, he wanted to put his mouth on her. But instead, she made him kneel on the bed and then took him in her mouth. She held him behind the buttocks and felt him tremble as she caressed him.

He was so tender that it quite astonished her—unhurried even in his desperation to have her, gentle even as his shaking fingers opened her. And when he was finally upon her, he waited until she reached down and guided him.

Then, patiently, he helped her into the rhythm. It was done so generously, it seemed as though no man had ever been so tender with her before. He put himself up on one elbow and slid one hand under her head and raised it softly to him. Adoringly, he cupped her breast in his other hand. Then he whispered, "Come with me." And when she was ready, he put his mouth softly against hers and let her sink her nails into his back so that they spent together.

They lay like that a long while after, him between her parted legs, one of her heels behind his knee, his head down on her chest, her arms holding him dearly. And then he heard her whimper, and when he looked at her in the last slow evening light through the ruffled curtains, she was weeping softly to herself.

"Did I hurt you?" he asked.

She shook her head and tried to catch her breath. "Oh, no," she said. "You're such a pretty lover."

"What, then?" he said. "Sally?"

"I want to love you so much that it hurts."

9:45 P.M. SAM BAKER WAS a little bit tipsy. He hadn't been that way since—well, he wasn't quite sure. New Year's Eve, perhaps. He had forgotten how good it felt. Or maybe it was only good to be tipsy because he felt so relieved.

After the press conference and the question-and-answer period, he'd thanked Mancuso and gone back to the Oval Office with Bender, O'Donnell, and Harrison for a postmortem. But when they walked in, his steward, Michael, was just opening a magnum of Hanns Kornell, and the three men shook his hand warmly and drank his health.

It had gone well. The press conference had all the drama of a Broadway opening night. And he'd handled the questions perfectly by all accounts. He'd even managed to sidestep the issue of how this would affect his relationship with Dan Eastman. It was just what Lou Bender had predicted, exactly what he'd wanted. And there was no doubt that tomorrow's polls would show a significant bump in the right direction.

After another bottle and another hour of small talk and big plans, Sam Baker had said good night and walked upstairs to the family quarters of the White House. He went into the green study, hung his jacket over a door knob, and loosened his tie and sat in the green chintz chair that he liked so well. Jack Kennedy had picked the furniture and decorated this room— well, Jackie actually. And Nancy Reagan had repapered the walls and recovered the sofa and chairs. But he had always thought of it as Wilson's room—because it was the room where Woodrow Wilson lay-in during his long illness.

Sam Baker put his feet up, his head back, and thought of his wife, Catherine, and how much he missed her and how much he wished he could share this moment with her. She had been a Newport Golden Girl in her time. She loved champagne and she loved to dance, from the day they met right up to the end. It was just like her to die on Christmas Day, leaving him with gifts and gay decorations to console him. Her passing had dimmed the season in a way that was beyond his capacity to express. But he saw that it was all just as she might have wished: the family gathered together, the house cheery and full of light. He thought, for her sake, he'd have one more glass of champagne before he went to bed. He pressed the button for his steward, and almost before he had released it, Michael knocked at the door and entered.

Baker looked up and smiled. "Michael, you're a mind reader."

"Admiral Rausch is here to see you, sir."

For a moment, the president didn't understand. Then he said, "Here? Now?"

"Downstairs, sir. In the conference room."

Sam Baker put his jacket on and went downstairs to the conference room on the second floor. Lou Bender was sitting at the far end of the long, gleaming mahogany table with his jacket slung over the back of his chair and no necktie and his sleeves rolled up. He looked like someone had just pulled him out of bed.

At the far end of the room sat two men Sam Baker didn't recognize. Rausch was in the corner, speaking on the phone. They all rose as the president entered.

"Good evening, gentlemen," he said. Then he turned to Bender.

But Bender opened his hands as though he hadn't a clue.

Rausch hung up the phone and came back to the table. Clearly, he was at a high level of excitement. "Mr. President," he said, "may I present Mr. Lewin Vander Pool. Lewin is head of the company's Office of Global Issues. He also supervises H-and-A."

They shook. "H-and-A?"

"Hypotheses and Assumptions," Vander Pool said, with a little bow of his head.

"War games," Bender said behind him.

"I see. A pleasure to meet you."

"And this is Jim Renwick. Head of our Latin American desk."

The president shook his hand. "I think we've met."

"Yes, sir. From time to time."

"Please. Be seated," the president said. And when they all sat down, Rausch opened a manila folder on the table before him.

"We believe we know who hired Petersen to assassinate Octavio Martinez," Rausch said.

The president shot a startled glance at Bender. Bender shrugged as though the whole thing were a big surprise.

Then Rausch said, "Jim?"

Renwick opened his folder and slid copies of a document across the table to the president and Bender.

"This is a list of the ten men who started the FSLN and the Sandinist revolution. You will recognize some of the names."

The president ran his eye down the list. Some of the names were familiar.

"Only Borge survived the twenty years of insurgency," Renwick said. "Eventually, he became a leader of the Marxist army that ousted Somoza and supplanted his government. The other nine died in the struggle. Eight in combat. One by assassination."

"The one who was assassinated was Carlos Fonseca," Rausch said.

The president shook his head to indicate that he didn't grasp the significance.

Renwick said, "Fonseca was the ideologue of the revolution. The father of the revolution, if you will. It was his idea they call themselves Sandinistas after the old guerrilla leader of the Thirties." He turned a page and went on. "By the time the Sandinistas kicked Somoza out in 1979, almost all the old revolutionaries were dead and many of the younger ones were disaffected. Some split over Ortega's close ties with the Soviet Union, others because they feared Nicaragua would become a Cuban proxy in Central America. Fonseca's romantic dream of a free, liberal, socialistic Nicaragua was long forgotten by the time Ortega marched into Managua."

Renwick closed his folder and took off his glasses. "But Ortega never forgot how Fonseca had used Sandino's memory to rally the *campesinos*. And when he came to power, Ortega ordered one symbolic act in the old man's name. They hunted down and killed the army officers who murdered Sandino in 1934. Two of the three who were still alive, anyhow."

"This is all quite interesting," the president said, and he was trying to be polite. "But I'm not sure I see the point."

"Wait until you hear the name of the third murderer," Rausch said.

Renwick said, "His name was Colonel Julio Ramirez."

"What?" Bender said, and his astonishment was real. "The old man who's spokesman for the Nicaraguan government-in-exile?"

"Yes."

"I don't believe it."

Vander Pool raised an index finger. "Yes, yes," he said. "You think of him as a blind old man, frail and poetic." He chuckled to himself and laced his hands across his belly. "But Julio Ramirez was not always an old man. You see, gentlemen, he was a colonel in Somoza's army. He was the commander of the death squads. For almost forty years, he systematically murdered the enemies of Somoza. He is, perhaps, the closest thing the Americas have ever produced to a Mengele or Eichmann."

"Are you telling me that the United States is sheltering a man like that?" the president said.

"It's a . . . convenience."

"It's an outrage."

"Mr. President," Vander Pool said gently, "it is a fact of political life."

Then Renwick said, "It's obvious to us that Ramirez and the Contra leaders hired Rolf Petersen to assassinate Martinez."

That drew a breath from everyone in the room.

Then Bender said, "Nonsense. That's idiotic."

"Not at all," Rausch said. "He was losing the war. We knew it. Why shouldn't they?"

"Goddamit," Bender said. "Martinez was the patron saint of the Contra movement! Are you telling me that his own people wanted him dead?"

"*We* did," Rausch said, softly.

"Pardon me, gentlemen," the president said. "Perhaps it would be opportune to ask Mr. Vander Pool and Mr. Renwick to excuse us at this time. That is, if they have nothing further to report."

Vander Pool and Renwick shuffled their papers together and rose to go. "Thank you, gentlemen," the president said. They nodded and went out.

When they had gone, the president turned on the two men left at the table. "Now, I want something understood," he said, and his voice was deep and sober. "What is said in this room stays in this room. And if I get even a hint that either of you have acted on anything said tonight without my express consent and permission, it will go hard with you. Do you hear me?"

"Yes," Bender said.

"Yes, sir," Rausch said.

The president sat where he could watch them both. "Now, Admiral Rausch," he said, "I want you to tell me what you believe happened to Octavio Martinez. I want it point-blank. Nothing held back."

"All right," Rausch said. He closed his folders and sat up and put his elbows on the table. "Martinez was losing the war. We knew it. Other leaders of the Contra movement knew it. We wanted Martinez out. So did they. And they knew—as we did—that the only way to get him out was feet first."

"Talk sense," Bender said. "If they'd wanted him out, they could have cut his throat in the jungle. Made it look like he'd died in combat."

"Sure, they could," Rausch said. "But they thought they could get a double-dip out of it. So, they hired a former CIA agent to do the killing— not to fool the peons or the press, but to fool us—the three of us—into thinking it was Ortega. If we believed that, they knew we'd step up the war. They fooled us. We stepped up."

The president sat, stunned.

Bender said, "You can't prove that. There's no hard evidence to prove that."

"Is there?" the president said. "Do you have any hard evidence? Or is this just another Company pipe dream?"

"Sometimes you have to draw conclusions without hard evidence," Rausch told them.

"Answer my question."

Rausch sighed and shook his head. "All right. There's no hard evidence."

Bender said, "I rest my case."

And Rausch said, "But there is circumstantial evidence—strong circumstantial evidence that ties Petersen to Ramirez."

Bender snorted. "That's preposterous. He was Ortega's hit man. You said so yourself."

"I was wrong."

"Christ, what else is new?" Bender said.

"Mr. President—"

"That's enough, Lou," the president warned.

Bender sat back away from the table and crossed his arms.

Rausch said, "Look, we knew that Petersen went freelance. And we assumed that he went over to the Marxists. He didn't. He went to work for Somoza. He went to work for Julio Ramirez."

Bender sat forward. "Prove it."

"He murdered Carlos Fonseca."

"What!"

"In 1976, Fonseca was in Honduras. Where the Nicaraguan army couldn't get at him. Petersen lured him into a cantina. He shot him in the face." Rausch slid a manila folder across the table to the president. "It's all here."

Bender rose and stood behind the president as he thumbed through the contents of the folder. There were two affidavits in Spanish with English translations. There was a photograph of a man's corpse, stripped naked and laid out on a bare board floor. There was a photocopy of a cashier's check for $50,000 drawn on the First National Bank of Tampa, its back endorsed "R. Peters."

"I don't buy it," Bender said. "Fonseca was killed in combat in the mountains of Nicaragua. It's in all the history books."

"Lou, that man was the George Washington of the Sandinist movement. What did you expect them to write about him? They put that story around to make him more of a hero," Rausch said. "He died in a whorehouse. In a dirty little fishing village called Cabo Gracias a Dios. Period."

"Shot by Rolf Petersen," the president said.

"Exactly."

The president closed the folder and got up and walked the length of the room. Then he stopped and looked back at Bender. "If it's true that Ramirez hired Petersen . . . what do we do about it?"

"Nothing," Bender said. "Not a goddam thing. We know it. We use it when we deal with Ramirez and the rest of those little rats. Other than that, we take it to our graves. If we let it go public, we tear the Contra movement in two—and you can kiss a democratic Nicaragua goodbye for the rest of this century."

"Excuse me, gentlemen," Rausch said, "but isn't going public with this the only chance we've got to stop the AIDS story from getting out?"

The president didn't answer. Rausch looked at Bender.

"Yes, Bill, I suppose it is," Bender said softly.

"Well, don't we want to—" Rausch broke off. He looked back and forth between the two men. Then Rausch realized that Bender had trapped him. "Now, wait a second. Just a damn second! If you think I'm taking that rap alone, you're goddam crazy!"

"Admiral Rausch!" the president said sharply. "You forget yourself."

"The hell I do," Rausch replied, and got up and came around the table to stand beside the president. He leveled a finger at Bender. "That little son-of-a-bitch set up the physical at Walter Reed. And approved the use of the virus."

"I think you're mistaken," Bender said. "We offer complete physicals to all visiting dignitaries from developing nations. And the virus was only authorized for laboratory testing—not for political murder."

"Goddamit, you knew it was going to be used on Martinez!"

"I knew nothing of the kind." Bender said.

Rausch stood facing the two men, his fists clenched, his face red with fury. "God damn you," he said "God damn you both."

Then he turned and slammed out the door.

Lou Bender put his hands behind his head and laced his fingers and rocked back in his chair. "Checkmate," he said.

10:20 P.M. WHEN SALLY FINISHED bathing, she toweled off and brushed her hair, sprayed her body with Shalimar, wrapped up in her big yellow terry robe, and slipped on her yellow fuzzy slippers and went out into the bedroom. Ross was lying on his back under the downy white coverlet, his hands behind his head and the fine black hair on his chest looking very male. There hadn't been a man in Sally's bed in so long, she had to stop and remember when Terry had been there last. But Terry looked so different from Ross, very russet and reddish and leaner and taller. Ross had thick patches of black hair in his armpits, and they kept a dark scent that aroused her when he held her. He had long, rolling muscles in his biceps and his forearms widened below the elbow, looking powerful and strong. But he had delicate wrists, and his palms were soft, and his fingers gentle and caressing. She had been astonished at his delicacy when he touched her. He touched her as she would have touched herself, soothingly, sensuously—as if he could feel the sensations he created in her body. It had been delicious, and when she thought of his touch, a warm wave of desire rolled over her.

"What are you doing?" she said.

He went on staring up at the ceiling. "Thinking."

"About what?" She went over and sat lightly on the edge of the bed. She was starting to want him again and she could feel the stirring in her belly.

"If I knew why that shell was black, I'd break this thing."

"Oh . . . really?" She was hurt that he was not thinking of her.

"I just—" Then he looked up and realized what he had done. He put his hand out to her and she took it. "I'm sorry," he said. "Do you . . . do you feel all right?"

"I feel—" And then she didn't know another way to say it. "I feel wonderful. I thought I was going to feel guilty. I thought I was going to be sick about. . ."

"Fallon?"

She nodded. "I thought I would be eaten up with guilt. But I'm not. I'm sorry. I'm just not."

"Me either. And I feel like I just broke rule number one. Do we have a chance?"

She smiled and looked wistful. "I don't know."

He said, "What you've got isn't working."

Then a chill came over her. "I know that," she said softly.

"Has he got that kind of grip on you?"

She rose and went to the far side of the bedroom and stood in the corner near the window. Then she said, "Yes."

"What is it?" he said. "How can he own you the way he does? I don't understand. You're a—"

"I love him," she said.

They stayed as they were a moment, staring at each other down the length of the room.

"You're afraid of him, aren't you?" Ross said. And when she didn't answer, he said, "That's it, isn't it? You're afraid of him."

She looked back at him.

"Why?" he asked. "Why are you so frightened of him? Are you afraid of what he might do if he found out about . . . us?"

"I don't know what he'd do," she said.

"What could he do?"

She lowered her head.

"He's dangerous," Ross said. "Fallon is dangerous, isn't he?"

She stared at him.

"Listen, Sally," he said, and sat up in bed. "Come here." He patted the edge of the bed beside him. And when she sat down, he took hold of her shoulders. "Nobody's going to hurt you as long as I'm around," he said. "Not Terry Fallon, not anybody." He held her close. "I know he's got you tangled up in something. Doesn't he?"

She swallowed hard, but she didn't deny it.

"And I know you've got to get away from him."

"I can't."

"You have to."

"I can't."

"What about us?"

But she didn't have an answer for him.

"Have you had a lot of men?" he said.

That made her stiffen. "Are we going to have that conversation now?"

"No. Only—"

"I've had enough men," she said. "But I've meant it every time. I don't make love the way some people do–for sport or to build a collection. I make it count. I make it matter."

"Do we matter?"

She said, "I wish we could." And she said it with all her heart.

He sat back, smiling. "For days I've been looking at you on the videotape," he said. "Watching you and wondering what it would be like to touch you. Looking at you and seeing how beautiful you are."

She laughed self-consciously. "I'm not beautiful," she said. "I'm a mess." Shyly, she put her hands to her face.

"You're beautiful even when you hide behind your ha—" He broke off there and stared at her, open-mouthed. He had seen her cover her face like that before—and, suddenly, he remembered where.

There was such a strange look in his eyes that it startled her. "What is it? David? What's the matter?"

"Nothing," he said. "Look. I have to go." He threw the covers back and began to swing his feet out of the bed.

"Wait," she said and caught at his hand. "What's wrong?"

"Nothing's wrong. I just have to go."

She looked at the clock on the nightstand. It read 10:35.

"It's not late."

"No, it's just—" he was hunting through the bedclothes for his undershorts.

She stretched back on the pillows and pulled one knee up so that her robe fell open. "Take me around again."

He had found his shorts, was hurrying to step into them, one leg after another. "I gotta go. Really."

"You can go later." She opened the top of her robe so that the cleavage of her breast peeped through.

"No. I really have to go now." He sat down on the end of the bed and started pulling on his socks.

"Wait," she said. She pulled open the drawer of her nightstand and drew out a handful of shiny multicolored ribbons, the kind of ribbons young girls wear in their hair.

He looked at the ribbons, then at her. "What's that for?"

"Don't you know?" She reached out and put the colored strips in his hand. He stared at them, puzzled.

"Like this." She opened her robe and slipped it out from under her body and tossed it onto the floor. Then she took one of the cotton strips from him and knotted it around her ankle and tied it to one of the brass stanchions at the foot of the bed.

"What are you doing?" he said.

She took another strip and tied her other ankle to the other stanchion. Now she was sitting up with her legs tied apart. He stared, dumb. She chose two more strips and knotted them around her wrists. And when she lay back, he could see that she meant him to tie her wrists to the brass pillars of the headboard.

"Sally, this is—"

"Do it," she said. "Please." And there was a look of lust in her eyes that he had never seen in any woman before.

When he had tied her wrists, she said, "There are some things in that drawer." And when he looked and saw the contents of the drawer, he was startled, even shocked.

"Start with my mouth," she said, and pulled all four ribbons until the bedposts moaned and he could see how helpless she was.

10:40 P.M. DAN EASTMAN STARED at the .38 revolver on his desk pad. It was hard to kill yourself. Even when it seemed like death was the only decent way out for everyone concerned. Even when death seemed to be the only satisfactory ending, the mind made it hard.

There was, after all, the matter of technique. In the ear? In the mouth? In the temple? There was the question of pain. Would it hurt? For how long? And what sort of mess would he leave on the walls and floor? Then there were the practical questions: a note, a will, insurance.

The mind had a clever way of expressing its will to live.

Dan Eastman sat for a long time—it seemed hours, and it was—staring at the revolver on his desk, trying to put the gun to his head and pull the trigger.

There was one thing that kept nudging him to act: the blinking lights on his telephone. All eight lights had blinked on as soon as the president had concluded his prepared remarks at the press conference. They blinked on and stayed on.

He knew that behind each of those lights was a reporter or a politician—

some shrewd man or woman with questions that would cut him to the quick. Would he resign? How could he have made such hollow allegations? Had the president reprimanded him? Had the president demanded he step down? And he knew those questions wouldn't end. They would go on as long as he was in politics, as long as he was in public life. And then they would take another form.

Even if he were to resign, the disgrace and humiliation would follow him forever. His friends—and his wife's friends—would whisper about him endlessly. At the club. After church. His children, who had lived their lives as privileged offspring of a state and national leader, would become objects of curiosity and, worse, sympathy. Like a chronic illness, like a foul odor—the ignominy would follow him and his family forever. And it would surround them like a fog, something that could not be confronted or faced down: eternal, ineradicable stigmata.

So, Dan Eastman brooded deep upon his death and life. And he had come to no resolution when his secretary, Dale, began knocking loudly on his study door. That reached him. In the nine years that she had served him, he had never once seen her lose her composure. Just then, he realized that she needed him—and that something of great moment was at hand.

He leaned back in his chair and blew a long breath at the ceiling. Then he opened the bottom drawer of his desk, and locked the revolver away. He stood up and brushed his shirt front, went to the door and opened it.

When Dale saw him, she blanched. It may have been because he looked like a man who had just returned from the dead. Or she may have been reacting to the astonishment on Dan Eastman's face when he saw, standing behind her, the director of the CIA.

11:35 P.M. LOU BENDER OWNED six white shirts and four black ties and wore a Timex watch. His old housekeeper, Charlotte, bought everything they needed for the apartment at Sears, J.C. Penney, or K-Mart. He didn't own a car and hoped he never would again. If he were home during the weekends, he was perfectly satisfied to have a can of tuna for lunch. But there were two things Lou Bender indulged in, and he was indulging in them tonight.

Somewhere back up the trail, when Howard Hughes was trying to get close to Senator Sam Baker, he'd sent him a Dunhill humidor—a big, square box made of matched grain rosewood, rubbed to a mirror sheen. The box was built to hold 200 massive Churchills. Under the lid, there were two humidifiers that were charged each month with distilled water. Between them was a hygrometer that measured humidity in the box to a perfect seventy-five percent. The box now commanded a place of honor in Lou Bender's living room, on a small Queen Anne table in a quiet corner, away from drafts and direct sunlight. In it, Lou Bender kept his everyday cigars and, for special occasions like tonight, a few Partagas *Lusitanias*—in his opinion, the best of the cabinet grade Havanas.

The other pleasure that Lou Bender esteemed above others was his brandy—Hennessy *Extra*, which he kept in a silver-mounted Baccarat decanter that his mother had sent him on his fiftieth birthday.

Tonight Lou Bender was savoring President Baker's triumphant press conference in his den, watching the television set with the huge Partagas in his teeth and his snifter of Hennessy at his hand. He was well satisfied with the coverage that the local station gave the conference on its eleven o'clock news. And he was actually looking forward to *Nightline*. He went out to the living room while the commercials were on, poured himself another brandy, and picked up a copy of the early edition of tomorrow's *Post* and wandered back toward the den.

When he returned to the set with his refill of brandy, *Nightline* had already started. The first thing Bender saw was a close-up of Vice President Dan Eastman and he heard Ted Koppel's voice say, ". . . what you call reliable sources?"

"Sources within the intelligence community who cannot be identified at this time," Eastman said.

For a moment, Lou Bender thought he must be watching a rerun. Or, perhaps, the Hennessy was simply getting the better of him.

"But if you knew this, Mr. Vice President," Koppel said, "why didn't you raise this issue at your press conference on Sunday?"

Eastman set his jaw. "Because I felt it might do irreparable damage to the foreign policy of the United States."

"You mean our policy of supporting the Contras?"

"Not just the Contras, Ted. What popular revolution would ever trust us again . . . if they knew that Colonel Martinez had been poisoned?"

At that moment, the red telephone rang.

11:55 P.M. ROSS WAS FULL of complicated feelings when Sally kissed him goodbye at the door. It was a soft kiss and a delicate one. And he looked down at her in the soft chiffon nightgown, all freckles and blue eyes and hair brushed back like a shy little girl. He thought what a mystery it was that one woman's body could contain all those appetites and desires and dark, unfamiliar passages.

Then he went out into the sticky night, walked to where he had parked his car. It was late, but he was going back to the office. He had an idea. And he had things to do.

He crossed into the street toward the door of his car and hefted his briefcase from hand to hand, digging in one pocket and then another for his car keys. And when he found them, he stood in the street, with his briefcase between his knees, bending over the lock of the car while he picked through the key ring for the right one. Then he heard a shoe scuff the pavement behind him, and when he looked around three young Latino men in their twenties were walking toward him. They looked like a street gang, cruising for trouble.

"Easy, boys," Ross said. "I'm a federal officer." He unbuttoned his jacket.

One of the boys lunged at him, shoving him hard into the side of his car, so hard that when his head hit the molding over the door frame, Ross almost lost consciousness. His briefcase fell to the pavement and another boy grabbed for it—and when Ross tried to stop him, the third boy hit him in the back, under the left shoulder blade, and knocked him down.

Then he heard their running feet behind him and car doors slamming and a squeal of tires. When he looked up, two headlights on high beams were roaring toward him. He rolled over, wedged himself under the edge of his car as the screeching wheels shot past. Then he rolled back out into the street with his revolver extended and fired six shots at the fleeing tail lights. The rear window of the car shattered. The old Ford bounced off cars left and right and came to a stop at the corner.

Ross ejected the empties from his revolver and reached for a reload on his belt. And while he snapped the bullets into the chambers, he squinted at the license plate of the car. He was dizzy from the blow and his back hurt. He couldn't quite focus, but he could make out a Virginia plate with the number BRB-627. He raised his revolver to fire, but the Ford lurched around the corner and out of sight.

He lay down, breathing heavily, and rested his cheek against the damp cobblestones. He was dizzy and light-headed, as though he might pass out. He thought of that number: BRB-627. He burned it into his memory even as he felt himself drifting into unconsciousness. BRB-627. When he saw Mancuso, he would have to remember to tell him. Joe would know what to do.

The gunshots that broke the quiet Georgetown night sent a barrage of calls to 911. And it was less than five minutes before a black-and-white turned off Wisconsin Avenue onto P Street to investigate, its spotlight sweeping back and forth and its cherrytop spinning.

When the two uniformed cops saw Ross by the side of the road, they parked the black-and-white so that it blocked the street and fixed the spotlight on him. And when they saw he was holding a gun, they challenged him. But when he didn't respond, one of them covered him while the other cop slid up along the row of parked cars. When he was close enough, he kicked the gun out of Ross's hand.

Then they turned him over and saw that he had been stabbed once below the left shoulder blade with some thin instrument that barely made a wound. There was only a dot of blood at the entry, but its placement indicated a cardiac puncture and massive internal hemorrhaging. Ross's breathing had stopped and they could not feel a pulse in his throat. But he was warm and not brain dead.

By the time the ambulance arrived, he was.

THE EIGHTH DAY

2:10 A.M. SALLY LURCHED IN her sleep and opened her eyes and listened. Then she knew it was the silence that had awakened her. That was odd.

She'd had no trouble falling asleep, even when the sirens passed the house and stopped a few blocks away. She had heard their approaching, rising whine and the falling Doppler effect as they went by. Then they settled in at a note and moaned on like a lost child for a long, long time.

She heard the helicopter overhead and imagined its searchlight sweeping down on the streets and houses of Georgetown. Then she heard the motors of the vans and their generators as the news crews gathered. But she was used to all of that. She unplugged the phone, turned over, plumped the pillow under her head, pulled the comforter to her chin, and drifted off to sleep. Now the silence itself had roused her, and she lay awake, thinking how much she had changed.

There had been a time in Memphis when sirens in the night would have set her heart pounding. The jungles of Honduras had ended all that. In the first months at Lagrimas, she had wept each time she helped lower the body of an old man or a newborn baby into the earth. Each time she had performed the simple ritual, she had cried bitter tears. But before the year was out, she felt nothing when a grown man or woman died. And when a child died, she felt only frustrated rage.

The change began that night the Honduran army had raided the village and shot two men. She had watched the barbaric murders with a kind of tempered curiosity—had watched the hog-tied men weeping and praying and begging for mercy. She had watched the soldiers shoot them— the first one in the ear, the other, who kept turning his head, in the mouth. And then she had watched them mutilate the bodies. It wasn't until they turned on the children of Lagrimas that she confronted the officer in charge, and got a crack in the face and was thrown onto the road for her trouble.

She could remember very clearly the day in 1976 when Terry took her to La Riserva, the mansion in the Florida Everglades, and introduced her to Colonel Julio Ramirez. He was in his early sixties then, a slim, patrician man in a white uniform and dark glasses, courtly and deferential to her in the way Latins often are to another man's woman.

Ramirez had spoken with passion about the pain and suffering of Nicaragua as the Sandinista war dragged on. And he tried to convince her—as he and Terry were convinced—that if the Somocistas could only talk to the Sandinistas, only sit down and reason together with them, that many lives could be spared. But, of course, by then there were decades of deceit and vendetta separating the two sides. There was no common ground, no meeting point. And so the pointless war dragged on, and the men died, and the old ones, and, of course, the children.

That night, together in the upstairs bedroom, she pressed herself to Terry and whispered, "I don't trust him. Let's go back to Houston."

"We have to trust him," Terry said. "It's the only chance for peace down there."

"I don't believe it."

"I need him," Terry said. "I need his help to get what we want. Don't deny me."

"Have I ever denied you anything?"

The next morning, she went. She took a plane from Miami to Tegucigalpa, took a wheezing, creaking DC-3 to Cabo Gracias a Dios, the place she had fled from five years before. She went back to the steaming damp nights, the whir of insects about the candle, the sounds of frogs in the hollows of the trees, the cool, drifting stink of the swamp that followed the land breeze eastward to the sea.

She was there a week in a two-dollar room above El Parador before the man she was waiting for finally came. She was having dinner on the rickety veranda when she saw him. He was just standing there in the little plaza wearing a soft brown fedora with a dark ring of sweat at the bottom of its crown. He'd grown a beard that was speckled with trail dust. He was wearing a blousy white *cotona* shirt—the kind the *Ladinos* wore—that hung almost to the knees, and baggy white cotton pants and moccasins. There was a wide, crackled leather belt around his middle and a machete stuck under it, the kind with the hooked tip that the *campesinos* used for cutting cane. She did not recognize him until he looked up at her and she noticed his eyes. Then she saw that he had the eyes of Carlos Fonseca—patient eyes, eyes that seemed certain of their destiny.

When they had made love and he had bathed and it grew dark and the heat of the day went down, they took a walk along the quay, through the rancid odors of the port, listening to the sad creaking of old steamers, and the moaning of their hawsers as the tide began to turn. They spoke softly, in Spanish.

"How did you know I had come back?" she said.

"They told me."

"Who?"

"Everyone. They remember you . . . *La Putita*."

She smiled and looked down at her bare feet on the concrete sea wall.

"It goes well?" she said.

"Poorly. Many are dead."

"And the Somocistas?"

"Stronger every day. They have helicopters now. They can be everywhere at once."

"Why don't you talk?" she said. "Negotiate?"

"They cannot be trusted."

"Then what can be done?"

"Nothing. But to go on."

"On to what?"

"To nothingness."

He stayed in the room that evening, and she went out and bought some fresh flowers and a bottle of *Flor de Caña*. The old woman from El Parador fixed them platters of *bocaditos*. And they were sitting at the table in the corner of the room with the candle flickering between them when the bullet struck. It was without warning, but she remembered it very clearly.

Through the window behind her, she heard a pop like a champagne bottle being opened on the terrace. There was a quick whisper in her left ear as though someone were trying to get her attention. Fonseca was sitting across from her, chewing, and then he jumped a little and sat still again. But there was a black mark on his right temple. Then his heart beat, and a spurt of blood shot out of the hole and spattered on her white linen night dress. He looked at the red stain, cocked his head as though he were embarrassed that he had made a mess of such a pretty gown and wanted to apologize. Then his body convulsed and he smashed his face down into the plate, spattering food and wine and blood over her.

Someone kicked in the door, men swarmed into the room, men in a uniform she didn't recognize. They threw Fonseca's body on the floor, kicked it until they had broken the jawbone and ribs and the pelvis. But he was already dead and beyond feeling the pain. Then they began to strip him. One of the soldiers stood beside her and put the barrel of a revolver to her temple.

But she didn't resist. She didn't look up at the man with the gun. All the while they were beating and kicking and stripping the dead Carlos Fonseca, she sat where she was at the table, the food and wine and blood running down her face and arms. When the soldier beside her put his hand down the front of her gown and roughly fondled her breasts, she sat unmoving in silence. The men were shouting and laughing and tearing through her belongings. Then the soldier who had been molesting her grabbed her elbow and dragged her to her feet and threw her on the bed and she lay there while he fumbled with the buttons of his fly. Then he lay down on her and pushed between her legs, but she was tense and dry and he could not penetrate her. So he threw his whole weight upon her and pressed the gun barrel into the middle of her forehead so hard that it pushed her head down into the mattress and he said, *"Senorita, acuérdate de mí cuando estás en el paraiso con Jesús. Amen."* He thumbed back the hammer of the gun.

Sally looked into his dull, sadistic eyes. It was always the same face that the murderers wore: the sweaty, heavy brow, the wide flat nose and thin mustache, the dark, cratered skin and slitted, bestial eyes. She had seen that face many times. And she knew it was a face that had no name and a hundred thousand names.

"Chinga usted," she said. And she spit in his face and closed her eyes and prepared to die.

Someone shouted, *"¡Basta¡ Basta ya!"* And the men stopped tearing the room apart and fell silent. The man on top of Sally began to fumble with his clothes and slipped off her. Then someone was pulling down the skirts of her gown, and helping her to sit up, and through the closed lids of her eyes she sensed flashes of light. When she opened her eyes, the body of Carlos Fonseca lay on the bare floor boards and a man with a camera was standing over it, snapping flash pictures.

"Are you going to be all right?" the man beside her said.

"Yes. In a moment."

"I've missed you."

She was just staring, dull-eyed, at the body on the floor.

"This is nothing personal," the man said. "Just a cash transaction. You understand."

"I understand."

"I work for anyone who has the money now."

"I'll remember that."

He wanted to kiss her, but she turned her face away. Then he shouted to the soldiers and they stole what they could carry and left her. The old woman from the cantina called the police, who took the body and questioned her. But, clearly, she knew nothing. They drove her to the airport under guard, passed her through customs, and left her. She cabled her flight number to Terry and flew home.

But there was no one to meet her at the airport in Houston. And when she arrived at the apartment on Faculty Row, he was out at a basketball game. And it was very late and she had been asleep for hours when he slipped into the bed beside her.

"Terry—"

"I'm glad you're home," he said, and folded her to him. "That was a very brave thing you did."

She pressed her cheek against the wiry hair of his chest. "Tell me you love me, for God's sake," she said.

"Did you sleep with him?"

And when she didn't answer, he said, "Tell me about it. Did you suck his cock? Sally?"

"Terry. They killed him."

"Did you suck him?"

Reluctantly, she nodded.

"Did he come in your mouth?"

"Terry, please. They—"

"Tell me."

"Yes."

"And did you go down on him? Or did he straddle your chest?"

"Please, don't," she said. "Not tonight."

"Which way?"

"Both . . ."

"Tell me."

And she told him all, told him step-by-step, every detail, while he masturbated until he came on her belly.

She didn't like to admit it, but he had meant something to her, Fonseca had. He was a fool and an impractical dreamer. But he had meant something to her. And she had loved him.

Perhaps it *was* nothing personal. But she had waited twelve years to send the note to Rausch and take her revenge on Rolf Petersen.

And it had been worth every blessed minute of the wait.

6:00 A.M. LOU BENDER WAS now entering phase three of the defense.

When Bender's red telephone rang just before midnight, it had been the president.

"Are you watching it?"

"Yes."

"And?"

"It's Rausch," Bender said. "He's . . . shall we say, transferring his allegiance."

"I see. How bad is it?"

"They've got nothing."

"Nothing?"

"They haven't got the body. They haven't got the autopsy report. The doctor from Walter Reed was killed. You heard about that?"

"Yes. I heard about that."

"I'd say we're in good shape and Eastman's made his final blunder."

"What are you going to do?" the president said.

"I've got some things to take care of," Bender said, but he didn't say what. "You'll have to ask Eastman for his resignation, you know."

The president hesitated. Then he said, "Yes. I know."

"I'd say it's more important now than ever to lock Fallon in on your ticket."

"That's impossible," the president said.

"It's inevitable," Bender said. "Sam, either you run with him—or you don't run."

"Is that your assessment?"

"It's the only assessment."

The president sighed. "I understand." He hung up.

The next thing Bender did was to cut off Rausch's only line of retreat. It took him almost an hour to track down chief of Naval Operations Fleet Admiral James Otis at Claridge's Hotel.

"What do you want?" Otis said when his wife woke him and handed him the phone.

"I want to know if Admiral William Rausch has a lot of friends in the navy."

"That's why you're calling me in London at five o'clock in the morning?" But Bender knew that Otis had already caught his drift.

"I can't think of a better reason," Bender said. "What's the answer?"

"Not many since the Walker purge."

"Jim, do you think that Rausch would be suitable for return to active duty?"

"What do you think?"

"I'm not so sure."

"Neither am I," Otis said.

"See to it," Bender said.

"I'll make some calls in the morning."

"It won't wait till morning."

"All right." Otis groaned, and Bender could hear him rolling out of the bed. "Consider it done."

The third phase required a luncheon meeting in New York. Bender set his alarm for 5:00 A.M.—and started on the calls at 5:30. By 6:00, the four guests had been summoned and the venue agreed. Then Bender called Andrews Air Force Base and booked the presidential G-3 for 11:15. With luck, he could be in and out of New York by 2:15 and back in his White House office by 3:30.

It was just coming up on 6:10 in the morning when he padded out to the kitchen in his bathrobe and slippers, poured himself another cup of coffee, and took the morning edition of the *Washington Post* into the den and sat down. By the cold, gray light of the gathering rain clouds, he read the banner headline.

Lou Bender sighed and shook his head. It was not as neat as he had made it sound when the president called. The FBI doctor who performed the autopsy on Martinez had removed the reference to AIDS from his report. Once he signed a falsified report, he was effectively neutralized. But the two agents had seen the original. One way or another, he would have to silence them. The awkward part was that he might need Rausch to get it done. He leafed through his newspaper. Then something caught his eye and made him laugh out loud.

6:15 A.M. SALLY HAD JUST stripped the *Washington Post* out of its plastic wrapper when the phone rang.

It was Steve Chandler. "Comment?" he said.

Sally stared at the headline:

EASTMAN SAYS MARTINEZ WAS POISONED

"Sally? Are you there?"

Quickly, she composed herself. "Yes," she said. "No comment."

"Off the record?"

"Nope."

"Background?"

"No chance."

"Deep background?"

"Pass."

"Miss Crain," Chandler said, and there was an edge in his voice, "is it true that Senator Fallon kicked you out on your pretty ass?"

"You know, Steve, I almost used to like you."

"You know, Sally, I'm just trying to do my job. And you're making it real hard for me."

"Am I? Good."

"You gave Fallon to the other guys exclusive for Thursday at eight."

"Wasn't my call."

"Who?"

"Chris Van Allen."

"The little fruit basket? So, you are out on your ass."

"Just a momentary setback, Steve-o. Don't hold a wake for me yet."

"Then I suppose I'll see you at the convention?"

It was a cruel and leading question. But Sally didn't blink. "You bet you will."

"They're saying that if this poisoning thing has any legs, your boy may have a chance to go all the way."

"Could be."

"All right," Chandler said, and Sally knew that the fishing expedition was over and that he was getting down to it. "Let's do business."

"I'm listening." She pushed a pillow up against the headboard and leaned against it.

But Chandler hesitated. Then he said, "Let me call you back on another line. Two minutes."

"Done." She hung up and ran her eye down column six of the front page of the *Post*.

It was an incredible story that had unfolded while she slept. Eastman had called Sandy Rogers, the producer of *Nightline,* and asked him if he would bump his scheduled show for a one-on-one interview about new revelations in the death of Martinez. Rogers grabbed the chance and ABC got an exclusive on the story of the alleged poisoning.

Sally could imagine the flurry of midnight phone calls as NBC and CBS executives castigated their staffs for getting beat on a major news break. That was half the reason for Chandler calling this morning. But as Sally followed the jumped story to an inside page, her hands began to tremble with excitement. She understood why Steve Chandler believed Terry might have a shot at the number one spot on the ticket.

In his *Nightline* interview, Eastman had quoted "unnamed but highly placed" sources who alleged that Martinez had been dosed by an army doctor with AIDS virus provided by the army's medical research center at Fort Deitrich, Maryland. A Pentagon spokesman had confirmed that the army, like many civilian research organizations, was working on an AIDS vaccine, but denied that any experimental strain of the virus had been furnished or could have been stolen. Although Eastman stopped short of placing the blame for the poisoning, the clear implication was that the order must have originated in the Baker White House.

If there were a grain of truth to the story . . . if the allegations gained currency, even if they were ultimately disproved, they might be enough to panic the convention. It might send the delegates in a headlong search for a white knight, a Mr. Clean. They just might hand Terry Fallon the presidential nomination.

She looked at the phone and longed to call Terry and talk it out. But she didn't want to miss Steve Chandler's call. When the phone rang she grabbed it.

"Yes, Steve?"

"Steve who?"

It was Terry. "I was just going to call you," she said.

"Steve who?"

"Steve Chandler. From the *Today* show. I'm waiting for him to call me back."

"You saw?"

"Yes."

"What do you think?"

"It could be the chance of a lifetime."

"What are you talking about?" he said, and his voice was strangely puzzled.

"The Eastman story. What else?"

"Did you see page five?"

"Page five?"

"Bottom right."

She turned to the page. Then she saw what he meant.

OFF-DUTY FBI AGENT
MUGGING VICTIM

It was two short paragraphs in the lower right-hand corner of the page. How cold it looked in black and white, how small. Like a little paper tombstone. A pennysworth of ink and paper that blotted out a life. She pictured him: his eyes-down, self-conscious smile, the way his hands shook the first time he held her. She looked again at the printed report. Such a brief knell for a life that could have brought her so much. Like another life she remembered that had flickered out too soon. She had wept for Carlos Fonseca. She would weep for Ross. But she could weep for neither before Terry Fallon.

"Oh," she whispered. "I didn't know. My God, it's terrible, isn't it?"

She put her hand on her belly as though she could still feel Ross moving within her.

"Yes," Terry said. "Terrible."

"When can I see you?"

"I'm very busy today. I'll have to call you."

"When?"

"When I'm not busy."

"Terry?"

"Yes?"

"Tell me you love me."

"I'll call you later." He hung up.

When the phone rang again, it was Chandler.

"Sorry," he said. "I wanted to find an empty office. Are you alone?"

"Yes."

"Nobody around to pick up an extension?"

"Steve, you're really getting into this secrecy bit, aren't you?"

"Listen, Sally, this is real hot. You know Mike Marshall, our investigative guy? The one who did the Mafia story with the hidden camera?"

"I've met him."

"You think he's solid?"

"When he's sober."

"Well, he's been in Honduras for the last three months. And he has documents that purport to show that Rolf Petersen—you know, the guy who shot Martinez?"

"Yes?"

"—that Rolf Petersen has been working for the Contras. He's been working for what's-his-face, Ramirez, the old guy who's their spokesman."

Sally held her breath. "And?"

"Well," Chandler said. "You know all the players. You think Ramirez could have ordered Petersen to hit Martinez?"

She tried to sound nonchalant. "No way."

"Why so sure?"

"Because Martinez was the only leader they had with the spine to stand up to the CIA and give the Contras some semblance of independence."

"Who do you think ordered the hit?"

"I don't know. But Ortega's in this somewhere."

"Not according to Ortega. He keeps swearing up and down that he's not guilty. He gave us another interview Friday."

"I saw it."

"Guy says he's innocent."

"So does Khadaffi."

"Our bureau chief in Managua believes him."

"Get another bureau chief."

"You really think they're all dirty, don't you?"

"They are all dirty," she said. "Don't forget—I've been there. I know how they smell."

"Okay, kid," Chandler said, and there was real gratitude in his voice. "I appreciate it."

"*Por nada.*"

"Buy you a drink in St. Louis?"

"Maybe two," she said. They hung up.

Sally dropped the newspaper and lay back. It would not be easy to keep three network news divisions off balance. She could not hope to cover the Ramirez connection for very long if they picked up the scent and decided to dog it. But if she could just keep them off balance for a few more days . . . then it might not matter. Steve Chandler's warm tone of gratitude had a sweet irony about it. It was always so tempting to a reporter to befriend someone in government, to get close to them, build a relationship with them. Every young reporter saw that as a shortcut to the big story, the real break, the personal exclusive. But it was also a trap. Because every reporter who relied on a relationship with someone in government got used. Sooner or later, they all got used.

She picked up the receiver and dialed a local number.

"Carter."

"Crain."

"Well . . . hello." There was a deep ripple in his voice. "How nice of you to call."

"Are you keeping up with the news?"

"Just heading over to the office now."

"Are you coming to visit me today?" She was purring.

"Hey," he said. "Give me a moment. How about—how about noon?"

"Noon is good," she said. "Park around back and don't be late. I've got something special to show you."

"Something I'll like?"

"Something you haven't seen in a long, long time."

"I can't wait," he said, and she could tell by his voice that he was already aroused.

After she put the phone down, she took her shaving cream and razor and ran herself a hot bath.

7:55 A.M. THE PARTY BRAIN TRUST had asked Charlie O'Donnell to breakfast at the Cosmos Club. But it wasn't an invitation. It was a summons. When he arrived, there were six men already seated at the long mahogany table, including Bill Wickert. It was the power of the party, if not the glory.

The stewards entered and served fresh orange juice all around and took orders. When they went out, Wickert said, "Charlie, you know what we want."

"No, Bill." O'Donnell tucked his napkin under his chin. "You tell me."

DeFrance reached over and put his hand on O'Donnell's. There was something so genteel about the man that you had to be more than careful around him. "Charlie, what we don't want is a quarrel. Not this morning. Not at the convention. You understand."

"I do."

"Then tell us, Charlie," Longworth said. "Tell us about your progress toward placing Terry Fallon on the ticket."

"Yeah. Tell us," Wickert said.

"Quiet, please, Bill," deFrance said.

Wickert slouched in his chair at the head of the table.

"I've got nothing to report," O'Donnell said.

"Nothing?" Hugh Brown said. He was a Connecticut Yankee, a descendent of one of the signers of the Constitution. He wore little round rimless glasses and carried a pocket watch in his breast pocket, hung from a gold chain in his lapel. "But surely after last night, everyone realizes that the president and Mr. Eastman can no longer be expected to serve another term together."

"The president is evaluating the situation," O'Donnell said.

"But, surely," Brown said, "the man has to resign."

"Does he?"

The men at the table looked at each other.

Longworth spoke for them. "Yes, he does. Sunday, Eastman told the country that the president might be guilty of obstruction of justice. And the FBI proved that he was either a liar or a fool. Now he's invented some fairy tale about Martinez being poisoned. I'm beginning to think he's a certifiable lunatic."

"Now just a minute," Wickert said. "Are you telling us that Baker isn't going to demand Eastman's resignation?"

"I don't know," O'Donnell said. "My compliments, Bill. This juice is fresh."

"Answer the goddam question!"

DeFrance sighed. "Bill, you are common," he said wearily.

"I want an answer," Wickert said, unfazed. "This party wants an answer."

O'Donnell looked at the men around the table. Wickert's manner was impertinent, but his question was not. "I'm sorry," O'Donnell said. "I don't have that answer for you this morning."

"Why the hell not?"

"Because I don't know it, Bill."

"Holy shit," Wickert said. "Is this whole administration out of its mind?"

DeFrance said, "Bill, be quiet."

"Yes, Bill," Longworth said. "Right now."

"For Christ's sake," Wickert said, "am I the only man at this table who understands that Eastman accused the president of the United States of murder?"

It was very quiet for a moment. Then there was a knock at the pantry door and the stewards entered and served breakfast.

When they had gone, Brown cleared his throat. "Is there any evidence to support the allegation that Colonel Martinez was poisoned?"

"None that I'm aware of," O'Donnell said.

"Has there been a proposal to exhume the body and conduct an examination?"

"That's impossible," O'Donnell said. "Colonel Martinez was cremated. A Contra plane scattered his ashes over Nicaragua. Joe, pass me the butter, please."

Some of them fell to eating.

"Well, what about the autopsy after the shooting?" Wickert said. "Who's seen a copy of that?"

No one spoke.

"Don't you think it would be a good idea if we did?"

"I believe we're losing sight of the issue, gentlemen," Swartz said. Whenever he spoke, people knew it was important. "Whether or not Colonel Martinez was poisoned is germane to our discussion, of course, but it is not the central question." Most of the men around him went on with their breakfast. But O'Donnell had stopped eating. He was listening, and watching.

"The issue is that Sam Baker is no longer electable on his own," Swartz said. "Without Terry Fallon on the ticket, he can't win."

At the far end of the table, Bill Wickert raised his head. He had found his first ally, and he was a powerful one.

"It's ludicrous to believe that Eastman can survive this kind of public humiliation. Whether he resigns is moot," Swartz went on. "He must resign and Sam Baker must accept Fallon."

"Or take a walk," Wickert said. "Charlie, are you listening?"

Charlie O'Donnell scanned the faces of the men on both sides of the table. Wickert was speaking the truth. If he couldn't deliver a Baker-Fallon ticket, his grip on the party leadership was lost. If that went, his position as Speaker went with it. Then he would have only two choices: a back bench in the House, or retirement.

"I'll know the sentiment of the room," O'Donnell said.

The words fell heavily.

Some of them looked down at the table. Some fidgeted with their silverware. The brave ones looked him in the eye.

"All right, Charlie," Wickert said. "If that's the way you want it." He sat up. "Resolved that the Speaker shall ask the president to accept Terry Fallon as his running mate . . . or not to seek renomination."

Hugh Brown said, "Aye."

Every head in the room turned to him.

Brown looked back at them. "That's what I believe. That's my vote."

Wickert said, "Roland?"

DeFrance put down his coffee cup. "Excuse me saying this, but I believe this gesture is premature."

Johnson said. "So do I."

"There's a motion on the table," Wickert said. "Roland? Yea or nay?"

DeFrance wet his lips. "Aye," he said.

"Gideon?"

But before Longworth could answer, Congressman Johnson put his napkin on the table, pushed his chair back and stood up. "Gentlemen, this resolution is infamous. And I say *no* to you. And good morning." He nodded to O'Donnell, went to the front door, and let himself out.

Senator Longworth cleared his throat. "Aye," he said.

"Abram?" Wickert said.

Swartz stared hard at O'Donnell.

"Abram?" Wickert said again.

"Aye," Swartz said. "God forgive me. Aye."

Charlie O'Donnell sighed and pulled his napkin from under his collar and set it on the table before him. "Oh, ye little men," he said softly.

"We're resolved then," Wickert said. "The Speaker will convey to the president the party's wish that he—"

"And when Eastman is gone and Sam Baker refuses your ultimatum?" O'Donnell said bitterly. "Then what?"

"Then," Wickert said, and his mouth curled in a leering smile, "Fallon."

8:30 A.M. THEY MET, AS had been their habit, in the study just off the Oval Office. There was something so imposing about the Oval Office, something so portentous in every word spoken between its walls, that they had decided early on in their administration that they would use the study when they had to put their heads together. And even though the subject of their meeting would be grave, the president kept his bargain and waited for Dan Eastman there.

When the vice president arrived, he looked rested and relaxed, like a man who had put down a great burden.

"Coffee?" the president said.

"No, thanks," Eastman said. "Let's keep this short and sweet."

"All right."

They sat in armchairs in a corner of the room.

"You've created quite a commotion this week, Dan," the president said. "First the issue of the FBI. Now this business about Martinez and the army."

"I call them as I see them, Sam. You know that."

The president smiled. "It was your most endearing quality. But now you've gone too far."

"Can you deny that the army dosed Martinez with AIDS?"

The president leaned back in his chair. "I can neither deny nor confirm that, Dan. And I can't let that become the focus of our conversation now."

"But it is the focus. And if it's true, I'm going to campaign on it."

"If you can prove it, you should do so."

"I will prove it. Don't worry."

"And you may campaign on any issue you choose. But you cannot campaign as vice president of the United States."

Eastman leaned forward and stuck out his chin. "Says who?"

Sam Baker sat back and crossed his legs. "Dan, we have a very unpleasant set of circumstances before us. I'll ask you, as a friend and a colleague, not to make them any more unpleasant than they have to be."

"Cut it out, Sam," Eastman said, and stood up. "You think I'm going to resign just for the sake of good form?"

"No. But I do want your signed, undated letter of resignation on my desk this morning."

"Undated?"

"I'll decide when it's appropriate for you to step down."

Dan Eastman laughed. "You are a dreamer, aren't you? You're in a death struggle with me for control of the convention and the White House. And you think you're going to win by a peremptory strike? Without a fight?"

The president spoke very quietly. "I'd hoped I wouldn't have to say this to you, Dan. . . ."

"Say what?"

"It took me a long time to understand why you came forward with the story of the Secret Service man. But I believe I understand it now."

"Understand what?"

"You've been trying to hide in plain sight. And it's so obvious that everyone overlooked it."

"Overlooked what?"

The president stood up. "I think we understand each other," he said. "Goodbye, Dan. I'll be waiting for your letter." He opened the door to the Oval Office and went out.

10:50 A.M. "GO 'WAY," MANCUSO moaned. He tried to pull his pillow over his head, tried to shut out the light and the banging at the door. "Go away. Nobody home."

But the knocking grew even louder and then he could hear Mrs. Weinstein on the other side of the door hollering, "Mr. Mancuso, your office is calling!"

"Tell 'em I'm sick. Tell 'em I died and went to heaven."

The banging stopped. "It's your office. They say it's an emergency."

"Fuck," he said, and swung his feet out of bed and pulled on his old blue-and-white bathrobe. He shuffled to the door.

Mrs. Weinstein stared at him when he opened the door. "You look like death *varmed* over."

"And a very nice morning to you, Mrs. Weinstein."

He went down the stairs to the telephone in the foyer. He'd slept half the night on the park bench, until a D.C. cop roused him and made him move along. His back was killing him.

"Yeah?"

"Joe . . . Jesus Christ, he's dead. . . ."

It was the secretary, Jean, and she was hysterical.

"Who is? What the hell are you talking about?"

"Dave. Dave Ross. He's dead."

He wrote down the address of the funeral home and hung up the phone.

Mancuso had left his car downtown; still, he could have called a cab. But he didn't. He walked. Even though the sky threatened rain, he walked.

He walked all the way across town to the funeral parlor, a low, modern, concrete building with curved walls. He stood across the street for a while, watching people going in, some alone, some in couples, some of the women weeping. When he finished his second cigarette, he realized he couldn't put it off forever. He made the sign of the cross over himself, kissed his thumbnail, and went inside. There was a pale, middle-aged man in a black suit standing at a little podium in the foyer like a restaurant maitre d'.

"May I help you, sir?"

Mancuso looked around. "I dunno. I—" He unfolded the piece of paper with the address.

"Which party are you with?" the man asked gently.

"Party?"

"Which funeral?"

But Mancuso didn't understand. "I thought. . . ." He looked at the paper again.

"The name of the deceased," the man said. "What is the name of the deceased?"

"He's my partner. Ross."

The man checked his book. "David Michael Ross. Yes. You'll find him in the Zion Room." He gestured to the doorway on the right. Mancuso turned to go and then the man cleared his throat, and held out a black handkerchief.

"I got one," Mancuso said, and touched the handkerchief in the breast pocket of his jacket.

"No, no," the man said "This is a yarmulke."

"A what?"

"A yarmulke—a hat."

"You wear a hat in there?" Mancuso said and pointed toward the room.

"Always," the man said. "Indoors." He turned his head and Mancuso could see that the man was wearing one.

"Me, too?"

"Please."

Mancuso shrugged and took the hat and put it on. Then he signed the book at the door and went inside.

Three rows of benches faced the plain maple coffin, and men and women in black were sitting here and there among them. Some were bent forward as if they might be praying. There was a soft sound of recorded organ music and, from time to time, someone sighed or blew his nose.

A little round man in a dark blue suit and a white yarmulke came up to him. "Welcome," he said and took Mancuso's hand and pumped it. Mancuso was surprised that he seemed so cheerful. "I'm Dave's uncle, Doctor Aronowitz. Call me Lenny. And you're?"

"Joe Mancuso. I work with him."

The man leaned back and looked him over and his face lit up. "You're Joe?"

"Yeah."

"Well, *shalom,* Joe. I'm delighted to meet you."

"Yeah," Mancuso said.

"Wait. Wait here," Lenny said.

Then he turned toward a group of women standing at the back of the benches and went "Psst! Psst! Tessie!" When a chubby, gray-haired lady looked up, he beckoned her over.

"Tess, this is Joe Mancuso," Lenny said, but it didn't seem to register. "Tess, it's Davey's partner from the FBI. Agent Mancuso from the FBI."

Instantly, her face lighted. "You're Joe? *Oi-yoi-yoi!* Did he love you!" She grabbed Mancuso in both her arms and pulled his head down and kissed him. Then she turned to the other women. "Marge. Ceil. Come. Come." And she waved them over. "This is Agent Mancuso from the FBI. Davey's partner. The man who taught him all the things."

And the two other women shook his hand and clucked and murmured over him until Lenny came back and said, "Enough already, leave the man live," and shooed them away. "Come on, Joe. Say hello to the folks, huh?"

He walked Mancuso down the aisle between the pews. And when they had come to the front, he motioned him to wait. Then he squatted down beside a couple in the front pew and whispered to them. They looked up, and then they stood up. Mancuso was astonished at how young they were. Neither one was as old as he was. The husband was tall and athletic. His wife looked a young woman. They were clear-eyed and did not seem to have been crying. Each had a little strip of black ribbon pinned above the heart.

"I'm Howard Ross," the man said and offered his hand. "This is my wife, Sylvia."

"Joe Mancuso." He shook the man's hand and then the woman's.

"We know you were very good to our boy," the father said. "We know you taught him a great deal."

Mancuso shifted his feet. "Yeah, well—"

"He talked about you all the time," the mother said. "He thought you were a great detective. And very funny. Very funny." She had that sweet, sad smile on her face that deep grief summons, and Mancuso thought she would burst into tears. But she set her jaw and held on to the smile.

"We're very grateful to you for everything you did for Davey," the father said. "If we can ever do anything for you, Mr. Mancuso, I hope you'll call on us."

"Yes," the mother said. "Come and see us some time. And tell us about what you and David did together."

Mancuso didn't know what to say. He reached up and scratched his head and the little round hat fell off and he and the father bent for it and almost collided.

"Sorry."

"Sorry."

They stood up and Mancuso put the hat back on.

"Well," the father said, and Mancuso could see he was biting his lower lip. Then he put his hand out in a manly way and Mancuso took it and the grip was strong and sure. "God bless you, Mr. Mancuso."

Then the mother opened her arms to him. And when she embraced him, her body shook with silent sobbing. But when she stepped back, she held herself erect and forced a brittle smile.

Mancuso nodded goodbye and then Lenny got him by the elbow. As they walked, he said, "They're so strong. It's amazing, isn't it?"

"Yeah," Mancuso said. "What was that thing they were wearing? The ribbon?"

"They cut that," Lenny said. "Then they pin it on. The immediate family anyhow. Symbolic of rending the clothes."

"And the box," Mancuso said. "They close the box?"

Lenny opened his hands. "Mostly. It depends."

"He wasn't cut up or nothing?"

Lenny leaned in close. "Stabbed. Once in the back. Muggers, they say." Then he clucked his tongue. "What a world."

"Yeah," Mancuso said.

Then Lenny patted him on the back and turned him around. "Well, maybe you'd like to spend a minute with Davey." And he walked Mancuso down to the coffin and shook his hand and let him stand there alone.

Mancuso thought it was about the dumbest fucking wake he'd ever been to. Nobody was crying. Not really crying. Not the way Italian women can cry. And there was nothing to eat. Not that he could see. Or to drink, neither. People just kind of drifted in and out, mumbled some words maybe, shook hands around and beat it out the door. Dumb fucking way to treat a guy who died.

And yet, as he stood looking at the closed cover of the coffin that contained David Ross—the closed, polished cover with the seam so fine that it was almost invisible—he felt tears welling in his eyes. He didn't know whether they were tears for Ross, but he wasn't going to be a jerk bawling in front of a lot of dry-eyed strangers. He took his handkerchief from his breast pocket and dabbed at his eyes, bending over a bit so that no one could see him blow his stuffy nose. And he felt like a fucking moron, getting choked up while they were all probably watching him. So, he sucked wind until he got his breath and gave a big sigh. And when he was sure that he wasn't going to make an asshole of himself, he pushed the handkerchief into his pocket and tried to primp it back into three neat points.

But the handkerchief was all balled up and came out again and he had to stuff it back down. And then it wouldn't make points because it was wet. Then he looked at the pocket a moment. It looked naked and empty without the three points of white handkerchief. Mr. Hoover had liked a man who showed some nice, fresh linen. For more than thirty years, Mancuso had.

Then he reached up and took the hem of his pocket in his fist and tore it straight down. It ripped straight down with a sharp noise of shredding cloth, baring the white ticking within the suit jacket, baring the stitching, baring the places where the linings were folded back and sewn. He tore it all the way down to the bottom hem of the jacket and let it hang. And then he turned around and looked at all the quiet people in the pews staring at him and the rip in his jacket and the strip of tweed that hung almost to his knee. He wiped the back of his hand across his runny nose and walked up the aisle toward the door and he didn't give a fuck what they thought.

There, standing in the doorway, was a woman dressed in black.

She was a tall woman in a black suit with black sequin trim that glittered in the light, black patent shoes and clutch, black hose and gloves, and a small black hat with a dark veil that hid her face but did not cover the cold yellow of her hair. Darkly, through the veil, Mancuso could see darts of light glistening in her eyes. And when she lifted her black-gloved fingertips, it stopped him.

"I came as soon as I heard," she said.

Mancuso stared at her as though she were the angel of darkness. Then he took the little round hat from his head, tenderly folded it and put it in his pocket.

"He was nothing to me," he said, and went by her and out the door.

When Mancuso pushed through the door of Gertie's Bar, it was almost noon and the lunchtime lushes were already beginning to assemble. But there was no gaiety in their welcome now. Some said "Hey, Joe" and some said "Jeeze" and "I'm sorry" and some said "He was a good guy." But nobody got down off a stool and nobody mentioned the long strip of cloth hanging loose down the torn front of his jacket.

He went down to the end of the bar and sat and Gertie came over. "We just heard," she said. "Jesus Christ."

"Don't give me no conversation," Mancuso said.

She went down the bar and got the bottle of Jack Daniel's and a glass full of ice and poured him a big shot and left the bottle in front of him. "On the house, Joey," she said. "God bless."

Noon SALLY WAS STILL veiled and dressed in black when she opened the door for Tommy Carter.

"I parked around the back," he said. "Hey, what are you dressed up for?"

"I had to go to a funeral this morning. I just got home."

Carter took off his jacket. "Who?"

"One of the FBI agents working on the case. He was mugged, killed."

"Jesus," Carter said. He put his hands on her waist. "Kiss?"

"A little one." She raised the edge of her veil. When he bent to kiss her, she let his lips brush hers, then she turned away. "Sit," she said. "Drink first."

There was a large whisky waiting on the end table beside the easy chair. He sat and raised the glass. "To our new . . . understanding." She nodded. He drank.

She sat on the couch across from him. "I want to talk terms."

"What?"

"Of our arrangement."

"Shoot." He kicked off his loafers and loosened his tie.

"I want you to destroy that backgrounder you wrote."

"Hey. No problem." He reached over and fished the folded yellow sheets out of the inside breast pocket of his jacket. He handed them to her. "Tear them up yourself."

"I mean the original. The file in your word processor."

"Sweetie, I pecked that out on my old 1948 Royal. You're holding the original."

She looked at the paper and she could see that it was typewritten. "No copies?"

"What do I need a copy for? I've got a draft right up here." He tapped his temple and smiled.

She put the papers down on the coffee table. "And I don't want anyone to know you're coming here or to my room in St. Louis or anywhere you see me."

"Sally, listen," he said. "Have you ever met the Washington correspondent of the *Jornal do Brasil*?"

"No."

"Well, if you'd ever met her, you'd understand why I want to keep this arrangement very, very private."

"What about your secretary?"

"All she knows is I'm out to lunch. That's all she'll ever know." He sipped his whisky. "You want this to be private. I want this to be private. It's a nice fit. Now. You said you had something to show me."

"Oh, yes," she said. "That's right." She leaned back on the couch and put one black, high-heeled shoe up on a cushion. And as she did, her skirt slipped up and he could see the top of her stocking and the black lace strap of her garter. "I remembered something that we used to do together," she said. Slowly, provocatively, she slid the skirt higher until he could see where she had shaved.

"Oh, Christ," he said.

She put her hand between her legs and there was a little wet click when she touched herself. "Come here, Tommy," she said. "Show me how much you want me."

He put his drink down and went over to kneel in front of the couch and put his mouth on her. She eased her skirts up so that she could watch him and ran her hand gently over the back of his head. She could feel him trembling with excitement.

She moaned and caressed him. "You're hot," she said. "Make me hot." And she moved her hips and let him suck her. But when he began to put his tongue inside, she took his head gently in her hands and held him away. "Wait," she said. "Let me show you."

She stood up and let him kneel there on the carpet beside the couch. Then she unzipped her skirt and stepped out of it. She unbuttoned her blouse and lay it aside. And she stood before him in her black veil with the soft flesh of her breasts swelling over the cups of her bra, and the black lace garter belt and stockings, and tall black heels. He wiped his mouth with the back of his hand and looked up at her, red-eyed, panting.

"Come with me," she said, and took his hand and helped him up. But she didn't lead him to the bedroom. Instead, she opened the door to the cellar.

"What's down there?" he said.

"I thought we could have a little adventure." She held the door ajar.

At the bottom of the stairs a candle was burning in the darkness. There was a blanket on the concrete floor beside it, and some leather straps laid neatly across it.

"Jesus," he said softly.

"Don't be afraid. You'll like it when you understand."

She went ahead of him down the stairs, and he watched the soft ripples in her buttocks as she descended. At the bottom, she turned and looked back at him and he could see all the voluptuous curves of her framed in black. She ran her hand down and rubbed herself between the legs. "Come," she said. "Come, Tommy." But he hung there, watching the red and yellow flicker of the candlelight wash over her. "Come," she said again.

At last he descended, one stair at a time. It was cold in the cellar, dark and quiet. And as his eyes adjusted to the gloom, he could see that it was a kind of playroom. But a playroom of a darker sort than he had ever imagined.

"What kind of place is this?" he said. "Sally?"

Just then the candle flickered out.

"Sally?"

Something glinted in the slant of daylight from the open door at the top of the stairs.

"Sally? Wha—"

12:20 P.M. SPEAKER CHARLIE O'DONNELL sat on the corner couch of the Oval Office, his jacket off and his shirt sleeves rolled up, and his little black book open on his lap. Pat Flaherty, the political pollster, sorted through the long green sheets of computer runs and pushed the buttons on his portable calculator. When Flaherty finally ran his total and pulled the tape out of the machine, O'Donnell said, "Seven hundred and seventy-eight."

Flaherty looked up blankly.

"Well?" the president said. He was sitting at his desk, watching the two of them.

"Exactly," Flaherty said. "Amazing."

"Just common sense." O'Donnell closed his little black book and set it down.

"With what significance?" the president said.

"You can't win on the first ballot, Sam," O'Donnell said. "Do you agree, sir?"

Flaherty shrugged. "Mr. Speaker, if IBM made little books like that, I'd be out of work."

"All right, Pat," the president said. "Thank you very much."

Flaherty gathered his papers and went out. O'Donnell leaned back into the cushions of the sofa. "It's a sad day for the party when it falls into the hands of vermin like Wickert," he said. "Have you spoken to Eastman?"

"Yes."

"And? What happens next?"

"What happens next is between Dan Eastman and his conscience." The president got up and came around his desk and stood behind the sofa facing O'Donnell. "Wickert's challenging your leadership. Isn't he?"

"I've been challenged before. Most went away with a bloody nose." O'Donnell sat up. "You're the one in serious trouble, Sam."

"Am I?"

"If you won't accept Fallon. . . . Well, they want me to ask you not to seek the nomination."

"I see." The president nodded once. "Are you asking?"

"I'm reporting."

"Reporting and asking?"

"I'm reporting," O'Donnell said again.

"And what's your recommendation?"

"If you don't mind, Sam, I'd like Lou Bender in on this."

"He's out-of-town. On business."

"Picked a poor day to be out-of-town."

"I gather it was essential."

"I see." O'Donnell shifted his great bulk and stood, flexing the straps of his suspenders. "I have a recommendation. I don't think you want to hear it."

"Fallon?"

"Yes, Fallon. Now, Sam, listen to me," O'Donnell said. "They're going to ask him to make the keynote speech."

"Without my approval?"

"Ah, Sam, why won't you understand? They don't give a damn for your approval anymore. They think you can't win the election on your own, so you've got to grovel."

"To hell with them," the president said.

"Sam, they're giving you a chance. Take it."

"What chance?"

"Kick Eastman out and name Fallon vice president tomorrow. He can't very well refuse. You're offering him the job, not the nomination. Then, at the convention, you become a one-two ticket that everyone can live with."

"Everyone but me."

"Sam . . . Sam."

"Charlie, hear me now. I am not going to prepare this country to be led by Terry Fallon."

"Ah, Sam, be reasonable. If you don't take him as vice president, they may bypass you and nominate him for president. Think, man. Think." O'Donnell crossed the room and stood very close to him. "He'll be on national television for the keynote. And he'll give one of those flag-waving, bully-bully addresses of his and drive the delegates into a frenzy. He'll just roll over you and crush you like an insect. Either you make Terry Fallon vice president, or I predict the party will give him the presidential nomination. And if they do, I don't think anything short of an act of God can keep him out of the White House."

The president stood where he was a moment. Then he put one hand to his forehead and kneaded his temples with his fingertips.

"Sam, you must be reasonable," O'Donnell said.

"I can't do it, Charlie. I can't do it. And I won't do it."

"They're going to demand the autopsy report," O'Donnell said.

The president looked up. "What?"

"The autopsy report on Martinez. They're going to demand a look at it. And if the man had AIDS, there could be an investigation . . . and prosecutions."

The president sat down on the couch. "So, that's it. That's their ace. If I accept Fallon, all's well. If I don't, the witch hunt begins."

O'Donnell put his hands in his pockets. "Yes," he said.

The president sat on the couch, silent, staring at the wall.

"Reconsider," O'Donnell said.

"No."

"Sam. Think about it. At least let me tell them you'll think about it."

"Charlie," the president said, "I think of little else."

O'Donnell sighed. He rolled his sleeves back down, took up his jacket, and slipped it on. "I'm sorry," he said.

"As am I."

O'Donnell went out.

1:00 P.M. THE DINING ROOM in the brownstone on Manhattan's East 82nd Street was an eclectic jewel. The walls were painted with a *trompe-l'oeil* of the garden of a Medici villa. But the round, green marble table was set for five with a vermeil art deco service and delicate fluted Venetian glassware. The plate was Flora Danica and the linen Belgian lace.

There were four Old Master paintings on the walls, and even before Lou Bender sat down, he had catalogued, provenanced, and evaluated them.

It was remarkable, Bender thought as he sat down, how the most delicate of treasures were always collected by the most venal of men. But the four men he faced around the table were a more interesting assemblage than the paintings: Lucas MacDougal, fifty, a corporate privateer who had greenmailed his way to an empire of television, radio and magazines; Oliver Greisman, a dark, small, fortyish man—an electronics entrepreneur who had bought into the network game as a hedge against Japanese technology; Roger Wainwright, sixty-five, a self-made plutocrat who had started out peddling radio spots and wound up chairman of the third network; and Halsey Bruton, thirty-seven, hereditary publisher of one of the world's most prestigious newspapers, and by far the wealthiest man in the room, thanks to a favor his great-grandfather did for President Grover Cleveland in 1894.

"And how is the president?" MacDougal said.

"He's well. He asked me to extend his greetings. And to thank you all for finding time to meet with me today." Bender swept the room with his best smile. Next to the Oval Office, there was probably not a single room in the United States that held such power at that moment. In the four chairs sat men who controlled three television networks and the world's most influential newspaper. Because of the way reporters cannibalized their own medium, what was said and decided at that table would influence the reporting of most of the television stations and all of the leading newspapers and news magazines in the United States and Western Europe. It was a card not to be turned lightly.

Bender knew well that there was a secret to dealing with such men, a technique to be followed, a rubric to be respected. The less one said, the more closely they listened. Understatement and innuendo were more persuasive than detailed exposition. And never ask for anything directly, always by implication. In all conversations with men of this stature, less was more.

"Gentlemen, we have a developing situation," Bender said. "It's a situation that the president has asked me to share with you on a personal and private basis. I hope I need not elaborate upon the need for extreme confidentiality."

He paused and looked around the table and saw that he had been understood.

"No doubt you've followed the recent erratic behavior of the vice president. His unprovoked tirade during the photo session with the ambassador from Gabon. His groundless allegation that the president and the FBI

were in collusion to obstruct justice during the investigation of the assassination of Colonel Martinez. And this latest episode, last night—unsupported
and wholly untrue allegations that Colonel Martinez was poisoned by—''
he paused and shook his head for sarcastic emphasis ''—unnamed clandestine forces within the army. I trust you can appreciate that there is only
one conclusion to be drawn from these events about the vice president's
state of mind.''

The men around the table nodded.

''Is Eastman a crackpot or what?'' Baumgarten said.

''In these matters, I can only offer a layman's opinion,'' Bender said.

''Well?'' Greisman said. ''What?''

''I think it's clear that Vice President Eastman is confused and, perhaps, disturbed,'' Bender said. But then he hurried on. ''I don't think it's
fair for anyone who isn't a health professional to speculate about the man or
the pressures he may be under. I'm sure you'll agree that such judgments
have to be left in the hands of trained therapists.''

''Are you telling us that the vice president requires a psychiatrist's
care?'' MacDougal asked.

''I cannot make any statement about any treatment the vice president
may be receiving or may require in the future. But I think the facts speak
for themselves.''

''Well, that's plain enough,'' MacDougal said. ''All right. What's the
plan?''

''At the moment, gentlemen, discretion is the plan,'' Bender said. ''For
humanitarian reasons, the president would like the vice president to come
forward and tender his resignation.''

''Has he demanded it?'' MacDougal said.

''No. We're concerned that might aggravate the symptoms.''

''If you don't mind me saying so,'' Greisman said, ''that's wrong-
headed. If a man's sick, he needs care. And this country needs a vice
president, not a gibbering idiot.''

MacDougal said, ''I think I see his game,'' and the other heads turned
his way. ''It's quite simple. At the convention, Eastman will not be
renominated as vice president. Once a new vice presidential nominee has
been chosen, Eastman becomes a lame duck. I believe that he will grasp his
situation and wish to make a conciliatory gesture.''

Lou Bender sat back and smiled as the watercress salad was set before him. It was so much easier to talk to the men who controlled America's press now that the age of conglomerates had come to the media
business.

By the time the coffee was served, they were long past the matter of Dan

Eastman, and Baumgarten was telling them about a four wood he hit on the twelfth hole at Bel Air.

Then, Lou Bender looked at his wristwatch. "Gentlemen," he said, "I have a plane to catch. The president wanted you to be able to make an assessment as this situation develops. And he asked me to express his deep gratitude for your kind attention today."

"We're all very grateful to you for making the trip to fill us in, Lou," MacDougal said, and looked around the table as the others nodded.

When they were standing in the lobby of the house shaking hands and saying goodbye, Greisman leaned over to Bender. "Send your car away, Lou," he said. "I'll give you a lift to the airport."

And when they had settled in the back seat of Greisman's limousine, he pressed a button and a tray of Davidoff *Dom Perignon* cigars slid out of the console. "Try one of mine?"

"Thanks," Bender said, and lit up. The car headed over the 59th Street bridge.

Greisman sat back and unbuttoned his vest. "Stuffy bunch of assholes, aren't they?"

"Makes the world go round," Bender said. "Good cigar, Ollie. Thanks."

"You know, Lou," Greisman said. "I've always admired the way you get a grip on the big picture."

"Well, thank you," Bender said, and settled back into his seat. The limousine turned up 21st Street in Long Island City and headed for the Grand Central Parkway.

"You get the big picture," Greisman was saying. "And you tackle head-on. That's as rare as it is important."

The man was going somewhere and he had Bender's full attention.

"Can you and I have a conversation without it going any further?" Greisman said.

"Yes."

"I mean, not to the president, not to your family, not to anyone?"

The car swung onto the Grand Central.

"Ollie, I think you know you can trust me to be discreet."

Greisman nodded. "This company of mine is at a crossroads, Lou. And it's going places our stockholders and our competitors can't even dream. If we play our cards right, we'll be the dominant force in American broadcasting by 1995. And MacDougal and Wainwright will be a memory."

"You mean prime time and news?"

"No, Lou. I mean something bigger. I'm talking about completely bypassing the affiliate station system and going direct from our stages and studios to the home. We have the technology to build satellites for direct-to-home transmission. We've got the technology to build the encoders—and build the decoders right into the television sets we sell. When the financial interest rule sunsets, we'll buy MCA or Warners and produce half our shows ourselves. We could be the first vertically integrated broadcast news and entertainment system on the planet. And right now we're looking at DBS in Europe and South America, too. We're going to be one hell of a company in a few years. And we could use a man like you on our side of the table in Washington.''

Bender puffed on his cigar. "Ollie, you flatter me. But I'm a strategist, not a lobbyist."

"We've got a million lobbyists," Greisman said. "I'm talking about a Washington-based corporate EVP for planning and development with the clout and perks of a division president. Options for 100,000 shares to start. Salary commensurate. Staff, secretaries, use of one of our planes. Five-year contract. That sort of thing."

Bender whistled softly through his teeth. It was the brass ring.

"Ollie, you tempt me. But I've got a convention to manage and a campaign to run."

"There's no reason you couldn't take this job and keep your lines open to the president. As a matter of fact, I'd want you to do that. If you help him, it would help us."

Bender considered. It was, by any standard, an offer that could not be easily refused.

"I'll have to give it very serious consideration."

"Look, Lou," Greisman said. "Let's spare the niceties, shall we? Sam Baker can't win in November. You know it. I know it. The boys know it. Hell, he might not even get the nomination next week."

Bender crossed his arms. "Step lightly, Ollie. I've been with Sam a long time."

"I respect your sense of loyalty," Greisman said. "This isn't a question of loyalty. It's a question of practicalities. If you grab this now, you're stepping out while you're still on top. Wait a week and Baker doesn't get the nomination and you're damaged goods. Just another Washington has-been."

Bender bit down hard on the end of the cigar.

"Sorry, Lou, but those are the facts of life."

The limousine halted. Bender nodded grimly.

"Give me a call tomorrow," Greisman said.

The chauffeur came around and opened Bender's door. But he didn't move to step out. He sat, staring out the side window, looking across the tarmac to the storm clouds swinging up from the south. It would be raining in Washington by the time he got back, a hard rain that would last through the night. What Greisman said was true. But to hear it spoken out loud gave the facts a cold, bitter reality.

"What time tomorrow?" he said.

1:15 P.M. WHEN SUPERVISORY AGENT BARNEY Scott stood up at the altar to give away his last daughter in 1981, he wasn't losing a daughter, he was selling a house. One day later the huge, old rambling Victorian monster in Mount Vernon was on the market. The next day it was sold and the Scotts bought a townhouse near Washington Circle. Barney Scott kissed 110 minutes of daily commuting goodbye and joined the walk-to-work, home-for-lunch crowd.

Now he came in the door of his house, whipped off his rainhat and coat, and called, "Claire? Honey? I'm home." He pulled open the door of the closet to hang his things away. But a foot came out and kicked him so hard in the nuts that he gasped, and doubled over on his knees.

Mancuso came out of the closet and knelt beside him. He had a silencer screwed on the front of his revolver and he pushed the barrel against Scott's neck.

"You make a sound and I'll blow your fucking head off," Mancuso hissed.

But Scott was too busy gasping for breath, heaving up and down, and clutching his groin with both hands. He looked at Mancuso out of the corner of his eye and groaned, "Ehhh . . . you . . . fuck."

But Mancuso jabbed the gun in under his chin. And when he spoke, his voice was cold with rage. "You had him killed."

"Wha—?" Scott groaned and rocked back and forth.

"You killed him, you fuck. And I'm gonna kill you."

"Whaddya—who?"

Mancuso grabbed the knot of Scott's necktie, pulled him closer. "Don't lie to me, you son-of-a-bitch!"

Scott looked up at Mancuso. He was in pain, but he wasn't afraid. "Whaddya talking? Ohhhh, Christ." He rolled his head and moaned.

"Say your prayers, you motherfucker," Mancuso hissed in his ear.

But Scott wasn't buying it. He groaned and said, "Come on, come on. Fuck . . . fuck . . ."

"Ross was getting close to something."

"What are you talking about? Oh, Jesus, you broke my nuts . . ."

"He was on to something and you shut him up."

420

"He was mugged . . . For Christ's sake, he was robbed." Scott tried to wriggle free, but Mancuso held him.

"He had something. Now he's dead and his briefcase is missing."

Scott was catching his breath now. "What briefcase? What are you talking about?"

"With his notes on the Martinez shoot."

Scott stretched back as the shock of the blow began to subside. "Aw, Jesus, notes my ass." Then he twisted his head and pulled his tie knot free. He looked at Mancuso and the huge flap torn out of his jacket where his breast pocket used to be. "What are you talking about, you dumb fucking guinea? Let me up. Jesus Christ, you could have put me in the hospital."

Mancuso pushed the barrel of the silencer against his throat. "I'll kill you," he said.

But Scott shoved his hand and the revolver away. "You'll kill shit." He put his hand on Mancuso's shoulder, got up on one knee, got to his feet and slowly straightened up. All the while he was doing that, he was muttering, "Never had the brains God gave little apples, dumb fucking son-of-a-bitch." And when he had straightened up, he leaned back and stretched and said, "I'll bust you out for this, cocksucker."

"Try it," Mancuso said. "And we'll go together."

He thumbed back the hammer of the revolver.

Scott looked at the pistol—and then back at Mancuso's eyes. Fear flickered across Scott's face like a death mask. Then he looked at the flapping front of Mancuso's jacket and shook his head and snorted.

"For Christ's sake, Mancuso, put that away and get a safety pin for your diaper. Your buddy Ross was mugged going home from a pussy party with Fallon's press bimbo. Your secretary saw them sucking mouth."

"What?" Mancuso said.

"Jesus Christ," Scott said. "Why don't you wake up and smell the coffee?"

Mancuso's arms fell limp and useless at his sides. And the sad, pathetic truth of it rolled in upon him. "Oh, no," he said aloud.

"Oh, yes," Scott said without looking back at him. "Now, put the fucking gun away and get out of here."

But Mancuso stood where he was and murmured, "No, no . . . in the name of Christ . . . no."

That made Scott look up. "What's the matter with you—you crazy old fuck?"

But Mancuso knotted his hands and shut his eyes and hunched his shoulders as a child might and put his head back and cried out, "No!"

Scott stood there, looking at the old fool shaking with emotion, and there was only contempt and disdain in his eyes. He poked Mancuso once in the chest. "Go on. Get out of here, you bum."

But Mancuso stood, fists clenched and trembling, and great spasms searing up his throat. Because in that moment of recognition, he knew who had killed Dave Ross. He had.

"Jesus Christ," Scott said, smirking in disgust. "He was a smartass kike with a chip on his shoulder. He had a jerk for a partner and a bump in his pants. How'd you expect him to wind up?"

Mancuso's eyes snapped open. His arm flashed out and grabbed Scott's hand at the wrist, and bent it back so suddenly and fiercely that it crackled. Scott went down, hard, on one knee. But as he opened his mouth to shout, Mancuso shoved the barrel of the silencer and revolver into his mouth.

"Don't." Mancuso hissed through the tears streaming over his lips. "Don't you talk about him that way, you ugly little bastard."

Scott was in agony, choking for breath.

"He cracked it," Mancuso whispered. "And I'm gonna close it."

Then he flung Scott, gasping, to the floor, opened the front door of the house, and slammed out.

2:05 P.M. TERRY FALLON LEANED back against the redwood slats of the sauna and breathed a chestful of the hot, dry air. When he turned, his side still ached where the bandage covered his wound. There was a knock at the door and then the door opened.

"Come in, Bill," Terry said.

Bill Wickert was still fumbling with his towel, trying to double it back so that it would hang at his waist. He straightened when the blast of hot air hit him.

"Man, I don't know how you take this," he said, and shut the sauna door behind him.

"It's relaxing, once you get the hang of it."

"Sure it is." They shook hands. Wickert sat down and then stood up again. "Jesus Christ, that's hot."

"Just sit down and take your time," Terry said. "Once your body adjusts . . ."

"We met with O'Donnell."

Terry motioned with his hands. "Sit, Bill. Please. Relax. Here."

Terry handed him another towel.

Wickert spread it on the redwood bench, then gingerly set his butt on it.

Terry shut his eyes and leaned back. "God, that's good," he said. Then he winced and put his hand against the adhesive bandage covering the wound.

"Still bothering you?"

"Feels like I got kicked by a horse."

"Going to have any after-effects?"

"Not according to the doctor. I get the stitches out after the convention."

"We want you to look sharp when you deliver the keynote."

Terry smiled at him. "Am I delivering the keynote?"

"It's all agreed."

"O'Donnell agreed?"

"O'Donnell didn't get a vote."

"The president?"

"He didn't get a vote, either. The president and O'Donnell don't run the party, Terry. Not any more." Wickert leaned back against the slats and sat up abruptly. "Shit! This place is a goddam oven."

"That's the idea, Bill." Terry leaned back and shut his eyes again.

"Well?" Wickert said. "Are you pleased?"

"I'm reflecting."

"On what?"

"On what the future of this country will be."

"And what will it be?"

"There will have to be a lot of changes."

"There are going to be a lot of changes in the party," Wickert said. "A lot of changes that are long overdue."

Terry nodded, smiling, his eyes shut, his shoulders resting against the boards.

"I've been thinking," Wickert said. "You know, it's time the vice presidency became a real job—not just some honorific waiting room."

"Really."

"President *pro tem* of the Senate only counts when there's a tie vote. That's once in a blue moon. But I see the vice president having a real voice in government. Maybe running the National Security Council, that kind of thing."

"Good thinking."

"And wrapping up all the key social programs into a kind of super agency—a metropolitan council, with HUD and all the those programs rolled up under it. There's a lot of fat in those giveaways. They need cutting.''

"Yes. I guess they do,'' Terry said.

"Well, I'd like to stay, but we've got a press conference to announce your selection as keynote speaker,'' Wickert said. "Want to give me a hint about what you're going to say? Not for publication, I mean. Just so that I know where we're going.''

"We're going to step into the future,'' Terry said without opening his eyes. "We're going to be the power that we were, the power we were chosen to be.''

"Yeah. Well. Meet me in St. Louis,'' Wickert said and smiled. He was so glad to get out of the sauna that he didn't wait for a handshake.

When the door shut behind him, Terry Fallon sat with the heat of the sauna prickling his skin, drawing his perspiration and evaporating it before it could bead. He would need some very fine words for the keynote speech, words that were far beyond his capacity or the limited gifts of Chris Van Allen. There was only one person he knew who could find the words to prepare America for the coming of a new age. And, luckily, she could not refuse him.

3:10 P.M. WHEN LOU BENDER got back to his office, he hung his jacket over the back of his chair and sat down to his mail. The door opened. It was the president. Bender got to his feet.

"Please,'' Sam Baker said. He shut the door behind him and sat down on the couch on the other side of the room.

"Lou, where've you been?''

"I had some things to take care of. Did you meet with Eastman?''

"Yes.''

"And?''

"Dan Eastman is a stubborn man.''

"Pigheaded, if you ask me. And stupid.''

"How much can he trouble us?''

"Not too much anymore.'' Bender leaned forward and put his elbows on his desk. "He's got to go, Sam.''

"Lou, one of the niceties of the Constitution is that the vice president can't be fired.''

"If he won't resign, he'll have to be impeached.''

"Put that out of your mind.''

Bender sat back. "All right. For the moment."

"O'Donnell came to see me."

That got Bender's attention. "What did he have to say?"

"The party leadership has asked me to accept Fallon or not seek renomination."

Bender looked up. But he wasn't surprised. "Well . . . there are worse things that could happen, Sam. The man brings you—"

"They've asked Terry Fallon to make the keynote address at the convention."

"Really?" And Bender couldn't hide his pleasure at the news. "You okayed that?"

"They didn't ask me."

"What?" Bender stood up. "What the hell is going on?"

"It's Wickert."

"That son-of-a-bitch!" Bender gritted his teeth. "I'll teach him to try and push us around." Bender pressed the intercom button on his phone.

"Yes, sir?" his secretary said.

"Maggie, get me the list of Bill Wickert's chief campaign donors. Get it for me right now."

He let the button go.

"I don't want any of that, Lou," Sam Baker said. "We're way beyond that."

"It doesn't hurt to get ready," Bender said. "If Wickert wants a street fight, he'll get one he can't handle."

"I said I don't want any of that, Lou. Call your secretary and tell her not to get that list."

"Sam—"

"Lou, I insist."

"Shit," Bender said. He pressed the button on his intercom. "Maggie, cancel that request," he said. Then he let the button go. "Goddamit," he said.

"The party leadership is going to ask to see the autopsy report on Martinez," Sam Baker said.

Bender just stopped and stared. Then he said, "What?"

"It's clear what they're up to. If I seek renomination without Fallon, they press an investigation. If I accept him or stand down, they'll let it go."

Bender shrugged. "Like I said. There are worse things than having a second term with Terry Fallon as your vice president."

"Never."

Bender thought a moment. "All right, then—fuck 'em. Let 'em have the goddam report. It's clean."

"But it wasn't clean when it was written. Was it?"

"How would I know? I never saw it."

Baker just stared. It was the first time in their thirty years together that he knew Lou Bender had told him a lie.

"Well," he said, "who did see the report?"

Bender opened his hands. "I suppose . . . the doctor who wrote it. And O'Brien. And those two clowns he put on the case."

"One of those men is dead."

"Yes. I saw that."

"And if the doctor changed the report and perjured himself, then he's no longer a credible witness," the president said.

"Which leaves O'Brien and what's-his-name, Mancuso."

"I see." He was watching Bender and he could see that his mind was racing.

"Look," Bender said, casually. "We don't know what the original report said, do we? Maybe it wouldn't hurt to take out a little insurance, right?"

"What kind of insurance?"

"You say a word to O'Brien. I'll take care of Mancuso."

"I've spoken to O'Brien."

"Good. Good," Bender said. "Then I'll take care of the rest."

3:15 P.M. MANCUSO SLAMMED THE office door open and then slammed it closed behind him. And while he was locking it, the new in-out boxes on the filing cabinet behind the door caught his eye. In the bottom wire tray on the right was a message slip:

PLEASE CALL MISS CRAIN.

He balled the paper, threw it in a corner, pulled off his jacket, and sat down at Ross's desk. There was a big stack of black videocassettes of the assassination, all neatly labeled 1 through 22, and the dumb white cardboard with the squares numbered 1 through 7. He pulled the ON switch of the television monitor.

He pushed the button on the cassette machine labeled PLAY. But nothing happened. Then he realized there was no cassette in the machine.

So he pried one of the boxes open and pulled out the cassette and shoved it into the slot. The machine cycled and seemed to suck in the cassette. But before he could hit the PLAY button, it spit the cassette back out. Mancuso turned the cassette over and pushed it in again. Same shit. So, he turned it around and this time it went in and stayed.

"Fucking thing," he said.

Then he pressed the button marked PLAY.

4:05 P.M. ADMIRAL RAUSCH WAS looking out the front parlor window of his Bethesda house when the black limousine pulled into the driveway and Lou Bender got out. He went to the front door and let him in.

"What the hell do you want?" he said when Bender came inside.

"I want to talk to you."

"Talk."

"Not here."

They went out into the garden behind the house and sat on a stone bench under a grove of chestnut trees.

"All right. Go ahead," Rausch said.

"I hear you long to go to sea again," Bender said.

"What about it?"

"Don't tell me you've had enough of Washington?"

"Get to the point," Rausch said.

"You told Eastman the army poisoned Martinez. Didn't you?"

"What if I did?"

"Bill, Eastman can't protect you."

"He can if he's elected president."

Bender sneered and shook his head. "Dan Eastman has a better chance of being elected president of the Congo."

"You blackballed me with the navy," Rausch said.

Bender smiled his oily smile. "I just didn't want you rushing off before the party was over."

"Bullshit. You were going to make me the scapegoat when the AIDS thing came out."

"Bill, Bill . . . who said the AIDS thing has to come out? The only people who saw the report are O'Brien and the two agents. And you've already taken care of one of them."

"What are you talking about?" Rausch said.

"Ross. The FBI agent who tracked the virus to the army. That day on the golf course.'' Bender smiled. "I knew you made up your mind to kill him.''

"I didn't.''

"Don't lie to me, Bill,'' Bender said. "For Christ's sake, the game's over!''

Rausch was staring at the ground. "All right, so we tried for him in Miami.'' He looked up. "But you had the FBI covering him, you fuck!''

"We had to know what he was up to. Anyhow, what are you crying about? You got him last night.''

"Wasn't our party.''

Bender looked him over. "Don't sit there and try to tell me that his murder was a coincidence. I don't believe in coincidence any more than you do.''

"Lou, if you're trying to trap me again—''

"Wait a second,'' Bender said. "Are you telling me you didn't mark the two FBI agents?''

Rausch took a long breath. "The old guy—Mancuso. His friend, Wilson, passed him Petersen's location. Then we had him followed when he landed at Baltimore. When we figured he was moving in on Petersen, Wilson called Petersen on the phone.''

"And the SWAT team?''

Rausch blinked. "I figured you sent them.''

"I sent them?'' Bender said, his voice rising. "You sent them. And you had Ross killed last night.''

"The hell I did,'' Rausch said angrily.

"Then who—?''

But Bender broke off there, and the two of them sat, looking in opposite directions, each with his own thoughts. The conclusion was inescapable.

"Lou, I got a bad feeling we're playing in a three-handed game.''

Without responding, Bender got up and paced. Then he said, "Look, I've come here to make you a proposition. You want out and I'm blocking the door.''

"Okay,'' Rausch said. "Let's hear it.''

"Take care of Mancuso and I'll see you back on active sea duty with full military honors.''

"You can't deliver that.''

"Sam Baker can.''

"But he won't. Lou, we've been down this road before,'' Rausch said, bitterly.

"He's already talked to O'Brien. He told me so himself.''

"I don't believe it."

"You don't know Sam Baker as well as I do," Bender said, and the oily smile bent his mouth. "He sometimes seems a little too honest for his own good. But he is, don't forget, a politician."

Rausch sat back, thinking.

"Does Mancuso know that Wilson sandbagged him?" Bender said.

"I don't think so."

"Well, why don't they have a little meeting? Maybe take a little trip together. Someplace nice and quiet. And maybe only one of them comes back. Arrange that. Then we'll talk about ships. Agreed?"

Rausch lowered his head. "All right. Agreed."

Bender turned to go.

"You know, Lou. You're a slimy little bastard."

Bender stopped and looked back at him and smiled. "I don't make the rules, Bill. I just play to win."

5:20 P.M. A COUPLE OF the barflies looked up and one nodded and said, "Hey, Joe," when he pushed his way through the door at Gertie's, but the rest of them didn't acknowledge him, pretended that he wasn't there. He went down to the end of the bar and sat on his stool, feeling like the invisible man. Grief was like that. It was a mantle of invisibility. Others turned from it.

Gertie was sitting at the end of the bar. She was reading her newspaper. The headline read:

FALLON TO KEYNOTE CONVENTION

"Hey, Joey," she said softly when she looked up and saw him. "Starting to rain?"

"Yeah."

He sat down and she poured him a double of Jack Daniel's. And while he kicked it back, she tapped the front of the paper with her fingernail. "This guy Fallon is cute."

"You can say that again." Mancuso stood up and looked down the length of the bar. "Seen Mandy?"

Gertie shrugged. "Doing a trick."

"Her key here?"

"Sure."

Mancuso put his hand out for it.

"Happy hour?" Gertie said.

"Yeah." Mancuso put the key in his pocket.

"Glad you're feeling better," she said. He went off down the bar.

5:30 P.M. SALLY LEFT THE bundle she was struggling with on the cellar stairs, ran up the rest of the way, and caught the phone on the fourth ring. "Yes?" she said, breathlessly.

"Did I catch you at a bad time?" It was Terry.

"No. I was . . . just packing."

"Packing for what?"

"The convention. We're leaving tomorrow, aren't we?"

"Oh. Yes."

"Terry, I am going with you."

"Of course you are, dear," he said. "But right now I need your help. I've been asked to make the keynote address."

"Terry, my God! That's wonderful! The president asked you to—"

"Not the president. The party leadership."

"Really?" She sat down and pulled the skirts of her robe around her.

"I think they're sending a signal."

"And a loud one," she said.

"I have the governors' caucus dinner tonight. I think by the time that dinner's over, we'll know where we stand."

"Oh, Terry. I'm so—"

"I want you to write the keynote."

She was stunned. "Terry, I—"

"Can you do it?"

She looked toward the back door. Tommy Carter's car was pulled up outside, its trunk open and waiting. "You mean, today? Now?"

"Of course, today."

She had things to do. Things that couldn't wait. "Terry, I—"

"Sally, please. I need you. And, Sally?"

"Yes?"

"I love you."

Her shoulders sagged forward, and she felt herself go limp as though he had just swept her up in his arms.

"Can I count on you?" he said.

"Yes," she said. "Yes, yes." And there was nothing more important to her in the world—not even herself.

"Call me when you have something," he said. "I'll send a messenger."

"I'll just bring it over."

"No. No, call me. You stay at your typewriter. We'll let the messenger service do the running."

"All right. Yes. Maybe you're right. I'll start on it right away."

"I knew I could count on you." Then he hung up.

She went into her den and switched on her IBM-AT in a state of total euphoria.

5:40 P.M. WHEN MANCUSO PUSHED the door open, he heard a little voice calling "Mamamamamama," and he heard little bare feet slapping on the wood floor. And by the time he had shut the door and turned the bolt, the little boy was standing in the hallway, naked except for his diaper, his eyes like saucers.

Mancuso knelt down. "Hey, Stanley," he said. "Hey."

But the little boy turned and waddled back off around the corner into the kitchen.

"That you, Joe?" the woman's voice called out.

Mancuso took his hat off. "Yes, Miz Robinson."

"You set," she said. "I'm makin' some in-fusion."

He looked over at the whisky bottles and glasses on the television set in the parlor. "Think I'll have a belt."

"Never you mind no liquor," she said, and came out of the kitchen, carrying a wicker tray with a teapot and two cups. "You done had enough liquor to last you some lifetimes."

Mandy's mother was a chubby little woman in a black dress printed with red and green flowers. She had nubby hair and a round face with little brown patches under her eyes. She looked him over. "You go hang your coat. Don't you go drippin' on the rug, hear?"

"Yes'm."

And when he took his raincoat off and she saw his torn lapel pinned up with a safety pin, she said, "What happen to your jacket?"

"Had an accident."

"Set down. Gimme that there." She put her hand out. "Gimme that, now."

He took his jacket off and gave it to her. "My, my," she said and shook her head. "Go on. Set." And when he did, she poured him a yellowish cup of tea and went out for her sewing box.

431

Mancuso took his cup in both his hands and looked at the yellow fluid. It looked like piss and didn't smell much better.

"That's rosemary," Mrs. Robinson said. "And mint. It's good when you down."

Mancuso looked longingly at the bottle of Jack Daniel's on the tray atop the television. Then he screwed up his face and sipped the tea.

Mrs. Robinson unpinned the torn flap of his jacket and shook her head. "There ain't no way to make this right." Then she got out a needle and some black thread and started basting the torn fabric together. "So, they killed your boy," she said.

"Yeah."

"I liked that boy." She was sewing now, eyes close to her work, talking to herself more than to him. "Don't fret none over him. He's with Jesus now. Praise the Lord."

"He was a Jew," Mancuso said.

She looked up at him, looked at him over the tops of her glasses. "Honey, that don't mean nothing after you dead."

Then they heard a key in the door and looked up and Mandy came in. "Mama. Hey, Joey," she said. She opened her red umbrella and stood it out in the hall and came back inside. "Where's Stanley?"

"On his bottle," Mrs. Robinson said.

Mandy hung her coat behind the door. "I'll see him. I'll be right back, honey."

Mancuso looked over at Mrs. Robinson. But she had gone back to her sewing. And when Mandy came out and stood in the hallway, Mancuso put his cup down and stood up.

"Go on, go on," Mrs. Robinson said without raising her eyes. "Lemme finish this here."

He followed Mandy into the bedroom.

"Oh, it's cold." She rubbed her hands together. She nodded toward the bed. "You go on. I gotta wash."

But he was still standing there in the last dying light through the window when she came out in her long blue housecoat and blue satin slippers with pom-poms on the toes.

"Whattsa matter?" she said.

"Nothin'."

She went over to him and started to undo his tie.

"Nah."

"Oh, sugar," she said, and slipped the tie out from under his collar. "Come on. I'm gonna hold you."

And after she had undressed him and made him lie down and held him a while, she slid down and put her mouth on him and made him hard. Then she dabbed herself with oil and pushed him inside.

They humped a long time in silence. There was only the soft hissing of the rain against the darkened window, and the soft murmur of Mrs. Robinson singing a lullaby to the baby in the room next door.

Finally, Mancuso rolled over, unspent. Mandy slid her hand down his belly.

"That's okay, sugar," she said softly. "Let me do it."

"Maybe later." He eased her hand away and started to get up. "Lemme get your dough."

She took his shoulders and held him, gently restraining him. "Joey . . . once in your life. Be smart."

"Aw, whaddya talking?"

She put her arms around his shoulders and held him against her bosom. "I liked the kid, too. He was okay. But you got to forget him."

He leaned against her quietly for a time, and she could hear the beating of his heart. Then he said, "I don't want to."

She chuckled tenderly, deep in her throat. "You never gonna get the guys who pushed the button on him. They too big for you."

Mancuso sighed and sat up. He took her arms away from his neck and set them at her sides. "I'm through trying to get them. Now I'm gonna help them get each other."

He reached over and switched on the lamp beside the bed. She squinted in the glare and put her hands up to cover her bosom.

"I got to go out for a while," he said. "When I come back, can I stay tonight?"

"Sure, honey. Whatever you need."

He looked toward the door of the bedroom. "Can your mother stay someplace else with the baby?"

"Sure, if you want."

He looked down at her body. She was no longer the young girl she had been the first time he had bought her. Now, her breasts were sagging and her nipples hung almost straight down.

"You want to make fifty bucks?" he said.

She lowered her eyes. "Sure, Joey. Here you get whatever you pay for."

7:20 P.M. THE FIRST THING the maitre d' did when Joe Mancuso came in the front door of the Cosmos Club was to try to send him around the back. He didn't like the look of the dumpy man in the rain-soaked hat and coat. But Mancuso knew that his FBI shield and ID were the best membership cards in America. Still, the governors' caucus was having dinner upstairs with the illustrious Senator Fallon and the lobby of the club was crawling with Secret Service. The maitre d' motioned to one of the colorless men in a stiff tuxedo jacket with a wire plugged into his ear.

The Secret Service man nodded to Mancuso. "Okay, let me see it." He waggled a finger at him.

Mancuso held out his ID. Fucking Secret Service.

The young man looked it over and then him. Then he handed it back and waved to someone at the top of the stairs.

"You need a fucking invitation to see this guy, or what?" Mancuso said.

The Secret Service looked back at him without emotion.

They made him wait, of course. They put him in a little office off the second floor lobby for fifteen minutes just to prove what a bunch of assholes they were. Then the door opened, he heard the sound of laughter and music, and another man in a tuxedo came in.

"I'm Chris Van Allen," he said. "Senator Fallon's aide. Now, what's so important?"

"I gotta talk to your boss."

"The senator's engaged."

"Yeah. And married, too, I suppose."

Chris put his hands on his hips and stared. He was just the kind of limp-wristed little faggot that Mancuso couldn't stand.

"I don't much care for your attitude, Agent Mancuso."

"Listen, Tinker Bell, why don't you go fly around with the rest of the fairies before I rap you off two walls."

Chris glared. "Why you common, garden variety—"

"Tell him it's about Sally Crain," Mancuso said. "Go on. Get lost before I pull your daisy."

Chris went out and slammed the door behind him.

After that, Mancuso didn't have to wait long.

The door opened and a Secret Service man came in with Terry Fallon behind him. Terry looked Mancuso up and down and shook his head. Then he turned to the Secret Service man. "It's all right," he said. The man nodded, "Yes, sir," and went out.

When the door closed, Terry said, "This had better be important, pal."

"It's about Sally Crain."

"What about her? Is she all right?"

"Yeah, she's fine."

"Then what do you want?"

Mancuso looked at Fallon. Jesus Christ, he sure was a picture. Big, tall, handsome guy in a monkey suit.

"Sally Crain hired the guy who shot you and Martinez."

Terry stared at him.

The door opened. It was Chris. "Senator, the governor of Ohio—"

"Get out!" Fallon said.

The door slapped closed.

Then Terry turned on Mancuso and his voice was low and menacing. "What the hell are you talking about?"

"She set up the whole thing."

"Nonsense. I don't believe it."

Mancuso shrugged and a little circle of water fell off the hem of his raincoat onto the marble floor. He looked down at the puddle under his feet and smiled rather wistfully. "You will," he said.

Mancuso signed Terry in at the guard's booth on the ground floor of the Hoover Building. Then they took the elevator to the third floor—Mancuso, Fallon, and four Secret Service men. But when they reached the videotape room, Mancuso held up his hand.

"They wait outside."

"It's all right," Terry said.

"May we inspect the area?"

"Shit, go on," Mancuso said. He pushed through the door. Inside, there was an elaborate editing console with a bank of eight video monitors facing it. The technician was sitting with his feet up, reading a paperback. The ashtray beside him was full of butts.

"Hey, Joe," he said, and sat up. "Come on, man. I get off at six. It's going on eight."

"Hold your water," Mancuso said. "This here is Senator Fallon."

The technician jumped up and stubbed out his cigarette. "Larry Harris," he said. "Pleased to meet you, Senator."

Terry didn't shake his hand.

"And those are the area inspectors of the U.S. Secret Service." Mancuso waved in the general direction of the four men who were casing the room and wandering around behind the console.

There was a rolling table against the wall with a sheet draped over it. The Secret Service man lifted one end. On the table lay an automatic rifle.

"What the hell is this?"

"That's part of the show," Mancuso said.

The man looked at Fallon. He nodded.

"All right. We'll be on the doors, Senator." He spoke into his lapel mike. "Outside," he said.

In a moment, they were alone.

"All right," Terry said. "I'm here. Show me."

Mancuso beckoned Terry to hold out his hand, and when he did, Mancuso poured the contents of a plastic bag into it.

"What's this?" Terry said.

"These are the cartridges Petersen fired." Mancuso leaned over and picked through them with his index finger. "Lemme see. There's . . . ah . . . six the same. And this here one."

Mancuso held up the black cartridge between his thumb and index finger.

Terry shrugged his shoulders. "And?"

Mancuso leaned in closer. "Well, Senator, you know, this guy Petersen was a pro hitter. I mean, he was major league."

"So?"

"Well, these major league hitters, they're like priests. Everything's a ritual. They don't leave nothing to chance. For instance." He held up one of the plain brass cartridges. "See how scratched this one is? This Petersen loaded his own. Nothing to chance. May I?"

He took Terry's hand and turned it over so that the shells fell into the plastic evidence bag. He zipped it closed. Then he peeled back the sheet and hefted the HK-91 carbine. "See?" Mancuso said. "The last thing Petersen would have done before he opened fire was to check that he had one in the chamber. Now, watch."

Mancuso raised the rifle and pulled the breech half-open. In the gap between the glistening steel jaws, a black shell casing was visible.

"When you pull the breech, you can only see the casing. You wouldn't have thought of that, would you?"

"What the hell are you driving at?" Terry said.

"The bullet. The load. You can see the casing, but not the load." Mancuso let the breech slap closed, and it rang with a deadly, metallic clang. "By painting one casing black, he could be sure he had the right load under the hammer."

436

Mancuso put the carbine down and stood there, seeming very pleased with himself.

"Agent," Terry said, "is this why you dragged me down here tonight?"

"You don't get it, do you?" Mancuso looked over to Harris and opened his hands. "He don't get it."

Terry stood, seething.

"Look, Senator," Mancuso said. "What I'm trying to tell you is that all the bullets weren't the same. See? Six were soft-nosed slugs that tear up a guy's guts. Makes a little tiny wound going in. Then—" Mancuso made a fist and suddenly popped his fingers open. "When it hits bone—bango! We couldn't understand why the last round was different."

"Why was it?"

"It wasn't." Mancuso stood, smiling. "It was the first one that was different." He held up the empty black shell casing. "This here was a full steel jacket. Cuts a clean wound in and out and keeps on going. We weren't looking for it, so we never found it. This is like getting poked with an ice pick. Put it in the right place and it hurts like hell. But it won't fragment and tear up the guts. This is the first round Petersen fired."

Mancuso leaned over and put the black shell into Terry's hand.

"This one was for you."

Terry stared down at the black shell casing in his hand.

Then he looked at Mancuso. There was a bead of sweat on his upper lip. "That's . . . that's preposterous."

Mancuso smiled. "Wanna bet?"

He sat down and swiveled around in his chair so that he faced the console and its eight blank monitors. "Show him."

Harris hit a button and five of the monitors blinked alive. On each was a frozen picture: five different angles of the rostrum on the Capitol steps on the morning of the assassination. In each still picture Terry and Martinez were shaking hands and beaming at each other. It was a strange panorama of the living and the dead, five views of the two dashing young men. Mancuso looked over at Terry. He seemed to have aged years in the past week. Was it only a week?

"Now, what we've done here, Senator," Harris said. "What we've done is to synchronize tapes from five different news crews. Videotape runs at thirty frames a second. That rifle fires ten rounds a second. So, even if the assassin held the trigger down, we would have twenty-one frames to look at."

Terry nodded.

Mancuso said, "Go ahead."

Harris hit the space bar on the console. All five monitors blinked as the tape began to roll. Then the pictures locked up and, in slow motion, Terry and Martinez reached out and turned their handshake into an embrace.

"Let him hear it," Mancuso said.

Harris pushed a slide up and the bizarre slow-motion grinding sound of applause came through the speakers like the groaning of a wounded animal. The time code counter at the bottom of the central monitor slowly ticked off the frames.

"Coming up," Harris said.

Suddenly, all five screens showed the waist of Terry's jacket exploding. As he twisted in pain, six small explosions struck Martinez, spattering tissue and baring the bones in his back. Then, in terrifying and graphic slow motion, the two men fell toward the floor.

"That's enough," Mancuso said.

Harris hit the space bar of the console and the five monitors went dark.

Terry Fallon sat at the desk before the monitors in cold, stony silence. Mancuso watched him. Then, slowly, Terry turned and looked at Mancuso. "It can't. It's— There must be a reason."

"There is," Mancuso said. He leaned over to Harris. "Show him the other way."

Harris typed a number into the CMX, and the center monitor lit with a frozen picture of the crowd standing below the rostrum. They were looking up, hands frozen apart in midapplause, the sunlight falling on their beaming faces as they watched the hero's welcome at the podium above.

"This is the cutaway angle that the network was shooting," Harris said, "so that they could edit the speeches for the evening news."

"Get in on the blond," Mancuso said.

Harris flicked a switch that activated the digital video effects board. As he pushed the joy stick forward, the picture zoomed in on a pretty blond woman standing among the reporters and onlookers.

"Recognize her?" Mancuso asked.

Fallon nodded silently.

"Go ahead," Mancuso said.

Slowly, the tape crept forward, and slowly Sally's hands went to her face as her look and the faces of the people about her changed from joy to horror.

Harris stopped the tape.

Terry shrugged his shoulders. "I don't see—"

"Again," Mancuso said. "Real slow."

Harris typed a message into the CMX. This time, the tape machine reracked and ran in super slow motion.

"With the sound," Mancuso said. Harris turned up the audio.

"Watch her hands," Mancuso said. "And listen."

Through the dull, grinding roar of the crowd and applause, they watched as Sally's hands slowly moved to her face. Just as her fingertips came to rest against her cheeks, the first shot sounded. The machine stopped.

"Want to see it again?" Mancuso said.

Terry swallowed once. Then he nodded once.

As the tape ran again, there could be no doubt about it. Sally's hands had begun to move to cover her mouth and her expression had changed from excitement to fear before the first shot was fired.

Mancuso put his hands on the desk before him.

"She knew."

Terry sat unmoving, the color drained from his face, his lips pressed tight. Darkness hung over his eyes.

"Thanks, Larry," Mancuso said. He nodded toward the door. "See you."

"Sure." Harris stood up and went out.

When the door closed behind him, Terry said softly, "Will that . . . stand up in court?"

Mancuso shook his head. "Nah."

"Are you going to . . . arrest her?"

"Hell, no. I wanna grab the guys she's working for."

"Who?"

Mancuso shrugged. "Don't know."

Terry got up. He walked to the end of the room as if in a daze. Then he turned. "But it's insane. Why? Why would she do a thing like that?"

Mancuso lit a cigarette. "Publicity stunt," he said.

Terry looked like he wanted to spit. "Why you sick, depraved—"

Mancuso snapped the match away. "It worked. Didn't it?"

Terry looked around as though he were lost. He muttered to himself, "She wouldn't. She. . . ."

Mancuso walked to Terry, took him by the arm. Then he leaned in so that he could speak softly and not be overheard.

"Look, Senator," he whispered. "You got to help me."

Terry stared at him. "Help you? How?"

"You got to go on treating her the same. Don't let her guess we're on to her. Don't do anything to put her on her guard."

"But our . . . our relationship is. . . ."

Mancuso winked and nodded. "Yeah, yeah. I get it. Look. When you hump her, just tell yourself you're doing it for Old Glory."

Terry set his teeth in anger. "Is that supposed to be funny?"

Mancuso just sighed.

They stood a while like that, Mancuso nodding, Terry standing stoop-shouldered, his body bent in despair.

Then Terry cleared his throat. "All right," he said. "All right. Thank you, Agent Mancuso."

They nodded to each other and Terry shuffled toward the door. Mancuso looked after him. And what he saw was a weary, broken man.

8:40 P.M. FALLON SAT IN his darkened office on the third floor of the Russell Building. The glow of the night lighting on the Capitol across the street threw horizontal blades of darkness on the mock-up of a campaign poster pinned to the wall. It was a huge blown-up photograph of Terry in shirtsleeves, with a Rocky mountain sunrise breaking behind him. It was a stunning image of a young, vigorous man—a leader, a hero, someone to believe in.

When his campaign began, that poster would be distributed all over the country—and in each region, the background would change, sometimes an eastern city skyline, a wheat field, the Rockies, the Cascades, the pride and heritage of America. It worked for everything. It was Sally Crain's idea.

He had asked her why she chose that image of him.

"It's how I first saw you," she had said. "On that afternoon in the Houston barrio. It's how you looked the moment I fell in love with you. I want all America to see you as I do. And to love you."

Terry Fallon sighed and put his elbows on the desk. Then someone snapped on the lights.

It was Chris Van Allen, about to boil over with excitement.

"Terry! I've been calling everywhere for you!" He pulled off his raincoat and threw it on a chair. "I talked to Ames from Virginia. And Geary from Ohio. They're drafting a letter to the president, demanding he take you on as his running mate. A delegation of governors is coming to the airport in St. Louis to welcome you to the city and the convention!"

But Terry just sat, staring back at him with dull and vacant eyes.

"For Christ's sake, Terry!" Chris shouted. "The governors' caucus is endorsing you for vice president! Terry, we're over the top!"

Just then, the door opened and Sally burst in, stripping off her raincoat. Terry got to his feet.

"Terry, the governors' caucus endorsement is all over town! Terry! We made it!"

Chris glared at her. "What are you doing here?"

"It's all right, Chris," Terry said.

Chris looked back and forth between them. "Hey, I've got to leak this to the AP. Back in a flash!" He rushed out.

Sally came around the desk to where Terry was standing and took his hand with both of hers. She was breathless and her eyes were shining with the thrill of it. "Terry, it's all coming true . . . It's really going to happen!"

He stared dully down at her, his face expressionless and remote.

Puzzled, she looked at him. "Terry, what is it? What's wrong?"

He let go of her hand and walked away from her, walked to the other side of the desk as though he wanted to keep her at a distance. He stood, looking at her as though she were a stranger.

"Terry, what is it?" His face was cold and hard as she had never seen him before. "Terry?"

"It's Mancuso," he said.

"What about Mancuso?"

"He knows."

It was as though a gust of wind had suddenly swirled through the office and whipped her face. The look of exulted wonder left her eyes. They darkened and narrowed. A snarl like a tongue of flame licked back along her lips and curled them.

"All right, all right," she whispered. "Leave him to me."

Terry stood, staring at the transformation in her.

Her slow smile was full of malice. "Don't worry, love," she said and started to slide around the desk toward him. "There's no need for concern." She ran her fingernails along the desktop. "Nothing to be afraid of." She was almost purring now. "I will take care of it."

Terry edged backward.

"You had Petersen shoot me," he said, suddenly.

That stopped her. She stood, eyeing him. "That's absurd."

"Don't lie to me, Sally! I saw it. On the tape." There was such cold fire in her eyes that it frightened him.

"I thought it would be more effective," she said. "It was."

"My God . . . Sally. . . ." His voice was choked, barely audible. "First it was Weatherby. Then Martinez. Then Petersen and Ross. When does it end?"

She hissed at him, "When we're in the White House."

He looked down at her with fear and loathing, as though she were inhuman. "Sally, in the name of heaven. . . ."

"You forgot Fonseca," she said. Then she stepped close to him, put her hand on the front of his shirt, caressing him. "You forgot you taught me."

He shrank from her touch. "My God, Sally. You're a monster."

Suddenly, she lashed out at him, cracked him across the face with a blow that might have felled him if it hadn't thrown him against the desk. He staggered and caught himself. Then he put the back of his hand to his face, half to soothe his flesh, half to protect himself.

She stood before him, flushed and beautiful, her blond hair streaming back off her head like sheets of flame.

"And you," she said. "You are a simpering fool."

9:20 P.M. THE TEXT READ:

WE HAVE AN OBLIGATION TO OURSELVES. WE HAVE AN OBLIGATION TO OUR PARTY. BUT MOST IMPORTANT—WE HAVE AN OBLIGATION TO THE AMERICAN PEOPLE. THAT OBLIGATION BEGINS WITH TRUTH . . . AND ENDS IN THE PERFECTION OF THE AMERICAN DREAM.

Dan Eastman crossed out the last phrase. In its place, he wrote:

. . . and continues with honor.

He looked at the words and shook his head and sat back in his desk chair and stared at the ceiling. It wasn't coming right. And the more he fiddled with it, the further the speech seemed to drift from what he wanted to say.

In two days, he would ascend to the rostrum and stand at the podium before the thousands of massed delegates to the convention. While the backroom politicking and jawboning seethed behind the closed doors of hotel suites all over St. Louis—while President Baker waited in Washington for his letter of resignation—Dan Eastman would have one chance to position himself before the convention and the entire nation as a man who could wipe the slate clean for the party. All that had happened—his open quarrel with President Baker, his two stunning announcements on television— all that provided the springboard for him to appear as a white knight, a charismatic hero, a prince of the Constitution. What he needed desperately were fine words that could capture the simpleminded faith of the American people. If only he and his script writers could find those words. . . .

He leaned over the page and scratched out the last line in exasperation. Then the door opened and his secretary, Dale, came into his office.

"What is it now?"

"Mr. Vice President, there's a man who insists on seeing you. He said to give you this."

She put a clipping torn from a newspaper on his desk. It was the police artist's sketch of the woman at the Four Seasons Hotel. Someone had written alongside the drawing: I KNOW HER.

Eastman lay the clipping on his speech and closed the folder over both of them. "All right," he said. "Send him in."

She went out. Then the door opened and Mancuso came in, his hat in his hand, his raincoat soaked and dripping. When the door closed behind him, Eastman said, "Who the hell are you?"

"Mancuso. FBI. I got something for you."

Eastman swung around in his desk chair to face him. "What?"

"The name of the girl at the Four Seasons."

"Why don't you give it to the District police?"

"They'd just arrest her. I got a better idea."

Eastman smirked and rocked back in his chair. "What?"

Mancuso reached into the pocket of his raincoat. He took out an old yellow envelope tied with string. He slipped the string and dropped the envelope on Eastman's desk and the contents spilled all over the folder containing the speech.

"What the hell is—"

Eastman broke off. He picked up one of the photographs. It was a young and very pretty blond woman, a girl in her early twenties perhaps. She looked very much like the woman in the drawing.

But the girl in the photograph was lying naked on rumpled bedsheets. Her wrists were tied to her ankles with leather thongs.

"What do you mean coming in here with this—"

"You're not looking close enough," Mancuso said. He spread the photographs across the desk.

It was the same girl in every photo. In some she was alone, her arms tied behind her back or bound to a bedpost, with harsh, cutting ropes lashed across her breasts. In others, her hands were tied behind her knees and she was hunched up on the floor, smiling back at the camera. In most of the photographs there was an object violating her. In a few of the photographs, another woman was in bed with her.

Dan Eastman stared at the photographs. They were grotesque beyond anything in his experience. But the girl was hypnotically beautiful. She was a flawless blond with earnest blue eyes and a wonderful open, freckle-faced expression. He stared at the frank blue eyes and he knew, suddenly, where he had seen those eyes before.

"God Almighty," Eastman said. "That's . . . that's—"

"Yeah," Mancuso said. "How 'bout that?"

Eastman turned his head away in disgust. "Where did you get this filth?"

"The wife of a friend of mine." Mancuso looked at his watch. "If you move your ass, you can still make the morning editions."

Eastman closed his fists. "You son-of-a-bitch," he said. "What do you think I am?"

Mancuso took his hand out of his pocket and dropped some little metallic objects that rang on the glass desktop. Eastman looked down. There were four little lapel pins: circle, square, the letter "S," and the American flag. Then Mancuso leaned in over the desk.

"You put a guy from your Secret Service protection staff into political espionage," he said. "That's a felony. And the guy got his ass killed. That's second-degree murder."

Eastman looked up, his face sickly, ashen with fear. A muscle twitched under his left eye. He wiped the back of his hand across his mouth. "Look," he said. "We should talk and—"

Mancuso picked up the flag pin and put it in his pocket. "Just do it," he said. "And then find another job."

He turned and went out.

10:10 P.M. LOU BENDER QUIETLY let himself into the president's study and sat in the big leather armchair under the window, sipping a brandy. When Sam Baker finally closed the book he was reading and looked up, Bender said, "Have you heard?"

"What?"

"The governors' caucus has endorsed Terry Fallon for vice president."

"Why?" Sam Baker said.

Bender stared at him. "Excuse me?"

"Why? Why have they endorsed him? Don't they think I'm competent to make that decision?"

Bender shrugged and shook his head. "Sam, I don't think that's the issue here."

"I'm asking a question. Am I the president of the United States and leader of the party or not?"

"Of course you are. They're just sending you a message that, without them, you may be neither."

Sam Baker folded his arms and lowered his head to his chest.

"You're going to have to face facts, Sam. You can't win without Fallon. If he takes you on for the nomination at the convention, he might be able to push you out then and there. You either offer Fallon the vice presidency or. . . ." He paused.

"Or what?"

"Or you might as well not go to St. Louis."

Sam Baker sat a while, thinking. Then he said, "Lou, has it ever occurred to you that Ramirez and his murderers might be after more than control of the Contras?"

Bender looked up. "Like what?"

"If Ramirez hired Petersen to shoot Martinez, perhaps his plan wasn't simply to change the leadership of the Contras. Perhaps he wants to name the next president of the United States."

"Who?"

"Fallon. You'll admit it's not completely implausible."

Lou Bender shook his head. "Sam, I think you're getting carried away."

"Humor me."

"Well," Bender said, "if this is an exercise in dialectic, then you must believe that Terry Fallon was in on it."

"It's possible."

"Sam. Really. Are you saying that you believe that Terry Fallon stood on a platform with Martinez and let a man shoot him—in the hope that the wound wouldn't be fatal?"

"Maybe Fallon's wound was an accident."

"Sam, please. This is a fantasy."

"Or maybe Fallon really believes he's been chosen."

Bender snorted. "Chosen?"

"He told me that fate chose him to be on that rostrum."

Bender put his drink down and the lightness left him. "He told you what?"

"Fate—"

"Fate? He talked about fate?"

"Yes. He said that fate chose the place for the Martinez shooting."

Bender was sitting up, tense, alert. "What else did he say?"

" 'Fate chose the place. I was ambitious. I was—' "

Bender continued it for him. " 'I was there. And I was lucky enough to survive. I can't apologize for that.' "

The president stared at him. "How did you know he said that?"

"For Christ's sake!" Bender got to his feet. His glass fell to the floor, but he didn't notice. "For Christ's sake, the whole thing's an act!"

STEVE SOHMER

Bender was holding his forehead with one hand, leaning with the other on the back of his chair.

Suddenly, he knew who had been playing the third hand.

"It's a fucking act, Sam. It's all written and rehearsed. 'Fate chose the place.' He actually said that?"

"Well . . . yes."

"Sam, listen to me!" Bender went across the room to the president's chair. "I watched him on television that morning. I watched him get up and stagger to the microphone with a bullet wound in his side. And what he said—the words—I thought, Christ, this guy is a miracle. But it wasn't a miracle. It was rehearsed. It was an act."

The president shook his head. "Lou, now you're being ridiculous."

"Listen to me, Sam. That son-of-a-bitch knew that Petersen was going to shoot Martinez. Goddamit, he knew. He planned it. He had the speech already written out. For Christ's sake, Sam, Terry Fallon murdered Octavio Martinez. He and Ramirez hired Rolf Petersen and then had him killed. There's no telling how many people he's murdered to get where he is. Sam, for Christ's sake—" Then, quite suddenly, Bender stopped cold.

"Lou," the president said softly. "Even if that's true, there's nothing we can do about it without evidence."

Bender's voice dropped, and his tone was ominous, deadly. "Who said you should do anything about it?"

Bender crossed the room, rubbing his hands together. "This is good, Sam. This is very good." Then he turned around. "Now hear this. You give Fallon the number two spot on the ticket. You campaign together. You win the election. How the hell can you miss with a hero like that at your side?"

"Lou, have you lost your mind?"

But Bender went on as though he hadn't heard. "You win the election. Then you put the screws to Ramirez and those other little Contra rats. You grind them until they cough up everything they know about Fallon." Bender laughed. "Then all you have to do is wave it under Fallon's nose and he resigns and goes back to teaching history. You've got four more years and we'll find some rookie to fill the vacancy."

The president looked at Bender with blank, expressionless eyes. "Lou, are you serious?"

"Dead serious."

"Have you any idea what you're saying?"

"There's no other way, Sam," Bender said. "There's just no other way."

446

Sam Baker sat back. "You'll have to let me think about it." He looked at his watch. "Getting late," he said.

"We'll talk tomorrow." Bender went to the door. "And don't worry, Sam. We've got them by the throat." He socked his fist hard into his open palm. Then, he went out.

Sam Baker slouched in his chair and looked down at the book resting on the end table beside him. Then he picked up the phone. "I'd like Speaker O'Donnell, please."

"Yes, sir." In a moment, O'Donnell was on the line.

"Yes, Mr. President?"

"Charlie, you heard about the governors' caucus endorsement?"

"Yes."

"Come over early tomorrow morning," the president said. "I'll tell you my decision then."

O'Donnell took a breath. "I'll be there." They hung up.

11:50 P.M. SALLY HAD JUST fallen asleep when the phone rang. She groaned and rolled over. She could hear the wind and the rain moving on the Georgetown street below her window. The phone rang again. She juggled it to her ear.

"Yes . . . I'm here . . ."

"Sally Crain?" It was a woman's voice, one she didn't recognize. But it spoke her name with a lilting southern drawl.

"Yes. Who—"

"Your friend just cut your throat," the woman said.

"Wha . . . ?"

"You hired Petersen. Then you sent the SWAT team to burn him."

Sally sat up, cold, clear, fully awake. She snapped on the lamp beside the bed. "Who is this?!"

"You put out the contract out on Ross."

"That's a lie!"

But the woman only chuckled in her throat. "You been pulling up your skirts for Fallon ever since you was a reporter on the *Houston Post*. Now ain't that a fact?"

Sally clenched her fist. "Who said that?"

The woman's voice was cooing now. "Why, honey, the man who knows all. The Honorable Terrence Fallon hisself."

Sally stood up and shouted, "You lying bitch!"

"Am I?" The woman laughed, a dark, throaty laughter. "Well, sweetie, he done told me the cutest little secret. He said that one night back in Houston, he took a friend home to help him rape his wife and put her in the funny farm.''

Sally's mouth fell open. Her breathing stopped.

"And this friend?'' the woman said. "Well, this friend wasn't what you might expect, honey. You see, this friend was a pretty little girl. You know? The kind who likes a little leather in her loving.''

Sally's legs began to tremble, so that she had to lean against the edge of the nightstand to keep from losing her balance.

"His little wife never seen this girl before, never seen her since. She don't even know her name.'' The woman laughed. "But you know, don't you, honey?'' Then her tone turned to ice. "Because it was you, honey. It was you, bitch. It was you, Sally Crain.''

Sally opened her mouth to speak. But there was no breath in her.

"See the morning paper, darling,'' the woman said sweetly. "Pleasant dreams.''

Sally screamed, "Who the hell is this!''

But the phone went dead.

She stood a moment, staring through the curtains and venetian blinds out into the rainy, swirling night. Then she threw the phone to the floor, tore her bathrobe from a hanger, and ran for the door.

Mandy let the disconnect button go and put the receiver down. Then she turned and looked at Mancuso.

He was sitting beside her on the edge of her bed, wearing only his undershorts. He was not looking at her, but staring at the wall, lost in some reverie. By the light of the lamp on the nightstand, he looked older than she'd ever seen him.

"Joey,'' she said gently.

Mechanically, without looking at her, Mancuso opened his hand. When she looked down, she could see that he was holding a fifty-dollar bill.

She put her hand around his and closed his fingers. "No, no, honey. That was for love.''

He sat as he was, stony and unmoving, his expression unchanged.

She leaned against him then, leaned in and buried her face under the stubbly wrinkles of his neck. Then she pressed her body tenderly against him.

"Oh, you poor baby,'' she said softly. "Don't you never feel nothin'?''

Sally flung the front door open and dashed out into the icy, rainswept night. It was a driving, hammering rain, a cold rain that beat against her as she ran in and out of puddles, splashing down the broken sidewalk toward

Wisconsin Avenue. The chilling water soaked her bathrobe and matted her hair and froze her bare feet. At the corner, she dashed across the cobbled street, straight into the oncoming headlights of a car. The driver slammed on his brakes, pounded his horn, and skidded past her as she ran on, down the last block toward the glitter of the avenue, wiping the rain from her eyes.

She ignored the people gaping at her, threw a dollar at the newsseller, tore a paper from the pile he was opening, ripped aside the front page, and held the pictures on page three up to the light. Desperate, she stared.

The photos had been carefully retouched and cropped, but she knew them. They were photos she had posed for once, many years ago, in a Houston apartment on Faculty Row. They were pictures she had let herself be used for, one of many ways she had let herself be used. She knew they had given pleasure to a man she had been obsessed with, a man she had to have, no matter what the price. And as she scanned down the page to the police artist's sketch and a picture of her as she looked today, her smoking breath hissed through gritted teeth.

She stood on the street corner in the beating, driving, icy rain, her breath condensing in a throbbing cloud before her face. Someone else might have found those photographs. Ramirez knew about her and Petersen. But only one man knew what she had done to Harriet Fallon—the man who had watched her do it.

Her yellow hair was dark with beading water and hung down over her forehead. And her face became the mask of Medusa as her fingernails tore the newspaper to shreds.

12:10 A.M. WHENEVER HE HAD something big to celebrate, Chris Van Allen would have his Jamaican houseman, Maurice, order a kilo of Beluga caviar and a magnum of *Dom Perignon*. Then he'd send Maurice upstairs to change, and when he came back down in something long and slinky, they'd party until drink and exhaustion claimed them. They were partying like that when the phone rang. And they didn't stop when the machine picked up. "Hello, this is Chris. Sorry I'm not here to take your call—"

It wasn't until Chris heard Terry's voice say, "Goddamit, Chris. If you're there, pick up the phone," that he dived for the receiver.

"I'm here. Terry?"

"Did you see—goddamit, did you see the goddam paper?"

"No. Terry, what is it?"

"It's—" Then he broke off. "See the paper. And get something ready. Now. Do it right now!"

When Terry hung up, Chris ran down the stairs and pulled open the front door. The blustery wind blew the cold rain into his face and turned his skin to gooseflesh. He looked everywhere, but the stoop of the house was empty.

He slammed the door, went to the foot of the stairs and shouted, "Maurice!"

"Yes, lover?"

"Goddamit! Get over to the Avenue and get me a newspaper?"

"Which newspaper, my dear?"

"Goddamit, I don't know. Get them all!"

12:15 A.M. WHEN SALLY PUSHED through the front door of her house, the phone was ringing. She only paused long enough to shrug off the freezing, rain-drenched robe. Then she grabbed the receiver.

"Sally? It's Aud. My God. . . ." It was her friend from the *Washing-*

ton Post, the woman who had joined the paper in the same week she had, the one reporter in town she could really trust.

"Sally, is it true? Are those—is that you in those pictures?"

"Aud, please don't ask me that."

"God, Sally . . . when were they taken?"

Sally stiffened. "Aud, is this on or off the record?"

"Sweetie, it's a big story—"

Sally slammed the receiver down. Now she knew what to expect. In an hour—maybe less—the street would be swarming and the house surrounded with reporters and news vans, the vultures swooping down upon the helpless prey. She didn't have much time.

She grabbed a dry robe from her closet, wrapped her soaking hair in a towel, went to the cellar door and snapped on the basement lights. For a moment, she hesitated, and looked down the wooden steps to the concrete floor below. It was no time for delicacy.

She raced down the steps, past the dark form rolled in the blanket in the corner. She had meant to take care of that this afternoon—but Terry had called and asked her to begin work on his keynote speech. Now reporters and police would be all over her within the hour. There was no time to deal with that secret, and she couldn't let it shake her nerve.

She grabbed the handle of the old footlocker that lay among the shadows and the cobwebs under the stairs. It was heavy and its metal corners grated on the concrete as she dragged it out under the light. There was a thick layer of dust on the lid, obscuring the name she had lettered there a hundred years and a hundred lifetimes ago. The old Yale padlock was rusted and she had long ago lost the key.

She took a hammer from a shelf, struck the lock, again and again, but it held. Finally, she grasped the hammer in both hands, knelt beside the trunk, and smashed down on the lock. It sprang open. The dark scent inside rolled over her like a heavy, swollen sea.

Green it was—fetid with decay. Black it reeked—like rotted bark and decomposing leaves. It smelled of putrefying mud, of mouldering ferns and wormwood. It was the jungle smell along the Rio Coco, the very spoor of death that had lain in wait for her these many years. And it enveloped her like a benediction.

She rocked forward on her knees as though in prayer and slowly slid her hands across the coarse, canvas jacket painted black and green and brown with camouflage. It was cold and clammy, damp with years of mildew. She could smell the degenerative bacteria eating through its fibers. She could feel the slick decay. She knelt, her head bowed, her hands reaching out to the mystery and the power of the jungle.

Upstairs, the phone rang incessantly. The wind battered at the shutters and the rain pounded on the roof. But, deep in the cellar, she took two fistfuls of the fabric as though squeezing out the memories woven there.

Yes, yes. As her hands fondled the contents of the footlocker, the memories sloshed and spilled out around her.

She could see the young nurse who had gone to Honduras, all innocence and light. She could see her cracked fingernails and the lines of care weathering her freckled face as the jungle hissed and steamed above her head. She watched her birthing the babies and laying them in their miniature graves. She watched the brutal army dispensing murder in the bushes. She watched the faceless *gringos* in their short-sleeved white shirts and khaki trousers plotting the destruction of the poor, illiterate *campesinos*.

There in her footlocker, buried among the camouflage gear, among the belts and boxes of cartridges and the weapons . . . the memories were tucked, taking no space but writhing and rising as they tumbled out and struck the floor.

In 1971 they had sent Rolf Petersen to turn her, to find out what she knew when she made her way back from her first encounter at Cabo Gracias a Dios with Fonseca. They had wanted to sift her, to see if she could be of any use to them in crushing the Sandinist rebellion. And in their supreme unvarnished cynicism—because she was only a pretty, impressionable young girl, because she was *La Putita*—they had sent a tall man, a fair-haired man with huge swelling muscles in his arms and chest.

But the morning he stepped off the dirty river steamer and onto the shaky board-and-bamboo dock of Santa Amelia, she recognized him. He was one of them, like the man who had sat in the Ambassador's office in Tegucigalpa, his eyes hidden behind the silver reflective lenses of his sunglasses, listening to her pathetic protest of the murders in Lagrimas.

Standing there on the dock in bare feet and blue jeans, naked to the waist and hefting his duffle over his shoulder, he might have been another Peace Corps volunteer. But he was not. He had a killer's eye and no smile. She didn't hesitate a moment. On his first night there, she took him to her bed and drained him and began her scheme to make him hers. Fonseca had taught her well; a shallow vessel is easily filled.

All winter, she fascinated him with the witchcraft of her body. Until at last, obsessed with her, he sat in the doorway of her hut, hunched under his poncho through the endless rains of winter, watching as she worked among the poor—midwifing the women through their sweaty labors, nursing the feverish babies, cleansing the running sores of the sick. All through the gray rains, he squatted at the door while she stitched closed the machete wounds, dressed the ulcers of gonorrhea, injected the penicillin, and cut away the gangrenous toes.

And in the spring, when the ragged men of Fonseca's FSLN dragged

STEVE SOHMER

themselves across the Nicaraguan border after their despairing clashes with
the forces of Somoza, she ministered to their wounds and healed them while
he sat, silent, on a bench by the door, with a huge red poster of Ho Chi
Minh on the wall behind him.

That summer, when the Honduran army finally swooped down upon
Santa Amelia as they had upon Lagrimas, he was hers—and they fought
together for the *campesinos*.

She could remember lying out all night in the oppressive summer
darkness, never daring to sleep, hearing the murky jungle moving about
her, listening for the crackle of a twig, or a cough, or the gulping sound
that a boot made in water. And when it came, they filled the air with hot
lead and screaming.

After they killed, they fucked and rubbed his semen on their bellies as
though it were a balm to reanoint their life. Then he went off to be hunted
among the hunted men. And she went home to find a way to turn the war in
their favor.

Years passed. And time had played its little shell game with the meaning
of good and evil. The world had turned and when they met again in 1976, she
was the bait to lure Fonseca to his death. And Rolf Petersen was the assassin.

Then what sweet irony it was a month ago when she learned Ramirez
was sending the same Rolf Petersen north to butcher Martinez for Terry
Fallon. What sweet irony it was to meet him at the Holiday Inn just south
of Baltimore, to feel him moving in the darkness on top of her again, to
hear him grunt and spend and groan. And all the while they sat together
plotting the wounding of Terry Fallon and the death of Martinez, she was
waiting to revenge herself for what he had done to Carlos Fonseca.

"Can you do it?" she said.

"Of course."

"You won't kill him. You'll just wound him."

"Martinez?"

"No. Martinez must die. I'm talking about Fallon."

"He's your lover."

"No."

"I don't believe you, *La Putita*."

"All right. He's my lover."

"Then it's a hundred thousand."

"To wound him?"

"No. Not to kill him."

Then the ring had closed.

It was perfect: the wound, the speech, the fools they sent to track him
down. Everything the government attempted, everything they did—all of it
seemed to rise like an unstoppable wave to carry Terry Fallon up out of the
Senate, past the vice presidency, roaring forward at blinding speed to the

456

White House and the reins of invincible power. They had the nation at their feet. And, once in the White House, she would show those cowards how to run the war.

She had herself to blame for Ross. He was an innocent, playing a deadly game he never grasped even at the end. The witchery of her body had mesmerized him, as it had all the men who had really loved her. It was only Fallon who was immune. And now she knew why. He had never cared for her—not really cared, not the way Ross, Fonseca, Carter, or Petersen had.

Fallon had never been her love. He had been her obsession. And now she understood why: because she had been able to mold and lead him—but she had never been able to touch him. She had never once reached beyond the facade and touched the man inside. He cared about only one person: himself. He had only one passion: power. And his coldness had bred in her an obsession as dark as night, as irresistible as fire.

She took a long parcel wrapped in plastic from the bottom of the trunk and sat back, cradling it in her arms, remembering. She was sorry about Ross. She missed him. But if she hadn't cozened Ross, she would never have known that Mancuso was on his way to Baltimore. She would never have had time to provoke the SWAT team with her phone call about an armed terrorist who planned to strike at Friendship Airport in the morning. And if she hadn't hired the *Ladinos* who killed Ross, he might have found her out.

Still. Still, she hurt for him. But she shook the hurt away.

She had herself to blame for Mancuso. She should not have let herself be used as bait again. His bumbling ignorance had deceived her—and he had trapped her in a squalid little crime. If only he had come with her after Ross's funeral, she would have put him out of the way.

Even with all that, if Terry had only listened to her, if she had only had her way, it would have worked. But from the moment that the murder of the Secret Service man became public, Terry Fallon began to lose his nerve.

At the thought of him, her mouth filled with spit. He was, after all, a fake, a phoney, a limp imitation of a man driven by hollow ambition, a man who couldn't give a woman pleasure, but only lusted to degrade the women who adored him. She had tried to make something of him, to stiffen his resolve. But at the first alarm, he had retreated. And now he had peddled the photographs and thrown her to the wolves. And what was worse, he had shared their darkest secrets with another woman.

The rage blazed in her. She pulled hard on the edges of the plastic packet in her arms, let its contents roll out on the floor. It was an M-16 carbine and it clattered on the concrete and lay, black and still. She lifted it, and the feel of cold gunmetal and wood surged through her body. It smelled of burned powder and death. She pulled on the action and it thunked open. It was still oily, still clean, and the steel retractors glistened.

Dressed in the drab canvas, her damp hair in a pony tail, she put two clips of ammunition in her pockets, pulled on her socks and boots, and went upstairs. She set the carbine near the back door of the house, and set her raincoat and hat beside it. Then, she went to the front windows.

The street was still clear. The vultures had not yet settled. As she started back, she saw Tommy Carter's jacket hung on the chair where he had left it. She took the jacket to the cellar door, flung it down the stairs, and closed the door after it. But when she reached to shut off the bedroom light, she caught a glimpse of herself in the mirror on her vanity.

Slowly, like a woman walking in a dream, she made her way across the room to the vanity table and sat down on the lacy white cushion. Behind her, she could see a frilly white bedroom—perhaps the bedroom of a young girl she had once known long ago. But the woman in the mirror was no stranger. She wore a faded brown cotton undershirt, olive combat fatigues, no makeup. And her lips were thin, her jaw set with purpose. But there was something in the mirror that was not her, something that didn't belong. She drew the brutal, gleaming serrated knife from the sheath that hung on her belt. Then she pulled up her long, blond pony tail. She stared and nodded goodbye.

Then she cut at the roots.

5:50 A.M. PRESIDENT SAMUEL BAKER was already dressed in a smart blue three-piece suit when his steward, Michael, set the tray of coffee on the table in his private dining room. There was an envelope on the tray. Inside, was a sheet of paper headed with the seal of the vice president of the United States. There was a typewritten line on the paper:

I hereby resign the vice presidency.

It was signed Daniel J. Eastman and undated. The president folded the paper back into the envelope and slipped it into his jacket.

"Michael, is the director here?"

"Yes, sir. In your study."

When the president went downstairs, Admiral William Rausch was waiting for him in the room off the Oval Office.

"Good morning, sir," Rausch said, and stood up.

The president closed the door. "Please be seated. Have you brought your appointment calendar as I asked?"

"Yes, sir." It was a red desk diary and it lay on the polished mahogany table before him.

"In a moment, I'm going to send my secretary in here," the president said. "You are to dictate to her everything you know about the plot to poison Colonel Martinez with AIDS. I want no ellipses."

Rausch didn't reply.

"If you do this, I will give you an immediate transfer to noncombatant sea duty for one year. After which, you will retire from the navy without the customary promotion in rank. Do you understand?"

"Yes, sir," Rausch said softly.

"Do you agree?"

"Yes, sir."

The president pressed a button under the edge of the table. In a moment, the door of the room opened and a marine sergeant entered and braced.

"This officer is not to leave this room without my permission," the president said. "If he tries to do so, you are to place him under close arrest. If he resists arrest, you are to shoot to kill."

The marine sergeant stared straight ahead. Then he pulled in his chin. "Yes, sir."

"That is all."

The sergeant went out.

"Now," the president said. "What orders did Mr. Bender give you at your meeting with him yesterday afternoon?"

Rausch wet his lips.

"For the last time, what orders?"

"He instructed me to . . . to have Agent Mancuso murdered."

The president stiffened. "When? How?"

Rausch looked at his wristwatch. "It's too late already," he said.

6:10 A.M. WHEN THE PHONE rang, Mancuso sat up sharply in bed. Mandy opened her eyes and stared at him. The phone rang again. He cleared his throat. "Okay," he said. "Go on."

Mandy lifted the receiver. "Yeah?" Then she handed the phone to Mancuso.

"Joey? That you?" It was Gertie's voice.

"What?"

"Friend of yours came in late last night."

"Who?"

"I dunno. Said his name was Wilson."

Mancuso swung his feet out of bed. "Did you tell him where I was?"

"Yeah. Didn't see no harm. Then I got to thinking."

"Thanks."

"Yeah." She hung up.

Just then, someone began pounding on the doorway to the tenement hall. Mancuso slapped his hand over Mandy's mouth to keep her from calling out. He slipped naked out of bed, took the .38 from under his pillow, and went into the hall. He leveled the revolver at the door and thumbed the hammer back. Mandy stood in the doorway to the bedroom, the bedsheet pulled across her nakedness.

"Joey," she whispered. "My God. . . ."

Suddenly, the pounding stopped. Then a voice called out, "Agent Joseph Mancuso?"

It wasn't Wilson's voice.

"Mancuso, if you're in there, open up."

"Touch that door again and I'll kill you," Mancuso said softly.

There was shuffling in the hallway, then silence.

"Look, pal, don't get excited," the voice said. "I'm just supposed to escort you over to the White House."

"Sure," Mancuso said. "The president wants to have breakfast with me."

"Not the president. Mr. Bender."

Mancuso thought about that. Then he said, "Stand across the hall. Stand where I can see you." He waited a moment, then he slid up to the door and put his eye to the lens of the peephole. It was a wide-angle glass and he could see up and down the hall. There was one of those typical, beautiful-but-dumb Secret Service creeps in a neat gray suit, standing against the far wall with his hands held away from his body so that Mancuso could see he wasn't holding a gun. He didn't look like he was more than twenty-five.

"What's your name, kid?"

"Halvorsen. Howard E."

"Lemme see your ID. Hold it up real close here. And no funny stuff, or I'll blow your fucking balls off."

The kid took his laminated ID out of his breast pocket and held it close to the peephole. It was legit.

"Okay," Mancuso said. "Now, slide that under the door."

"Hey, man. I need this."

"Me, too. Cause if this don't go right, friend of mine gotta know who to put in a box. Okay?"

"Shit," the kid said, but he slid the card under the door.

"Now just go stand against the wall till I'm ready."

Mancuso went back, dressed, and gave the ID to Mandy. Then he took the angle gun he always carried against the small of his back, cocked it, and handed it to her. "You know how to use this?"

She nodded.

"Anybody tries to come in after I leave, you give 'em the whole six. Understand? And when I call you to say I'm clear, you drop this card in a mailbox. Then you go stay somewhere else for a week. You get me?"

She bit her lip and nodded quickly.

"Hey, I'm sorry I got you into this," he said.

"Never no mind."

He kissed her. "Come on."

She followed him to the door. When he looked through the peephole, the Secret Service agent was still standing against the far wall. "Lock this as soon as I'm out," Mancuso said.

He put his revolver into his coat pocket with his finger on the trigger. Then he opened the door. The kid looked down at the bulge in Mancuso's jacket and went white.

"Hey, man," the kid said. "Be cool."

"You be cool," Mancuso said. "Anybody even farts and I'm opening up. You got me?" He pulled the door closed and heard Mandy lock it behind him.

"Sure. Sure."

"Come on, princess. Let's go," Mancuso said, and he followed him down the hall and the stairs.

At the front door, he made the kid wait while he looked up and down the street. There was a boy riding his paper route, two athletic young men jogging in cutoffs and football jerseys, a bag lady and an old man walking a bulldog. There was an unmarked car double-parked at the curb with another lily-white boy sitting behind the wheel.

"That your partner?" Mancuso said.

"Yes."

"Where do they find you guys? Fantasyland?"

"What do you mean?"

"You're all so fucking pretty. Why don't you look like regular people?"

The kid cocked his head sidelong. "Hey, fuck you, pal," he said. "Enough bullshit. You coming or not?"

Mancuso chucked him lightly on the shoulder. "Now you're talking. Go sit in the front seat. Tell your partner to watch his hands."

He followed the agent to the car. When he opened the door and slid into the rear seat behind them, the partner looked up and said, "What's happening, Chick?"

The kid thumbed back at Mancuso. "That asshole's got a gun on us."

"Hey, man," the partner said. "What is this? Some kind of fucking joke?"

Mancuso put the revolver in the driver's ear. "You want to hear the punchline, you just say the word."

461

"Hey. No offense. Be cool."

"What are you guys? A fucking weather bureau? Come on. Drive."

The car pulled away into traffic and Mancuso shouted, "Stop! Right now!"

The driver slammed on the brakes and the two men in the front seat hit the floor.

But Mancuso wasn't looking at them. He was looking across the street at a man standing in the shadow of a doorway. It was Wilson.

Mancuso rolled his window down. "Hey, you! Yeah, you—you fucking scumbag!" he yelled. Wilson shrank back in the doorway. "You blew your chance, you fucking creep! You shit-eating bum—you couldn't spy on your old lady taking a dump!"

The boy on his paper route stopped his cycle and the two joggers stood, running in place and looking on. The bag lady stood right in front of the doorway where Wilson was standing, staring up at him. And the old man with the bulldog started to laugh out loud.

Mancuso kept shouting. "Fuck you, Wilson! Big fucking CIA hot-shot! Yeah, mister—" he shouted to the man with the dog, "I mean him over there! That cocksucker in the doorway! Yeah! That one! That's Harry Fucking Wilson! Big fucking CIA spy—caught with his cock in his hand!"

In spite of themselves, they were all laughing now—the boy, the joggers, the old man, even the bag lady.

Wilson looked around, embarrassed. Then he pushed his dark glasses up his nose, pulled his hat down over his eyes, and hurried around the corner.

"Go on! Run! You fucking shit-heel! Goddam fucking pansy hit man! You couldn't hit my fucking maiden aunt, you dick-face!"

When Mancuso pulled his head back inside the window, the two Secret Service men were still cowering on the floor.

"Hey," Mancuso said. "What's the matter with you guys? You just saved my life."

7:10 A.M. WHEN MANCUSO CAME through the door of the office, Bender had the newspaper open before him on his desk. The headline read:

VICE PRESIDENT IDENTIFIES MYSTERY WOMAN

And under that:

Fallon Aide Implicated in Sex Ring Murder

"You did this, you son-of-a-bitch!" Bender snapped.

"Eastman did it. Says so right at the top."

"You did it. And you're going to pay for it."

"Maybe," Mancuso said. "And maybe you'll be out on the street, come November."

Bender smirked at him. "Don't bet on it, Mancuso. This isn't going to work. Terry Fallon's the Teflon candidate. This is going to slide off him like the dirty slur it is. In two days, he'll be nominated for vice president and there's nothing you can do to stop it."

Mancuso shrugged. "We'll see."

"You're to report to Supervisory Special Agent Scott's office, mister. You're washed up. Finished. Right now."

"Yeah. I know," Mancuso said. "I just came by to give you a going-away present." He put a square of paper on Bender's desk.

Bender's mouth curled in disgust. It was another photograph of Sally, bound in leather, lying naked on her side, one leg pulled up. But in this photograph a man in leather harness was sodomizing her. The man was young and muscular and redheaded. It was Terry Fallon.

Bender looked up sharply. "Do you have any more of these?"

"Anything funny happens to me, you're gonna find out."

Bender nodded, grim. Then he took out his lighter, touched it to a corner of the photograph. "You stupid bastard," he said as the flames blackened the picture. "You should have given this one to the papers. This would have ruined Fallon's career as well as the girl's." He dropped the curling cinders into an ashtray.

Mancuso stood, watching it burn. "I know that," he said, softly.

Bender looked at him.

"Somehow that didn't seem enough." Mancuso put his hat on and went out the door.

It was a moment before Bender understood. Then he pounded his fist down on the desk in front of him and shouted, "Mancuso!"

Bender was still steaming when he got in to see the president.

"Those photographs?" Bender said.

"Yes?"

"Mancuso."

The president rocked back in his chair. "Really?"

"That son-of-a-bitch O'Brien. . . ." Bender dropped down into the chair across from the president's desk. "In his supreme ignorance, he put the one man on the case who could solve it. A lonely, despicable misanthrope with no respect for authority."

"Lou, have you seen this?" the president said, and slid a lengthy, typewritten memo across the desktop toward him.

"No. I don't think—" Bender broke off. He read a page. Then he turned to the second and read that. Then he leafed back to the date and signature at the end.

Then he looked at the president. "This is. . . ."

"A confession. Yes," the president said. "I'm holding it for O'Brien."

Bender smiled. "But you're not going to give it to him, of course."

"Lou—yes, I am. I have every intention of giving it to him."

Bender sat forward. "But, Sam—my name's in there. I'm mentioned . . . implicated. You can't—"

"I suppose the Intelligence Oversight Board will want to ask you about some of the details."

The color drained from Bender's face. "But I'll be disgraced, Sam. I'll have to resign. I won't—" Then he broke off. "The job," he said.

The president sat where he was.

Bender leaned back in his chair and chuckled to himself and shook his head. "The job," he said again. Then he laughed out loud.

"What job, Lou?"

"You arranged that," Bender said. "Yesterday, Greisman offered me one of those rich, do-nothing jobs, high up on some corporate shelf. And I didn't know why. It was you, wasn't it?"

"It's the least I could do," the president said.

"And Rausch?"

"A noncombatant at sea for a year. Then retirement."

"Very neat," Lou Bender said. "So, when the full report goes to the Oversight Board, the guilty have already been kicked out. Which proves that the system works. So, the story of how the CIA poisoned Martinez remains a national security secret. And the Board goes back to sleep. Right?"

"Lou, I have a very busy morning," the president said and stood up.

"Well," Bender said and got to his feet. "I take it I've resigned to accept a position in the private sector?"

"The press room will issue the release at 9:00 A.M."

Bender looked at his wristwatch. "That doesn't give me much time. I have to clear my desk and—"

"We'll send your things after you."

"I have to call Greisman and—"

"He's at his New York office waiting for your call."

Lou Bender stood, staring. Then he chuckled again. "I see the time I spent on you was not wasted."

"No," the president said. "And, Lou—there were good times. And I have much to thank you for. This country has much to thank you for."

Bender put his hands in the pockets of his trousers and pulled up his cuffs and looked at the shine on his shoes. "Then what purpose does this exercise serve?"

"If you don't understand that," the president said, "I am not the man to instruct you."

They stood like that a while, two men who had shared much and shared nothing. Then Bender opened the door and went out.

7:20 A.M. TERRY WAS STANDING in the bay window of the living room of the house in Cambridge, reading a typescript by morning light. He wore a gray suit and a red and blue regimental tie. He looked very Eastern, very smart, very right.

Chris Van Allen rushed in, carrying his bag, his chubby face gleaming with perspiration. "Sorry I'm late. The traffic—"

"This is good, Chris. Very good," Terry said, and held up the pages. "It sets the issue of Sally and the photographs to rest. Permanently."

Chris just stared.

Then Terry said, "You wrote this, didn't you?"

Slowly, Chris shook his head.

Terry looked at the pages in his hand. "It came by messenger this morning. I assumed you. . . ." He broke off there, staring down at the neatly typed text. Then he smiled, fondly. "The strange things people do in the name of love. . . ."

"We know she can write," Chris said.

"Have you heard from her?"

"No." Then Chris opened his notebook. "Here's the agenda. A quick televised press conference at station WRC. I'll introduce, you'll do your talk, take a few questions. Then I'm going to cut them off and say we'll take more questions in St. Louis this afternoon."

"Good."

"We limo to National. I've moved the flight back one hour. We arrive at 11 A.M. local time." He closed the book, pleased with himself.

"Okay," Terry said and began to fold the pages into his pocket. "By the way," he said casually, "make sure the Secret Service have a recent picture of Sally."

7:40 A.M. WHEN MANCUSO GOT to the Bureau, he went directly to Captain Scott's office. The secretary waved him inside.

"What now?" Mancuso said when he shut the door.

"You're out, Joe!" Scott yelled. "Today. Right now. You're gone. Finished, you motherfucker!"

"I got three months yet."

"You're done. This minute."

Mancuso set his jaw. "I'll appeal. You're not busting my pension."

"That's right. I'm not."

He held up a sheet of paper. Mancuso took it, held it out at arm's length and further, trying to make out the small print.

"What's this?"

"Early retirement, pal. In a search through its files, the benevolent Bureau has found that you have a shitload of unused sick leave and vacation days."

"No, I don't."

"As of today, you do. And it's enough to take you out, buddy. You're paid, you're pensioned, you're history. Sign it."

"With pleasure."

Mancuso took a ballpoint from the desk and leaned over to sign. And when he did, Scott sat forward and said, very softly, "You iced a guy from Secret Service, you fuck."

Mancuso looked up at him. They were eyeball to eyeball. "He was working two jobs. Eastman sent him to ruin Terry Fallon. You want that in the papers, too?"

For a moment, Scott glared at him. Then he slumped back in his chair and the grit seemed to go out of him. "Jesus Christ," he said, "it was supposed to be clerical work. You knew that, Joe. Why the fuck did you turn it into a nightmare? What was it to you?"

Mancuso stared at him. "Nothin'," he said. "Maybe I'm just an old-fashioned idealist."

Scott's face turned bitter. "See the cashier, asshole."

Mancuso dropped the pen and paper on his desk, and went out.

7:50 A.M. STEVE CHANDLER WAS as busy as an octopus with athlete's foot. Between the regular *Today* show in New York and the remote Fallon press conference at WRC, he felt like he had a flying circus on the air. So, when his private line rang in Control Room 3B, he was in no mood to mince words. "What is it?"

"How would you like an exclusive interview with a woman who's been kicked out on her ass?"

It took a moment for the voice to register. "Where are you? I've been trying to reach you all night?"

"Somewhere safe."

"Is it true?"

"Do I get on the air?"

"Anytime you want," he said.

"What time is Fallon on?"

"The usual. Eight-eleven."

"Okay," Sally said. "I'll give you the rebuttal right after the commercial. Fair?"

"Done. Where?"

"Where's he coming from?"

"Studio 1 at WRC. We can do it from there."

"No, thanks. Can you get a remote crew to the Senate press gallery?"

"We've got one there now. For comments on the Fallon speech."

"Tell them to leave a pass at the door. In the name of Susan Lane."

"They all know you there."

"Well, I look different," she said. "I had a haircut."

"Women," Chandler said. "Okay. Whatever you want." He scribbled out the name. "Listen," he said. "There's something I should tell you. When nobody could get through to you last night—"

"What?"

"The police got a search warrant for your house. There's a report on the wire that—"

"See you on the air after Fallon," she said. Then she hung up.

8:05 A.M. WHEN CHRIS VAN ALLEN stepped to the podium on the rostrum in Studio 1 at WRC, he was facing a hornet's nest. The vast studio had been set with thirty rows of metal folding chairs—almost 400 in all—and every seat was filled. News crews packed the rear of the room and lined the walls along both sides. It seemed that every reporter in Washington had fought his or her way into the room. From under the black glass of the announcer's booth jutting out of the rear wall, to the very foot of the rostrum, reporters were milling about, working each other, engaged in loud, agitated conversation.

Chris leaned into the microphones. "May I have your attention, please?" he said and his amplified voice cracked with stage fright. Only a few reporters looked around. Some of them sniggered. "Please!" he said. "Ladies and gentlemen! Please, be seated!" The public address system seemed to amplify not only his voice but everything that was effete about him.

The reporters reluctantly began to find their seats.

"Please," Chris said again. "Please, ladies and gentlemen. Be seated. Thank you."

They settled uneasily, rustling and unquiet.

Chris opened a slip of paper on the podium before him. "Senator Fallon will have a brief statement," he said. "The senator regards the revelations in today's newspapers as a personal matter pertaining only to Miss Crain."

Someone shouted, "Don't you mean *intimate*?" and someone else shouted "Has Sally Crain been fired?" and suddenly the roof seemed to come off. Reporters in the front row jumped up, shouting angry questions. When they rose, so did the row behind them. And in a moment, the entire room was standing. Those who weren't shouting were laughing.

"Please! Everyone! Please!" Chris shouted into the microphone. "Unless you take your seats, the senator will go to the airport and this press conference will be held in St. Louis! Please!"

Gradually, with deep grumbling, they began to seat themselves again.

Chris cleared his throat. "The published photographs clearly predate Miss Crain's association with the senator's office—"

"Yeah," someone shouted. "They're her baby pictures!" and the room exploded into gales of laughter.

Chris went on, shouting over them, "—and these photographs have no connection with either the senator or this campaign!"

A reporter in the back called out, "Did he know she had an affair with Weatherby?" And a dozen or so voices called out and the room was on its feet again.

Steve Chandler sat before the remote feed monitor in Control Room 3B at 30 Rockefeller Center. It was 8:08 A.M. and the fat little clown had three minutes to get the room settled and get Fallon to the podium. If he didn't, when *Today* put the feed from WRC on the air, America was going to watch the press corps tear Chris Van Allen into dog meat. Chandler leaned over and nudged the technical director with his elbow.

"Why is it that the best television shows never get on the air?"

When Mancuso got to the cashier's office on the third floor of the Hoover Building, he tapped on the bulletproof glass, and Myrtle, the old, white-haired lady who was the benefits supervisor, waved and buzzed him in. She was a sweet little dame, with apples in her cheeks and a smile for everyone and an old-fashioned, upside-down pendant watch pinned over her heart.

"Come on in, Joey," she said, and nodded at the chair alongside her desk.

"How you keeping, Myrtle?" Mancuso sat down and put his hat on the desk beside him.

"So, you finally pulled the plug?"

"Yeah."

"I'm gonna miss you, kid," she said.

Mancuso shrugged. "Yeah."

"Well, let's see what we got here." She put on her glasses and opened the manila folder on the desk before her. "This one you'd better read before you sign it."

It was the usual small fucking type and Mancuso had a hard time making it out. "What's it about?"

"That you forfeit your pension and benefits—the whole thing—if you tell any secrets."

Mancuso started to laugh. The phone rang.

Myrtle answered it. Then she said, "It's for you," and passed the receiver to Mancuso.

"Yeah?"

"Joe?" It was the big blond secretary, Jean.

"What?"

"You quit?"

"I'm retiring, yeah."

"Well. . . ." She sounded congested, like she was coming down with a cold.

"Hey, what do you want? I got all these papers and stuff to sign."

Her voice was very small. "Aren't you . . . coming up to say goodbye?"

He looked at Myrtle, then away, out the window. "Yeah, sure," he said. "When I get my things."

"I'm transferring a call," Jean said.

"Who?"

"I don't know. Says it's important. Won't say who it is."

Mancuso thought about that. "All right. Go ahead." There was clicking in his ear, then a voice said, "Joe, are you there?"

Mancuso started to stand up. Then he saw Myrtle looking at him and sat down. "Yeah, this is Joe."

"You went to Eastman last night, didn't you?"

"What if I did?"

"And you told Bender you knew about . . . about the poison. You panicked him."

"So?"

"You know they tried to kill you?"

"Yeah, I know."

"They won't anymore. I've seen to that."

"They weren't too good at it anyhow."

"Joe, I'd like to ask you why?"

"Why what?"

"You could have walked away from the whole thing. Why didn't you?"

Mancuso shrugged. "No reason."

"I don't believe that."

"Maybe I figured this country should have a second chance."

There was silence at the end of the phone.

"You there?" Mancuso said.

"There is no way we can repay even part of what we owe you," the voice said. Then he hung up.

Mancuso put the receiver back into its cradle. Then he sat, staring at it.

"What was that all about?" Myrtle said.

Mancuso lit a cigarette. "Nothing," he said. "Just some guy I once did a favor."

A man at the side entrance of the studio gave the thumbs-up, and Chris Van Allen stepped to the podium again. "Roll tape," he said.

On the NBC network, Bryant Gumbel was looking directly into the camera and saying "—to NBC affiliate WRC in Washington, where Senator Terry Fallon is about to hold a live press conference to discuss events that have shocked the political establishment."

Today cut to a picture of Chris Van Allen at the podium. He said, "Ladies and gentlemen, the senator from Texas, the Honorable Terrence Fallon." As though by magic, the roomful of reporters fell silent.

"What happened to his blond honey?" the TD said to Chandler.

"I think he may be about to tell us," Chandler said, and sat back smugly with his styrofoam container of coffee.

Terry crossed the front of the studio, stepped up on the rostrum and took his place at the podium. "I have a short statement," he said. "This morning I received a sad and disturbing telephone call from a woman who has been an important part of our office throughout my years in the Senate."

There was pain in his eyes, and all across America, millions who were watching could believe that the pain was real.

Myrtle laid the forms out for Mancuso one by one, patiently explaining each, showing him where to sign.

"Now this," she said, and opened a blue folder. "This moves your health insurance to retirement basis. And this is your major medical."

"What's that?"

"If you get real sick."

"What's the difference?"

"Well, you've been paying for it all these years. Now you get it and you don't have to pay."

"All these years I paid and I didn't need it. Now I might need it and I don't have to pay no more?"

Myrtle smiled. "This is the government, Joey. Nobody said it had to make sense."

"Tell me about it." He signed in both places.

"Now, this one here—" and she swapped the forms before him "–this one cancels your bond-a-month plan."

"How come?"

She shrugged. "You don't have to cancel it. But you'll be on your pension now, you know."

"How much is it?"

"$12.50 twice a month."

"Leave it," he said. "Maybe Uncle Sam needs the money."

They smiled at each other.

The rear door of the office opened and one of the bookkeepers stuck her head in. "Myrtle, he's on. Fallon's on television."

"You go ahead, Dot. I'll be along."

"Do you want to see it?" Mancuso said.

"Don't you? It's about that poor girl."

"Nah," Mancuso said. "I'm done with all that now."

It was a rare experience for Terry Fallon, standing before the grim faces of unfriendly reporters. "I want to leave no doubt that I regard the revelations in today's newspapers as indecent and notorious," he said, and looked them in the eye.

"How Sally Crain comported herself as a young woman—or in her recent private life—raises questions that defy easy explanation. These are forms of behavior for which I have no sympathy, toward which no decent person can feel anything but revulsion. And yet," he said, and his tone deepened, "I am dismayed, ladies and gentlemen, that the personal tragedy and real significance of these events has, so far, been ignored."

He paused a moment and scanned the faces that were hardened against him. His eye was keen, and dauntless. He had the look of a man who knew the truth and was about to speak his mind, no matter if the sky fell around him. Then he unfolded the speech Sally had written for him, and began.

"Today, a young woman has had her career destroyed. Because once, in the distant past, she fell into the hands of unscrupulous men who exploited her in the cruelest way imaginable. What happened to Sally Crain was her fault—and she must answer for it. But it was not hers alone—and I will not allow her to become the scapegoat for a guilt others must share. Sally did not fall alone. There were accomplices."

The reporters shifted uneasily in their seats.

*　　*　　*

471

"Now, this here," Myrtle said. "This is nice." She put a government paycheck in front of Mancuso, and he whistled through his teeth.

"That for me?"

"Yes, sir." She leaned over and touched the boxes and the numbers as she described them. "This is your lump-sum payment for unused vacation days and sick leave. Less FICA. See that?"

"Yeah."

"Less federal. Less District taxes. And this is the net. Now you fold that up and put it in your wallet."

He did as he was told. "Should have got one of these every week. I'd have been set."

She opened the next set of papers. "Have you thought about what you're going to do?"

"About what?"

"When you're retired."

"I don't know," Mancuso said. "Maybe go to Hollywood and get in the movies."

Myrtle smiled.

"Hey, don't laugh," Mancuso said. "I'm a pretty good actor."

Steve Chandler had Fallon on the remote feed monitor in Studio 3B. But the monitor he was watching now was the feed from the Senate press room. Stagehands were moving in a single chair and audio was testing a patch so that Bryant Gumbel could interview Sally Crain live. It was the kind of exclusive that newsmen prayed for and dreamed about. Just as Fallon finished washing his hands of her, Sally Crain would open up with what had to be years of dirty laundry. It would not only help the ratings, but the whole *Today* staff could dine out on it for a month.

Chandler picked up the open line to the press room floor manager.

"Is she in makeup?"

"She hasn't shown yet," the floor manager said.

"Call down to security. Make sure they hustle her right upstairs. Fallon isn't going to stand there forever."

Terry said, "Sally Crain had everything a girl could ask for—intelligence, personality, a loving family, and a fine education. She grew up believing in the American dream, in our Constitution and in the sincerity of our government. She was to be bitterly disappointed."

He looked up from the pages on the podium before him.

"Many of you knew Sally. Many of you admired her." His eyes settled on the faces of the reporters, moved among them one-by-one. "And, like her, you witnessed how deceit and perjury stained one American administration after another—from Watergate to the Iranian arms-for-hostages deal."

"Shit, he's breaking my heart," Steve Chandler said.

Sam Baker was watching Fallon speak on television when Charlie O'Donnell arrived.

"Don't let me interrupt you," O'Donnell said.

"That's all right," the president said. He pressed the remote and the set clicked off. "Fallon's trying to dig his way out of the situation with that woman."

"Disgusting."

"Sad."

"Well, I came as soon as I could," O'Donnell said, trying to prod the conversation forward.

"Yes, I appreciate that, Charlie. I wanted you to be here in person to hear my decision."

O'Donnell folded his hands in his lap.

"I have decided to seek the nomination," the president said. "And go all out to have it."

O'Donnell swallowed hard. "With . . . whom?"

"Not with Fallon."

"Then Fallon may seek the presidential nomination himself."

"That's why I'm stepping up, Charlie. I must deny him."

O'Donnell shook his head. "I don't think the convention will have you, Sam. Not with Eastman."

"Charlie, I have Dan Eastman's letter of resignation in my pocket."

"What?"

"It's undated. I will make it official when I choose. That's our arrangement."

"Mary, Mother of God," O'Donnell said softly.

"Once I've selected a running mate, Eastman will step down and the ticket can campaign as incumbents."

O'Donnell smiled. "It's clever, Sam, but it won't work. I'm not sure you can win, no matter who runs with you."

"Then we'll have to pick some qualified party regular who has the courage to lose."

O'Donnell shrugged and opened his hands. "I don't know anyone who'd be willing."

The president sat, silent.

Suddenly, O'Donnell understood.

"It'll be a hard fight, Charlie," the president said. "And a bitter pill to swallow when all is said and done. I can't promise you anything but rancor at the convention and disappointment after. But we'll have done something courageous. And I'm willing to go out on that."

O'Donnell hung his head and he seemed to be muttering. But he was chuckling softly to himself.

"Vice President O'Donnell," he finally said. "Ah, me."

O'Donnell leaned back and hooked his thumbs under the straps of his suspenders. "Oh, sure," he said. "I've been in Congress long enough. The mongrels are nipping at my heels. It's time I kicked back at the dogs. I say, let's give 'em hell, Sam. If you want me, I'm yours." He held his big hand out across the table and the president took it. "Who says we're too old to fight?"

"God bless you, Charlie," the president said, and clasped his hand. "But there's one other issue. And you have to know the truth about it before you sign on."

O'Donnell nodded darkly. "Martinez."

"Yes." The president pressed the button on his intercom. "Katherine," he said, "ask the director to join us."

The door opened and Henry O'Brien came in.

"Mr. President. Mr. Speaker."

"Please, Henry," the president said. "Be seated."

O'Brien took a chair at the end of the table. He looked uneasy. Clearly, no one had prepared him for this appearance.

"Henry, I want you to tell the Speaker about the autopsy on Colonel Martinez. Particularly, what was found in the blood tests."

O'Brien sat dumbfounded for a moment. Then he felt through all his pockets, but his little spiral notebook wasn't there. "The . . . blood tests?"

"Yes." The president leaned forward in his chair. "Henry, do you remember when we talked together in the ADR? When you told me I could count on you?"

"Yes."

"Well, I'm counting on you now." The president sat back and waited.

O'Brien looked back and forth between the two powerful men. Then, he thought of Joe Mancuso. Mancuso had been right: O'Brien *shouldn't* have let them do it.

O'Brien drew a breath. Then he said, "Colonel Martinez had AIDS."

In the hush that followed, O'Donnell whispered, "My God in heaven. So . . . it's true."

The president smiled. "Thank you, Henry," he said. "Thank you for telling the truth." He turned to O'Donnell. Not in all his years in government had he seen the great Speaker of the House so shaken.

"Yes," Sam Baker said. "It's true. Executives of the government of the United States conspired to poison Octavio Martinez." He got up and went to the desk and picked up two copies of a typewritten document and handed one to each of them. "This is Admiral Rausch's report on the attempted murder by poisoning of Colonel Martinez. It's all there. Who ordered the AIDS virus used, how it was obtained, the name of the doctor who administered it—everything. Henry, I want you to deliver this on Friday to the Intelligence Oversight Board. Along with your own complete report."

O'Brien was blinking a mile a minute. "Yes, sir . . ."

O'Donnell had already scanned the first few pages. "For God's sake, man. This is—" He flipped another page. "Rausch, Bender—"

"Admiral Rausch is returning to active duty with the navy for one year before he retires," the president said.

"And Bender?"

"Mr. Bender will—" But the president stopped there.

"What is it, Sam?"

"Nothing." Then Sam Baker smiled sadly to himself. "I just realized how much I'm going to miss him."

"There isn't one of us—" Terry Fallon was saying "—not one of us who has lived in America in the last forty years, who doesn't have some stake in the tragedy of Sally Crain. This is no isolated act of exploitation. This is one more brutal proof of the erosion of our values. Think of these last forty years. Think of what we've seen.

"We've seen our government lie to our nation and our allies, carry on clandestine dirty wars while preaching a doctrine of peace. We've seen our agents infiltrate and destroy popular liberation movements here and abroad, trade with terrorists and create a mass-market in the weapons of destruction. Our government has made right into wrong and wrong into right so many times over these past four decades—who is able to tell good from evil any more?

"This immorality that infects the highest offices in our land is a disease contagious and virulent. It infects more than our foreign policy—it infects and sickens the very heart of the American people. Were we so arrogant? Were we so blind? Did we think we could spread this infection throughout the rest of the world and remain, ourselves, immune?"

He looked directly into the television cameras, directly into the eyes of millions of people across the country.

"What has become of our ideals, America? What has become of the truths we hold to be self-evident? What has become of our dreams?"

He paused, and the accusation hung in the silence. Then he lowered his voice and went on. "The despicable photographs published today are unfit to be seen. But I ask you to seek them out and look at them with your own eyes. Look closely at the face of the woman in these photographs.

"And when you see them, remember that she was a girl baptized in Christ, a heroic nurse who served the sick and needy in the darkest, foulest jungles of Central America. She was a girl who returned home with a vision of what our role in our hemisphere should be. This is a woman who contributed. Who dreamed of a better world. And believed it could be achieved."

He shook his head. "And, yet . . . when you look into the face of the girl in those ghastly photographs, you will see nothing but confusion and despair. Because—like this country—under the veneer of success and achievement, dwelt a soul in torment. She was a girl—we are a nation— that lost touch with its ideals. And when you look at these ghastly pictures, remember—they are not merely a spectacle. They are a warning."

Behind the black glass of the announcer's booth at the back of the studio, in the cool darkness of the padded acoustic walls, a figure waited. It might have been a young boy with short-cropped blond hair, wearing baggy Army surplus clothes. But it was not. It was Sally Crain.

Methodically, she slipped her arm through the sling of the carbine and set the parallax on the telescopic sight for fifty meters. Then she slid the breech half open. Between its steel jaws, the brass casing of a cartridge gleamed golden yellow.

Myrtle divided the documents into two piles—one set for Mancuso, the other for file. Then she flipped through the calendar on her desk, counting out the weeks. Mancuso looked over her shoulder. "Now then," she said. "Your first pension check will mail on November 8. No . . . November 9. The eighth is Election Day."

He smiled at the irony.

"You gonna vote this year, Joe?"

"I already did," Mancuso said.

Steve Chandler was getting anxious. Fallon was winding up, and still the chair in the Senate press room sat empty. He grabbed the direct line to the floor manager.

"Any sign of her?"

The man on the screen shook his head and opened his hands. Then he turned suddenly to the sound of a door slamming and heated voices off-camera.

"What the hell is that?" Chandler said. "Camera one, let me see it."

The camera swish-panned right, and in the shadows behind the light stands and the technicians, he could see that a group of uniformed police-men with drawn sidearms had entered the studio. Through the open line, Chandler could hear a man in plainclothes arguing with the floor manager.

"Where is she?" the policeman demanded.

"Goddamit," Steve Chandler muttered under his breath.

"I told you, buddy," the floor manager said. "She's not here."

"We got a call that you're expecting her." He stepped out into the bright stage lights, and blinked and shaded his eyes, and looked around the room. "Hey, you," he said to the camera. "Is there a—" he looked at a slip of paper in his hand. "Anybody here named Steve Chandler?"

Chandler hit the talk-back button and his voice boomed out in the press room. "I'm Steve Chandler."

"I'm Lieutenant Driscoll of the D.C. police. You get out here, mister. I want to talk to you."

"I'm in New York."

"The fuck you are."

"You bet your ass I am. Now go on. Talk. And I hope you've got a warrant."

"I got a warrant for Sally Crain's arrest for first-degree murder. Now if you know where she is, mister, talk up."

Steve Chandler caught his breath. ". . . murder?"

"Some guy named Carter. Her fingerprints were all over him."

"Sally Crain . . . murdered Tommy Carter?"

"She stuck a screwdriver in the back of his brain. Now if you know where she is, let's have it!"

Steve Chandler put his hand to his mouth to control his retching. Then he threw off his head set and pushed through the control room door into the hall. When he got there, he vomited.

Terry Fallon lowered his eyes. "I will make a confession to you," he said, and the reporters stirred. "I knew something of Sally Crain's past when I came to the Senate. I knew she had been an idealistic young woman who had gone into the world full of hope—and instead of finding a way to love and honor, she had lost part of her soul. I knew that she had erred. I knew that she had suffered. And I knew, most of all, that she wanted nothing more than a chance to redeem herself.

"I believe in the forgiveness of sin. Who among you does not?" Terry paused and looked deeply into the faces of the newsmen and women before him. They were no longer angry. Now, they were sitting like penitents, alone with their thoughts. "Those of us in government, and you in the press, know better than most that the world trembles on a precipice over the darkness. And all that will save this nation from drifting into the maelstrom is the tenacity with which we cling to our ideals."

As he scanned their faces, he could see that he was reaching them. Because they were thinking not only of Sally now, but of themselves and the world they had helped to create. Across the nation, men and women watching Terry Fallon on the network morning news knew that he was speaking the truth. They had, each of them, neither given enough nor demanded enough of themselves and the people who led them.

Now, they gazed at their television sets as into a mirror, and saw their own shame reflected.

Terry straightened his spine and spoke out. "I believe in this nation and what it stands for. I believe in the fundamental ideals we adore. I believe in a world of equal peoples and free nations. And I believe America must stop lying to itself and to the world."

There was a scattering of applause from among the reporters.

Sally lowered the rifle and listened. They were her words. And they sang.

Myrtle shuffled the papers on her desk into a large manila envelope, clipped it shut, and handed it to Mancuso.

"Well, that just about wraps it up, kid," she said.

Mancuso stood up and took his hat and put the envelope under his arm. "Thanks, Myrtle."

"Wait, wait," she said. "I almost forgot. One more thing." She opened her desk drawer and handed him a wallet-sized laminated card.

Mancuso squinted at it. It was a new FBI ID card with his picture. Across the face of the card in large red letters was the word RETIRED.

"Might help if you get stopped going through a red light," Myrtle said.

"I am not here to apologize for Sally Crain," Terry said. "But I am here to accuse this country of complicity in her crimes against herself."

He paused and drew a heavy breath. "And, today, I pledge myself that this nation will have a rebirth in courage and honor, feared by our enemies, admired by our friends, a bright light of conscience and hope for the world."

Terry's eye swept the room. "Sally Crain was one of the most devoted friends of this hemisphere in the Federal establishment. However history may judge her, she will be missed. The poor people of the Americas have lost a champion and a benefactor. And if she were standing here before you today, she would say to you and to them: *valentia*—courage; *resilencia*—persistence; *esperanza*—faith."

Terry folded the papers before him and raised his face. "For my part, I am committed to an America in which this tragedy can never happen again. And with all my heart, Sally, I wish you Godspeed to a new and productive life."

He stood there in the hush that followed, stood under the halo of studio lights. The reporters sat in numbed silence—some sharing the bitter taste of repentance, all sitting awestruck by the miracle that had happened before them. Terry Fallon had turned the scandal into a moral victory for himself and his candidacy.

In the announcer's booth above the last row of chairs, Sally Crain pressed the wooden stock of the carbine to her cheek. Her eye burned red into the telescopic sight. Under the crosshairs, she saw Terry Fallon smile and look up, look straight back at the announce booth as though he could see her. And her finger slackened on the trigger.

Once more, she marveled at his poise and stature. Once more, she warmed in the glitter of his smile. He was, after all, a beautiful creation. She had found him a raw, ambitious young man. And she had nurtured and coached him until he was the equal of any charismatic leader on the planet. She had taught him, written for him, and toiled for him. She had killed for him. He had been her obsession.

And he obsessed her still.

She lowered the carbine.

Terry Fallon was what she had made him. He was going to be president of the United States.

And she? What was she?

Sally looked down at her hands holding the carbine. She looked at the faded, mildewed, ridiculous camouflage gear. Without Terry Fallon, she was nothing—nothing but a river captain's dirty joke—nothing but a misbegotten creature of the Nicaraguan night.

She stared down at the weapon in her hands. And in that moment, she knew. She knew exactly what she was.

She was the thing she had been born to be.

She was Carlos Fonseca's messenger.

She was Carlos Fonseca's whore.

She pulled the carbine's stock hard against her cheek. Then she screamed her vengeance. Then she opened fire.

The wall of one-way glass that separated the booth from the studio exploded outward and disintegrated into thousands of sharp, razor-edged fragments that showered down on the screaming, diving reporters below. The burst of bullets hit Terry Fallon squarely in the chest and threw him back off the rostrum against the wall of the studio. His shirt erupted in a scarlet mass of blood and bone and shredded flesh. He opened his mouth to scream. Just before he died, he realized what had happened. When his corpse slid jerking to the floor, it left a long streak of bloody tissue on the wall.

The Secret Service men around the room dropped to their knees, swung up their weapons. But by the time their concentrated fire shattered what remained of the booth and tore through the plaster of the walls, Sally had kicked the back door open and started running down the third floor hallway toward the fire exit.

Two uniformed cops came rushing around the end of the hall, revolvers drawn. Sally pulled the trigger and fired from the waist. The spray from the automatic rifle sent the two men sprawling in a bloody tangle on the linoleum. She hit the spring that ejected the empty ammunition clip, slapped a full one home.

A Secret Service man with an Uzi opened up from a doorway at the other end of the hall. Sally sprawled into a prone firing position as plaster from the walls and ceiling rained down about her. Then she squeezed the trigger and the volley ripped through the door frame and the wall. There was a scream and the door slammed closed. She came up on all fours and crawled, breathless, to the end of the hall and pushed through the steel fire door.

She was in a concrete air shaft with three flights of steel steps that led down to the street at the rear of the building. She ran down the stairs and threw her body at the bar that controlled the release mechanism of the fire door. It was locked. She stepped back and threw her body at the bar again. But it held fast. She swung the rifle around and hammered its butt against the bar. But it wouldn't budge.

On the landing three floors above her, she heard a door open, shouting, and running feet. She stepped back from the fire door, leveled the carbine at the lock, closed her eyes and emptied the whole clip into it. The mechanism disintegrated and hot metal ricocheted past her face and bounced madly around the bottom of the air shaft.

She threw the empty carbine aside, drew the .45 automatic from her belt, and kicked with her boot at the door. It stuck. She kicked again. She could hear the men gathering upstairs. She cried out and kicked with all her might. Then the door crashed open and the concrete walls were washed in bright sunlight. She shielded her eyes and stepped out.

Someone cried, "Look out! It's the terrorist!"

People on the curb and in the parking lot screamed.

"There he is!"

They shouted and ran and ducked for cover.

Then a voice shouted, "Hey, it's only Sally!"

And another said, "That's no terrorist. That's Sally Crain!"

"Sally? Is that you?"

"Hey, look!"

"Look, everybody! It's Sally Crain!"

They stopped running and stuck their heads up from behind the cars parked in the lot. Sally shaded her eyes and looked back and forth for her route to Tommy Carter's car and escape.

"Hey, guys! It's Sally Crain!"

And as her eyes adjusted to the blinding daylight, she saw the sidewalk and driveway filling with reporters and news crews and still cameramen rushing toward her.

They shouted, "Hey, Sally! Sally!"

Then the tungsten lights switched on and the strobes began to flash. She blinked and shielded her eyes from the blinding lights that surrounded her.

"Over here! Sally! Please!"

They pushed in around her for a better shot, a better angle. Someone stuck a microphone in her face.

"Sally, what was it like to kill Senator Fallon?"

"Did he give the pictures to the papers?"

"Was he your lover?"

"Jeeze, what a great get-up."

Over the heads of the tangled ring of reporters, she could see Secret Service men rushing out the front door of the television station, running up the street toward her, guns drawn.

She stepped back and fired her .45 into the air. Some of the reporters ducked, but the herd kept closing in, circling her, cutting off any chance of escape.

"That's great!" someone shouted.

"Again!" a cameraman yelled. "Shoot again!"

She tried to push through the solid ring of reporters and break away. But they pressed toward her in an ever-closing knot, their cameras glaring at her, their microphones thrust into her face. There was no way out. There was no time. She looked into the lenses of the cameras, and she could see this was her last chance to speak her heart, to tell what she had seen and learned in those nights along the Rio Coco.

She said, "Senator Fallon was killed as a revolutionary act on behalf of the poor and—"

"Aw, come on, Sally, give us a break."

"Give us the real stuff, babe."

"Did he do trios?"

"Were there orgies?"

She cried out, "Senator Fallon was killed as a revolutionary act to—"

But the reporters shouted her down. They didn't want to listen. Like everyone else, they didn't care.

"Who was the other woman? Do you know her name and address?"

"Sally, one more." Flash. "Just one more." Flash.

"Were there just the three of you?"

"Did other senators join the fun?"

It was no use. The ring of reporters pressed against her and she stood, silent and cornered, her hands and the automatic pistol hanging limp at her side. On the outside of the group, the Secret Service men tried to push through the reporters, tried to fight their way through the tangle of bodies and cameras and microphone booms. But the surging crush of the newsmen was impenetrable.

"Give us the low-down, Sally."

"Where was the love nest?"

"Is there any film?"

There was a blond girl standing right in front of Sally. A young reporter who just stood staring at her with gentle blue eyes. Sally looked at her. She could have been a farm girl with freckles across the saddle of her nose, or a stringer for one of the papers in the upper Midwest. She was a girl who hadn't been touched by Washington yet. She was a girl who had all of life before her. Perhaps she was someone who would listen.

"Did you love him?" the girl said.

Sally stopped. "No," she said. "Never." Then one of the Secret Service men managed to push through the ring of reporters and shove the girl aside. He grabbed roughly at Sally's arm.

Sally looked hard into his face. "Take your filthy hands off me," she said. "Pig." Then she put the barrel of the .45 into the socket of her right eye and pulled the trigger.

8:55 A.M. THE IMAGE ON the screen was Terry Fallon, slumped in a bloody mass between the rostrum and the studio wall. The voice was Bryant Gumbel's, and he was saying, "If you've just joined us, Senator Terry Fallon, the vice presidential hopeful, was shot and killed this morning. His assailant was Sally Crain, a member of his own staff. Yesterday, newspaper reports identified her as an accomplice in the murder of Secret Service Agent Steven Thomopolous—and as the mistress of a Washington sex ring of which the senator may have been part."

The picture cut to tape of Sally surrounded by the reporters in the parking lot, waving a pistol and calling out—but her words were unintelligible, lost in the shouted questions of the newsmen. Gumbel said, "Police have characterized this as a crime of passion, and there is speculation that Miss Crain was despondent over the breakup of her love affair with Senator Fallon. However, her bizarre appearance and a garbled statement before she took her own life suggest that she was psychologically disturbed."

Sally's picture vanished as *Today* cut to Gumbel seated on the studio couch between Jane Pauley and Willard Scott.

Gumbel said, "Tonight at 11:00 eastern, 10:00 central and mountain time, NBC News will present a one-hour special report: 'Capitol Crimes'—a historical look at Washington's scandals and illicit affairs and how they have changed the course of government. *Today* will stay on the air for one additional hour this morning to cover further developments on this story."

"Yes," Jane said, "but *Wheel of Fortune* will be seen at its regular time."

9:00 A.M. JOE MANCUSO WALKED out the front door of the Hoover Building, down the short flight of steps to Pennsylvania Avenue. He was carrying a snazzy blue gym bag with the handle of a squash racquet sticking out through the top. He stopped on the last step and squinted at his new ID card. The picture looked more like his father than it did like him. Fucking FBI. Couldn't even take a ten-cent ID picture right. He put it in his jacket pocket. As he did, he felt something sharp prick the end of his finger. He fumbled around and pulled it out.

It was the little American flag pin—the one he hadn't wanted to leave on Eastman's desk last night. He thought a moment. Was it only last night?

He looked at the pin in the August sunlight. It was painted blue and red and white enamel. Some of the blue had slopped over on the red, and some of the red had seeped in among the blue field of white stars. It was a forlorn little flag. But it suited him. It suited him just fine. He pinned it to his lapel. He felt like he'd earned it.

Then, he picked up the gym bag and looked one way down the street and then the other. People were rushing up and down the street, everyone hustling, everyone with somewhere important to go. But he didn't have to be anywhere this morning. Not this morning. Not any morning ever again. Then he looked at his watch. The sunlight hazed the scratched crystal, and he could barely make out that it was just coming up on nine. One of these days, he was going to have to get a new crystal for that watch. Maybe even a new watch. But not today.

Today he was just going to walk down to the Lincoln Memorial and maybe sit on the steps until noon and get some sun and watch the mothers and fathers telling their kids about Washington and what a great country this is. That's what he was going to do. And he was just about to head out when he heard the sirens over in the north part of town. Not one siren, but more like fifty. Like every police car and paramedic unit in the District was roaring toward the north side. The government workers rushing to their offices didn't look up, didn't pay the sirens the least attention. But Mancuso raised his head and listened to the sound, listened as if to music. He dug the ID out of his pocket and took another look at the face on the card. Dumb old guinea bastard who couldn't find his pecker to pee. Yeah. He sure looked the part.

Then he headed off down the block, humming to himself no-song-in-particular. At the corner, he paused just long enough to toss the ID into a litter basket. Then he crossed the street and was lost among the rush hour crowd.

ACKNOWLEDGMENTS

Thanks to Steve Rubin, whose vision and conviction caused *Favorite Son* to be written. To editor Fred Klein. To expert advisors Shirley Christian, Charles W. Bailey II, Norman Sandler, Dr. Paul R. Sohmer. And to early commentators Elizabeth McKee, Mark Wells, Gail Gordon Kamer, Barbara Alpert, Paul Wang, Raymond J. Timothy, Lynda Farmer, Raeanne Hytone, Andrea Merkel, and Martin Cutler.